MORDENKAINEN'S TOME OF FOES

CREDITS

Lead Designers: Mike Mearls, Jeremy Crawford
Designers: Adam Lee, Ben Petrisor, Robert J. Schwalb, Matt Sernett, Steve Winter
Additional Design: Kim Mohan, Christopher Perkins, Kate Welch
Guest Designer: Nolan Whale (oblex, Balthran Ireheart)

Managing Editor: Jeremy Crawford
Editors: Kim Mohan, Michele Carter

Art Director: Kate Irwin
Graphic Designer: Emi Tanji
Additional Art Direction: Shauna Narciso
Cover Illustrator: Jason Rainville
Cover Illustrator (Alternative Cover): Vance Kelly
Concept Artists: Richard Whitters, Shawn Wood
Interior Illustrators: Dave Allsop, Tom Babbey, Mark Behm, Eric Belisle, Michael Berube, Zoltan Boros, Aleksi Briclot, Filip Burburan, Christopher Burdett, Matt Cavotta, Sidharth Chaturvedi, Jedd Chevrier, Ed Cox, Olga Drebas, Wayne England, Justin Gerard, Lars Grant-West, Leesha Hannigan, Jon Hodgson, Ralph Horsley, Lake Hurwitz, Tyler Jacobson, Julian Kok, Daniel Landerman, Olly Lawson, Howard Lyon, Warren Mahy, Brynn Metheney, Aaron Miller, Scott Murphy, Jim Nelson, William O'Connor, Efrem Palacios, Adam Paquette, Claudio Pozas, Vincent Proce, Rob Rey, Richard Sardinha, Chris Seaman, Ilya Shkipin, Craig J Spearing, Zack Stella, Philip Straub, Bryan Syme, David A. Trampier, Cory Trego-Erdner, Richard Whitters, Anthony S. Waters, Shawn Wood, Ben Wootten, Min Yum, Xi James Zhang

Project Management: Stan!
Production Services: Cynda Callaway, Carmen Cheung, Jefferson Dunlap, David Gershman

Other D&D Team Members: Bart Carroll, Trevor Kidd, Christopher Lindsay, Shelly Mazzanoble, Hilary Ross, Liz Schuh, Nathan Stewart, Greg Tito

Playtesters: Adam Hennebeck, Adam Pearson, Alex D'Amico, Alex Kammer, Alexander Forsyth, Andrew Norman, Andrey Sarafanov, Arthur Wright, Ashleigh Bishop, Beau Coker, Ben Rabin, Brian Dahl, Brittany Schoen, Bryan Gillispie, Bryan Harris, Burt Beegle, C. McGovern, Cait Davis-Pauley, Caleb Zutavern, Cameron Scruggs, Charles Benscoter, Chloe Urbano, Chris Garner, Chris Presnall, Cody Helms, Daniel "KBlin" Oliveira, Dave Rosser Jr., Davena Oaks, David Callander, David Gidcumb, David Krolnik, David Merritt, David Morris, Derek DaSilva, Derek Gray, Emre Cihangir, Enrique Bertran, Eric Weberg, Evan Jackson, Garrett Colon, George Strayton, Gerald Wan, Grant Fisk, Gregory L. Harris, Grigory Parovichnikov, J. Connor Self, Jacob DelMauro, James Schweiss, Jared Fegan, Jawsh Murdock, Jay Anderson, Jay Elmore, Jay White, Jenna Schmitt, Jeremy Nagorny, Jerry Behrendt, Jia Jian Tin, Jim Berrier, Jimmer Moeller, Joe Alfano, Joe Reilly, Jonathan Longstaff, Joseph Schenck, Joshua Hart, Justin Donie, Karl Resch, Keith Williams, Kerry Kaszak, Kevin Engling, Kevin Grigsby, Kevin Moore, Kevin Murphy, Kevin Neff, Kirsten Thomas, Kyle Turner, Justin Hicks, Lawrence "Bear" Beals, Lou Michelli, Marcello De Velazquez, Marcus Wiles, Mark Merida, Matt Maranda, Matthew H Budde, Matthew Roderick, Matthew Shurboff, Matthew Warwick, Michael Long, Michael Obermeier, Mike Mihalas, Nel Pulanco, Nichola Sobota, Nicholas Giovannetti, Oleg Suetnov, Paige Miller, Paul Hughes, Phil Morlan, Pieter Sleijpen, Randall Harris, Randall Shepherd, Richard Chamberlain, Robert Alaniz, Russ Paulsen, Russell Engel, Sam Robertson, Sam Shircel, Samuel Sherry, Scott Beck, Scott Chipman, Shane Leahy, Stacy Bermes, Stephen Lindberg, Stephen Morman, Sterling Hershey, Tashfeen Bhimdi, Teos Abadia, Timothy Hunt, Travis Fuller, Travis Woodall, Troy Sandlin, Wayne Chang, Zachary Pickett

This book is dedicated to artist William O'Connor, who passed away during its creation. Since 2001, his work has graced numerous D&D products, including this one. Like his art, his was a spirit of vibrancy and warmth.

ON THE COVER

Using an intricate orrery, the wizard Mordenkainen observes conflicts across the D&D multiverse, in this painting by Jason Rainville.

ON THE ALTERNATIVE COVER

The sinister shadows of adversaries emerge under the shrewd gaze of the archmage Mordenkainen, illustrated by Vance Kelly.

620C4594000001 EN
ISBN: 978-0-7869-6624-0
First Printing: May 2018

CE

Disclaimer: We asked Mordenkainen to write a humorous disclaimer for this book, and we got this response: "The day I start writing frivolous disclaimers for game manuals—particularly one riddled with text stolen from my notes—is the day I retire from wizardry and abandon all self-respect."

9 8 7 6 5 4 3 2

Contents

Index of Monster Stat Blocks

PREFACE

You have in your hands that which you covet, just as I promised. It is indeed the true work of that Oeridian wizard Mordenkainen, although penned in large part by his apprentice, Bigby. You didn't know that? Yes—the work of two great wizards for the price of one! You should pay me extra.

Bigby wrote as dictated by his master, burdened by the chains of a charm spell. Eventually, Mordenkainen released Bigby from the spell once he had turned Bigby away from his evil ways and Bigby had earned Mordenkainen's trust. The last few chapters are thus in Mordenkainen's own hand. But you'll see the voice of the author is the same throughout.

Funny, isn't it? How all the stories say that Mordenkainen rescued Bigby from evil? Does Mordenkainen seem like the kind of person whose virtues outweigh his villainy? Do you think him capable of saving a soul? Does he seem like someone who'd even care?

Perhaps it's no accident that this book contains Mordenkainen's first expression of the Balance. In here, he starts to describe the multiverse as a collection of opposing forces, each one trying to tip the scales of fate in its favor. He posits that if any side in a struggle grows too powerful, it becomes tyrannical. But where does that leave us—all the soldiers in all these wars? Surely for the soldiers of all sides, a war is better when it is over.

Are you a soldier? What war do you fight? Whose side are you on? Law or Chaos? Evil or Good? Can you be sure that Mordenkainen would judge you as you judge yourself? When he puts his thumb on the scales to preserve the Balance, can you be certain that the weight of that finger will not crush you?

All this might seem odd coming from a yugoloth, but you should believe me, because I am in the best position to know: endless wars profit only mercenaries and arms dealers. Think on this as you peruse the wise words of Mordenkainen.

—The words of Shemeshka the Marauder, upon delivering *Mordenkainen's Tome of Foes*

I've included Shemeshka's words in this copy of my master's seminal work because they have haunted me from the moment she uttered them. I know her kind exists to twist truth and to deceive, and she in particular has a reputation for ruthlessness in pursuit of her ends. But what was her end here?

Am I to believe my tutor and friend Mordenkainen was actually twisted to evil by Bigby? Am I to believe that the ideals of the Circle of Eight are self-serving, merely a way for them to justify murder and plunder?

I cannot do so. Mordenkainen has no need for ever more magic and treasure. He is not a cruel man.

And yet ... I must confess that I paid Shemeshka to purloin the book without Mordenkainen's knowledge. My desire to preserve the works of my master is not one he shares. But this treatise on the conflicts of the multiverse has many important insights, and its value as a historical document—as the birthplace of Mordenkainen's philosophy of the Balance—cannot be overstated.

I hope that once he learns of this small betrayal on my part, Mordenkainen will see that disseminating the results of his scholarship serves his ends. If more people understood his quest, surely his work would be made easier.

—Qort

There are no small betrayals.
—Mordenkainen

ABOUT THIS BOOK

In the worlds of DUNGEONS & DRAGONS, conflicts rage within mortal realms and in the very domains of the gods. This book explores some of the greatest conflicts in the D&D multiverse and delves into the cultures of the peoples and monsters involved in those conflicts. Why do dwarves and duergar hate each other? Why are there so many kinds of elves? What lies at the heart of the Blood War, the great cosmic struggle between demons and devils that threatens to destroy everything if either side were ever to emerge victorious? This book provides answers to those questions and many more.

The first five chapters present material for a Dungeon Master to add depth to a campaign that involves the ongoing conflicts described there. Options for players are provided as well, including new character races.

Chapter 6 contains game statistics for dozens of monsters: new demons and devils, several varieties of elves and duergar, and a vast array of other creatures from throughout the planes of existence. The appendix lets you look up stat blocks in this book by challenge rating, creature type, and environment.

A companion to the *Monster Manual* and *Volo's Guide to Monsters*, this book contains the musings of the renowned wizard Mordenkainen from the world of Greyhawk. In his travels to other worlds and other planes of existence, he has made many friends, and has risked his life an equal number of times, to amass the knowledge contained herein.

CHAPTER 1:
THE BLOOD WAR

T HROUGHOUT HISTORY, THE TEEMING HORDES of the Abyss and the strictly regimented legions of the Nine Hells have battled for supremacy in the cosmos. In the mortal world, the scant few scholars, arcanists, and adventurers who know the conflict for what it is refer to it as the Blood War.

The fighting takes place across the Lower Planes, on the Material Plane, and anywhere else that demons and devils might congregate. From time to time, demons spill out of the Abyss to invade Avernus, the uppermost layer of the Nine Hells. While the devils defend their home turf, they also make strikes against locations in the Abyss. Although the intensity of the conflict waxes and wanes, and the front lines of the war can shift drastically, a moment never goes by when demons and devils aren't battling each other somewhere in the multiverse.

THE GREAT DANCE

WE MEASURE OURSELVES BY THOSE WE FIGHT, AND MY *company faces the greatest threat to the cosmos.*

—Veritus Wrath, commander, Flawless Execution

The battle lines in the Blood War undulate like a writhing snake. Each time one side gains an advantage, invariably its lines weaken somewhere else.

Demons enter the Nine Hells by following the River Styx from the Abyss into Avernus. By hiring skilled merrenoloth pilots to navigate the river, a demon lord can transport an invasion force of enormous size.

Mimicking a complex dance, the two sides shift their attacks and trade positions with each passing day. About once every thousand years, the demons close in on the lower reaches of the Styx and portals leading deeper into the Hells. Invariably, the legions of the Nine Hells boil up from below to repel the invaders out of Avernus, back to the juncture where the Styx enters the Hells. This drive by the devils attracts the attention of more demons from the Abyss, which pushes the front line back into Avernus. The process repeats itself time and time again.

To the good fortune of the rest of the multiverse, almost all the battles in the Blood War take place in the Abyss and the Nine Hells. Whether by cosmic chance or the design of some unknown power, the dark waters of the Styx provide passage between the two planes, but pathways to other realms are at best fleeting and unreliable. Despite the difficulty of escaping the Lower Planes, combatants on both sides find their way to the Material Plane and other realms from time to time. Although the conflicts on these other planes are little more than skirmishes in the Blood War, even a small number of demons and devils can wreak havoc and bring destruction wherever they see fit to do battle.

MORTALS AND MINIONS

Devils and demons are far from the only combatants in the Blood War. Both sides exploit the Material Plane's most abundant resource—mortal creatures, whose bodies and souls are both useful to the cause.

Devils constantly strive to recruit mortals into their ranks by offering them rewards in return for their service. While they live, these cultists carry out the wishes of their archdevil masters, whether raiding an enemy outpost or gathering more members for the cult. When a cultist dies, its soul emerges in the Nine Hells and becomes another of the Blood War's immortal soldiers. Most of the evil souls consigned to an afterlife in the Nine Hells become lemures, which make up the vast majority of the hellish forces, but some mortal recruits who willingly accept a contract offer from a powerful devil can arrive as a lesser devil.

Demons generally have no regard for mortal souls and do not solicit them, but living creatures do have their uses. Groups of corrupted cultists dedicated to one of the demon lords exist all across the realms of the material world. For as long as these mortals do the bidding of their lord, they are allowed to live. From a demon's perspective, all other living creatures are nothing more than sheep ripe for slaughter, and demonic cultists share this view. These fanatics don't hesitate to slay other mortals if given the chance—and if their victims happen to be in league with devils, so much the better.

A casual observer might suppose that two forces of evil bent on exterminating each other would be an advantageous situation for the forces of good, but the combatants in the Blood War have no regard for collateral damage—and on the Material Plane, they can cause a lot of it. If agents of Asmodeus discover a thriving demon cult in a city, they might deal with the threat by starting a fire that not only destroys the cult but burns through several neighborhoods and kills hundreds of innocents. A demon might unleash a plague to kill every person in a town, just for the sake of claiming from its library an old book containing a map to a lost artifact. The fiends on both sides of the Blood War take the path of least resistance to their goals, heedless of consequences that don't affect them.

AGENTS OF TREACHERY

Both sides in the Blood War employ spies and soldiers drawn from the ranks of other evil creatures of the planes. The devils are generally more successful at this tactic because of the discipline they can bring to bear on these ostensible allies. Even so, powerful, intelligent demon lords such as Graz'zt can also force their agents to do their bidding under threat of annihilation.

As creatures that don't favor either cause, because they care nothing for the philosophical concerns of law and chaos, other fiends including incubi, succubi, and night hags work for whichever side offers the best compensation. Demons use them as insurrectionists in the Nine Hells, inciting rebellion and defiance. The devils employ such creatures as scouts, who use their magic and other abilities to navigate the Abyss and gain intelligence about the demons' activities. Adventurers hired by an agent of the Nine Hells to make a foray into the Abyss are customarily guided by such a mercenary.

THE SEARCH FOR SECRETS

The Blood War has all the characteristics of an eternal stalemate, in part because the two sides are so familiar with each other. Every time the Abyss belches forth some new variety of horror, the disciplined and well-trained legions of the Nine Hells reorganize, rally, and counterattack. The devils continually dream up variations on their attack strategies, only to be checked by the overwhelming chaotic force of the Abyss. Little true advancement occurs under the angry red sky of Avernus or in any other realm where the forces clash.

The leaders of each side recognize that the introduction of some unexpected factor could permanently affect the balance of power. Accordingly, demons and devils constantly send their agents across the planes in search of artifacts, powerful creatures to recruit, and other resources that could lead to a key advantage in the war. Adventurers of great repute might get involved in such a quest, either as unwitting pawns or as an independent force pursuing its own ends.

COSMIC BATTLEFIELD

The Blood War rages along the length of the River Styx. Direct confrontations between demons and devils erupt along its banks, making any of the Lower Planes the Styx touches a potential battleground.

The devils view fighting demons on Avernus as a net benefit for their cause. Although most devils slain there are destroyed forever, ready access to supplies and support from the Nine Hells tilts the tide heavily against in-

---

There are many theories about why it is called the Blood War, but I believe it is because the branches of the River Styx act like blood vessels that circulate the conflict throughout the Lower Planes.

SAILING THE STYX

The River Styx frustrates every attempt to map it or predict its course. Although anyone can try to navigate it, only merrenoloths, the yugoloth ferrymen of the Styx, can faultlessly negotiate the Styx's treacherous waters. For a price, merrenoloths will carry anyone safely and swiftly across planar boundaries. The greater the distance and the more perilous the passengers to be ferried, the higher the price.

Getting lost while sailing the Styx isn't the only danger the river presents. Merely tasting or touching its waters causes most creatures to become stupefied, and drinking fully or being immersed for too long can render that condition permanent, robbing a creature of all its memories. Fiends don't fear being momentarily exposed to the Styx, but—with the notable exception of hydroloths, merrenoloths, and amnizus—even they can't retain their memories if they drink from the River Styx or swim for too long in its waters.

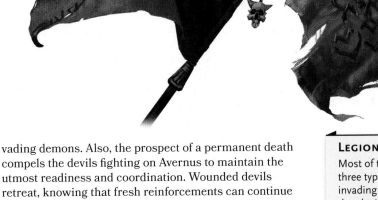

vading demons. Also, the prospect of a permanent death compels the devils fighting on Avernus to maintain the utmost readiness and coordination. Wounded devils retreat, knowing that fresh reinforcements can continue the fight. Hordes of lemures, devils that are permanently destroyed only if subjected to holy energies, are used to blunt demonic incursions. The terrain of Avernus is thoroughly mapped and festooned with ambush points, strongholds, and other defensive measures.

More important, demons that are slain and sent back to the Abyss return to their chaotic wanderings in that realm. A demon lord is thus hard pressed to keep a horde cohesive as it takes casualties. If the devils extended a tenacious defense out to the planes beyond Avernus, they could keep the demons away from Hell's doorstep, but such a strategy would place a great strain on supplies, reinforcements, and unit integrity. Although the devils killed in such places would recover, their weapons, armor, and other materials would remain lost.

THE DEVILISH POINT OF VIEW

MY LEGIONS ARE THE ONLY THING STANDING BETWEEN *your precious Seven Heavens and the bottomless hunger of the Abyss. I did not fall into the clutches of evil. I rose to shoulder a cosmic burden.*

—Zariel, Archduchess of Avernus,
former angel of Celestia

Although the basic facts of the Blood War aren't subject to debate, a host of theories exist that attempt to explain why the conflict erupted in the first place.

The devils fight as a matter of pride mixed with burning resentment for a cosmic order that refuses to acknowledge their role as overseers of the multiverse.

LEGIONS OF THE DAMNED

Most of the forces of the Nine Hells are grouped into three types of legions that each play a role in repelling the invading demons. Incompetent or weak devils fill out the dreg legions, composed mainly of hordes of lemures and nupperibos. They are deployed as a delaying tactic, serving as fodder to slow down an advancing horde of demons while sword legions organize their counterattacks and shield legions establish their defenses. Each legion within a category has a distinctive, fearsome-sounding name in the Infernal tongue. When translated into Common, these names are often descriptive of the legion's status or battle-worthiness, such as the ones given below.

Dreg Legions. Bugs in the System, Momentary Lapse of Progress, Casualties Imminent, Last in Line for Healing, Not Worth the Effort

Shield Legions. Moment of Silence, Welcome to the Hells, Pleased to Meet You, Front toward Enemy, End of the Line

Sword Legions. Flawless Execution, Damned Good, The Hanging Blade, Inevitable Outcome, A Taste for Carnage

---

To the devils' way of thinking, the Nine Hells are the front line in the demons' war against all of creation, and the fate of the cosmos depends on the devils' ability to blunt the invasion and send the demons back to the Abyss.

In fact, devils believe that the demons would have long ago swept across the multiverse but for the unflinching rule of law that underlies the actions of the infernal leaders and their armies. If necessary, a general must not hesitate to sacrifice entire legions to stall an enemy advance or punch a hole through an enemy phalanx. Iron discipline combined with a ruthless focus on victory at any cost is what fuels the devils' war machine.

Every devil takes a grim pride in its service in the Blood War. Talk to one for a short time, and it will reveal the scars earned during its time in Avernus and tell tales of the great battles it has seen. Talk to one for a little longer, and it will inform you that you are alive only because of the devils' heroic efforts. If there was truly justice in the world, it would tell you, the multiverse would bend its knee to the Nine Hells in thanks for the devils' role in preserving the cosmos.

THE DEMONIC POINT OF VIEW

WHY DO WE DESCEND UPON THE DOMAIN OF OUR HATED *enemies? Because that's where the fighting is!*

—Zaadaaak, demon of the Abyss

Most other creatures believe demons to be little more than mindless engines of destruction and violence. If that supposition were true, the Blood War should have ended long ago, since the tactical and strategic genius of the archdevils would have made quick work of the hordes that erupt from the Abyss. In fact, even though demons are quintessentially chaotic, their evilness combines with that outlook to produce a fiendish, subtle shrewdness. Demon lords and other powerful entities exert control over their armies that enables the forces to accomplish goals that would be beyond the capabilities of a leaderless mob. To the demons that have intelligence enough to appreciate their role in it, the Blood War offers an endless source of diversion underscored by resentment of a cosmic order that refuses to admit their superiority.

As the devils have surmised, the demons invade Avernus because it is easily accessible from the Abyss. But some sages and demonologists maintain that even if that were not the case, the Nine Hells would still be the demons' prime target. If the demons sent out a large force to invade a different plane, this theory holds, the devils would be able to marshal allies from across all the planes to rise up against the Abyss and end its threat forever. Instead, as long as the demons focus most of

YUGOLOTHS: FICKLE ALLIES
Yugoloths are major players on both sides of the Blood War. The death of a yugoloth is meaningless when it occurs in the Abyss or the Nine Hells, and thus these mercenaries freely give their all in any battle even when it means fighting other yugoloths. Demons and devils both know that a yugoloth's loyalty is constantly for sale—even during a conflict on the battlefield—and a yugoloth never agrees to a contract that prohibits it from seeking a better offer. This set of circumstances prompts hellish and abyssal armies to carry war chests with them in the hope of buying the services of the yugoloths on the other side. The war chests themselves thus become highly prized targets, which in turn leads to protective measures, such as valuables hidden in *bags of holding* or empty treasure containers used to lure the enemy into a trap.

Regardless of the side that hires them, yugoloths almost never fight on their home plane of Gehenna despite the fact that both sides sometimes traverse it and many battles of the Blood War are fought there. A yugoloth killed in Gehenna can't be restored to life except through an exceptional ritual, so the sums required to entice one to fight on its home plane are astronomical ... and making such a bargain always draws the attention of the ultroloths.

their efforts on the doorstep of the Nine Hells, realms such as the Seven Heavens and Bytopia are loath to commit aid to defend a plane that is inimical to everything they stand for by aiding the devils directly.

Therefore, the demons assault the Nine Hells over and over not only because it is the greatest threat to their dominion, but also because striking in force anywhere else would play into the devils' hands.

THE BALANCE

The demons and the devils both foresee their own versions of the future of the multiverse—a cosmos in which one side or the other triumphs in the Blood War and rules for the rest of eternity. A third point of view exists, held by those who take both sides at their word and strive to make sure that neither outcome ever comes to pass.

The adherents of this viewpoint refer to the concept they espouse as the Balance, and they seek to maintain equilibrium across the cosmos above all. Mordenkainen and his compatriots are among its most notable devotees. Since a true appreciation of the Balance and its implications requires a grasp of events on a cosmic level, very few people or entities fully embrace the idea. Those few, however, make up a formidable force that can mix martial and magical power to keep the extremists of the Blood War in check.

To an outside observer, a disciple of the Balance might act cruelly or heartlessly one day, and benevolent and caring the next. A follower might aid in consigning one city to domination by a devil cult while driving demonic cultists from another. For the sake of the Balance, the cosmos must remain in a static state where neither demon nor devil can permanently gain the upper hand.

Keepers of the Balance sometimes resort to strategies that seem inexplicable to those who don't grasp the whole situation. A crusading paladin might be discouraged from seeking out and defeating Demogorgon, because doing so could weaken the Abyss enough to allow the forces of the Nine Hells to gain a firm foothold there. An adherent of the Balance might vie with a great arcanist as both search for knowledge of a ritual that would cripple Asmodeus for a short time. The arcanist correctly believes that performing the ritual would free a world of the Material Plane from the devils' taint, but doesn't appreciate that it also would bring a grievous setback to the forces that had been keeping the demons from overrunning Avernus.

Those who vow to maintain the Balance make enemies wherever they go, because their full reasons for acting as they do aren't always apparent. The fact that some of these adherents embrace the Balance to further their personal quests for power makes it impossible to count on them as allies with complete certainty.

LORDS OF THE NINE

From his throne at the bottom of the Nine Hells, Asmodeus commands a sprawling bureaucracy tied to a massive war apparatus dedicated to turning back the demons that invade the uppermost realm of Avernus, and to taking the fight to the other planes, including the Abyss, whenever the opportunity arises.

Asmodeus and the other archdevils rule over the nine layers that comprise the Hells. The devil lords make up a hierarchy that is both rigid and fragile. Although Asmodeus is more powerful than any other lord, he has to be constantly wary of treachery within his ranks. It could be said that the true ruler of the Nine Hells is the immense body of rules and regulations that dictate how all devils, even Asmodeus, must conduct themselves.

LAYERS AND RULERS OF THE NINE HELLS

Layer	Layer Name	Ruler
1	Avernus	Zariel
2	Dis	Dispater
3	Minauros	Mammon
4	Phlegethos	Belial and Fierna
5	Stygia	Levistus
6	Malbolge	Glasya
7	Maladomini	Baalzebul
8	Cania	Mephistopheles
9	Nessus	Asmodeus

ASMODEUS

I LITERALLY SIT BENEATH EIGHT TIERS OF SCHEMING, *ambitious entities that represent primal law suffused with evil. The path from this realm leads to an infinite pit of chaos and evil. Now, tell me again how you and your ilk are the victims in this eternal struggle.*

—Asmodeus addresses the celestial jury, from *The Trial of Asmodeus*

Asmodeus is an unmatched strategist and orator. The most epic of all his achievements is chronicled in *The Trial of Asmodeus*, a play based on purportedly true events as researched by the aasimar bard Anodius.

In ancient times, as the Blood War raged, the angels of law and good that dwell on Mount Celestia issued a decree accusing Asmodeus of terrible crimes. Outraged by such claims, the Lord of the Nine Hells petitioned for the right to answer the charges before his accusers. The angels, although shocked at his impudence, accepted his petition and agreed to hear the bargain he proposed. Both sides, he suggested, would present their case to Primus, leader of the modrons. As a creature of absolute law, Primus could be trusted to issue a fair and impartial verdict. Asmodeus drafted a contract to seal the deal, and the angels—after carefully scrutinizing the terms—agreed to the trial.

When he testified before Primus, Asmodeus attributed his actions to the dictates of law and the survival of the cosmos. He admitted that he swayed mortals to evil, but he and his minions never breached a contract and explained the terms clearly. Had they not obeyed the rule of law in doing so? Was it not mortal ambition, rather than infernal deception, that led so many souls astray?

Asmodeus also pointed out that the souls harvested from the Material Plane went on to serve in the infernal legions that repel the endless tide of the Abyss. Were not such souls put to good use against the demonic hordes, a power that if unchecked would scour the universe of all lawfulness and goodness?

He further asserted that he was bound to the rules and traditions of the Nine Hells, compelled to adhere to law and to maintain the devils' trafficking in souls. If he violated those laws, he would be no better than the demons he fought. Mortals who refused a devil's offer were left alone, in accordance with the law. Those who struck deals with his followers and then somehow turned the contracts against the devils were freed from their debts. A contract is the law, and the law is a contract.

Primus weighed Asmodeus's words and listened patiently as angel after angel testified to his crimes. Hours turned to days and days into weeks as more and more of his sins entered the court record.

Even Primus's patience has its limits, and in time, the remaining angels who were eager to testify were told that only a few more would be allowed to speak. A brawl broke out when one angel, Zariel, pushed her way to the front and demanded to be heard. As the scuffle turned into a battle, Asmodeus looked on with a smirk.

In the end, Primus declined to issue a definitive judgment. He rebuked the angels for their descent into infighting, but didn't punish Asmodeus for his evil ways. He did, however, order Asmodeus to forever carry a mighty artifact, the *Ruby Rod*, that would guarantee his adherence to law. The artifact, which has remained at Asmodeus's side ever since, grants him and his underlings the right to enter into contracts with mortals for their souls but unleashes an inescapable punishment upon any devil that breaches such a contract.

He Who Would Rule

Asmodeus wants to rule the cosmos. Under his watch, he believes, the universe would take on a pristine, perfect state, with every living creature assigned a place in the infernal hierarchy. Wars would end, and every creature would have a purpose to fulfill. The universe would be a utopia, at least as Asmodeus views such a thing.

Of course, as he sees it, Asmodeus is the only being with the charisma, strength, and insight necessary to shepherd in this ideal future. His rivals are inferiors who, if left to their own devices, will turn the cosmos into a demon-infested maelstrom. The powers of good are sentimental fools, too delicate and soft to do what must be done. In his mind, Asmodeus has been chosen by the universe to protect it from annihilation.

If Asmodeus were any less capable, his arrogance would have led to his undoing long ago. Yet still he sits atop his throne, having thwarted every conspiracy mounted against him. He once walked into the lair of one of his enemies in Mount Celestia and survived using nothing more than his words and his wits. Even his most ardent enemies must grudgingly admit that his skill and competence are unparalleled.

Power without Limit

Unlike the other Lords of the Nine, Asmodeus has no quota of souls to fill. Any soul recruited by any denizen of the Nine Hells is also pledged in his name, and a cult dedicated to any other devil is also dedicated to him. Because he doesn't need to spend his time courting mortals, he concentrates on manipulating demigods and beings of similar station. Occasionally, he lures such a being into a contract and adds a new, unique devil to the ranks of the Hells. His most recent recruit is Zariel, a former angel. His supposed daughter, Glasya, is thought by some sages to be a godlike entity of unknown origin.

Lord of Nessus

Asmodeus resides in Nessus, the bottommost layer of the Nine Hells. By design, the place is devoid of activity, since Asmodeus values his privacy and safety. The environment is a rocky wasteland, crisscrossed by deep fissures and lacking roads, bridges, and other means of passage. Asmodeus dwells in a great fortress somewhere in the wasteland, at the bottom of its deepest pit. Only his most trusted followers and most important advisors know the route to it. He remains inside, relying on messengers and magic to convey his dictates.

Zariel

Keep wasting my time with your pointless words *and die, or join my war band and live. Choose swiftly. I have a plane to conquer.*

> —Zariel addressing emissaries from Dis

Zariel was once an angel, but her impetuous nature and love of battle led to her fall. In her previous life, she was charged with observing the battles on Avernus and tracking their progress. From this exposure, she grew obsessed with the Blood War, and a thirst for battle grew within her that she couldn't ignore. In time, she became frustrated that she and the other angels were forced to remain spectators while the demons and devils battled. The hosts of Mount Celestia, she believed, could descend upon Avernus en masse and wipe both hordes of evil from the cosmos if they so desired.

After her repeated requests to join the fray were denied, her frustration overtook her, and she launched herself into the Blood War. Accompanied by a mob of mortal followers, she cut a swath through a legion of devils before their numbers overwhelmed her. A delegation of bone devils later dispatched to the site by Asmodeus recovered her unconscious form beneath a small mountain of her slaughtered enemies. After allowing her to recover in the depths of Nessus, Asmodeus installed her on Avernus as his champion and new lord of that layer.

A Fighting General

When Zariel supplanted the pit fiend Bel as the ruler of Avernus, that change signaled a major shift in the devils' tactics. Zariel's fiery temperament and reckless maneuvering stand in stark contrast to Bel's approach, which relied on his expertise in logistics and defensive tactics to make steady but slow advances. Bel remains one of her chief lieutenants, and he doesn't discourage her reckless tactics in the hope that she will overextend her forces and suffer a defeat that leads to her removal.

For now, though, the devils are fighting with a berserker fury under her charge. Zariel leads their offensives herself, and her unyielding resolve coupled with the fighting skill of her underlings has pushed nearly all the demonic invaders out of Avernus.

THE WARRIOR'S GENERAL

Zariel is no politician. She lives to fight, and she bases her assessment of those she meets on a combination of their combat skills and their willingness to use those skills. In Zariel's eyes, zeal and fury are as important in a fight as iron discipline and extensive training.

That outlook has made her something of a political pariah, since she has spurned overtures of alliance from other Lords of the Nine and elected to swell the ranks of her armies through the aggressive recruitment of mortal souls. Her agents offer gifts of martial skill and courage to any who are willing to bargain. Zariel needs souls that yearn to prove their worth on the battlefield.

LADY OF RUIN

Zariel rules over the ruin that Avernus has become. Once it was a bustling realm filled with cities, trade outposts, and other features, but recent activity in the Blood War has reduced it to a blasted wasteland. The few structures still standing are citadels constructed by the devils to repel attackers, to be rebuilt each time the front line of the war moves. The devils are in control of Avernus at present, though the fighting goes on (as it always does) in isolated locales throughout the layer.

Adventurers able to avoid the other occupants can find treasure within some of the ruins, though they must venture to the fringes of the active conflict to have any hope of finding places that have not yet been looted.

Many of the active citadels on Avernus loom over the River Styx or surround portals to other planes or to Dis. An amnizu presides over each location, directing the lemures that emerge from the Styx, marshaling forces against invaders, and preventing unauthorized travel.

DISPATER

THE COSMOS IS A GRAND GAME. HE WHO KNOWS ITS *rules the best shall win the prize.*

—Dispater

Dispater is the foremost arms dealer of the Nine Hells, and perhaps the greatest weapons supplier in all the planes. As the lord of Dis, he oversees a mining and smelting operation that continually churns out weapons and armor. Using some of the great number of secret techniques Dispater has unearthed over his lifetime, the foundries of Dis produce deadly armaments that help to stem the abyssal tide. The fighting requires constant reinforcements, creating a voracious appetite for the products of the iron mines on Dis and the workshops in the sprawling metropolis that shares the name of the layer.

Dispater trusts no one and dislikes surprises. Since Zariel's rise to power, he has taken to dwelling in the libraries inside his iron palace. He employs a network of spies and informants to watch over anyone that might threaten him, a measure of his deep paranoia. Dispater has created an impenetrable suit of adamantine armor for himself, imbued with charms designed to foil spells and keep him safe in any environment, no matter how hostile. No one can guess at all of its features, since he crafted it using methods that only he has mastered.

Dispater's paranoia affects everything he does. For example, he often dispatches orders and other missives by branding his message on the back of an imp. The imp wears a leather vest that conceals the message, and the laces of the vest are knitted into the imp's heart. If the vest is removed by anyone other than the intended recipient, that act kills the imp and causes its body to disintegrate before the message can be read.

The lord of Dis measures everything in terms of the knowledge it contains and the secrets that can be gleaned from it. He yearns to solve every mystery of the cosmos, a quest that might seem foolhardy for anyone other than an immortal being. Any hint of a secret that remains hidden draws his attention, and a discovery that could tip the scales in his favor might be enough to entice him to act against his fellow Lords of the Nine.

Given his reclusive nature, gaining an audience with Dispater is difficult at best, with no guarantee that any correspondence truly reaches him.

THE GREATEST GAME

Dispater's trade in souls is concerned mainly with the acquisition of secrets. His imps scour the Material Plane in search of any lost lore that could help to turn a soul to Dispater's service. Such a secret could be a lost spell sought by a mighty archmage, who pledges fealty to Dispater in return for the knowledge, or it could be the identity of a petitioner's secret admirer. Dispater and his minions know that the perceived value of a secret is a highly subjective matter. A farmer has no use for an arcane spell that could incinerate a legion of warriors, but the promise of knowing which crops will sell best over the coming years might persuade him to enter into an infernal compact.

To Dispater, all of reality is a contest played out under secret rules. If he can discover the principles that define the true nature of the cosmos, he can learn how to ascend to the top of the Nine Hells' hierarchy and then eventually the entire planar order. He covets the souls of those who seek secrets and those who have useful, secret information of their own that he can bargain for.

If you must make a deal with a devil, Mammon might be your best option. Unfortunately, you need the wealth of a dozen kingdoms to close the deal if you don't want to offer your soul.

MAMMON

THE COUNT OF MY COINS IS MORE RELIABLE THAN ANY *roster of mortal hearts or immortal souls.*

—Mammon

Mammon is the foremost merchant and miser of the Nine Hells, and perhaps the richest entity in all the planes. As the lord of Minauros, Mammon oversees the soul trade. While those who pledge their souls are claimed by the devil they bargained with, lawful evil creatures that aren't bound by any contract emerge from the River Styx as lemures. Roving bands of soul-mongers patrol the river's banks, harvesting the newly created devils. On its arrival, each soul passes through the capital of Minauros, the Sinking City, and is recorded. The soul is then distributed to whoever should claim it, according to contracts in force and laws in effect. Mammon appropriates any extra lemures for himself and sells them for profit.

Mammon has accumulated a great treasure hoard, but spends only a small portion of it on maintaining his domain. As a result, Minauros is a fetid, wretched place, its structures characterized by cheap construction, flimsy materials, and shoddy artisanship.

EVERYTHING HAS A PRICE

Mammon measures everything in terms of its value in gold. He cares only for the material gain that a transaction can provide for him. He never rests, and spends every waking moment pursuing schemes to fatten his treasury. He looks for every opportunity to make his processes more efficient, so that he can rake in more and more gold in a given span of time.

Mammon's obsession with wealth and efficiency make him a dangerous entity to entreat. He enters any bargain with the goal of making a profit. Those who waste his time or tarry in their dealings with him are likely to incur his wrath. If he can't make an acceptable profit in

return for the time he has spent, he can at least vent his frustration by grinding the offending party into a thick, bloody sludge.

FINANCIER OF THE HELLS

Mammon's wealth is his primary way of exerting power and influence. He offers monetary loans to other devils in return for service, favors, or items he desires. From time to time, he dips into his coffers to attract mercenaries to ensure that a particularly virulent demonic advance is stopped—always in the expectation that the current lord of Avernus turns loot and booty obtained from the defeated demons over to him.

When they bargain with mortals, Mammon and his minions can offer irresistible wealth. Devils that are tasked with harvesting souls for Mammon carry with them *The Accounting and Valuation of All Things*, a manual that guides them in assessing the value of a soul in gold or other goods. The amount of gold that is needed to incite the greed of mortals is a minuscule drain on Mammon's treasury, but the transactions that he and his followers consummate draw in more souls than the efforts of any other Lord of the Nine.

A SHABBY KINGDOM

The layer of Minauros teeters on the edge of ruin. The realm is a great swamp, interspersed with cities and fortresses that are in constant need of repair, upkeep, and replacement. Time and again, structures built on this layer are left untended and are eventually drawn into the bottomless muck of the swamp.

Mammon refuses to spend any more coin than necessary to keep the soul marketplace in the Sinking City functioning. Devils and fiends from across the planes gather here to trade souls. The place bustles with activity as caravans arrive and depart and merchants haggle over their wares. Buildings rest haphazardly atop the ruins of those that have sloughed into the muck. The roads are little more than huge stones sunk into the swamp, needing constant replacement as they slowly submerge until the mud consumes them.

FIERNA AND BELIAL

A PALADIN? HOW EXQUISITE! SIT, PLEASE. REST. TELL ME *about the god that would send such a bright soul on so long and dark a journey.*

—Fierna

In the flaming realm of Phlegethos, Fierna and Belial rule in strange tandem. They are variously thought of by mortals as mother and son, daughter and father, wife and husband, or ruler and consort, but none of those terms can capture the paradoxical nature of their partnership. The Nine Hells is a hierarchy in which two individuals can't normally hold the same position as ruler of a single layer. Yet Asmodeus allows these two to claim dominion over Phlegethos as partners and rivals.

Fierna's charisma, equaled only by that of Asmodeus, makes her a brilliant manipulator capable of filling mortal and immortal hearts with whatever emotion she chooses to evoke. Belial, meanwhile, doesn't attempt to sway others with his interpersonal skills and focuses on the duties of ruling a layer of the Nine Hells. The two seem to hate and admire one another in equal measure and are in constant competition. Every time Belial outthinks Fierna, she talks her way out of whatever trap he has devised. Fierna stages insurrections against Belial, but his contingency plans rescue him from possible disaster. Other devils might gain a brief advantage over the two lords because of their infighting, but whenever any true threat to their rule arises, the seeming enemies cooperate to dispatch pretenders to their shared throne.

Fiery Realm of Dark Delights

The pair rules over Phlegethos, an expanse filled with immense volcanoes that expel rivers of lava into a sea of molten rock. The fires that burn throughout Phlegethos seem to be sentient. They leap at intruders, appearing to take delight in setting creatures and objects aflame.

At the same time, the fires of Phlegethos do no harm to any denizens of the Nine Hells. Even devils that are susceptible to fire suffer no injury or pain from exposure to them. The realm's primary city, Abriymoch, is a pleasure palace of sorts for devils that are enjoying a respite from their duties. Abriymoch is filled with devilish versions of taverns, theaters, casinos, and other entertainments. In contrast to the stiff regimentation of the rest of the Nine Hells, the laws that govern Abriymoch allow the place to operate as a carnival in which any wanton desire can be fulfilled.

Justice in All Its Forms

Phlegethos is the center of the Nine Hells' judicial system, which is overseen by Belial. Any disputes regarding contracts, accusations of cowardice in battle or dereliction of duty, and other criminal charges are resolved here. The Diabolical Court is an independent institution, answering only to Asmodeus. That fact doesn't discourage devils from constantly plotting to introduce new laws or to set precedents that they find advantageous. The court's function and its decisions are wholly dependent on the intricate laws of the Nine Hells, an impossibly complex code marred by a multitude of loopholes and exceptions that can cause any legal dealings to drag out for years before a resolution is reached.

Belial and his underlings also administer the procedure that determines the fate of devils that are in line for promotion or demotion. At the culmination of the process, the candidates are made vulnerable to the fires of Phlegethos through a special ritual designed for this purpose. The flames either bring searing agony that reduces a devil to a weaker form, or ecstatic joy that transforms it into a mightier being.

Soul Searching

Like the rulers of the other layers, Belial and Fierna have a quota of souls they must meet. Belial largely leaves this task to Fierna, even turning over to her the mortals that directly contact him. Fierna offers her supplicants the gift of personal influence, endowing them with a glib tongue and the ability to mold others' emotions as they see fit. Her agents typically concentrate on swaying mortals who already seek to manipulate others. Mortals who are desperate to attain positions of power

and status entreat her, as do those who—for whatever reason—need to be loved, feared, or respected.

Fierna takes a direct interest in the soul trade. Her prodigious intellect allows her to glean the best information from the mountains of reports generated by her agents on the Material Plane. Fierna sometimes personally takes a role in bending a mortal's emotions to her will, as a way to better understand the workings of mortal hearts and minds. What she or Belial intends to do with their accumulated knowledge none can definitively say, but rumors exist that Fierna has stolen the secret of how to travel freely between the Nine Hells and the Material Plane from the archlich Vecna. The fact that the denizens of the Nine Hells take such rumors seriously is a clear indication of their respect for Fierna's power.

Levistus

Though ice might hold my body in place, it has *done nothing to contain my ambition.*

—Levistus

Even by the otherworldly standards of the Nine Hells, the realm of Stygia and its lord, Levistus, both occupy strange positions in the hierarchy. Stygia is a frozen wasteland of mysterious origin, a churning, murky sea covered in a thick layer of ice. Where the ice gives way to open water, immense icebergs drift on the unpredictable currents. Levistus is trapped within one of these bergs, imprisoned there by Asmodeus for reasons that few can even guess about.

As part of Levistus's punishment, Asmodeus decreed that he must offer escape and safety to the desperate, especially those who fear for their lives. A criminal might entreat Levistus on the eve of his execution, for instance, agreeing to exchange his soul for a boon that enables him to escape to safety. With nothing to do in his tomb other than answer distant entreaties from the Material Plane, Levistus has attracted the devotion of a wide variety of criminals, rascals, and ne'er-do-wells across a multitude of worlds. He continues to meet his quota of souls, both despite his lack of mobility and because of it. Being imprisoned means that Levistus can focus his full attention on such matters, which allows him to excel at what he does.

A Contested Realm

Levistus was not always the lord of Stygia. The archdevil Geryon previously ruled over the layer. The two constantly vied for control of Stygia. The conflict ended when Asmodeus brought down his punishment on Levistus, who was frozen just after his latest victory over Geryon. The displaced lord still schemes to supplant Levistus as ruler of the realm, but he can't directly affect his foe, since the ice that imprisons Levistus is impervious to harm.

Violence does, however, remain a viable option for Geryon against Levistus's servants. As such, Stygia has become a war-wracked realm. Any devils bound to either of the archdevils that aren't needed for service in the Blood War engage in constant skirmishes across the ice, and yugoloths and other mercenaries from across the planes play a key role in the struggle. Both sides sometimes employ adventurers to seek out knowledge that could free Levistus or allow Geryon to vanquish him and ascend to the lordship.

Geryon fulfills his responsibilities in the soul trade by continuing to court mortals through his agents, offering them superior strength and great physical prowess in return for their allegiance.

A Frozen Wasteland

Every other layer of the Nine Hells has a function related to warfare, industry, administration, or commerce, but Stygia is an expanse of untamed, unimproved territory. Even so, it has its uses. All manner of unlikely beasts wander the frozen terrain and swim the seas, including remorhazes, krakens, mammoths, and even a few tribes of frost giants. These denizens have no fear of any other creatures, including devils, which makes the place an ideal proving ground. Lesser devils that need to sharpen their combat skills or improve their endurance before reporting to Avernus for duty in the Blood War spend time in Stygia. The cruelly cold environment, combined with the constant threat of attack, helps commanders assess their troops and place them into the various legions as appropriate for the skills they demonstrate.

The presence of so many creatures native to the Material Plane has led to speculation that Stygia was not always a layer of the Hells, but was previously a world on the Material Plane. Its inhabitants, facing annihilation, are said to have pledged their souls and their world to Asmodeus in return for a safe haven—whereupon Asmodeus kept his end of the bargain by transporting the world into the Hells. The archmage Tzunk has researched the topic extensively but has yet to find any evidence that truly confirms the account. If the supposition is true, then the riches of that world might lie under miles of ice and beneath frigid, monster-infested seas.

Glasya

OF COURSE I LOVE MY FATHER. WITHOUT HIM, WHOM *would I have to strive against?*

—Glasya

Malbolge is the prison of the Nine Hells, and on this layer dwells its most infamous criminal. Glasya, the rebellious daughter of Asmodeus, rules the place and oversees the punishments doled out to devils that stray from their assigned tasks. These lawbreakers are put on trial in Phlegethos, and if they are found guilty they are dispatched to Malbolge to endure years of torment. That Glasya is both prison warden and the Nine Hells' most notorious criminal is evidence that in the infernal realms, crime pays as long as you avoid being convicted.

Prison and Torture Chamber

Malbolge comprises one infinitely large, steep-sloped mountain. Boulders and other debris rain down from its heights in frequent avalanches. Some of the structures here are erected atop pillars of adamantine embedded in the mountain that can withstand the constant battering, though the platforms they support sway under the

---

Devils and Gender

To a devil, gender is insignificant. Devils can't create new life through physical means; a new devil comes into being only when a soul is corrupted or claimed in a bargain, and the gender of the mortal that provided the soul is immaterial. Devils that represent themselves to mortals are likely to adopt an appearance (including an apparent gender) that conforms with what those mortals believe to be true. Gender (and the assumptions that mortals make about it) is just another tool for devils to use to get what they want.

Devils that are known to and named by mortals often accept the gender assigned to them, but they aren't bound by that label. Stories of the Lords of the Nine told by mortals might speak of Glasya as Asmodeus's daughter and Belial as Fierna's consort, but such expressions can't encompass the complexities of the strange relationships formed by beings of immortal evil.

---

force of the onslaught. Condemned devils are typically trapped in cages, which are lowered on chains to hang beneath the platforms. From such a vantage, the prisoners are continually battered by Malbolge's avalanches, causing injuries that are agonizing but never fatal.

Some locations on the mountain are shielded from the rockfall by structures that have projections pointing upslope so that avalanches wash around the protected areas beneath. Roofed trenches and tunnels make travel between locations possible, if perilous.

A Singular Iconoclast

Of all the Lords of the Nine, Glasya is the most unpredictable. She flaunts the rules of tradition and bends the law without breaking it. She delights in shocking others by springing gambits that catch them unaware. Mortals who go up against overwhelming odds with an audacious plan attract her attention and could win her respect and patronage.

The reason behind Glasya's rise to lordship is the subject of much whispered debate in the Nine Hells. It is generally known that Asmodeus presented Glasya to the Lords of the Nine as his daughter, and she toured the Nine Hells on his behalf. While doing so, she put her own plans into motion, much to the surprise of the other archdevils. Even before Glasya assumed the rulership of Malbolge, she established the Hells' first organized crime syndicate, using her followers to purchase souls on her behalf while paying for them with what amounted to worthless coin.

Was it Asmodeus's intent all along that Glasya should strike out on her own, or was Glasya rebellious and clever enough to successfully defy her father? Was Glasya's rise to power an unforeseen benefit of her machinations, or is it a great embarrassment to Asmodeus? Likely only the two of them know the truth.

Coin Legions

Taking a cue from the sword, shield, and dreg legions into which the devils' armies are grouped, Glasya established a new category of "legion" to realize her plans for profit and power: the coin legions.

The members of Glasya's coin legions operate in the manner of thieves' guilds on the Material Plane. They have one critical advantage compared to their mortal contemporaries: Glasya's knowledge of the law. She knew that in many cases, procedures that devils observed and obeyed as laws were merely traditions, and failing to observe a tradition carries no penalty according to the law of the Hells.

Glasya's scheme involved using counterfeit currency to buy souls in Minauros, then selling them soon after to turn an incredible profit. When the truth of her dealings became apparent, she defended her actions based on the legal definition of a coin as minted in Minauros.

According to law, the gold composition of a coin was strictly defined at the time of the coin's creation, but no law governed a coin's state after it left the mint. As long as it was made in the mint, it was legal currency.

Glasya got around the law by transmuting lead to gold, then having coins minted from the substance. After she claimed her currency and her coin legions spent it on her purchases, the magic expired and the gold became lead once more.

Asmodeus, although he couldn't punish Glasya for breaking the law, decided to discipline her by doing something only he could do: making her an archdevil. He reasoned that, now that she was effectively tied to a single layer of the Hells and saddled with responsibilities in her capacity as prison warden, her ambitions would be kept in check.

An Ironic Sphere of Influence

To make Glasya's workload even more onerous (and to serve as an ironic form of punishment), Asmodeus decreed that Glasya could entice souls into the Nine Hells only through delving into matters of contracts, bargains, and legalities. She and her agents offer mortal petitioners advice on how to manipulate or circumvent the law, or to identify escape clauses—all to ensure that whatever they desire can be obtained without violating a legal precedent.

Her petitioners want power, money, and love, but they want to come by it within the bounds of the law. An ambitious prince who is entitled by law to inherit his parents' wealth but doesn't want to murder them might ask for help, and Glasya's agents provide it by arranging for them to die in an accident.

A notable portion of Glasya's petitioners are souls who have pledged themselves to another Lord of the Nine and want out of the bargain. Her minions scour every contract struck with another devil and approach mortals whose contracts contain loopholes. In return for giving their souls to her instead, such individuals learn how to break the contract and negate whatever price the contract says they must pay.

Baalzebul

THROUGH SUFFICIENT PENANCE AND GRACE, EVEN THE *lowliest can redeem themselves. Am I not a living testament to that fact?*

—Baalzebul

Maladomini was once a bustling realm of vibrant cities and a panoply of roads, gardens, and bridges. It was the center of the Hells' bureaucracy, where every edict, law, and order was dutifully copied and filed away. With each

Never forget that devils can speak lies to you at will, even though one might promise not to. Only a contract with the devil—one that it will try to get you to sign—can make it speak true. Even then, its talk will be leavened with vagueness to lead you to draw the wrong conclusions.

passing year, the devils would add more fortresses and archives to Maladomini to house all their records.

Then came the single greatest act of treachery in the annals of the Nine Hells. At the time, the archdevil Baalzebul was so powerful that he ruled two layers of the Hells, Maladomini and Malbolge. He conspired to topple Asmodeus and replace him, which in itself was not a crime. But in order to work his plans, he knowingly altered documents that passed into his care with the intent of confounding the apparatus of the bureaucracy. Before his scheme could come to fruition, he was caught and subjected to the most bizarre of punishments.

In that time long past, Baalzebul believed that he could cast Asmodeus as incompetent and amass a force to replace him before Asmodeus's allies could act, but his calculations failed to take into account the unpredictability of the Blood War. A sudden offensive from the Abyss struck Avernus just as Baalzebul was about to put his plan in motion. Baalzebul directed most of his shield legions to stay out of the fight, instead of helping to hold the line against the demons, so that he could use them in staging his coup. The absence of those legions, however, enabled the horde to push close to the doorstep of Dis.

Baalzebul was forced to abandon his plans, realizing that the Nine Hells would be of little use to him if it was overrun with demons, and ultimately he united with the other archdevils to turn back the invasion. But when an investigation of the events uncovered his treachery, Baalzebul didn't submit to punishment, and Maladomini was wracked with fighting as the other Lords of the Nine took to the field against the conspirator. The resulting devastation left much of the layer in ruins.

After Baalzebul was overwhelmed and defeated, Asmodeus stripped him of his rulership of Malbolge but left him in charge of Maladomini, albeit with a new set of duties. Asmodeus knew that Baalzebul's superior intellect and propensity for lying would make him the ideal representative of the bureaucracy of the Hells in the worlds of mortals. So, to ensure his loyalty while taking advantage of his talents, Asmodeus enacted two laws concerning him.

First, whenever Baalzebul lied to a devil, he would transform into a slug-like creature, hideous to all who beheld him, for one year. This penalty was retroactive, covering several millennia of deceptions and untruths—and only recently has Baalzebul worked off all those transgressions and been returned to his former humanoid form. In all that time, he has not told a lie to another devil, and his continued honesty is motivated by his desire to keep his current appearance.

Second, Asmodeus decreed that any deal Baalzebul strikes shall end in disaster for the other party. For this reason, other devils avoid forming alliances with him, even though they know he is compelled not to lie to them. Mortals, on the other hand, know nothing of the situation and still offer their souls to him.

His ability to scheme neutralized by these limitations, Baalzebul continues to ensure that the devils' bureaucracy runs smoothly. He focuses most of his attention on gathering souls from the Material Plane, a task to which his talent for lying is well suited.

A MAZE OF INFORMATION

Every edict, policy statement, scientific treatise, and other document in the Nine Hells is recorded, copied, and filed away in Maladomini's archives. These storehouses are buried deep underground, so that they would remain intact if the layer is ever again hit by the sort of devastation that occurred when Baalzebul was brought to heel.

Each document in the archives is important in its own way, and all these sites are heavily guarded by devils and traps. Even if would-be thieves could get around the defenses, they would have figure out how to navigate the complex classification system that marks the precise location of each bit of paperwork stored within.

THE PRICE OF REDEMPTION

Baalzebul and his agents recruit mortals that are desperate for redemption of some sort, perhaps the restoration of lost status or the recovery of resources that were lost because of treachery or incompetence. To these people who have been humbled by unfortunate events, Baalzebul offers a supernatural means of regaining one's reputation or riches. The failed merchant desperate for another chance at making his fortune or the once-traitorous knight eager to restore her honor are examples of the individuals he deals with.

What those folk don't know is that Baalzebul is a master manipulator. He directs his agents to embed clauses and specifications in contracts that trip up the unwary. Because Baalzebul's targets are typically desperate, he almost always bargains from a position of strength.

Although Baalzebul claims a great number of unsuspecting souls, almost all of them are pathetic, incompetent wretches best suited for the dreg legions, whose only task is to die as slowly as possible so that they might delay the advance of an abyssal army.

MEPHISTOPHELES

THERE ARE FEW PROBLEMS THAT CANNOT BE SOLVED *through the application of overwhelming arcane firepower.*

—Mephistopheles

Cania, like Stygia above it, is a bitterly cold realm of glaciers and howling ice storms. Mephistopheles holds court here with the ice devils that make up his retinue. Operating from his great tower, the icy citadel of Mephistar, he conducts a never-ending series of experiments that expand his understanding of arcane magic and of the planes of existence.

Devils bargain with mortals to upend the divine order. They stake claims on souls that would otherwise go to the gods or be cast adrift somewhere other than the Nine Hells. If you are already a creature of Law and Evil devoted to no other entity, your damned spirit is of meager value.

Mephistopheles keeps his realm churning with punishing storms. He doesn't entertain visitors, and Asmodeus has charged him with maintaining a stout security force around Nessus. Travelers that aren't protected against the environment, which is cold enough to kill a creature in seconds, have little hope of surviving.

The foremost wizard in the Hells, Mephistopheles suffers nothing that would compromise his intellectual focus. He hates distractions and allows only particular devils to speak to him without first being spoken to. He has been known to disintegrate minions for the smallest transgressions, and sometimes carries out an execution simply because he suspected that a devil was about to do something to annoy him.

Mephistopheles is able to devote almost all his time to his research thanks to the loyalty of Hutijin, his top lieutenant. Even though Hutijin commands enough power to threaten his master's position, he is content to remain at the right hand of the throne, at least for the time being.

EXPERIMENTS IN THE UNKNOWN

Cania is essentially an enormous laboratory. Mephistopheles and his devotees prefer to conduct their studies in a wasteland where they can unleash gouts of arcane energy without destroying anything important. Experiments involving new spells, new magic items, and other innovations for the infernal arsenal regularly cause localized cataclysms in this place.

This activity attracts numerous spies despite the inhospitable environment. Merely observing Mephistopheles's disciples at work can provide insights into the nature of their research and the discoveries they have made. His court is constantly alert for agents from Dis, since it greatly pains Dispater that Mephistopheles might come across a scrap of information that he doesn't possess. A number of renowned archmages, including Mordenkainen, have at times found their way into this realm on a search for forgotten lore or in the hope of confirming a theory of arcane magic.

KEEPER OF ARCANE SOULS

Mephistopheles and his followers specialize in luring wizards and sages into making compacts with the Nine Hells. Of all the Lords of the Nine, he has the lowest quotas but the highest standards. He harvests the souls of skilled wizards and cunning sages, exactly the sort of folk he needs to further his research. Curiosity and ambition are motivating factors that entice such souls into his service—often, a mage who gets an opportunity to join the cause of Mephistopheles sees that invitation as proof of one's ascension to greatness.

The downside to this arrangement is the true nature of Mephistopheles, which is apparent only after a new contract is signed. He can be charming when he recruits a soul directly, and his agents are careful to avoid making any promises about his actions or attitudes. But once a soul arrives in the Nine Hells to serve him, it invariably faces decades of routine work or tedious study.

Thus, few who join his stable of arcanists remain happy with their decision, but they would be well advised not to show any discontent. Mephistopheles fills his contracts with cleverly worded clauses that allow him to annihilate any of his servants with a word. As further protection against dissent, he isolates his minions, allowing them to gather in small groups only when needed to carry on their work. Even then, the law of Mephistopheles prohibits all but the most vital communication, limited to why they have come together. Some of the most skilled but most gullible former wizards of the Material Plane now toil eternally in Cania, alone except for their books, their tools, and their regrets.

STOREHOUSES OF LORE

Libraries and other places where arcane knowledge is recorded or contained are scattered across Cania, mainly to ensure that a single disastrous experiment at one location can't destroy the evidence of all the work conducted at other sites. In his pursuit of ever more lore, Mephistopheles combines his prodigious intellect with his obsessive nature. This combination of traits enables him to delve far more deeply into a topic than most ordinary wizards can even conceive of. Even the tiniest of trivialities is fascinating to him.

Sometimes, however, the business of the Nine Hells forces him to relinquish direct oversight of a project. When he returns to his research, a new mystery might capture his fancy, while the older project continues to move forward without his oversight or interference.

Here and there, tucked away in Cania's terrible environment and similarly buried in the immense bureaucracy of the Hells, stand long-isolated citadels occupied by sages and spellcasters toiling away at some seemingly forgotten endeavor. The supervisors of these projects might have achieved incredible results that they patiently wait to share with Mephistopheles the next time his attention points in their direction.

THE RANK AND FILE

While the Lords of the Nine set the overall direction of the Hells, it is the rank and file—uncounted numbers of lesser devils—that drive their schemes forward. Denizens of the Material Plane deal primarily with devils from the lower tiers of the hierarchy.

ALL CREATURES IN THEIR PLACES

Status is all-important to devils. Every devil knows its place in the hierarchy, and each devil has a unique name to ensure that no cases of mistaken identity occur when a devil is called to account for its actions.

A devil's form usually corresponds to its status, but circumstances can allow for variations. A pit fiend, for instance, might take the form of an imp in order to personally infiltrate a kingdom on the Material Plane.

The hierarchy of the Nine Hells has thirteen tiers or ranks. A devil of a higher rank can potentially compel those beneath it to obey its orders, but it must still abide by the law when exercising its authority. In most cases, a devil can demand the obedience of another devil only if both are in the hierarchy of the same archdevil. For example, a devil in service to Dispater can't command a lower-ranked devil among the forces of Levistus.

Lowest of the Low. At the bottom of the hierarchy are lemures and nupperibos, creatures that qualify as devils only by the most generous of definitions. Although they are individually worthless, they constitute an effective fighting force when gathered into a teeming horde that floods the battlefield.

Lesser Devils. The next six higher tiers are occupied by the lesser devils: imps (rank 2), spined devils (rank 3), bearded devils and merregons (rank 4), barbed devils (rank 5), chain devils (rank 6), and bone devils (rank 7). These devils are specialists, typically assigned to tasks that best suit their capabilities. Imps are used as spies and messengers rather than combatants, and they are the infernal agents most often encountered on the Material Plane. Lesser devils rarely command other devils, aside from specific, short-term assignments for which they are invested with authority.

Greater Devils. Grouped in the four tiers above the lesser devils are the greater devils: horned devils and orthons (rank 8), erinyes (rank 9), ice devils and narzugons (rank 10), and amnizus and pit fiends (rank 11). Lesser devils deal with these leaders on a daily basis. Ice devils are combat commanders, equivalent to captains and colonels, while pit fiends are the Hells' generals and nobles.

Archdevils. The mightiest devils of all are the unique and uniquely powerful archdevils. Those who don't presently serve as lord of a layer hold the title of Duke or Duchess (rank 12). Atop the hierarchy at rank 13 stand the Lords of the Nine, arrayed from topmost layer to bottommost, with Asmodeus holding sway over all.

RULES FOR EVERYTHING

Devils are evil schemers by nature, but they must operate within the bounds of the Nine Hells' intricate legal code. A devil's attitude toward the law is in part driven by its personal attitude and situation.

For instance, devils that fight in the Blood War rely on military regulations and their officers' directions to dictate their actions. They obey orders without question, and take part in drills when off duty to ensure that they act to the exact parameters of their instructions.

Some other devils, particularly those of higher ranks and those tasked with infiltrating the Material Plane, see the law as a puzzle to be decoded or an obstacle to be circumvented. For instance, a devil might be bound by law never to withhold aid from its commander except under rare and specific circumstances. A clever upstart that wants to annihilate its superior could manipulate events to bring about one such circumstance, then look on as the commander succumbs while it cites the law that "prevents" it from offering help.

Devils look at mortals as sheep, just as demons do, except devils see themselves not as wolves but as shepherds. Shepherds fleece sheep by the season and slaughter them as needed. A shepherd likely kills the wolves that threaten its sheep. But then again, shepherds always expect to lose a few sheep.

If you were a sheep, would you trust your shepherd?

THREE PATHS TO POWER

Rank-and-file devils have three ways of ascending through the ranks. The Nine Hells uses a complex system of rules to quantify and recognize a devil's deeds.

Souls. Each time a devil signs a contract that pledges a mortal's soul to the Nine Hells, that devil receives credit for the achievement. A stronger soul, such as a mighty warrior who leaves mortality behind to become an ice devil, is worth more than a simple peasant likely to be consigned to existence as a lemure.

Glory. All devils are required to fight in the Blood War. Every low-ranking devil spends at least some time on the front lines as part of a legion. Some find combat enticing and volunteer for extra missions. Others are content to do only the minimum needed to fulfill their obligations, but they fight just as furiously when they are engaged. A devil receives credit for each foe it slays, based on the worthiness of the opponent and whether the devil scored the kill alone or with the help of others.

Treachery. Just as the law has complex rules for the promotion of devils under normal circumstances, it also includes contingencies for how to fill a sudden vacancy in the upper ranks. Vaulting into the position formerly occupied by one's superior is the fastest means of advancement available to a devil. A devil that successfully arranges for a superior's death can immediately step into the vacant role, as long as the devil is aware of the rules of succession and positions itself as next in line.

DIABOLICAL CULTS

Cults dedicated to infernal beings are the foes of adventurers throughout the D&D multiverse. This section gives the DM ways to customize the members of cults dedicated to the powers of the Nine Hells.

Every archdevil attracts a certain type of person based on the gifts the devil offers. In the following cult descriptions, stat blocks from the *Monster Manual* are suggested in a cult's Typical Cultist entry to help you represent those people.

Each description also includes a list of signature spells associated with the cult. If a cult member can cast spells, you can replace any of those spells with spells from that list, as long as the new spell is of the same level as the spell it replaces.

The customization options here will typically have no appreciable effect on the challenge rating of a creature that gains them.

CULT OF ASMODEUS

Asmodeus demands the loyalty of all cultists who gain power and leadership in the cults of the Nine. His cult subsumes all the others.

Any NPC who leads a diabolical cult must acknowledge the power of Asmodeus. In return, the most worthy of those leaders gain the Demands of Nessus trait.

Demands of Nessus. At the start of each of this creature's turns, this creature can choose one ally it can see within 30 feet of it. The chosen ally loses 10 hit points, and this creature regains the same number of hit points. If the creature is incapacitated, it makes no choice; instead, the closest ally within 30 feet is the chosen ally.

CULT OF BAALZEBUL

Goals: Restoration of honor and respect, at the cost of those who stole it
Typical Cultist: Any NPC or monster that has suffered a fall from grace
Signature Spells: *Minor illusion* (cantrip), *disguise self* (1st level), *phantasmal force* (2nd level), *major image* (3rd level)

Baalzebul typically recruits individuals rather than cults. He offers hope to those whose failures drive them to seek redemption.

He grants a boon, the Path of Baalzebul trait, that allows a favored cultist to look good in the aftermath of an ally's failure.

Path of Baalzebul. As a bonus action on its turn, this creature can choose one ally it can see within 30 feet of it. Until the start of this creature's next turn, it gains advantage on all ability checks and attack rolls, while the chosen ally suffers disadvantage on all ability checks, attack rolls, and saving throws.

CULT OF DISPATER

Goals: Power gained and used in secret, influence exerted via blackmail, control of people and organizations through knowledge of their weaknesses and shames
Typical Cultist: Acolyte, bandit, bandit captain, cult fanatic, cultist, mage, noble, spy
Signature Spells: *Guidance* (cantrip), *identify* (1st level), *see invisibility* (2nd level), *clairvoyance* (3rd level)

Dispater trades in secrets, offering them in return for a creature's soul. His cults typically trade secrets to devils in return for other information. They often hatch conspiracies aimed at toppling and replacing governments or religious orders.

Renegade mind flayers sometimes strike pacts with Dispater in search of the secrets needed to forever escape an elder brain's domination.

Cultists can gain the Infernal Insight trait. Cult leaders might also have the Vexing Escape trait.

Infernal Insight (Recharges after a Short or Long Rest). As a bonus action, this creature gains advantage on all ability checks and attack rolls it makes until the end of the current turn.

Vexing Escape (1/Day). As a reaction when this creature takes damage, it reduces that damage to 0 and teleports up to 60 feet to an unoccupied space it can see.

CULT OF FIERNA

Goals: Control over the emotions of others, turning them into puppets and playthings

Typical Cultist: Acolyte, archmage, bandit captain, cult fanatic, cultist, knight, noble, priest, spy

Signature Spells: *Friends* (cantrip), *charm person* (1st level), *suggestion* (2nd level), *hypnotic pattern* (3rd level)

Fierna is a master manipulator. Mortals who desire success in love or who seek to become beloved leaders at the head of a band of fanatics are drawn to striking bargains with her.

Her cultists can gain the Infernal Loyalty trait. Cult leaders can also gain the Loyalty beyond Death trait.

Infernal Loyalty. This creature has advantage on saving throws while it can see a creature within 30 feet of it that has the Loyalty beyond Death trait.

Loyalty beyond Death (Recharges after a Short or Long Rest). As a reaction when an ally this creature can see is reduced to 0 hit points, that ally is instead reduced to 1 hit point and gains temporary hit points equal to this creature's Charisma score + half its number of Hit Dice.

CULT OF GERYON

Goals: Physical prowess, domination of others through strength, destruction of all opposition

Typical Cultist: Bandit, bandit captain, berserker, cult fanatic, cultist, gladiator, thug, tribal warrior, veterans

Signature Spells: *Shillelagh* (cantrip), *wrathful smite* (1st level), *enhance ability* (2nd level), *aura of vitality* (3rd level)

Despite being deposed, Geryon still has the ability to strike bargains. He deals especially with those who seek brute strength. Any warlike monster—such as orcs, ogres, and trolls—can be lured into Geryon's cult.

His cultists typically form fighting companies and bandit gangs, proving their strength by defeating others in battle and taking what they want as loot.

Members of the cult can gain the Crushing Blow trait. Cult leaders can also gain the Indomitable Strength trait.

Crushing Blow (Recharges after a Short or Long Rest). As a bonus action, the creature gains a bonus to the damage roll of its next melee weapon attack that hits within the next minute. The bonus equals its Strength modifier (minimum of +1).

Indomitable Strength (Recharge 5–6). As a reaction when this creature takes damage, it can roll a d10 and subtract the number rolled from the damage.

CULT OF GLASYA

Goals: Power gained by turning a system against itself, yielding power that isn't only absolute but legitimate on a cultural and legal basis

Typical Cultist: Bandit, bandit captain, cult fanatic, cultist, knight, noble, spy, thug

Signature Spells: *Friends* (cantrip), *charm person* (1st level), *invisibility* (2nd level), *haste* (3rd level)

As an expert in finding loopholes and exploiting the law for her own good, Glasya is a patron of thieves and other criminals, especially corrupt nobles. Her influence is supposed to strengthen family bonds, but she has taken a liberal interpretation of that and offers gifts that can be turned against family members.

Goblins who risk insurrection against their hobgoblin masters make pacts with Glasya, as do kenku who form criminal gangs.

Glasya grants the Step into Shadows trait. Cult leaders can also gain the Infernal Ring Leader trait.

Step into Shadows (Recharges after a Short or Long Rest).
As an action, this creature, along with anything it is wearing and carrying, magically becomes invisible until the end of its next turn.

Infernal Ring Leader. As a reaction when this creature is hit by an attack, it can choose one ally it can see within 5 feet of it and cause that ally to be hit by that attack instead.

CULT OF LEVISTUS

Goals: Survival and eventual revenge against those who wrong them

Typical Cultist: Assassin, bandit captain, cult fanatic, cultist, mage, noble, spy, thug

Signature Spells: *Blade ward* (cantrip), *expeditious retreat* (1st level), *spider climb* (2nd level), *gaseous form* (3rd level)

Levistus has no cult in the traditional sense. Instead, he offers favors to those who are desperate to escape a seemingly inevitable fate.

Drow are sometimes worshipers of Levistus, as their cruel society often pushes them into situations they feel they can't escape.

WHY DEVILS WANT CULTS

For all their might, most devils are effectively trapped in the Nine Hells. While other planar creatures use magic to move between planes, devils require either a portal they can physically walk through or a summoning conducted by an entity on a distant plane. They have little will in determining where they go.

Because of this restriction, on the Material Plane most devils work through cults. Cults typically consist of folk who have used rituals to contact devils and pledge their souls to them in return for power. The Lords of the Nine drive most of the soul trade, and the gifts they can offer are determined by Asmodeus's decrees.

Levistus usually grants those who pledge their souls to him a single chance to escape from danger, but some cunning folk strike a deal with Levistus, pledging their souls to him in return for escape at a future date. This boon takes the form of the Path of Levistus trait.

Path of Levistus. This creature magically teleports to a location of Levistus's choice within 1 mile of its location. Using this ability also restores all of the creature's hit points. This ability can be invoked as an action by the creature or when the creature would die. Once the creature uses it, the creature can't use it again.

CULT OF MAMMON

Goals: Wealth, secured not only to promise personal comfort and power but to deny wealth and its benefits to others.

Typical Cultist: Bandit, bandit captain, cult fanatic, cultist, noble, spy, thug

Signature Spells: *Mending* (cantrip), *Tenser's floating disk* (1st level), *arcane lock* (2nd level), *glyph of warding* (3rd level)

Mammon's greed overwhelms everything else. He deals with mortals who desire material wealth and provides them with the ability to spread that greed like an infection.

The greedy duergar and even some dragons are prone to falling prey to Mammon's temptations, and merchants and trade guilds are vulnerable to his bargains.

Mammon's cultists can gain the Grasping Hands trait. Cult leaders can also gain the Promise of Wealth trait.

Grasping Hands (Recharges after a Short or Long Rest). As a bonus action, this creature makes a Dexterity (Sleight of Hand) check contested by the Wisdom (Insight) check of a creature it can see within 15 feet of it. If this creature succeeds, one hand-held item of its choice that it can see on the target magically teleports to its open hand. The item can't be one that the target is holding, and it must weigh no more than 10 pounds.

Promise of Wealth (Recharges after a Short or Long Rest). As a bonus action, this creature chooses one creature it can see. Up to five allies of its choice become convinced that the target carries great wealth. Until the end of this creature's next turn, those allies gain advantage on all attack rolls against the target.

CULT OF MEPHISTOPHELES

Goals: Magical skill and power, backed with the will to use it to crush rivals

Typical Cultist: Archmage, cult fanatic, cultist, mage, priest

Signature Spells: *Fire bolt* (cantrip), *burning hands* (1st level), *flaming sphere* (2nd level), *fireball* (3rd level)

As a master of the arcane arts, Mephistopheles finds eager recruits among those who study magic. Any monsters that use spells, such as storm giants and oni, might follow him, and wizards' guilds and conclaves of sages are the most likely to come under his influence.

Mephistopheles's cultists can gain the Spell Shield trait. Cult leaders can also gain the Spell Leech trait.

Spell Shield. This creature gains advantage on saving throws against spells. If it succeeds on such a saving throw, it gains temporary hit points equal to the spell's level.

Spell Leech. As a bonus action, this creature chooses one ally it can see within 30 feet of it. The target loses its lowest-level spell slot, and this creature gains it.

CULT OF ZARIEL

Goals: Conquest, glory in battle, fame and fortune derived from military victory

Typical Cultist: Berserker, cult fanatic, cultist, gladiator, guard, knight, veteran

Signature Spells: *True strike* (cantrip), *heroism* (1st level), *spiritual weapon* (2nd level), *crusader's mantle* (3rd level)

Zariel's cult offers martial training and talent. It flourishes in areas wracked by war. Refugees with the will to fight but lacking experience are drawn to Zariel, as she can provide them with the skills needed to survive. Established warriors looking for an edge are otherwise her most common recruits.

Knightly orders, fighters' guilds, and mercenary companies are the most likely to come under her sway. Hobgoblins sometimes turn to her, but only if they have escaped the influence of Maglubiyet and his priests.

Zariel's cultists can gain the Ferocious Surge trait. Cult leaders can also gain the Infernal Tactics trait.

Ferocious Surge (Recharges after a Short or Long Rest). When this creature hits with an attack that isn't a critical hit, it can turn the hit into a critical hit.

Infernal Tactics. This creature has a keen eye for seizing a tactical advantage. Immediately after rolling initiative, it can choose itself and up to three allies it can see if it isn't incapacitated. It can swap the initiative results of the chosen creatures among them.

INFERNAL CAMBIONS

Some archdevils consort with mortals to produce cambion offspring. While most have the typical abilities for a cambion (as detailed in the *Monster Manual*), some gain abilities reminiscent of their archdevil parent.

SIGNATURE SPELLS

Cambions have the Innate Spellcasting trait. When customizing an infernal cambion, you can replace spells in that trait with ones of the same level from the list of signature spells in the cult entry of the devilish parent. The cambion can use these spells once per day each.

SPECIAL TRAITS

A cambion linked to a specific devil typically gains any special traits conferred to that devil's cultists.

Some devils grant a unique ability to their spawn that replaces the cambion's Fiendish Charm trait; Zariel and Geryon have a penchant for spawning cambions to serve as war leaders among their followers. The two of them grant the Fury of the Nine ability in place of Fiendish Charm.

Fury of the Nine. As a bonus action, the cambion chooses another creature that can see or hear it within 120 feet. That creature gains advantage on all attack rolls and saving throws for the next minute or until the cambion uses this ability again.

TIEFLING SUBRACES

At the DM's option, you can create a tiefling character who has a special link to one of the Lords of the Nine Hells. This link is represented by a subrace.

SUBRACE TRAITS

If your tiefling has a subrace, choose one of the following options—whichever one corresponds to the infernal being connected to the tiefling's family.

The traits of the chosen subrace replace the tiefling's Ability Score Increase and Infernal Legacy traits given in the *Player's Handbook*. There is one exception: tieflings connected to Asmodeus. Those tieflings use the traits in the *Player's Handbook*.

ASMODEUS

The tieflings connected to Nessus command the power of fire and darkness, guided by a keener than normal intellect, as befits those linked to Asmodeus himself. Such tieflings use the Ability Score Increase and Infernal Legacy traits in the *Player's Handbook*.

BAALZEBUL

The crumbling realm of Maladomini is ruled by Baalzebul, who excels at corrupting those whose minor sins can be transformed into acts of damnation. Tieflings linked to this archdevil can corrupt others both physically and psychically.

Ability Score Increase. Your Charisma score increases by 2, and your Intelligence score increases by 1.

Legacy of Maladomini. You know the *thaumaturgy* cantrip. When you reach 3rd level, you can cast the *ray of sickness* spell as a 2nd-level spell once with this trait and regain the ability to do so when you finish a long rest. When you reach 5th level, you can cast the *crown of madness* spell once with this trait and regain the ability to do so when you finish a long rest. Charisma is your spellcasting ability for these spells.

DISPATER

The great city of Dis occupies most of Hell's second layer. It is a place where secrets are uncovered and shared with the highest bidder, making tieflings tied to Dispater excellent spies and infiltrators.

Ability Score Increase. Your Charisma score increases by 2, and your Dexterity score increases by 1.

Legacy of Dis. You know the *thaumaturgy* cantrip. When you reach 3rd level, you can cast the *disguise self* spell once with this trait and regain the ability to do so when you finish a long rest. When you reach 5th level, you can cast the *detect thoughts* spell once with this trait and regain the ability to do so when you finish a long rest. Charisma is your spellcasting ability for these spells.

FIERNA

A master manipulator, Fierna grants tieflings tied to her forceful personalities.

Ability Score Increase. Your Charisma score increases by 2, and your Wisdom score increases by 1.

Legacy of Phlegethos. You know the *friends* cantrip. When you reach 3rd level, you can cast the *charm person* spell as a 2nd-level spell once with this trait and regain the ability to do so when you finish a long rest. When you reach 5th level, you can cast the *suggestion* spell once with this trait and regain the ability to do so when you finish a long rest. Charisma is your spellcasting ability for these spells.

GLASYA

Glasya, Hell's criminal mastermind, grants her tieflings magic that is useful for committing heists.

Ability Score Increase. Your Charisma score increases by 2, and your Dexterity score increases by 1.

Legacy of Malbolge. You know the *minor illusion* cantrip. When you reach 3rd level, you can cast the *disguise self* spell once with this trait and regain the ability to do so when you finish a long rest. When you reach 5th level, you can cast the *invisibility* spell once with this trait and regain the ability to do so when you finish a long rest. Charisma is your spellcasting ability for these spells.

LEVISTUS

Frozen Stygia is ruled by Levistus, an archdevil known for offering bargains to those who face an inescapable doom.

Ability Score Increase. Your Charisma score increases by 2, and your Constitution score increases by 1.

Legacy of Stygia. You know the *ray of frost* cantrip. When you reach 3rd level, you can cast the *armor of Agathys* spell as a 2nd-level spell once with this trait and regain the ability to do so when you finish a long rest. When you reach 5th level, you can cast the *darkness* spell once with this trait and regain the ability to do so when you finish a long rest. Charisma is your spellcasting ability for these spells.

MAMMON

The great miser Mammon loves coins above all else. Tieflings tied to him excel at gathering and safeguarding wealth.

Ability Score Increase. Your Charisma score increases by 2, and your Intelligence score increases by 1.

Legacy of Minauros. You know the *mage hand* cantrip. When you reach 3rd level, you can cast the *Tenser's floating disk* spell once with this trait and regain the ability to do so when you finish a short or long rest. When you reach 5th level, you can cast the *arcane lock* spell once with this trait, requiring no material component, and regain the ability to do so when you finish a long rest. Charisma is your spellcasting ability for these spells.

MEPHISTOPHELES

In the frozen realm of Cania, Mephistopheles offers arcane power to those who entreat with him. Tieflings linked to him master some arcane magic.

Ability Score Increase. Your Charisma score increases by 2, and your Intelligence score increases by 1.

Legacy of Cania. You know the *mage hand* cantrip. When you reach 3rd level, you can cast the *burning hands* spell as a 2nd-level spell once with this trait and regain the ability to do so when you finish a long rest. When you reach 5th level, you can cast the *flame blade* spell once with this trait and regain the ability to do so when you finish a long rest. Charisma is your spellcasting ability for these spells.

ZARIEL

Tieflings with a blood tie to Zariel are stronger than the typical tiefling and receive magical abilities that aid them in battle.

Ability Score Increase. Your Charisma score increases by 2, and your Strength score increases by 1.

Legacy of Avernus. You know the *thaumaturgy* cantrip. When you reach 3rd level, you can cast the *searing smite* spell as a 2nd-level spell once with this trait and regain the ability to do so when you finish a long rest. When you reach 5th level, you can cast the *branding smite* spell once with this trait and regain the ability to do so when you finish a long rest. Charisma is your spellcasting ability for these spells.

DEVIL CUSTOMIZATION TABLES

This section provides tables useful for DMs who want to create devil NPCs.

DEVIL HONORIFICS

d20	Title	d20	Title
1	the Perceiver	11	the Infiltrator
2	Veteran of Avernus	12	the Voluminous
3	the Insightful	13	the Stoic
4	Collector of Debts	14	the Shatterer
5	the Summoner	15	the Keeper
6	Speaker of Profit	16	the Faithful
7	Chainer of Demons	17	the Clever
8	the Conqueror	18	the Chanter
9	Glory Seeker	19	the Indomitable
10	the Victorious	20	the Vicious

DEVIL PERSONALITY TRAITS

d6	Trait
1	I always have a scheme to make a profit.
2	Nobody is as smart as me, and I need to prove that all the time.
3	There's a rule for everything.
4	If I can't seize control, I'll serve in the meantime.
5	I'm a bully who backs down when faced with any sort of resistance.
6	Every problem can be solved with the use of force.

DEVIL IDEALS

d6	Ideal
1	**Loyalty.** I keep my vows to my superior and respect those who do the same.
2	**Law.** I might not like the rules, but I obey them.
3	**Ambition.** The need to improve my station drives my every action.
4	**Conquest.** I am equal to the sum of the foes I have defeated in combat.
5	**Cunning.** Those who can see an advantage in the direst situation deserve respect.
6	**Brutality.** Overwhelming violence, and those who can deliver it, are worthy of obedience.

DEVIL BONDS

d6	Bond
1	I and my comrades fought well in the Blood War, and our service demands respect.
2	Evil without law is a pointless exercise in destruction. Rules make us what we are.
3	Those who follow me rely on my wisdom to ensure their prosperity.
4	One day I will have revenge on those who defied me.
5	If I do my duty, in time I will be rewarded.
6	We don't corrupt mortals. We teach them enlightened self-interest.

DEVIL FLAWS

d6	Flaw
1	My frustration boils over into violence.
2	I obey the law, but I strain at its limits to the point of heresy.
3	I put the minimum effort possible into anything that isn't my own idea.
4	A low profile is the best defense of all.
5	I'm so reliant on the laws of the Nine Hells that I panic without their guidance.
6	I am secretly jealous of the freedom that mortals enjoy.

PRINCES OF THE ABYSS

The Abyss is a vast wound in the cosmic order, a bottomless pit teeming with creatures that exist only to rend, tear, and destroy. The demon princes, individual demons of great power and determination, bend and shape the Abyss and its inhabitants to meet their every whim. These mighty beings imagine themselves at the center of the cosmos. Each demon prince believes that the universe will one day be theirs to command, its laws and structure twisted and warped to match the demons' ideal of perfection.

The demon princes' arrogance is exceeded only by their ambition. While any rational being would dismiss their goals as empty ambitions sparked by madness, the truth remains that the demon princes and their thralls are among the mightiest forces in the planes. It is conceivable that, if the Blood War turns dramatically in their favor, the demon princes could put the rest of their apocalyptic plans in motion.

SCOURGE OF WORLDS

YOU MUST UNDERSTAND THAT MY AMBITIONS DO NOT *stop here in Doraaka, or even at the doorstep of Greyhawk or the Amedio jungles beyond. Oerth is but the first of many worlds that will fall.*

—Iuz the Old

The Abyss and its demonic inhabitants are akin to a virus. While most other factions across the planes spread their influence into other realms through conquest, conversion, or diplomacy, demons infect a world by traveling there and beginning to transform their environment to resemble the malleable, chaotic substance of their home plane. If demons dwell in a place for a significant amount of time, the area starts to warp in response to the abyssal energy that churns within it. If a demonic infestation is left unchecked, a portal to the Abyss is the result, and more and more of the essence of the Abyss pushes its way through. In time, a plane or a world could become a colony of the Abyss, overrun with demons and devoid of all other forms of life.

INITIAL INFECTION

A full-fledged demonic incursion takes time to develop. A demon prince might rampage across a world for a few days or weeks before returning home, but that event doesn't qualify as an incursion. After the demon is banished, the world suffers no long-term effects, aside from the destruction wrought by the demon.

But if demons can dwell undisturbed on a plane for a period of time, their continued presence begins to erode the barriers between their location and the Abyss. It can take a few years for weaker demons to warp their environment, while changes begin to occur around the location of a demon prince in about a month.

To bring about these changes, the invaders must remain in the same location for some time, usually an area no more than six miles on a side, to combine their influence. Fortunately for their would-be victims, the chaotic evil nature of demons means that they rarely

organize in a way to cause such a disturbance. Demons that enter the world are bent on destruction, not concerned with greater matters, and inclined to go their separate ways unless a powerful leader can keep them under control long enough for the virus to take hold.

During the first stages of an abyssal incursion, the natural world recoils from the demonic presence. Plants become twisted versions of themselves. Leering faces appear in leaf patterns, vines writhe of their own accord, and trees grow foul-smelling tumors instead of leaves as their branches wither and die. Bodies of water in the area become tainted and sometimes poisonous, and the weather might feature extremes of heat, cold, wind, rain, or snow that aren't typical of the normal climate. Living things in the area flee or are killed by the demons.

At this stage, natives can stop the incursion by killing or driving away the demons that infest the area. The effects of the event might persist for a few months or even centuries, but the barriers between the Abyss and the world remain intact.

A GROWING MENACE

If the first stage of the infection continues long enough, a portal opens in the corrupted environment that connects to a random location in the Abyss. Demons that happen to be near the portal can travel through it and into the world, while the raw stuff of the Abyss also begins to seep through the passage.

Even at this stage, the infection has almost no chance of developing into a true incursion. The immensity of the Abyss means that a portal's random location is more likely to be an empty, uninhabited place than anything else, and demons can't make use of the portal unless they can locate it. The incursion might be long delayed as a result, but the portal's opening on the other plane remains a lurking threat until it is closed.

As more demons find and use the portal, the Abyss becomes strongly linked to the world, and the region's transformation grows more extreme. The odd but still mundane weather gives way to storms that drop burning embers, or winds that shriek in all directions, seizing living creatures and hurling them against the ground. The environment becomes inimical to all living things.

At this point, the incursion is still in a state of flux. The demons aren't yet directed by a single will. Unless a powerful demon dominates all the others, the area is wracked by fighting as one demon after another claims primacy, only to be overcome. The tie to the Abyss is still fragile enough that, as demons are slain, the portal grows smaller and weaker. If the invaders are reduced to about half the number that were present when the portal was created, the opening winks out of existence.

A STAIN ON REALITY

In its third phase, the demonic virus invades fully and becomes a part of the world. Simply killing the demons in an afflicted area is no longer enough to remove the Abyss's stain.

The size of the region begins to grow, the effects of the lethal environment expanding from the original area. The demons likewise begin to roam, and a small force capable of establishing its own incursion might travel far. If enough of these groups splinter off, the incursion could spread into a network of similar sites, each opening its own portal and drawing in more demons.

Slaying all the demons in an infested area ends their direct threat, but the terrain remains twisted and accursed, the portal dormant but still in place. To repel the incursion at this stage, the defenders must not only slay the demons but also establish a permanent watch over the portal, to ensure that it remains unused. Ambitious cultists, or even a random confluence of planar energy, could awaken the portal and start the infection anew.

Apocalypse Now

If the incursion remains unchecked or grows strong enough, it enters its fourth and final phase with the entrance of a demon lord. As a portal continues to shunt demons and abyssal energy into the world, it begins to attract the attention of the lords. Two or more of them might fight for control of it, or in the worst case, several might travel through the portal in rapid succession.

The visitation of a demon lord to the Material Plane is a cataclysmic event. The lord's presence overwhelms the minds of other beings to keep them from resisting, and the lord's power enables it to command the other demons already present in the world. They form a horrid army that sets about stripping the world of life and clearing the path for the lord's dominance.

At this point, a besieged world's only hope for survival is the expulsion of the demon lord. The lord's defeat leaves the other demons again leaderless, and they react by warring against each other, which makes them susceptible to attacks from the world's defenders. The longer a demon lord remains in control of all the other fiends, the more the world around it becomes irrevocably changed. When a demonic incursion runs its course, no vestige remains of the world that existed before—in effect, the realm has become another layer of the Abyss.

Chaos Incarnate

Although sages group demons into types according to their power, the Abyss knows no such categories. Demons are spawned from the stuff of the Abyss in a near-infinite variety of shapes and abilities. The common forms that are familiar to demonologists represent broad trends, but individual demons defy those tendencies. For instance, a vrock might crawl out of an oil slick in the Demonweb Pits with three eyes and vestigial wings. A chasme might appear on the layer of Azzagrat possessing the ability to belch forth clouds of flies.

If a demon survives for centuries, it accumulates changes to its form due to interaction with the energies of the Abyss. These long-lived demons often become demon lords, beings of such power that they can hold sway over entire realms within the Abyss. A few demon lords have come to the attention of mortals and are even worshiped as gods in some places, but the vast majority of demon lords remain unknown to scholars and sages.

THE UNKNOWABLE ABYSS

The Abyss is a puzzle to those who study demons and an attraction for those who seek power. It isn't as purely chaotic as Limbo nor as pliable, and yet demon lords can shape its essence by their subconscious will. Some demon lords emerge from the planar stuff, others seem to have been in existence since the start of time, and still others are interlopers from outside the Abyss. Several theories exist about what principles dictate who can gain a demon lord's power, or, if no such principles exist, how that power might be seized.

Most mortals would rather be annihilated than have their souls travel to the Abyss, but some see its chaos as something that can be harnessed and manipulated by those of sufficient will. A powerful soul might be able to dominate demons, retrieve weapons of the Blood War to use in mortal conflicts, or discover spells known only in the Abyss—and the madly ambitious might even seek out the means of becoming a demon lord.

EVER-CHANGING LAYERS

The physical nature of the Abyss is something that few mortal minds can understand. Those who discuss such matters use the term "layer" to define a certain part of this infinite expanse. That nomenclature, to the extent that it implies a particular configuration, is misleading.

The Abyss is a chaotic tangle of miniature worlds, each one shaped by the demon lord that claims primacy over it. Within the layers it controls, a demon lord manipulates conditions to match its view of how that world best serves the lord's desires.

Of course, keeping control of a layer involves fighting off other demons that are looking to expand their domains. From time to time, a layer changes hands or is seemingly obliterated in a battle (perhaps to be reborn in another location). For this reason, imposing a sense of order on the relationship between the Abyss's layers is a fool's errand. All that can be determined at any given time is which lord holds sway over which parts of the Abyss, and which areas are being contested by two or more lords. And as soon as such a fact becomes known, it might already be obsolete.

GETTING AROUND

Portals connect various locations in the Abyss, but these passages are as unreliable as anything else in this environment. Most of them fluctuate, sometimes winking in and out of existence or connecting to different layers at random. Rituals exist that travelers can use to attune a portal to a certain domain. However, the exact specifications of such a ritual vary for each potential destination.

Those who would navigate the Abyss always enter the place in a random location. From there, they must locate a portal and then perform the ritual that enables them to find a specific destination. Escaping the Abyss likewise requires knowledge of the specific ritual needed to do so. Without it, visitors are trapped unless they have access to magic that permits travel between planes.

EVIL INCHOATE

I WILL BE THE LAST CREATURE WHEN I AM DONE. THE cosmos will then be perfect, free of the braying abominations that are all other living things.

—Orcus

As beings of utter chaos and absolute evil, demons have no concept of empathy. Each demon believes that only its needs and desires matter.

This self-centeredness applies even with regard to other demons. These fiends have no particular affinity for their own kind, which is the biggest reason why they seldom cooperate with one another unless they are forced to submit to a demon lord or other leader.

Going even farther, every demon sees itself as the rightful inheritor of the cosmos. It is driven to destroy all other living creatures, or at least command their absolute loyalty. In due time, the laws of the universe will bend to its will, shifting to bring about its vision of a world of absolute perfection with the demon at its center.

ONE COSMOS, INFINITE VISIONS

All demons seek to satisfy their whims and force others around them to serve their purposes. What specifically motivates a demon varies greatly from one to another and often changes within the same demon, but it is always attached to fulfillment of its desires.

Less intelligent and less powerful demons typically have correspondingly modest visions for what it means to be the center of their universes. All demons have an instinctive sense of their own status, and they typically don't set impossible goals—a lesser demon, for instance, might simply run amok when unleashed into the world, its only desire to spread chaos, but a marilith or other powerful demon usually has an intent that goes beyond merely causing carnage, and a plan to achieve it.

DEMONIC AMULETS: BLESSING AND CURSE

Some demon lords have a way of cheating death, but this great benefit doesn't come without its own perils. A demon that stores part of its essence in a demonic amulet can avoid being destroyed even if it is killed in the Abyss. On the other hand, anyone else who lays claim to such an item can command the demon to do as they wish.

For this reason, demon lords hide their amulets away and trust no one, not even their followers, with knowledge of the location. Such a site is usually protected with intricate traps, mindless servants, and other defenses that bring no risk of subversion or betrayal.

If an archdevil were ever to acquire a demonic amulet, that event could signal a tipping point in the Blood War. If Asmodeus held Demogorgon's amulet, for instance, the demon lord might find itself in a position from which there is no escape.

LORDS AND THEIR THRALLS

While the demons fight for domination among their own kind in the Abyss, the Material Plane is the most fertile ground for demons to acquire followers. Even a relatively weak demon can demand obedience and worship from humans and other mortals through the threat of force. In turn, its magical abilities allow it to impart boons to its servants, making them more useful and better able to pursue the demon's goal in the world.

Sects dedicated to the worship of the various demon lords are spread across the mortal worlds of the multiverse as well as the Abyss. In return for a cult's adoration, a demon receives allies in its struggle against its rivals. To show their reverence, cultists might offer sacrifices of treasure and magic items that the demon can use. Taking advantage of that same reverence, a demon might send its cultists into battle to soften up an enemy before the demon enters the fray itself.

Many cultists gravitate to a demon lord out of a desire for power. Others find themselves captivated by a demon's narcissism, so that their minds and worldviews become twisted into a pale version of their master's.

BAPHOMET

Known as the Horned King, Baphomet divides the creatures of the world into two groups. Those who acknowledge his power are his servants, and he endows them with savagery and a hunter's cunning. The rest are prey, creatures to be hunted and slaughtered. His aim is to transform the cosmos into his personal hunting ground.

Baphomet is a savage entity, but he tempers his ferocity with shrewdness. He loves the hunt and the sense of impending doom that comes over prey that can't escape his pursuit. His fondness for labyrinths, instilled in the minotaurs he created, reflects this aspect of his personality. Baphomet studies every detail of the mazes he creates and exults in the dread that overcome those who become lost in them. He tracks them at his leisure, striking only after the maze's contorted corridors have exhausted the energy and the hope of his victims.

Cultists. The cult of Baphomet attracts those who see themselves as superior to everyone else, to the extent that they consider other people little more than animals. Baphomet's teachings reinforce these beliefs, appealing to the ego and justifying narcissism. Bigots are also drawn to Baphomet's doctrine of individual superiority.

Cultists of Baphomet include nobles who use their vassals as playthings, assassins who practice their murderous art for the sheer love of hunting intelligent creatures, and paranoid humans who combine a hatred of outsiders with bloodthirstiness.

Typically, a cult builds a maze beneath a castle, a guild hall, or some other place it controls. The cultists drug their victims, strip them of their weapons and armor, and place them in the labyrinth before they wake up disoriented. Then the cultists stalk their prey in the maze. They howl as they chase their quarry, striking fear into their victims' hearts before descending for the kill. If the hunt claims a particularly powerful creature, Baphomet might bestow boons on the cultists as a reward.

> ### LOLTH EXTENDS HER WEBS
> The Demon Queen of Spiders and her brood rarely take part directly in the Blood War; rather, her agents in the Abyss contrive to lure her enemies into throwing themselves into the struggle. Her servitors spy on both sides, playing demon and devil against each other.
>
> Lolth's plan, as far as those who study the Abyss understand it, is to tempt her rival demon lords into venturing onto other planes or to send them away with powerful magic. Because it is in the demons' nature to spread and destroy, they rampage in their new environs instead of seeking revenge on Lolth. Lolth, in turn, delights in filling the vacancy left by a departed rival, expanding the reach of the Demonweb Pits and claiming those servants her enemies have left behind as new spies and informants for her.

DEMOGORGON

The Prince of Demons is a being of unfettered violence and rage, the mightiest of the demon lords. His twin heads, Aameul and Hathradiah, compete in some ways and cooperate in others. The result is an entity that is capable of devising and enacting the most clever strategies, paranoid at all times about threats to his rule (which certainly exist in the chaos of the Abyss), and possessed of immense physical power.

Demogorgon prefers to meets every challenge with overwhelming force and to ferret out enemies long before they can marshal the strength to make a serious stand against him. He sees every living creature as a potential threat—and only those who debase themselves before him have a chance of escaping his wrath.

His ultimate goal is to empty the multiverse of all other creatures, even his cultists. Free from any prospect of being betrayed or insulted, he can finally rest in a perfectly peaceful cosmos. According to one hypothesis, if Demogorgon were ever to achieve this end, his two heads would finally fight to the death, each devouring the other and leaving behind nothing but a void.

Cultists. Demons comprise the majority of Demogorgon's cultists, since he commands unmatched power in the Abyss. The mere sight of him anywhere in that realm can transfix lesser demons and instantly compel them to do his bidding.

In mortal realms, people can fall under his sway simply by laying eyes on a true copy of his symbol, crafted either by Demogorgon or one of his most powerful demonic followers. An individual exposed to such a symbol becomes an agent of Demogorgon, dedicated ever after to a life of lurking in the shadows, lashing out against unsuspecting victims and striking fear into those who discover the bodies left behind.

I studied Demogorgon's symbol. I thought that, by looking at it through a mirror, I might avoid its effects. If anything, viewing its reflection made its effect more potent and more subtle. It was Rary who saved me, and I thought he had been spared the symbol's effects. I don't have many regrets, but underestimating that symbol is one of my greatest.

Fraz-Urb'luu

The most deceptive of all demons, Fraz-Urb'luu is a master illusionist and weaver of lies. He thrives by luring his cultists and his enemies alike into lives of self-delusion. He can take on nearly any form, usually appearing in whatever shape is most pleasing to a potential cultist.

Fraz-Urb'luu considers himself the smartest entity in the cosmos, the only one who can see through all of reality's lies and understand the truth that lies beyond them. Yet the truth that he sees remains known only to him. He utters cryptic remarks about a grand design that guides the cosmos toward some unknown end, but none can say whether these statements are another layer of deception or evidence of a true insight.

Cultists. Those who worship Fraz-Urb'luu fall into two camps. Most of his so-called "cultists," rather than being true volunteers, are unfortunates duped into honoring him because they listened to his lies. Fraz-Urb'luu might appear to a desperate paladin and claim to be a saintly figure, or contact a wizard while in the guise of a wise sage. He tells these folk whatever stories and promises they want to hear, playing to their needs and slowly drawing them into his circle of influence. He especially enjoys using the arrogance and vanity of good folk against them, helping to bring about their downfall.

A few of his followers are illusionists, deceivers, and con artists who seek him out. Fraz-Urb'luu makes use of their talents, and rewards these supplicants appropriately, as long as they follow his example in the campaign to bring about the downfall of all that is lawful and good.

Graz'zt

The lord of pleasure and limitless indulgence, Graz'zt is the ultimate hedonist. He incites lust and uncontrollable urges in both his cultists and his enemies.

In Graz'zt's eyes, the universe is a great plaything, and one day he will be its master. All other creatures and things will be allowed to exist only if they give him pleasure. When he ascends to dominate the cosmos, all who are left will love and worship him.

Despite his extreme self-indulgence, Graz'zt isn't blind to what goes on around him. He can curb his lust when he needs to plot against an enemy or counter an attack. When he must contend with an enemy, he fights with a

Graz'zt's Murky Past

Sages have put forth ideas for why demons consider the denizens of the Nine Hells as the greatest threat to their designs for the cosmos. Some researchers claim to have uncovered evidence that the animosity between demons and devils has its roots in a primeval time when Graz'zt, now a demon lord, was a member of the devils' hierarchy.

As the hypothesis goes, Graz'zt wasn't satisfied with the prospect of being eternally subservient to Asmodeus in the Hells, where only one devil can claim absolute rulership. The Abyss offers greater freedom to those who are powerful enough to carve out a realm for themselves—and, after forsaking his status in the Hells, that's exactly what Graz'zt did.

Those who find this idea plausible hope that Graz'zt's defection is a unique event, never to be repeated. If that turns out not to be the case, another such shift could be a major turning point in the Blood War.

detached, thoughtful demeanor, channeling his frustration at being distracted from pleasurable pursuits into the actions of a cool, efficient killer.

Cultists. Graz'zt attracts most of his followers from the ranks of those who seek pleasure above all else. He promises dark delights and forbidden ecstasies, in return for total submission to him. His cult gathers new members by circulating tracts, poems, and other works of art that depict encounters with him. Upstanding folk regard these works as vulgar, wretched, and obscene, but the delights they depict or describe sometimes lure a curious soul into learning more about the demon lord.

When a cult beseeches him during the induction of new members, Graz'zt sends an emissary or an avatar to preside over the proceedings, which conclude with the new followers being treated to a night of debauchery.

JUIBLEX

The Faceless Lord is a truly alien creature, said to be responsible for spawning the oozes found throughout the world. Those who study such topics theorize that every such creature has a connection to Juiblex, and the demon lord sees and knows all that its minions encounter.

Wherever Juiblex wanders, it leaves trailings in its wake that coalesce into new slimes and oozes. Most sages believe that if Juiblex and its spawn were given free rein, they would one day overrun the universe, turning every realm into an ooze-infested wasteland.

Cultists. Juiblex has few cultists, and most of them are incurably disturbed or delusional. His mortal cultists preach of the glorious day to come, when a tide of slimes and oozes will swallow the world. These wretched followers believe that by aligning with Juiblex, they can avoid the fate that awaits all other living creatures.

The lord's followers dwell underground, where they maintain a stable of oozes and slimes that help to protect their gathering place. They use traps to capture sentient creatures, then feed them to the oozes in a simulation of what awaits all who don't revere Juiblex.

ORCUS

The bloated Demon Prince of the Undead seeks to end all life in the cosmos, replacing the living with immortal, undead creatures that answer only to him. In this grim future, the many suns of the Material Plane are extinguished, and all hope has faded away. All that remains is the eternally static realm of the living dead.

Orcus is the universe's staunchest advocate of stagnation. He sees the activity of life as noisy, crude, and maddening. It rakes at his senses like the claws of a rat scratch across a hard floor. In his view, the universe can know peace only when life's incessant hum is replaced with the peace and quiet of the world of the dead.

Cultists. Worshipers of Orcus are heretics and blasphemers who see the gods of the multiverse as cruel, unjust creatures. They resent that mortals must suffer and die at the whims of these entities. In Orcus, they see the promise of release from pain without the demand of obedience. In the state of undeath that Orcus offers, they will be free from hunger, fear, and worry.

People who have lost a loved one to a tragic death are especially susceptible to his appeal. A father stricken with grief after the death of his child might seek Orcus's intervention in returning his child to the world after the gods cruelly snatched her away.

All who would become cultists of Orcus must be willing to become undead. Those who commit to the cause are admitted to the cult. Those who have second thoughts and attempt to decline are destroyed, their souls condemned to the Outer Planes while their bodies are animated as skeletons and zombies.

YEENOGHU

Also known as the Beast of Butchery, Yeenoghu inspires his followers to devour any creatures they meet. In his mind, the cosmos is made up only of predators and prey.

To sate his blood lust, Yeenoghu often rampages across the Abyss, killing everything in his path. Only those demons that join him in wreaking carnage can avoid his wrath. Yeenoghu's wanderings across the Abyss are like the meanderings of a storm. He and his cultists pass through an area like a monstrous hurricane whose course can never be predicted.

Of all the demon lords, Yeenoghu has made the greatest mark on the Material Plane. During his rampage across the world eons ago, the race of gnolls sprang up in his wake. Every gnoll is a miniature embodiment of Yeenoghu's rage and hunger. They mimic their creator, killing any creatures that cross them and respecting only those that can withstand their fury.

Cultists. Yeenoghu rarely acquires cultists other than gnolls, leucrottas, and the other creatures spawned by his incursions across the planes. The few humanoids that take up his worship are disaffected loners, many of them outcasts driven away from civilization. A cult of Yeenoghu operates like a pack of gnolls, regardless of what creatures make it up. Yeenoghu infuses them with a cannibalistic hunger, and they know that each victim they claim draws them closer to his presence.

ZUGGTMOY

The Demon Queen of Fungi has many traits similar to those of Juiblex. Some sages believe she is the originator of all fungi and molds, from the mushrooms that grow in the forest to the deadliest forms of yellow mold. Those who study demons argue that Zuggtmoy isn't merely a patron of fungi, and that her ultimate goal is to meld all living creatures into one great organism, an entity that she will then join with and rule over.

Cultists. Most of Zuggtmoy's cultists are hapless mortals that have been infested with the demonic spores she cultivates in the fungi she created. The spores slowly devour these creatures' brains, leaving them with enough functionality to spread malevolent fungi but robbing them of the will to turn against their master.

A few mortals freely enter her service. Most are druids who want to exterminate civilization and replace it with wild plants and fungus, or deluded, power-hungry individuals who believe that they would retain their identities while they bring others under Zuggtmoy's thrall. Zuggtmoy allows these zealots to retain their existing forms if doing so furthers her aims and helps to spread her children far and wide, but they are destined for the same fate as all the others.

Demonic Boons

Wicked folk who seek power from demons are scattered across the multiverse. Some of them gather in cults, but many of them act on their own or in small groups. Whatever their organization, they are united in their desire to draw power from the bottomless evil of the Abyss.

The following entries outline boons that a DM can grant to monsters and NPCs dedicated to a particular demon lord. The entries also list signature spells associated with a demon lord. If the monster or NPC can cast spells, you can replace any of those spells with spells from that list, as long as the new spell is of the same level as the spell it replaces.

A typical demon can impart boons to a number of creatures equal to the demon's number of Hit Dice. In contrast, demon lords have no limit on the number of creatures that can receive their boons.

Boons from demons are fickle gifts. They remain in place only as long as the demon is pleased. Accepting such a boon is a damning act that corrupts the soul and drives a person toward acts of chaos, evil, and madness. Rejecting a boon likely provokes a demon's wrath.

Baphomet

Ability Score Adjustment: Up to a +4 bonus to Strength, Wisdom, or both
Signature Spells: *Hunter's mark* (1st level), *beast sense* (2nd level), *slow* (3rd level)

Baphomet grants the gifts of cunning and physical power. He grants his rank-and-file followers the Unerring Tracker trait, and cult leaders gain the Incite the Hunters trait. All of his devotees also gain the Labyrinthine Recall trait.

Unerring Tracker. As a bonus action, this creature magically creates a psychic link with one creature it can see. For the next hour, as a bonus action this creature learns the current distance and direction to the target if it is on the same plane of existence. The link ends if this creature is incapacitated or if it uses this ability on a different target.

Incite the Hunters (Recharges after a Short or Long Rest). As an action, this creature allows each ally within 30 feet of it that has the Unerring Tracker trait to make one weapon attack as a reaction against the target of that ally's Unerring Tracker.

Labyrinthine Recall. This creature can perfectly recall any path it has traveled.

Demogorgon

Ability Score Adjustment: Up to a +4 bonus to Strength, Charisma, or both

Signature Spells: *Charm person* (1st level), *enlarge/reduce* (2nd level), *vampiric touch* (3rd level)

Demogorgon's followers are typically lone killers driven by the whispering voice of their master. His most blessed followers gain the Two Minds of Madness trait.

Two Minds of Madness. This creature has advantage on all Intelligence, Wisdom, and Charisma saving throws.

Fraz-Urb'luu

Ability Score Adjustment: Up to a +4 bonus to Wisdom, Charisma, or both
Signature Spells: *Minor illusion* (cantrip), *disguise self* (1st level), *invisibility* (2nd level), *hypnotic pattern* (3rd level)

As a master of deceit, Fraz-Urb'luu teaches his initiates the secrets of lies and illusions. They can also gain the Liar's Eye trait.

Liar's Eye. This creature has advantage on Wisdom (Insight or Perception) checks.

As a bonus action, it automatically detects the location of all illusions and hidden creatures within 15 feet of it.

Graz'zt

Ability Score Adjustment: Up to a +4 bonus to Constitution, Charisma, or both
Signature Spells: *False life* (1st level), *hold person* (2nd level), *fear* (3rd level)

The Lord of Forbidden Pleasures grants his cultists the ability to transform even the most hideous pain into pleasure. His cultists gain the Joy from Pain trait, while his cult leaders gain the Master of Pleasures trait.

Joy from Pain. Whenever this creature suffers a critical hit, it can make one melee weapon attack as a reaction.

Master of Pleasures. As a reaction when this creature takes damage, it can magically grant 5 temporary hit points to itself and up to three allies within 30 feet of it.

Juiblex

Ability Score Adjustment: Up to a +8 bonus to Constitution, with an equal penalty to Intelligence, Wisdom, and Charisma
Signature Spells: *Grease* (1st level), *web* (2nd level), *gaseous form* (3rd level)

The Faceless Lord's followers are bizarre loners who prefer the company of slimes and oozes to other creatures. They gain the hardiness of a slime at the cost of their minds. Lesser followers gain the Liquid Movement trait. The most dedicated devotees of ooze also gain the Slimy Organs trait.

Liquid Movement. As an action, this creature can move up to 20 feet through spaces no more than an inch in diameter. It must end this movement in a space that can accommodate its full size. Otherwise, it takes 5 force damage and returns to the space where it began this movement.

Slimy Organs. This creature has resistance to bludgeoning, piercing, and slashing damage from nonmagical attacks.

Whenever this creature suffers a critical hit or is reduced to 0 hit points, all creatures within 5 feet of it take acid damage equal to its number of Hit Dice.

The Abyss's infinite varieties of evil are not born only from the souls of mortals dedicated to Chaos and Evil. In addition, the Abyss makes its own demons from nothing more than the foul essence that pervades the place. By this means, it has the potential of countering all the forces that stand against it.

ORCUS

Ability Score Adjustment: Up to a +4 bonus to Intelligence, Wisdom, or both

Signature Spells: *False life* (1st level), *ray of enfeeblement* (2nd level), *animate dead* (3rd level)

In most cases, Orcus transforms his followers into undead creatures such as ghouls and wights. Sometimes he needs his followers to retain their mortal forms, to more easily infiltrate a kingdom or city. He grants rank-and-file cultists the Undying Soul trait, and his cult leaders gain the Aura of Death trait.

Undying Soul (Recharges after a Short or Long Rest). If this creature is reduced to 0 hit points, it immediately makes a DC 10 Constitution saving throw. If it succeeds, it is instead reduced to 1 hit point.

Aura of Death. This creature emanates a deathly aura that extends 30 feet in every direction from its space while it isn't incapacitated. The aura is blocked by total cover. While in the aura, the creature and any friendly undead are immune to the frightened condition and have resistance to radiant damage. Enemies suffer disadvantage on death saving throws while in the aura.

YEENOGHU

Ability Score Adjustment: Up to a +4 bonus to Strength and Dexterity, with an equal penalty to Intelligence and Charisma

Signature Spells: *Tasha's hideous laughter* (1st level), *crown of madness* (2nd level), *fear* (3rd level)

Yeenoghu's followers form packs of cannibalistic marauders. They grow more like gnolls in temperament with each passing day. His most devoted followers gain the Gnashing Jaws action option and the Rampage trait, while cult leaders gain the Aura of Bloodthirst trait.

Gnashing Jaws. *Melee Weapon Attack:* bonus to hit equal to this creature's proficiency bonus plus its Strength modifier, reach 5 ft., one target. *Hit:* 1d4 + this creature's Strength modifier piercing damage.

Rampage. When this creature reduces a creature to 0 hit points with a melee attack on its turn, it can take a bonus action to move up to half its speed and make its Gnashing Jaws attack once.

Aura of Bloodthirst. If this creature isn't incapacitated, any creature with the Rampage trait can make its Gnashing Jaws attack as a bonus action while within 10 feet of this creature.

ZUGGTMOY

Ability Score Adjustment: Up to a +4 bonus to Constitution, with an equal penalty to Intelligence, Wisdom, and Charisma

Signature Spells: *Ray of sickness* (1st level), *suggestion* (2nd level), *plant growth* (3rd level)

Zuggtmoy's followers are primarily mindless victims of her children's strange spores. The spores burrow into a victim's brain, turning it into a fanatic servitor. Each victim gains the Spore Kissed trait.

Spore Kissed. This creature is immune to the charmed and frightened conditions. In addition, if it is reduced to 0 hit points, each creature within 10 feet of it takes poison damage equal to its number of Hit Dice.

DEMONIC CAMBIONS

OTHER DEMONS

Demons of sufficient cunning and power can bestow boons, using the boons' recipients as pawns. A demon can grant a special trait based on its type, as shown below.

BALOR

Fiery Soul. This creature has resistance to fire damage. When it dies, it explodes; each creature within 10 feet of it takes fire damage equal to its number of Hit Dice.

GORISTRO

Labyrinthine Recall. This creature can perfectly recall any path it has traveled.

MARILITH

Serpentine Reaction. This creature can take an extra reaction each round, but this reaction can be used only to make an opportunity attack.

NALFESHNEE

Guarded Mind. This creature is immune to the frightened condition.

DEMONIC CAMBIONS

Cambions spawned by demon lords sometimes manifest different abilities from a typical cambion. Graz'zt is notable among demon lords for the many cambions he has spawned across the multiverse. Most famous among them is Iuz, who combined his father's abyssal heritage and his mother's peerless arcane tutelage to become a demigod.

SIGNATURE SPELLS

Cambions have the Innate Spellcasting trait. When customizing a demonic cambion, you can replace spells in that trait with ones of the same level from the list of signature spells in the boon entry of the demonic parent. The cambion can use these spells once per day each.

SPECIAL TRAITS

A cambion descended from a demon can have the special traits conferred to that demon's cultists, as described in the demon's boon section.

Few demons consort with mortals, and those with the charm or desire to usually grant their cambion children the Fiendish Charm ability. Cultists of Baphomet and Orcus can also use foul rituals to infuse their master's strength into a young or unborn child, yielding a cult champion who can wield special abilities; a cambion linked to Orcus replaces Fiendish Charm with Spawn of the Grave, and one linked to Baphomet replaces it with Horned One's Call.

Horned One's Call. When the cambion targets only one creature with the attacks of its Multiattack, it can choose one ally it can see within 30 feet. That ally can use its reaction to make one melee attack against a target of its choice.

Spawn of the Grave. At the end of each of the cambion's turns, each undead of its choice that it can see within 30 feet gains 10 temporary hit points, provided the cambion isn't incapacitated.

In addition, this cambion can use its Innate Spellcasting ability to cast *animate dead* three times per day.

Demon Customization Tables

This section provides tables useful for DMs who want to customize certain demons.

Demon Personality Traits

d6	Trait
1	I enjoy telling lies.
2	Threats are my only language.
3	I fawn over others to make my betrayal more unexpected.
4	I crush those I can defeat, and lie in wait to weaken and overwhelm those I must respect.
5	I will do anything to survive. Anything.
6	Someday all will worship me. Until then, I track their insults with obsessive attention.

Demon Ideals

d6	Ideal
1	**Self-Preservation.** It's everything and everyone for themselves in this cruel world.
2	**Might.** The world is divided into the strong who rule and the weak who obey or die.
3	**Cunning.** Always have a backup plan ready, especially if it involves betraying someone.
4	**Strength.** Strength is the one coin accepted in all realms and by all folk.
5	**Ambition.** We reach the station in the cosmos that we deserve due to our drive and talents.
6	**Cruelty.** Strength without regular demonstrations of its potential is an empty weapon.

Demon Bonds

d6	Bond
1–6	I am a perfect product of creation, destined to one day shape the cosmos to my whims. Everything I do verifies my destiny.

Demon Flaws

d6	Flaw
1	I act based on instinct, rarely with a plan.
2	I am cowed by threats, and even preposterous ones make me pause.
3	Deep down, I know I am doomed to anonymity.
4	My natural inclination is to grovel and beg for the favor of those stronger than me.
5	I rage, but I use anger to distract from my fear of confrontation.
6	I become entangled and betrayed by my own machinations.

Unusual Demon Features

d20	Feature
1	**Belches Flies.** Once per day, the demon can use an action to belch enough flies to create an effect as though it cast *fog cloud*.
2	**Tiny Wings.** The demon gains a flying speed of 10 feet. If it could already fly, its flying speed becomes 10 feet.
3	**Ever-Open Extra Eye.** The demon gains advantage on Perception checks related to sight.
4	**Bleeds Wasps.** The first time in each combat the demon is reduced to half its hit points or less, a swarm of insects (wasps) forms around it. The swarm considers creatures other than the demon to be enemies.
5	**Extra Arm.** The demon gains advantage on Sleight of Hand checks.
6	**Enormous Ears.** The demon gains advantage on Perception checks to hear sounds.
7	**Silver Bones.** The demon's natural weapons are considered silvered.
8	**Snake Hair.** Creatures that grapple the demon or are grappled by it are poisoned until the grapple ends.
9	**Endlessly Mumbling Second Mouth.** The demon suffers disadvantage on Stealth checks against creatures that can hear.
10	**Huge Feet.** The demon suffers disadvantage on Stealth, Athletics, and Acrobatics checks when they involve moving its feet.
11	**Translucent Skin.** The demon's skin is slimy and translucent. It has advantage on attempts to escape a grapple.
12	**Oily Boils.** Each time the demon takes bludgeoning, piercing, or slashing damage, the area within 5 feet of it becomes difficult terrain until the end of the demon's next turn.
13	**Thick Lead Skull.** The demon can't use telepathy or be contacted by telepathy. It can't be charmed, frightened, or stunned.
14	**Worm Tongue.** The demon can't speak any language.
15	**Head Hands.** The demon has heads where its hands should be and uses the heads' mouths to manipulate objects. If the demon had claw attacks, they become bite attacks that deal piercing damage.
16	**Blimp Body.** The demon can float at will as if under the effect of the *levitate* spell (no concentration required). While it has half its hit points or less, it loses this ability.
17	**Immaterial.** The demon has resistance to all damage except psychic damage, and all damage it deals is halved.
18	**Long Arms.** The demon's reach is 5 feet longer than normal.
19	**Eyeless.** The demon is blind. It has blindsight with a radius of 60 feet.
20	**Vestigial Demon.** A miniature vestigial twin of the demon grows from its body. The demon can't be blinded, deafened, or stunned.

Fiendish Cults

The following tables can be used to generate random cults dedicated to fiends. Roll on the tables in the order in which they appear to build up the cult's traits.

1. Cult Goals

d6	Goal
1	Political power, control over the local area
2	The death of a hated enemy or rival
3	Control of a guild or similar institution
4	Recovery of an artifact or magic item that could prove useful in the Blood War
5	Revenge for an insult, wrong, or past defeat
6	Personal power and comfort for its leaders; the rank and file are disposable

2. Cult Resources

d6	Resource
1	The cult uses a respectable guild, business, or institution as a front.
2	The cult thrives through the support of generations of a powerful noble family.
3	The cult controls the local officers of the law.
4	The cult has access to a cache of powerful magic.
5	The cult can open a direct portal to the Outer Planes, allowing fiends to intercede on their behalf.
6	The cult's leader is a renegade fiend seeking to evade its enemies.

3. Cult Organization

d6	Organization
1	**Conspiracy.** Members use passwords and double-blind communication.
2	**False Front.** The cult puts on an elaborate deception to appear as a harmless civic group.
3	**Criminal Enterprise.** The cult is organized through a thieves' guild.
4	**Network.** The cult has a secret alliance of members who have infiltrated the lower ranks of every organization of note in the region.
5	**Cult of Personality.** The cult leader is a beloved figure renowned for great, benevolent deeds.
6	**Entrenched.** The cult is part of the local culture, a tradition that established decades ago and kept secret from outsiders.

4. Cult Hardship

d6	Hardship
1	The cult is wracked with infighting.
2	A rival cult strives to destroy this group and replace it.
3	The cult struggles to rein in its dark, violent impulses in order to remain undetected.
4	Murder and betrayal leads to a constant turnover in cult leadership.
5	The cult leader is a figurehead. The real power is a crime lord behind the scenes.
6	The cult is a disposable pawn manipulated by its master.

CHAPTER 2: ELVES

THE MOST ANCIENT TALES SPEAK OF ELVES as the children of the god Corellon. Unlike many similar myths involving other races, these tales are true. Elves are all descended from a deity, and their origin led to a tragedy that shapes their culture to this day.

The gulf between the elves and Corellon, and the split between Corellon and Lolth, arose from the same transgression. That one incident set all the many races of elves on their present paths, determined their unique life cycle, and triggered an unflagging hatred between the drow and the elves of the Material Plane. No other event has had such momentous impact on elven history as the one that began it all.

A RACE DIVIDED

ONCE WE FOLLOWED IN CORELLON'S FOOTSTEPS, BUT *we strayed from that path. For our whole existence, we pay penance for a misstep. It is just? Mayhap not, but when is love just? Is loss and longing a matter for judges to decide? The heart knows what the soul wants.*

— Amlaruil Moonflower, Last Queen of Evermeet

Long before elves existed, Corellon danced from world to world and plane to plane. A being of consummate

mutability and infinite grace, Corellon was a god like no other—able to take the form of a chuckling stream, a teasing breeze, an incandescent beam, a cavorting flame, or a crackling bolt of lightning. On nothing more than a whim, Corellon's body could become a school of fish, a swarm of bees, or a flock of birds. When consorting with other gods, Corellon often adopted their appearances—male, female, or something else—but just as often kept their company in the form of a rose blossom or a delicate doe.

Corellon's flamboyant, mercurial personality showed through no matter which form the entity took. Corellon loved wholeheartedly, broke oaths without reservation, and took pleasure from every encounter with the other divine beings of the multiverse.

Most of the gods accepted Corellon's mutability and passionate behavior, but these traits infuriated Gruumsh, the greatest of the orc gods. Gruumsh's wrath was almost universally respected, even among the divine powers, but Corellon blithely took no heed of him. Perhaps it was this seeming hauteur that enabled Gruumsh to get close enough to wound Corellon, igniting the legendary conflict that cost Gruumsh one of his eyes. Depending on who does the telling, the battle was a clash of titans fought across many planes and worlds, or it was little more than an annoyance to Corellon. But the legends all agree that the first elves emerged from the blood that Corellon shed.

These primal elves were much akin to Corellon, not nearly as powerful but just as changeable and audacious. Splendid fey creatures, they traveled in Corellon's shadow, sparkling like the reflections from a finely cut gem. When Corellon came to notice these glorious echoes, the god tarried with them in the place that became the realm of Arvandor. While enjoying the company of these primal elves, Corellon came to appreciate their ideas, which were both novel and familiar, and singled out those of great repute for special treatment. Corellon gave each of these luminaries a unique name—Aerdrie, Keptolo, Solonor, Naralis, Erevan, Hanali, Tarsellis, Rillifane, Zandilar, Labelas, and many more—and with each name uttered, a new elf god was born.

One of these beings, although privileged to be elevated above the rest of the primal elves, was not satisfied with being one of Corellon's trusted underlings. She—for she had declared herself thus—saw in the multiverse around them other beings making an impact in various worlds. The entity who called herself Lolth spoke to the other new gods and wove an enticing tale of how the elves could attain superiority if only they could relinquish a bit of their individual freedom. Together, united in purpose, the gods could be the vanguard of this effort. Wasn't losing freedom to achieve greatness worth the price? Through this argument, Lolth persuaded the primal entities to take static forms, largely resembling what elves look like today, and thereby turn away from the example of Corellon's wild, ever-shifting ways.

As these primal reflections of Corellon changed their nature and defined themselves, they came to see Corellon and Lolth in new lights. They now viewed Corellon as their father, the one who had sired them, and Lolth as their mother, the one who set them on the path to their destiny. Each of the other primal elves, as children will do, favored one parent or the other. Corellon was revolted by this perceived betrayal and railed against Lolth's intrusion. Some of the primal elves rose to her defense. They argued that no entity who sprang from Corellon, no matter how rebellious, should be attacked. Those who remained advocates of Corellon insisted that their sire also wanted greatness for the elves and that such greatness could be achieved if all the primal elves followed Corellon's lead.

The primal elves gathered in great hosts around Lolth and Corellon as each entity pleaded its case. At a time when Corellon became distracted and lost in thought, Lolth crept up on him and sought to strike a mortal blow. The elves who favored Corellon helped to blunt the attack, but those in Lolth's camp remained aloof and detached, doing nothing to prevent her onslaught.

This act rent the elves asunder. Lolth and Corellon parted ways, Lolth to become a demon lord in the Abyss and Corellon to become the de facto leader of a pantheon that could no longer be trusted. The elf gods who sided with Corellon became the Seldarine, and those who fled along with Lolth became the Seldarine's dark reflection. Save for those who had been named gods, Corellon cast out the primal elves from Arvandor and consigned them to a physical existence on the Material Plane and other worlds of the multiverse such as the Feywild and the Shadowfell. From then on, all elves would be mortal, fixed in the forms they had adopted in defiance of Corellon's will. The elves who most revered Lolth became drow, and the others divided themselves into a multitude of surface-dwelling groups, each worshiping some or all of the Seldarine in their respective enclaves.

As a consequence of this rift, no elf would ever fully return to Corellon's embrace to enjoy life eternal in Arvandor. Instead, when an elven soul returns to Arvandor, it is adopted by the other gods of the Seldarine and given respite from the world for a time, during which it is left alone to contemplate its creator's disappointment. Then the soul emerges from Arvandor, to be reborn into a lissome, graceful body that lives for an incredibly long time—evidence that their creator holds a love for them that, deep down, is boundless.

THE ELVEN DIASPORA

The primal elves cavorted on various planes of existence before the rift between Corellon and Lolth. Outside the glory of Arvandor, their favorite place was the Feywild, also called Faerie—a realm of unbridled passion. It is to that place of splendors that the elves fled after they were flung from Corellon's presence. It is in that place where they transformed from fey creatures into humanoids. Afterward, they often wept as they realized what they had lost, their sorrow made even deeper by the influence of the Feywild. But it was also in the Feywild where they discovered the potential joys of being a person in a world of fixed forms.

Most of the elves eventually spread from the Feywild to other worlds, as wanderlust and curiosity drove them to the far reaches of the multiverse. In those other worlds, the elves developed the forms of culture and society that are now associated with their people. In some places, the name Corellon has passed from the memory of the elves, but the god's blood flows within them still, even if they know nothing of its source.

No matter where they are in the multiverse, elves of all sorts feel a special connection to the realm of Faerie, for it was their race's first home after they were cast adrift. Even if they can't name that realm or don't know how to return there, vestigial memories of the place sometimes glimmer in their minds when they trance.

One group of elves, the eladrin, never left that first refuge. After being exposed to the pervasive magic of the Feywild for centuries, these elves have a supernatural quality not shared by their cousins on the Material Plane. Some eladrin have been transformed so thoroughly that they have become fey creatures again and have been permitted to return to Arvandor, where they are a fascination and a delight to the Seldarine.

LIVING IN REVERIE

HISTORY, MY YOUNG FRIENDS? JUST BECAUSE YOUR *lives are as fleetingly swift as a hummingbird's flight is no cause to say mine constitutes history. History is the weave of things outside life, not for those still within its loom. Still I shall tell you of my lifetime and my clan's lifetime, as my clansong has not been sung in over a century. In reverie, the People may learn all that has passed for them and their predecessors. Now, in songs that were once only sung in celebration, I may teach you brief candles of humanity of the People and your own place among us.*

—Cymbiir Haevault, Lorekeeper of House Haevault

A memory is a curious thing. One can come into consciousness unbidden, evoked by an unexpected scent or the words spoken by a friend. A memory can also be elusive, foiling all attempts to recall it and sometimes remembered only after the hunt is abandoned, like a word on the tip of one's tongue. Some memories pull at the heart, weighing it down and holding it there as an anchor moors a ship. Others buoy it up or make it flutter joyously like the wings of a bird. Some memories lie in wait like predators, ready to leap out when the mind or the heart is vulnerable. Some linger like scars, not always visible but ever-present.

Perhaps more so than any other race, elves are familiar with all aspects of memory. From birth, elves don't sleep but instead enter a trance when they need to rest. In this state, elves remain aware of their surroundings while immersing themselves in memories. What an elf remembers during this reverie depends largely on how long the elf has lived, and the events of the lives that the elf's soul has experienced before.

CHILDHOOD

Much has been made of the relative fecundity of humans compared to elves. Ignorant folk wonder how elves can live so long, yet have so few children. They cannot know what it means to an elf to usher a child into the world. They cannot understand how a birth is both a joy and a sorrow, a reunion and a parting.

Each birth represents an elf soul that has been to Arvandor and returned. Mortal elves cannot know if it is the soul of someone recently dead or someone who died millennia ago. They cannot even be certain it is an elf of the same world. The only assurance they have is that it is an elf of their own kind, for when the primal elves went against Corellon and took permanent shapes, they chose this fate for themselves.

How many elves are born to which parents or in any given generation is a topic studied by elves in the hope of discerning some sign from Corellon or others of the Seldarine. Aerdrie Faenya, the winged goddess of air and sky, is thought to ferry souls from Arvandor into the world, bringing them down from the heavens to begin their mortal lives anew. A decade in which many elves are born across the world is thought to be a harbinger of danger that great numbers of elves will be needed to withstand. In contrast, if an elven community goes a century or longer without a new birth, members take this as a sign that the community has stagnated and must disband.

Because of the rarity of elf births, siblings might be separated in age by decades, or even a century or more. Thus, few elves grow up playing with brothers or sisters of similar age and instead rely on friends for the development of their social skills. In exceedingly rare cases, a birth might produce twins or—scarcer yet—triplets. These offspring, which the elves refer to as soul siblings, are believed to have a special, intertwined destiny

HALF-ELF, HALF SOUL?

From the elven perspective, the birth of a half-elf represents a disruption of the natural order of reincarnation. Elves in different communities and across different worlds have numerous ideas about the nature of the disruption, because the gods have never given an answer that seems applicable to all. The soul of a half-elf might be an elf soul whose connection to the Seldarine has been weakened, or it might be a true elf soul trapped in the body of a half-elf until death, or the soul that lies beneath one's elf-like visage might be human.

Many elves, especially the younger ones, view the existence of half-elves as a sign of hope rather than as a threat—an example of how elf souls can experience the world in new ways, not bound to a single physical form or a particular philosophy.

that can be fulfilled only if they are raised together. Elf legends are filled with tales of misfortune and tragedy that comes to pass when twins are separated and kept too long apart. One might be compelled to reunite with the other, at risk of life and limb; identical twins could become entangled in a case of mistaken identity; or the siblings might grow up as opposites, each determined to seek out and defeat the other.

During a young elf's first few years, the memories evoked during trance are drawn not from current life experiences, but from the fantastic past adventures of the elf's immortal soul. Parents of young elves and priests of Erevan Ilesere encourage the youths to explore these memories and talk about them with one another, but they aren't to be discussed with adults until a memory of waking life first intrudes upon a youngster's trance. This experience, called the First Reflection, marks the end of childhood and the start of adolescence.

ADOLESCENCE

Most elves experience their First Reflection in their second or third decade. It marks the beginning of the period when an elf must focus on acquiring the knowledge and skills needed for the elf's role as an adult.

As a means to this end, elves in adolescence learn how to use trance to evoke memories of their waking lives, giving them opportunities to reflect on the joys of the mortal world and to reinforce the principles of any training or practice undertaken while awake. At the same time, the memories of long ago that came so easily during childhood now arise less and less frequently. The Drawing of the Veil is the name that elves give to the occasion when a young elf no longer experiences primal memories during trance but instead recalls only the events of its current mortal existence.

ADULTHOOD

The Drawing of the Veil marks an elf's passage into adulthood, which typically occurs at the end of the first century of life.

Losing access to one's primal memories can be a traumatic experience. Elder elves look for signs of this change in young elves and try to guide them through it. Most elven cultures mark the Drawing of the Veil with a ceremony of pride or celebration, as a way of offsetting an individual's melancholy. For some young adults, this might be a time to contemplate Labelas Enoreth, while in another community the Drawing of the Veil is occasion for a celebration that invokes gods such as Alobal Lorfiril and Zandilar.

After the Drawing of the Veil, an elf enters the prime of life, a span of centuries during which most elves strive to engage with the world. An adult elf learns how to control the memories that bubble up during trance, choosing to recall experiences from its waking life that enhance its training or give it solace in bad times.

This is the stage of elven life that others are most familiar with because it's the age when elves move outside their reclusive communities and interact with the larger world. They strive to have a permanent effect on the world, to change things for the better (as they see it). Elves want to leave a mark on the world that future generations will remember.

Over time, an adult elf can become accomplished in many endeavors while pursuing its destiny. It isn't unusual among elves to meet someone who is expert in disparate disciplines, such as a battle wizard who also is a settlement's best vintner and famous for creating delicate wood carvings. This versatility speaks to every adult elf's eagerness for new experiences, because memories of adventures, escapades, and accomplishments will fuel the next and possibly longest phase of one's life.

ELDER ELVES

At some point during adulthood, the reverie of an elf's trance is first interrupted by a new form of unbidden thought. This seemingly errant memory arises not from the elf's personal experience, nor from the memories of the elf's primal soul, but comes from another life and another time. An elf's first experience of this sort is often referred to as the Remembrance and attributed to the influence of Labelas Enoreth. Or it is called the Revelation, and Araleth Letheranil is honored for its occurrence. Regardless of its label, this event marks the start of a new phase in an elf's life.

DREAMS FROM BEYOND MEMORY

Elves can sleep and dream just like any human, but almost all surface elves avoid doing so. Dreams, as humans know them, are strange and confusing to elves. Unlike the actual memories of one's primal soul, present life, or past lives, dreams are uncontrolled products of the subconscious, and perhaps the subconscious minds of those past lives or primal souls as well. An elf who dreams must always wonder whose mind these thoughts first arose from, and why. Priests of Sehanine Moonbow are an exception: they sleep and dream to receive signs from their god, and elves consult such priests to interpret their own dreams.

An elf who begins to experience these other-life memories might live on as normal for decades, but as the intrusions become more frequent, they take their toll on the individual's outlook. Eventually, an elf's thoughts start drifting away from worldly accomplishments and turning more and more inward. This change is gradual at first, but it becomes more and more severe until it can't be ignored. When that happens, an elf loses interest in the outside world and wants nothing more than to return home, to be surrounded by others of their own kind, to explore the memories they've accumulated in this life and keep them separate from the ever-increasing number of other-life memories that are resurfacing.

Most elves undergo this experience in their third or fourth century. Elves who led extremely active and dangerous lives, such as adventurers, seem to be affected earlier than those who pursue more sedate occupations. Notably, elves who have been revived from death by magical means seem to experience their first other-life memory earlier than they otherwise might.

Regardless of how soon or how often elves experience such memories, most consider them a blessing from the gods. The experiences of other lives that are revisited during trance can be examined for lessons to be applied during one's waking life, signs from the gods, or ways to open an elf's perspective to other points of view.

A handful of elves in any generation never experience an other-life memory during trance. It's hypothesized that these select few might be reincarnations of the original primal elves who sprang from Corellon's blood and were allowed to stay in his company. Although most elder elves become more serene, these rare folk spend the rest of their lives throwing themselves into dangerous situations, as if daring death to try to take them.

AGING AND DEATH

Most elves don't age outwardly as other humanoids do. The skin of adults remains smooth, their hair does not gray, and their bones do not ache. Even the oldest elves look similar in age to a human of perhaps 30 years.

Yet there is one sure sign that an elf is nearing the end of life: cataracts in the shape of crescents, points down, that appear over the pupils of both eyes when the elf is in trance. This change, commonly known as Transcendence, is evidence that Sehanine Moonbow has opened the door to enable the elf's soul to return to Arvandor—a direct sign from the gods that it's time to get one's affairs in order.

How much time an elf's body has left is never certain. Whether hours or years, the period is marked by both intense joy and great sadness. Most mortal elves accept their upcoming fate with optimism or resignation, but some react by throwing themselves back into the labors of life with a frenzy other elves consider unbecoming.

Elves who die of old age without experiencing Transcendence are believed to have been denied admission to Arvandor, and thus their souls pass on to other planes and are never reincarnated. The living are left to guess why this might be true, but an elf's conduct during life often offers a clue. Drow never experience Transcendence, for example, and the same is true for elves who turn to the worship of gods other than the Seldarine.

THE ELVEN OUTLOOK

The elves of the surface realms have a unique perspective on the workings of the world and their place in it that is a mixture of all the factors that shape their nature, dating back to the rift between the primal elves and Corellon in the time before time.

CULTURAL MELANCHOLY

The reason that elves are seldom frivolous and carefree is rooted in an inborn malaise or sorrow that infused the primal elves when they chose to stop following Corellon's path. These feelings of regret and sadness grip all elves at various times in their lives and impact every aspect of their society.

Priests among the elves typically believe that the broken link can never be healed unless Corellon has a change of heart. And as changeable as Corellon is, the god has been adamant on one point: as long as Lolth remains in existence, the responsibility for her betrayal falls on all elves. When the primal elves cast aside formlessness and impermanence for the promise of greatness, they forsook the part of their nature that Corellon most cherished—and, worse still, by doing so they somehow compromised Corellon's mutability as well.

Whether or not Lolth tricked the primal elves, to Corellon's mind, is beside the point. They chose to follow her lead, which precipitated the schism between Corellon and Lolth, even if many of them ultimately remained loyal to Corellon. Now the elves of the world must forever live and die and live again, suffering the consequences of their ancestors' poor judgment. In this one regard, Corellon is as inflexible and unchanging as the foundation of the world. And all elves grieve over the memories of the irreparably broken bond between themselves and their creator.

THE LONG VIEW

Elves have a natural life span of seven centuries or longer. Not surprisingly, this trait affects their attitude and outlook toward every aspect of mortal life.

Events from centuries ago that are distant or even ancient history to humans might have been experienced firsthand by many elves who are still alive. And an elf's memory of such events is likely more accurate than a well-researched historian's account, because the elf can revisit the memory over and over during trance, fixing it more firmly in mind each time.

The elven sense of value as it relates to time is hard for humans to comprehend. An elf seldom becomes sentimentally attached to physical objects such as manufactured structures and furnishings, except those of personal significance, for the simple reason that the object is likely to become decrepit before the elf does. Even fine jewelry and steel swords become tarnished and pitted, succumbing to the ravages of age long before the years of their elven owners come to an end.

Paradoxically, elves pay special interest to the ephemeral: a cloud of mayflies, bubbles in water, illusions, eclipses, rainbows, artistic performances, and so forth. They are fascinated by any thing of beauty—an object, creature, scene, or event—that might be experienced only once, but which can be captured in an elf's memory and revisited during trance for the rest of their lives.

It's a rare elf who forms strong relationships with people of other races, particularly those whose life spans are much shorter. Humans like to believe that elves don't form close bonds with them because the elves are saddened whenever they lose a human friend to death, but that's only a portion of the truth. From the elven view, humans' lives are over too soon for elves to forge what they consider a real friendship. Among elves, a hundred years of acquaintance between individuals is considered a good foundation for a close relationship.

In keeping with their seeming aloofness, elves can appear cold and emotionless in the face of tragedy. They do feel the same pain that others feel, and they do mourn their losses. But they also understand, in a way that other creatures can't, that all worldly pain is fleeting. Also, if an elf becomes too emotionally invested in a loss, the experience might be relived during trance for centuries to come. Keeping some distance between themselves and the concerns of others serves elves best.

Even though they are stingy with their affection for others, most elves are excellent judges of character. Thus, they can form superficial associations with other creatures very quickly. An elf often knows within minutes of meeting someone whether that new acquaintance would be a fitting companion for a journey or an adventure, and their first impressions are seldom wrong—though it might be decades later before the relationship becomes deeply personal.

The quality of patience, as other races define it, is so ingrained in elves that it goes beyond second nature.

The elves of Oerth are a sorry sort, abused by their past conquerors, often in hiding, and much divided. Although I have found evidence of greater elven empires in other worlds, these too seem shattered. In so many worlds, the rise of humanity seems to follow the fall of elves. What will follow, should humanity fall? Orcs. There is evidence of this already in the world of Eberron, a place where humanity lost a war with itself.

When enemies threaten to invade their domain, elves are just as often satisfied to wait out the danger in their concealed strongholds as to come forth and fight. Remaining out of harm's way for a year or even a decade is a small price to pay to avoid bloodshed—because elves, after all, have all the time in the world.

CRIMES AND PUNISHMENT

Consistent with their long perspective on the world and their knowledge of its history, elves have a special view of morality. They abide by the traditional definitions of good and evil, but tinged with elven sensibilities. When someone takes the life of another, for instance, the elves have a unique way of delivering justice.

Like most civilized beings, elves consider murder a serious crime, but their reasoning concerning punishment is their own. Mortal creatures, such as humans, condemn murder and those who commit it because it snuffs out a life. Where a mortal's life is concerned, elves see things the same way. Even if a murdered creature is brought back to life with magic, that doesn't negate the crime any more than replacing stolen gold makes up for the original act of thievery. But elves aren't truly mortal in the way that humans and other creatures are. If an elf is killed, the soul is reincarnated into a new body after some indeterminate time. Only the deceased elf's ambitions and current life goals are cut short; the soul will eventually receive another chance at life and fulfillment.

Because elves are reincarnated, their society treats the family and friends of a slain elf as the real victims of the murder. The survivors must carry on in life without a beloved parent, child, partner, sibling, or companion, and might feel that loss for centuries. Justice in such cases is geared toward their benefit rather than toward avenging the individual whose life was ended. Punishment for the murderer depends to some extent on the nature of the crime and whether it was premeditated. It can take the form of being exiled from the community, paying a great sum to the survivors, or being forced to carry on whatever unfinished work the slain elf was engaged in. Of these, exile is the most severe punishment.

The surface elves' attitude toward murder—which some races see as bordering on blasé—is carried to the extreme by the drow, who have elevated the assassination of both enemies and friends to an art and who consider killing to be just another tool for resolving disputes and clearing the way for social advancement.

Property crimes such as theft are usually considered evidence of significant character flaws, because elves don't value material goods as highly as shorter-lived races do. An item's intrinsic value is secondary to its historical and sentimental value, which can be considerable. An elf who steals a pouch full of gems would be pitied, but someone who steals a dried flower presented to an elf by her long-gone sister would be seen as a monster and likely exiled from the community.

Passion vs. Restraint

The elven personality is a mixture of two opposing forces, which vie for dominance throughout an elf's life. How an elf handles the tension between passion and restraint colors their life experiences.

When they're young, elves approach life with great enthusiasm. Their joy is as intense as roaring flame, their sadness as deep as the sea. They dive into endeavors with seemingly inexhaustible energy, yet they typically do so without much display of emotion.

The reserve and patience of elves is well known among other races, but what a dwarf or a human doesn't see is the conflict taking place inside an elf's mind. Elves keep their passion internalized because they learn at a young age that such feelings can become destructive when they are allowed to take control. Elves who let passion overtake their behavior can be consumed by it. They stop caring about friendships, alienate family members, and take foolish risks in pursuit of gratification that a cooler head would never hazard.

This passion wanes as an elf ages, but it never disappears entirely. One of the most important responsibilities of elder elves is teaching youngsters the danger of letting their passions loose and showing them how to develop a long-lasting self-discipline.

Primeval Hatred

One of the most fervent passions in an elf is the animosity that surface elves and drow hold for one another. This hatred dates back to when the primal elves surrendered their mutable forms in response to Lolth's promises. They split into two factions: the drow, who believed that Corellon had held them back and that Lolth's betrayal was justified, and all other elves, who felt bereft of Corellon's presence and believed Lolth had manipulated them from the very beginning. To the drow, every elf who basks in Corellon's light is a weakling and a fool. To most other elves, every drow is a traitor.

Despite the rift between them, drow and other elves can deal with each other when necessary, avoiding violence for the sake of a common cause. They won't like it—they might even hate themselves for a time afterward—but they'll do what must be done according to the circumstances of the situation.

Some elves do manage to transcend this hatred. They have met or heard of dark elves, like Drizzt Do'Urden, who find their own paths in life and view each elf as an individual, not as the representative of one side or the other in a cosmic struggle.

Elf Adventurers

Most surface elves embark on a period of adventuring during their early adulthood. An adventure to an elf, however, isn't always the same as what humans mean when they think of adventure. Humans tend to equate adventurers with people who battle monsters, explore dangerous ruins, delve into deep caverns, and generally stir up trouble, usually in pursuit of gold and glory. Elves have been known to do all those things, but more typical elf adventurers are simple travelers.

Elves know that once they experience Transcendence, the memories they have accumulated will contribute to their eternal contentment. So they seek out experiences that will produce exciting, beautiful, or satisfying memories. A few battles against monsters certainly could qualify, but such activities aren't usually the focus of an elf's endeavors. Much preferred are memories of faraway places, excellent meals, and fascinating people. As such, most elf "adventurers" are primarily sightseers, not valiant crusaders or heroes for hire.

This aspect of elven life isn't as well known among other races as it might be, because elves spend much of their "adventuring" years in places far away from other societies. They're more interested in remote forests, lonely valleys, high mountains, and other natural places than in cities. Traveling elves want to meet people, but not too many.

A small fraction of elves are born with or develop the qualities that mark them as potential adventurers, as other races define the term. Many traditional adventuring groups are happy to count an elf among their members, and some elves take to this life enthusiastically. Elves have a reputation for remaining unruffled in the face of danger, a very good quality to have among folk who regularly find themselves in difficult situations.

On extremely rare occasions, an elf might join an adventuring party for reasons that are based in fear. A tiny percentage of elves develop an irrational fear of the serene, contemplative life that awaits them in their

later years. Even if such a future life seems tepid and unbearably dull during an elf's prime, the psychological changes that come with age make this peaceful period of existence the most satisfying experience possible for an elf's later years. Nevertheless, this fear is immune to logic when it arises in adult elves. To avoid the fate they dread, consciously or subconsciously, they throw themselves into dangerous situations, not caring whether they survive or perhaps even hoping they don't. In effect, they're looking for another chance, seeing their current life or perceived future as unbearable and hoping to stop the clock on this mortal body and start afresh.

Elves and Magic

Magic infuses the elves' world. Even so, they aren't born with an innate understanding of magic. To master spellcasting, an elf must devote years of study and practice to it, the same as most folk. But from the moment they're born, elves are surrounded by a culture, a philosophy, and an artistic style that incorporates and subtly reveals the mysteries of magic to someone who is receptive to the message—which elves certainly are.

Wizardry

There's a reason most powerful wizards are old. The special formulas of action, item, and sound that produce wizardly magic require precision, and such precision comes only from long practice. More than that, each spell a wizard might cast requires a portion of one's powerful intellect to be dedicated to the task, with the necessary patterns of thought and proper mindset kept in stasis, ready to be unleashed. Even after these concepts are mastered, new knowledge of magic remains elusive, and a wizard must progress steadily through deeper levels of understanding, breaking through mental barriers in order to achieve ever greater mastery.

Of all peoples, elves are perhaps best suited to wizardry. They have centuries of life to devote to their studies, and their trance effectively gives them extra time to practice, as lessons learned during study can be reinforced by recalling them during resting periods. The rigidity and studiousness required by wizardry would seem anathema to a people who can recall a life of unfettered exploration and free expression of form, but magic provides a means of regaining that power. The patience and restraint for which elves are well known serves them well in this pursuit.

Not all elven communities embrace wizardry, but most worlds of the multiverse have at least one community of elves in which the spellcasters are renowned as masters. In some worlds, elves are even credited with the invention of the art of wizardry.

Mythals

Great works of magic are by no means unique to elves, but the creation of *mythals* seems to be knowledge that did originate with them. Known by different names on different worlds, a *mythal* is a persistent magical field that changes how reality works over a large area. Creating the most powerful of *mythals* requires many wizards of great renown and long experience to engage

Elves are often seen as masters of magic because of how easily it comes to them, but the mightiest of their mages are always those folk who burn with ambition. The path to power is never smooth. Anyone who tells you otherwise is a fool or an enemy.

in the same ritual, while lesser wizards feed spells into the growing webwork of magic. Such a ritual can take a long time to perform and sometimes requires the sacrifice of lives in order to achieve its purpose, but the results can be utterly miraculous.

The *mythal* that protected the mighty city of Myth Drannor on the world of Faerûn prevented the entrance of enemy races such as dragons, illithids, drow, and doppelgangers. It negated spying magic and teleportation, and every elf within its bounds gained the power to fly and a multitude of magical protections.

Similar magic allowed the elves of Krynn to raise a *mythal* at Qualinost. A city of moon-pale stone, its many towers stand hundreds of feet tall, and bridges of alabaster arc impossibly through its sky like pale rainbows.

A *mythal* can't be dispelled or suppressed by any conventional means, nor can its effects. Once one is in place, it seemingly lasts forever, since none are known to have dissipated. A *mythal*'s nature can only be warped or changed, and that can be accomplished only through the use of magical energy equal to that required for its creation.

The metropolis of Waterdeep, which lies on the Sword Coast of Faerûn, benefits from *mythals* that were created to protect the capital of a great empire of elves that stood on the spot over two thousand years before the city's founding. The elves left for Evermeet upon the order of their leader, who commanded the wizards of the city to alter the *mythal* so that evidence of the empire's existence was wiped from the surface of the world.

Bladesong

Those who see a bladesinger in battle never forget the sight. Surrounded by chaos and blood, the bladesinger moves in an otherworldly dance. Spells and sword act in concert, meshing awe-inspiring beauty with fearsome deadliness. When the bladesinger's sword whirls through the air so swiftly that it keens and the air hums and whistles in chorus, the bladesong has begun—and it might be the last thing the bladesinger's enemy hears.

The elves and half-elves who practice the art of the bladesinger, a tradition found primarily on the world of Faerûn, appear to be almost casual in combat, deflecting opponents' blades while elegantly moving into position to score hits in return. A bladesinger wields a weapon one-handed, leaving the other free for spellcasting or to manipulate a wand that can be incorporated into the fighting style. This technique gives a bladesinger the freedom of movement necessary for the dancelike motions of the various forms of martial art, which allow both magical and physical attacks to flow freely.

ELF DEITIES (THE SELDARINE)

Deity	Alignment	Province	Suggested Domains	Common Symbol
Aerdrie Faenya	CG	Air, rain, fertility, birth	Life, Tempest, Trickery	Bird silhouetted against a cloud
Angharradh	CG	Wisdom, growth, protection	Knowledge, Life, War	Three interlocking circles
Alathrien Druanna	N	Runes, writing, spellcasting	Arcana,** Knowledge	A quill or glyph
Alobal Lorfiril	CG	Revelry, mirth	Life, Trickery	Wine glass
Araleth Letheranil	CG	Light, stars, revelations	Knowledge, Light	Shaft of light
Corellon Larethian	CG	Primary god of elves	Arcana,** Life, Light, War	Quarter moon or starburst
Darahl Tilvenar	LN	Fire, earth, metalwork	Forge,* Light	Flame between hands
Deep Sashelas	CG	Creativity, knowledge, sea	Knowledge, Nature, Tempest	Dolphin
Elebrin Liothiel	CG	Abundance, gardens, the harvest	Life, Nature	Acorn
Erevan Ilesere	CN	Mischief, change	Trickery	Asymmetrical starburst
Fenmarel Mestarine	CN	Solitude, outcasts	Nature, Trickery	Two peering elven eyes
Gadhelyn	CN	Independence, outlawry	Nature, Trickery	Leaf-shaped arrowhead
Hanali Celanil	CG	Love, beauty, the arts	Life	Golden heart
Kirith Sotheril	NG	Divination, illusion	Knowledge, Trickery	Rainbow sphere
Labelas Enoreth	CG	Time, history, memory	Arcana,** Knowledge, Life	Setting sun
Melira Taralen	CG	Poetry, songs	Knowledge, Life, Trickery	Lute
Mythrien Sarath	CG	Abjuration, mythals	Arcana,** Forge,* Knowledge	Row of three intertwined rings
Naralis Analor	NG	Healing, suffering, death	Life, Grave*	White dove
Rellavar Danuvien	NG	Winter, harsh weather	Tempest	Spear between two circles
Rillifane Rallathil	CG	Nature, beasts, the seasons	Nature	Oak
Sarula Iliene	CG	Lakes, streams	Tempest, Trickery	Three lines symbolizing waves
Sehanine Moonbow	CG	Dreams, death, travel	Grave,* Knowledge, Light	Full moon under a moonbow
Shevarash	CN	Vengeance, loss, hatred	War	Broken arrow over a tear
Solonor Thelandira	CG	Archery, hunting, survival	Nature, War	Silver arrow with green fletching
Tarsellis Meunniduin	CN	Mountains, rivers, wild places	Nature, Tempest	Mountain with a river
Tethrin Veraldé	NG	Battle, sword fighting	War	Crossed swords beneath a quarter moon and above a full moon
Vandria Gilmadrith	LN	War, grief, justice, vigilance	Grave,* War	Weeping eye
Ye'Cind	CG	Music, enchantment	Life, Trickery	Recorder
Zandilar	CN	Romance, lust, dance	Life	Lips

*Appears in *Xanathar's Guide to Everything*
**Appears in *Sword Coast Adventurer's Guide*

Few among the elves, and an even smaller number of half-elves, have the honor of being inducted into the ranks of the bladesingers. One must have the mind necessary to be a great wizard, and also the agility of the greatest dancers.

THE SELDARINE

The pantheon of elven deities, called the Seldarine, includes Corellon and the group of primal elves whom he graced with divinity. These gods were the ones who brought word to Corellon of Lolth's radical ideas, and their creator rewarded them with a vast increase in their divine power. When Lolth lured some of the primal elves away from Corellon with her promises, this high-ranking core of divine entities remained loyal. Because they rejected Lolth's treacherous ways, they retained their primal power and their immortality.

Surface elves, and other elves who dwell in the light, revere these entities for remaining true to Corellon. In practice, this reverence is expressed more as the honoring of an ancestor than the worshiping of a god, for all the elves are descended from the Seldarine.

The Elf Deities table enumerates the members of the Seldarine. For each god, the table notes alignment, province (the god's main areas of interest and responsibility), suggested domains for clerics who serve the god, and a common symbol of the god. Several of the gods in the table are described in this section.

CORELLON LARETHIAN

The creator of all elves is both chaos and beauty personified. Corellon is as fluid and changeable as a breeze or a brook—quick to anger, but equally quick to forgive and forget. The god loves magic, artistry, nature, and freedom. Anyone who has felt the mystical presence of Corellon describes it as a joy like no other, followed by a deep melancholy when his presence is no longer felt.

Corellon doesn't expect much from followers—no complex rituals or frequent ceremonies or even regular

PRIEST OF CORELLON

and all these luminaries have ever been able to glean is that it is a secret gathering of elves dedicated to Corellon where a magical replaying of the elven myths of creation is communally experienced.

The truth is that the Mysteries of Arvandor is a phenomenon that elves recognize as a summons from their creator, which they can choose to accept or disregard. The event occurs on one plane or multiple planes within the multiverse in a single moment, and there is no guarantee that it will ever occur again; the ability to hear the call is a rare gift. Depending on Corellon's need, the god might call a few dozen or several thousand elves to gather, each elf returning to Corellon's body temporarily for some task that only the god can comprehend.

Before this gathering begins, the elves who have been selected start to have powerful dreams and waking visions, urging them to travel to a certain location. At this point, each of the summoned elves must choose whether to follow the visions, because it is known that not every elf returns from an encounter with Corellon. It's true that to be absorbed into the god once more, and returned to awareness before the Drawing of the Veil, is the fulfillment of every elf's longing, but some elves have grown attached to the mortal and mundane world, and thus they turn away from their god's summons. Those who answer the call of Corellon are telepathically guided to their destination, often for hundreds of miles across unknown terrain, or even across planes.

Most elves who return to their homes from the Mysteries are forever transformed. These participants generally remain silent about their experience, out of reverence and appreciation. Those who speak about the Mysteries of Arvandor struggle for the right words, but they all say in one way or another that experiencing the Mysteries is a way for elves to join with Corellon, gifting the god with their life force—and in return, they revert back to their free, formless nature for a time. After this mystical communion, many elves have a deeper under-

prayer. Corellon wants them to enjoy life, to try new things, to imagine what they desire and then pursue it, and to be kind to others. In return for this freedom from the usual requirements of religion, Corellon expects them to address their own problems and not pray for aid in every crisis. These precepts are instilled within every elf, since all elves are ultimately descended from fragments of Corellon. When elves ask their priests how one might become able to sense Corellon's presence, the priests often say, "First, truly know yourself. Only then can you feel our creator near."

Services in Corellon's honor are typically conducted in natural stone amphitheaters or bowl-shaped forest clearings. In keeping with Corellon's chief commandment for everyone to be free, all who attend are allowed to show their obeisance however they choose, as long as their way of contributing combines with the others to form a grand display of reverence. Such a gathering has the atmosphere of a festival rather than of an organized worship service.

Many elf wizards honor Corellon and adorn their spellbooks and towers with the god's symbols. Some of them speculate that Corellon is the personification of raw magic itself, the primal force that underlies the multiverse. Corellon is not magic tamed or shaped—not the Weave, as some name it—but magic in its original form: a well of endless, splendid possibilities.

The Mysteries of Arvandor. Only those long-lived scholars who have researched the elves with the greatest tenacity have heard of the Mysteries of Arvandor,

THE BLESSED OF CORELLON

Ever changing, mirthful, and beautiful, the primal elves could assume whatever sex they liked. When they bowed to Lolth's influence and chose to fix their physical forms, elves lost the ability to transform in this way. Yet occasionally elves are born who are so androgynous that they are proclaimed to be among the blessed of Corellon—living symbols of the god's love and of the primal elves' original fluid state of being. Many of Corellon's chief priests bear this blessing.

The rarest of these blessed elves can change their sex whenever they finish a long rest—a miracle celebrated by elves of all sorts except drow. (The DM decides whether an elf can manifest this miracle.) Dark elves find this ability to be terrifying and characterize it as a curse, for it could destabilize their entire society. If Corellon's blessing manifests in a drow, that elf usually flees to the surface world to seek shelter among those dedicated to Corellon.

standing of their origin and a firmer grasp of magic, and some enjoy a lingering telepathic connection with others who have been initiated into the Mysteries.

Cryptic shrines to the Mysteries of Arvandor appear throughout the planes, mostly sites where carved or painted stars cover the ceiling of a cave. On the planes that have hosted one of these rare events, elf priests consecrate and maintain temples devoted to the Mysteries. Often these sacred sites are natural spaces that have intrinsic magical properties.

Stories about the Mysteries are preached by many theologians as examples of Corellon's abiding love for his wayward children. Some sages imagine that, one day, all elves will be given this opportunity, after Corellon is satisfied by the completion of some great cosmic quest, and elves will once again be a people of unfettered form and unimaginable joy.

HANALI CELANIL

Hanali is the elven god of beauty and love. Usually depicted as a beautiful female, in some stories the god appears to mortals as a gorgeous male. Hanali's gender in a story seldom matters, for no matter how much heartache and confusion the stories contain, they end with affairs of the heart properly sorted out and everyone in love with the person, or persons, they were fated to be with. Stories of Hanali's romantic adventures among elves and other mortals are perennial favorites when sung by elf bards and poets.

In Arvandor, Hanali maintains a hidden pool called Evergold. She bathes in it at least once a day. It's said that the water of Evergold keeps her young and breathtakingly beautiful, but this is certainly a poetic myth, since all the Seldarine appear young and beautiful, with or without having bathed in this fountain. Mortal elves who are invited to join Hanali in the pool are said to retain their youthfulness and to delay the onset of Transcendence by at least a century. More than a few elves claim to have experienced this benefit, and the truth of it is attested by many bards—sometimes in all earnestness, sometimes with a knowing wink.

Priests of Hanali perform weddings between elves and preside over most other family-related ceremonies. Other than nuptials and a spate of spring celebrations, the priests conduct few observances.

Pools of Beauty. Those who worship Hanali Celanil build shrines in her honor around natural pools of clear spring water—a representation of the purity and power of Evergold. Her priests often surround such an area with flowers or arrange stones in a way that accentuates the natural beauty of the place. In a shrine dedicated to the worship of several elven deities, an alabaster bowl of water, usually with yellow flowers or petals floating in it, is left in reverence to Hanali.

Hanali's pool is a symbol of rejuvenation, and its water has significance as well in representing the ever-flowing force of love. To Hanali's followers, love is a living thing that flows like a river, moving around obstacles with ease, and, if it must, carving a path through bedrock to reach the sea of unity where all love gathers to become one with the cosmos. As one would navigate a river, the faithful of Hanali are known for following their hearts, unwilling to deviate from the pursuit of ultimate beauty.

Devotees of Hanali Celanil are known for taking the initiative in beautifying their surroundings without asking or expecting others to follow suit. If a shrine to the gods is beginning to look somewhat untidy, her followers will straighten things up, bring fresh flowers, and refresh offerings of food, water, and wine. Especially vigilant individuals might even decide to clean up after others who carelessly spill a drink in a tavern or leave their dinner table in a slovenly condition, all in humble service to their god.

LABELAS ENORETH

Even though elves live far longer than most other humanoids, they show few physical signs of aging until they become very old. By the time an elf's hair turns to silver and wrinkles appear around the eyes, the elf has lived for centuries and probably has only a few decades remaining. For this longevity and long-lasting vitality, they thank and revere Labelas Enoreth.

Labelas is portrayed as an elderly elf with silver hair, still-active eyes that once were bright blue but now are clouded and gray, fine wrinkles around the eyes and mouth, and a right hand slightly impaired by the effects of age. If anything, these symptoms of mortality make the god even more handsome and stately in the eyes of his followers than he was in his youth.

Elves tend to give Labelas little regard until they experience Remembrance. Like Corellon and Hanali, Labelas makes few demands on his followers. A few minutes each day spent thanking him for his gift of long life and good health, and occasionally placing a fresh flower in one of his shrines, is generally all that's expected. When an elf develops unusual ailments in old age and appears headed for decrepitude, other elves might wonder if these are the repercussions for not paying Labelas his due.

Most settlements have only one or two priests of Labelas. These individuals are elves well past their prime but who have not yet begun to withdraw into themselves. Their duties involve guiding elves who have recently experienced Remembrance, and are thus beginning the journey into introversion in the waning days of one's mortal life. The priests also preside over funeral celebrations, since Labelas is also honored for his role in seeing that elves experience beneficial reincarnations.

Eternal Witness. Shrines and temples to Labelas Enoreth are mostly made of or decorated with ephemeral things. Patterns and images made with colored sand, cut flowers, precariously stacked stones, and images made from thin paper are all commonly found there. These places of veneration are usually located in desolate, high places where the ever-changing sky and the setting sun can be seen and contemplated. Along with the setting sun, images of clouds are a major motif for followers of Labelas, who often tattoo such designs on their bodies or embroider them on their robes to signify the ephemeral nature of the physical world.

Labelas Enoreth is the custodian of time, monitoring its passing and making sure that the warp and weft of history isn't torn asunder by powerful maniacs and errant demigods. He is also the eternal witness, watching the souls of the elves as they dance from incarnation to incarnation, each mortal lifetime representing a role an actor would take in a play. From his cosmic perspective, Labelas looks on each elven life as a story to be written, nudging wayward souls toward incarnations that he deems suitable for their overall development, and thus weaving the life of each elven soul into a tapestry that spans the ages. In acknowledgment of this gift, priests and devotees of Labelas often weave modest tapestries of their own and donate them to shines in his honor.

Despite Labelas's influence in the Seldarine, elves can become psychologically immersed in their mortal incarnations, forgetting about the tick of time and the eventual end of their physical forms. Even Labelas's appearance, with his obvious signs of aging, isn't enough to dissuade some elves from growing attached to their youthful features, long life, and worldly treasures. But all such naive behavior is brought to heel when the Remembrance occurs, and an elf's inward examination begins as one journeys toward death and a new beginning. Priests of Labelas smile with compassion when these wide-eyed elves show up at their temples, suddenly full of contrition and offerings for Labelas, still shaken from the vision of their Remembrance and the gravity of its meaning.

To enhance an elf's Remembrance, the priests of Labelas use a special mirror made of polished black onyx. Small versions of these can be seen at many shrines dedicated to the Seldarine, as a reminder to the passing faithful of the importance of Remembrance. The priests advise those in their care to look into the mirror in order to deepen the trance of Remembrance. In the black void of the mirror, they see the faces of their former selves and scenes from their past lives—a glimpse into the grand tapestry of the each soul's existence as Labelas begins to weave yet another incarnation.

RILLIFANE RALLATHIL

Like the other elven deities, Rillifane Rallathil was once a primal elf sprung from droplets of Corellon's blood.

The original primal elves—and indeed, Corellon himself—have no "true form." Their common, elf-like portrayals are a convenience adopted after the elves took on permanent humanoid form.

When the other elven deities decided on humanoid forms, Rillifane took a different approach. He took as his principal form that of an enormous oak tree, taller and wider than any other. Its roots are so deep and far-reaching that they touch the roots of every other plant in the world, or so it's said. Through this network of tendrils, Rillifane remains aware of everything that happens in the forest.

When he chooses to travel to other planes and worlds, Rillifane takes the appearance of an uncommonly tall and strong wood elf with dark skin, handsome features, and twigs and leaves protruding from his hair.

In either guise, his main concerns are the welfare of forests and prairies, the passing of the seasons, and the lives of beasts. Most of his followers and priests are elf druids. They're just as insular and secretive as any other druids, which means their motives are often not clear to those around them.

Energetic debates have been held over whether Rillifane's oak tree exists only on Arvandor; has roots that extend to all worlds; is duplicated fully on every world that has plant life; or is only a metaphor for Rillifane's deep connection to nature. A growing sentiment among Rillifane's druids holds that the correct answer is "All of the above or none of the above, depending on Rillifane's mood."

Roots Run Deep. Ancient trees are almost always incorporated into shrines to Rillifane Rallathil. Many forests in elven lands have sacred groves where such trees stand as silent witnesses to the events of the world. At the base of such a tree, amid its immense, gnarled roots, the druids of Rillifane place their offerings. Carvings of animals, golden acorns, snowdrops, and sprigs of holly or witch hazel are all common offerings to the god of the passing seasons and the beasts of the forest. Often a shrine to Rillifane contains resting places where one can bend knee and meditate at the base of the great tree.

The druids of Rillifane consider trees to be symbolic of the connection between the mental and the physical, between what is illuminated and what remains mysterious. Trunks and branches reach high into the expanse of the mind and the realm of revelation, while roots sink deep, anchoring themselves in the known and enwrapping what remains hidden. When Rillifane's druids meditate at the site of a great tree, they can receive visions that afford them a new way of seeing the world. Often these flashes compel the devotee to undertake a quest to bring balance to the natural order by delivering a vital message or completing some other task.

SEHANINE MOONBOW

Sehanine is Corellon's beloved; Corellon is Sehanine's creator. Sehanine is Corellon's shadow; Corellon is Sehanine's reflection. Sehanine is the moon; Corellon is the moon's crescent. Sehanine is the night sky; Corellon is the sun and all the stars.

No god of the Seldarine is as intertwined with Corellon or presents so many paradoxes for worshipers to unravel, but this role befits Sehanine, for she is a god of mysteries as much as anything else. Many non-elves find it easiest to think of Sehanine as the companion of Corellon and the god of the moon, but to elves she is much more than that. The moon passes from one phase to the next, and Sehanine watches over all such cycles, be it from season to season or cradle to grave. She is midwife to elf mothers, ushering souls into the world. She is also thought to stand beside dying elves, to greet their departing spirits and set them on the path to Arvandor. Sehanine serves as patron of the lost and any who travel, as well as those who seek meaning. Elves beseech her to provide relief from madness, and they mark her symbol on graves and tombs to invoke her protection of the dead. In these comforting aspects, Sehanine is often imagined as a willowy, gentle male elf with shining eyes that reveal both melancholy and tenderness in their gaze when depicted alongside his beloved Corellon.

In stories of the Seldarine, Sehanine is Corellon's steadfast companion, the one being who can persuade Corellon to pause and reflect rather than allow his emotions to rule him. Corellon can be resplendent with joy or shaking with anger, but a word or a look from Sehanine is enough to check or subtly alter Corellon's mood and behavior, redirecting the god to a less extreme course of action. Some elven legends treat Sehanine as Corellon's spouse or as a favored child, but other stories hint at a deeper truth. They say Sehanine was formed from the first drop of blood spilled from Corellon's body, and so she reminds Corellon that even as a divine being, he can be harmed.

Sehanine's priests often seek her guidance by entering into a state of true sleep and sifting through their dreams for signs. But Sehanine has another way of sending messages to the elves of the world. The crescent-shaped cataracts that appear in the eyes of an elderly elf at Transcendence are symbolic of the moonbow, an astronomical phenomenon with which she is associated. It appears in the night sky above the moon as a luminous arc of refracted light, no brighter than the moon itself. Only elves and some half-elves can perceive this sign, for it is meant only for Corellon's people. What it signifies depends on the phase of the moon. Above a full moon, when it is most often detected, it means that an elf of great importance and advanced age will soon journey to Arvandor. Elves who see the sign might be compelled to seek out this individual to commune with and learn from before the elder departs the world. The moonbow appearing above the moon during its other phases can be interpreted in many ways, depending on the season and the timing of its appearance. A moonbow appearing above a new moon is the most dreaded sign, for it is said to signal a coming period of great upheaval and many deaths.

Lunar Worship. Temples to Sehanine Moonbow are almost always aligned with the heavens to enable the priests to track the motion and phases of the moon. The sleeping quarters of the priests are positioned such that a shaft of light from the full moon falls on them while they are sleeping, and this silver light of Sehanine can influence their dreams and impart messages to them.

Offerings to Sehanine are mostly made from silver, often shaped in a way that is reminiscent of the full moon. Cups, bowls, cloak pins, and plates of silver are found at her shrines, as well as those dedicated to the Seldarine collectively. The weapons and gear used by her followers, such as silver arrowheads, knife blades, and wooden shields, are often decorated with a stylized image of Sehanine's eye with rays coming out of it—a warning to the elves' enemies that Sehanine's gaze has fallen upon them.

Deep Sashelas

Deep Sashelas, sometimes known just as Sashelas, is the elven deity of the sea, seafaring, and knowledge. Sashelas is called the Knowledgeable One. His awareness of all lore, not only that about the sea, is seemingly limitless. He is especially beloved by sea elves, dolphins, and elf sages.

Most of Sashelas's most devoted followers are sea elves, as are his priests. Many seafarers toss offerings of gold and jewels overboard, beseeching Sashelas to calm storms or provide favorable winds, and he is inclined to aid them even if they aren't fully dedicated to his worship. His sea elf priests often lurk in the water beneath ships when these offerings are made. They catch the treasures as they sink and use them to decorate Sashelas's underwater shrines, to purchase items from coastal merchants that can't be manufactured underwater, and to bribe dragon turtles into their service. Ceremonies honoring Sashelas are held underwater at times of uncommonly high tides or during electrical storms, when flashes of lightning above the waves provide illumination to the calmer realm below the surface.

Sea of Knowledge. Over time, much of the world sinks to the depths of the oceans and is thought to be lost forever, but it isn't lost to everyone. Sashelas gleans much about the world above the waves from that which sinks beneath them: every shipwreck, every offering, and the wealth and knowledge of every seaside city swallowed by a giant wave are added to Sashelas's ever-expanding library of lore. Knowledge that has disappeared from the surface world might still be known to the priests of Sashelas, gained through communion with their god. Messengers who never reached their destination, ships filled with scrolls from an ancient library, scholars whose works were lost at sea—all of these add to Sashelas's storehouse.

Away from the open sea, many lagoons, reefs, and grottoes have shrines devoted to Sashelas. Many come in reverence to bathe in the waters in the hope of receiving visions from the god, since it is known that Sashelas is fond of sharing knowledge with those who are true seekers. Scholars, monks, and clerics visit these elaborately decorated seaside temples, immersing themselves in the blessed waters and looking for enlightenment. Because the god also dispenses lore through dreams and reveries of memory, many artists and poets worship Sashelas. They seek his creative insight by spending time floating on the waves, then return to shore to write down or sketch out the gifts bequeathed to them.

Arvandor

Arvandor is the ancient elven name for the home of the Seldarine, one of the realms on the Outer Plane of Arborea. It is a place where the unfettered passions of elves run free. Joy, lust, rage, contentment, jealousy, and love in all their extremes are on spectacular display

there. Lifelong friends might share a laugh over food and wine, cross blades over a mutual lover, and write songs celebrating each other's courage and integrity, all in a single evening. Elves who live on Arvandor are no different from elves living anywhere else, except for the intensity of their passion. All manner of elves can be found there, including eladrin and even a few extraordinary drow. The splendor of the Seldarine illuminates their days, and their trances are filled with the intoxicating, blissful feeling engendered by their nearness to Corellon's magnificence.

When an elf's soul reincarnates, the elf might return to life on any world or on Arvandor. As a result, many elves alive today have latent memories of a previous life spent on Arvandor. Because of the deep feelings associated with those memories, they are often among the first previous-life recollections to resurface at the beginning of an elf's Remembrance. Recalling such an existence can stir up a great longing to visit the place once again.

Like most Outer Planes, Arvandor can be perilous for outsiders, including mortal elves who were not born in the place. The native elves are boisterous, tempestuous, and ready to draw blood over the slightest insult or lapse of tradition. The plane's beauty is both overpowering and bewildering. Fey spirits lurk everywhere, and they're even more unpredictable and more easily provoked than the elves.

Those are the obvious dangers. The subtle danger of Arvandor is that it can act like an addictive drug on visitors: the longer they remain, the more likely they will never want to leave. Anyone who stays more than a month might need to be dragged back to their home plane by well-meaning friends, then guarded or confined until Arvandor's pull on the person wanes.

Because of all these difficulties, many elves resist the urge to visit Arvandor and instead make a pilgrimage to the Feywild, which feels like a realm very similar to the home of their gods.

Evermeet

Uaul'Selu'Keryth. In your tongue, the name might *be translated as "At War with the Weave." When twelve High Mages last performed this ritual, the world was torn asunder. It is a power no mortal should possess and no god should use.*

— Ecamane Truesilver, High Mage of Silverymoon

At one time or another, every surface elf, during every lifetime, pines for Arvandor. They might not know of Arvandor or be able to fully define the longing, but they can't escape it. Getting to Arvandor, on the other hand, is extraordinarily difficult for most mortal elves, requiring magic far beyond what most practitioners are capable of. Yet even if one could manage to open or find such a pathway, Corellon doesn't look favorably on elves from the mortal world who get near to him in this way. He suffers their presence only for a short time, forcing them to vacate the realm or be overcome by it.

It was, in part, this situation that led to the creation of Evermeet. By means of a cataclysmic ritual, the greatest elf wizards of Faerûn summoned into the world a piece of Arvandor and bound it there. Their intent was to craft a new homeland for the elves, a place protected from the outside world and so similar to their afterlife as to allow elves to live in a virtual heaven on earth.

Although the performance of the ritual was an act of supreme sacrilege, it didn't bring divine retribution down on those responsible. Perhaps the Seldarine deemed the consequences of the act to be punishment enough. The ritual ripped continents apart. It shifted seas. The lives lost couldn't be counted. Even time and space were, for a time, torn asunder. This event was the first Sundering of Faerûn, and the world was forever changed by it.

Millennia later, Evermeet still exists, although now it is unmoored from the world, somewhere in the space between the Feywild, Arvandor, and the Material Plane. By using secret pathways, entering a fairy ring on special nights, or traversing a moonlit sea by following certain stars, elves of many worlds can get to Evermeet—if they're lucky. Even from Faerûn, for instance, one can sail to Evermeet only on a ship captained by an elf who has been there before. And if the captain slips up, the ship might become adrift on the Astral Plane.

Despite all these obstacles, when elves feel the pull of Arvandor, some find the way to assuage that feeling by traveling to Evermeet instead. Unlike on Arvandor, elves who visit Evermeet can do so for as long as they like and leave when they want—or can choose to stay, as many elves do in the later decades of their lives.

The arrival of elves from worlds other than Faerûn is a phenomenon of just the last few decades. When Evermeet became detached from Faerûn, it also lost its great queen, Amlaruil Moonflower, said to have been invested with powers by all of the Seldarine. Her throne has sat empty ever since. The consensus of the ruling houses in Evermeet is that the Seldarine now want Evermeet to be open to all elves and not ruled by any single mortal.

Eladrin and the Feywild

The Feywild exists separate from but parallel to the Material Plane. It's a realm of nature run amok, and most of its inhabitants are sylvan or fey creatures. In these respects, the Feywild has certain similarities to Arvandor. First-time visitors might be excused for not being sure which of the two planes they're on for a time after arriving. Unlike Arvandor, however, which is a plane of good, the Feywild leans toward neither good nor evil; both are equally prevalent and powerful there. For that reason, parts of the Feywild where evil holds sway are substantially more dangerous than any place in Arvandor.

All kinds of elves live in the Feywild, but one subrace—the eladrin—has adopted it as their home. Of all the elves, eladrin are closest in form and ability to the first generation of elves. Some could pass for high elves, but most are distinctly eladrin in appearance: very slender, with hair and skin color determined by the season with which they feel the closest affinity. And their eyes often glimmer with fey magic.

Continued exposure to the Feywild, over a century or more, hastens the onset of Remembrance significantly among most elves. Elves who have spent most of their lives in the Feywild can experience their first other-life memory as early as the age of 200 years. Eladrin aren't affected this way.

Because of their link to the primal elves, eladrin tend to be haughty around other elves. They're proud of their heritage and equally proud of their ability to thrive in the Feywild, a land full of threats that would overwhelm and destroy weaker creatures. Some eladrin trade haughtiness for a tender kindness toward their elf cousins, knowing that many elves have never felt the ecstasies of a life amid the fey and of years spent near the ancient shrines and other glories created by the primal elves who first arrived in Faerie. These kinder eladrin take a special pleasure in introducing their realm to others.

Eladrin cities represent the pinnacle of elven architecture. Their soaring towers, arching bridges, and gracefully filigreed homes are a perfect blend of construction, natural elements, and magic-inspired motifs. Streams and waterfalls, gardens and copses, and structures of stone and wood are commingled in ways that are original and yet completely natural-looking.

Eladrin culture is older than any other elven civilization, and it's also the most decadent. Most elves are impetuous to some extent, but eladrin are known for their fickleness. Many of them change their minds on the spur of the moment without giving reasons. Their system of justice vacillates between capriciously harsh and whimsically mild, depending on the mood of the eladrin passing judgment, and eladrin are more susceptible to flattery than other elves are.

Elves from the Material Plane who have researched eladrin culture blame these traits on the influence of the Feywild. As part of their argument, they point out that eladrin who spend a significant amount of time on the Material Plane—adventurers and scholars, primarily—still demonstrate these attitudes, but to a lesser degree.

Although eladrin have the closest connection to Corellon because of their ancestry, they are alone among elves in feeling little affinity for Arvandor. Eladrin don't long to end their cycle of rebirth and rejoin Corellon, but rather to meld with the Feywild when they are reincarnated. They believe that an eladrin who excels in life throughout a series of incarnations can eventually come back as a member of the Seelie or Unseelie court or, in extreme cases, even as an archfey.

DROW

When the primal elves chose to take the forms of mortals, they were one people split by conflicting loyalty to gods who reviled each other. The schism led to a conflict that ended with Lolth retreating to the Abyss and her adherents exiled to the Underdark. This banishment enabled the victors to once again live in peace on Arvandor but did nothing to heal the rift.

The vanquished elves weren't seen or heard from again for centuries. Throughout that age of residing in the darkness, absorbing the unhealthy emanations of the Underdark, subsisting on its tainted water and food, and always beseeching their god for guidance and following her poisonous dictates, Lolth's worshipers gradually transformed into the drow: the cruel, predatory, and wicked offshoot of the elf race.

REFLECTIONS OF LOLTH

From the time they're old enough to understand, drow are taught that they're superior to all other creatures, for they remain steadfast in their devotion to Lolth despite the hardships of their existence. Any creature that isn't a drow is useful only as a sacrifice to Lolth, as a slave, or as fodder for the giant spiders that the drow train to patrol their cities and tunnels.

Among these other, lesser forms of life, the elves that live in sunlight are especially despised because they are descended from the primal elves who betrayed Lolth so long ago. First they accepted Lolth's offer of mortality in return for destiny, but then they turned against her in a pathetic effort to win back Corellon's favor. Drow view the elves of the surface world as cowardly children who defy their parents when they're not around but cower in the corner when their parents return, terrified of having their bad behavior found out.

Reverence for Lolth touches every aspect of drow life. All dark elves constantly watch for signs of her favor. Any incident or physical feature can be interpreted as such a sign, and priestesses are quick to attach meanings to obscure omens that benefit their own interests.

All this effort to please Lolth is a wise precaution. Though she resides in the Abyss, the Spider Queen isn't a distant god. She sometimes tests her most faithful by drawing their spirits to her in the Demonweb to undergo her judgment. Followers never know when or if they are to be tested. One who claims to have undergone the test and passed it is rewarded with respect and elevated status. Even someone who successfully lies about having taken the test can earn the respect of their peers, since perpetrating this falsehood is a way of proving one's worth to Lolth. Lying and conniving can't save those who fail the test, however, because the evidence of such an outcome is immediately obvious—a drow whose spirit has failed its test in the Demonweb Pits becomes transformed into a drider.

When Lolth is well served, she rewards her faithful with favors. When she is defied, she visits the Underdark in one of her forms and takes a direct hand in punishing the malefactor in a manner that discourages anyone who might be contemplating a similar kind of disobedience. Perhaps making an example of malcontents in this way is simply an aspect of how Lolth's cruel personality

The so-called descent of the drow isn't one moment in history, but the result of conflict between godly powers in an era that has become myth to mortals. My investigations indicate it occurred in different worlds of the Material Plane at different times. I have even discovered one world, Krynn, where it has yet to come to pass.

works. It also might be evidence of a lesson that she learned all too well from the way Corellon reacted to her betrayal of him: the smallest flame of resistance must be snuffed out before it grows into a conflagration.

Society of Blood and Poison

The principal organization in drow culture and society is the house, an extended clan that comprises many related families, plus a number of lesser families who have pledged loyalty to the house. A house's membership also includes some (potentially very large) number of indentured drow servants and slaves of other species. A house usually specializes in a business, a service, or a craft that supports by providing income.

Houses are in constant competition with one another. They vie for money, for prestige, and, more than anything else, for power over others—the surest sign of Lolth's approval.

No tactic is outside the rules in this ongoing conflict. Raids against another house's outlying property (farming caverns, trade caravans, or hunting parties) are commonplace. Rumors about disloyalty, conspiracies with surface elves, or heresy against Lolth are circulated so frequently that no one knows what to be sure of. Assassinations, both by blade and by the use of special drow poisons, are a constant threat. Bodyguards and food tasters are as necessary to the survival of a high-ranking drow as air and water. Squabbles within a house also occur from time to time as relatives jockey for position. It's a rare occurrence, though far from unknown, for drow to assassinate their own parents or siblings if that's what it takes to create a path for advancement.

Cities without Sunlight

The drow might have not chosen to live in the Underdark, but just the same they consider it their home, not a prison. Just as the sea elves adapted to their aquatic realm, the drow have long been accustomed to the harsh conditions of life in the Underdark. They've lived away from sunlight for so long that they can't bear the touch of it on their flesh, and thus they prefer to visit the surface only at night.

Even though they live underground, drow are much more than cave-dwellers. Their cities are as magnificent as anything built by surface elves, and their defenses are even more secure. Their most important sites are located inside immense, hollowed-out stalactites and stalagmites, with entrances well guarded.

Driders: Lowest of the Low

Much confusion and misinformation exists about driders among non-drow, but all dark elves know exactly what driders are: failures. They have either fared badly in Lolth's test or displeased her in some other way.

Once its transformation has taken hold, a newly created drider is shunned by its house and exiled from the community, with nothing but a few meager supplies and its knowledge of the Underdark to protect it. Drow congregate to throw stones at the still-dazed creature and drive it into the tunnels beyond the city's environs. If it's unlucky, it's attacked by a roper, a carrion crawler, or another drider. If it's lucky, the new drider finds a safe place to hide while its wounds heal.

So begins a drider's life in exile. Another widespread misunderstanding about driders is that they serve the drow as pickets, elite troops, or even suicide squads. They do none of those things. They are despised outcasts who live on the fringes of drow territory. Even though drow revile driders, they don't kill them, because a drider's punishment is to live a long life in wretchedness. Killing one would cut short Lolth's judgment and possibly earn the same sentence for the perpetrator.

Driders that survive for a long time can become accomplished hunters and navigators in the Underdark. Nothing will reopen the doors of drow society to them, but sometimes a drider can find a place in another community. Someone who needs a guide through the Underdark might not find a better one than a centuries-old drider that has faced every hazard those tunnels hold.

Rule of Matriarchs

Females are the top figures in drow society. At the head of each house is someone who is a shrewd business operator, a skilled tactician, a high priestess of Lolth, and probably also a merciless assassin with blood on her hands. Unlike with many other races, female drow are typically taller and more robust than males.

To rise to the top echelons of power, a female must first become a priestess of Lolth. Then, to ascend to the status of high priestess, she must take advantage of powerful connections or craft special alliances. The path to ultimate power in drow society is never direct and is always paved with death.

A male drow can advance in standing as a combatant, a consort, or both. Physical beauty and fitness are highly prized in male drow, and those who are especially favored in this regard can earn protection and gifts from their matrons. A few males can attain high status in their society, especially those who serve as mages, but they never overshadow the females of their houses. Even the most intelligent, strong-willed, and devious male will never be more than a second-class citizen in any drow city or house. That situation will never change as long as Lolth reigns as their queen.

Nocturnal Raiders

If the drow kept to themselves in their subterranean cities and fortresses, few other creatures would care. The dark elves could indulge their evil practices until their caverns were heaped with corpses and awash in blood. Even the surface elves might be content to overlook their hatred for their kin and leave the drow alone,

as long as they never had to lay eyes on the drow or view the results of their efforts.

But drow society is predicated on a foundation of terror and slavery, and the most desirable slaves live on the world's surface: humans, dwarves, and best of all, other elves. To the dark elves, raiding the surface for captives and treasure isn't just a cultural and military tradition, but also an economic necessity.

Some raids are major operations that involve hundreds of warriors, mages, priestesses, and giant spiders, a large enough force to overwhelm a community. The invaders would sweep through the town in the dark of night, shackle the best potential slaves into long trains of chattel, kill everyone who resisted, burn everything to the ground, and set their sights on the next town in line.

Most of the dark elves' raids, however, are small, stealthy, one-night missions. The drow scout their targets in advance, then strike on a night when the moon is new or its light is obscured by thick clouds. They might kill indiscriminately to spread terror, while at other times they slip into a village, knock out their targets with poison, and spirit their captives away without even waking the neighborhood dogs. Sometimes a raid uses both tactics; one squad sets fires or sets off alarms to focus the defenders' attention on one area, as another team strikes at the real target on the other side of town.

Loot is a secondary goal on almost all raids; taking prisoners is the primary objective. Some of the dark elves' victims become slaves, some end up as food for giant spiders or other monsters that the drow have trained to serve them, and some are laid out across blood-stained altars and sacrificed to Lolth.

The drow know how vulnerable they are during daylight, so they typically plan raids that can be executed within the span of a single night. As a rule, that means their target must be no more than a few hours' march—eight to twelve miles is typical—from an entrance to the Underdark. Ideally, they'll have more than one return path mapped out; if an escape route is blocked, they can switch to another and get safely home.

Once the raiders get inside their escape tunnel, they're usually safe. Opposing forces seldom pursue the drow below ground for good reason—beyond the light lies unmapped enemy territory where everything they meet is likely to be hostile. In special circumstances, such as if one of the raiders' captives is a royal heir or the scion of a wealthy family, adventurers might be hired to mount a rescue mission. Otherwise, it's rare for any rescuers to follow the kidnappers' trail deep into the deadly darkness without becoming victims themselves.

SLAVES AND STATUS

The drow are known and feared throughout the world for their practice of slavery, but those who have visited their cities report that slaves aren't as prevalent as the dark elves' reputation would suggest. In general, only powerful houses hold significant numbers of slaves, and the slaves of a house are never more numerous than its population of drow.

Slaves are often kept as signs of status as much as for their intrinsic worth as laborers. When they are put to work, they are also put on display, doing jobs that enable everyone on the street or in an audience chamber to see that their drow master owns and subjugates powerful enemies. As such, the creatures are commonly used as litter bearers, banner carriers, servers, and footstools.

Slaves without appreciable value as status symbols are used for strenuous or dangerous jobs such as tending farms, hauling cargo, or hollowing out giant stalagmites and stalactites to make new dwelling spaces. When they become too weak or dispirited to work, they might be staked out as bait during a hunt, fed to the spiders, or sacrificed to Lolth (and then fed to the spiders).

Although all slaves are at the bottom of the dark elves' social hierarchy, the lowest-ranking drow are considered little better than slaves themselves. A weak house that doesn't ally itself with a protector will be preyed on and victimized into extinction. If it does swear allegiance to a more powerful house, it avoids being persecuted by other houses but becomes effectively a clan of indentured servants. Only the most exceptional females in such a clan have any chance of rising above their low station, and those who do advance end up hurting rather than helping their families because they are adopted into the more prestigious house, leaving their original house even weaker than before.

THE DARK SELDARINE

Lolth demands the lion's share of worship from the drow, according to her wishes and by the command of her priestesses. The Spider Queen isn't, however, the only entity venerated by drow. They revere a host of divine entities, which they refer to as the Dark Seldarine in mockery of the surface elves' deities. The Dark Seldarine are mighty, immortal beings, survivors from the original group of primal elves who revolted against Corellon to remain at Lolth's side.

The Drow Deities table lists the members of the Dark Seldarine. For each god, the table notes alignment, province (the god's main areas of interest and responsibility), suggested domains for clerics who serve the god, and a common symbol of the god. The gods in the table are described below.

LOLTH

Unlike Corellon, who asks very little of his followers, Lolth is a demanding mistress. What she demands most of all are sacrifices of treasure and blood. Time and time

DROW TRANCE: ENTERING THE VOID

Drow enter trance just as other elves do, but they do not experience memories of a primal soul or of past lives. Often they recall nothing at all, but simply dwell for a time in darkness and silence, a respite from the dangers of their daily lives. When drow do dream, whether in trance or in sleep, they look for signs from Lolth or others of the Dark Seldarine. That drow do not experience trance the way other elves do lends credence to the idea that their souls do not reincarnate. Did Corellon forever bar the souls of dark elves from Arvandor and change them in some fundamental way? Or does Lolth somehow weave new souls for her followers, in the way that Moradin forges new spirits for dwarves? Only those entities know for certain.

again, the screams of sacrificial victims echo through Lolth's lightless temples as they fall under the knives of her priestesses. Her altars are piled with skulls picked clean of flesh by the giant spiders that lurk in the web-draped stalactites overhead.

In return for victims and adoration, Lolth grants signs of her favor, such as great success during a slave raid on the surface, the matron of a rival house being struck down by an inexplicable illness, or an heiress to the house being born under propitious omens.

GHAUNADAUR

This entity is most often referred to as That Which Lurks, because uttering its real name risks attracting its attention. Its actual form, if it even has one, is unknown; it's most often represented as an ooze-like creature with many tentacles or a purple pupil surrounded by black instead of white. The liquid nature of Ghaunadaur is symbolic of its unpredictable nature, which is what makes attracting its attention so risky. It occasionally rewards its followers with supernatural powers or wealth, but it's equally likely to curse its faithful with hideous torments and afflictions. A subterranean hunter who whispers Ghaunadaur's name might stumble into a forgotten treasure trove, while a devoted priestess who offers long prayers and valuable sacrifices is consumed by a gelatinous cube. The entity's random behavior can be an attraction to drow who lack status and are desperate to achieve it. A small sacrifice and a prayer to That Which Lurks might simply go unnoticed by Ghaunadaur, or it might punish the petitioner, but there is also a chance of receiving a great reward.

DROW DEITIES (THE DARK SELDARINE)

Deity	Alignment	Province	Suggested Domains	Common Symbol
Eilistraee	CG	Freedom, moonlight, song	Life, Light, Nature	Sword-wielding, dancing female drow silhouetted against the full moon
Ghaunadaur	CE	Oozes, slimes, outcasts	War	Purple eye with black sclera
Keptolo	CE	Beauty, hedonism, fertility	Nature, Trickery	Mushroom
Kiaransalee	CE	Necromancy	Arcana,* Death	Drow hand wearing many silver rings
Malyk	CE	Chaos, rebellion, wild magic	Tempest, Trickery	A flame in a tear or a multihued vortex
Lolth	CE	Primary god of drow, spiders	Trickery, War	Spider
Selvetarm	CE	Warriors, slaughter	War	Spider over crossed sword and mace
Vhaeraun	CE	Arrogance, thieves	Trickery, War	Black mask with blue glass lenses inset over eyes
Zinzerena	CN	Assassination, illusion, lies	Trickery	Shortsword draped with cloth

*Appears in *Sword Coast Adventurer's Guide*

Worship of That Which Lurks is widespread in the Underdark. Not just drow pay respect to it. Even creatures that are considered to be mindless, such as oozes and jellies, sometimes behave in ways that seem consistent with reverence for That Which Lurks.

Those who are faithful to Lolth often oppose Ghaunadaur's cultists, driving them into hiding or forcing them into open conflict. Some priestesses and scholars believe that this enmity exists because Ghaunadaur betrayed Lolth shortly after she betrayed Corellon. In these legends, Ghaunadaur tried to curry favor with Corellon and recapture his earlier formless nature by turning on Lolth. Ghaunadaur's double act of betrayal brought retribution from both gods, and he was cast down into the world as a skinless, boneless mass. Other stories portray Ghaunadaur as an incredibly ancient and ineffable deity, one of the so-called Great Old Ones. Both claims might have merit, because the truth about the time of the birth of gods can never be known for certain.

KEPTOLO

KEPTOLO SHOWS THE WAY. FEED THE VANITY OF YOUR *mistress, and all her treasures shall be yours. Be careful whom you offend, and keep an expendable companion nearby to hold culpable for your crimes. Gossip can be as deadly as the venom on an assassin's blade. Use the poison of words to destroy your rivals, that you may claim for yourself all they once presumed was theirs.*

—Tezzeryn, Head Consort of House Bhaerynden, instructing his son

The ideal of what a male drow can become, Keptolo is handsome, stylish, witty, hedonistic, an outrageous flatterer, and sought after as a lover. He is also dangerous in his aspects as a subtle assassin and a whisperer of rumors. For those attributes, he is worshiped by ambitious males who hope to emulate him. Some succeed admirably and achieve great things beyond the reach of most males, but many more succumb to excesses of the flesh, dissipation, and disease, or they are ruined or murdered by a rival—who is also a true disciple of Keptolo.

In most myths, Keptolo resides in the Demonweb Pits alongside Lolth, whom he serves as consort, more than a plaything but much less than an equal. Keptolo is a bitter enemy of Zinzerena, who deceives and uses him as a tool in many of the stories about the Dark Seldarine.

KIARANSALEE

The drow god of vengeance and undeath, called the Revenancer, is portrayed in some legends as a fierce female clad in silver and translucent veils, and in others as a banshee. In either version, her hands bear many glittering silver rings, and this image is recognized as her symbol.

Drow see Kiaransalee as the patron of vengeance because she is said to have died and returned from death to get her revenge, bringing an army of the dead back with her. Various communities of her worshipers have differing ideas about who killed her and why, but typically the murderer is portrayed as having the features

Give no quarter to drow, for none shall be given to you. Capture by drow means certain death, either as a sacrifice or after a life as a slave or a plaything.

of some kind of creature the drow have great hatred for. Followers of Kiaransalee don't trouble themselves greatly over these details, because all the stories could be true: the Revenancer is believed to have returned from death over and over again.

Vengeance is the aspect of Kiaransalee that appeals to most drow, because it becomes a necessity in every ambitious drow's life—usually more than once. The state of undeath is of less concern to them, but those who practice necromancy turn to Kiaransalee for guidance and for protection from undead. Some of her most fervent followers seek out the secret of attaining undeath for themselves. Kiaransalee favors them by bringing them back as undead, but unlike other gods of similar sort, Kiaransalee doesn't offer the undeath of lichdom but a lowly existence as a banshee, a revenant, or a wight.

Drow believe that Kiaransalee was driven mad by returning from death as a god so many times, but her followers aren't discouraged by this assessment. Despite her madness, her actions are guided by a deep and devious cunning—a trait that drow attach more importance to than they do to sanity.

MALYK

Malyk embodies rebellion and chaos. Drow know of his influence from the appearance of wild mages among their number. Such an individual, possessed of sorcerous powers seemingly bestowed at random, is often seen as a threat to the established order. Many drow, especially males and even females of low station, try to attract Malyk's attention by secretly making sacrifices to him. Meanwhile, house matrons and others steeped in the faith of Lolth attempt to purge Malyk's worship from drow society—at the same time that some of them pray to him for power.

Malyk is associated with rebellion because when a wild mage's true nature is revealed, the individual often has no recourse but to openly attack others and create chaos. Most other drow vie to receive Lolth's blessing by being the one to bring such a blasphemer to justice. In order to survive, a wild mage must defeat or elude all attackers and forge an alliance with those who can be threatened or bribed to provide a safe haven. Most wild mages who are discovered are put to death, some survive as outcasts, and a rare few rise to positions of status, declaring their allegiance to Lolth—or at least pretending to.

SELVETARM

Drow regard Selvetarm as the Champion of Lolth and the patron of drow warriors. He is portrayed as an eight-armed drow that represents the epitome of fighting prowess. But Lolth rarely looses her champion to do her bidding, keeping him snared by unbreakable webs that she removes only in times of direst need.

The dark elves believe that Selvetarm walked in solitude for many centuries, spurning both Lolth and Corellon, for he was not wholly given over to evil but neither was he fully aligned with the forces of light. Eventually his path crossed that of Eilistraee, and he began to appreciate the goodness of the Dark Maiden, as exhibited in her teachings and deeds. By aiding in Selvetarm's redemption, Eilistraee hoped to begin to heal the breach between drow and the Seldarine. That hope was dashed, however, by the insidious plotting of Lolth.

The Queen of Spiders had long resented the existence of Zanassu, a minor demon lord that competed with her for divine authority over spiders. She hated almost as much the possibility of Eilistraee's winning an ally among the drow pantheon. A prime opportunity arose when the spider demon lost much of its power in a conflict on the Material Plane. Lolth convinced Selvetarm to destroy Zanassu in its depleted state and seize the spider demon's burgeoning divine power. She did so by suggesting to Selvetarm that a victory would win him favor in the eyes of Eilistraee, whom he greatly admired. But when Selvetarm prevailed in battle over the spider demon, the wholly evil and chaotic nature of the divine power he absorbed overwhelmed Selvetarm's innate goodness and weakened him enough that the Spider Queen could bound his will tightly to her own.

Enraged by Lolth's duplicity, Selvetarm is an engine of destruction, an eight-limbed maestro of slaughter. If allowed to operate unchecked, he could rend his way through an entire drow city in a berserk rage. Keeping him restrained is one of the few acts of Lolth that can be described as merciful.

Because of his status as a captive, Selvetarm draws little attention from drow of high status. Low-caste drow warriors who are themselves slaves or indentured servants, or who have no chance to rise in rank, can beseech Selvetarm for prowess in battle without suffering any shame. Anyone of high standing or who hopes to attain high standing shies away from openly expressing reverence for Selvetarm, though such an individual might still beg his aid privately.

VHAERAUN

Vhaeraun stands for the dark elves' superiority over other races and for the primacy of individual drow over other drow. He is a god of arrogance, and thus he condones all acts of avarice, fair and foul alike. Those who take what they want from whom they wish, whether through stealth or bullying, pay homage to Vhaeraun. He is patron to thieves and often the object of prayer before drow embark on a raid.

Among the male gods of the Dark Seldarine, he is as widely recognized and accepted as Keptolo. But Vhaeraun represents a different aspect of drow masculinity: strong, silent, obedient, swift, and deadly. He is thought of as Lolth's favored son, in contrast to Keptolo's role as her beautiful consort.

Due to his high status in the Dark Seldarine (for a male) and because of his arrogance, a few of his worshipers look on him as an advocate of equality between male and female drow. That heresy, when it is expressed openly, is liable to be savagely crushed by the priestesses of Lolth. So most of Vhaeraun's male followers honor him simply by trying to carve out better lives for themselves, and that activity is tolerated. Even so, adherents of Vhaeraun don't appear in public without wearing masks. This practice exists in part because Vhaeraun is never portrayed unmasked, and partly because anonymity is a wise precaution when one challenges the social structure of the drow in even a small way.

To quash any challenge to the matriarchy that Vhaeraun might inspire in his followers, some drow communities preach that he wears a mask to hide the terrible scars from the wounds inflicted on him by Lolth as punishment for his arrogance. His silence, too, is part of his punishment, for his tongue was removed for questioning Lolth's orders. Worshipers of Vhaeraun who believe this dogma sometimes ritually scar and silence themselves as signs of their devotion, and then serve as voiceless, masked bodyguards for the matrons of their house.

ZINZERENA

As the patron of assassination, illusions, and lies, Zinzerena personifies cruelty, stealth, misdirection, and survival by any means necessary. In some ways, Malyk is her reflection, and in many interpretations of the age-old stories, the two gods are siblings or lovers. But Zinzerena is more palatable to female drow than Malyk, and she condones the study of arcane magic.

The liturgy of Zinzerena is passed on in the form of folk tales, for her faith has no place among the leadership of drow society. Her tales usually describe her hiding and waiting until her foes are weakened or lax in their attention before she attacks. Those who respect or revere Zinzerena are almost always of modest social status, or worse. Even the most prestigious of noble estates, where a high priestess reigns supreme, might have a number of her followers among the commoners who work as servants and staff. Only the most capricious of nobles would enter her priesthood, though some have done so. Inevitably, when such traitors are discovered, they are cast out from their houses. Ironically, these maverick nobles often become leading figures in Zinzerena's cult, for they are the best educated and most politically experienced of her followers. Her adherents come from a wide range of occupations, including common thieves, laborers, guides, physicians, poets, and nearly any other profession. What they all share is a rebellious spirit and a desire for change.

In some stories, Zinzerena is Lolth's daughter, who was spirited away and hidden from her by illusions. In other tales, she begins life as a mortal elf who uses glamors to trick her way into the company of the gods. Regardless, Zinzerena always has some element of illusion magic about her, and she uses it and other de-

ceptions to get the better of more powerful opponents. Deceit and taking advantage of others' weaknesses are recurring themes in the tales of her exploits. The only figure in the Dark Seldarine immune to Zinzerena's deceptions is Lolth, although even the Queen of Spiders is sometimes tricked when Zinzerena shifts blame for her actions onto others.

Not many female drow devote their lives to the study of magic, because it's held to be a low-status avocation more suited to males. Most females who pursue it seriously do so in secret. Even rumors that a drow matron practices arcane magic, if they aren't quashed, can sabotage her standing in society. Yet there's no denying that knowledge of arcane magic could be a great boon to an ambitious female. Zinzerena's worshipers encourage this pursuit and offer tutelage and tools in exchange for a candidate's alliance with Zinzerena's secret cult.

EILISTRAEE

Most drow know nothing of Eilistraee. Matron mothers of the most powerful houses closely guard the scrolls that chronicle her existence. They retain them for the sake of remaining aware of the enemy they describe: a drow god who would spirit away all of Lolth's worshipers to the surface world.

The matron mothers warn those who go to the surface on raids to retreat if they can see the moon—practical advice, it would seem. But an equally important reason is that Eilistraee is known to work her wiles under the light of the moon, so that drow are more susceptible to her lure at such times. The matrons also direct the raiders to flee back underground if any of their number hear music they find appealing, such as a parent's lullaby or the chorus of a rousing song carried on the mind, because Eilistraee's call to drow who would be free of Lolth's web is often delivered within dulcet tunes that aren't of otherworldly origin.

Eilistraee is a god of moonlight, song, dance, and, most important, the rejection of the evil ways of Lolth. Drow who feel like outsiders in their society, who react with disgust to the evils perpetrated by their kind, who come to the surface and fall in love with the stars—these are the ones who might be pleased to hear Eilistraee's call. If they respond to it by going to the surface and staying there, Eilistraee offers no guarantee of their safety and no promise of acceptance in the world above. But she opens her followers' hearts to the wonder of the nature in the night, and her songs and signs can show a drow how to persevere in that alien environment.

The scrolls that the matron mothers guard so closely attest that Eilistraee turned against Lolth but knew better than to seek solace among the Seldarine. Her position among the other drow gods remains uncertain, as is the fate of the souls of those who turn to her worship. Drow who are beloved by Eilistraee sometimes appear to vanish when they die, as the body dissolves into pale light and leaves no clue to where the soul has gone.

VULKOOR

Drow of the world of Eberron worship a scorpion-god named Vulkoor, which is their world's equivalent of Lolth. Vulkoor is often portrayed or envisioned as a giant scorpion or as a hybrid creature with the head, arms, and upper torso of a strong male drow and the lower body of a scorpion. The dark elves of Eberron revere scorpions, seeing spiders and other arachnids to be lesser servitors of Vulkoor. Many drow believe that Vulkoor and the Mockery (one of the group of evil deities known as the Dark Six) are one and the same. Drow from the jungle continent of Xen'drik ritually tattoo themselves using scorpion venom, leaving white scars etched into their skin.

Drow of other worlds rarely know of Vulkoor. Those who are familiar with his name consider him one of the weakest of the Dark Seldarine, a subordinate of Lolth who is disregarded by the other gods. Both visions of Vulkoor might be accurate, since Lolth seems to have little influence in Khyber but the drow there bear many similarities to the Lolth-worshiping drow of other realms throughout the multiverse.

THE DEMONWEB CONNECTION

Lolth's personal realm is a layer of the Abyss known colloquially as the Demonweb Pits. Far from being intimidated by their deity's connection to the Abyss, the drow revel in it—sometimes literally.

Drow have respect for the power of demons, but they don't fear them the way most other mortal creatures do. A drow who calls up a demon from the Abyss into the Underdark wants something from it, typically a means of improving one's status or gaining leverage against enemies. A demon that answers the call wants something in return: an opportunity to spread carnage, to curry Lolth's favor, or to accomplish something more devious. As long as both sides get what they want, these arrangements conclude without further incident.

Every so often, a demon summoning goes badly. Perhaps the drow intended to trap the demon into servitude but took inadequate precautions, or the demon was wilier than usual, or the call was answered by a being more powerful than the summoner could handle. Calling forth a demon and failing to rein it in is a capital crime in most drow communities—an uncontrolled demon often spells disaster not only for the drow who pulled it from the Abyss but for the summoner's entire house.

A demon is the highest form of slave a drow house can own. There's no better display of a house's power than a demon kept shackled as it serves its master, and few more potent ways of striking fear in an enemy's heart. Demons are also sometimes sought after as house guests. The occasion of a major sacrifice, the dedication of a newborn daughter to Lolth, or even a lavish banquet takes on greater significance and imparts more status when one or more demons are in attendance. In addition, any "peaceful" gathering of drow and demons has the potential to descend into a riot of hedonism, even more raw and debased than the orgies drow engage in on their own. Stories of such encounters have spread all the way to the surface world, where listeners dismiss them as exaggerations—but they're not. Draegloths, the offspring of drow and glabrezu, serve as proof enough that when demons and drow consort with one another, the result can be truly horrific.

YOCHLOLS

The shape-changing demons known as yochlols are the personal servants of Lolth. They seem to be numberless in the Demonweb Pits, but where they arise from is unknown. Are they spawned from drow souls that became trapped in Lolth's web? Or do they spring directly from the queen herself? Regardless of their origin, yochlols respond to the will of Lolth alone. No other demon or demon lord can command them.

Because yochlols can assume the form of a female drow or a giant spider, and because they serve Lolth without hesitation, all drow assume that some number of their friends and neighbors are actually yochlols in disguise, spying for Lolth. The higher a drow's standing, the more worrisome this prospect becomes. After all, Lolth has little reason to care about those at the bottom of society, but those who lead her people and direct her worship must be closely watched to be sure they remain devout, unquestioning, and afraid.

DROW RENEGADES

Drow society is, paradoxically, extremely open-ended and extremely oppressive. All drow have a chance, at least theoretically, to improve their station in life, and movement does occur throughout the hierarchy all the time. But, naturally, those in power are determined to put down any threat against them—and the penalty for insubordination is death.

As things work out in practice, indentured drow at the bottom of the ladder spend their lives laboring for another house's gain, and powerful drow at the top of society spend their time trying not to be assassinated or framed for heresy, while clinging to the power and prestige they've wrested from other houses.

A dark elf who challenges another for superiority and fails, or who fails to respect the hierarchy in some other way, has just three options: agonizing death on an altar, virtual enslavement, or fleeing for their lives. Some of those who choose to run succeed in escaping into the Underdark, despite the odds against them.

Survival for a solitary drow underground is nearly impossible. The main routes through the Underdark are dotted with drow guard posts, and the back ways are prowled by ropers, mind flayers, duergar, and other killers. To make matters worse, the renegade's former house offers a bounty that entices drow assassins to take up the chase. Of those who run, only a small fraction get to the surface. And even that achievement is no guarantee of safety, because a lone drow above ground is likely to be attacked on sight by surface dwellers.

Those who find a way to survive in the painful world of sunlight either live as recluses or find a community where their heritage and upbringing give them an advantage, such as an assassins' guild or a company of adventurers. Even in such cases, these traitorous drow spend the rest of their lives looking over their shoulders, hoping to spy the black hood and flashing blade of a bounty-hunting drow assassin before it's too late.

THE RAVEN QUEEN AND THE SHADAR-KAI

THE RAVEN QUEEN IS TRAPPED BY HER FASCINATION *with the past. She sits in her fortress, amidst all the memories of the world, looking at the ones that please her most as though they were glittering jewels. Many great wizards have attempted to understand her motives, but like a raven she has always remained cryptic, keeping her cache of secrets just out of their reach.*

—High Lady Alustriel Silverhand

The Raven Queen is a being of dark mystery. Accomplished wizards talk about her in hushed tones, and with no small amount of fear, for even they can't say what power she wields in her realms, too subtle for mortal minds to sense. Rumors abound as to her current form, most coming from claims made by lunatics who have described an array of disturbing images: a terrible shadow that clawed at their innermost thoughts, a pale and regal elf who exploded into an untold number of ravens, a shambling tangle of slick roots and sticks that overwhelmed them with dread, or an unknown presence that pulled them screaming blindly into the gloom.

Despite all attempts to demystify her, the Raven Queen has remained enigmatic and aloof, immersed in a sea of questions. She rules from her Raven Throne within the Fortress of Memories, a mazelike castle deep within the bleakness of the Shadowfell. From there she sends out her ravens to find interesting souls she can pluck from various planes of existence. Once they are in the Shadowfell, she watches as these souls attempt to unravel the mystery of their being—and ultimately go mad in the process.

ORIGIN OF THE RAVEN QUEEN

For those who seek to unravel the enigma of the Raven Queen, the story of her origin comes from the ancient history of the elves. It is said that she was once an elf queen, whose people loved her more than they loved the gods. Her true name has been lost to time.

But from the fragments that have been found of her history, it was she who, when Corellon and Lolth were locked in conflict, tried to use the souls and magic of her people to elevate herself to godly status, thus salvaging the fractured pantheon of the elves. Afterward, the legends suggest, she would attempt to implore Corellon and Lolth to come to their senses. But the information in these fragments was woefully incomplete, and the queen's true motives were never fully understood.

I have heard tales of drow who have forsaken the evil ways of their kind. I give these stories no credit, though Elminster himself swears they have validity. Never trust a drow, or the word of an archmage.

DESCENT INTO SHADOW

As the queen rose in power, many elves became inspired by her, freely offering their souls and their magical abilities to help her achieve her goal. This group of devoted followers called themselves the shadar-kai, and they gathered others like themselves around their queen in hopes that, once she achieved divinity, she would unify all the elves. The queen's plan was to use the souls of the shadar-kai to forge a pathway through the Feywild to Arvandor, all the while increasing her influence.

As the numbers of shadar-kai grew, a consortium of evil wizards among her followers saw an opportunity to siphon off the energy of the shadar-kai for themselves by performing their own self-serving ritual, which would impart to them magical powers beyond those of the greatest elven wizards of legend. But as the queen approached the entrance to Arvandor, she realized what the wizards were doing and brought all her wrath down upon them as the ritual was under way. Because she was by now a quasi-divine entity, her supernatural rage corrupted the ritual into a phenomenon that took on a terrible strength of its own.

By the time the queen realized her error, she could feel the now-twisted magical energy grabbing hold of her, and she was powerless to stop it. In a panic, she reached out to the souls of the shadar-kai for more power, hoping to save herself, but the gravity of the spell had become irresistible. It pulled the queen, and all who were under her sway, into the Shadowfell, where she was instantly killed. From her ruined mind and body, the Raven Queen was born.

THE CREATION OF THE NAGPAS

When their ritual failed with catastrophic results, the wizards in the consortium were pulled into the Shadowfell along with the queen and the shadar-kai, but their misfortune didn't end there. Their former queen arose from the center of a maze of ash and let loose a scream of ebon smoke that penetrated the flesh and minds of the wizards, turning their bones black and lacerating their souls. Their cries of agony merged with her own, and when her scream faded, the wizards had been mutated and warped into the scabrous, vulturish creatures known as nagpas. Now they wander the planes as wretched monsters, marked forever by the Raven Queen's curse and banished from her presence.

AFTER THE FALL

After the nagpas were created and then banished by the Raven Queen, the shadar-kai watched as she fell deeper and deeper into a divine madness. Her pain and turmoil over the betrayal of her wizards, the destruction of her kingdom, and her failure at attaining godhood all con-

tributed to her descent into an unquenchable sorrow. At the same time, the energy of the corrupted ritual was still transforming her, breaking down her form from a physical one into an entity composed of symbols, images, and perceptions. To keep herself from dissipating entirely into nothingness, the queen used the last vestiges of her personal power to pull dead memories from the Shadowfell about her, creating a cloak of identities that sustained her. Over centuries, those dark memories accumulated and coalesced to give shape to the entity now known as the Raven Queen.

The Fortress of Memories

Since achieving divinity, the Raven Queen has filled her realm with shadows and memories, obsessively collecting such essences from remnants of dead gods and mortals that were strewn throughout the Shadowfell. From these metaphysical fragments she formed her new home, a twisted castle that the shadar-kai call the Fortress of Memories. The fortress is a mournful place, filled with incessant echoes of the past. Flocks of ravens that act as her eyes and ears darken the skies around it when they emerge from within, bearing her cryptic messages and omens far and wide across the multiverse.

Bizarre Menagerie. Within the Fortress of Memories are trinkets and items that the Raven Queen finds irresistible, memories plucked from people's pasts that have been invested with deep feelings of pain, sorrow, longing, guilt, or remorse. These items are brought to her as gifts from the shadar-kai. These trinkets can include furniture, clocks, mirrors, jewels, and toys. Also appearing in the fortress are ghostly visions of people, places, and pets. Any of these things can spontaneously appear about her lair, every object and apparition being a metaphoric representation of some story—great or small—that was saturated with raw emotion.

Encountering the Raven Queen

Mortals that enter the Raven Queen's realm are almost instantly confronted with a glimpse into their own internal landscape. Because she is fascinated with emotions, the Raven Queen worms into the unconscious minds and memories of her visitors, bringing forth visions from the deepest reaches of their psyches. Some of these visitors are the unwitting souls of departed people who have been pulled into the Raven Queen's clutches, others are astral travelers who are caught and trapped within the Shadowfell by her magic—but a rare few come of their own volition, seeking knowledge or freedom from a dark past.

A Quest to the Fortress of Memories

Because the Raven Queen has godlike power, she can put an adventuring party inside a demiplane that is created from the psyche of one of the characters. On entering the Fortress of Memories, or encountering the Raven Queen, a character can find themselves transported to a strange fairy tale world pulled from their experiences, filled with metaphors, parables and allegories, all of which challenge that character's frailties, fears, and desires. Much can be learned from adventuring within the fortress and undergoing the Raven Queen's test, but much can also be lost. Many adventurers never return from the fortress, forever trapped within a world created from their own experience.

Many of these daring individuals are adventurers who know of the Raven Queen's terrifying power yet nevertheless travel to the Shadowfell to undergo her trial, letting the secrets of their souls be unfolded and revealed. The reasons why folk would subject themselves to this dangerous experience are numerous, including:

- To free themselves from a dark and terrible past. It is said that the Raven Queen can make you confront your fears; some find a way to move beyond them, but others can be driven mad.
- To discover a secret of someone who is dead. Adventurers might need to go to the Shadowfell to find a soul that has been claimed by the Raven Queen, hoping to unlock its memories.
- To seek answers that only the Raven Queen might know. The Raven Queen's realm contains innumerable memories from all over the multiverse. Desperate adventurers might seek her out as a last resort or be led to her realm by a series of tempting clues.

Method or Madness? Some wizards and other scholars have speculated that the Raven Queen is simply insane, that there is no method to her madness other than a nervous pecking apart of a psyche with no more motive than a curious child pulling the legs off an ant. Others have speculated that the Raven Queen needs the gravity of emotions to hold her eternally decaying identity together. But a few sages have postulated that the Raven Queen's purpose is of greater importance, that she serves as a filter of sorts, cleansing souls that cling to fear and pain, forcing them to confront their unfinished business so that they are freed of their mortal baggage and can rise to explore higher planes of existence.

The Raven Queen's Influence

The Raven Queen's desire to interfere with the affairs of the gods and her subsequent failure was taken as nothing less than treason by both Corellon and Lolth. As a result, the physical reality of her kingdom was shifted to the Shadowfell, and the memory of her existence was wiped from the minds of elves. Initially, no mortals knew of her, but over the centuries, those who have journeyed to the Shadowfell and those who have encoun-

tered shadar-kai in the world have seen, or heard tales of, a dark fortress, a mysterious figure surrounded by gaunt servants, and scores of seemingly sentient ravens. Most folk who have heard of the Raven Queen view her through a lens of superstitious fear, attributing to her all kinds of strange occurrences, mishaps, and coincidences. But those who seriously study the arcane—warlocks, wizards, sorcerers, and the like—know that her effect on the world is farther-reaching than that.

Audience after Death. Some adventurers claim to have been visited by the Raven Queen after their deaths—before their stalwart friends paid to have them resurrected. While they were in the afterlife, the Raven Queen enlisted them for a quest to complete a task, acquire a particular item, or perhaps to travel to a location and simply wait. Most of those who have talked about these visitations say they felt compelled to do her bidding, because the visions imparted by the Raven Queen made it apparent that the quest was in some way part of their greater purpose.

The Raven Queen's reason for communing in this way is a matter of some dispute. Some sages posit that she is using people as pawns in an inscrutable game, the rules of which are known only to her and the Lady of Pain. Others suggest that she is balancing the multiverse by having mortals complete various tasks, and some say that it is in these moments of obeisance to her that the Raven Queen recalls a fragment of her former self.

Servants of the Queen

The shadar-kai are bound to the Raven Queen, cursed to forever serve her in the Shadowfell. They dwell in places outside the Fortress of Memories, usually too terrified of the place to enter it willingly. In their communities they reenact their old rituals and ceremonies, in a pale imitation of the days when they dwelled in the life and light of their now-lost kingdom.

When shadar-kai are in the Shadowfell, their bodies and faces are old and withered, displaying the full effects of the terrible magic that stripped them of their former elven beauty. To hide their visages, they often wear masks made of metal or wood, but even these coverings are melancholic in appearance. When shadar-kai are sent away from the Shadowfell to do the Raven Queen's bidding, they take on youthful features similar to those of other elves, although their skin remains deathly pale.

Immortal Servants. The shadar-kai know that when they die, the Raven Queen captures their souls and returns them to the Shadowfell, where they are resurrected to serve her yet again. Thus, they consider death to be a temporary condition, and many shadar-kai care little for the physical shell they currently inhabit.

Shadar-kai know that those who come willingly to the Raven Queen's tower are there to beseech her for something, and thus they try to prepare such visitors for what they will face. The queen's servants talk to any inquiring adventurer about the gravity of emotion, how sorrow weighs on the soul as it travels through the Shadowfell, and how best to persevere in the Raven Queen's test.

Follow the Ravens. When the Raven Queen sees a soul or a piece of information she wants, she sends her ravens to alert the shadar-kai. Her minions then put

---

Vecna's Obsession

One evil mind is fixated on wresting away the Raven Queen's power: the archlich Vecna. Vecna has long coveted her ability over knowledge and souls; to steal souls would give him the ability to amass an army of the dead large enough to conquer the Shadowfell and turn it into his own kingdom of death. There he would rule from the Fortress of Memories, and through the Raven Queen's power have access to all the lost knowledge stored within the souls she has trapped over the millennia. But to this day, all his attempts to gain a foothold there have been thwarted.

Because of his obsession with usurping the Raven Queen, and claiming the Fortress of Memories, Vecna has embroiled himself in a terrible conflict, leading his armies into relentless battles against the Raven Queen and her shadar-kai fanatics and against the vampire lord Kas, Vecna's former lieutenant, whom Vecna wants to see destroyed over all other enemies. Some say this war is just another of the Raven Queen's beloved tragedies playing out for her amusement.

---

their trust in these cryptic, cawing guides to lead them to where the barriers are weakest so they can then slip across planes to their destination. Once at their destination, the shadar-kai watch and wait, looking for the tragedies their queen wishes them to collect. Sometimes they are small: a spurned lover, a lost item, a betrayal. But some tragedies are much graver: a murder, a war, a diabolical bargain. To bring back a trinket for their queen, the shadar-kai use their shadow magic. If a target is living, they magically infiltrate the person's mind and excise the desired bits of emotion, or if the target is close to death, the shadar-kai capture the whole soul to bring back to the Raven Queen.

Sediment of Memory. Shadar-kai are very interested in the magical silt at the bottom of the River Styx that holds the memories and identities of lost souls. Any adventurers who travel to the Nine Hells to procure a vial of this powder will likely draw the attention of the shadar-kai, who will attempt to steal or barter for it. Adventurers might also bring a bit of the sediment as a gift to the Raven Queen. What she would give in return is never known ahead of time, but her boons come in many wondrous forms: the restoration of a lost soul, the rediscovery of a missing memory, or a glimpse into the forgotten knowledge of the ancients.

ELF SUBRACES

At the DM's discretion, you have access to more subraces for elf characters, in addition to the subraces in the *Player's Handbook*. When you choose the subrace of your elf, you can choose one of the following options: eladrin, sea elf, or shadar-kai.

RANDOM HEIGHT AND WEIGHT

Subrace	Base Height	Base Weight	Height Modifier	Weight Modifier
Eladrin	4'6"	90 lb.	+2d12	× (1d4) lb.
Sea elf	4'6"	90 lb.	+2d8	× (1d4) lb.
Shadar-kai	4'8"	90 lb.	+2d8	× (1d4) lb.

Height = Base Height + Height Modifier (in inches)
Weight = Base Weight + Height Modifier (in pounds) × Weight Modifier

ELADRIN

Eladrin are elves native to the Feywild, a realm of beauty, unpredictable emotion, and boundless magic. An eladrin is associated with one of the four seasons and has coloration reminiscent of that season, which can also affect the eladrin's mood:

Autumn is the season of peace and goodwill, when summer's harvest is shared with all.
Winter is the season of contemplation and dolor, when the vibrant energy of the world slumbers.
Spring is the season of cheerfulness and celebration, marked by merriment as winter's sorrow passes.
Summer is the season of boldness and aggression, a time of unfettered energy.

Some eladrin remain associated with a particular season for their entire lives, whereas other eladrin transform, adopting characteristics of a new season.

When finishing a long rest, any eladrin can change their season. An eladrin might choose the season that is present in the world or perhaps the season that most closely matches the eladrin's current emotional state. For example, an eladrin might shift to autumn if filled with contentment, another eladrin could change to winter if plunged into sorrow, still another might be bursting with joy and become an eladrin of spring, and fury might cause an eladrin to change to summer.

The following tables offer personality suggestions for eladrin of each season. You can roll on the tables or use them as inspiration for characteristics of your own.

AUTUMN

d4	Autumn Personality Trait
1	If someone is in need, you never withhold aid.
2	You share what you have, with little regard for your own needs.
3	There are no simple meals, only lavish feasts.
4	You stock up on fine food and drink. You hate going without such comforts.

d4	Autumn Flaw
1	You trust others without a second thought.
2	You give to others, to the point that you leave yourself without necessary supplies.
3	Everyone is your friend, or a potential friend.
4	You spend excessively on creature comforts.

ELADRIN OF AUTUMN

Winter

d4	Winter Personality Trait
1	The worst case is the most likely to occur.
2	You preserve what you have. Better to be hungry today and have food for tomorrow.
3	Life is full of dangers, but you are ready for them.
4	A penny spent is a penny lost forever.

d4	Winter Flaw
1	Everything dies eventually. Why bother building anything that is supposedly meant to last?
2	Nothing matters to you, and you allow others to guide your actions.
3	Your needs come first. In winter, all must watch out for themselves.
4	You speak only to point out the flaws in others' plans.

Spring

d4	Spring Personality Trait
1	Every day is the greatest day of your life.
2	You approach everything with enthusiasm, even the most mundane chores.
3	You love music and song. You supply a tune yourself if no one else can.
4	You can't stay still.

d4	Spring Flaw
1	You overdrink.
2	Toil is for drudges. Yours should be a life of leisure.
3	A pretty face infatuates you in an instant, but your fancy passes with equal speed.
4	Anything worth doing is worth doing again and again.

Summer

d4	Summer Personality Trait
1	You believe that direct confrontation is the best way to solve problems.
2	Overwhelming force can accomplish almost anything. The tougher the problem, the more force you apply.
3	You stand tall and strong so that others can lean on you.
4	You maintain an intimidating front. It's better to prevent fights with a show of force than to harm others.

d4	Summer Flaw
1	You are stubborn. Let others change.
2	The best option is one that is swift, unexpected, and overwhelming.
3	Punch first. Talk later.
4	Your fury can carry you through anything.

Eladrin Traits

Eladrin have the following traits in common, in addition to the traits they share with other elves. Choose your eladrin's season: autumn, winter, spring, or summer.

Ability Score Increase. Your Charisma score increases by 1.

Fey Step. As a bonus action, you can magically teleport up to 30 feet to an unoccupied space you can see. Once you use this trait, you can't do so again until you finish a short or long rest.

When you reach 3rd level, your Fey Step gains an additional effect based on your season; if the effect requires a saving throw, the DC equals 8 + your proficiency bonus + your Charisma modifier:

Autumn. Immediately after you use your Fey Step, up to two creatures of your choice that you can see within 10 feet of you must succeed on a Wisdom saving throw or be charmed by you for 1 minute, or until you or your companions deal any damage to it.

Winter. When you use your Fey Step, one creature of your choice that you can see within 5 feet of you before you teleport must succeed on a Wisdom saving throw or be frightened of you until the end of your next turn.

Spring. When you use your Fey Step, you can touch one willing creature within 5 feet of you. That creature then teleports instead of you, appearing in an unoccupied space of your choice that you can see within 30 feet of you.

Summer. Immediately after you use your Fey Step, each creature of your choice that you can see within 5 feet of you takes fire damage equal to your Charisma modifier (minimum of 1 damage).

Sea Elf

Sea elves fell in love with the wild beauty of the ocean in the earliest days of the multiverse. While other elves traveled from realm to realm, the sea elves navigated the deepest currents and explored the waters across a hundred worlds. Today, they live in small, hidden communities in the ocean shallows and on the Elemental Plane of Water.

Sea Elf Traits

Sea elves have the following traits in common, in addition to the traits they share with other elves.

Ability Score Increase. Your Constitution score increases by 1.

Sea Elf Training. You have proficiency with the spear, trident, light crossbow, and net.

Child of the Sea. You have a swimming speed of 30 feet, and you can breathe air and water.

Friend of the Sea. Using gestures and sounds, you can communicate simple ideas with any beast that has an innate swimming speed.

Languages. You can speak, read, and write Aquan.

Shadar-kai

Sworn to the Raven Queen's service, the mysterious shadar-kai venture into the Material Plane from the Shadowfell to advance her will. Once they were fey like the rest of their elven kin, and now they exist in a strange state between life and death. Eladrin and shadar-kai are like reflections of each other: one bursting with emotion, the other nearly devoid of it.

SHADAR-KAI TRAITS

Shadar-kai have the following traits in common, in addition to the traits they share with other elves.

Ability Score Increase. Your Constitution score increases by 1.

Necrotic Resistance. You have resistance to necrotic damage.

Blessing of the Raven Queen. As a bonus action, you can magically teleport up to 30 feet to an unoccupied space you can see. Once you use this trait, you can't do so again until you finish a long rest.

Starting at 3rd level, you also gain resistance to all damage when you teleport using this trait. The resistance lasts until the start of your next turn. During that time, you appear ghostly and translucent.

ELF TABLES

This section provides tables for players and DMs who want to choose or randomly generate details about elves.

ELVEN TRINKETS

d8	Trinket
1	A small notebook that causes anything written in it to disappear after 1 hour
2	A crystal lens made of ivory and gold that causes anything observed through it to appear to be surrounded by motes of multicolored light
3	A small golden pyramid inscribed with elven symbols and about the size of a walnut
4	A cloak pin made from enamel in the shape of a butterfly; when you take the pin off, it turns into a real butterfly, and returns when you are ready to put your cloak back on again
5	A golden compass that points toward the nearest portal to the Feywild within 10 miles
6	A small silver spinning top that, when spun, endlessly spins until interrupted
7	A small songbird made of enamel, gold wire, and precious stone; uttering the songbird's name in Elvish causes the trinket to emit that bird's birdsong
8	A small enamel flower that, when put in one's hair, animates, tying back the wearer's hair with a living vine with flowers; plucking a single flower from this vine returns it to its inanimate form

Drow Adventurer Story Hooks

d8	Hook
1	You overheard members of your own house plotting to poison you, so you fled from the Underdark to save yourself. You won't return until you've amassed enough fortune to surround yourself with loyal mercenary bodyguards.
2	You were enslaved as punishment for trying to poison an influential rival, but you escaped and fled to the surface. If you return to the Underdark and are captured, you'll be re-enslaved.
3	You were the lover of a high-ranking priestess of Lolth as a means of enhancing your status. When she tired of you, the loss of status was humiliating, so you left.
4	You killed a drow from a more powerful house in a duel over a public insult. The slain drow's house vowed to destroy your house unless you were handed over. Your kin urged you to leave the Underdark. You wonder what became of them.
5	A close friend of yours was revealed to be a worshiper of Eilistraee. Suspicion fell on everyone in her circle. Running was a tacit admission of guilt, even though you knew nothing about it, but you'd have been sacrificed to Lolth if you stayed.
6	You were among a group of surface raiders that was ambushed, and you were captured. During years of captivity, you learned that most of what Lolth's priestesses taught about the outer world was lies. Now you're experiencing the truth for yourself.
7	All your life, you were alienated and terrified by the cruelty of your kin. The first chance you got, you volunteered to go on a surface raid, then deserted the group and remained behind. Now you're hated and feared wherever you go, but at least you've found a small group of adventurous friends who trust and support each other.
8	You were part of a delegation carrying diplomatic messages to another drow city when duergar attacked the caravan for slaves and treasure. Only you and one other guard escaped. If you'd returned home, you'd have been poisoned or worse for failure. Becoming a mercenary was your best option.

Elf (Non-drow) Adventurer Story Hooks

d8	Hook
1	You believe the key to reuniting the elves with Corellon lies somewhere in the wider world, not within elven society, and you're determined to find it.
2	Your sibling was killed by a rampaging monster. You won't rest until you track it down and slay it.
3	A raven brought you a cryptic message from an old friend who needs your help, but the message was vague about the friend's location. You're trying to follow a years-old trail and save your friend.
4	A beautiful elf won your heart, then broke it. If you earn enough gold and glory by adventuring, perhaps you can win back your love.
5	Your father thought you too weak to survive as an adventurer, but he's wrong, and you'll prove it.
6	Only those who perform great deeds are remembered long after their death. Bards will honor your exploits for generations to come.
7	You're secretly in love with one of the other members of your adventuring group, and you can't bear the thought of any harm befalling that person.
8	When you were born, your grandmother prophesied you would one day rule a human kingdom. You've gone in search of that destiny.

Drow House Specialty

d10	Specialty
1	Adamantine weapons
2	Assassinations
3	Giant spiders subject to magical control
4	Hallucinogenic substances
5	High-status slaves and sacrificial victims
6	Items taken from surface world in raids
7	Low-cost, humanoid slaves
8	Maps of the Underdark
9	Poisons
10	Reptilian beasts of burden

CHAPTER 3: DWARVES AND DUERGAR

To impartial observers, the tale of the ancient war between dwarves and duergar is at its heart a tragedy, the story of a people turned against each other by bitterness and resentment. Once the dwarves were unified in their worship of Moradin, the deity who crafted the first dwarves from metal and fire. Today, the race is splintered into those who still embrace him as their father and creator—and those who have sworn to topple him from his divine throne.

While the dwarves loyal to Moradin take joy in the art of crafting and form strong family bonds, the duergar are joyless, hateful creatures who create their works out of an urge to build and acquire. They come closest to feeling true joy when they raid dwarven strongholds to satisfy their lust for blood and treasure.

THE DEEP ROOTS OF WAR

Take this message to your doddering fool of a god. His turn is coming, Laduguer willing.

—Duergar assassin Vozala Spikefist, before slaying the dwarf king Umbrag Hammerthorn

The conflict began in ages past, when the world was new. Almost all the dwarves were more than content to make their homes inside the mountains and hills that were filled with ore and other valuables, not digging too far beneath the surface. The dwarves of clan Duergar, however, became obsessed with delving deep into the Underdark. The clan's miners continually insisted that a great trove of gold and iron lay just beyond where the clan had explored. The next strike of a pick, they said, could reveal wealth beyond imagining.

This obsession took root and spread throughout the clan. Soon, all other activity in the community ceased; the forges grew cold, and the temples to Moradin stood empty. Every dwarf old enough to hold a pick or shovel worked the mines.

The dwarves relentlessly dug, hacked, and tunneled. The weakest among them fell dead from exhaustion, the rest pausing only long enough to push the corpses aside so they could continue the digging.

Only the hardiest and most iron-willed individuals of the clan survived this brutal campaign. When their delving finally broke through into a cavern, the dwarves found the cause of their obsession. A great elder brain and its mind flayers waited there, ready to take the next step in the subjugation of clan Duergar. The monsters had sent out a psychic lure that played on the dwarves' greed, and the never-ending work schedule that was the product of their obsession weeded out all but the best specimens for their slave pens. The illithids had no trouble overwhelming the remaining dwarves with their psionic power and soon put them to work.

The dwarves proved to be able slaves, but the elder brain saw within them another kind of usefulness. The dwarves' innate ability to resist the effects of harmful substances such as poison made them suitable subjects for a variety of grisly experiments. Generations of psychic surgery and physical alterations mutated the captives into creatures that had special powers of their own.

In time, a leader arose among the enslaved dwarves. Named Laduguer, he struck a deal with Asmodeus, pledging the assistance of clan Duergar against Lolth's ambitions in the Underdark. With the help of the Lord of the Nine, the dwarves overthrew their illithid masters in a great uprising. At last, Laduguer could bring his clan upward to rejoin the world they had left behind.

TRIUMPH TURNED SOUR

When Laduguer and his people returned to the dwarves of the upper world, they were shocked by the hostility they faced. As Laduguer quickly learned, the priests of Moradin had long ago labeled the lost clan as heretics, spoken of now only as an object lesson concerning the fate of dwarves who stray from Moradin's teachings.

When Laduguer protested this treatment, the priests insisted that Moradin had sent omens and warnings to the lost dwarves, but they went unheeded. Envoys from the other clans had found clan Duergar's stronghold abandoned, with no evidence of invasion, plague, or other calamity. Even worse, the temples of Moradin had been left untended. Only laziness, greed, and contempt for the All-Father could account for the clan's fate.

Laduguer, in response, tried to explain that his people had been lured into a trap by the mind flayers, but his assertions fell on deaf ears. Thus, with no other apparent choice, the lost clan fled back to the Underdark. Laduguer focused his fury on Moradin. The dwarves' supposed father had turned a blind eye as they fell into the mind flayers' trap, then sat idle as the clan suffered unspeakable abuses. Laduguer and his followers swore that they wouldn't rest until the father of the dwarves lay dead and Laduguer sat upon his throne.

Of course, by declaring his intent to destroy Moradin, Laduguer created a state of war between the duergar and the other dwarves in the world. Since that time, the duergar have not eased up on their hostility, and the dwarves have not relaxed their vigilance.

CONFLICT WITHOUT END

Few others aside from the dwarves and the duergar understand or appreciate the true scope and intensity of the battles between these two races. Viewed on a grand scale, the conflict is a great war of attrition—the combatants don't often gain or lose territory as the result of battle. But on a personal scale, combat is brutal, with no quarter given or expected.

The duergar fight a persistent guerrilla war of sudden raids and brutal attacks against isolated groups of dwarves. Duergar often begin an attack by burrowing into a dwarf settlement from below, then bursting out in a vicious assault that leaves few survivors. If robbery rather than murder is the goal, a duergar war party might surreptitiously dig for weeks to penetrate a dwarf treasure vault, hoping to seize a clan's riches from beneath its noses.

For their part, the dwarves keep safety and defense uppermost in their priorities, realizing that there is little to be gained from trying to mount a large-scale assault against the duergar. They actively protect their strongholds, keeping careful watch for signs of tunneling, and—dwarven pride being what it is—send bands of warriors out from time to time to deal reprisals to duergar camps and fortresses. In addition to these rare offensive thrusts, dwarves sometimes send small squads of explorers or scouts into the Underdark to learn about duergar activity or to recover stolen treasures if they can do so without attracting too much attention.

This eternal enmity between duergar and dwarves doesn't consume either side; both have other concerns and needs that take much of their time and attention, At the same time, the never-ending state of war is never out of mind—every dwarf knows that a chance encounter with a duergar could be fatal, and every duergar would like nothing better than to have such an opportunity.

DWARVES

The dwarf god Moradin forged the first dwarves in his great workshop, causing them to spring to life from inert metal when he cooled the heated castings with his breath. Since then, the dwarves have revered Moradin and sought to follow in his footsteps. Through constant, steady work, they strive to emulate the perfect example set by the originator of the arts and skills the dwarves pursue.

To the dwarves, Moradin is the Creator. With his impeccable skills, he crafted the first dwarves and imbued them with a sense of relentless purpose, driven to apply their own crafting skills to the raw materials around them and thereby unlock the beauty that hides within.

Moradin is also worshiped as the All-Father, in acknowledgment of his role as the progenitor of the dwarven race. In this aspect as well, he is credited not only for the birth of the dwarves but for fostering in them a deep appreciation for clan and family. He demonstrates how dwarf parents should raise their children, instilling in them the urge to further not only themselves but to contribute to the success of the larger group. Just as Moradin looks out for all dwarves, all dwarves in a clan look out for one another.

THE PATH TO PERFECTION

EVERY FALL OF THE HAMMER ON THE ANVIL, EVERY FIRE *stoked in the forge, is a step on a journey set before me by Moradin himself. It isn't work. It is a challenge to achieve greatness.*

—Balifra Eversharp

Dwarves have a strong sense of their progress, and each day that goes by must bring them closer to the standard set by Moradin. Acutely aware of their mortality, they see the many centuries afforded to them as too short a time to risk wasting even a single day in indolence.

Dwarves pursue perfection. This chase is foolish. There is no one pure truth of anything.

Moradin crafted the dwarves' sturdy bodies, giving them the strength to work for long periods of time. Rather than imparting his skills to them, he fueled their spirits with a burning desire to follow his example. His gifts of durability and purpose gave the dwarves all they needed to devote their lives to steady work, refining their skills and improving their inner selves while they transform rock and ore into wondrous creations.

LIFETIMES OF GLORIOUS LABOR

Dwarf artisans regard the fruits of their labors with the same love that members of other races reserve for their children. A dwarf's works are built to last for centuries, to carry a legacy into the world long after the dwarf is gone. Each item a dwarf crafts is a milepost on the path to perfection, a step taken toward mastering a technique. All of one's works taken together are the physical representation of a dwarf's accomplishments. A dwarf who has lived a good, fruitful life leaves behind a rich legacy of wondrous goods—gleaming metal goblets, gem-encrusted stone sculptures, tapestries made of ores and minerals, finely honed weapons, or the end result of any other endeavor that enriches the crafter while it pays homage to the Creator.

Dwarves guard their personal creations with the vigilance and ferocity of a dragon protecting a treasure hoard. Such protectiveness isn't often called for in the company of friends and family—but just as a parent doesn't leave a child unattended, a dwarf doesn't craft an item and then knowingly leave it vulnerable to being stolen (or worse). A dwarf who loses an item to thievery pursues the item's recovery or seeks vengeance against the thieves with the same fury that parents direct against those who kidnapped their child.

At the other extreme, a dwarf's gift of a personal item to someone else is a deep expression of commitment, love, and trust. The beneficiary of the gift is expected to provide the item with the same careful stewardship exhibited by its creator—never letting it fall into an enemy's hands and sparing no effort to recover it if is stolen.

MINDS AS RIGID AS STONE

Although the dwarves' obsessive pursuit of perfection in the arts of crafting leads them to produce great works, it comes at a price. Dwarves value stability, repetition, and tradition above all else. Chaos and change cause distractions from the task at hand. Dwarves crave predictability, routine, and safety. A mind not fully focused can't give a task its proper attention.

This rigidity in outlook, though a fundamental part of the dwarven psyche, can sometimes be a disadvantage. Dwarves don't change their minds easily, and once set on a course rarely alter their strategy. Their commitment to following a plan serves them well when they build a stone bridge designed to last for centuries, but the same inflexibility can bring problems when applied to the unpredictable dangers of the world. A clan might continue to depend on the same plan for defending its stronghold that has been used for centuries, without considering the possibility that its enemies have discovered how to overcome those defenses.

The dwarves' way of thinking leads to difficulties in their relationships with humans and elves. From their long-lived perspective, dwarves can't understand the speed with which human communities and civilizations rise and fall. If a trade delegation from a dwarven stronghold were to visit a human town once every twenty or thirty years—not a long time to a dwarf—the community's leaders would likely be different every time, and for the dwarves the experience would be akin to making first contact all over again. Establishing trade with this "new" human outpost would require forming new relationships, a process that could take weeks or months.

The elves' chaotic nature and love of the wilderness baffle the dwarves, who think of them as somewhat mad. Dwarves typically find elves too flighty to ever fully trust them, believing that creatures that thrive on change and chaos can't possibly be reliable allies.

In particular situations, of course, the benefits of cooperating with humans or elves can override the dwarves' concern about the shortcomings of those races. When dwarves, humans, and elves have a common enemy, they all find a way to work together for the common good.

All for One: The Clan

So the barman isn't a relative, and you don't even know the names of any of the folk here? How can you possibly sleep peacefully in this inn, surrounded by strangers? We'll be lucky to see the morning.

—Tordek

The clan is the basic unit of dwarven society, an extended family that dwells together. Everything a dwarf does in life is devoted to improving or helping the clan, bringing security and stability to its members and greater glory to the group.

The most important clan members to any dwarf are the members of one's immediate family, because the instinctive connection between parent and child is stronger than the attachment between unrelated clan members. Nevertheless, the distinction is so slim as to be unnoticeable to outsiders—dwarves will endure hardship or lay down their lives for any of their clan mates, whether related to them by blood or by the devotion that holds the clan together.

The Greatest Legacy
The life of a dwarf is all about doing good work and leaving behind a fitting legacy that continues to bolster the clan even after its creator has passed on—a legacy counted not only in objects, but also in dwarven souls. Dwarves who become parents rightfully think of their children as the greatest legacy they can leave the clan, and they raise them with the same care and attention to detail that they give to the items they create. A dwarf's

Dwarves are creatures of stone, and like stone they change only in response to extremes. The dwarves of the many worlds share much in common, but never allow those similarities to blind you to their unique traits.

direct descendants—beloved sons, daughters, and grandchildren—are often the ones who inherit the inanimate works their ancestor leaves behind.

Marriage is a sacred rite among the dwarves, taken very seriously because it requires two children to move away from their homes to start a new family in the clan. The affected families feel a sense of loss that is healed only when a new dwarf child enters the world—an event that calls for great celebration.

Few dwarves develop romantic feelings for their spouses, at least not in the way that other races do. They view their spouses as collaborators and co-creators, their elders as respected experts to be obeyed, and their children as their most treasured creations. The emotion that underlies all those feelings might not be love, as others would term it, but it is just as intense.

Roles in the Clan
Every clan calls upon its members to fill three principal roles, each of which contributes to the group's welfare.

First, many dwarves support the clan by working at an occupation that sustains the community—brewing ale, tending crops, and preparing food, for instance. Not everyone can be a master artisan or a vigilant warrior; the clan needs a wide range of labor and talents to meet all the needs of the group.

Filling the second role are an equally large number of dwarves whose occupations involve the crafting of items and other forms of creation—smelting, smithing, gem-cutting, sculpture, and similar tasks. These artisans are responsible for making the items that help the clan protect its stronghold.

The third function is performed by those who navigate the space between the clan and the chaotic creatures of the outside world. These dwarves are merchants, warriors, and envoys, tasked with representing the dwarves in dealings with other races and with providing a buffer between the clan and the potential threats of creatures and communities in the vicinity of the stronghold.

A dwarf assigned to a role takes years to master it. A weaponsmith starts work in the forge, providing manual labor to haul ore from the mines and learning how to repair tools. The dwarf might then work in the mines, pushing carts and learning to pick out the best ore samples from a lode. Slowly but surely, a dwarf masters every aspect of a task or an occupation from start to finish.

Leadership and Government
A clan is led by a king or a queen who sits at the head of a noble family. Dwarf nobles are members of families that claim direct ancestry to the first dwarves crafted by Moradin. To the dwarves, leadership is a craft like any other activity, calling for careful practice and constant

attention to detail in order to yield the best, most satisfying results.

Young nobles apprentice for a time with masters of every profession in the clan. This period of work and education has two important results. First, the apprenticeships expose a young noble to each part of the clan's operation and create personal ties between the apprentice and every group in the clan's society. By the time a noble takes on a leadership role, the noble has a clear overview of all the clan's interrelationships and has formed friendships with people from every spot on the spectrum of roles within the clan.

More important, a young noble's conduct while pursuing a variety of tasks gives the elder nobles a chance to assess the youth's character. Ideally, a noble who ascends to the leadership of a clan demonstrates an even temperament and an affinity for the clan's key functions. A noble who particularly enjoys fighting might become a minister of war or a general, while one who loves smithing might become an overseer of the crafters' work.

ONE FOR ALL: THE STRONGHOLD

I LIVE HERE AMONG MY FOLK, AND I SWEAR THAT IF NEED
be I will die here atop a mountain of my enemies' corpses.
—King Ulaar Strongheart

Every dwarf clan maintains a stronghold, typically a series of chambers dug out beneath a mountain or inside a hill. The stronghold is a haven from the chaos of the outside world, allowing the dwarves to toil in peace. The first concern of any stronghold is defense, but older and prosperous strongholds can grow to become wondrous underground cities filled with generations of exquisite dwarven artisanship.

Regardless of a clan's size and status, its stronghold is a stony personification of the clan itself—what's good for the clan is good for the stronghold, and vice versa. If a stronghold fails from within, or falls victim to outside forces, such an event is often the clan's death knell.

A LIVING MONUMENT

The masons and stone carvers in a clan consider the stronghold to be their greatest work. In a typical stronghold, stone bridges arc over chasms, their surfaces embellished with fine carvings and intricate patterns. The great stone doors leading outside can withstand a battering ram when secured, but glide open at the touch of a child when they are unlocked. While some other races erect statues or build special structures to honor their heroes or commemorate momentous events, the dwarves live and work within their greatest memorial.

A clan's stronghold holds the record of its history and accomplishments. A work that an outsider regards as "merely" intricate stone carving might actually be a carefully composed recounting of deeds, events, and important persons. Dwarves combine their runes into patterns, present pictorial histories in seemingly unconnected murals and images, and otherwise leave their clan's legacy of accomplishments hiding in plain sight. The story of the clan is meant to be appreciated by clan members and fellow dwarves, not the few outsiders who might be allowed inside the stronghold.

ISLAND OF STABILITY

A well-built stronghold is an easily managed, tranquil environment where dwarves focus on rearing their families and pursuing their craft. Since the beginnings of their existence, dwarves have carved out their strongholds underground for a variety of reasons. Their unmatched prowess in mining and stonework makes them ideal candidates to use the subterranean realm for living quarters—and considering their outlook on the rest of the world, the dwarves wouldn't have it any other way.

The stronghold's remoteness isolates the dwarves from the vagaries of politics and other forms of turmoil in the surface world. Underground, they don't have to contend with the changing of the seasons, or even daily variations in the weather, so that one day inside a stronghold is much like any other day. The activities of the clan are governed by a firm schedule that provides every member with daily time for work, family, and personal enrichment. The forges are never allowed to go cold, and the mines around the stronghold are worked every hour of every day.

BEAUTIFUL ON THE INSIDE

Dwarves are acutely aware that their reputation as skilled miners and crafters of beautiful works of art makes any stronghold a prime target for thieves and raiders. For that reason, the entrance to a stronghold doesn't broadcast its presence by being a stellar example of dwarven stonework. The outer precincts of a clan's home are plain and functional, decorated minimally or not at all, to give visitors and those passing

nearby no reason to suspect what lies in the deeper chambers. From what they see, a dwarven stronghold is well built but austere.

The greatest treasures crafted by a clan are sequestered in the innermost chambers of the stronghold, behind secret doors in areas that are open to clan members but forbidden to all outsiders. Even dwarves from other clans are granted access to such a place only after earning the trust of their hosts.

These inner precincts hold the stuff of a thief's wildest dreams. In one chamber, gold foil lines the ceiling of an immense hall, carefully worked with diamonds that mimic the stars at night. In another, jewels are used to form wondrous murals that tell of the clan's greatest deeds. A clan's feasting hall might be stocked with utensils and place settings made of silver and gold.

DEFENSE COMES FIRST

Every dwarf knows instinctively that clan and stronghold are inextricably tied together—if one comes undone, the other fails as well. As such, defending the stronghold is a concern that the dwarves address even in the earliest stages of construction. They plan and then build with the goals of safety and security uppermost in mind. And the only way that a home can be truly safe and secure is if it is protected against intruders.

Dwarves use a variety of approaches and devices in setting their defenses. The strongholds of many clans are honeycombed with secret passages designed to enable the dwarves to ambush and flank enemies. Dwarves also make liberal use of secret doors fashioned by dwarf artisans, slabs of stone that fit so precisely in their openings that no one but a dwarf knows how to locate and open one.

Unlike some other races that guard their territory by creating features that actively deter invaders, dwarves rarely use arrow traps, pit traps, and other such measures that could cause harm to clan members. They see little sense in risking injury if a trap of that sort malfunctioned or was accidentally triggered by a dwarf. A defensive measure isn't doing its job if it ends up hurting those it was meant to protect.

Dwarves of the Multiverse

Like any race, dwarves display a wide array of skin tones, hair colors, and other physical traits. Adding to this diversity, they have a variety of cultural identities from world to world across the multiverse.

Dwarves of Greyhawk

The hill dwarves and mountain dwarves of war-wracked Oerth have endured many centuries of turbulence. Their outlook on the world is shaped largely by how they perceive outsiders and how much of a threat those outsiders might pose.

Hill Dwarves. Most of the dwarves on Oerth are hill dwarves. Compared to the mountain dwarves, they have a relaxed and open attitude toward the outside world. Because they dwell in regions that lack the towering peaks that their mountain kin favor, they build stone fortresses that start above ground and end in chambers that tunnel deep beneath the surface. A typical clan's settlement features stout walls and a sturdy gate, inside which are living quarters, community areas, and a well-protected treasure vault.

Hill dwarves are more perceptive and empathic than their kin. They rely on their intuition and insight to guide them in relationships with other races. To offset the disadvantage of not being protected by mountains, they frequently form defensive pacts with humans, gnomes, and elves that live nearby.

Although the best artisans are revered for their skills, just as in any dwarf clan, hill dwarves put special emphasis on diplomacy and trade as key elements in the clan's survival. They appreciate the value of creating high-quality goods to trade with others, both to enrich the clan and to form bonds with neighbors.

Mountain Dwarves. As tough and strong as the natural stoneworks they dwell among, mountain dwarves see themselves as the true progenitors of their race and the exemplars of their gods' traditions and teachings.

Mountain dwarves maintain a strong martial tradition. They know that the great wealth they accumulate in their vaults makes them prime targets for raiders. As a result, all the adults in a typical mountain dwarf clan are trained in the use of armor and weapons.

Miners are among the most revered members of a clan, since the tunnels and shafts they dig in search of ore are considered works of art in themselves—as much a part of a clan's legacy as any treasure chamber heaped with gold and gems.

The mountain dwarves' militancy and the need to protect their mines leads them into frequent clashes with Underdark monsters. Creatures or raiding parties that enter the mines from below invite retributive raids by dwarf war parties. The dwarves will mount an ambitious assault to reclaim even a single miner captured by attackers. Even the cruel drow are reluctant to raid mountain dwarf settlements, since they know a single attack will ignite the flames of war.

Hill dwarves view their mountain cousins as overly grim shut-ins who refuse to believe that life is anything but a constant battle for survival. Mountain dwarves view their hill-dwelling relatives as painfully naive optimists who risk losing their precious works because of their overexposure to the outside world.

Dwarves of the Forgotten Realms

In an age long since passed into myth, the dwarves of Toril were one people dwelling in the mountains where three continents—Faerûn, Kara-Tur, and Zakhara—met. A gradual diaspora over millennia spread them across the world, giving rise to diverse types of dwarves. In Faerûn, the two most numerous subraces are gold dwarves and shield dwarves.

The dwarves of Faerûn traveled north from the southern mountains and founded an extensive subterranean empire called Bhaerynden, which lay beneath a hot savannah now known as the Shaar. A rift in the leadership of the dwarves caused a schism among their people. One group left Bhaerynden and built new kingdoms in the North and the Heartlands, becoming the shield dwarves. Those who remained became the gold dwarves.

Gold dwarf scholars point to Abbathor as the cause of this division, claiming that the deity's influence weakened Bhaerynden and left it vulnerable to the dark elves that threatened its borders. That claim might well be true, but shield dwarf scholars point out that those who abandoned Bhaerynden did so two millennia before the drow conquered the place. They put the blame for its fall on the complacency that drove their ancestors to leave. "Gold dwarves endure. Shield dwarves adapt." That is a truism that both subraces of dwarves repeat with pride and derision, each extolling the qualities of their own kind.

Gold Dwarves. The conquest of Bhaerynden by the drow spurred its survivors to create many separate outposts in southern lands. During the same period, the dark elves fell victim to infighting, which culminated in the collapse of the great cavern. Emboldened by this development, armies of gold dwarves returned to drive the drow from the region. At the site that would come to be known as the Great Rift, they shaped the underground canyons and passages to their needs, and from there they tunneled under the Shaar for miles around, carving a new empire from stone.

Gold dwarves consider themselves the true keepers of dwarf culture. More so than shield dwarves, they prefer to dwell underground. Many gold dwarves live their lives without seeing the sun. Surrounded by the artistry and wealth that earlier generations have drawn from the earth, they are accustomed to flaunting their fortune, dressing in bejeweled and glittering garments. Gold dwarves who interact with other races (including shield dwarves) tend to be suspicious, taciturn, and secretive, and especially distrustful of anyone who doesn't show outward signs of wealth.

Shield Dwarves. The ambition to seek new horizons that led the first dwarves to leave Bhaerynden still runs strong in shield dwarves today. Over thousands of years, many kingdoms of shield dwarves have risen, often at the whim of one enterprising individual who decided to found a new clan. So too have many kingdoms of shield dwarves fallen and been forgotten, leaving behind wondrous landmarks and mysterious dungeons.

Shield dwarves who occupy a stronghold can be as clannish and insular as gold dwarves, but shield dwarves are far more likely than gold dwarves to dwell in surface communities, forming trade relationships and alliances with neighboring nations. The openness of the shield dwarves as a people manifests on a personal level as well, with individuals being far more likely to travel among and make friends with other races.

DWARVES OF DRAGONLANCE

Most dwarves on the world of Krynn trace their ancestry to a single great empire known as Kal-Thax. They have long been split into several clans based on traditional roles that were established in Kal-Thax and its successor settlements. Yet, as with much on Krynn, the fate of the dwarves has been shaped by the Cataclysm.

Before the Cataclysm, the dwarves that dwelt on the surface, called the Neidar, interacted with other races and provided foodstuffs and goods for their subterranean cousins that couldn't be acquired underground. The great city of Thorbardin was the most prominent of the dwarves' underground settlements, where several clans lived and worked together.

But when the anger of the gods struck the world, mountains fell and seas rose. Although many settlements of dwarves were wiped out, Thorbardin survived. When the famine and plagues caused by the Cataclysm swept the world, the Neidar and their human allies sought succor from Thorbardin, which the Neidar knew held stores of food that could last generations. But the king wouldn't let any citizen of Thorbardin suffer to ease the anguish of the supplicants at its gates.

The result of that refusal was the Dwarfgate Wars, a series of sieges and battles that ended when a magical explosion and conflagration consumed both armies on the battlefield. Thorbardin's gates remained shut, and the hatred between the Neidar and the other clans has festered for centuries. Although some families among the Neidar eventually founded new communities, many of the surface dwellers drifted apart to take up life with humans or as lone traders and crafters.

Meanwhile, within Thorbardin, disagreements over the treatment of the Neidar, the loss of Thorbardin's army in the war, the distribution of supplies, and other disputes drove the clans farther apart. The Hylar are Thorbardin's best engineers and crafters, and that clan continues to rule despite its increasingly autocratic policies. Although the subservient clans continue to perform their traditional roles in the hierarchy, they have largely segregated themselves into separate districts within Thorbardin. The ambitious and vicious Theiwar clan

maintains its influence through the use of mysterious magic. The Daergar grudgingly work as Thorbardin's miners when they aren't taking out their aggression on each other or antagonizing other clans. The Daewar long ago submitted to the rule of the Hylar and have the privilege of being Thorbardin's merchants and builders. Driven mad by their love of quicksilver, the wild Klar serve as Thorbardin's scouts and fiercest warriors.

Gully Dwarves. The Aghar clan is an anomaly among the dwarves of Krynn, having retained a foothold both in out-of-the-way locations inside Thorbardin and on the surface. Referred to by others as gully dwarves, the Aghar are derided as stupid, smelly, and dirty. Most dwarves consider them a form of vermin, unsuitable even as servants. The Aghar in Thorbardin have carved out living space for themselves from the massive piles of tailings left over from the excavations of the Daergar. They have no role in sustaining the city.

DWARVEN RELIGION

OUR FOREBEARS INSTILL WITHIN US THE POTENTIAL FOR *everything that made them great. It is our responsibility to refine that gift into something wonderful.*

—Vistra Frostbeard

The religion of the dwarves is at the root of the societal roles that dwarves follow. Where most other creatures view their deities as ultrapowerful beings who stand forever apart from their worshipers, the dwarves see their gods as exemplars who blaze a path for their lives to follow. Dwarven deities exist in a wide variety, with a few common across many worlds. They are collectively known as the Mordinsamman.

Moradin is foremost among the dwarven pantheon, the epitome of everything dwarves strive to be. The rest of the group consists of those first dwarves who performed their labors so well that they could almost duplicate Moradin's level of skill.

The Dwarf Deities table lists the members of the Mordinsamman. For each god, the table notes alignment, province (the god's main areas of interest and responsibility), suggested domains for clerics who serve the god, and a common symbol of the god. Several of the gods in the table are described below.

MORADIN

The father of the dwarves crafted his children from metal and gems and imbued them with souls as he cooled them with his breath.

Moradin is the master of every craft practiced by the dwarves and the patron of artisans. He expects his children to follow in his footsteps, studying his techniques and aspiring to one day match his expertise.

Priests of Moradin are responsible for judging and assessing the work of a stronghold's artisans. They keep great volumes that describe various crafting techniques in detail, and use the guidelines in them to judge the quality of individual works.

The priests also evaluate young dwarves to determine the youths' vocations. The decisions of the priests are accepted without question.

Dwarves like to blame the gods for their obsessions, whether craft, ale, or gold. There is a simpler explanation for the divine inspiration they claim to experience. Dwarves are neurotic.

ABBATHOR

The Great Master of Greed exerts an influence, no matter how subtle, over every dwarven heart. Abbathor teaches that greed isn't only desirable, but necessary to keep the dwarves in a strong and safe position.

Abbathor has no skill in crafting. Instead, he relies on his ability as a thief to take ownership of what he wants. Why work so hard to manufacture something when a much easier path to riches lies open?

Abbathor is the only advocate for change within the dwarven pantheon. He can inspire dwarves to seek shortcuts, normally frowned upon, but sometimes those methods turn out to be efficient techniques that improve a clan's capabilities.

BERRONAR TRUESILVER

The Matron of Home and Hearth is the patron of family, honor, and law. She lays out the rules for managing a dwarf clan.

Berronar's code establishes the laws of the dwarves, including contracts, trade agreements, and every other kind of bond forged through words and deeds. As Moradin provides the example that dwarves strive to match, Berronar provides the bonds that create dwarven society and culture.

Berronar's priests arrange marriages, using a process that finds the best matches and is designed to ensure that each generation of a clan is stronger and more talented than the last. Their dictates in this respect are sacrosanct, and a dwarf designated for an arranged marriage must obey the priests or risk exile.

CLANGEDDIN SILVERBEARD

Known as the Father of Battle, Clangeddin Silverbeard is the patron of dwarf warriors. Impetuous and brave yet a cunning strategist, Clangeddin embodies the warrior's spirit that makes dwarven armies such formidable foes.

Clangeddin encourages dwarf warriors to venture out of the stronghold in search of foes to defeat. He particularly hates goblinoids, giants, and dragons. He compels his followers to seek out and dispatch such enemies before they can become a threat to the stronghold.

Clangeddin's faithful are mainly full-time warriors assigned to weapon training from an early age and expected to take the fight to the enemy. The two axes he wields embody his attitude, since he forsakes the added protection of a shield for the chance to deal more damage to his enemies.

Clangeddin's priests are warriors who lead from the front. When defending a stronghold, they guard the walls and lead sorties against enemy positions. When an external threat is near, the priests plan guerrilla raids to disrupt invaders before they can besiege the stronghold.

DWARF DEITIES (THE MORDINSAMMAN)

Deity	Alignment	Province	Suggested Domains	Common Symbol
Abbathor	NE	Greed	Trickery	Jeweled dagger, point down
Berronar Truesilver	LG	Hearth, home, truth	Life, Light	Intertwined silver rings
Clangeddin Silverbeard	LG	War, strategy	War	Crossed silver battleaxes
Dugmaren Brightmantle	CG	Discovery	Knowledge	Open book
Dumathoin	N	Buried secrets	Grave,* Knowledge	Gemstone in a mountain
Gorm Gulthyn	LG	Vigilance	War	Bronze half-mask
Haela Brightaxe	CG	Combat prowess, luck in battle	War	Upright sword with blade sheathed in flame
Hanseath	CN	Festivity, brewing, song	Trickery, War	Beer stein
Marthammor Duin	NG	Explorers, wanderers, the lost	Nature, Trickery	Upright mace in front of a tall boot
Moradin	LG	Primary deity of dwarves	Forge,* Knowledge	Hammer and anvil
Muamman Duathal	NG	Storms, travel	Tempest	Mace held in gauntlets
Mya	NG	Clan, family, wisdom	Knowledge, Life	A faceless mother figure
Roknar	NE	Lies, intrigue	Trickery	Hands filled with coins
Sharindlar	CG	Healing, love	Life	Burning needle
Thard Harr	CG	Wilderness, hunting	Nature	Two clawed gauntlets
Tharmekhûl	N	Fire, forges, molten rock	Forge,* Light	Fiery axe
Thautam	N	Mysteries, darkness, lost treasures	Knowledge, Trickery	Blindfold
Ulaa	LG	Mining, quarrying	Forge*	A miner's pick
Valkauna	LN	Oaths, birth, aging, death	Grave,* Life	A silver ewer
Vergadain	N	Luck, wealth	Trickery	Gold coin bearing a dwarf's face

Appears in Xanathar's Guide to Everything

OTHER DEITIES

The dwarven pantheon is quite large. The four deities discussed above are acknowledged by occupants of almost every stronghold, while the following gods are worshiped by some clans and ignored by others. These deities include Dugmaren Brightmantle, the Gleam in the Eye; Dumathoin, the Keeper of Secrets under the Mountain; Gorm Gulthyn, the Golden Guardian; Haela Brightaxe, the Lady of the Fray; Marthammor Duin, Watcher over Wanderers; Sharindlar, Lady of Mercy; and Vergadain, the Merchant King.

THE DUAL ROLE OF ABBATHOR

A LITTLE ACT OF SELFISHNESS NOW AND THEN IS TO BE *expected even from the wisest of folk.*

—Tenelar, Outcast of Five Peaks

Dwarves have rigid principles and lofty ambitions. They devote their lives to the pursuit of perfection, and the best come close to realizing that goal. But for all their dedication, dwarves are mortal, which means they are fallible. And that's where Abbathor comes in.

The dwarves' attachment to their creations has a dark side: many of them fall victim to feelings of selfishness and greed. The culprit is Abbathor, the black sheep of the dwarven pantheon. Abbathor is an advocate of change, not stability—an attitude normally regarded with suspicion by dwarves. But in this case, the god delivers his message inside the embrace of avarice.

Greed is at the heart of change. Greedy individuals aren't content with their own accomplishments and seek to undermine the works that others have made, sometimes going so far as to take credit for their creation, or actually steal them. Greed distorts the joy that dwarves normally take from their work. It focuses on the value of the end result, rather than the importance of the process of creation. A dwarf tempted by Abbathor might sabotage a rival's work or uncover a wondrous treasure and pass it off as something they created.

Abbathor does, however, play a positive role in helping the dwarves discover new methods and techniques. Although he espouses greed and treachery, he is also the standard bearer for revision and innovation. His guidance is especially critical when a clan faces an unanticipated situation that requires quick, decisive action.

In that vein, dwarf emissaries and merchants are expected to use Abbathor's tricks when they deal with humans, elves, and other races. When a dwarf offers a piece of merchandise for sale to an outsider, that merchant is expected to drive a hard bargain, even if the item is in truth an inferior example of its kind.

Fortunately for the other party in the arrangement, the dwarves' idea of "inferior" means that a product they consider substandard is still far superior to any such item that outsiders might create. The dwarves might laugh among themselves at a human farmer who bought a shovel from them that will last only a few decades. To the dwarves, that's a shoddy tool; to the farmer, it's a purchase that lasts a lifetime.

ENEMIES ALL AROUND

If the dwarves weren't so good at accumulating treasure, it's likely that they wouldn't have as many enemies. As things stand, however, almost every variety of marauding humanoid or greedy monster lusts after the riches that dwarves keep in their strongholds. The biggest threats to their security are dragons and giants, but other humanoids such as orcs and the hated duergar are their most numerous foes.

Dragons

Chromatic dragons, by their nature, are often attracted to the treasures that dwarves gather in their fortresses. Although such a place might be too stout for a dragon to assault and take over, an evil dragon that makes its lair near a dwarven stronghold can be a threat to the occupants in many ways.

Black Dragons. Since black dragons prefer to dwell in swampland, one rarely makes a lair close to a stronghold. When a black dragon does cross paths with dwarves, it might attempt to isolate a settlement by making the roads leading to it impassable. The terrain around the dragon's lair is transformed into a riot of vegetation and patches of mud, slowing travelers and making caravans vulnerable to attack by the dragon's followers. When a stronghold becomes cut off, the dragon might start to test its outer defenses in advance of mounting a larger assault. This strategy can take years to come to fruition, but from the dragon's perspective it is time well spent.

Blue Dragons. Blue dragons are the least likely of their kind to tangle with dwarves, since their lairs are always far from where dwarves typically settle, and a blue dragon almost never gives away the location of its lair. One might appear before a band of dwarves traveling through the area and demand a toll for safe passage through its territory, expecting payment in the form of gems—and particularly sapphires.

Green Dragons. Dwarves and green dragons don't often interact, and when they do, the dragon doesn't usually threaten them directly. A typical green dragon has no burning desire to possess the material goods in a stronghold's hoard, and would much rather snatch up living treasure. Using its powers of deception, a green dragon might try to entice dwarves it encounters to ally with it in return for the promise of great wealth. Dwarves who have been touched by Abbathor might succumb to this temptation—only to find themselves im-

---

Dwarves and Ale

Dwarves have a reputation for being able to consume great quantities of ale. Although drinking plays a significant role in their culture, it is a mistake to assume that intoxication has the same effect on them as it does on humans.

Humans drink to forget, while dwarves drink to remember. A dwarf deep in his cups is overcome by powerful, vivid memories of his past, especially events tied to lost kin, great deeds, or monumental failures.

When dwarves drink in a group, this effect spreads among them. The clan might joyfully sing of triumph as they reminisce over the defeat of a dragon, or weep as they recall the death of a beloved elder.

In contrast to clan gatherings, dwarves who drink alone invariably become morose and sullen—when separated from their clan mates, they can't avoid dwelling on unpleasant memories. It's the wise traveler who leaves alone the sole, drunken dwarf in the corner.

In my experience—for all their long-winded rambling about lineage and tradition—dwarves are greedy and devious folk. I write this not to insult them in any way. I have found greed to be a useful motivator both for myself and my underlings, and I prize the trickery that some members of that race demonstrate.

prisoned in the dragon's lair, sentenced to a lifetime of crafting new items for the dragon's treasure collection.

Red Dragons. Even though dwarves and red dragons compete for the same terrain, they don't come into conflict as often as they once did. Nowadays, red dragon lairs and dwarven strongholds are far enough apart that the dwarves don't have to worry constantly about being attacked. But occasionally, a young red dragon sets out to establish its own legacy—and what better place for a lair than one that comes with its own treasure hoard?

To begin its campaign, the dragon sends out followers and minions to lay siege to the stronghold. If this effort succeeds and the defenders withdraw deeper inside, the dragon comes forth to lead the assault into the tunnels. In those cramped quarters, only a few dwarves at a time can be brought to bear against the dragon's teeth, claws, and fiery breath. But the dwarves know that if they allow the dragon access to the fortress's innermost chambers, the fight is all but over.

White Dragons. Dwarves who live in cold climates don't usually have to cope with as many predators and marauders as do their kin in more hospitable terrain. But a white dragon patrols its territory relentlessly, neither subtle nor shrewd in its methods, often using natural camouflage to ambush its prey. A dragon that lairs nearby might be willing to leave a dwarven settlement unmolested if its appetite is sated by creatures it can catch in the open, including the travelers that enter and exit the place.

On occasion, this state of (relatively) peaceful coexistence is shattered when a devious rival dragon with designs on a white dragon's territory enters the picture. Taking advantage of the dragon's limited mental faculties, the rival secretly sends its minions out to harass the dragon. Convinced that the dwarves must be to blame, the dragon engages them in a wider conflict, and the dwarves respond in kind. Even if neither side destroys the other, both will be severely weakened, after which the rival moves in to finish the job.

Giants

Giants have no special enmity toward dwarves, but they do consider them ideal slaves. Even when captured and put to work against their will, dwarves are innately driven to bring their full effort to a task at hand. Even simple toil brings dwarves some relief from captivity. Fire giants are more likely than other giants to enslave dwarves expressly for their talents. Many tribes of hill giants have discovered the value of dwarves as workers and now seek to capture them rather than devour them.

Giants don't launch direct attacks on dwarven strongholds except under extraordinary circumstances. Their size is a great disadvantage in the underground passages of a fortress, potentially turning any such assault into a suicide mission.

Orcs

Every orc tribe dreams of overrunning a dwarven stronghold and returning to the caves with a war wagon laden with gold, gems, stout armor, and sharp weapons. Given the orcs' propensity to rely on brute force rather than cunning, they can overcome only severely weakened dwarven strongholds. Unfortunately for the dwarves, orcs seem to receive omens from Gruumsh bidding them to invade a stronghold just when it is wracked with plague, riven by infighting, or otherwise at its weakest. The all-seeing eye of Gruumsh is ever vigilant for signs that Moradin's children have faltered.

Duergar

The evil dwarves of the Underdark are responsible for the constant undercurrent of peril in the life of any clan. Although the duergar don't come near the surface in sufficient numbers to invade and occupy a stronghold, they send out raiding parties to set upon any dwarves they find on the loose and to pull off occasional acts of sabotage or guerrilla activity. Though no dwarven fortresses are currently at risk of succumbing to a duergar onslaught, none of them are immune to the treachery that a small group of gray dwarves can commit.

When Clans Collapse

WE HAVE BUT ONE DESIRE—REVENGE AGAINST THOSE
who drove us out of our home.

—Queen Helgret Deephammer,
of the Deephammer clan in exile

For all the attention dwarves pay to their defenses and the security of their homes, no clan is immortal and no stronghold unassailable. Threats to a clan can come from the outside or the inside, and it's often the latter variety that proves more difficult to defeat.

Every clan is aware that there are plenty of unprincipled creatures in the world that would love to steal its cherished works or even obliterate the dwarves and take over their home. Formidable though they may be, these are enemies that can be prepared for. More insidious are the forces that can tear apart a clan from within.

Festering Rivalries

It's not unusual for individuals in a clan to fall prey to occasional bickering and infighting. Abbathor's influence affects some dwarves more than others, and even those with the strongest resolve can be tempted to compromise their principles from time to time.

Minor turmoil of this sort rarely leads to civil war or a rapid decline of the clan's strength. But in the worst cases, a clan's collective lack of dedication to its goals strains the bonds between elements that must work together for the clan to prosper. Feuds between artisans drive wedges between families. Dwarf traders strike

---

> ### Friendly from a Distance
> Even though dwarves have a natural affinity for one another, different clans keep a comfortable distance between their strongholds. Anyone not of the clan, even another dwarf, is considered an outsider.
>
> Relations between neighboring clans are cordial, if not warm. They might exchange messengers to share lore and news that can prove useful against the vagaries of the outside world, but that is likely to be the extent of their contact. Under normal circumstances, dwarves prefer to be left alone. Interacting with neighbors brings unpredictability and change, things dwarves prefer to avoid.
>
> Circumstances cease to be normal when a clan faces an external threat. When word gets out that one of their own is in danger, dwarves of other clans rally against the threat without question. The standoffish diplomacy that marks their normal relations gives way to an unshakable alliance. An attack on one dwarf clan is an attack against them all.

deals that fail to benefit the clan, and stone carvers start using short cuts that compromise their constructions.

If such a decline continues for too long and becomes too severe, the result could be a schism within the clan. The quarreling factions might segregate themselves in different parts of the stronghold; in an extreme case, some clan members might leave to found a new community. In either event, a divided clan is weaker than it was before the unrest occurred, and thus it's an easier target for outside enemies. If selfishness and greed were not enough to bring the clan to utter destruction, the horde of orcs waiting to attack will be happy to finish the job.

A Life in Exile

If the worst comes to pass and the loss of a clan's stronghold to invaders is inevitable, most of the dwarves would be willing to die while making a last stand for their home. But the clan must survive, even if only as a shell of its former self, and so every clan has a contingency plan to secure a safe escape for the stronghold's children and enough adults to care for them.

If the survivors are able to get away, they tend to seek shelter in a human city or kingdom. Their skill as artisans ensures that almost any community would welcome their contribution to the workforce, and they can eke out a comfortable existence for themselves.

A group of refugee dwarves seeking residence in a community will do whatever they can to live together, keeping the clan intact. They recreate what they can of their former lifestyle, living underground when possible and remaining isolated from their neighbors.

Dwarf Adventurers

THE MOUNTAINS WERE HOME ONCE, BUT NEVER AGAIN.

—Tenelar, Outcast of Five Peaks

A dwarf who leaves the stronghold to pursue a life of adventuring does so for one of two reasons. Some dwarves set out with the blessing of the clan to undertake an important mission. Others depart, willingly or otherwise, because they simply don't fit in.

When a situation calls for such drastic action, the nobles or priests select one or more clan members to venture forth. These dwarves are charged with a specific quest, such as recovering a stolen artifact or discovering

Clanless dwarves present an opportunity for wise employers and recruiters. They seek purpose and a firm footing. Give a clanless dwarf these things, and you will have a lifelong ally.

the fate of an allied stronghold that has fallen silent. They are held in high esteem by their clan mates, since they have dared to forsake the safety of home for the uncertainty of the upper world. When their mission is over, they return to the stronghold and are hailed as heroes.

Other dwarves turn to a life on the outside because they are misfits who found the stronghold stultifying or outcasts who were forced to leave the clan because of criminal behavior. Not all dwarves are born with the same strong sense of community, and the strictures of society can prove difficult for some to accept. Such an individual might protest an arranged marriage or insist that the priests of Moradin have erred in deciding their vocation. The rest of the clan views these malcontents with mistrust, and those who remain disruptive can find themselves exiled.

HAZARDOUS DUTY

Some dwarves leave the stronghold to serve the clan in nontraditional ways as envoys, explorers, crafters, and merchants. Although a human wouldn't think of all these folk as adventurers, in the dwarves' view they are undertaking a dangerous mission.

Even when dwarves volunteer for a life in the outside world, whether to take up true adventuring or to pursue a mundane occupation, they remain members of the clan, and their duties almost always include some responsibility to the clan. A blacksmith working in a human village, for instance, might report news of the outside world back to the clan.

Dwarves who reside in surface communities prefer to keep to themselves when not plying their trades, but over time they might develop close relationships with neighbors of other races—much in the same way that dwarves who join an adventuring party learn to trust their companions.

CASTOFFS AND CRIMINALS

Of course, not every dwarf is destined for a long life in service to the clan. A few are born with a tendency to think and behave in ways that undermine the clan rather than supporting it, and those who don't change their ways are cast out.

Some of these independent dwarves, especially those who espouse the moral and ethical standards of their kin, end up becoming adventurers. Their companions and allies satisfy every dwarf's innate need to belong to a clan, and those folk become the beneficiaries of the dwarf's industriousness and loyalty.

For dwarves of evil temperament, the place of one's clan is liable to be taken by a group such as an assassins' guild or an outlaw gang. Those who understand their role in the organization and abide by its hierarchy are some of the most loyal followers a would-be conqueror could acquire.

MAGIC: GODS' GIFT TO DWARVES

Dwarves are of two minds on the topic of magic.

They view divine magic as a gift from their gods, a direct helping hand meant to aid them in their effort to follow their gods' examples. Indeed, many forms of divine magic are essential for the smooth operation of any stronghold and the continued survival of the clan. For that reason, clerics are more common among the dwarves than in other races. Dwarves who are especially devoted to the clan are believed to have a special connection to the deities, and often learn how to use that conduit to bring forth divine magic.

Arcane magic in all its forms is a different matter. Dwarves have no innate fear or hatred of such things, but arcane magic has no true patron among the dwarven deities. As such, the dwarves ignore it in their daily lives, and clan members who take up the practice are exceedingly rare. Using arcane magic to assist in the creation of one's works is anathema to almost all dwarves, because the act amounts to nothing more than cheating. The few dwarves who embrace arcane magic tend to venerate Abbathor, if only in secret.

Evil dwarves with no respect for authority or community are few and far between. Shunned by the rest of their race, they take perverse delight in raiding villages, enslaving or killing innocents, and otherwise venting their rage against the world.

DUERGAR

Duergar see themselves as the true manifestation of dwarven ideals, clever enough not to be taken in by the treacherous deceptions of Moradin and his false promises. Their period of enslavement and the revolt against the mind flayers led by their god, Laduguer, purged the influence of the other dwarven gods from their souls and thus made them into the superior race.

Duergar have no appreciation for beauty, that ability having been erased from their minds by the mind flayers long ago and any thought of recapturing it obliterated by Moradin's betrayal. The duergar lead bleak, grim lives devoid of happiness or satisfaction, but they see that as their defining strength—the root of duergar pride, as it were—rather than a drawback to be corrected.

A DARK REFLECTION

WORK OR DIE. IN THE FIRST CASE, YOU ARE USEFUL. IN *the second, you are entertaining.*

—Vozala Spikefist

Duergar society is a dark mirror of the dwarven clan. Where dwarves toil for love of industry, duergar do so out of a drive to create and own as much goods and treasure as possible. Their priests assign vocations and arrange marriages, but only to ensure that a clan continues to exist, not out of any sense of creating a legacy.

In many ways, the culture of the duergar is fundamentally hollow. For all their wars, and all the treasures they have accumulated, duergar feel no happiness or satisfaction. They simply continue to exist, ever-turning cogs in an engine of destruction that is the antithesis of the dwarves' joyful cycle of creation.

Laduguer Claims His Due

Our three rules come from the actions of Laduguer himself, as he quested through the Nine Hells on his mission to bring glory to the duergar.

First, the devils sought to turn his greed against him. They offered as much treasure as he could carry, thinking that he would take too much and collapse in exhaustion. Instead, Laduguer used his cunning magic to twist his pockets into bottomless pits, so that there was no limit to the treasure he could carry.

Then, in their frustration at his stratagem, the devils fell upon him with claw and blade. They didn't understand that with each treasure he claimed, Laduguer's will to win grew stronger and stronger. With so much to fight for, he lashed out and broke the backs of Hell's legions.

Finally, Asmodeus confronted Laduguer. The Lord of the Nine laughed, joked, and cajoled with all his guile, but Laduguer remained grim and stoic, refusing to be affected even when the mightiest celestials might have admitted some grudging amusement at the devil's antics. Laduguer was resolute because he wanted one final treasure: the allegiance of Hell in the coming war against the mind flayers. Asmodeus offered a world's worth of other temptations, but Laduguer's countenance never changed. Even when Asmodeus relented at last, Laduguer accepted the arrangement as nothing less than his due and refused to display any reaction.

Thus did Laduguer deliver the three rules that govern our people. These principles liberated our people from the illithids, and to this day they keep us strong.

—Felstak Goldgrief, Tyrant of Goethelskar

Three Rules of Conduct

Duergar psychology, culture, and society are predicated on three principles set down by their god Laduguer. Adherence to these precepts is now enforced by Laduguer's chief lieutenant, Deep Duerra.

Our Pockets Are Never Full

The duergar are fueled in all their actions by two pervasive feelings: ambition that never flags and greed that can never be satisfied. Though they might scheme and plot at great lengths to gain treasure or prestige, success is never a cause for celebration. Each acquisition, once in hand, is like a meal that quickly loses its appeal, leaving the duergar hungry for more. No matter how much wealth or power they gain, it's never enough.

Our Fight Is Never Done

As duergar acquire treasure and prestige, they need to become ever mightier to hold on to what they have. When the duergar wage war on other races, they demonstrate that the weak aren't fit to possess that which is meant for the strong. And to the duergar, no creatures are more unworthy of holding wealth than dwarves. When duergar have an opportunity to strike at dwarves, especially in their strongholds, they fight with utmost viciousness and cunning, matching the value of the spoils to be gained with the intensity of their onslaught.

Our Resolve Is Never Shaken

Any show of weakness is a mortal sin among the duergar, and that stricture extends to personal conduct as well as to the workings of a duergar clan. Displays of happiness, contentedness, and trust are forbidden. The duergar are bound together in a rigid society, but it is a marriage of necessity rather than choice. In the Underdark, they must cooperate to survive. Within their society, each individual fills a role assigned to them and must perform it to the best of their abilities.

Duergar warriors epitomize the race's abandonment of emotion and individuality. In battle, they wear heavy armor and hateful, scowling masks that hide their identities. When assembled in ranks, the duergar move forward like army ants. They are an implacable, relentless foe, marching over the corpses of their fallen comrades to press the attack.

DUERGAR DEITIES

OUR GODS SPRANG FROM AMONG US. THEY ENDURED our hardships and carved a path to our salvation. What has your god done for you?

—Morkai Ashlord

Two mythic figures who were long ago responsible for the duergar's liberation have achieved divinity in the eyes of their supplicants.

The Duergar Deities table provides basic information about each one: alignment, province (the god's main areas of interest and responsibility), suggested domains for clerics who serve the god, and a common symbol of the god.

DEEP DUERRA

According to legend, Deep Duerra stole the power of psionics from the mind flayers and gifted it to her people. Her command of it was so great that she dominated a mind flayer colony and turned the illithids into her slaves.

Deep Duerra's followers stand at the forefront of the duergar's attacks on their most hated enemies. Inspired by her mythic deeds, her priests are especially eager to find and annihilate dwarf communities and mind flayer colonies.

The priests of Deep Duerra maintain a training ground and armory inside each duergar stronghold. All duergar are required to learn the basic skills of combat, and the nobles are obliged to contribute weapons, armor, and followers to the stronghold's defensive force. The priests honor their deity by planning, equipping, and launching holy crusades against their enemies.

LADUGUER

Also known as the Grim One, Laduguer was a mighty duergar warrior who liberated his people from the illithids. Laduguer entered into a pact with Asmodeus, pledging the duergar to an alliance against Lolth and

The mental power that duergar wield was given to them by the illithids, no matter what the adherents of Deep Duerra might claim. Why, then, would the illithids create slaves that could turn invisible or grow to ogre size? Most likely because those slaves would excel at herding their masters' other chattel. In retrospect, it seems arguable that the duergar escaped bondage because their jailers had already given them the keys.

the demons of the Abyss in exchange for which Laduguer received a spark of divinity from Abbathor himself.

Laduguer's teachings stand in direct opposition to everything Moradin represents. He is the dwarf god's dark opposite, a shadow that seeks to rise up and consume its original creator.

Duergar don't worship Laduguer in any traditional way; their communities include no temples or formal services. They honor their deity by acquiring more power and wealth through any means possible. Priests of Laduguer maintain the internal functions of duergar society but have no role that is expressly religious.

INSIDE A STRONGHOLD

Duergar strongholds are best defined in terms of how they compare to the underground fortresses of the dwarves. Both places constantly bustle with activity, forges and picks and hammers always at work, but that's where the similarity ends.

In a dwarven stronghold, the atmosphere is one of optimistic industry. Dwarves enjoy what they do, and their dedication to furthering the clan and leaving a proper legacy shows through in every aspect of a clan's operation.

In contrast, the duergar care nothing for the dwarven ideal of achieving utmost mastery of a craft. For this reason, they pay no mind to their environment or the aesthetics of their creations. In a duergar stronghold, the atmosphere is one of unrelenting drudgery. Quantity, not quality, is at the heart of their efforts, as the duergar strive to craft as many items as possible in the shortest period of time. Duergar goods aren't flawed or substandard, but are plain to the point of austerity. To the duergar, a manufactured object is useful only for the function it performs.

In a typical stronghold, the workshops occupy the central chamber. The smoke that belches from them fills the air and drifts into surrounding passages.

DUERGAR DEITIES

Deity	Alignment	Province	Suggested Domains	Common Symbol
Deep Duerra	LE	Conquest, psionics	Knowledge, War	Mind flayer skull
Laduguer	LE	Labor, slavery	Death, Forge*	Broken arrow

*Appears in *Xanathar's Guide to Everything*

The outer edges of the stronghold are honeycombed with mining operations. The duergar wrest rock from the cavern walls and process the chunks in search of useful ore, pulverizing them with powerful mechanical devices and sorting out the metals, minerals, and gems.

Between the mines and the workshops stands a ring of fortresses, each ruled by a noble and occupied by the noble's followers. The stronghold's king commands the largest edifice, five times the size of the next biggest.

The priests of Deep Duerra reside in the second largest fortress, which houses the duergar army. The priests organize patrols and guard duty and oversee the settlement's armory.

Steeders, spiders that are used as mounts and war beasts by the duergar, are housed in stables that stand between the workshops and the fortresses. Each enclosure is virtually an individual prison, since the violent creatures must be kept apart lest they tear into each other or wreak havoc in some other way. Only careful supervision and brutal discipline keep them in line when they are out of their cages. Each noble is responsible for maintaining a set of steeder pens, and a squad of duergar are assigned to train and supervise the beasts.

POWER OF THE MIND

THE MIND IS BUT ANOTHER MATERIAL, SET BEFORE US TO *shape into a weapon.*

—Gargosa Ironmind

During their period of slavery under the mind flayers, the duergar were the subjects of a variety of bizarre experiments that endowed them with psionic abilities.

Every duergar is born with some amount of psionic talent. The typical warrior can turn invisible or increase in size, and some duergar take up a more formal study of psionics to enhance or augment their capabilities. These individuals push their abilities beyond the normal limits, using what they learn to create new talents that they can then teach to others.

Despite these efforts, duergar still have a limited understanding of the true extent of their psionic capabilities. From the perspective of most other creatures, such abilities are seen as merely another flavor of magic. After all, they reason, what does it matter if a duergar turns invisible by using magic or a psionic ability? The outcome is the same either way.

Those duergar who delve into psionic research describe the process as accessing a dimensional space in which they can tap into the energy exerted by living minds. Using this power source, a small number of duergar can alter their bodies and those of other creatures, tap into thoughts and bend them as they see fit, and impart a spark of locomotion and even basic intelligence into objects. Duergar of truly exceptional skill can move

DUERGAR AND ALE

Unlike their dwarven kin, duergar drink alcohol only in moderation and avoid overindulgence. The duergar have learned from bitter experience that those who drink too much risk awakening deep racial memories of their ancestors' cruel treatment at the hands of the mind flayers. The psychic agony that these memories evoke manifests in a severe flight-or-fight response. An intoxicated duergar might flee in panic and search for a safe place to hide until the effect wears off. A different one might respond by brawling with anyone in the vicinity, venting the rage the duergar harbor against their former masters.

> *Consider that the duergar began as homeless outcasts, and today their fortresses are some of the most impregnable strong points in the Underdark. The question might not be if they will conquer the realm below, but when.*

objects without touching them, view creatures from a great distance, and push their bodies to achieve incredible feats, such as lifting a boulder or transforming into liquid to flow through a crack in a wall.

BUILDING BETTER SLAVES

For generations, duergar relied on humanoid captives to perform unskilled labor in their workshops. Only the lowest, most miserable duergar would consent to do grunt work that requires no artifice or skill.

In recent decades, however, the duergar have begun to move away from the practice of slavery. Some of them have discovered that mechanical servitors powered by psionic energy are more durable and more efficient than slaves. Thus, various kinds of automatons have been developed, each designed to fill a role within a duergar stronghold. Some clans have created models to make raiding parties more formidable. Other forms include digging and tunneling machines, golem-like monstrosities that tear through rock and extract ore from it.

DUERGAR CHARACTERS

Those duergar who become adventurers are almost invariably exiles from their society. The duergar have no patience for those who fail to conduct themselves with an appropriate amount of ambition and cruelty.

Any gray dwarves who leave the Underdark and take up adventuring, after having been raised among their own kind, are paranoid about possible treachery from within the party. One might insist on sleeping separately from the rest of the group, never displaying or sharing treasure, and trying to hoard treasures that can help

---

A PSIONIC AWAKENING

I performed the ritual just as the book described. As the magic turned the aboleth's brain to dust, I inhaled deeply of the leavings, and a nearly infinite roll of years began to unspool before my eyes.

I saw a red sun hanging in the sky over a desolate land, where the ruins of a castle slowly sank into a sea of dust.

I saw an alien empire in a formless, silver realm vanish in the wink of an eye, its slaves left to fend for themselves.

I felt the pull of a force more ancient than the gods, one that remained beneath the surface of my consciousness but was ready to receive a new disciple.

Since the day of my awakening I have felt a presence in the back of my mind, something that pushes to be set free as I struggle to stifle it. It grows, even as my ability to keep it inside falters. Will there come a day when my mind is no longer my own?

Final journal entry of Garral Longseer, once of Candlekeep, whereabouts now unknown

---

survival, such as potions and items or spells that can allow the user to teleport to safety.

At the DM's discretion, you can play a duergar character. When you choose the subrace of your dwarf, you can choose duergar, using the following rules to create your character.

DUERGAR TRAITS

Duergar have the dwarf traits in the *Player's Handbook*, plus the traits below.

Ability Score Increase. Your Strength score increases by 1.

Superior Darkvision. Your darkvision has a radius of 120 feet.

Extra Language. You can speak, read, and write Undercommon.

Duergar Resilience. You have advantage on saving throws against illusions and against being charmed or paralyzed.

Duergar Magic. When you reach 3rd level, you can cast the *enlarge/reduce* spell on yourself once with this trait, using only the spell's enlarge option. When you reach 5th level, you can cast the *invisibility* spell on yourself once with this trait. You don't need material components for either spell, and you can't cast them while you're in direct sunlight, although sunlight has no effect on them once cast. You regain the ability to cast these spells with this trait when you finish a long rest. Intelligence is your spellcasting ability for these spells.

Sunlight Sensitivity. You have disadvantage on attack rolls and on Wisdom (Perception) checks that rely on sight when you, the target of your attack, or whatever you are trying to perceive is in direct sunlight.

DWARF TABLES

This section provides a number of tables useful for players and DMs who want to choose or randomly generate details about dwarf characters or settlements.

In the tables, a name in bold refers to a stat block in the *Monster Manual*.

DWARVES ON THE MOVE

When dwarves journey away from their strongholds, they prefer to move in substantial, heavily defended groups. Use the following tables to generate a band of dwarf travelers and some additional details of their situation. Roll once on each line of the Group Composition table and once on each table that follows it.

GROUP COMPOSITION

Members	Number Present
Dwarf **guards**	2d4 + 10
Dwarf **scouts**	1d8 + 2
Dwarf **veterans**	1d6 + 1

GROUP LEADER

d6	Leader
1	Dwarf **priest**
2–4	Dwarf **noble**
5–6	Dwarf **knight**

BALTHRAN IREHEART

SPECIAL ALLIES

d8	Ally
1–4	1d4 dwarf **acolytes**
5	1d3 **earth elementals**
6	1d4 trained **griffons**
7	1d4 **azers**
8	1 dwarf **mage**

PURPOSE OF TRAVEL

d6	Purpose
1	Merchant caravan
2	Seeking a specific enemy
3	Patrolling to keep roads safe
4	Delivering ransom for captive clan member
5	Fleeing attack on stronghold
6	Diplomatic mission

SPECIAL CIRCUMSTANCES

d4	Circumstance
1	Suspicious of all outsiders
2	Carrying secret message
3	Pursued by foe
4	Returning home laden with treasure

DWARVES IN THE CLAN

The following tables can be used to create basic information about a clan of dwarves: the group's current status, a trait or a fact that sets that clan apart from others, and the vocation of a given clan member.

CLAN'S STATUS

d6	Status
1	**Prosperous.** Clan occupies original stronghold, currently flourishing
2	**Growing.** Stronghold expanding; glory days lie ahead
3	**Declining.** Clan population stagnant or decreasing
4	**Beleaguered.** Victimized by goblinoid and dragon attacks, intact but severely weakened
5	**Scattered.** Stronghold recently lost, many folk slain, survivors scattered
6	**Refugees.** Stronghold lost, survivors occupy a neighborhood or ward in human city

CLAN'S NOTABLE TRAIT

d10	Trait
1	Founder was one of the greatest artisans in history
2	Clan owns a powerful artifact, such as an *Axe of the Dwarvish Lords*
3	Clan noted for expertise in a specific craft, such as brewing or armorsmithing
4	Clan has a sinister reputation, history plagued by scandal and mark of Abbathor
5	Militaristic clan, known for excellent fighting skills
6	Unusual stronghold, such as an undersea castle, a former cloud giant fortress, or an aboveground city
7	Prophecies indicate clan is destined to play a pivotal role in history
8	Heretical clan has rejected dwarf teachings in favor of human deities
9	Unique marker or curse, such as all clan members are hairless
10	Clan is known for its evil ways or a particularly sinister, notable member

CLAN VOCATIONS

d20	Vocation	d20	Vocation
1	Armorer	11	Merchant
2	Blacksmith	12	Messenger
3	Brewer	13	Miner
4	Carpenter	14	Potter
5	Cook	15	Scout
6	Envoy	16	Sculptor
7	Farmer	17	Shepherd
8	Hunter	18	Warrior
9	Jeweler	19	Weaponsmith
10	Mason	20	Weaver

Dwarves in the World

The tables below are designed to add depth to a dwarf character by offering possible reasons why the character left the clan for the life of an adventurer and a set of personality quirks tailored for dwarven sensibilities.

Dwarf Adventurer Story Hooks

d6	Hook
1	You were accused of stealing a fellow artisan's item and claiming it as your work. Innocent or guilty, you were made an outcast.
2	Your wanderlust prompted you to shirk your duties as a crafter in favor of wandering the world. Your clan isn't pleased with this choice.
3	You became separated from your clan due to an earthquake, a drow slave raid, or similar event and hope to return home.
4	You were assigned to become a merchant by the priests of Moradin and have yet to forgive them for their mistake. You should be working a forge, not wandering the outside world!
5	You are a spy, traveling incognito to gather information for the clan elders.
6	You struggle to resist the lure of Abbathor, but can't hold it at bay. Better to walk the world and sate your greed on non-dwarves.

Dwarf Quirks

d8	Quirk
1	Water from the sky! It always surprises you.
2	You have a fascination with the ocean and its chaos.
3	Any creature larger than a human makes you nervous.
4	You prefer to travel with a parasol or similar item that puts a comforting shelter over your head.
5	You prefer to sleep during the day.
6	You speak Common or any other non-dwarf language only if you must.
7	For you, relaxation is putting in a day at the forge.
8	You avoid contact with other dwarves, since you mistrust those who would leave their strongholds.

Duergar Tables

Most of the tables in this section are duergar-themed versions of the information for dwarves that's presented above and in the *Player's Handbook*.

In the tables, a name in bold refers to a stat block in the *Monster Manual*.

Duergar Raiding Parties

When duergar emerge from the Underdark, they generally do so in the form of small but vicious raiding parties. Use the following tables to generate a band of duergar raiders and some additional details of their situation. Roll once on each line of the Group Composition table and once on each table that follows it.

Group Composition

Members	Number Present
Duergar	2d6 + 5
Duergar stone guards	1d4 + 1
Duergar kavalrachni	1d4
Steeders, male	1d4

Group Leader

d6	Leader
1	Duergar stone guard
2–4	Duergar warlord
5–6	Duergar despot

Special Allies

d20	Ally
1–3	1d4 steeders, female
4–6	1d3 duergar hammerers
7	1 duergar mind master
8	1d3 duergar screamers
9–10	1d3 duergar soulblades
11	1d6 duergar xarrorn
12	1d6 **bearded devils** bound to service
13	2d4 allied evil **azers**
14	3d20 enslaved **goblins**
15	1d4 summoned **earth elementals**
16	1d6 + 2 **gargoyles**
17	1d8 **hell hounds**
18	1 trained **rust monster**
19	1 **shield guardian** bound to group leader
20	1d4 enslaved **trolls**

Purpose of Raid

d6	Purpose
1–3	Collecting slaves
4	Pursuing a specific enemy
5	Patrolling for expansion opportunities
6	On a rampage for loot

Special Circumstances

d4	Circumstance
1	Special hatred for dwarves, will attack them first
2	Exiles, willing to bargain
3	Laden with loot from raid, tries to flee
4	Seeks to take hostages for ransom

Duergar in the Clan

The following tables can be used to create basic information about a clan of duergar somewhere in the world: the group's current status, and a trait or a fact that sets that clan apart from others.

Duergar Clan Names

d12	Name	d12	Name
1	Ashlord	7	Mindeater
2	Battlegore	8	Necksnapper
3	Doomfist	9	Orehammer
4	Earthlord	10	Runehammer
5	Firetamer	11	Thundermaster
6	Knifemind	12	Underearth

Clan's Status

d6	Status
1	**Mighty.** Conquered several dwarven strongholds, dominates Underdark region
2	**Growing.** Stronghold expanding; glory days lie ahead
3	**Declining.** Clan growing stale, population falling
4	**Beleaguered.** Surrounded by drow and illithid foes
5	**Scattered.** Torn apart by slave rebellion or civil war
6	**Refugees.** Defeated by enemies, few survivors

Clan's Notable Trait

d12	Trait
1	Stole a mighty dwarven artifact
2	Has bound many devils to service
3	Experts in building mechanical devices
4	Conducts trade with the City of Brass
5	Notable for defeating many dwarves
6	Conquered and occupied a drow enclave
7	Is secretly controlled by mind flayers
8	Has enslaved a colony of troglodytes
9	Have interbred with devils
10	Known for its extensive spy network on surface
11	Masters of psionics
12	Dominated by a coven of warlocks

Duergar in the World

The tables below are designed to add depth to a duergar character by offering possible reasons why the character left the clan for the life of an adventurer and a choice of personality quirks that are tailored for duergar.

Duergar Adventurer Story Hooks

d6	Hook
1	You are a heretic, drawn to worship of Moradin.
2	Caught stealing, you escaped imprisonment but not before torture left you with a scar or lasting injury.
3	You were enslaved by drow or mind flayers but escaped to the surface.
4	You seek only to test yourself in battle with monsters.
5	Profit is all that matters to you.
6	The best way to defeat the folk of the surface is to study them firsthand.

Duergar Quirks

d6	Quirk
1	A separate personality in your mind provides advice and guidance to you.
2	Your gear must be perfectly arranged, otherwise someone must bleed.
3	When there isn't a roof over your head, you keep your eyes on the ground.
4	You don't talk unless you absolutely must.
5	The outside world is a giant cave, and nothing will convince you otherwise.
6	Humans fascinate you, and you collect odd trinkets of their culture.

Chapter 4:
Gith and Their Endless War

HE STORY OF THE GITH IS ROOTED IN A CRUEL twist of cosmic fate. Inspired by the great leader for whom the race is named, the gith rose up to overthrow the mind flayers that held them in servitude. But after they won their freedom, two factions among the gith disagreed on what kind of civilization they would forge. That disagreement quickly flared into open hostility, and the two groups distanced themselves from one another to pursue their separate agendas. They remain bitter enemies today, each side willing to fight to the death whenever they cross paths.

The githyanki were motivated by revenge and convinced that they deserved to take whatever they wanted from the worlds they traveled. Ranging out from the titanic city of Tu'narath on the Astral Plane, they send raiders out to plunder the Material Plane and other worlds, bringing treasures and slaves back to their ageless realm. At the same time, they hunt down and kill mind flayers whenever possible, as recompense for what the illithids did to them.

The githzerai believed that the path to an enlightened civilization lay in seclusion, not conflict. Their dedication to the principles of order is so strong that they can manipulate the stuff of chaos and use it to their benefit; thus, they have carved out a stronghold for themselves on the plane of Limbo that is virtually impervious. Though the githzerai are pacifists by nature, they share the githyanki's racial hatred for mind flayers, and from time to time they send out squads to destroy illithid outposts.

If the two races were ever to team up against the illithids, a combined force of gith could conceivably tip the balance in their favor. But as long as the githyanki and githzerai stay at each other's throats, their goal of ultimate victory over their original common enemy will likely remain unachieved.

Githyanki

Since winning their freedom from the mind flayers, the githyanki have become corrupt raiders and destroyers under the rulership of their dread lich-queen, Vlaakith. They dwell on the Astral Plane in the city of Tu'narath, a metropolis built on and in the corpse of a deity.

Vlaakith commands the loyalty of the githyanki from her personal stronghold, Susurrus, also called the Palace of Whispers, which is located deep inside the floating city. She sits on her Throne of Bones, a mighty artifact fueled by the intellects of mind flayers and elder brains that were defeated by her minions. It is crafted from mind flayer skulls and extremities, and the cushion she sits on is made of leather produced from the cured remains of an elder brain. A grand statue of Gith, an obsidian monument over 100 feet tall, stands beside the palace.

THE REVERED QUEEN

TO SLAY IN HER NAME IS OUR GREATEST SERVICE. TO DIE
in her name is our last act of reverence.

—Meldavh, githyanki knight

Vlaakith sits at the center of everything concerning the githyanki. She is their ruler in every sphere of activity and, as such, demands and receives utter obedience.

During the war with the illithids, Vlaakith urged Gith to seek out allies from among the planes and in particular advised her to seek counsel with Tiamat. Gith agreed to venture into the Nine Hells to forge an alliance with the Queen of Dragons. She didn't return. Instead, the great red dragon Ephelomon brought news to the gith: Tiamat had pledged many of her red dragon servants to the gith cause. They would refrain from attacking gith and would provide support against the illithids and protection for the gith's outposts on the Material Plane. In return, a few select young dragons would serve alongside the gith for a time, for purposes known only to Tiamat. Ephelomon also proclaimed that Vlaakith was to rule in Gith's place until she returned.

After the gith overthrew the mind flayers and Zerthimon's followers began to emerge as a threat to Gith's preeminence, Vlaakith played a critical role in ensuring that the githyanki under her rule were protected from an immediate, direct assault by their kin. Using her mastery of arcane magic, she helped the githyanki establish a permanent stronghold on the Astral Plane. From there, she began making plans to strike back at both the hated mind flayers and the traitorous githzerai.

THE GRAND PROCLAMATION

Vlaakith cemented her position as the supreme ruler of the githyanki with a grand proclamation that defined the githyanki's all-encompassing mission. They had been bred and trained for war by their one-time masters and had never known anything other than a martial existence. They needed a clear purpose and a forceful commander to spur them on, and Vlaakith provided both.

Vlaakith decreed that, having defeated the mind flayers, the githyanki would take the place of the illithids as sovereigns of the Material Plane. The many worlds of the Material Plane would be the githyanki's gardens, prime for harvesting as they saw fit. The Astral Plane would be their home domain, because in that timeless realm they could ignore the need for food, water, and other mundane concerns that plague lesser races.

Vlaakith also proclaimed that githyanki who proved themselves skilled in battle would ascend to an even greater paradise. A long lifetime of service would earn any githyanki a journey to the boundless delights of her innermost court—the wondrous realm that Gith discovered in her journeys, and where she awaits those who have proven themselves worthy.

THE BITTER TRUTH

In the time since Vlaakith made this promise to her people, she has called many of the most formidable githyanki warriors to their reward. At the culmination of a grand ceremony that supposedly readies them for

Imagine you lack any concept of family. You're constantly told that other races are inferior and that only faith in the Revered Queen preserves your people from the traitorous githzerai and the brain-eating illithids. You undergo years of hard labor and study and then embark on a perilous illithid hunt. Failure means death, but if you succeed, you're brought to the Astral, where you are welcomed into a society of people just like yourself.

I'll say this for Vlaakith: she knows how to build fanatics. But alas, fanatics are good for nothing of lasting consequence.

their journey to where Gith awaits, the supplicants enter her inner sanctum and are never seen again.

In truth, instead of sending them to paradise, Vlaakith drains their souls and absorbs their strength, gaining more power with every "ascension." Her knowledge of arcane magic equals that of a conclave of archmages, while her combat skill matches the combined talents of hundreds of sword masters.

Perhaps the lich-queen's promise isn't a complete fabrication, but no others can say for sure. If Vlaakith knows anything more, she has taken drastic measures to keep it secret. A few sages and spellcasters have sought to learn the truth about Gith's fate using arcane magic, only to fall victim to a bizarre curse that transforms them into the formless creatures known as allips.

All attempts to learn about Gith through divine magic return utter silence. Those who try experience a strange sensation, as if their minds were teetering on the edge of a great abyss, one that spans time, space, and memory.

BORN TO SERVE

UNDER THE ILLITHIDS, WE AND THE GITHYANKI FOUGHT *and died across a thousand worlds for implacable masters. Under Vlaakith, our kin fight and die across a thousand words for an implacable master. And they call that liberation?*

—Adaka Fell Hand, githzerai monk

From birth, githyanki are conditioned to fight and die for their queen. Children endure a brutal upbringing that constantly preaches devotion to Vlaakith. Each of the fortified settlements where young githyanki are raised and trained is a combination of military academy and cult headquarters.

ONLY THE BEST SURVIVE

The githyanki raise their young in hidden crèches that they construct in far-flung places on the Material Plane. Such measures are necessary because birth and growth are impossible on the Astral Plane, whose occupants don't age. The adult overseers in these places train young githyanki to harness their psychic and physical abilities.

Githyanki hatch from eggs. Each newborn enters the world alongside other eggs deliberately laid so that all hatch at the same time. Since githyanki adults must return to the Astral Plane to keep from aging significantly, the roster of instructors continually changes, with no adult staying longer than a few months and none ever returning for a second stint.

The instruction that young githyanki undergo is unrelenting and unforgiving. As a crop of youngsters grows older, more and more is demanded from each student, and the penalties for failing to keep up become more and more severe. In the early stages, combat practice lasts only until a wound is scored. Later, near the end of training, a drill of the same sort might be a fight to the death—the ultimate way of weeding out all those who don't meet Vlaakith's standards. To the githyanki, it's better for a weakling to die in training than to undertake a mission and imperil a war band.

FINAL TEST OF LOYALTY

By the time a group of githyanki come of age, they have heard years of stories of Vlaakith and her immortal warriors dwelling in the silvery void. The young are told they are on the verge of entering the queen's realm, each one of them destined to take a special place in the society. Their skills have proven them worthy, and now only their loyalty to the Revered Queen remains to be determined.

As their last test, a group of githyanki entering adulthood must slay a mind flayer as a sacred rite of passage before they are permitted to join their people on the Astral Plane. When the victors enter Tu'narath for the first time, they carry the bounty of their hunt directly to Vlaakith. She accepts the gift and intones a ritual chant that marks the youngsters' induction into githyanki society.

VLAAKITH'S DILEMMA

Long gone are the days when the gith race was fully embroiled in conflict. When the githyanki settled Tu'narath and took up residence in the Astral Plane, they no longer had to fight constantly for survival, and in that respect the lives of all githyanki became easier.

The mission laid out by Vlaakith in her grand proclamation remains of utmost importance. Her rule remains absolute, in part because she suffers no competition or divergent viewpoints. And her regime is in no danger, yet to an outsider in Tu'narath it might seem as though the place is in decline.

Indeed, in a way the githyanki are victims of their own success. After centuries of staging lucrative raids throughout the multiverse, the folk of Tu'narath have become spoiled and decadent. Vlaakith can still summon her people to action, and when she does so they obey her willingly. But when they aren't otherwise occupied, many of the citizens of the city spend their time in self-indulgent activities.

For all her seeming invincibility, Vlaakith finds herself in an awkward situation that—in her paranoid mind—has no easy resolution. If she keeps her people busy more often by ordering an increase in raids, she risks her best warriors and marauders becoming experienced and powerful enough to challenge her rule. Also, if she sends out too many raiding parties at one time, the security of Tu'narath might be compromised. So she addresses the problem by not dealing with it directly, but by trying to encourage her indolent followers to find purpose in meaningful activities that don't involve plundering and killing. She isn't always successful in that effort.

Merciless Marauders

When Vlaakith decrees that another githyanki raid is in the offing, Tu'narath comes alive with anticipation. The knights and other soldiers selected for the mission consider it a high privilege. All the raiders do their best to honor Vlaakith by savaging their target—killing creatures indiscriminately, taking whatever treasures catch their fancy, and leaving destruction in their wake.

When one of the githyanki's astral vessels returns home after a raid, it is laden with the spoils of the incursion. Vlaakith makes no specific demands but allows each individual raider freedom of choice in what they bring back. Some might seek exotic spices and herbs, while others pillage to find scrolls or tomes of knowledge. As a result, Tu'narath is cluttered (if not crowded) by a nearly infinite variety of objects that the githyanki have pirated from other planes, ranging in size from enormous buildings down to the smallest pieces of exquisite jewelry.

Indolent Dilettantes

As a race bred and shaped by the mind flayers for a life of fighting, the githyanki never knew anything else while they were enslaved. Now that they aren't constantly at war, keeping her people occupied is perhaps the greatest challenge Vlaakith faces.

When githyanki aren't on raids or other missions for Vlaakith, they enjoy a languid existence in Tu'narath. Since time doesn't pass on the Astral Plane, the githyanki have no need to labor for food or water. To keep their minds sharp, Vlaakith orders them to pursue a variety of arts and studies. She regularly arranges contests, scavenger hunts, and other trials to keep her servants involved in purposeful activity, but the attraction of such diversions wears off after a brief time. Most of the citizens of Tu'narath, when they haven't been called for duty on a raid or for some other mission, indulge themselves in any way they see fit.

Githyanki, with an infinite amount of time on their hands, crave novelty. They expect every returning raid to provide new forms of entertainment. This preoccupation with newness stands at the hollow center of githyanki culture. They dabble in creating art, but never master it. They stand among treasures taken from countless worlds but are never truly appreciative of them. The githyanki flit from topic to topic, craft to craft, never settling on one endeavor for long. Tu'narath is littered with

A silver sword in motion is a liquid thing, as much a weapon of the mind as a piece of metal in the hand.

half-built sculptures, partially completed frescoes, and other unfinished works of all sorts. The githyanki simply abandon personal projects that bore them, and every such endeavor they undertake ends in this manner.

A Blade Kept Sharp

Despite the decadent lifestyle the githyanki indulge in, they remain in fighting shape. All are required to attend weapon and combat drills, which serve as a brief respite from their boredom.

Vlaakith, of course, stands atop the githyanki military hierarchy. Under her serve the supreme commanders, each of whom oversees a regiment of one thousand githyanki warriors. Ten kith'rak, each responsible for a company of one hundred, answer to a commander. Each kith'rak in turn commands ten sarths, each of whom leads a party of ten warriors. A githyanki war leader retains that status in times of peace, looking after her underlings and maintaining their discipline and combat training.

Knights: A Breed Apart

I am her will made manifest.

I am her unsheathed sword.

I am a master of dragons.

I am the fate of all worlds.

I am a knight of Vlaakith.

Ever may she reign.

—Battle hymn of the githyanki knights

Githyanki knights are warriors, spellcasters, and scouts of exceptional ability devoted to the unflagging service of Vlaakith. Knights report directly to the queen and aren't part of the military hierarchy. The personnel for any important mission includes at least one knight, and every githyanki fortress or outpost across the multiverse is administered by at least one knight in residence. Knights are selected for their roles based on their martial and psionic potential, and young githyanki who pass muster are inducted into service soon after they enter Tu'narath for the first time.

Knights are always involved in important decisions, and it is forbidden to keep secrets from them. They act as commissars and enforcers of Vlaakith's will. They are the rough equivalent of religious figures in githyanki

The Spoils of War

An individual githyanki's weapons and armor are ornate and decorated with trophies taken on raids. With each new victory, a warrior brings home a token to serve as a memento. Anything might strike a githyanki's fancy, from a jewel taken from the pommel of a fallen opponent's sword to colorful banners taken from a plundered castle that, preserved by the timeless nature of the Astral Plane, keep their original vibrant hue for centuries. The more baroque and ostentatious a raid token is, the more likely it is to be admired by one's fellow warriors.

culture, although the githyanki have no priests or clerics of normal sort.

Two aspects of their nature set knights apart from other githyanki. Each knight wields a cherished silver greatsword that imparts special powers to its owner, and the knights are among the few githyanki who can not only travel psionically between planes, but can also take allies along with them. Knights often emerge from planar travel astride the backs of red dragons, which have been serving the githyanki as allies ever since their time of enslavement under the mind flayers.

Silver Swords

The first silver swords were created eons ago, when the gith were still a single race, by those who would become the first githyanki knights. A silver sword, which functions as a *+3 greatsword*, is a conduit through which its wielder can assail a foe both physically and psychically. The weapon is particularly effective on the Astral Plane against any travelers who are connected to their physical bodies by a silver cord—a strike against such an enemy has a chance of severing the silver cord, causing instant death.

Knights and their silver swords are inseparable, and a knight will fight to the death to prevent the loss of its weapon. If a silver sword falls into the possession of someone other than a githyanki, Vlaakith sends a squad of knights out from Tu'narath to destroy the malefactor and recover the weapon.

Dragon Steeds

The relationship between githyanki and red dragons has remained basically unchanged since ancient times. Under the terms of the alliance with Tiamat, a small cadre of dragons serve as cohorts and mounts for knights and other high-ranking githyanki. The dragons remain above githyanki politics. They obey the orders of their riders and fulfill their terms of service without offering opinions or advice.

Red dragons typically serve the githyanki during their younger years. Once a dragon reaches adulthood, it is dismissed and replaced with a younger dragon, taking with it the loot it has accumulated on raids.

Since dragons don't age while on the Astral Plane, they don't grow in size or capability. In order to become both stronger and richer, they prefer to spend as much time as possible engaged in raids on the Material Plane or other realms. The best duty of all for a dragon is being tasked to guard a githyanki crèche on the Material Plane, a posting that could last for years. Not only does it receive treasure as compensation, the dragon ages normally while completing its service, so that it reaches adulthood sooner than the dragon cohorts that are stationed in Tu'narath.

The dragons that are bound to serve githyanki consider their assignment an irritant but aren't hostile. They resent their masters, but the promise of loot makes them eager to participate in raids. As part of the compact with Tiamat, the githyanki are forbidden from using psionics or magic to compel their dragon allies' actions or read their minds. A dragon remains a loyal ally as long as its riders and handlers treat it with respect and it gets plenty of opportunities to pillage.

TERROR FROM THE SKY

WE PRAISED PELOR WHEN WE REALIZED THE SHAPES *above us were not dragons. We cursed him when we saw they were the airships of the githyanki.*

—Lord Kedrek Thoroden,
Marshal of the Eastern Reach

During the great war between the mind flayers and the gith, one of the githyanki's greatest achievements was their discovery of the magic that mind flayers used to produce and propel the flying vessels that the illithids used to travel between worlds.

Now, the githyanki scour the worlds of the Material Plane in their versions of those craft. Their astral ships are ideal for carrying troops and the spoils of their raids. Their wizards' divination magic seeks out great treasures. Under the guidance of Vlaakith, the supreme leaders organize raiding parties and dispatch them to return with the spoils of war.

The githyanki sky ships attack from above in the dead of night, gaining an instant advantage since communi-

ties on the surface rarely offer strong defenses against attacks from the air. Red dragons ridden by knights accompany the vessels, serving as outriders and shock trips to pave the way for the githyanki warriors to descend en masse.

In battle, the githyanki use mobile tactics combining psionics and magic to devastate their foes. They hit hard, setting buildings aflame and killing all in their path, to foster a panic among their victims that cripples any hope of an organized defense.

Because the githyanki strike to plunder rather than conquer, raiders linger over their target for no more than a few hours. By daybreak the attackers are gone, purposely leaving behind enough survivors to rebuild the ruined community—so that the githyanki might visit the place years or decades later and lay it low all over again.

THE HELM

To enable them to traverse the skies and travel between planes, each githyanki ship is powered by a helm, a magical device in the form of a throne-like chair that converts psychic energy into motive force.

THE GITH ALPHABET

The gith use a written language composed of alphabetic symbols arranged in circular clusters called tir'su. Each "spoke" on the wheel corresponds to a letter of the alphabet. Each cluster of characters represents a single word, and multiple tir'su connect to form phrases and sentences.

Githyanki and githzerai both speak Gith, but each race has a distinct dialect and accent. Similarly, the two races of gith differentiate their language by how they write it. Githyanki write a tir'su clockwise, starting at the top. Githzerai use the same letter symbols but write their tir'su counterclockwise, starting from the bottom.

A gish, a githyanki who excels as both a warrior and a spellcaster, most commonly occupies the helm. A gish uses its combination of abilities to pilot the ship and also take part in the inevitable battle that awaits the vessel at the end of its voyage. The rest of a ship's crew is made up of warriors who manage the craft's weapons and serve as lookouts.

ASTRAL SKIFF

An astral skiff is operated by a crew of three and carries up to a dozen passengers. The githyanki employ this small vessel, 30 feet long and 10 feet wide, for patrols in the Astral Plane and for quick raids in pursuit of specific objects on the Material Plane. A skiff has a top speed of 15 miles per hour. It lacks weapons aside from those carried by its passengers and has a limited amount of storage space.

ASTRAL BRIG

The astral brig is the standard githyanki military vessel. It requires a crew of five and can transport up to sixty passengers. A brig is 90 feet long and 30 feet wide, with two levels below decks for quarters and storage space. It is equipped with two ballistae, each one operated by a pair of crew members, and has a top speed of 12 miles per hour.

PLANAR RAIDER

The largest of the githyanki ships, the planar raider serves as a mobile headquarters during a major attack on the githyanki's enemies. It needs a crew of ten and can carry more than a hundred passengers. A planar raider can travel up to 12 miles per hour. It is 40 feet wide and 120 feet long, with two levels below decks, and is equipped with three ballistae and a catapult.

I have been to Tu'narath. A heaven for the githyanki it is not. Their apathy and frustration manifest as a visible fog, which clears only when the githyanki ready for war.

TU'NARATH

THEY CALL IT THE CITY OF DEATH. I WOULD MOCK SUCH *a tired excuse for a name, but if it fits, who am I to argue?*

—Gimble, gnome bard

When the githyanki fled from the illithids, Vlaakith led them to safety on the Astral Plane inside the floating corpse of a six-armed deity. This being's body long ago calcified into a great slab of rock, its lower half smashed by some ancient disaster. A trail of debris, some of the stones larger than a castle, extends from the corpse's lower end.

The city of Tu'narath is built on and in the corpse's upper body, with a central district in the area corresponding to its chest and ancillary districts radiating outward along its six outstretched arms and toward its head. Despite the body's partial destruction, the occasional tremor that echoes through its rocky mass suggests that some spark of life might still linger deep within.

Anyone who visits the city does so either at the behest of the githyanki or in stealth. Fortunately for those who try to enter clandestinely, the place is immense enough that a small group can sneak in with relative ease.

If uninvited visitors arrive openly, they can expect a sharp reception from githyanki patrol vessels. If that's not enough to bring them to heel, the call goes out for a squad of dragon-mounted knights.

THE STREETS OF TU'NARATH

Tu'narath is a jumble of crooked streets that run between buildings and other structures that are ripped

---

TU'NARATH IN BRIEF

Here are some key details of Tu'narath.

Population. Roughly one hundred thousand folk dwell in Tu'narath. The vast majority are githyanki, but visitors from other planes aren't uncommon. Individuals who come to deal with the githyanki reside here. Residents also include captives that the githyanki have taken on raids.

Law and Order. Warriors patrol above the streets in astral skiffs to keep the peace. Githyanki who cause unwarranted conflict are disciplined, but such punishment is rarely lethal. Any visitor who causes a ruckus, however, is likely to be slain on the spot, unless Vlaakith has specifically forbidden such action.

Inns. Tu'narath has no taverns or inns in the traditional sense. The githyanki expect visitors to carve out their own accommodations; they can choose from among any number of abandoned structures. As an alternative, a small troupe of renegade modrons maintains a crumbling citadel called the Iron House that has rooms for rent. Visitors can pay with interesting trinkets from across the planes.

Markets. There are no organized markets in Tu'narath. The githyanki don't offer goods for sale to visitors, and they don't purchase items offered to them—they simply take what they want.

---

from the worlds of other planes. Many githyanki raiders have a particular obsession for architecture, which they satisfy by seizing buildings from the Material Plane and other locales and relocating them in Tu'narath.

Often, these prizes don't remain intact for long. When residents become bored or find themselves in the mood for debauchery, the githyanki's natural propensity for violence manifests in the form of a great brawl or wild celebration that causes serious damage to their surroundings. When a structure has served its purpose and is no longer useful (or even recognizable), the githyanki tear the debris from its resting place and throw it into a refuse pile or cast it adrift into the astral sea, to be eventually replaced by a new specimen.

Nonetheless, the city does have a great number of permanent structures, and a system of districts in which particular functions or activities are concentrated.

Queen's District. Susurrus, the queen's stronghold, is protected by thick, obsidian walls. Only one gate leads into it, located on a path that passes beneath the statue of Gith. Beyond the statue, the path becomes a labyrinthine maze designed to prevent attackers or visitors from gaining access to the queen. Vlaakith's throne room, a gargantuan hall supported by obsidian pillars, sits at the center of the labyrinth. Guarded by two red dragons, Vlaakith sits upon her Throne of Bones and holds court over her supplicants.

Glathk District. A muddy field that extends as far as the eye can see is the githyanki equivalent of a labor camp. The glathk district, named after the Gith word for "farmer"—a term of derision—is where githyanki are taken when they violate society's rules. Punishments are nonlethal, and often don't involve physical harm. Instead, offenders are forced to submit to the mind-numbing sameness of performing one task interminably—a fate that, for some, might feel worse than death. For instance, a warrior might be sequestered here after slacking off during weapons practice, sentenced to a prison term and charged with moving piles of mud from one end of the field to the other. Elsewhere, a squad of warriors stands at attention for an indeterminate time, after their failure to maintain proper formations during drills.

Those incarcerated here are rarely supervised closely, but knights patrol the area regularly.

District of Discards. The githyanki dispose of loot that they have no use for in a space on the outer surface of Tu'narath set aside for the purpose. Such items can range from trophies and treasure to prisoners of other races that have been set free and left to fend for themselves. The few githyanki who dwell here maintain a semblance of order amid the wreckage by categorizing the castaway items, making it easier for other githyanki to locate objects related to their personal interests.

Creatures seeking to infiltrate Tu'narath have had success in using this place as a base, since the warriors and knights seldom patrol it, and several groups of freed captives—humans, elves, hobgoblins, and other sorts—make their homes here.

Military Districts. Soldiers and officers occupy several areas around the city, most of which contain defensive works and armories. The githyanki also maintain barracks that serve as mustering points in advance of raids. All githyanki are required to report to one of these districts regularly for weapon practice. Non-githyanki that venture into these areas are attacked on sight unless accompanied by a knight who can vouch for them.

Mlar District. This area passes for an artisan's district. Githyanki engaged in distractions that involve artistry or creation gather here, both to share their skills and to show off their goods. Outsiders can pass through the district if appropriately disguised; the githyanki bring captured artisans here to provide insight and tutelage, but rarely keep a close watch on them. After all, they have little chance of escaping the city.

Shipyards. The githyanki store and maintain their vessels at docks and outcrops that adjoin the military districts. Those who are assigned to ship maintenance enjoy a high status and are allowed to consider their work as part of their military service. Githyanki warriors provide labor as needed.

Dragon Caves. The shattered lower body of the dead god contains an abundance of natural caves and fissures. Each of the red dragons that serve the githyanki has a lair deep within this region, jealously guarding its hoard until it is called for service. No one has ever successfully mapped out the strange passages and tunnels, and a variety of scavengers, astral predators, and other creatures lair here, some of them likely dating from the time before the githyanki came along. The residents of Tu'narath don't typically spend time in the caves, except as necessary to tend to the dragons. On occasion, a githyanki craving a new experience might venture into this area for a respite from boredom. Those who don't return, it can be assumed, found what they were after.

Rumors persist of an enormous dungeon that lies beyond the caves, a hidden fortress occupied by a mighty demigod who claimed The One in the Void as its home before the githyanki occupied it. Coteries of Red Wizards from the land of Thay on Faerün, accompanied by githyanki knights, have ventured into this area in recent years. Supposedly, the Thayans once emerged with a huge adamantine container that rumbled and shook, as if to the beat of a monstrous heart.

SURVIVOR COMMUNITIES

As befits a society of conquerors, the githyanki have no regard for the victims of their raids. They take lives to assert their dominance, not out of anger or because they feel threatened. From time to time, instead of killing everyone they encounter on a raid, they bring captives back to Tu'narath for various reasons.

The githyanki treat prisoners with the same detachment and disdain they show for those they slay. When captives are no longer useful, their masters might end their lives, or they might simply stop caring about their possessions and leave the creatures to fend for themselves.

The hardiest and most elusive of these folk make their way to the District of Discards, where they can take refuge from the threats that face them in other parts of the city and live in relative obscurity. The githyanki care nothing for what goes on in these survivor communities, unless a disruption becomes serious enough to attract their attention. A group of would-be infiltrators might be able to get a foothold in Tu'narath by stealthily entering the district and blending in with a community of survivors.

Githzerai

The githzerai were born as a race at the end of the gith's bloody, genocidal uprising against the mind flayers. A gith named Zerthimon, who had gained a significant following during the conflict, challenged Gith's plans and her leadership. Gith was evil, the newcomer proclaimed, and she would lead the people into darkness and tyranny not unlike the one imposed by the illithids.

Thus, no sooner had the gith defeated their sworn enemies than they were plunged into a bitter civil war. In the ensuing conflict, Zerthimon was killed and his followers, naming themselves githzerai, relocated their civilization to the plane of Limbo.

Today, under the leadership of the Great Githzerai, Zaerith Menyar-Ag-Gith, the githzerai continue to stand fast against the githyanki, as well as taking their revenge on the mind flayers. Through forays into the Material Plane and other realms, they provide stiff opposition to their enemies' plans for world domination.

Order in a Sea of Chaos

WE GITHZERAI CRAVE A CHALLENGE, SO THAT WHEN *Zerthimon returns he shall find us ready. Thus we traveled to howling Limbo to make our new home.*

—The Teachings of Menyar-Ag

Strong-minded philosophers and austere ascetics, the githzerai pursue lives of rigid order. Their society focuses on enhancing the potential of the mind through meditation, education, and physical tests. The most accomplished among them stand as exemplars of the githzerai's monastic principles, but even those who perform mundane duties in a community have a significant measure of the same mental fortitude.

Living in the ever-turbulent churn of Limbo requires all githzerai to harness the power of thought to counteract and hold at bay the chaos-stuff of the plane. If they were not relentless in this effort, the tides of Limbo would overwhelm and destroy them.

The githzerai have a unity of purpose that comes from their reverence for their great heroes and their desire to emulate the virtues of those figures in their everyday lives.

Menyar-Ag, the Great Githzerai

Menyar-Ag led the githzerai into Limbo at the culmination of the conflict between Gith and Zerthimon. Thanks to unimaginable arcane and psionic power, he has survived far beyond the life span of an ordinary githzerai. Time has nevertheless taken its toll, and Menyar-Ag today is a decrepit, corpse-like entity—capable of tremendous feats of magic and psionics but barely able to move a finger or lift his own eyelids. A host of servants constantly attend to Menyar-Ag and see to his every need.

Although Menyar-Ag is no longer capable of physical actions of any consequence, his mind is as active and sharp as ever. He never sleeps, using a rotating staff of attendants to spread his commands and counsel to all githzerai. If needed, he can call upon his own psychic energy to contact his people, even across the planes.

Anarchs

A githzerai community works constantly to maintain a stable base of operations protected from the wilds of Limbo. The mental energy of the collective that keeps the plane's forces of chaos at bay is funneled through the exceptional githzerai known as anarchs. One or more anarchs maintain each community by serving as both the receptacle for the psychic power of other githzerai and the means by which that power is employed.

Anarchs have a special gift for stabilizing and controlling the chaos-stuff of Limbo. In their communities on Limbo, they can create matter and energy out of nothingness with a thought. They can control the direction of gravity. The environment around them can be whatever they want it to be.

Anarchs are exceedingly rare among githzerai. When a githzerai in an existing community demonstrates the ability to become an anarch, that individual might leave the community to found a new colony or might remain where it is and ascend to a leadership position.

Zerths

Zerthimon's mortal form died in battle, but his sacrifice freed the githzerai from Gith's dark designs. They believe that Zerthimon, in his new godly form, will return someday and usher them into new age of freedom. Until that happens, the githzerai known as zerths fill the symbolic role of Zerthimon in society, as accomplished wielders of psionic power who can move themselves and others between planes.

The githzerai believe that when Zerthimon returns, he will first gather all the zerths and take them to their new paradise to prepare it for those who follow. Zerths are similar to what other races would call priests, although githzerai don't have a religion as such, beyond their admiration for Zerthimon and Menyar-Ag.

Fortress Cities

The monasteries of the githzerai are massive outposts of stability that sail through the chaos of Limbo. Githzerai anarchs keep the fortresses stable and control their interior design, opening portals to the outside only as needed. Most fortresses drift through Limbo at random, but none of them are ever isolated. When Menyar-Ag sends out a call to them, the anarchs of the other communities can instantly communicate with him.

Aside from its inhabitants, the most well-defended element of a githzerai fortress is its food supply. Because Limbo provides no sustenance, the githzerai rely on crops and livestock they appropriate from elsewhere. Plants are grown in hydroponic chambers, and livestock are raised in pens where light, temperature, and other conditions are tailored to their needs.

A community's activity is overseen by monks who assign duties to each occupant. Everyone participates in mock combats and ongoing academic instruction, and each fortress allocates personnel and resources as needed. Every fortress is designed to be self-sufficient, even though no two of them are ever out of psychic contact.

Shra'kt'lor

Shra'kt'lor is a fortress city that houses the largest concentration of githzerai. It serves as both the capital of the civilization and the headquarters of the githzerai military forces. The greatest generals, spellcasters, and zerths of the race meet here to plan or refine their strategy for battling the githyanki and the mind flayers.

Shra'kt'lor is the most well defended of the githzerai outposts—no force in Limbo could readily threaten the city or its inhabitants. Teleportation circles are barred except on the fringes of the place, at always-guarded locations beyond the city's outermost defenses. Those who use plane-shifting magic to arrive at these sites or who approach through the chaos of Limbo aren't admitted to the city without the approval of an anarch.

Beyond the entrance to the city wait six layers of nested defenses. Each one is dominated by a fortress maintained by a powerful anarch chosen by Zaerith Menyar-Ag-Gith, who dwells at the heart of it all.

Githzerai in the World

ZERTHIMON DOES NOT EXPECT US TO WAIT IN PATIENCE *for his return. Instead, we must pave the way for his efforts, so that we can hasten the coming of our golden age.*

—The Teachings of Menyar-Ag

It's natural for githzerai to prefer to remain in Limbo. They have carved out a well-ordered civilization in an environment that they can freely manipulate with their minds. When they visit other realms, particularly the Material Plane, githzerai feel sluggish and aren't comfortable functioning in a landscape that they see as being locked in immutability. Despite their disinclination toward travel, the githzerai send groups away from Limbo on a regular basis to keep from giving ground in their battles against the githyanki and the mind flayers.

Adamantine Citadels

When githzerai travel, they sometimes bring a sliver of Limbo along. Before they set out, a cadre of powerful anarchs craft a citadel of adamantine out of the chaos-stuff around them. Inside the structure is more of Limbo's essence, left in raw form until it's needed. Then, in an eruption of psionic and arcane power that only Menyar-Ag can produce, the citadel and its accompanying githzerai are transported to another plane.

After the transfer is complete, at least one anarch must always attend the citadel to maintain its form and shape as well as to utilize the chaos-stuff within. When a citadel is ensconced on another plane, the githzerai create a teleportation circle inside it to facilitate travel between that plane and Limbo.

The appearance of an adamantine citadel on another plane creates a blot on the natural world. Life, the one thing that can't be spontaneously created from the stuff of Limbo, is driven away from the location in a wave of dread. Depending on the size of the citadel, the affected area can have a radius of between several hundred feet and several miles. Birds avoid flying over or near it, other animals flee the area, and plants in the vicinity wither and die. Intelligent creatures can act normally, but being in the affected area is unnerving to them, and if they investigate, they soon identify the citadel as the cause. The githyanki, however, find it in their best interest to keep their citadels safe from discovery. Menyar-Ag prefers to plant them in desolate and rarely frequented places such as barren deserts or remote locations in the Underdark.

The primary purpose of an adamantine citadel is to watch over the activity of some foe of the githzerai, such as an illithid colony, and to provide a base of operations for a possible attack. Citadels are also used to collect foodstuffs and other material goods for transport to Limbo. When the githzerai are finished with a citadel, they vacate it and return to Limbo. Immediately after the last anarch teleports away, the citadel vanishes, leaving only a scarred landscape to indicate where it once stood.

SPREADING THE WORD

The githzerai see their cause as not just a provincial concern, but one that they strive to impress upon others. As such, they have taken the initiative in preaching the philosophy of Zerthimon and sharing their knowledge of how to fight illithids and githyanki. To this end, zerths sometimes venture to other planes with the intent of founding a new monastery or joining an existing one.

These "missionaries" are always looking for those with psionic potential who can bring those powers to bear against the githzerai's foes. Most often, they operate in secret or behind the scenes as they pursue their agenda and try to swell the ranks of their allies. Who can say how many monasteries are in truth secret recruiting stations for the githzerai?

GOING ON THE ATTACK

The githzerai know full well that they can't make progress in the war against their enemies by staying inside their fortresses on Limbo. To check the advances of the illithids and the githyanki and keep their foes' numbers down, squads of githzerai often travel to other planes with the express intent of destroying the objects of their hatred.

Githyanki. Githzerai rarely confront githyanki on their home turf in the Astral Plane, but on other planes they maintain steady surveillance, always on the lookout for githyanki plots to foil and crèches to exterminate. During a mission of this sort, the githzerai don't intentionally endanger the natural denizens of the plane, but they never compromise a planned attack on the githyanki just to protect innocent bystanders. In battling githyanki, the end justifies the means.

Githzerai sometimes employ mercenaries on the Material Plane to aid them in battling the githyanki, primarily to keep their enemies off-balance or to provide reinforcements. For those who need such enticement, they offer the promise of sharing the bounty of great treasures held by the githyanki.

Mind Flayers. Though they devote most of their military efforts to the constant campaign against the githyanki, the githzerai's enmity for the illithids is even older. On one thing the githyanki and the githzerai can agree: the mind flayers must pay for what they did to the gith eons ago.

As their means of vengeance against the mind flayers, the githzerai send bands of warriors called rrakkmas—illithid hunting parties—to other planes to do battle with any mind flayers they come across. It is in these circumstances that the natives of the plane most often encounter githzerai away from their monastery. With their attention focused only on their mission, the githzerai pay little heed to those around as long as they don't interfere with the hunt.

GITH CHARACTERS

At the DM's option, you can create a gith character, using the following traits.

GITH TRAITS

Your character shares the following traits with other gith.

Ability Score Increase. Your Intelligence score increases by 1.

Age. Gith reach adulthood in their late teens and live for about a century.

Size. Gith are taller and leaner than humans, with most a slender 6 feet in height.

Speed. Your base walking speed is 30 feet.

Languages. You can speak, read, and write Common and Gith.

Subrace. There are two kinds of gith, githyanki and githzerai. Choose one of these subraces.

GITHYANKI

The brutal githyanki are trained from birth as warriors.

Ability Score Increase. Your Strength score increases by 2.

Alignment. Githyanki tend toward lawful evil. They are aggressive and arrogant, and they remain the faithful servants of their lich-queen, Vlaakith. Renegade githyanki tend toward chaos.

Decadent Mastery. You learn one language of your choice, and you are proficient with one skill or tool of your choice. In the timeless city of Tu'narath, githyanki have bountiful time to master odd bits of knowledge.

Martial Prodigy. You are proficient with light and medium armor and with shortswords, longswords, and greatswords.

Githyanki Psionics. You know the *mage hand* cantrip, and the hand is invisible when you cast the cantrip with this trait.

When you reach 3rd level, you can cast the *jump* spell once with this trait, and you regain the ability to do so when you finish a long rest. When you reach 5th level, you can cast the *misty step* spell once with this trait, and you regain the ability to do so when you finish a long rest.

Intelligence is your spellcasting ability for these spells. When you cast them with this trait, they don't require components.

GITHZERAI

In their fortresses within Limbo, the githzerai hone their minds to a razor's edge.

Ability Score Increase. Your Wisdom score increases by 2.

Alignment. Githzerai tend toward lawful neutral. Their rigorous training in psychic abilities requires an implacable mental discipline.

Mental Discipline. You have advantage on saving throws against the charmed and frightened conditions. Under the tutelage of monastic masters, githzerai learn to govern their own minds.

Githzerai Psionics. You know the *mage hand* cantrip, and the hand is invisible when you cast the cantrip with this trait.

When you reach 3rd level, you can cast the *shield* spell once with this trait, and you regain the ability to do so when you finish a long rest. When you reach 5th level, you can cast the *detect thoughts* spell once with this trait, and you regain the ability to do so when you finish a long rest.

Wisdom is your spellcasting ability for these spells. When you cast them with this trait, they don't require components.

RANDOM HEIGHT AND WEIGHT

Race	Base Height	Base Weight	Height Modifier	Weight Modifier
Githyanki	5'0"	100 lb.	+2d12	× (2d4) lb.
Githzerai	4'11"	90 lb.	+2d12	× (1d4) lb.

Height = Base Height + Height Modifier (in inches)

Weight = Base Weight + Height Modifier (in pounds) × Weight Modifier

I studied for a time with the githzerai in Limbo. Their adamantine citadels inspired a spell I created.

GITH TABLES

This section provides tables for players and DMs who want to create githzerai and githyanki characters.

GITHYANKI NAMES, MALE

d10	Name	d10	Name
1	Elirdain	6	Quith
2	Gaath	7	Ris'a'an
3	Ja'adoc	8	Tropos
4	Kar'i'nas	9	Viran
5	Lykus	10	Xamodas

GITHYANKI NAMES, FEMALE

d10	Name	d10	Name
1	Aaryl	6	Quorstyl
2	B'noor	7	Sirruth
3	Fenelzi'ir	8	Vaira
4	Jen'lig	9	Yessune
5	Pah'zel	10	Zar'ryth

GITHYANKI PERSONALITY TRAITS

d4	Trait
1	When I'm bored I make my own excitement, and I'm always bored.
2	I treat others as if they were animals that simply don't know any better.
3	Violence is a spice that makes life worth living.
4	Old age is a concept that I find fascinating. Maybe someday I too will be aged.

GITHYANKI IDEALS

d4	Trait
1	**Fidelity.** Warriors are only as good as the vows they keep.
2	**Power.** The weak rule the strong.
3	**Duty.** It is by Vlaakith's will alone that I act.
4	**Freedom.** No strong soul should be enslaved. Better to die first than live as another's puppet.

GITHYANKI BONDS

d4	Bond
1	There is no greater duty than to serve the Revered Queen.
2	Humanity thrives only because we conquered the illithids. Therefore, what is theirs is ours.
3	Without battle, life has no purpose.
4	Life is but a spark in the dark. We all go dark, but those who dare can burn bright.

GITHYANKI FLAWS

d4	Flaw
1	Hunger and thirst are unbearable pains to me.
2	I can't see a non-githyanki as a real threat.
3	I follow orders, regardless of their implications.
4	I start projects but never finish them.

GITHZERAI NAMES, MALE

d10	Name	d10	Name
1	Dak	6	Kalla
2	Duurth	7	Muurg
3	Ferzth	8	Nurm
4	Greth	9	Shrakk
5	Hurm	10	Xorm

GITHZERAI NAMES, FEMALE

d10	Name	d10	Name
1	Adaka	6	Izera
2	Adeya	7	Janara
3	Ella	8	Loraya
4	Ezhelya	9	Uweya
5	Immilzin	10	Vithka

GITHZERAI PERSONALITY TRAITS

d4	Flaw
1	All energy must be expended to a useful end. Frivolity is the first step to defeat.
2	Patience in all things. The first step in any venture is the most treacherous.
3	Emotions are a trap, meant to weaken the intellect and disturb the nerves. Pay them no heed.
4	Begin only those tasks you will finish. Strike only that which you will kill.

GITHZERAI IDEALS

d4	Ideal
1	**Faith.** Zerthimon shall return, and I will be worthy to walk beside him.
2	**Courage.** The mind can master anything if it is unfettered by fear.
3	**Duty.** My people survive only because those like me place their needs above our own.
4	**Freedom.** No strong soul should be enslaved. Better to die first than live as another's puppet.

Githzerai Bonds

d4	Bond
1	Zerthimon provides an example of conduct that I strive to duplicate.
2	Menyar-Ag hand-picked me for my duties, and I will never betray the trust he showed in me.
3	Vlaakith and her toadies will be defeated, if not by me then by those who follow in my footsteps.
4	I will not rest until the last elder brain is destroyed.

Githzerai Flaws

d4	Flaw
1	I see githyanki machinations behind every threat.
2	I believe in the supremacy of the gith and that githzerai and githyanki will align to rule the multiverse.
3	I respond to even minor threats with overwhelming displays of force.
4	The next time I laugh will be the first. The sound of merriment takes me to the edge of violence.

Githyanki Raiding Parties

Use the following tables to generate a band of githyanki raiders and some additional details of their situation. Roll once on each line of the Group Composition table and once on each table that follows it.

In the tables, a name in bold refers to a stat block in the *Monster Manual*.

Raiding Party Composition

Members	Number Present
Githyanki warriors	2d6
Githyanki knights	1d4
Young red dragons	Roll a d6. On a result of 6, the group includes 1d3 dragons.

Raiding Party Leader

d6	Leader
1	Githyanki supreme commander
2–3	Githyanki knight
4–5	Githyanki kith'rak
6	Githyanki gish

Special Allies

d10	Ally
1–3	None
4–5	1d4 githyanki knights
6–7	1d4 githyanki knights, 1 githyanki gish
8–9	1d4 githyanki gish, 1d4 githyanki knights
10	1d4 githyanki gish, 1d4 githyanki knights, 1 githyanki kith'rak

Raiding Party Transport

d6	Transport (with crew)
1–2	One astral skiff carrying entire group
3–4	Two astral skiffs, each carrying half of group
5	Astral brig carrying entire group plus an additional 30 githyanki warriors
6	Planar raider carrying entire group plus an additional 60 githyanki warriors

Purpose of Raid

d6	Purpose
1–2	Wanton destruction; the githyanki want to fight and loot to relieve their boredom
3	Revenge; the githyanki seek a stolen silver sword
4–5	Mind flayer hunt; the githyanki are seeking mind flayers and their thralls
6	Vlaakith's orders; the githyanki have been dispatched to seize a specific item or person

Githzerai Groups

Use the following tables to generate a band of githzerai and determine their reason for being away from Limbo. Roll once on each line of the Group Composition table and once on each table that follows it.

In the tables, a name in bold refers to a stat block in the *Monster Manual*.

Group Composition

Members	Number Present
Githzerai monks	2d8
Githzerai zerths	1d4

Group Leader

d6	Leader
1	Githzerai anarch
2–3	Githzerai enlightened
4–6	Githzerai zerth

Special Allies

d8	Ally
1–3	None
4–5	1d4 githzerai zerths
6	1d4 githzerai enlightened
7	1d4 githzerai zerths, 1d4 githzerai enlightened
8	1 githzerai anarch, 1d4 githzerai enlightened

Purpose of Mission

d4	Purpose
1	Hunting a specific mind flayer colony
2	Seeking news on mind flayer activity; 20% chance they suspect the characters are hiding something
3	On a training mission, seeking to hone their skills and learn of the world
4	Seek to ally with party on a raid against mind flayers; group has something characters want

Chapter 5: Halflings and Gnomes

Creatures of many races and cultures are embroiled in struggles that flare up across the multiverse. Other folk survive in the face of all this turmoil by keeping a low profile and avoiding the wars and other depredations that keep the outside world in a state of flux.

Halflings and gnomes are two groups that have survived by remaining largely unnoticed by the aggressive powers of the cosmos. Both races are exceptions in a multiverse wracked by conflict—peaceful folk who have found niches for themselves away from the battles and rivalries that fill the lives of the larger folk.

Halflings

I DON'T HAVE ENOUGH FINGERS AND TOES TO COUNT THE *times I saw our little rogue cheat death, but I remember them all. Let's see ... there was the enraged roper, the flaming lava stream, the catapulted gelatinous cubes, the Ten Tilting Corridors of Death, the exploding toad trap, the Hall of the Spinning Scimitars ...*

—Magnificus, wizard extraordinaire

Anyone who has spent time around halflings, and particularly halfling adventurers, has likely witnessed the storied "luck of the halflings" in action. When a halfling is in mortal danger, it seems as though an unseen force intervenes. If a halfling falls off a cliff, her britches will snag on a root or a sharp outcrop of rock. If a halfling is forced by pirates to walk the plank, he will catch a piece of flotsam and use it to stay afloat until he is rescued.

Halflings believe in the power of luck, and they abide by a great number of superstitions that they believe bring good or ill fortune. They attribute their unusual gift to the favor of Yondalla, believing that, now and then, the divine will of the goddess tips the balance of fate in their favor (or gives it a hearty shove when the occasion warrants).

Naturally Innocent

Scholars, wizards, druids, and bards of other races have different ideas about how halflings escape peril, suggesting that by virtue of something in their nature, they occupy a special place in the multiverse.

One such hypothesis cites a legend that speaks of a document containing ancient elven writings—a series of essays spanning centuries. Among the many arcane and mundane topics addressed in this tome, the elves set down thoughts regarding the power of innocence. They recounted how they had long observed the halfling race, watching as the chaos of the world swept around them and left their villages untouched. While orcs, dwarves, and humans struggled, fought, and spilled blood to expand their territory, the elves noted that the halflings dwelled in a state of placid disregard, uncaring of the events of the world. They remarked on how the halflings enjoyed the simple pleasures of the moment, such as food and music, family, and friendship, and how they seemed to desire no more than that. The writers concluded that the halflings' seemingly innate ability to sidestep turmoil and ill fortune could in fact be a special boon of nature, in recognition of the value of protecting the halflings' worldview and to ensure that their unique place in the cosmos will be forever preserved.

FRIENDLY TO A FAULT

Halflings easily warm to creatures of other races that don't try to do them harm, in large part due to the lack of guile that goes along with their innocent nature. Appearance doesn't matter; what counts is a creature's fundamental character, and if the halflings are convinced of a creature's good intentions, they respond well. Halflings would welcome an orc with a good heart into their company and treat it as politely they would as an elf visitor.

This openness doesn't extend all the way to naiveté. Halflings won't be taken in by merely a promise of good intentions, and their instinct for self-preservation makes them wary of any new "friend" that doesn't come across as genuine. Although they might not be able to define the feeling, halflings sense when something isn't quite right, keeping their distance from a questionable individual and advising others to do the same.

This aspect of the halfling mind-set accounts for what members of other races often characterize as courage. A halfling about to enter the unknown doesn't feel fear as much as wonderment. Instead of being frightened, the halfling remains optimistic, confident of having a good story to tell when it's all over. Whether the situation requires a rogue slipping into a dragon's den or the

---

> *I don't believe in luck. None of the ridiculous superstitions halflings put their faith in has any value whatsoever.*

local militia repelling an orc attack by refusing to yield, halflings surprise larger folk again and again with their unflappable nature.

HAPPY WITH TODAY

Throughout recorded history, halflings have never sought to expand their reach beyond the borders of their isolated communities. They live their lives satisfied with what the world has to offer: fresh air, green grass, and rich soil. They grow all the food they need, taking pleasure in every poached egg and piece of toast. Halflings aren't known for great works of literature or elaborate written accounts of their history. Scholars who study their behavior speculate that halflings realize—consciously or otherwise—that the past is a story that can only be retold, not changed, and the future doesn't yet exist, so it can't be experienced. Only by living in the moment can one appreciate the wonder of being alive.

LIFE AS A HALFLING

On the surface, halflings seem to be simple folk, but those who have lived with them or who have had a halfling in their company know that there is much more to the lives of these small folk than meets the eye. The members of a halfling community have a set of shared values and purposes, whether they are tucked away in a hillside burrow or occupying a neighborhood of their own in a city or town dominated by another race.

EVERYTHING HAS A STORY

As do many other races, halflings enjoy accumulating personal possessions. But unlike with most other races, a halfling's idea of value has little if anything to do with monetary concerns. A typical halfling's most prized possessions are those that have the most interesting stories attached to them. Indeed, entering an elderly halfling's home is much like opening a book of tales. Every nook and cranny contains some quaint curio or another, and its owner is more than happy to tell the story of where it came from. A halfling who has retired after a life of adventuring might own mementos as diverse as a spoon from Sigil's Great Bazaar, a pan pilfered from an elven kitchen in Evermeet, a rake received as a gift from a svirfneblin mushroom tender in the Underdark, and the scale of a white dragon acquired from its lair.

Of course, most halflings' possessions aren't so exotic in origin. But even a stay-at-home halfling strives to collect everyday objects that played a significant role in an exciting story (such as "the rolling pin that Aunt Hattie used to chase away a bugbear" or "the shoes that Timtom wore when he escaped from the wolf"). Halflings believe that an item has a "spirit" of its own—the more dramatic or incredible its story, the stronger its spirit. This outlook prompts them to ask probing questions about the possessions of other folk they encounter—queries that can make them seem nosy to those who don't understand where they're coming from.

HALFLING SUPERSTITIONS

Halflings might perform the following actions, among many others, to ward off bad luck or to bring good fortune. Villages or even families might have superstitions observed by no one else, such as the following:

- For a safe journey through a forest, leave a few seeds or a cloverleaf for Sheela Peryroyl.
- A large silvery squirrel could be Yondalla in disguise. Be on your best behavior and offer a treat when you see her!
- A spring is a sacred place full of good luck. Take a moment to pause and reflect in such a place, or stop for a quick snack.
- Set flowers in your cap or hair to protect against evil faeries.
- When the hair on your neck stiffens or the skin on your arm looks like a plucked chicken, know that Charmalaine is near—and heed her warning.
- Put a frog under your cap to bring good luck, but not for too long, or it's bad luck for a fortnight.
- If you step on a butterfly, you'd best not leave the safety of your house for three days.
- When you plant a row of turnips or radishes, be sure to bury a nice round stone for Yondalla at the head of it, and she'll help bring you some big fellers.
- Always keep a fairy circle on your left when you pass by, and be sure to tip your cap. Never enter or stand in the center of one.

Keeping History Alive. The halflings' penchant for storytelling has another outlet, in the form of gatherings in which an elder holds court or several tale-tellers try to outdo one another as they pass on their experiences. Witnessing a halfling storytelling session is a rare treat for an outsider, for halfling elders can spin a yarn like no one else. A tale with all the trappings told by an elder can cause listeners to howl with laughter, long for home, sit on the edges of their seats, dream of far-off shores, choke up with emotion, or smile from ear to ear.

Some of the most often-told tales concern the origin of a halfling clan's name. Generally, such appellations come about because in the distant past, a halfling matriarch or patriarch performed a memorable feat or displayed some amazing skill that led to a name that stuck. Clans with evocative names such as the Cavecrawlers, the Hogtrotters, and the Fishskippers all have a story to be told about how they came to be.

HIDDEN IN PLAIN SIGHT

Although halflings aren't reclusive by nature, they are adept at finding out-of-the-way places to settle in. It takes a combination of luck and persistence for an ordinary traveler to find such a place, and often that's not enough. For those who subscribe to the idea that Yondalla actively shields her worshipers from harm, this phenomenon is easily explained—she looks out for their homes just as she protects their lives. Whatever the reason, travelers might look for a halfling village, but they fail to notice a narrow path that cuts through the underbrush, or they find themselves traveling in circles and getting no closer to their goal. Rangers who have encountered halflings or lived among them know of this effect, and they learn to trust their other senses and their instincts rather than relying on sight.

A typical halfling village is a cluster of small, stone houses with thatched roofs and wooden doors, or burrows dug into hillsides with windows that look out onto gardens of flowers, beans or potatoes. Since a halfling community usually has less than a hundred members, cooperation is critical to their society, and each resident performs regular chores or offers benefits that support the population. One family might provide baked goods, while another one cobbles shoes or knits clothing. Generally, halflings in a village don't produce goods for sale to outsiders, but they do love to trade, especially with visitors who have interesting items to swap.

Life of Leisure. Halflings rarely consider leaving the security of their villages, because they already have all the comforts they could want—food, drink, laughter, family, friends, and the satisfaction of doing a good day's work. When all their necessities have been taken care of, halflings take it easy—and many of them find a way to turn idleness into an art form. Every halfling has a favorite spot for doing nothing—in the shade of a large stone, on the fringe of a sun-dappled meadow, or nestled in a comfy crook high in a tree. When they're not dozing off and dreaming of chasing butterflies, halflings spend time on simple creative activities, such as whittling a pipe from a branch, braiding yarn into a thick rope, or composing a jaunty tune on a second-hand mandolin.

Serious Business. The oldest members of a halfling community are its leaders, although that role has

HOW THE FISHSKIPPERS GOT THEIR NAME

From the gentle waters,
Amid the swaying reeds,
There rose a hairy villain,
A troll called Snobble Sweed.

He came to gobble children,
To line his lair with bones,
And pick his teeth with talons,
And grind their flesh with stones.

But on that day a-fishing
Was a halfling brave and true,
The first of the Fishskippers,
Grand-kin to me and you.

When he saw old Snobble Sweed
A-sharpening his knives,
He knew that all his family's folk
Were in danger of their lives.

In that moment of grave peril,
Fishskipper caught a bream
And hurled it by its silvery tail
Across the glassy stream.

Ten times the bream did swiftly skip,
And like a clap of thunder
It smote old Sweed upon his head,
And tore the beast asunder.

—"Tale of the Fishskippers," by Harkin Fishskipper

a special application. A clan's elders aren't authority figures in the traditional sense; they are respected, and their words are heeded, because of the stories they tell. Their best tales deliver practical knowledge within the framework of a mythic saga. An elder doesn't simply announce, "We must be always ready for a goblin attack." Instead, that advice is delivered in a story about how a village long ago turned back a goblin invasion, which both entertains the villagers and teaches them what to do if goblin raiders find the village.

For the most part, halflings aren't the targets of warring nations. Their villages are of little tactical value, nor are they likely to be coveted by evil wizards or to become the object of wrath for some dark force. The only enemies that a halfling village must watch for on an ongoing basis are roving bands of orcs or goblins, and the occasional hungry ogre or other solitary monster. And, as halfling luck would have it, these incidents are so rare that a single one might be talked about for generations. In one village, the story of the ogre that ate Farmer Keller's billy goat is a cautionary tale that will be repeated and embellished for decades.

HOMES AWAY FROM HOME

An individual halfling or a family might leave its community behind for a number of reasons. A clan that is forced to relocate (perhaps because of invading creatures or a natural disaster) might decide to seek refuge or opportunity in a city or town, rather than trying to find another secluded spot in the wilderness.

A city or a large town is likely to have a halfling neighborhood already, meaning that newcomers have a place to go that they can call home. Often, they join other halflings who have set up shop and support whatever enterprises their newfound friends have created, making a living as storytellers, bakers, chefs, or shopkeepers.

BAD APPLES

Although most halflings are energetic and jovial, as with any other race individuals among them can be dour or curmudgeonly, standoffish or suspicious. Such traits might appear in someone who ends up turning fully to the cause of evil—an event that is rare in the extreme, but has happened often enough that every community tells at least one story of this sort.

A halfling who turns evil usually severs all links to their family, friends, and village. Slowly, over time, halflings who pursue a dark path—especially those who break too many oaths or hurt other halflings along the

Halfling settlements survive wars because halflings are so irritating. Why conquer something you want nothing to do with?

way—lose the protection of Yondalla and the other halfling gods. Some say that the minds of these halflings eventually become twisted, and they turn into cruel, paranoid creatures wracked by misery and despair.

HALFLING GODS AND MYTHS

Halflings see their gods more as extended family members than as divine beings. They don't worship them in the same way as elves and dwarves revere their gods, because the halfling gods are viewed as folk heroes— mortal beings who ascended to divinity, rather than divine entities who descend from their realms to influence the world. Because of this outlook, halflings rarely worship a single deity exclusively; they revere all the gods equally and pay their respects in modest ways.

Halflings speak of Yondalla the way humans would describe a strong and protective parent. They talk about Brandobaris as others might refer to a mischievous and dashing uncle. They don't beseech the gods for daily favors, and they have no sense of metaphysical distance or separation between them and their gods. To halflings, their gods are part of the family. And as family members do, the gods set an example that is reaffirmed through the stories of their heroic deeds, with each tale helping to teach important lessons to the next generation.

The Halfling Deities table lists the members of the halfling pantheon. For each god, the table notes alignment, province (the god's main areas of interest and responsibility), suggested domains for clerics who serve the god, and a common symbol of the god. Each of the gods in the table is described below.

YONDALLA

The story of Yondalla begins at the dawn of the world, when halflings were timid wanderers, scraping out a meager existence. The goddess Yondalla took note of them and decided to adopt the halflings as her people. She was a strong leader with a vision for her people, and she dedicated her life to gathering them together and protecting them. Over time, she elevated to godhood those halflings who were the most adept at the skills halflings needed to survive. Those legendary halflings comprise the rest of the pantheon.

HALFLING DEITIES

Deity	Alignment	Province	Suggested Domains	Common Symbol
Arvoreen	LG	Vigilance, war	War	Crossed short swords
Brandobaris	N	Adventure, thievery	Trickery	Halfling footprint
Charmalaine	N	Keen senses, luck	Trickery	Burning boot print
Cyrrollalee	LG	Hearth, home	Life	An open door
Sheela Peryroyl	NG	Agriculture, nature, weather	Nature, Tempest	A flower
Urogalan	LN	Earth, death	Death, Grave,* Knowledge	Silhouette of a dog's head
Yondalla	LG	Primary goddess of halflings	Life	Cornucopia

*Appears in *Xanathar's Guide to Everything*

Yondalla created the first halfling villages and showed the people how to build, plant, and harvest. She knew that the bounty of a halfling village would be tempting plunder for any brigand or monster, so she used her powers to conceal their homes from easy discovery, blending them into the landscape so that most travelers would pass by without a second glance.

To the halflings, Yondalla is responsible for the spring in their step and the bubbly excitement they feel from knowing that luck is on their side. When a pumpkin grows to enormous size or a garden yields twice as many carrots as usual, credit goes to Yondalla. When a halfling trips, slides down a hillside, and lands on a nugget of gold, that's Yondalla turning bad luck into good.

Arvoreen

From time to time, halflings must fight to defend their friends or their village. In those moments, the tales of Arvoreen come to the fore in every halfling's memory. Every youth hears over and over again the stories of the hero's bravery and cunning, his clever tactics in battle, and his ability to use speed and smallness to defeat a much larger foe. The elders know that the world outside is dangerous and that their kin must understand how to deal with those dangers. Stories about Arvoreen are told in such a way that youngsters are inspired to act out his epic battles. In this way, the halflings get practical experience in executing measures that are designed to help the halflings defeat kobolds and goblin raiders, or even take down an ogre. When the time comes to put those tactics to use in earnest, everyone will be ready.

Cooperation is a fundamental principle in how halflings fend off their enemies. Every community practices its own version of Arvoreen's favored tactics:

Scatterstrike. The halflings run in every direction as if in a panic, but then they regroup and circle back to attack with a concentrated effort.

Turtle Shell. Halflings cluster together and cover each other with shields, washtubs, wheelbarrows, coffer lids, or anything else that can deflect a blow.

Troll Knocker. A few halflings act as bait to lure a troll or other large creature into a clearing where the rest of the group can hurl stones at it from concealment to confuse the monster, persuading it to seek other prey.

Swarming Stickwhackers. Halflings rush an intruder in waves, swatting the enemy with sticks on all sides.

Fiddle and Crack. A halfling fiddler lures the monster into a trap, usually a net or a pit, followed by several burly halflings wielding large sticks and hitting the monster from a safe vantage.

Sheela Peryroyl

Every halfling village sets aside a place for paying respects to Sheela Peryroyl. In a grove of trees, a raspberry patch, or a swath of wildflowers, villagers leave a small offering whenever they walk by, or tip their caps, or whisper a blessing in her honor. A village counts itself lucky if this place is cared for by a druid. Creatures that attack a village under the protection of the god's druids soon learn the error of their ways when all manner of plants lash out to grapple and sting the intruders, as though nature herself were aiding the halflings' cause.

On nights when the moon is full, especially during the planting and harvesting seasons, the elders tell stories about Sheela Peryroyl. After becoming a hero though her glorious adventures, Sheela joined with the earth, fusing her spirit with the flowers, plants, and trees so she could better provide for her kin. A halfling who accidentally steps on a flower often says, "Begging your pardon, Sheela." Before halflings cut down a tree to use its wood for a new house, it is customary for them to stand before the tree with their caps doffed, humbly asking permission from Sheela to continue.

Charmalaine

Charmalaine is an energetic and spontaneous deity, unafraid of danger, for she expects to be able to detect it as it approaches and evade it before it brings her harm. The stories of her accomplishments read like an adventurer's wildest dreams: she escaped from an army of sahuagin, solved the Chamber of a Thousand Traps, and took treasure from the lair of Tiamat. Halflings envision her as a young adult who moves so fast that her boots smoke and sometimes even catch fire. She carries a mace that has a head that shouts out warnings, and she is accompanied by her ferret friend, Xaphan.

Halflings sometimes call Charmalaine the Lucky Ghost because she can send her spirit out of her body to scout ahead, and thus she is able to warn halfling adventurers of danger while in her incorporeal form. Halflings who favor Charmalaine are usually adventurers or those who pursue other risky professions such as hunting, beast training, scouting, and guarding public officials.

CYROLLALEE

Cyrollalee embodies the spirit of friendship and hospitality that is part of every halfling's makeup and is represented by one's home and hearth. The home is a welcoming place, but it is also sacrosanct. Halflings honor Cyrollalee by opening their homes to visitors, and by respecting the home of one's host as if it were one's own.

Every halfling village tells its version of the legendary tale of Cyrollalee and the troll pies. Long ago, a large human town near Cyrollalee's village was regularly attacked by a vicious troll. Warriors from the town hacked at the troll, but even its most dire wounds would heal, and the troll would come back again. One day Cyrollalee presented herself at the town gate in apron and peasant clothes, and she offered to rid the town of the troll. The proud human warriors all scoffed at her, but the desperate mayor asked Cyrollalee for her help.

So Cyrollalee set all the people in the town to baking pies, but not just any pies. They were special troll pies. Into each one she put a pinch of magic to make them irresistible to trolls. While the warriors of the town grumbled and sharpened their steel, Cyrollalee created an atmosphere of fun, bringing cheer to the frightened people as they worked. When the day was done, she set off with a cart full of pies and laid them in a tasty trail far up into the mountains. When the troll came near the town and found the trail, it began to gobble up pie after pie, following the delightful smells up the mountain path until it walked right into the lair of a young red dragon. The greedy troll was swiftly incinerated.

Cyrollalee returned a hero, and from that day forward all the townsfolk remembered her with a word of thanks when baking pies.

BRANDOBARIS

Dashing trickster, patron of thieves, and star of fantastical fables and wild stories of adventure—that's the legacy of Brandobaris, the Master of Stealth. Stories of Brandobaris, full of artful trickery and narrow escapes, inspire many young halflings to play at roguish pursuits. In their imagination, a grain silo becomes a lofty wizard's tower to scale in search of treasures, or a rowboat becomes the setting for a swashbuckling adventure. And for some—the youngsters who are said to "have a bit of Brandobaris in them"—that play-acting is the prelude to a life of living as Brandobaris does: always on the lookout for the next challenge.

Brandobaris continues to wander in search of excitement, and now, as an ascended being, his travels span the planes of existence. His curiosity takes him to all corners of the multiverse in search of magical curios, rare treasures, and mystical puzzles. When Brandobaris moves stealthily, no mortal or god can hear his footfalls—an ability he uses not only for defense, but also to bestow unlooked-for treats upon those he favors.

Although he never seems to rest in his travels, Brandobaris always has time to reward halflings who dare to take risks and explore the world to make their own mark on it. He has been known to give a bit of aid to halflings in dire straits, turning them invisible for a time or intervening so that they can't be heard or tracked.

UROGALAN

In ancient times the halfling hero Urogalan left his village with his faithful hound to venture into the afterlife—and then, much to the villagers' amazement, he returned. They could see that Urogalan had been deeply affected by his experiences, since he didn't speak for a long time. He merely sat in a white robe with his hound by his side, watching the world go by. When he did speak at last, he told of a place he called the Green Fields, where the halflings' god-heroes live alongside mortals who have passed on, enjoying lush farmland, bright sunshine, and all the comforts of home.

Urogalan declared that all who have gone before still watch over their loved ones from this place of eternal peace, sending messages to the material world. In acknowledgment of this assertion, halflings look for signs from their departed loved ones. One might be thinking about catching butterflies with his grandmother long ago, when suddenly a butterfly lands on his hand—clear evidence that, as Urogalan promised, she is still looking out for her grandson from beyond the veil of death.

As a divine being, Urogalan can move freely through the earth and across the planes of existence. He holds aloft a magic lantern that protects him on his journeys. With his black hound leading the way, Urogalan scours the multiverse and shepherds deceased halflings to their eternal home in the Green Fields.

Unlike other halfling deities, Urogalan is surrounded by a cloud of melancholy. He is gaunt, with his dusky skin covered by white robes. Priests who venerate Urogalan emulate this practice of dress and demeanor.

THE HALFLING ADVENTURER

WHO KNOWS WHERE A HERO'S SPIRIT WILL GROW? EVEN *the smallest seed can produce the mightiest tree.*

—Elminster Aumar, Sage of Shadowdale

Everything about halflings, from their small stature to their easy demeanor, makes them unlikely candidates for taking up a life of adventure away from home. Yet every generation produces a handful of exceptional individuals who defy conventional wisdom and seek their fortunes in the wider world.

Opinions vary on what compels some halflings to leave home and set off over the farthest hill to explore the unknown. The simplest explanation is that some folk are born with an overabundance of curiosity. Some say that Arvoreen or Brandobaris is responsible for urging them on, and others point to the stories told by the elders that inspire some youngsters to take such risks. Whatever the reason, from time to time a halfling feels the call of adventure and sets off with a walking staff, a satchel, and a few biscuits. The first stop for many of these plucky souls is a faraway city where they hope to find some like-minded companions.

FANCY FEET

A halfling's potential for adventuring usually manifests early in life. When a child first wanders away from the village, seemingly by accident, or one day hops on a log and tries to set off down the river, the parents are

concerned but not alarmed. They attribute these acts of rambunctiousness to Brandobaris's meddling, and almost all children outgrow this tendency to put themselves at risk. But if one persists in these antics, the other villagers say the youngster has "fancy feet."

The term refers to the persistent urge to wander beyond the boundaries of the community—activity that is in the purview of Brandobaris, who is said to have "the fanciest feet of all." Each village has its own way of coping with this phenomenon. Some elders—especially those who once had fancy feet themselves—just shrug, smile, and say it is the way of things. Nevertheless, well-meaning villagers might try to dissuade a youngster from leaving the community. Other villages are much more supportive of one of their members who demonstrates the urge to adventure, likely because some of their elders have gone into the world and returned to tell about it. In one of these places, a youngster about to set out is celebrated with a rousing party that goes far into the night, during which the adventurer-to-be is regaled by tales of other "fancy-footed" heroes of halfling history.

HALFLINGS OF THE MULTIVERSE

In the worlds of DUNGEONS & DRAGONS, many kinds of halflings exist, and they vary greatly from place to place.

In the Forgotten Realms, halflings are of the lightfoot and strongheart varieties. Lightfoot halflings are taller and thinner than stronghearts, although "thinner" is a relative word by halfling standards. Lightfoots prefer to live on the move in traveling bands, and their members are most likely to take to a life of adventuring. Stronghearts are homebodies by nature, most of them likely to spend their lives tucked away in their secluded villages, and are also quite happy living in the communities of other races, working as farmers, innkeepers, cobblers and bakers.

In the Dragonlance setting, kender are the counterparts of halflings. Possessed of shorter life spans than their counterparts on other worlds, the kender have pointed ears and become wizened as they age. Great mimics and vocalists, kender are consummate storytellers, but they often speak too fast for other races not accustomed to their frenetic cadence.

Halflings in the world of Greyhawk live in underground burrows or small cottages in the grasslands or hills. They are lightly covered with hair over most of their bodies, especially on the backs of their hands and the tops of their feet, and they rarely wear shoes. The three subraces are the hairfeet, which are the most numerous; the tallfellows, which are the tallest and least athletic of the halflings, somewhat resembling elves; and the stouts, which are more akin to dwarves in temperament and stature than the other two.

On the world of Athas in the Dark Sun setting, halflings are feral creatures, prone to devouring the flesh of humans and elves. Small, furtive and sun-bronzed, they live a hard life under their chief, eking out a savage existence by hunting, foraging, and raiding. Outside their tribe, halflings are mistrusting, cynical, and often paranoid, since they think that all other races are as fond of devouring humanoids as they are.

LEGENDS IN THE MAKING

Halflings who take up a life of adventure are emboldened by the stories told by their elders—tales of halfling heroes slinking through human cities, plundering dungeons laden with treasure, and being received in the hall of a dwarven king. Each new would-be hero hopes to have adventures that merit exciting stories of their own, to inspire and delight new generations for years to come.

Of course, not every journey into the world involves risking one's life or claiming great riches. An adventure for a halfling could mean traveling with a caravan, sneaking on board a tall ship, serving as a messenger for a lord, or living with the dwarves for a few years as an apprentice. From the point of view of a halfling villager, going anywhere beyond home is an adventure, and anyone who does so must have a fine story or two to tell upon their return. Even on a dangerous mission, halflings find enjoyment all around them. If it's raining, a halfling is playing in the puddles; in a stiff wind, a halfling might fly a kite instead of seeking shelter.

HALFLING TABLES

This section provides a number of tables useful for players and DMs who want to choose or randomly generate details about halfling characters or villages.

HALFLING PERSONALITY TRAITS

d6	Personality Trait
1	You try to start every day with a smile.
2	Why walk when you can skip?
3	You make up songs about your friends that praise them for their bravery and intelligence.
4	You are extremely cautious, always on the lookout for monsters and other dangers.
5	You always see the bright side of a situation.
6	You like to collect mementos of your travels.

Halfling Ideals

d6	Ideal
1	**Courage.** You seek to prove that the bravest heart can be contained within the smallest of packages.
2	**Companionship.** You're pretty sure you can be friends with anyone or anything.
3	**Hopeful.** You will live a life of adventure and have many stories to tell.
4	**Protective.** You make sure to shelter the innocent.
5	**Honest.** Your mother told you to always tell the truth.
6	**Excitement.** Can you steal the sleeping giant's pouch? Of course you can!

Halfling Bonds

d6	Bond
1	The safety of your village is worth any sacrifice.
2	Nothing is more valuable than friendship and family.
3	You are following your own path through life. No one can tell you what to do.
4	You have a special heirloom that you never part with.
5	You won't rob or hurt those who are weaker or less fortunate than you.
6	No matter how small you may be, you won't back down from a bully.

Halfling Flaws

d6	Flaw
1	You can't resist poking your nose where it doesn't belong.
2	You are very fidgety. Sitting still is a major challenge.
3	You can't pass up a good time.
4	You hate to miss a meal, and become grumpy and ill-tempered when you must.
5	You are fascinated by shiny things and can't help "borrowing" them.
6	You never settle for just one slice when you can have the whole cake.

Reasons for Adventuring

d6	Reason
1	Peeling taters and herding goats all the time wasn't your cup of tea.
2	You fell asleep on a raft one day and woke up near a human city. You were so thrilled with the strange sights and tasty food that you never turned back.
3	What started off as simple pumpkin pillaging from nearby farms turned into your becoming a wandering rogue for hire.
4	You talked to a nice faerie in the woods, and all of a sudden you were a thousand miles from home.
5	Your village elder told you so many stories about being a rogue in an adventuring party that you couldn't resist the urge to try doing it yourself.
6	A friend dared you to jump on the back of a sleeping horse, which turned out to be a pegasus, and your life hasn't slowed down since.

Gnomes

And then the whole thing exploded into a million jillion pieces! [gasp] I never saw anything like it in my life!

—Griballix, gnome of Sigil

Love of discovery is the force that drives the life of a gnome, whether one is investigating the nature of magic or trying to invent a better back scratcher. Questions about the world fill a gnome's head: how an insect flies, a fish swims, or a grasshopper jumps—they want to figure it all out! But it's not just nature and its workings that intrigue them; gnomes become obsessed with all sorts of topics. In particular, they have a keen interest in mechanical devices, the natural world, and magical pursuits; a gnome might seek to invent a new garden tool, collect and categorize every type of butterfly, or develop a new method for cutting gemstones.

Drinking Deeply of Life

A gnome is rarely bored and tries to savor every minute, for life is full of opportunities to learn, to help others, and to have fun.

Gnomes are born with a fascination for learning fueled by an irrepressible curiosity. Most individuals settle on a specialized area of study such as an aspect of the natural world, a particular method of invention, or the patterns that underlie the multiverse.

Though this pursuit of knowledge might compel a gnome to spend long periods in the workshop or the laboratory, the activity is never seen as drudgery—quite the opposite. Gnomes enjoy making an unexciting aspect of life more enjoyable, such as inventing a shovel that whistles a tune to lighten the toil of digging, or creating a telescoping fork that can reach across the table to enliven mealtime.

Their fun-loving attitude also comes through in the form of jokes that gnomes tell to, or about, their companions, and in the good-spirited pranks that they play on each other—and on other folk (who might not always appreciate being the target of their humor).

The Journey Is the Destination

Gnomes aren't overly goal-oriented as they pursue their interests. To them, the journey and the destination are one and the same, and an achievement at the end of one journey is merely the first step toward the next accomplishment.

Even though failure, disappointment, and dead ends are recurring obstacles on the path to discovery, gnomes revel in the search. They savor the acquisition of new knowledge, realizing it might come at a cost, and even a series of bad results in experiments doesn't dissuade a gnome from following their chosen path.

Rock Gnomes

A visitor's first steps into a rock gnome warren are accompanied by the sounds of industry—hammers rapping on metal, chisels chewing wood, cauldrons bubbling, and a host of assorted squeaks, pings, and whistles. Against this backdrop, the halls echo with the voices of

rock gnome inventors jabbering at near unintelligible speed about their latest ideas, and the hubbub is occasionally punctuated by a big bang or the abrupt collapse of some unstable contraption.

To rock gnomes, life is a combination of scavenger hunts and periods of bold experimentation. First they mine materials from within the earth, and then they figure out what they can create or invent using those resources. The discovery of a new vein of metal—whether tin, copper, silver, or gold—makes rock gnomes clap their hands with glee, but they are happiest of all when they find a cache of gems, particularly diamonds.

Individual rock gnomes have different ideas about what sorts of inventions are the most satisfying to create, with some favoring practicality and others more interested in artistic expression. In each group, there are those who prefer to practice the alchemical arts and those whose talents lean toward the creation of mechanical devices. Every warren has members of each persuasion, and they are all bound by mutual respect for what they do despite their different perspectives.

Practical Makes Perfect

Rock gnomes who take a more scientific approach to inventing are the ones responsible for creating technological devices that make life easier. Even an invention as simple as a new kind of rake is celebrated, and that advance might later be superseded by someone who modifies it in a way that makes it more efficient or more enjoyable to use.

These inventors are rarely reluctant to try making devices of exceptional power, even if one might not work at first the way it was intended to. The gnomes know that it's always possible for someone else to learn from an inventor's mistakes, so even a failed experiment is a success in some way. Every minor explosion or other incident of turmoil in a rock gnome burrow serves as a clue about what not to do next time—unless, of course, the goal was to make something explode.

For Beauty's Sake

Imagination runs wild in the mind of a gnome. Any fresh idea can be the starting point for a new journey of ex-

---

Celestial Toymakers

A handful of master artificers exist among the rock gnomes who take the magic of their craft to new heights. These legendary gnomes usually reside in Bytopia and on other planes far from the Material Plane, locales where they can access and harness powerful energies. They have unlocked secrets of the multiverse that enable them to fashion mind-boggling creations—their so-called "celestial toys."

These master artificers are friendly to those who seek them out. They enjoy showing off their works and take great glee in watching visitors interact with their toys, while they scribble notes on how to refine their creations.

Celestial toys can do just about anything. Many of these objects have properties not unlike those of wondrous items, such as a toy that can increase an ability score or one that can show happenings on other planes.

artifacts that seem to have no purpose. The gnomes who produce these works of art are using new ideas and new approaches, breaking through old boundaries and advancing the frontier of knowledge. For instance, an artist might create a beautiful articulated sculpture whose pieces can be manipulated in a unique way. Another artisan might take that idea and apply it to a new form of invention—but no one forgets that it was the artist's idea that blazed the trail for that journey.

Alchemists

Rock gnome alchemists explore the nature of minerals and chemicals, curious to see what happens when they mix certain substances with other compounds or with raw magic. Most alchemists, even those who busy themselves with experimentation and new ideas, can produce a number of useful substances, such as alchemist's fire, antitoxin, super slippery goo, stone melting compound, stirge repellent, and glow-in-the-dark paint.

Artificers

Rock gnome artificers construct exquisitely tooled and enameled pieces of machinery, often weaving magical properties into their work. Artificers often develop a reputation for a particular style and type of work. For example, a friendly gnome artificer might create lovable mechanical pets and companions, while a grumpy gnome might make snapping critter constructs with sharp teeth and claws. Gnome artificers can become famous, with their works highly sought after by nobles, wizards, and other collectors.

An artificer's inventions might include items such as a lock box that opens with a verbal command or a series of gestures, a clockwork critter designed to respond to simple commands, or a common magic item (such as those introduced in *Xanathar's Guide to Everything*).

Tunnel Vision

When they are at work, rock gnomes hole up in their workshops with "Do Not Disturb" signs hung on the door. It isn't uncommon for gnomes who are working on their projects to spend most of their time in seclusion, and even when they emerge (for meals or other reasons), they are often deep in thought and oblivious of their surroundings. In the safety of the burrow, they seldom come to harm because of this vulnerability. But even city-dwelling gnomes can fall prey to this sort of obsession as they pursue their projects, and in such cases it's much safer for them to stay in their homes, since a gnome wandering the streets deep in thought is liable to walk into a moat or be run over by a wagon.

Forest Gnomes

As the companions of nature and its animals, forest gnomes learn from their surroundings as if from a master teacher. They evade incursions into their wooded realm by great numbers of humans and other races, but they aid individuals and small groups whom they deem worthy of their help. They create lovely gardens, organic sculptures, and wondrous emerald jewelry—that precious green stone being their favorite of all gems.

Tinker Gnomes

On the world of Krynn in the Dragonlance setting, rock gnomes take invention to extreme heights and are known for being purveyors of madcap mayhem. Despite losing body parts or gaining scars from various accidents, nothing stops the tinker gnomes' insatiable quest to experiment and discover.

Go Big or Go Home. The creations of tinker gnomes range from the ridiculous to the dangerous. They love to push the art of invention beyond its limits, and to explore the instability of volatile materials. They cackle with glee after an ear-splitting bang, and jump and cavort amid lethal sprays of lightning. Though it might be bizarre and unusual, a working tinker gnome creation is a rare thing, and highly prized. Such inventions include the following:

- A chain-driven tomato smasher that is also able to fly
- A lightning-powered portable rat-zapper—good for keeping out the vermin
- A floating metal facsimile of a beholder, complete with disintegrating eye rays
- A flock of exploding parrots

Fail Often, Fail Happy. These inventors are delighted by every explosion, every melted mess, and every heap of smoking wreckage. Failure is part of the eventual solution and something to be celebrated. A truly epic failure might be cause for a great celebration in the community.

perimentation and discovery. Even though rock gnomes appreciate the practical aspects of their endeavors, they also find satisfaction in creating items that have no true usefulness. Many an invention is celebrated just for being beautiful to behold or for being complex and intricate in its construction, and the artists who create such things are as esteemed as those who specialize in designing tools.

Exploration is a part of invention, as the gnomes see it, so there's nothing wrong with creating machines and

Forest gnome settlements often escape notice. Roving hunters can wander through without ever suspecting they are walking through anything but wilderness. A community of elves might be surprised to discover they have been neighbors of a forest gnome village for years.

Forest gnomes are good at making their homes vanish into the landscape. It helps that they are small folk, and that they fashion their homes by digging down and living within rather than building up and living above. Like the badgers and raccoons that are often their companions, they live in the hollows of trees and warrens dug into hillsides, each home connected to the others in the community by elaborate burrows.

Beyond the secret doors into their houses, the homes of forest gnomes are gaily decorated, tidy spaces that take advantage of natural features. A great glass bowl swimming with fish and frogs might serve as a skylight for a gnome burrow, while appearing to the world above as a small pond. The gnarled and tangled roots of a tree might be used for shelves, seats, tables, and bed spaces. Such houses often have many little channels open to the outside, allowing scraps of sunlight to dapple the walls and floors and providing a means of egress for the many animals that live with the gnomes. Similar small openings are used for their cleverly hidden chimneys, disguised as tree branches, which carry smoke from their small fires high into the treetops, reducing it to little more than a haze before it disperses.

ANIMAL HELPERS

Forest gnomes can communicate with many of the small animals of the woods. Squirrels, raccoons, foxes, weasels, owls, rabbits, robins, hummingbirds, and more are their allies and friends. Outsiders often think of these creatures as the gnomes' pets, but the gnomes treat them more like trusted neighbors.

When strangers approach a woodland inhabited by forest gnomes, the gnomes often know about it while such visitors are still miles away. Speedy squirrels run through the treetops, each trying to be the first to warn the gnomes and earn a sweet treat. Birds trill a special call that alerts the gnomes to danger. At night, nocturnal animals such as owls and bats carry word to the gnomes during times when they should be on their guard.

EXPERTS IN ILLUSION

Forest gnomes have innate magical ability, letting them create simple illusions. They practice the use of illusion magic from an early age. Most forest gnome communities include a full-fledged illusionist and an apprentice or two, and they use their talents in service of the community—designing longer-lasting or larger-scale illusions that help the community stay hidden from the world.

Gnomes use illusions for practically any reason—as a game, for defense, or for communication—and some-times for no reason other than artistic considerations. A simple illusion can often express a complex idea, such as when the memory of a location is triggered by the illusory sound of a babbling brook that runs through the place. A storytelling session conducted by a group of forest gnomes is a riot of sounds and images that helps give meaning and intensity to the tale being told. It is a kind of entertainment unfathomable by most other races, whose stories and performances are limited by whatever materials are on hand.

The forest gnomes' playful nature shows through in the illusions they create, even those that have a serious purpose. (An illusion that conceals the entrance to a tunnel by making it look like solid earth might not amuse other folk, but the gnomes get a good laugh out of it.) Forest gnomes spend their spare time experimenting with the creation of never-before-seen illusions, or embellishing the images and sounds they already know how to produce.

The number of ways in which forest gnomes use illusions to have fun is nearly limitless. A few examples: visual enhancements to a mythic tale told by an elder, new and interesting sounds, and false doors and hallways to fool intruders and lead them into traps. (Goblins just can't pass by a door that calls them names.)

DEEP GNOMES

Deep gnomes, or svirfneblin, are the pragmatic and often grumpy cousins of the gnome family, who live deep underground. The Underdark is full of danger, meaning that deep gnomes spend much of their time simply staying alive. They endure this life because the Underdark also holds incredible treasures: minerals and gemstones, gold, silver, and platinum. The svirfneblin mine these materials whenever they find a new deposit—especially rubies, which they prize above all other treasure. The svirfneblin do take pleasure from success in these mining operations. A thin smile emerges from the stonelike features of a deep gnome who finds a truly remarkable gem, and such a discovery lightens the mood in the enclave for a time.

Hidden but Homey

Deep gnomes protect their enclaves with labyrinthine tunnels, traps, and armed guards, all designed to make the entrance to a settlement uninviting. But inside its borders, a deep gnome settlement is a warren shaped and decorated by the svirfneblin to make the place welcoming and comfortable.

Although they are skilled stonemasons, svirfneblin appreciate the beauty of natural stone and prefer either to carve to accentuate its features or to leave it unchanged. Their architecture is marked by smooth, curving shapes rather than straight lines and hard edges.

Svirfneblin are intensely community-minded and have little concern about privacy among themselves. Thus, they don't close off living spaces with doors or window coverings. Most of their homes are sparsely furnished dwellings of one or two rooms. Bed spaces, often carved into the cavern walls, are strung with hammocks for each inhabitant, but often are otherwise empty except for stone coffers holding a few personal effects.

Gnome Gods

Who forged the chains that bind Tiamat in Avernus? Why do the modrons go on the Great March? Who is the Lady of Pain, really? I can't tell you, but the answers lie in the Golden Hills. And if Garl and his gang don't know, it can't be known.

—Griballix, gnome of Sigil

It shouldn't be surprising that gnomes, inveterate inventors that they are, have an incredible number of legends they tell about their deities. Every warren has its unique repertoire of tales—some of them no doubt grounded in fact, while others could be the products of imagination. The distinction isn't important to the folk who take inspiration and pride from the stories of their gods, because each legend is true in its own way.

> *Elminster calls gnomes the Forgotten Folk—an apt name for them in most worlds. I've walked many realms, and nary a one has even a hint of a gnome nation.*

Each deity in the gnome pantheon is an expert in multiple fields of activity who is capable of incredible feats. Yet these heroes also display shortcomings, such as hesitance or selfishness. Only the chief gnome deity, Garl Glittergold, can convince the others to set aside personal concerns to embark on a grand excursion or to work together toward a common goal. And according to the gnomes, it is proven that their gods can accomplish the impossible when they band together.

Perhaps because of each community's particular outlook or because the gods frequently use illusory guises, several diverse ideas exist about the membership of the pantheon. In some communities, the gods are thought to be all male or all female; in some they are animals, or constructs made by Garl Glittergold. Some gnomes say Garl has five allies, while others tally eleven.

A consensus of sorts emerges from the totality of these beliefs. Most gnomes believe that Garl Glittergold and his seven able assistants dwell on, in, or under seven summits known as the Golden Hills. This is the place from where new gnomish souls are sent out to experience the wider world, and to which they return to join the hallowed community of those who have come before them. Urdlen is the only gnome deity that doesn't dwell there, having been exiled by Garl for its refusal to cooperate with the rest of the group.

The Gnome Deities table lists the members of the gnome pantheon. For each god, the table notes alignment, province (the god's main areas of interest and responsibility), suggested domains for clerics who serve the god, and a common symbol of the god. Several of the gods in the table are described below.

Gnome Deities

Deity	Alignment	Province	Suggested Domains	Common Symbol
Baervan Wildwanderer	NG	Woodlands	Nature	Face of a raccoon
Baravar Cloakshadow	NG	Illusion, deception	Arcana,** Trickery	Dagger against a hooded cloak
Bleredd	N	Labor, craft	Forge,* Light	Iron mule
Callarduran Smoothhands	N	Mining, stone carving	Knowledge, Nature	Golden signet ring with six-pointed star
Flandal Steelskin	NG	Metalwork	Forge,* Knowledge	Flaming hammer
Gaerdal Ironhand	LG	Protection	War	Iron band
Garl Glittergold	LG	Primary god of gnomes	Trickery	Gold nugget
Gelf Darkhearth	CN	Frustration, destruction	War	Broken anvil
Nebelun	CG	Invention, luck	Forge,* Knowledge, Trickery	Bellows and lizard tail
Rill Cleverthrush	LN	Law, thought	Knowledge	Interlocking gears
Segojan Earthcaller	NG	Earth, the dead	Grave,* Light	Glowing gemstone
Sheyanna Flaxenstrand	CG	Love, beauty, passion	Light	Two silver goblets
Urdlen	CE	Greed, murder	Death, War	White-clawed mole emerging from ground

*Appears in *Xanathar's Guide to Everything*

**Appears in *Sword Coast Adventurer's Guide*

GARL GLITTERGOLD

When gnome children hear their first stories about the gods, they are introduced to a gold-skinned gnome with a wide grin and glittering gemstone eyes that shift colors like a kaleidoscope. The youngsters quickly learn to recognize that their favorite character, the god of the gnomes, is about to steal the show.

A joker and a prankster, Garl Glittergold reminds gnomes that life is to be taken lightly, and that a good laugh will serve them better than a grim attitude. When Garl cavorts with mischief on his mind, Moradin's beard might end up woven with giggling flowers, and Gruumsh's axe could sprout braying donkey heads at the most inopportune time.

Cooperation Is Key. The legends about Garl Glittergold inspire gnomes to work together. Garl knows that many heads and many hands make light work. Although he also plays many pranks on his own, Garl is the one who gathers the heroes together for an enterprise that requires all their talents. To provide specific guidance, Garl might send an omen to nudge a group of gnomes in a certain direction, or even manifest an avatar in the middle of a gnome burrow. When Garl makes one of these rare appearances, it is to resolve a dispute that threatens a community.

Brains over Brawn. Garl favors trickery and illusion over direct combat, preferring to use his mind to overcome a problem rather than his steel. For gnomes to thrive, they must use their intellect and ingenuity. But when push comes to shove, Garl uses Arumdina, his intelligent two-headed battle axe—capable of cleaving through any substance—to escape a perilous situation.

BAERVAN WILDWANDERER

Baervan Wildwanderer is the god of the forests and of those who travel, a peaceful soul whose explorations often turn into exciting adventures. Baervan's constant companion is Chiktikka Fastpaws, a mischievous giant raccoon who often gets the duo into trouble. Although Baervan isn't as much of a prankster as some of the other gods, she is often held responsible when Chiktikka does something outrageous, such as stealing Gruumsh's breakfast or peeing on Rillifane Rallathil's shoes.

Baervan can sing every bird's song, knows every type of plant that has ever grown, never gets lost, and can befriend anyone under the sun (as long as Chiktikka chooses to act pleasant rather than annoying). Forest gnomes believe that they can speak to the animals of the woods and on the wing because Baervan teaches their souls how to do so before they are born.

BARAVAR CLOAKSHADOW

When gnomes arrived in the world, Baravar protected them by teaching them how to hide, use magic, and deceive their foes. She was once entrapped by the goblin god Khurgorbaeyag, and after escaping and gaining her revenge, she began the practice of never wearing the same face twice, and she follows a different routine every day so no one can predict what she might do. When gnomes tell stories of their gods' adventures, Baravar is always the last to be found when the group forms, but she nevertheless swiftly agrees to support Garl's plans.

Forest gnomes and deep gnomes owe their innate magical abilities to Baravar, and all gnomes get their natural defense against magic from her shrewdness.

CALLARDURAN SMOOTHHANDS

Callarduran became the patron of the deep gnomes when he led them into the Underdark and taught them how to survive, but all gnomes see him as the embodiment of the drive to know more, to examine everything more minutely—and thereby make great discoveries.

Callarduran earned his moniker when, after stealing the heart of Ogrémoch, he rubbed his hands smooth as he polished the heart and turned it into a magical stone. The theft caused Ogrémoch to turn to evil, but it gave Callarduran the power to control earth elementals—which, it is said, he can confer to deep gnomes by rubbing the stone and saying their names.

FLANDAL STEELSKIN

The stories that gnomes tell of Flandal Steelskin typically feature some perfect item that he crafted or a misadventure that results from following his enormous nose, which can smell ore more easily than a wolf can scent a skunk. The most often told legend of Flandal includes both elements. Before creating Garl's marvelous axe, Arumdina, Flandal sniffed out the purest source of mithral: the heart of Imix. With the aid of the other gnome gods, he stole the heart and turned it into a mithral forge that now burns with an eternal furious flame.

The legends of Flandal portray him not only as the god of metalcraft, but also of fire and glass-work and alchemy. Rock gnomes attribute their knack for crafting devices and alchemical objects to Flandal's superlative skills in those areas.

GAERDAL IRONHAND

The Shield of the Golden Hills, Gaerdal Ironhand, has no use for amusements, and she doesn't deign to smile at any prank except those of Garl Glittergold. Gaerdal obsesses about defense and vigilance, and she is an expert in fortification, siege tactics, combat, and traps. Instead of bustling about as gnome deities normally do, Gaerdal has a tendency to dig in and hide out, and in many tales Garl finds it difficult to convince her to leave her home to join the others on adventures. Some legends say this reluctance is due in part to an escapade that cost her the loss of her hand. Flandal and Nebelun worked together to replace it with a stronger one made of iron, but her resentment over the mishap lingers.

Gnomes build their homes in hidden and defensible places because Gaerdal teaches them these techniques. Every secret door, spy hole, and intruder alarm in a gnome warren is a tribute to Gaerdal's principles.

NEBELUN

Nebelun, also known as the Meddler, is fearless, perhaps foolishly so. Every invention of Nebelun's starts with a wild idea, nothing goes entirely according to plan, and her greatest exploits often spring from mistakes. Who else would stroll in and steal Semuanya's tail as the lizardfolk god splashed in his favorite pool? Who else would use Thor's hammer to pound a nail and thus be inspired to invent the lightning rod? Garl never needs to persuade Nebelun to join an excursion, but he and the rest of the pantheon do have to focus her attention on the task at hand, so that her madcap inventiveness doesn't derail the effort.

All gnomes see Nebelun as the delightful spirit of invention and discovery, even those whose livelihoods have nothing to do with the construction of odd devices. Any accident that fortuitously results in a new discovery might be credited to Nebelun's benevolent meddling in the affairs of mortal gnomes.

SEGOJAN EARTHCALLER

The gnomes know Segojan Earthcaller as a kind, modest hero. He is said to be the best cook among the gnome gods and to have the power to heal any sickness, because he knows the medicinal and culinary uses of every creature and plant that lives underground. During the misadventures of the gnome pantheon, Segojan contributes to the group through his healing abilities and the restorative power of his meals, and on many occasions the other gnome gods call upon him to use his ability to burrow through any substance.

GIFTS FROM THE GODS

The gnome gods enjoy traveling about the multiverse in the guise of ordinary gnomes. Those who offer them aid or treat them with respect might receive a modest token of appreciation in return. Sometimes the deity reveals itself before giving the gift, and sometimes the item simply appears on the recipient's pillow or in a loot sack. Typical gifts include a golden whistle that can mimic any bird song, a clockwork beetle made of silver that can fly and obey simple commands, and a seed that, when planted, grows into a miniature fruit tree and bears fruit within a few hours.

Forest gnomes believe that their ability to speak with burrowing animals comes from Segojan. All gnomes see Segojan as a healer of the sick and a protector of the hearth. He is also revered in his role as a guide for gnomish souls after death, as long as the body is buried before worms claim it. If a gnome's body isn't entrusted to Segojan by interring it, the soul is forced to find its own way to the afterlife.

URDLEN

Many pantheons include in their number a miscreant or an outlier—someone not to be emulated in the customary way, and often an entity whose existence serves as an object lesson and an example of what befalls mortals who conduct themselves the same way. For the gnomes, this niche is filled by Urdlen, also known as the Glutton for its selfish and cruel behavior.

Though the details differ from telling to telling, all gnomes know the story of how Garl banished Urdlen from the Golden Hills because Urdlen refused to go on an important quest. Despite Garl's efforts and the pleas of the rest of the pantheon, Urdlen selfishly refused to set his own interests aside and contribute to the group. Every version of this story ends in some sort of tragedy—perhaps the loss of Gaerdal's hand, the affliction that caused Flandal to need new skin, or the disappearance of Baravar's shadow—and each one concludes with "And that is why Garl sent Urdlen into exile." In tales of his later life, Urdlen is no longer a gnome but has become a greedy and destructive monster, a great blind and hairless mole with iron claws and teeth.

Gnomes believe that Urdlen exerts influence on their lives when they experience jealousy, greed, petulance, or envy. Individuals are more likely to fall prey to these feelings when they don't spend enough time in activities with others, and so tales of Urdlen serve as a somber reminder of the importance of participating in society.

THE GOLDEN HILLS

Seven hills set in a ring on Dothion, the more pastoral half of the plane of Bytopia, are the homes of the gnome gods. Each one of the Golden Hills, described below, is the domain of a certain deity, except for Callarduran, who dwells deep beneath them all in a set of caverns called Deephome:

Glitterhome. Garl's hill is no larger than the rest, but it glows more brightly than the others beneath the light of the eternal sunset that gives the place its name. Yet the true "glitter" lies inside—treasures from Garl's many adventures, displayed in a hall tiled with gemstones.

The Mithral Forge. Mines containing every kind of mineral run throughout Flandal's hill, which also features tunnels that lead to large ore deposits on other planes. When Flandal is at work, the whole hill vibrates to the rhythm of his hammer working at the forge for which his hill is named.

The Hidden Knoll. Baravar conceals the entrance to her hill with illusions and riddles, never allowing any who visit her to enter twice by the same way. Those who persevere through her trickery to discover her inner sanctum might be rewarded with a treasure.

The Golden Hills is a realm burnished with soothing golden light at all times. Every hour is that of a warm autumn evening. It would be the most relaxing place in the multiverse, were not the hills each as busy as a beehive on the inside.

Whisperleaf. This hill takes its name from the impossibly large oak tree that grows from its top and spreads out to shade much of its slopes. Even when Baervan and Chiktikka aren't present in their cottage at the base of the tree, its boughs and roots and the grassy slopes of the hill are always alive with mischievous animals.

Stronghaven. Gaerdal's home is a fortress that contains a confounding maze of tunnels, designed to defy any attempt to invade or infiltrate. Gaerdal, ever watchful for any threat to the Golden Hills, is almost always inside, not to be found unless she wills it so.

The Gemstone Burrow. A small round door just below the summit of Segojan's hill opens onto a network of tunnels and burrows, illuminated by brilliant gems. All sorts of burrowing creatures live peaceably with gnomish souls here.

The Workshop. Nebelun's hill is festooned inside and out with structures and contraptions of mysterious purpose in various stages of completion. Only the Meddler can say how she plans for any of these inventions of hers to work. From time to time she gifts one of them to a worthy follower, promising that its use will bring success—but offering no guarantee that it will function the way it was supposed to.

GNOME ADVENTURERS

I DON'T KNOW HOW MANY TIMES I'VE SEEN A GNOME *turn a dead end into a wonderful opportunity.*

—Delaan Winterhound

When a gnome leaves the burrow, the force behind that decision is almost always curiosity—an insatiable need to seek out and experience what the world has to offer. Sometimes the adventuring life is the natural outgrowth of a gnome's research project or experiment. A rock gnome alchemist who discovers a new form of fungus growing in a nearby cavern might wander farther afield from the burrow, looking for knowledge about other fungi in the world. A forest gnome who hears about a master illusionist in a faraway realm could embark on a journey to find that person and learn new tricks. A rock gnome artificer might become determined to locate any deposits of a rare metal, willing to travel the world high and low in search of it. Even a deep gnome might be born with an irrepressible urge to leave the Underdark and join a group to pursue a life of shared purpose.

Some gnome communities make a practice of sending young adults away from the burrow as a rite of passage, encouraging them to explore the realms of humans, dwarves, and elves for a time, with instructions to bring back information and new ideas for the community. Most of these folk return to the burrow at the appointed time or even sooner, their curiosity having been satisfied. But a few of them take readily to life in the outside world and don't come back on schedule, returning to the burrow only after spending years or decades away as a member of an adventuring party.

THE PULL OF THE STARS

Because of their extensive travels, gnome adventurers often become fascinated with the grandeur of the cosmos as seen in the motion of the stars across the sky. They view the cosmic array as a giant machine of wonderful complexity—a banquet for a curious gnomish mind. Many renowned astronomers, wizards, and extraplanar travelers are gnomes, having undertaken those disciplines in the hope of better understanding the workings of the multiverse.

A GNOME'S ROLE

Gnomes are valuable members of an adventuring party for a number of reasons, derived from both their innate abilities and their unique mind-set.

Possessed of higher intelligence than most other races, a gnome can be an important source of knowledge, and can devise solutions for many problems an adventuring party encounters. A rock gnome rogue on a dungeon expedition, if not lost in thought, can steer a party clear of many obstacles. Even the most complex magical or mechanical traps can be disarmed by a rock gnome who takes pride in solving difficult puzzles.

A forest gnome's skills are invaluable in the wilderness. Forest gnomes can spot subtle tracks, uncover clues that others would miss, and locate the safest path. Their illusion magic taunts, deludes, and terrifies enemies at the same time it delights their friends.

Forest gnomes and rock gnomes also contribute to a party by being a source of optimism and levity. Even in the worst circumstances, a gnome can find something to be hopeful for—an attitude that is infectious and thus can keep the group from falling into despair.

A deep gnome, pragmatic and cautious, brings a sense of duty rather than a sense of humor to an adventuring group. With their grit and iron will, deep gnomes meet adversity with hammers, picks, and their dour, dry wit— or no wit at all—as their weapons of choice.

DEEP GNOME CHARACTERS

At the DM's discretion, you can play a deep gnome character. When you choose the subrace of your gnome, you can choose deep gnome, using the following rules to create your character.

DEEP GNOME TRAITS

Deep gnomes have the gnome traits in the *Player's Handbook*, plus the subrace traits below. Unlike other gnomes, svirfneblin tend to weigh 80 to 120 pounds.

Short-lived compared to other gnomes, deep gnomes mature at the same rate humans do and are considered full-grown adults by age 25. They live 200 to 250 years, although toil and the dangers of the Underdark often claim them before their time.

Svirfneblin believe that survival depends on avoiding entanglements with other creatures and not making enemies, so they favor neutral alignments. They rarely wish others ill, and they are unlikely to take risks on behalf of others, except those dearest to them.

Ability Score Increase. Your Dexterity score increases by 1.

Superior Darkvision. Your darkvision has a radius of 120 feet.

Stone Camouflage. You have advantage on Dexterity (Stealth) checks to hide in rocky terrain and underground.

Extra Language. You can speak, read, and write Undercommon.

OPTIONAL DEEP GNOME FEAT

If your DM allows the use of feats from chapter 6 of the *Player's Handbook*, your deep gnome character has access to the following special feat.

SVIRFNEBLIN MAGIC
Prerequisite: Gnome (deep gnome)

You have inherited the innate spellcasting ability of your ancestors. This ability allows you to cast *nondetection* on yourself at will, without needing a material component. You can also cast each of the following spells once with this ability: *blindness/deafness*, *blur*, and *disguise self*. You regain the ability to cast these spells when you finish a long rest. Intelligence is your spellcasting ability for these spells.

GNOME TABLES

This section provides several tables useful for players and DMs who want to create gnome characters.

GNOME PERSONALITY TRAITS

d6	Personality Trait
1	Once you develop a liking for something, you quickly become obsessed with it.
2	You live life like a leaf on the breeze, letting it take you where it will.
3	The world is a miraculous place, and you are fascinated by everything in it.
4	You study your friends and take notes about how they act, jotting down things they say that interest you.
5	Your curiosity is so wide-ranging that you sometimes have trouble concentrating on any one thing.
6	You like to make little objects and creatures out of twigs or bits of metal and give them to friends.

GNOME IDEALS

d6	Ideal
1	**Love.** You love little (and big) critters and go out of your way to help them.
2	**Curiosity.** You can't stand an unsolved mystery or an unopened door.
3	**Knowledge.** You are interested in everything. You never know when what you learn will come in handy.
4	**Compassion.** You never turn down a plea for help.
5	**Helpfulness.** Whether you see a broken contraption or a broken heart, you have to try to fix it.
6	**Excellence.** You strive to be and do the best you can.

GNOME BONDS

d6	Bond
1	You pledge to bring something of immense value back to your burrow.
2	Anything of great quality and artisanship is to be protected, respected, and cared for.
3	Kobolds have caused you and your people nothing but trouble. You will avenge those wrongs.
4	You are searching for your lost love.
5	You will recover a keepsake stolen from your clan.
6	You are willing to take risks to learn about the world.

GNOME FLAWS

d4	Flaw
1	You embody the typical absent-minded professor. If you could forget where you put your head, you would.
2	You prefer to hide during a fight.
3	There is no difference between what you think and what you say.
4	You can't keep a secret.

CHAPTER 6: BESTIARY

HIS BESTIARY PROVIDES GAME STATISTICS and lore for more than a hundred monsters suitable for any D&D campaign, including old favorites from past editions of the game as well as original creations. Among those returning to the fold are the berbalang, the iron cobra, the spirit troll, the meazel, and the vampiric mist, all of which trace their lineage back to the original *Fiend Folio* published in 1981.

Many of these monsters, old and new alike, are ideal for use with the earlier chapters of this book. For instance, the demons and devils presented here—lesser varieties as well as the greatest of the demon lords and the archdevils—can add even more chaos and savagery to a campaign based on the Blood War.

Similarly, you'll find a selection of specialized duergar to spice up a game that involves the characters in the struggle described in chapter 3.

The ranks of the drow and the shadar-kai are swelled by the addition of special individuals that can add depth—and danger—to adventures that take heroes into the Underdark or the Shadowfell.

Or, if you're interested in exploring either side of the conflict between the gith that's portrayed in chapter 4, the bestiary has new versions of githyanki and githzerai that supplement the *Monster Manual* entries for those creatures.

This chapter is a continuation of the *Monster Manual* and adopts a similar presentation. If you are unfamiliar with the monster stat block format, read the introduction of the *Monster Manual* before proceeding further. It explains stat block terminology and gives rules for various monster traits—information that isn't repeated here.

As with the monsters in the *Monster Manual*, we've tried to capture the essence of each creature and focus on those traits that make it unique or that encourage DMs to use it. You can do what you will with these monsters and change their lore to suit your game. Nothing we say here is meant to curtail your creativity.

The creatures in this bestiary are organized alphabetically. A few are grouped under a banner heading; for example, the "Demons" section contains stat blocks for various kinds of demons, which are presented alphabetically within that section.

Following this chapter is an appendix that contains lists of the creatures arranged by type, challenge rating, and environment. DMs can use these lists, in conjunction with similar information in the *Dungeon Master's Guide* and other sources, to choose monsters for a particular adventure or campaign.

Allip

When a mind uncovers a secret that a powerful being has protected with a mighty curse, the result is often the emergence of an allip. Secrets protected in this manner range in scope from a demon lord's true name to the hidden truths of the cosmic order. The allip acquires the secret, but the curse annihilates its body and leaves behind a spectral creature composed of fragments from the victim's psyche and overwhelming psychic agony.

Blasphemous Secrets. Every allip is wracked with a horrifying insight that torments what remains of its mind. In the presence of other creatures, an allip seeks to relieve this burden by sharing its secret. The creature can impart only a shard of the knowledge that doomed it, but that piece is enough to wrack the recipient with temporary madness. The survivors of an allip's attack are sometimes left with a compulsion to learn more about what spawned this monstrosity. Strange phrases echo through their minds, and weird visions occupy their dreams. The sense that some colossal truth sits just outside their recall plagues them for days, months, and sometimes years after their fateful encounter.

Undead Nature. An allip doesn't require air, food, drink, or sleep.

> ## Insidious Lore
>
> An allip might attempt to share its lore to escape its curse and enter the afterlife. It can transfer knowledge from its mind by guiding another creature to write down what it knows. This process takes days or possibly weeks. An allip can accomplish this task by lurking in the study or work-place of a scholar. If the allip remains hidden, its victim is gradually overcome by manic energy. A scholar, driven by sudden insights to work night and day, produces reams of text with little memory of exactly what the documents contain. If the allip succeeds, it passes from the world—and its terrible secret hides somewhere in the scholar's text, waiting to be discovered by its next victim.

Allip

Medium undead, neutral evil

Armor Class 13
Hit Points 40 (9d8)
Speed 0 ft., fly 40 ft. (hover)

STR	DEX	CON	INT	WIS	CHA
6 (−2)	17 (+3)	10 (+0)	17 (+3)	15 (+2)	16 (+3)

Saving Throws Int +6, Wis +5
Skills Perception +5, Stealth +6
Damage Resistances acid, fire, lightning, thunder; bludgeoning, piercing, and slashing from nonmagical attacks
Damage Immunities cold, necrotic, poison
Condition Immunities charmed, exhaustion, frightened, grappled, paralyzed, petrified, poisoned, prone, restrained
Senses darkvision 60 ft., passive Perception 15
Languages the languages it knew in life
Challenge 5 (1,800 XP)

Incorporeal Movement. The allip can move through other creatures and objects as if they were difficult terrain. It takes 5 (1d10) force damage if it ends its turn inside an object.

Actions

Maddening Touch. *Melee Spell Attack:* +6 to hit, reach 5 ft., one target. *Hit:* 17 (4d6 + 3) psychic damage.

Whispers of Madness. The allip chooses up to three creatures it can see within 60 feet of it. Each target must succeed on a DC 14 Wisdom saving throw, or it takes 7 (1d8 + 3) psychic damage and must use its reaction to make a melee weapon attack against one creature of the allip's choice that the allip can see. Constructs and undead are immune to this effect.

Howling Babble (Recharge 6). Each creature within 30 feet of the allip that can hear it must make a DC 14 Wisdom saving throw. On a failed save, a target takes 12 (2d8 + 3) psychic damage, and it is stunned until the end of its next turn. On a successful save, it takes half as much damage and isn't stunned. Constructs and undead are immune to this effect.

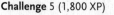

ASTRAL DREADNOUGHT

Enormous and terrifying monstrosities known as astral dreadnoughts haunt the silvery void of the Astral Plane, causing planar travelers to shudder at the very thought of them. They have been gliding through the astral mists since the dawn of the multiverse, trying to devour all other creatures they encounter.

As big as an ancient red dragon and covered from head to tail in layers of thick, spiked plates, a dread-

only by using magic that enables planar travel, such as the *plane shift* spell. The demiplane resembles a stone cave roughly 1,000 feet in diameter with a ceiling 100 feet high. Like a stomach, it contains the remains of the dreadnought's past meals. The dreadnought can't be harmed from within the demiplane. If the dreadnought dies, the demiplane disappears, and everything inside it appears around the corpse. The demiplane is otherwise indestructible.

Legendary Resistance (3/Day). If the astral dreadnought fails a saving throw, it can choose to succeed instead.

Magic Weapons. An astral dreadnought's weapon attacks are magical.

Sever Silver Cord. If the astral dreadnought scores a critical hit against a creature traveling through the Astral Plane by means of the *astral projection* spell, the dreadnought can cut the target's silver cord instead of dealing damage.

ACTIONS

Multiattack. The astral dreadnought makes three attacks: one with its bite and two with its claws.

Bite. *Melee Weapon Attack:* +16 to hit, reach 10 ft., one target. *Hit:* 36 (5d10 + 9) piercing damage. If the target is a creature of Huge size or smaller and this damage reduces it to 0 hit points or it is incapacitated, the astral dreadnought swallows it. The swallowed target, along with everything it is wearing and carrying, appears in an unoccupied space on the floor of the astral dreadnought's Demiplanar Donjon.

Claw. *Melee Weapon Attack:* +16 to hit, reach 20 ft., one target. *Hit:* 19 (3d6 + 9) slashing damage.

LEGENDARY ACTIONS

The astral dreadnought can take 3 legendary actions, choosing from the options below. Only one legendary option can be used at a time and only at the end of another creature's turn. The dreadnought regains spent legendary actions at the start of its turn.

Claw. The astral dreadnought makes one claw attack.

Donjon Visit (Costs 2 Actions). One creature that is Huge or smaller that the astral dreadnought can see within 60 feet of it must succeed on a DC 19 Charisma saving throw or be magically teleported to an unoccupied space on the floor of the astral dreadnought's Demiplanar Donjon. At the end of the target's next turn, the target reappears in the space it left or in the nearest unoccupied space if that space is occupied.

Psychic Projection (Costs 3 Actions). Each creature within 60 feet of the astral dreadnought must make a DC 19 Wisdom saving throw, taking 15 (2d10 + 4) psychic damage on a failed save, or half as much damage on a successful one.

ASTRAL DREADNOUGHT

Gargantuan monstrosity (titan), unaligned

Armor Class 20 (natural armor)
Hit Points 297 (17d20 + 119)
Speed 15 ft., fly 80 ft. (hover)

STR	DEX	CON	INT	WIS	CHA
28 (+9)	7 (−2)	25 (+7)	5 (−3)	14 (+2)	18 (+4)

Saving Throws Dex +5, Wis +9
Skills Perception +9
Damage Resistances bludgeoning, piercing, and slashing from nonmagical attacks
Condition Immunities charmed, exhaustion, frightened, paralyzed, petrified, poisoned, prone, stunned
Senses darkvision 120 ft., passive Perception 19
Languages —
Challenge 21 (33,000 XP)

Antimagic Cone. The astral dreadnought's opened eye creates an area of antimagic, as in the *antimagic field* spell, in a 150-foot cone. At the start of each of its turns, the dreadnought decides which way the cone faces. The cone doesn't function while the dreadnought's eye is closed or while the dreadnought is blinded.

Astral Entity. The astral dreadnought can't leave the Astral Plane, nor can it be banished or otherwise transported out of the Astral Plane.

Demiplanar Donjon. Any creature or object that the astral dreadnought swallows is transported to a demiplane that can be entered by no other means except a *wish* spell or this creature's Donjon Visit ability. A creature can leave the demiplane

A

nought has two gnarled limbs that end in razor-sharp pincer claws. Constellations appear to swirl in the depths of its single eye, and its serpentine, armored tail trails off into the silvery void.

An astral dreadnought lives a solitary existence. On the rare occasion when two dreadnoughts meet, they typically fight until one tires of the conflict and departs. Some mighty villains have enslaved astral dreadnoughts and used them to terrifying effect.

Antimagic Eye. Astral sailors claim that insanity awaits anyone who gazes into the eye of an astral dreadnought. What one sees reflected in that starry void is the sudden, terrifying realization of one's own mortality. Spellcasters have cause to fear the eye more than others, since it emits a continuous antimagic field. The dreadnought can shut off the effect by simply closing its eye, though it seldom has reason to do so.

Astral Predator. A remorseless, indiscriminate hunter, an astral dreadnought employs terrifying, if unimaginative, tactics. It uses its teeth and claws to tear apart its prey. Instinctively aware of how dangerous spellcasters can be, it maneuvers to keep as many opponents as possible within its antimagic gaze.

An astral dreadnought doesn't have a gullet or a digestive system. Anything it swallows is deposited in a unique demiplane—an enclosed space that contains eons worth of detritus, as well as the remains of dead planar travelers. The place has gravity and breathable air, and organic matter decays there. Although escape from the demiplane is possible with the aid of magic, most creatures arrive here only after they have died. When the dreadnought dies, its demiplane vanishes, and its contents are released into the Astral Plane.

An astral dreadnought doesn't communicate. It simply consumes any prey it finds, then continues its silent patrol. It can't leave the Astral Plane, nor would it want to.

Titans of the Chained God. Tharizdun, the Chained God, created astral dreadnoughts to devour planar travelers who were seeking portals that lead from the Astral Plane to the Outer Planes—portals they might use to gaze upon their gods or realize some dream of godhood.

Astral dreadnoughts don't procreate, so their population can't grow. Even though githyanki and other astral voyagers hunt the creatures, they rarely see any success, and the dreadnoughts aren't in danger of becoming extinct anytime soon.

Titanic Nature. Although it eats and sleeps if it so desires, an astral dreadnought doesn't require air, food, drink, or sleep.

Astral dreadnoughts exist for one reason: hubris. Not the hubris of mortals, but the hubris of gods who deem themselves too mighty to be approached and looked upon.

BALHANNOTH

Native to the Shadowfell, the vicious, predatory balhannoth alters reality in its lair to make the place appear inviting to travelers. Once they step inside, the balhannoth springs its trap.

False Hope. Thanks to a limited form of telepathy, a balhannoth can sense the desires of other creatures and identify images of places where they expect those desires to be met. The balhannoth then warps reality around it, remaking its environment so that it matches the appearance of the place the creature seeks. The balhannoth never quite gets all the details right, and plenty of incongruities might give away the deception, but the imitation is good enough to fool desperate creatures into stumbling into the monster's clutches.

Malevolent Entities. A balhannoth thrives on fear and despair, taking pleasure in the horror its victims experience. It terrorizes its prey by using its reality-warping powers to mask its presence until it can snatch the target. Then it teleports away to feed on its victims.

Useful Slaves. Drow hunting parties and other denizens of the Underdark sometimes venture into the Shadowfell to capture balhannoths. They install the creatures as guardians, protecting passages from enemy intruders and cutting off avenues of retreat or watching over slaves.

A BALHANNOTH'S LAIR

In the Shadowfell, balhannoths make their lairs near places inhabited by creatures they hunt. They typically haunt well-traveled roads and paths, snatching people who come along. A balhannoth that has been captured and exploited by drow might lair in caves near Underdark passages and guard the ways in and out of a drow enclave.

LAIR ACTIONS

When fighting inside its lair, a balhannoth can use lair actions. On initiative count 20 (losing initiative ties), a balhannoth can take one lair action to cause one of the following effects; the balhannoth can't use the same lair action two rounds in a row:

- The balhannoth warps reality around it in an area up to 500 feet square. After 10 minutes, the terrain in the area reshapes to assume the appearance of a location sought by one intelligent creature whose mind the balhannoth has read (see Regional Effects below). The transformation affects nonliving material only and can't create anything with moving parts or magical properties. Any object created in this area is, upon close inspection, revealed as a fake. Books are filled with empty pages, golden items are obvious counterfeits, and so on. The transformation lasts until the balhannoth dies or uses this lair action again.
- The balhannoth targets one creature within 500 feet of it. The target must succeed on a DC 16 Wisdom saving throw or the target, along with whatever it is wearing and carrying, teleports to an unoccupied space of the balhannoth's choice within 60 feet of it.

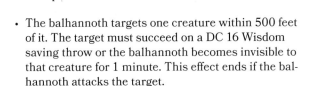

- The balhannoth targets one creature within 500 feet of it. The target must succeed on a DC 16 Wisdom saving throw or the balhannoth becomes invisible to that creature for 1 minute. This effect ends if the balhannoth attacks the target.

REGIONAL EFFECTS

A region containing a balhannoth's lair becomes warped by the creature's unnatural presence, which creates one or more of the following effects:

- Creatures within 1 mile of the balhannoth's lair experience a sensation of being close to whatever they desire most. The sensation grows stronger the closer the creatures come to the balhannoth's lair.
- The balhannoth can sense the strongest desires of any humanoid within 1 mile of it and learns whether those desires involve a place: a safe location to rest, a temple, home, or somewhere else.

If the balhannoth dies, these effects end immediately.

There are no virtues in the Shadowfell. Thanks to the balhannoth, even hope is punished with death.

BALHANNOTH
Large aberration, chaotic evil

Armor Class 17 (natural armor)
Hit Points 114 (12d10 + 48)
Speed 25 ft., climb 25 ft.

STR	DEX	CON	INT	WIS	CHA
17 (+3)	8 (−1)	18 (+4)	6 (−2)	15 (+2)	8 (−1)

Saving Throws Con +8
Skills Perception +6
Condition Immunities blinded
Senses blindsight 500 ft. (blind beyond this radius), passive Perception 16
Languages understands Deep Speech, telepathy 1 mile
Challenge 11 (7,200 XP)

Legendary Resistance (2/Day). If the balhannoth fails a saving throw, it can choose to succeed instead.

ACTIONS

Multiattack. The balhannoth makes a bite attack and up to two tentacle attacks, or it makes up to four tentacle attacks.

Bite. *Melee Weapon Attack:* +7 to hit, reach 5 ft., one target. *Hit:* 25 (4d10 + 3) piercing damage.

Tentacle. *Melee Weapon Attack:* +7 to hit, reach 10 ft., one target. *Hit:* 10 (2d6 + 3) bludgeoning damage, and the target is grappled (escape DC 15) and is moved up to 5 feet toward the balhannoth. Until this grapple ends, the target is restrained, and the balhannoth can't use this tentacle against other targets. The balhannoth has four tentacles.

LEGENDARY ACTIONS

The balhannoth can take 3 legendary actions, choosing from the options below. Only one legendary action can be used at a time and only at the end of another creature's turn. The balhannoth regains spent legendary actions at the start of its turn.

Bite Attack. The balhannoth makes one bite attack against one creature it has grappled.
Teleport. The balhannoth magically teleports, along with any equipment it is wearing or carrying and any creatures it has grappled, up to 60 feet to an unoccupied space it can see.
Vanish. The balhannoth magically becomes invisible for up to 10 minutes or until immediately after it makes an attack roll.

B

Berbalang

Berbalangs creep across the petrified remains of dead gods adrift on the Astral Plane. Obsessed with gathering secrets, both from the gods they inhabit and from the bones of dead creatures, they call forth the spirits of the dead and force them to divulge what they learned in life.

Speakers of the Dead. Berbalangs prefer to speak only to dead things, and specifically only to the spirits they call forth in the hope of learning secrets. They record their stories on the bones that once belonged to these creatures, thus preserving the information they gain.

Spectral Spy. The pursuit of knowledge drives everything berbalangs do. Although they mostly learn their secrets from the dead, they aren't above spying on the living to take knowledge from them as well. A berbalang can create a spectral duplicate of itself and send the duplicate out to gather information on other planes by watching places where the gods and their servants gather. When a berbalang is perceiving its environment through its duplicate, its actual body is unconscious and can't protect or nourish itself. Thus, a berbalang typically uses its duplicate for only a short time before returning its consciousness to its body.

Weird Oracles. The knowledge that berbalangs accumulate makes them great sources of information for powerful people traveling the planes. Berbalangs ignore petitioners, however, unless they come bearing a choice secret or the bones of a particularly interesting creature. Githyanki have found a way to coexist with berbalangs, and sometimes use the creatures to spy on their enemies and to watch over their crèches on the Material Plane.

BERBALANG
Medium aberration, neutral evil

Armor Class 14 (natural armor)
Hit Points 38 (11d8 – 11)
Speed 30 ft., fly 40 ft.

STR	DEX	CON	INT	WIS	CHA
9 (–1)	16 (+3)	9 (–1)	17 (+3)	11 (+0)	10 (+0)

Saving Throws Dex +5, Int +5
Skills Arcana +5, History +5, Insight +2, Perception +2, Religion +5
Senses truesight 120 ft., passive Perception 12
Languages all, but rarely speaks
Challenge 2 (450 XP)

Spectral Duplicate (Recharges after a Short or Long Rest). As a bonus action, the berbalang creates one spectral duplicate of itself in an unoccupied space it can see within 60 feet of it. While the duplicate exists, the berbalang is unconscious. A berbalang can have only one duplicate at a time. The duplicate disappears when it or the berbalang drops to 0 hit points or when the berbalang dismisses it (no action required).

The duplicate has the same statistics and knowledge as the berbalang, and everything experienced by the duplicate is known by the berbalang. All damage dealt by the duplicate's attacks is psychic damage.

Innate Spellcasting. The berbalang's innate spellcasting ability is Intelligence (spell save DC 13). The berbalang can innately cast the following spells, requiring no material components:

At will: *speak with dead*
1/day: *plane shift* (self only)

ACTIONS

Multiattack. The berbalang makes two attacks: one with its bite and one with its claws.

Bite. *Melee Weapon Attack:* +5 to hit, reach 5 ft., one target. *Hit:* 8 (1d10 + 3) piercing damage.

Claws. *Melee Weapon Attack:* +5 to hit, reach 5 ft., one target. *Hit:* 8 (2d4 + 3) slashing damage.

ness to be sliced apart or teleported elsewhere to be tortured to death.

Dark Reflections. A boneclaw's master might not want such a servant or even know it has one. Boneclaws bind to petty criminals, bullies, and even particularly cruel children. Even if the master is unaware of its new, horrid bodyguard, its local area will be plagued by disappearances and grisly murders, tied together by the common thread of the master's envy or hunger for revenge.

Undead Nature. A boneclaw doesn't require air, food, drink, or sleep.

Boneclaw

A wizard who tries to become a lich but fails might become a boneclaw instead. These hideous, cackling undead share a few of the lich's attributes—but where liches are immortal masters of the arcane, boneclaws are slaves to darkness, hatred, and pain.

The most important part of the transformation ritual occurs when the soul of the aspiring lich migrates to a prepared phylactery. If the spellcaster is too physically or magically weak to compel the soul into its prison, the soul instead seeks out a new master—a humanoid within a few miles who has an unusually hate-filled heart. The soul bonds itself to the foul essence it finds in that person, and the boneclaw becomes forever enslaved to its new master's wishes and subconscious whims. It forms near its master, sometimes appearing before that individual to receive orders and other times simply setting about the fulfillment of its master's desires.

Limited Immortality. A boneclaw can't be destroyed while its master lives. No matter what happens to a boneclaw's body, it re-forms within hours and returns to whatever duty its master assigned.

The boneclaw can serve only evil. If its master finds redemption or sincerely turns away from the path of evil, the boneclaw is permanently destroyed.

Cackling Slayers. Boneclaws delight in murder, and nothing pleases them more than causing horrific pain. They lurk like spiders in shadowy recesses, waiting for victims to approach within reach of their long, bony limbs. Once speared, a creature is pulled into the dark-

BONECLAW
Large undead, chaotic evil

Armor Class 16 (natural armor)
Hit Points 127 (17d10 + 34)
Speed 40 ft.

STR	DEX	CON	INT	WIS	CHA
19 (+4)	16 (+3)	15 (+2)	13 (+1)	15 (+2)	9 (−1)

Saving Throws Dex +7, Con +6, Wis +6
Skills Perception +6, Stealth +7
Damage Resistances cold, necrotic; bludgeoning, piercing, and slashing from nonmagical attacks
Condition Immunities charmed, exhaustion, frightened, paralyzed, poisoned
Senses darkvision 60 ft., passive Perception 16
Languages Common plus the main language of its master
Challenge 12 (8,400 XP)

Rejuvenation. While its master lives, a destroyed boneclaw gains a new body in 1d10 hours, with all its hit points. The new body appears within 1 mile of the boneclaw's master.

Shadow Stealth. While in dim light or darkness, the boneclaw can take the Hide action as a bonus action.

ACTIONS

Multiattack. The boneclaw makes two claw attacks.

Piercing Claw. *Melee Weapon Attack:* +8 to hit, reach 15 ft., one target. *Hit:* 20 (3d10 + 4) piercing damage. If the target is a creature, the boneclaw can pull the target up to 10 feet toward itself, and the target is grappled (escape DC 14). The boneclaw has two claws. While a claw grapples a target, the claw can attack only that target.

Shadow Jump. If the boneclaw is in dim light or darkness, each creature of the boneclaw's choice within 5 feet of it must succeed on a DC 14 Constitution saving throw or take 34 (5d12 + 2) necrotic damage.

The boneclaw then magically teleports up to 60 feet to an unoccupied space it can see. It can bring one creature it's grappling, teleporting that creature to an unoccupied space it can see within 5 feet of its destination. The destination spaces of this teleportation must be in dim light or darkness.

REACTIONS

Deadly Reach. In response to a visible enemy moving into its reach, the boneclaw makes one claw attack against that enemy. If the attack hits, the boneclaw can make a second claw attack against the target.

CADAVER COLLECTOR

The ancient war machines known as cadaver collectors lumber aimlessly across the blasted plains of Acheron until they are called upon by a necromancer, hobgoblin general, or other evil warlord to bolster the ranks of a conquering army. These fearsome constructs obey their summoners until being dismissed back to Acheron, but if a summoner comes to a bad end, a cadaver collector might wander the Material Plane for centuries, collecting corpses while searching for a way to return home.

Sweeping the Dead. Cadaver collectors respond to a summons from a mortal only when they are called to the scene of a great battle—either where one is in progress, where one is imminent, or where one once took place. They encase themselves in the armor and weapons of fallen warriors and impale the corpses of those warriors on the lances and other weapons embedded in their salvaged armor.

Conjured Berserkers. Corpses that accumulate on the construct's shell aren't just grisly battle trophies. A cadaver collector can summon the spirits of these cadavers to join battle with its enemies and to paralyze more creatures for eventual impalement. Although these specters are individually weak, a cadaver collector can call up an almost endless supply of them, if given time.

Constructed Nature. A cadaver collector doesn't require air, food, drink, or sleep.

CADAVER COLLECTOR

Large construct, lawful evil

Armor Class 17 (natural armor)
Hit Points 189 (18d10 + 90)
Speed 30 ft.

STR	DEX	CON	INT	WIS	CHA
21 (+5)	14 (+2)	20 (+5)	5 (−3)	11 (+0)	8 (−1)

Damage Immunities necrotic, poison, psychic; bludgeoning, piercing, and slashing from nonmagical attacks that aren't adamantine
Condition Immunities charmed, exhaustion, frightened, paralyzed, petrified, poisoned
Senses darkvision 60 ft., passive Perception 10
Languages understands all languages but can't speak
Challenge 14 (11,500 XP)

Magic Resistance. The cadaver collector has advantage on saving throws against spells and other magical effects.

Summon Specters (Recharges after a Short or Long Rest). As a bonus action, the cadaver collector calls up the enslaved spirits of those it has slain; 1d6 specters (without Sunlight Sensitivity) arise in unoccupied spaces within 15 feet of the cadaver collector. The specters act right after the cadaver collector on the same initiative count and fight until they're destroyed. They disappear when the cadaver collector is destroyed.

ACTIONS

Multiattack. The cadaver collector makes two slam attacks.

Slam. *Melee Weapon Attack:* +10 to hit, reach 5 ft., one target. *Hit:* 18 (3d8 + 5) bludgeoning damage plus 16 (3d10) necrotic damage.

Paralyzing Breath (Recharge 5–6). The cadaver collector releases paralyzing gas in a 30-foot cone. Each creature in that area must make a successful DC 18 Constitution saving throw or be paralyzed for 1 minute. A paralyzed creature repeats the saving throw at the end of each of its turns, ending the effect on itself with a success.

Chokers are cowardly and dim-witted creatures, useless as guard beasts, and utterly awful as servants. Yet for wizards of shorter stature, securing one as a familiar does negate the need for a ladder.

CHOKER

The choker is a subterranean predator far more dangerous than its small size and spindly, rubbery limbs would suggest.

Chokers have cartilage rather than a bony skeleton. This flexible internal structure enables them to easily slip into narrow fissures and niches in the walls of their cavern homes. They lurk in these spots, silent and unseen, waiting for prey to happen by.

Sly Trappers. A choker's usual method for luring prey involves positioning the body of its latest catch just outside its hiding spot. Whenever it gets hungry, it tears off a few chunks of flesh to feed itself. In the meantime, the corpse serves to entice other curious humanoids—explorers, drow, duergar, or the choker's favorite prey, goblins—to come within reach.

When a target presents itself, the choker's starfish-shaped hands dart out of its hiding spot, wrap around the victim's throat, and pin the unfortunate creature against the cavern wall while choking out its life. Because its arms are so long, the choker can keep its body deep inside the crevice where it hides, beyond the reach of most normal weapons.

Lone Hunters. Chokers tend to set their ambushes alone, rather than working in concert, but where one creature is found, others are likely to be nearby. They communicate through eerie, keening howls that travel long distances through rock but are difficult to identify or locate in a typical echo-filled cavern.

CHOKER
Small aberration, chaotic evil

Armor Class 16 (natural armor)
Hit Points 13 (3d6 + 3)
Speed 30 ft.

STR	DEX	CON	INT	WIS	CHA
16 (+3)	14 (+2)	13 (+1)	4 (−3)	12 (+1)	7 (−2)

Skills Stealth +6
Senses darkvision 60 ft., passive Perception 11
Languages Deep Speech
Challenge 1 (100 XP)

Aberrant Quickness (Recharges after a Short or Long Rest). The choker can take an extra action on its turn.

Boneless. The choker can move through and occupy a space as narrow as 4 inches wide without squeezing.

Spider Climb. The choker can climb difficult surfaces, including upside down on ceilings, without needing to make an ability check.

ACTIONS

Multiattack. The choker makes two tentacle attacks.

Tentacle. *Melee Weapon Attack:* +5 to hit, reach 10 ft., one target. *Hit:* 5 (1d4 + 3) bludgeoning damage plus 3 (1d6) piercing damage. If the target is a Large or smaller creature, it is grappled (escape DC 15). Until this grapple ends, the target is restrained, and the choker can't use this tentacle on another target. The choker has two tentacles. If this attack is a critical hit, the target also can't breathe or speak until the grapple ends.

Clockworks

The gnomes' efforts to invent and tinker with magic and mechanical devices produce many failed constructs, but also result in genuine advances, such as clockworks. Since their discovery, the methods used to craft clockworks have passed from one community of gnomes to another and down the generations.

Constructed Nature. A clockwork doesn't require air, food, drink, or sleep.

Bronze Scout

A bronze scout seldom emerges from below ground; thanks to its telescoping eyestalks, it can observe enemies at close range while most of its segmented, wormlike body remains buried. If it is detected, the bronze scout deters pursuers by sending electrical shocks through the ground while it retreats to safety.

Iron Cobra

An iron cobra is exactly what its name implies: a metal snake with a poisonous bite. In addition to standard poisons, gnomes load this clockwork with alchemical concoctions that can paralyze creatures and cloud their minds with paranoia.

Oaken Bolter

No ordinary ballista, an oaken bolter is a construct capable of striking at long distances. The bolts it launches can rend flesh, destroy armor, or drag enemies toward traps or melee-oriented clockworks—and at shorter ranges, burst with explosive force.

Stone Defender

Thick plates of stone riveted onto a stone defender give it substantial protection and allow it to conceal itself against a stony surface. Its chief role isn't as an ambusher, however, but as a bodyguard for gnomes and other clockworks.

Individual Designs

A gnome artisan values an individualized clockwork more highly than a perfectly functioning one that copies too much from another creation. For that reason, even clockworks that fit established designs, such as those described here, are seldom identical.

A clockwork can be customized by adding one of the following enhancements and one potential malfunction to its stat block. You can select randomly or choose a pair of modifications that fit the temperament of the clockwork's builder.

Clockwork Enhancements

d10	Enhancement
1	**Camouflaged.** The clockwork gains proficiency in Stealth if it doesn't already have it. While motionless, it is indistinguishable from a stopped machine.
2	**Sensors.** The range of the clockwork's darkvision becomes 120 feet, unless it is higher, and it gains proficiency in Perception if it doesn't already have it.
3	**Improved Armor.** The clockwork's AC increases by 2.
4	**Increased Speed.** The clockwork's speed increases by 10 feet.
5	**Reinforced Construction.** The clockwork has resistance to force, lightning, and thunder damage.
6	**Self-Repairing.** If the clockwork starts its turn with at least 1 hit point, it regains 5 hit points. If it takes lightning damage, this ability doesn't function at the start of its next turn.
7	**Sturdy Frame.** The clockwork's hit point maximum increases by an amount equal to its number of Hit Dice.
8	**Suction.** The clockwork gains a climbing speed of 30 feet.
9	**Vocal Resonator.** The clockwork gains the ability to speak rudimentary Common or Gnomish (creator's choice).
10	**Water Propulsion.** The clockwork gains a swimming speed of 30 feet.

Clockwork Malfunctions

d10	Malfunction
1	**Faulty Sensors.** Roll a d6 at the start of the clockwork's turn. If you roll a 1, the clockwork is blinded until the end of its turn.
2	**Flawed Targeting.** Roll a d6 at the start of the clockwork's turn. If you roll a 1, the clockwork makes attack rolls with disadvantage until the end of its turn.
3	**Ground Fault.** The clockwork has vulnerability to lightning damage.
4	**Imprinting Loop.** Roll a d6 at the start of the clockwork's turn. If you roll a 1, the clockwork mistakes one creature it can see within 30 feet for its creator. The clockwork won't willingly harm that creature for 1 minute or until that creature attacks it or deals damage to it.
5	**Leaking Lubricant.** Roll a d6 at the start of the clockwork's turn. If you roll a 1, the clockwork gains 1 level of exhaustion that it isn't immune to.
6	**Limited Steering.** The clockwork must move in a straight line. It can turn up to 90 degrees before moving and again at the midpoint of its movement. It can rotate freely if it doesn't use any of its speeds on its turn.
7	**Overactive Sense of Self-Preservation.** If the clockwork has half its hit points or fewer at the start of its turn in combat, roll a d6. If you roll a 1, it retreats from combat. If retreat isn't possible, it continues fighting.
8	**Overheats.** Roll a d6 at the start of the clockwork's turn. If you roll a 1, the clockwork is incapacitated until the end of its turn.
9	**Rusty Gears.** The clockwork has disadvantage on initiative rolls, and its speed decreases by 10 feet.
10	**Weak Armor.** The clockwork isn't immune to bludgeoning, piercing, and slashing damage from nonmagical attacks that aren't adamantine.

> *Never depend on something built by a gnome. You can always rely on a gnome to take a good idea and make it impractical.*

Bronze Scout

Medium construct, unaligned

Armor Class 13
Hit Points 18 (4d8)
Speed 30 ft., burrow 30 ft.

STR	DEX	CON	INT	WIS	CHA
10 (+0)	16 (+3)	11 (+0)	3 (−4)	14 (+2)	1 (−5)

Skills Perception +6, Stealth +7
Damage Immunities poison; bludgeoning, piercing, and slashing from nonmagical attacks that aren't adamantine
Condition Immunities charmed, exhaustion, frightened, paralyzed, petrified, poisoned
Senses darkvision 60 ft., passive Perception 16
Languages understands one language of its creator but can't speak
Challenge 1 (200 XP)

Earth Armor. The bronze scout doesn't provoke opportunity attacks when it burrows.

Magic Resistance. The bronze scout has advantage on saving throws against spells and other magical effects.

Actions

Bite. *Melee Weapon Attack:* +5 to hit, reach 5 ft., one target. *Hit:* 5 (1d4 + 3) piercing damage plus 3 (1d6) lightning damage.

Lightning Flare (Recharges after a Short or Long Rest). Each creature in contact with the ground within 15 feet of the bronze scout must make a DC 13 Dexterity saving throw, taking 14 (4d6) lightning damage on a failed save, or half as much damage on a successful one.

Iron Cobra

Medium construct, unaligned

Armor Class 13
Hit Points 45 (7d8 + 14)
Speed 30 ft.

STR	DEX	CON	INT	WIS	CHA
12 (+1)	16 (+3)	14 (+2)	3 (−4)	10 (+0)	1 (−5)

Skills Stealth +7
Damage Immunities poison; bludgeoning, piercing, and slashing from nonmagical attacks that aren't adamantine
Condition Immunities charmed, exhaustion, frightened, paralyzed, petrified, poisoned
Senses darkvision 60 ft., passive Perception 10
Languages understands one language of its creator but can't speak
Challenge 4 (1,100 XP)

Magic Resistance. The iron cobra has advantage on saving throws against spells and other magical effects.

Actions

Bite. *Melee Weapon Attack:* +5 to hit, reach 5 ft., one target. *Hit:* 6 (1d6 + 3) piercing damage. If the target is a creature, it must succeed on a DC 13 Constitution saving throw or suffer one random poison effect:

1. **Poison Damage:** The target takes 13 (3d8) poison damage.
2. **Confusion:** On its next turn, the target must use its action to make one weapon attack against a random creature it can see within 30 feet of it, using whatever weapon it has in hand and moving beforehand if necessary to get in range. If it's holding no weapon, it makes an unarmed strike. If no creature is visible within 30 feet, it takes the Dash action, moving toward the nearest creature.
3. **Paralysis:** The target is paralyzed until the end of its next turn.

OAKEN BOLTER
Medium construct, unaligned

Armor Class 16 (natural armor)
Hit Points 58 (9d8 + 18)
Speed 30 ft.

STR	DEX	CON	INT	WIS	CHA
12 (+1)	18 (+4)	15 (+2)	3 (−4)	10 (+0)	1 (−5)

Damage Immunities poison; bludgeoning, piercing, and
slashing from nonmagical attacks that aren't adamantine
Condition Immunities charmed, exhaustion, frightened,
paralyzed, petrified, poisoned
Senses darkvision 60 ft., passive Perception 10
Languages understands one language of its creator but can't
speak
Challenge 5 (1,800 XP)

Magic Resistance. The oaken bolter has advantage on saving
throws against spells and other magical effects.

ACTIONS

Multiattack. The oaken bolter makes two lancing bolt attacks
or one lancing bolt attack and one harpoon attack.

Lancing Bolt. Melee or Ranged Weapon Attack: +7 to hit, reach
5 ft. or range 100/400 ft., one target. *Hit:* 15 (2d10 + 4) piercing damage.

Harpoon. Ranged Weapon Attack: +7 to hit, range 50/200 ft.,
one target. *Hit:* 9 (1d10 + 4) piercing damage, and the target
is grappled (escape DC 12). While grappled in this way, a creature's speed isn't reduced, but it can move only in directions
that bring it closer to the oaken bolter. A creature takes 5 (1d10)
slashing damage if it escapes from the grapple or if it tries and
fails. As a bonus action, the oaken bolter can pull a creature
grappled by it 20 feet closer. The oaken bolter can grapple only
one creature at a time.

Explosive Bolt (Recharge 5–6). The oaken bolter launches an
explosive charge at a point within 120 feet. Each creature within
20 feet of that point must make a DC 15 Dexterity saving throw,
taking 17 (5d6) fire damage on a failed save, or half as much
damage on a successful one.

STONE DEFENDER
Medium construct, unaligned

Armor Class 16 (natural armor)
Hit Points 52 (7d8 + 21)
Speed 30 ft.

STR	DEX	CON	INT	WIS	CHA
19 (+4)	10 (+0)	17 (+3)	3 (−4)	10 (+0)	1 (−5)

Damage Immunities poison; bludgeoning, piercing, and
slashing from nonmagical attacks that aren't adamantine
Condition Immunities charmed, exhaustion, frightened,
paralyzed, petrified, poisoned
Senses darkvision 60 ft., passive Perception 10
Languages understands one language of its creator but can't
speak
Challenge 4 (1,100 XP)

False Appearance. While the stone defender remains motionless against an uneven earthen or stone surface, it is indistinguishable from that surface.

Magic Resistance. The stone defender has advantage on saving
throws against spells and other magical effects.

ACTIONS

Slam. Melee Weapon Attack: +6 to hit, reach 5 ft., one target.
Hit: 11 (2d6 + 4) bludgeoning damage, and if the target is Large
or smaller, it is knocked prone.

REACTIONS

Intercept Attack. In response to another creature within 5 feet
of it being hit by an attack roll, the stone defender gives that
creature a +5 bonus to its AC against that attack, potentially
causing a miss. To use this ability, the stone defender must be
able to see the creature and the attacker.

Corpse-flower seedlings are quite useful for various purposes. Simply kill and bury a necromancer, and you should have a good crop in about a week.

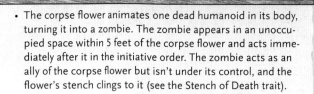

CORPSE FLOWER

A corpse flower can sprout atop the grave of an evil necromancer or the remains of power-ful undead. Unless it is uprooted and burned while it is still a seedling, the corpse flower grows to enormous size over several weeks, then tears itself free of the earth and begins scavenging humanoid corpses from battle-fields and graveyards. Using its fibrous ten-tacles, it stuffs the remains into its body and feeds on carrion to repair itself. The plant has a malevolent bent and despises the living.

Horrible Odor. With or without humanoid corpses nested in its body, a corpse flower exudes a stench of decay that can overwhelm the senses of nearby creatures, causing them to become nauseated. The stench, which serves as a defense mechanism, fades 2d4 days after the corpse flower dies.

CORPSE FLOWER
Large plant, chaotic evil

Armor Class 12
Hit Points 127 (15d10 + 45)
Speed 20 ft., climb 20 ft.

STR	DEX	CON	INT	WIS	CHA
14 (+2)	14 (+2)	16 (+3)	7 (–2)	15 (+2)	3 (–4)

Condition Immunities blinded, deafened
Senses blindsight 120 ft. (blind beyond this radius), passive Perception 12
Languages —
Challenge 8 (3,900 XP)

Corpses. When first encountered, a corpse flower contains the corpses of 1d6 + 3 humanoids. A corpse flower can hold the remains of up to nine dead humanoids. These remains have total cover against attacks and other effects outside the corpse flower. If the corpse flower dies, the corpses within it can be pulled free.

While it has at least one humanoid corpse in its body, the corpse flower can use a bonus action to do one of the following:

- The corpse flower digests one humanoid corpse in its body and instantly regains 11 (2d10) hit points. Nothing of the digested body remains. Any equipment on the corpse is ex-pelled from the corpse flower in its space.

- The corpse flower animates one dead humanoid in its body, turning it into a zombie. The zombie appears in an unoccu-pied space within 5 feet of the corpse flower and acts imme-diately after it in the initiative order. The zombie acts as an ally of the corpse flower but isn't under its control, and the flower's stench clings to it (see the Stench of Death trait).

Spider Climb. The corpse flower can climb difficult surfaces, including upside down on ceilings, without needing to make an ability check.

Stench of Death. Each creature that starts its turn within 10 feet of the corpse flower or one of its zombies must make a DC 14 Constitution saving throw, unless the creature is a construct or undead. On a failed save, the creature is incapacitated until the end of the turn. Creatures that are immune to poison damage or the poisoned condition automatically succeed on this saving throw. On a successful save, the creature is immune to the stench of all corpse flowers for 24 hours.

ACTIONS

Multiattack. The corpse flower makes three tentacle attacks.

Tentacle. *Melee Weapon Attack:* +5 to hit, reach 10 ft., one tar-get. *Hit:* 9 (2d6 + 2) bludgeoning damage, and the target must succeed on a DC 14 Constitution saving throw or take 14 (4d6) poison damage.

Harvest the Dead. The corpse flower grabs one unsecured dead humanoid within 10 feet of it and stuffs the corpse into itself, along with any equipment the corpse is wearing or carry-ing. The remains can be used with the Corpses trait.

DEATHLOCK

The forging of a pact between a warlock and a patron is no minor occasion—at least not for the warlock. The consequences of breaking that pact can be dire and, in some cases, lethal. A warlock who fails to live up to a bargain with an evil patron runs the risk of rising from the dead as a deathlock, a foul undead driven to serve its otherworldly patron from beyond the grave.

An extraordinarily powerful necromancer might also discover the dark methods of creating a deathlock and then bind it to service, acting in this respect as the deathlock's patron.

Obedient and Obsessed. An overpowering urge to serve consumes the mind of a newly awakened death-lock. All goals and ambitions it had in life that don't please its patron fall away as its master's desires become the purpose that drives the deathlock. The creature immediately resumes work on its patron's behalf. Accomplishing a difficult goal might mean the deathlock is forced to serve another powerful creature or might entail in gathering servants of its own.

Whatever the goal, it always reflects the patron's interests, ranging from small-scale concerns to matters of cosmic scope. A deathlock in the thrall of a fiend might work to destroy a specific temple dedicated to a good god, while one that serves a Great Old One could be charged with hunting for the materials needed to call forth a horrifying entity into the world.

Undead Nature. A deathlock doesn't require air, food, drink, or sleep.

PATRON-SPECIFIC SPELLS

You can customize a deathlock by replacing some or all of the spells in its Spellcasting trait with spells specific to its patron. Here are examples.

Deathlock

Archfey patron: *blink, faerie fire, hunger of Hadar, hypnotic pattern, phantasmal force, sleep*

Fiend patron: *blindness/deafness, burning hands, command, fireball, hellish rebuke, scorching ray*

Great Old One patron: *armor of Agathys, detect thoughts, dissonant whispers, hunger of Hadar, Tasha's hideous laughter, phantasmal force*

Deathlock Mastermind

Archfey patron: *blink, dominate beast, dominate person, faerie fire, greater invisibility, hunger of Hadar, hypnotic pattern, phantasmal force, seeming, sleep*

Fiend patron: *blindness/deafness, burning hands, command, fire shield, fireball, flame strike, hellish rebuke, scorching ray, stinking cloud, wall of fire*

Great Old One patron: *clairvoyance, detect thoughts, dissonant whispers, dominate person, Evard's black tentacles, hunger of Hadar, phantasmal force, sending, Tasha's hideous laughter, telekinesis*

DEATHLOCK
Medium undead, neutral evil

Armor Class 12 (15 with *mage armor*)
Hit Points 36 (8d8)
Speed 30 ft.

STR	DEX	CON	INT	WIS	CHA
11 (+0)	15 (+2)	10 (+0)	14 (+2)	12 (+1)	16 (+3)

Saving Throws Int +4, Cha +5
Skills Arcana +4, History +4
Damage Resistances necrotic; bludgeoning, piercing, and slashing from nonmagical attacks that aren't silvered
Damage Immunities poison
Condition Immunities exhaustion, poisoned
Senses darkvision 60 ft., passive Perception 11
Languages the languages it knew in life
Challenge 4 (1,100 XP)

Innate Spellcasting. The deathlock's innate spellcasting ability is Charisma (spell save DC 13). It can innately cast the following spells, requiring no material components:

At will: *detect magic, disguise self, mage armor*

Spellcasting. The deathlock is a 5th-level spellcaster. Its spellcasting ability is Charisma (spell save DC 13, +5 to hit with spell attacks). It regains its expended spell slots when it finishes a short or long rest. It knows the following warlock spells:

Cantrips (at will): *chill touch, eldritch blast, mage hand*
1st–3rd level (2 3rd-level slots): *arms of Hadar, dispel magic, hold person, hunger of Hadar, invisibility, spider climb*

Turn Resistance. The deathlock has advantage on saving throws against any effect that turns undead.

ACTIONS

Deathly Claw. *Melee Weapon Attack:* +4 to hit, reach 5 ft., one target. *Hit:* 9 (2d6 + 2) necrotic damage.

DEATHLOCK MASTERMIND

Though deathlocks exist to serve their patrons, they retain some freedom when it comes to devising particular tactics and carrying out their plans. Powerful deathlocks recruit lesser creatures to help them carry out their missions and, in this capacity, become the masterminds behind vast conspiracies and intrigues that culminate in the accomplishment of great acts of evil.

DEATHLOCK MASTERMIND
Medium undead, neutral evil

Armor Class 13 (16 with *mage armor*)
Hit Points 110 (20d8 + 20)
Speed 30 ft.

STR	DEX	CON	INT	WIS	CHA
11 (+0)	16 (+3)	12 (+1)	15 (+2)	12 (+1)	17 (+3)

Saving Throws Int +5, Cha +6
Skills Arcana +5, History +5, Perception +4
Damage Resistances necrotic; bludgeoning, piercing, and slashing from nonmagical attacks that aren't silvered
Damage Immunities poison
Condition Immunities exhaustion, poisoned
Senses darkvision 120 ft. (including magical darkness), passive Perception 14
Languages the languages it knew in life
Challenge 8 (3,900 XP)

Innate Spellcasting. The deathlock's innate spellcasting ability is Charisma (spell save DC 14). It can innately cast the following spells, requiring no material components:

At will: *detect magic, disguise self, mage armor*

Spellcasting. The deathlock is a 10th-level spellcaster. Its spellcasting ability is Charisma (spell save DC 14, +6 to hit with spell attacks). It regains its expended spell slots when it finishes a short or long rest. It knows the following warlock spells:

Cantrips (at will): *chill touch, mage hand, minor illusion, poison spray*
1st–5th level (2 5th-level slots): *arms of Hadar, blight, counterspell, crown of madness, darkness, dimension door, dispel magic, fly, hold monster, invisibility*

Turn Resistance. The deathlock has advantage on saving throws against any effect that turns undead.

ACTIONS

Deathly Claw. *Melee Weapon Attack:* +6 to hit, reach 5 ft., one target. *Hit:* 13 (3d6 + 3 necrotic damage).

Grave Bolts. *Ranged Spell Attack:* +6 to hit, range 120 ft., one or two targets. *Hit:* 18 (4d8) necrotic damage. If the target is Large or smaller, it must succeed on a DC 16 Strength saving throw or become restrained as shadowy tendrils wrap around it for 1 minute. A restrained target can use its action to repeat the saving throw, ending the effect on itself on a success.

DEATHLOCK WIGHT

Bereft of much of its magic, a deathlock wight lingers between the warlock it was and the deathly existence of a wight—a special punishment meted out by certain patrons and necromancers.

DEATHLOCK WIGHT
Medium undead, neutral evil

Armor Class 12 (15 with *mage armor*)
Hit Points 37 (5d8 + 15)
Speed 30 ft.

STR	DEX	CON	INT	WIS	CHA
11 (+0)	14 (+2)	16 (+3)	12 (+1)	14 (+2)	16 (+3)

Saving Throws Wis +4
Skills Arcana +3, Perception +4
Damage Resistances necrotic; bludgeoning, piercing, and slashing from nonmagical attacks
Damage Immunities poison
Condition Immunities exhaustion, poisoned
Senses darkvision 60 ft., passive Perception 14
Languages the languages it knew in life
Challenge 3 (700 XP)

Innate Spellcasting. The wight's innate spellcasting ability is Charisma (spell save DC 13). It can innately cast the following spells, requiring no verbal or material components:

At will: *detect magic, disguise self, mage armor*
1/day each: *fear, hold person, misty step*

Sunlight Sensitivity. While in sunlight, the wight has disadvantage on attack rolls, as well as on Wisdom (Perception) checks that rely on sight.

ACTIONS

Multiattack. The wight attacks twice with Grave Bolt.

Grave Bolt. *Ranged Spell Attack:* +5 to hit, range 120 ft., one target. *Hit:* 7 (1d8 + 3) necrotic damage.

Life Drain. *Melee Weapon Attack:* +4 to hit, reach 5 ft., one creature. *Hit:* 9 (2d6 + 2) necrotic damage. The target must succeed on a DC 13 Constitution saving throw or its hit point maximum is reduced by an amount equal to the damage taken. This reduction lasts until the target finishes a long rest. The target dies if this effect reduces its hit point maximum to 0.

A humanoid slain by this attack rises 24 hours later as a zombie under the wight's control, unless the humanoid is restored to life or its body is destroyed. The wight can have no more than twelve zombies under its control at one time.

D

DEMONS

Incarnations of chaos and evil, demons display endless variation in appearance and in how they go about wreaking havoc across the multiverse.

ALKILITH

An alkilith is easily mistaken for some kind of foul fungal growth that appears on doorways, windows, and other portals. These dripping infestations conceal the demonic nature of the alkilith, making what should be a dire warning appear strange but otherwise innocuous. Wherever alkiliths take root, they weaken the fabric of reality, creating a portal through which even nastier demons can invade.

Symptoms of Doom. The appearance of an alkilith in the world heralds a great wrongness and an imminent catastrophe. An alkilith searches for an aperture such as a window or a door around which it can take root, stretching its body around the opening and anchoring itself with a sticky secretion. If left undisturbed, the opening becomes attuned to the Abyss and eventually becomes a portal to that plane (see "Planar Portals" in chapter 2 of the *Dungeon Master's Guide*).

Spawn of Juiblex. Alkiliths spring from the cast-off bits of Juiblex's hideous, shuddering body, then gradually become self-aware and set out to find their way onto the Material Plane. Since most cultists consider them too risky for summoning—they can, after all, create portals to the Abyss—alkiliths must find other escape routes out of their native plane.

ALKILITH
Medium fiend (demon), chaotic evil

Armor Class 17 (natural armor)
Hit Points 157 (15d8 + 90)
Speed 40 ft.

STR	DEX	CON	INT	WIS	CHA
12 (+1)	19 (+4)	22 (+6)	6 (–2)	11 (+0)	7 (–2)

Saving Throws Dex +8, Con +10
Skills Stealth +8
Damage Resistances acid, cold, fire, lightning; bludgeoning, piercing, and slashing from nonmagical attacks
Damage Immunities poison
Condition Immunities charmed, frightened, poisoned
Senses darkvision 120 ft., passive Perception 10
Languages understands Abyssal but can't speak
Challenge 11 (7,200 XP)

Amorphous. The alkilith can move through a space as narrow as 1 inch wide without squeezing.

False Appearance. While the alkilith is motionless, it is indistinguishable from an ordinary slime or fungus.

Foment Madness. Any creature that isn't a demon that starts its turn within 30 feet of the alkilith must succeed on a DC 18 Wisdom saving throw, or it hears a faint buzzing in its head for a moment and has disadvantage on its next attack roll, saving throw, or ability check.

If the saving throw against Foment Madness fails by 5 or more, the creature is instead subjected to the *confusion* spell for 1 minute (no concentration required by the alkilith). While under the effect of that *confusion*, the creature is immune to Foment Madness.

Magic Resistance. The alkilith has advantage on saving throws against spells and other magical effects.

ACTIONS

Multiattack. The alkilith makes three tentacle attacks.

Tentacle. *Melee Weapon Attack:* +8 to hit, reach 15 ft., one target. *Hit:* 18 (4d6 + 4) acid damage.

ARMANITE

Great herds of armanites race across the blasted fields of the Abyss, bent on slaughter and death, driven by unrestrained bloodlust. Whether being controlled by more powerful demons or charging into battle for the sake of it, armanites use their claws, hooves, and long, whiplike tails to tear apart their foes.

Live for War. In the armies of the demon lords, armanites perform the role of heavy cavalry, leading the charge and tearing into their enemies' flanks. Armanites fight all the time, even among themselves if they can't find another enemy. They make ideal shock troops, courageous to the point of stupidity and utterly savage.

Walking Arsenal. Part of what makes armanites so fearsome is the number of weapons they have at their disposal. They possess sharp hooves, claws that end in

Armanite

Large fiend (demon), chaotic evil

Armor Class 16 (natural armor)
Hit Points 84 (8d10 + 40)
Speed 60 ft.

STR	DEX	CON	INT	WIS	CHA
21 (+5)	18 (+4)	21 (+5)	8 (−1)	12 (+1)	13 (+1)

Damage Resistances cold, fire, lightning
Damage Immunities poison
Condition Immunities poisoned
Senses darkvision 120 ft., passive Perception 11
Languages Abyssal, telepathy 120 ft.
Challenge 7 (2,900 XP)

Magic Resistance. The armanite has advantage on saving throws against spells and other magical effects.

Magic Weapons. The armanite's weapon attacks are magical.

Actions

Multiattack. The armanite makes three attacks: one with its hooves, one with its claws, and one with its serrated tail.

Hooves. *Melee Weapon Attack:* +8 to hit, reach 5 ft., one target. *Hit:* 12 (2d6 + 5) bludgeoning damage.

Claws. *Melee Weapon Attack:* +8 to hit, reach 5 ft., one target. *Hit:* 10 (2d4 + 5) slashing damage.

Serrated Tail. *Melee Weapon Attack:* +8 to hit, reach 10 ft., one target. *Hit:* 16 (2d10 + 5) slashing damage.

Lightning Lance (Recharge 5–6). The armanite looses a bolt of lightning in a line 60 feet long and 10 feet wide. Each creature in the line must make a DC 15 Dexterity saving throw, taking 27 (6d8) lightning damage on a failed save, or half as much damage on a successful one.

Bulezau

Medium fiend (demon), chaotic evil

Armor Class 14 (natural armor)
Hit Points 52 (7d8 + 21)
Speed 40 ft.

STR	DEX	CON	INT	WIS	CHA
15 (+2)	14 (+2)	17 (+3)	8 (−1)	9 (−1)	6 (−2)

Damage Resistances cold, fire, lightning
Damage Immunities poison
Condition Immunities charmed, frightened, poisoned
Senses darkvision 120 ft., passive Perception 9
Languages Abyssal, telepathy 60 ft.
Challenge 3 (700 XP)

Rotting Presence. When any creature that isn't a demon starts its turn within 30 feet one or more bulezaus, that creature must succeed on a DC 13 Constitution saving throw or take 1d6 necrotic damage plus 1 necrotic damage for each bulezau within 30 feet of it.

Standing Leap. The bulezau's long jump is up to 20 feet and its high jump is up to 10 feet, with or without a running start.

Sure-Footed. The bulezau has advantage on Strength and Dexterity saving throws made against effects that would knock it prone.

Actions

Barbed Tail. *Melee Weapon Attack:* +4 to hit, reach 5 ft., one target. *Hit:* 8 (1d12 + 2) piercing damage. If the target is a creature, it must succeed on a DC 13 Constitution saving throw against disease or become poisoned until the disease ends. While poisoned in this way, the target sports festering boils, coughs up flies, and sheds rotting skin, and the target must repeat the saving throw after every 24 hours that elapse. On a successful save, the disease ends. On a failed save, the target's hit point maximum is reduced by 4 (1d8). The target dies if its hit point maximum is reduced to 0.

D

curling talons, and long, serrated tails that can flense the flesh from a victim, and they use them all to carve through their foes. When they are up against tough formations, they can call on their innate magic to loose bolts of lightning and blow holes in the enemy ranks.

BULEZAU

Diseased manifestations of animalistic rage, bulezaus embody the violence of nature. Across the Abyss, bulezaus lurk in deep canyons and lofty crags, and many find a place in the ranks of the demon lords' armies, serving as foot soldiers in the Abyss's endless warring.

Bloodlust. Bulezaus crave violence. Their eagerness to kill and willingness to die make them common members of any demon lord's entourage. When not being corralled by larger and tougher demons, bulezaus gather into scrabbling mobs, wrestling and fighting among themselves until a better target comes along or until a stronger demon bullies them into subservience.

Repulsive. Disfiguring ailments plague bulezaus: crusted eyes, maggots wriggling in open sores, and a reek of rotten meat that follows them wherever they go.

DYBBUK

Dybbuks terrorize mortals on the Material Plane by possessing corpses and giving them a semblance of life, after which the demons use them to engage in a range of sordid activities.

Puppet Masters. In their natural form, dybbuks appear as translucent flying jellyfish, trailing long tendrils as they move through the air. They rarely travel in this fashion, however. Instead, a dybbuk possesses the first suitable corpse it finds, rousing the body from death so it can then indulge its hideous vices.

Dark Masquerade. By plundering a corpse's memories and accessing its capabilities, a dybbuk can impersonate the creature as it was in life. But the truth of the matter quickly becomes apparent to those around it, because a dybbuk can't resist pursuing its vices with a maniacal single-mindedness that betrays its true nature. Dybbuks delight in terrorizing other creatures by making their host bodies behave in horrifying ways—throwing up gouts of blood, excreting piles of squirming maggots, and contorting their limbs in impossible ways as they scuttle across the ground.

DYBBUK

Medium fiend (demon), chaotic evil

Armor Class 14
Hit Points 37 (5d8 + 15)
Speed 0 ft., 40 ft. (hover)

STR	DEX	CON	INT	WIS	CHA
6 (−2)	19 (+4)	16 (+3)	16 (+3)	15 (+2)	14 (+2)

Skills Deception +6, Intimidation +4, Perception +4
Damage Resistances acid, cold, fire, lightning, thunder; bludgeoning, piercing, and slashing from nonmagical attacks
Damage Immunities poison
Condition Immunities charmed, exhaustion, frightened, grappled, paralyzed, petrified, poisoned, prone, restrained
Senses darkvision 120 ft., passive Perception 14
Languages Abyssal, Common, telepathy 120 ft.
Challenge 4 (1,100 XP)

Incorporeal Movement. The dybbuk can move through other creatures and objects as if they were difficult terrain. It takes 5 (1d10) force damage if it ends its turn inside an object.

Innate Spellcasting. The dybbuk's innate spellcasting ability is Charisma (spell save DC 12). It can innately cast the following spells, requiring no material components:

At will: *dimension door*
3/day each: *fear, phantasmal force*

Magic Resistance. The dybbuk has advantage on saving throws against spells and other magical effects.

Violate Corpse. The dybbuk can use a bonus action while it is possessing a corpse to make it do something unnatural, such as vomit blood, twist its head all the way around, or cause a quadruped to move as a biped. Any beast or humanoid that sees this behavior must succeed on a DC 12 Wisdom saving throw or become frightened of the dybbuk for 1 minute. The frightened creature can repeat the saving throw at the end of each of its turns, ending the effect on itself on a success. A creature that succeeds on a saving throw against this ability is immune to Violate Corpse for 24 hours.

ACTION

Tendril. *Melee Weapon Attack:* +6 to hit, reach 5 ft., one target. *Hit:* 13 (2d8 + 4) necrotic damage. If the target is a creature, its hit point maximum is also reduced by 3 (1d6). This reduction lasts until the target finishes a short or long rest. The target dies if this effect reduces its hit point maximum to 0.

Possess Corpse (Recharge 6). The dybbuk disappears into an intact corpse it can see within 5 feet of it. The corpse must be Large or smaller and be that of a beast or a humanoid. The dybbuk is now effectively the possessed creature. Its type becomes undead, though it now looks alive, and it gains a number of temporary hit points equal to the corpse's hit point maximum in life.

While possessing the corpse, the dybbuk retains its hit points, alignment, Intelligence, Wisdom, Charisma, telepathy, and immunity to poison damage, exhaustion, and being charmed and frightened. It otherwise uses the possessed target's game statistics, gaining access to its knowledge and proficiencies but not its class features, if any.

The possession lasts until the temporary hit points are lost (at which point the body becomes a corpse once more) or the dybbuk ends its possession using a bonus action. When the possession ends, the dybbuk reappears in an unoccupied space within 5 feet of the corpse.

DYBBUK

MAUREZHI

MAUREZHI

When Doresain, the King of Ghouls, corrupted a society of elves, he created a new breed of demons to lead packs of ghouls and ghasts in the material world.

Horrid Infiltrators. When a maurezhi consumes the corpse of a humanoid it has slain—a process that takes about 10 minutes—it instantly assumes the creature's appearance as it was in life. The new appearance begins to rot away over the next few days, eventually revealing the demon's original form.

A Plague of Ghouls. Maurezhi are contagion incarnate. Their bite attacks can drain a victim's sense of self. If this affliction is allowed to go far enough, the victim is infected with an unholy hunger for flesh that overpowers their personality and transforms them into a ghoul.

MAUREZHI

Medium fiend (demon), chaotic evil

Armor Class 15 (natural armor)
Hit Points 88 (16d8 + 16)
Speed 30 ft.

STR	DEX	CON	INT	WIS	CHA
14 (+2)	17 (+3)	12 (+1)	11 (+0)	12 (+1)	15 (+2)

Skills Deception +5
Damage Resistances cold, fire, lightning, necrotic; bludgeoning, piercing, and slashing from nonmagical attacks
Damage Immunities poison
Condition Immunities charmed, exhaustion, poisoned
Senses darkvision 120 ft., passive Perception 11
Languages Abyssal, Elvish, telepathy 120 ft.
Challenge 7 (2,900 XP)

Assume Form. The maurezhi can assume the appearance of any Medium humanoid it has eaten. It remains in this form for 1d6 days, during which time the form gradually decays until, when the effect ends, the form sloughs from the demon's body.

Magic Resistance. The maurezhi has advantage on saving throws against spells and other magical effects.

ACTIONS

Multiattack. The maurezhi makes two attacks: one with its bite and one with its claws.

Bite. *Melee Weapon Attack:* +6 to hit, reach 5 ft., one target. *Hit:* 14 (2d10 + 3) piercing damage. If the target is a humanoid, its Charisma score is reduced by 1d4. This reduction lasts until the target finishes a short or long rest. The target dies if this reduces its Charisma to 0. It rises 24 hours later as a ghoul, unless it has been revived or its corpse has been destroyed.

Claws. *Melee Weapon Attack:* +6 to hit, reach 5 ft., one target. *Hit:* 12 (2d8 + 3) slashing damage. If the target is a creature other than an undead, it must succeed on a DC 12 Constitution saving throw or be paralyzed for 1 minute. The target can repeat the saving throw at the end of each of its turns, ending the effect on itself on a success.

Raise Ghoul (Recharge 5–6). The maurezhi targets one dead ghoul or ghast it can see within 30 feet of it. The target is revived with all its hit points.

D

MOLYDEUS

The most ruthless and dangerous of demons—more feared than the dreaded balor—the molydeus speaks with the authority of the demon lord it serves as it enforces its master's will. Standing some 12 feet tall, a molydeus has a red-skinned, humanoid body and two heads—one that of a slavering wolf and the other that of a serpent with dripping fangs perched atop a long neck. Molydei might guard their masters' possessions, roam the battlefields of the Abyss to ensure the loyalty of troops, or bring swift death to their enemies.

Branded and Bound. When a demon earns the attention of a demon lord through ferocity, cunning, or an act of surprising devotion, the demon lord might reward such service by snatching up the fiend and subjecting it to excruciating torments to remake it into a molydeus.

Voice of the Master. A demon lord has a direct link to its molydeus and uses the serpent head to communicate its wishes. A molydeus is, therefore, said to utter its master's will, commanding other demons to carry out orders and using violence to ensure they obey. A molydeus must constantly be ready for the scrutiny of its master, for the demon lord can decide at any moment to observe the molydeus through the serpent. Thus, there is no room for treachery in a molydeus.

> ## VARIANT: DEMON SUMMONING
>
> You can give a molydeus the ability to summon other demons.
>
> ***Summon Demon (1/Day).*** As an action, the molydeus has a 50 percent chance of summoning its choice of 1d6 babaus, 1d4 chasmes, or one marilith. A summoned demon appears in an unoccupied space within 60 feet of the molydeus, acts as an ally of the molydeus, and can't summon other demons. It remains for 1 minute, until it or the molydeus dies, or until the molydeus dismisses it as an action.

Special Weapon. As part of a demon lord's trust in its molydeus, it bestows a powerful weapon upon the guardian demon. The demon lord fashions the weapon from a portion of the fiend's essence, so that the demon and its weapon are forever bound. If the molydeus dies, the weapon dissolves into a pool of foul-smelling slime. It's possible to steal such a weapon, but a molydeus deprived of its weapon will stop at nothing to regain it.

The weapon a molydeus wields reflects the nature of its master. Those that serve Baphomet carry a glaive; Demogorgon, a whip; Fraz-Urb'luu, a battleaxe; Graz'zt, a greatsword; Orcus, a morningstar; and Yeenoghu, a flail. The weapon's form doesn't affect its capabilities.

MOLYDEUS

Huge fiend (demon), chaotic evil

Armor Class 19 (natural armor)
Hit Points 216 (16d12 + 112)
Speed 40 ft.

STR	DEX	CON	INT	WIS	CHA
28 (+9)	22 (+6)	25 (+7)	21 (+5)	24 (+7)	24 (+7)

Saving Throws Str +16, Con +14, Wis +14, Cha +14
Skills Perception +21
Damage Resistances cold, fire, lightning; bludgeoning, piercing, and slashing from nonmagical attacks
Damage Immunities poison
Condition Immunities blinded, charmed, deafened, frightened, poisoned, stunned
Senses truesight 120 ft., passive Perception 31
Languages Abyssal, telepathy 120 ft.
Challenge 21 (33,000 XP)

Innate Spellcasting. The molydeus's innate spellcasting ability is Charisma (spell save DC 22). It can innately cast the following spells, requiring no material components:

At will: *dispel magic, polymorph, telekinesis, teleport*
3/day: *lightning bolt*
1/day: *imprisonment*

Legendary Resistance (3/Day). If the molydeus fails a saving throw, it can choose to succeed instead.

Magic Resistance. The molydeus has advantage on saving throws against spells and other magical effects.

Magic Weapons. The molydeus's weapon attacks are magical.

ACTIONS

Multiattack. The molydeus makes three attacks: one with its weapon, one with its wolf bite, and one with its snakebite.

Demonic Weapon. *Melee Weapon Attack:* +16 to hit, reach 15 ft., one target. *Hit:* 20 (2d10 + 9) slashing damage. If the target has at least one head and the molydeus rolled a 20 on the attack roll, the target is decapitated and dies if it can't survive without that head. A target is immune to this effect if it takes none of the damage, has legendary actions, or is Huge or larger. Such a creature takes an extra 6d8 slashing damage from the hit.

Wolf Bite. *Melee Weapon Attack:* +16 to hit, reach 10 ft., one target. *Hit:* 16 (2d6 + 9) piercing damage.

Snakebite. *Melee Weapon Attack:* +16 to hit, reach 15 ft., one creature. *Hit:* 12 (1d6 + 9) piercing damage, and the target must succeed on a DC 22 Constitution saving throw or its hit point maximum is reduced by an amount equal to the damage taken. This reduction lasts until the target finishes a long rest. The target transforms into a manes if this reduces its hit point maximum to 0. This transformation can be ended only by a *wish* spell.

LEGENDARY ACTIONS

The molydeus can take 3 legendary actions, choosing from the options below. Only one legendary action option can be used at a time and only at the end of another creature's turn. The molydeus regains spent legendary actions at the start of its turn.

Attack. The molydeus makes one attack, either with its demonic weapon or with its snakebite.
Move. The molydeus moves without provoking opportunity attacks.
Cast a Spell. The molydeus casts one spell from its Innate Spellcasting trait.

Dark Guardians. One of the chief tasks of any molydeus is to help protect its master's amulet—the most prized possession of any demon lord. Each of these dangerous relics allows a demon lord to return to life in the Abyss if the unthinkable occurs and its abyssal form is destroyed. As useful as these amulets are, they are also liabilities—because, armed with an amulet, a creature can coerce the demon lord to which it belongs into doing its bidding, or can strand it in the Abyss if the amulet is destroyed.

Nabassu

The insatiable nabassus prowl the multiverse in search of souls to devour. If they think they can kill a creature and consume its soul, they attack—even if that other creature is a demon, including another nabassu.

Hated Outcasts. Demons have few rules, and the murder of other demons hardly raises an eyebrow among these fiends. The act of devouring souls is something else. For this reason, most demons shun nabassus and force them to live on the fringes of the Abyss. There, nabassus pick off weaker demons or, if the situation warrants, gather in packs to take down larger prey. Some especially powerful nabassus even search for demon lords' amulets.

Demonic Infiltrators. Whenever magic pulls demons from the Abyss to the Material Plane, nabassus try to get summoned so that they can embark on a feast of souls there. If a nabassu is summoned, it tries to break free so that it can devour the soul of its summoner and then set out to feed on the souls of whatever creatures it can catch. One way a summoner can avoid this fate is by

Nabassu

Medium fiend (demon), chaotic evil

Armor Class 18 (natural armor)
Hit Points 190 (20d8 + 100)
Speed 40 ft., fly 60 ft.

STR	DEX	CON	INT	WIS	CHA
22 (+6)	14 (+2)	21 (+5)	14 (+2)	15 (+2)	17 (+3)

Saving Throws Str +11, Dex +7
Skills Perception +7
Damage Resistances cold, fire, lightning; bludgeoning, piercing, and slashing from nonmagical attacks
Damage Immunities poison
Condition Immunities poisoned
Senses darkvision 60 ft., passive Perception 17
Languages Abyssal, telepathy 120 ft.
Challenge 15 (13,000 XP)

Demonic Shadows. The nabassu darkens the area around its body in a 10-foot radius. Nonmagical light can't illuminate this area of dim light.

Devour Soul. A nabassu can eat the soul of a creature it has killed within the last hour, provided that creature is neither a construct nor an undead. The devouring requires the nabassu to be within 5 feet of the corpse for at least 10 minutes, after which it gains a number of Hit Dice (d8s) equal to half the

creature's number of Hit Dice. Roll those dice, and increase the nabassu's hit points by the numbers rolled. For every 4 Hit Dice the nabassu gains in this way, its attacks deal an extra 3 (1d6) damage on a hit. The nabassu retains these benefits for 6 days. A creature devoured by a nabassu can be restored to life only by a *wish* spell.

Magic Resistance. The nabassu has advantage on saving throws against spells and other magical effects.

Magic Weapons. The nabassu's weapon attacks are magical.

Actions

Multiattack. The nabassu uses its Soul-Stealing Gaze and makes two attacks: one with its claws and one with its bite.

Claws. *Melee Weapon Attack:* +11 to hit, reach 5 ft., one target. *Hit:* 17 (2d10 + 6) slashing damage.

Bite. *Melee Weapon Attack:* +11 to hit, reach 5 ft., one target. *Hit:* 32 (4d12 + 6) piercing damage.

Soul-Stealing Gaze. The nabassu targets one creature it can see within 30 feet of it. If the target can see the nabassu and isn't a construct or an undead, it must succeed on a DC 16 Charisma saving throw or reduce its hit point maximum by 13 (2d12) and give the nabassu an equal number of temporary hit points. This reduction lasts until the target finishes a short or long rest. The target dies if its hit point maximum is reduced to 0, and if the target is a humanoid, it immediately rises as a ghoul under the nabassu's control.

providing a steady supply of souls to the nabassu, which can cause the demon to be cooperative—for as long as the supply lasts.

RUTTERKIN

The rutterkins, a breed of warped demon, roam the Abyss in mobs that constantly search for intruders to surround and devour.

Abyssal Defenders. Rutterkins protect the Abyss from non-demons. When they spot any interlopers, they gather in a crowd and surge forward, emitting a wave of fear in advance of their attacks that leaves their victims terrified and rooted in place.

Warping Plague. Creatures bitten by rutterkins are exposed to a terrible disease that infects them with the corrupting influence of the Abyss. Victims that succumb to the disease experience tremendous pain as their bodies become disfigured, flesh twisting around the bones, until they transform to join the mass of abyssal wretches that follow in the wake of the rutterkin mob that laid them low.

RUTTERKIN
Medium fiend (demon), chaotic evil

Armor Class 12
Hit Points 37 (5d8 + 15)
Speed 20 ft.

STR	DEX	CON	INT	WIS	CHA
14 (+2)	15 (+2)	17 (+3)	5 (–3)	12 (+1)	6 (–2)

Damage Resistances cold, fire, lightning
Damage Immunities poison
Condition Immunities charmed, frightened, poisoned
Senses darkvision 120 ft., passive Perception 11
Languages understands Abyssal but can't speak
Challenge 2 (450 XP)

Crippling Fear. When a creature that isn't a demon starts its turn within 30 feet of three or more rutterkins, it must make a DC 11 Wisdom saving throw. The creature has disadvantage on the save if it's within 30 feet of six or more rutterkins. On a successful save, the creature is immune to the Crippling Fear of all rutterkins for 24 hours. On a failed save, the creature becomes frightened of the rutterkins for 1 minute. While frightened in this way, the creature is restrained. At the end of each of the frightened creature's turns, it can repeat the saving throw, ending the effect on itself on a success.

ACTIONS

Bite. *Melee Weapon Attack:* +4 to hit, reach 5 ft., one target. *Hit:* 12 (3d6 + 2) piercing damage. If the target is a creature, it must succeed on a DC 13 Constitution saving throw against disease or become poisoned. At the end of each long rest, the poisoned target can repeat the saving throw, ending the effect on itself on a success. If the target is reduced to 0 hit points while poisoned in this way, it dies and instantly transforms into a living abyssal wretch. The transformation of the body can be undone only by a *wish* spell.

ABYSSAL WRETCH
Medium fiend (demon), chaotic evil

Armor Class 11
Hit Points 18 (4d8)
Speed 20 ft.

STR	DEX	CON	INT	WIS	CHA
9 (–1)	12 (+1)	11 (+0)	5 (–3)	8 (–1)	5 (–3)

Damage Resistances cold, fire, lightning
Damage Immunities poison
Condition Immunities charmed, frightened, poisoned
Senses darkvision 120 ft., passive Perception 9
Languages understands Abyssal but can't speak
Challenge 1/4 (50 XP)

ACTIONS

Bite. *Melee Weapon Attack:* +3 to hit, reach 5 ft., one target. *Hit:* 5 (1d8 + 1) slashing damage.

Sibriex

Thought to be as old as the Abyss itself, sibriexes haunt remote parts of the plane, where they use their vile abilities to breed new horrors and apprehend forbidden lore. Rivulets of blood and bile cascade from a sibriex's body. Where these noxious fluids hit the ground, the landscape becomes polluted.

Sibriex
Huge fiend (demon), chaotic evil

Armor Class 19 (natural armor)
Hit Points 150 (12d12 + 72)
Speed 0 ft., fly 20 ft. (hover)

STR	DEX	CON	INT	WIS	CHA
10 (+0)	3 (−4)	23 (+6)	25 (+7)	24 (+7)	25 (+7)

Saving Throws Int +13, Cha +13
Skills Arcana +13, History +13, Perception +13
Damage Resistances cold, fire, lightning; bludgeoning, piercing, and slashing from nonmagical attacks
Damage Immunities poison
Condition Immunities poisoned
Senses truesight 120 ft., passive Perception 23
Languages all, telepathy 120 ft.
Challenge 18 (20,000 XP)

Contamination. The sibriex emits an aura of corruption 30 feet in every direction. Plants that aren't creatures wither in the aura, and the ground in it is difficult terrain for other creatures. Any creature that starts its turn in the aura must succeed on a DC 20 Constitution saving throw or take 14 (4d6) poison damage. A creature that succeeds on the save is immune to this sibriex's Contamination for 24 hours.

Innate Spellcasting. The sibriex's innate spellcasting ability is Charisma (spell save DC 21). It can innately cast the following spells, requiring no material components:

At will: *charm person*, *command*, *dispel magic*, *hold monster*
3/day: *feeblemind*

Legendary Resistance (3/Day). If the sibriex fails a saving throw, it can choose to succeed instead.

Magic Resistance. The sibriex has advantage on saving throws against spells and other magical effects.

Actions

Multiattack. The sibriex uses Squirt Bile once and makes three attacks using its chain, bite, or both.

Chain. *Melee Weapon Attack:* +6 to hit, reach 15 ft., one target. *Hit:* 20 (2d12 + 7) piercing damage.

Bite. *Melee Weapon Attack:* +6 to hit, reach 5 ft., one target. *Hit:* 9 (2d8) piercing damage plus 9 (2d8) acid damage.

Squirt Bile. The sibriex targets one creature it can see within 120 feet of it. The target must succeed on a DC 20 Dexterity saving throw or take 35 (10d6) acid damage.

Warp Creature. The sibriex targets up to three creatures it can see within 120 feet of it. Each target must make a DC 20 Constitution saving throw. On a successful save, a creature becomes immune to this sibriex's Warp Creature. On a failed save, the target is poisoned, which causes it to also gain 1 level of exhaustion. While poisoned in this way, the target must repeat the saving throw at the start of each of its turns. Three successful saves against the poison end it, and ending the poison removes any levels of exhaustion caused by it. Each failed save causes the target to suffer another level of exhaustion. Once the target reaches 6 levels of exhaustion, it dies and instantly transforms into a living abyssal wretch under the sibriex's control. The transformation of the body can be undone only by a *wish* spell.

Legendary Actions

The sibriex can take 3 legendary actions, choosing from the options below. Only one legendary action option can be used at a time and only at the end of another creature's turn. The sibriex regains spent legendary actions at the start of its turn.

Cast a Spell. The sibriex casts a spell.
Spray Bile. The sibriex uses Squirt Bile.
Warp (Costs 2 Actions). The sibriex uses Warp Creature.

Keepers of Forbidden Lore. Sibriexes have spent eons amassing information from across the planes, hoarding knowledge for when it might be useful. Such is their incredible intellect that many seek them out, including demon lords. Some sibriexes act as advisors and oracles, manipulating demons into serving their ends, while other sibriexes cling to their secrets, parceling out lore only when doing so would advance their plans.

Demon Crafters. Sibriexes can channel the power of the Abyss to create new demons from other creatures. Over the course of days, they can create vast numbers of rutterkins to protect their lands and to ensure that the plane teems with destructive monsters. Some demons petition sibriexes for physical gifts, and if they are moved to do so, sibriexes can graft on new body parts to give the demons greater strength, vision, or stamina. Sibriexes never give aid freely; they demand a service or a treasure in return for the flesh-shaping they provide.

VARIANT: FLESH WARPING

Creatures that encounter a sibriex can be twisted beyond recognition. Whenever a creature fails a saving throw against the sibriex's Warp Creature effect, you can roll percentile dice and consult the Flesh Warping table to determine an additional effect, which vanishes when Warp Creature ends on the creature. If the creature transforms into an abyssal wretch, the effect becomes a permanent feature of that body.

A creature can willingly submit to flesh warping, an agonizing process that takes at least 1 hour while the creature stays within 30 feet of the sibriex. At the end of the process, roll once on the table (or choose one effect) to determine how the creature is transformed permanently.

FLESH WARPING

d100	Effect
01–05	The color of the target's hair, eyes, and skin becomes blue, red, yellow, or patterned.
06–10	The target's eyes push out of its head at the end of stalks.
11–15	The target's hands grow claws, which can be used as daggers.
16–20	One of the target's legs grows longer than the other, reducing its walking speed by 10 feet.
21–25	The target's eyes become beacons, filling a 15-foot cone with dim light when they are open.
26–30	A pair of wings, either feathered or leathery, sprout from the target's back, granting it a flying speed of 30 feet.
31–35	The target's ears tear free from its head and scurry away; the target is deafened.
36–40	Two of the target's teeth turn into tusks.
41–45	The target's skin becomes scabby, granting it a +1 bonus to AC but reducing its Charisma by 2 (to a minimum of 1).
46–50	The target's arms and legs switch places, preventing the target from moving unless it crawls.
51–55	The target's arms become tentacles with fingers on the ends, increasing its reach by 5 feet.
56–60	The target's legs grow incredibly long and springy, increasing its walking speed by 10 feet.
61–65	The target grows a whiplike tail, which it can use as a whip.
66–70	The target's eyes turn black, and it gains darkvision out to a range of 120 feet.
71–75	The target swells, tripling its weight.
76–80	The target becomes thin and skeletal, halving its weight.
81–85	The target's head doubles in size.
86–90	The target's ears become wings, giving it a flying speed of 5 feet.
91–95	The target's body becomes unusually brittle, causing the target to have vulnerability to bludgeoning, piercing, and slashing damage.
96–00	The target grows another head, causing it to have advantage on saving throws against being charmed, frightened, or stunned.

No creature embodies the chaotic nature of the Abyss so well as the sibriex. Although the realm of the demons is already a place of infinite horrors, sibriexes for some reason make even more of these monstrosities.

The corruption left behind when a wastrilith visits the world can persist for decades. If left unchecked, it can become a bridge to the Abyss.

WASTRILITH

Found in the waters of the Abyss and other bodies of water contaminated by the plane's fell influence, wastriliths establish themselves as lords of the deep and rule their dominions with cruelty.

Despoilers. A wastrilith contaminates the waters around it. Its noxious presence even affects nearby sources of water when the demon travels on land. The corrupted water, which contains a measure of the demon's essence, responds to its commands—perhaps hardening to prevent foes from escaping, or erupting in a surge that drags would-be victims into its reach.

Silent Corrupters. Creatures that ingest water that has been corrupted by a wastrilith risk their very souls. Those who drink the poisonous liquid might wither away until they finally die, or remain alive only to become a thrall of chaos and evil. To represent this defilement, you can use the optional rule on abyssal corruption in chapter 2 of the *Dungeon Master's Guide*, causing the poisoned creature to be corrupted.

WASTRILITH
Large fiend (demon), chaotic evil

Armor Class 18 (natural armor)
Hit Points 157 (15d10 + 75)
Speed 30 ft., swim 80 ft.

STR	DEX	CON	INT	WIS	CHA
19 (+4)	18 (+4)	21 (+5)	19 (+4)	12 (+1)	14 (+2)

Saving Throws Str +9, Con +10
Damage Resistances cold, fire, lightning; bludgeoning, piercing, and slashing from nonmagical attacks
Damage Immunities poison
Condition Immunities poisoned
Senses darkvision 120 ft., passive Perception 11
Languages Abyssal, telepathy 120 ft.
Challenge 13 (10,000 XP)

Amphibious. The wastrilith can breathe air and water.

Corrupt Water. At the start of each of the wastrilith's turns, exposed water within 30 feet of it is befouled. Underwater, this effect lightly obscures the area until a current clears it away. Water in containers remains corrupted until it evaporates.

A creature that consumes this foul water or swims in it must make a DC 18 Constitution saving throw. On a successful save, the creature is immune to the foul water for 24 hours. On a failed save, the creature takes 14 (4d6) poison damage and is poisoned for 1 minute. At the end of this time, the poisoned creature must repeat the saving throw. On a failure, the creature takes 18 (4d8) poison damage and is poisoned until it finishes a long rest.

If another demon drinks the foul water as an action, it gains 11 (2d10) temporary hit points.

Magic Resistance. The wastrilith has advantage on saving throws against spells and other magical effects.

Undertow. As a bonus action when the wastrilith is underwater, it can cause all water within 60 feet of it to be difficult terrain for other creatures until the start of its next turn.

ACTIONS

Multiattack. The wastrilith uses Grasping Spout and makes three attacks: one with its bite and two with its claws.

Bite. *Melee Weapon Attack:* +9 to hit, reach 10 ft., one target. *Hit:* 30 (4d12 + 4) piercing damage.

Claws. *Melee Weapon Attack:* +9 to hit, reach 10 ft., one target. *Hit:* 18 (4d6 + 4) slashing damage.

Grasping Spout. The wastrilith magically launches a spout of water at one creature it can see within 60 feet of it. The target must make a DC 17 Strength saving throw, and it has disadvantage if it's underwater. On a failed save, it takes 22 (4d8 + 4) acid damage and is pulled up to 60 feet toward the wastrilith. On a successful save, it takes half as much damage and isn't pulled.

D

DEMON LORDS OFTEN TURN AGAINST EACH OTHER.
HERE ZUGGTMOY WILL SOON FACE THE TREACHERY OF JUIBLEX.

Demons: Demon Lords

This section provides game statistics for the demon lords who are detailed in chapter 1. They are incredibly formidable opponents.

Baphomet

Civilization is weakness and savagery is strength in the credo of Baphomet, the Horned King and the Prince of Beasts. He rules over minotaurs and others with savage hearts. He is worshiped by those who want to break the confines of civility and unleash their bestial natures, for Baphomet envisions a world without restraint, where creatures live out their most savage desires.

Cults devoted to Baphomet use mazes and complex knots as their emblems, creating secret places to indulge themselves, including labyrinths of the sort their master favors. Bloodstained crowns and weapons of iron and brass decorate their profane altars.

Over time, Baphomet's cultists become tainted by his influence, gaining bloodshot eyes and coarse, thickening hair. Small horns eventually sprout from the forehead. In time, a devoted cultist might transform entirely into a minotaur—considered the greatest gift of the Prince of Beasts.

Baphomet appears as a great, black-furred minotaur, 20 feet tall with six iron horns. An infernal light burns in his red eyes. Although he is filled with bestial blood lust, there lies within him a cruel and cunning intellect devoted to subverting all of civilization.

Baphomet wields a great glaive called Heartcleaver. He sometimes casts this deadly weapon aside so that he can charge his enemies and gore them with his horns, trampling them into the earth and rending them with his teeth like a beast.

Baphomet's Lair

Baphomet's lair is his palace, the Lyktion, which is on the layer of the Abyss called the Endless Maze. Nestled within the twisting passages of the plane-wide labyrinth, the Lyktion is immaculately maintained and surrounded by a moat constructed in the fashion of a three-dimensional maze. The palace is a towering structure whose interior is as labyrinthine as the plane on which it resides, populated by minotaurs, goristros, and quasits.

Lair Actions

On initiative count 20 (losing initiative ties), Baphomet can take a lair action to cause one of the following magical effects; he can't use the same effect two rounds in a row:

- Baphomet seals one doorway or other entryway within the lair. The opening must be unoccupied. It is filled with solid stone for 1 minute or until Baphomet creates this effect again.
- Baphomet chooses a room within the lair that is no larger in any dimension than 100 feet. Until the next initiative count 20, gravity is reversed within that room. Any creatures or objects in the room when this happens fall in the direction of the new pull of gravity, unless they have some means of remaining aloft. Baphomet can ignore the gravity reversal if he's in the room, although he likes to use this action to land on a ceiling to attack targets flying near it.
- Baphomet casts *mirage arcane*, affecting a room within the lair that is no larger in any dimension than 100 feet. The effect ends on the next initiative count 20.

D

Regional Effects

The region containing Baphomet's lair is warped by his magic, creating one or more of the following effects:

- Plant life within 1 mile of the lair grows thick and forms walls of trees, hedges, and other flora in the form of small mazes.
- Beasts within 1 mile of the lair become frightened and disoriented, as though constantly under threat of being hunted, and might lash out or panic even when no visible threat is nearby.
- If a humanoid spends at least 1 hour within 1 mile of the lair, that creature must succeed on a DC 18 Wisdom saving throw or descend into a madness determined by the Madness of Baphomet table. A creature that succeeds on this saving throw can't be affected by this regional effect again for 24 hours.

If Baphomet dies, these effects fade over the course of 1d10 days.

Madness of Baphomet

If a creature goes mad in Baphomet's lair or within line of sight of the demon lord, roll on the Madness of Baphomet table to determine the nature of the madness, which is a character flaw that lasts until cured. See the *Dungeon Master's Guide* for more on madness.

Madness of Baphomet

d100	Flaw (lasts until cured)
01–20	"My anger consumes me. I can't be reasoned with when my rage has been stoked."
21–40	"I degenerate into beastly behavior, seeming more like a wild animal than a thinking being."
41–60	"The world is my hunting ground. Others are my prey."
61–80	"Hate comes easily to me and explodes into rage."
81–00	"I see those who oppose me not as people, but as beasts meant to be preyed upon."

BAPHOMET

Huge fiend (demon), chaotic evil

Armor Class 22 (natural armor)
Hit Points 275 (19d12 + 152)
Speed 40 ft.

STR	DEX	CON	INT	WIS	CHA
30 (+10)	14 (+2)	26 (+8)	18 (+4)	24 (+7)	16 (+3)

Saving Throws Dex +9, Con +15, Wis +14
Skills Intimidation +17, Perception +14
Damage Resistances cold, fire, lightning
Damage Immunities poison; bludgeoning, piercing, and slashing that is nonmagical
Condition Immunities charmed, exhaustion, frightened, poisoned
Senses truesight 120 ft., passive Perception 24
Languages all, telepathy 120 ft.
Challenge 23 (50,000 XP)

Charge. If Baphomet moves at least 10 feet straight toward a target and then hits it with a gore attack on the same turn, the target takes an extra 16 (3d10) piercing damage. If the target is a creature, it must succeed on a DC 25 Strength saving throw or be pushed up to 10 feet away and knocked prone.

Innate Spellcasting. Baphomet's spellcasting ability is Charisma (spell save DC 18). He can innately cast the following spells, requiring no material components:

At will: *detect magic*
3/day each: *dispel magic, dominate beast, hunter's mark, maze, wall of stone*
1/day: *teleport*

Labyrinthine Recall. Baphomet can perfectly recall any path he has traveled, and he is immune to the *maze* spell.

Legendary Resistance (3/Day). If Baphomet fails a saving throw, he can choose to succeed instead.

Magic Resistance. Baphomet has advantage on saving throws against spells and other magical effects.

Magic Weapons. Baphomet's weapon attacks are magical.

Reckless. At the start of his turn, Baphomet can gain advantage on all melee weapon attack rolls during that turn, but attack rolls against him have advantage until the start of his next turn.

Actions

Multiattack. Baphomet makes three attacks: one with Heartcleaver, one with his bite, and one with his gore attack.

Heartcleaver. *Melee Weapon Attack:* +17 to hit, reach 15 ft., one target. *Hit:* 21 (2d10 + 10) slashing damage.

Bite. *Melee Weapon Attack:* +17 to hit, reach 10 ft., one target. *Hit:* 19 (2d8 + 10) piercing damage.

Gore. *Melee Weapon Attack:* +17 to hit, reach 10 ft., one target. *Hit:* 17 (2d6 + 10) piercing damage.

Frightful Presence. Each creature of Baphomet's choice within 120 feet of him and aware of him must succeed on a DC 18 Wisdom saving throw or become frightened for 1 minute. A frightened creature can repeat the saving throw at the end of each of its turns, ending the effect on itself on a success. These later saves have disadvantage if Baphomet is within line of sight of the creature.

If a creature succeeds on any of these saves or the effect ends on it, the creature is immune to Baphomet's Frightful Presence for the next 24 hours.

Legendary Actions

Baphomet can take 3 legendary actions, choosing from the options below. Only one legendary action option can be used at a time and only at the end of another creature's turn. Baphomet regains spent legendary actions at the start of his turn.

Heartcleaver Attack. Baphomet makes a melee attack with Heartcleaver.
Charge (Costs 2 Actions). Baphomet moves up to his speed, then makes a gore attack.

Demogorgon

Prince of Demons, the Sibilant Beast, and Master of the Spiraling Depths, Demogorgon is the embodiment of chaos, madness, and destruction, seeking to corrupt all that is good and undermine order in the multiverse, to see everything dragged howling into the infinite depths of the Abyss.

The demon lord is a meld of different forms, with a saurian lower body and clawed, webbed feet, as well as suckered tentacles sprouting from the shoulders of a great apelike torso, surmounted by two hideous simian heads, named Aameul and Hathradiah, both equally mad. Their gaze brings madness and confusion to any who confront it.

Similarly, the spiraling Y sign of Demogorgon's cult can inspire madness in those who contemplate it for too long. All the followers of the Prince of Demons go mad, sooner or later.

Demogorgon's Lair

Demogorgon makes his lair in a palace called Abysm, found on a layer of the Abyss known as the Gaping Maw. Demogorgon's lair is a place of madness and duality; the portion of the palace that lies above water takes the form of two serpentine towers, each crowned by a skull-shaped minaret. There, Demogorgon's heads contemplate the mysteries of the arcane while arguing about how best to obliterate their rivals. The bulk of this palace extends deep underwater, in chill and darkened caverns.

Demogorgon
Huge fiend (demon), chaotic evil

Armor Class 22 (natural armor)
Hit Points 406 (28d12 +224)
Speed 50 ft., swim 50 ft.

STR	DEX	CON	INT	WIS	CHA
29 (+9)	14 (+2)	26 (+8)	20 (+5)	17 (+3)	25 (+7)

Saving Throws Dex +10, Con +16, Wis +11, Cha +15
Skills Insight +11, Perception +19
Damage Resistances cold, fire, lightning
Damage Immunities poison; bludgeoning, piercing, and slashing that is nonmagical
Condition Immunities charmed, exhaustion, frightened, poisoned
Senses truesight 120 ft., passive Perception 29
Languages all, telepathy 120 ft.
Challenge 26 (90,000 XP)

Innate Spellcasting. Demogorgon's spellcasting ability is Charisma (spell save DC 23). Demogorgon can innately cast the following spells, requiring no material components:

At will: *detect magic, major image*
3/day each: *dispel magic, fear, telekinesis*
1/day each: *feeblemind, project image*

Legendary Resistance (3/Day). If Demogorgon fails a saving throw, he can choose to succeed instead.

Magic Resistance. Demogorgon has advantage on saving throws against spells and other magical effects.

Magic Weapons. Demogorgon's weapon attacks are magical.

Two Heads. Demogorgon has advantage on saving throws against being blinded, deafened, stunned, or knocked unconscious.

Actions

Multiattack. Demogorgon makes two tentacle attacks.

Tentacle. *Melee Weapon Attack:* +17 to hit, reach 10 ft., one target. *Hit:* 28 (3d12 + 9) bludgeoning damage. If the target is a creature, it must succeed on a DC 23 Constitution saving throw or its hit point maximum is reduced by an amount equal to the damage taken. This reduction lasts until the target finishes a long rest. The target dies if its hit point maximum is reduced to 0.

Gaze. Demogorgon turns his magical gaze toward one creature that he can see within 120 feet of him. That target must make a DC 23 Wisdom saving throw. Unless the target is incapacitated, it can avert its eyes to avoid the gaze and to automatically succeed on the save. If the target does so, it can't see Demogorgon until the start of his next turn. If the target looks at him in the meantime, it must immediately make the save.

If the target fails the save, the target suffers one of the following effects of Demogorgon's choice or at random:

1. **Beguiling Gaze.** The target is stunned until the start of Demogorgon's next turn or until Demogorgon is no longer within line of sight.
2. **Hypnotic Gaze.** The target is charmed by Demogorgon until the start of Demogorgon's next turn. Demogorgon chooses how the charmed target uses its actions, reactions, and movement. Because this gaze requires Demogorgon to focus both heads on the target, he can't use his Maddening Gaze legendary action until the start of his next turn.
3. **Insanity Gaze.** The target suffers the effect of the *confusion* spell without making a saving throw. The effect lasts until the start of Demogorgon's next turn. Demogorgon doesn't need to concentrate on the spell.

Legendary Actions

Demogorgon can take 2 legendary actions, choosing from the options below. Only one legendary action option can be used at a time and only at the end of another creature's turn. Demogorgon regains spent legendary actions at the start of his turn.

Tail. *Melee Weapon Attack:* +17 to hit, reach 15 ft., one target. *Hit:* 20 (2d10 + 9) bludgeoning damage plus 11 (2d10) necrotic damage.
Maddening Gaze. Demogorgon uses his Gaze action, and must choose either the Beguiling Gaze or the Insanity Gaze effect.

Lair Actions

On initiative count 20 (losing initiative ties), Demogorgon can take a lair action to cause one of the following effects; he can't use the same effect two rounds in a row:

- Demogorgon creates an illusory duplicate of himself, which appears in his own space and lasts until initiative count 20 of the next round. On his turn, Demogorgon can move the illusory duplicate a distance equal to his walking speed (no action required). The first time a creature or object interacts physically with Demogorgon (for example, by hitting him with an attack), there is a 50 percent chance that the illusory duplicate is being affected, not Demogorgon himself, in which case the illusion disappears.
- Demogorgon casts the *darkness* spell four times at its lowest level, targeting different areas with the spell. Demogorgon doesn't need to concentrate on the spells, which end on initiative count 20 of the next round.

Regional Effects

The region containing Demogorgon's lair is warped by his magic, creating one or more of the following effects:

- The area within 6 miles of the lair becomes overpopulated with lizards, poisonous snakes, and other venomous beasts.
- Beasts within 1 mile of the lair become violent and crazed—even creatures that are normally docile.
- If a humanoid spends at least 1 hour within 1 mile of the lair, that creature must succeed on a DC 23 Wisdom saving throw or descend into a madness determined by the Madness of Demogorgon table. A creature that succeeds on this saving throw can't be affected by this regional effect again for 24 hours.

If Demogorgon dies, these effects fade over the course of 1d10 days.

Madness of Demogorgon

If a creature goes mad in Demogorgon's lair or within line of sight of the demon lord, roll on the Madness of Demogorgon table to determine the nature of the madness, which is a character flaw that lasts until cured. See the *Dungeon Master's Guide* for more on madness.

Madness of Demogorgon

d100	Flaw (lasts until cured)
01–20	"Someone is plotting to kill me. I need to strike first to stop them!"
21–40	"There is only one solution to my problems: kill them all!"
41–60	"There is more than one mind inside my head."
61–80	"If you don't agree with me, I'll beat you into submission to get my way."
81–00	"I can't allow anyone to touch anything that belongs to me. They might try to take it away from me!"

Fraz-Urb'luu

All demons are liars, but Fraz-Urb'luu is the Prince of Deception and Demon Lord of Illusions. He uses every trick, every ounce of demonic cunning, to manipulate his enemies—mortal and fiend alike—to do his will. Fraz-Urb'luu can create dreamlands and mind-bending fantasies able to deceive the most discerning foes.

Once imprisoned for centuries below Castle Greyhawk on the world of Oerth, Fraz-Urb'luu has slowly rebuilt his power in the Abyss. He seeks the pieces of the legendary *staff of power* taken from him by those who imprisoned him, and commands his servants to do likewise.

The Prince of Deception's true form is like that of a great gargoyle, some 12 feet tall, with an extended, muscular neck and a smiling face framed by long, pointed ears and lank, dark hair, and bat-like wings are furled against his powerful shoulders. He can assume other forms, however, from the hideous to the beautiful. Often the demon lord becomes so immersed in playing a role that he loses himself in it for a time.

Many of the cultists of Fraz-Urb'luu aren't even aware they serve the Prince of Deception, believing their master is a beneficent being and granter of wishes, some lost god or celestial, or even another fiend. Fraz-Urb'luu wears all these masks and more. He particularly delights in aiding demon-hunters against his demonic

adversaries, driving the hunters to greater and greater atrocities in the name of their cause, only to eventually reveal his true nature and claim their souls as his own.

Fraz-Urb'luu's Lair

Fraz-Urb'luu's lair lies within the abyssal realm of Hollow's Heart, a featureless plain of white dust with few structures on it. The lair itself is the city of Zoragmelok, a circular fortress surrounded by adamantine walls topped with razors and hooks. Corkscrew towers loom above twisted domes and vast amphitheaters, just a few examples of the city's impossible architecture.

The challenge rating of Fraz-Urb'luu is 24 (62,000 XP) when he's encountered in his lair.

Lair Actions

On initiative count 20 (losing initiative ties), Fraz-Urb'luu can take a lair action to cause one of the following effects; he can't use the same effect two rounds in a row:

- Fraz-Urb'luu causes up to five doors within the lair to become walls, and an equal number of doors to appear on walls where there previously were none.
- Fraz-Urb'luu chooses one humanoid within the lair and instantly creates a simulacrum of that creature (as if created with the *simulacrum* spell). This simulacrum obeys Fraz-Urb'luu's commands and is destroyed on the next initiative count 20.

Fraz-Urb'luu

Large fiend (demon), chaotic evil

Armor Class 18 (natural armor)
Hit Points 337 (27d10 + 189)
Speed 40 ft., fly 40 ft.

STR	DEX	CON	INT	WIS	CHA
29 (+9)	12 (+1)	25 (+7)	26 (+8)	24 (+7)	26 (+8)

Saving Throws Dex +8, Con +14, Int +15, Wis +14
Skills Deception +15, Perception +14, Stealth +8
Damage Resistances cold, fire, lightning
Damage Immunities poison; bludgeoning, piercing, and slashing that is nonmagical
Condition Immunities charmed, exhaustion, frightened, poisoned
Senses truesight 120 ft., passive Perception 24
Languages all, telepathy 120 ft.
Challenge 23 (50,000 XP)

Innate Spellcasting. Fraz-Urb'luu's spellcasting ability is Charisma (spell save DC 23). Fraz-Urb'luu can innately cast the following spells, requiring no material components:

At will: *alter self* (can become Medium when changing his appearance), *detect magic, dispel magic, phantasmal force*
3/day each: *confusion, dream, mislead, programmed illusion, seeming*
1/day each: *mirage arcane, modify memory, project image*

Legendary Resistance (3/Day). If Fraz-Urb'luu fails a saving throw, he can choose to succeed instead.

Magic Resistance. Fraz-Urb'luu has advantage on saving throws against spells and other magical effects.

Magic Weapons. Fraz-Urb'luu's weapon attacks are magical.

Undetectable. Fraz-Urb'luu can't be targeted by divination magic, perceived through magical scrying sensors, or detected by abilities that sense demons or fiends.

Actions

Multiattack. Fraz-Urb'luu makes three attacks: one with his bite and two with his fists.

Bite. *Melee Weapon Attack:* +16 to hit, reach 10 ft., one target. *Hit:* 19 (3d6 + 9) piercing damage.

Fist. *Melee Weapon Attack:* +16 to hit, reach 10 ft., one target. *Hit:* 22 (3d8 + 9) bludgeoning damage.

Legendary Actions

Fraz-Urb'luu can take 3 legendary actions, choosing from the options below. Only one legendary action option can be used at a time and only at the end of another creature's turn. Fraz-Urb'luu regains spent legendary actions at the start of his turn.

Tail. *Melee Weapon Attack:* +16 to hit, reach 15 ft., one target. *Hit:* 20 (2d10 + 9) bludgeoning damage. If the target is a Large or smaller creature, it is also grappled (escape DC 24). The grappled target is also restrained. Fraz-Urb'luu can grapple only one creature with his tail at a time.
Phantasmal Killer (Costs 2 Actions). Fraz-Urb'luu casts *phantasmal killer*, no concentration required.

- Fraz-Urb'luu creates a wave of anguish. Each creature he can see within the lair must succeed on a DC 23 Wisdom saving throw or take 33 (6d10) psychic damage.

REGIONAL EFFECTS

The region containing Fraz-Urb'luu's lair is warped by his magic, creating one or more of the following effects:

- Intelligent creatures within 1 mile of the lair frequently see hallucinations of long-dead friends and comrades that vanish after only a brief glimpse.
- Roads and paths within 6 miles of the lair twist and turn back on themselves, making navigation in the area exceedingly difficult.
- If a humanoid spends at least 1 hour within 1 mile of the lair, that creature must succeed on a DC 23 Wisdom saving throw or descend into a madness determined by the Madness of Fraz-Urb'luu table. A creature that succeeds on this saving throw can't be affected by this regional effect again for 24 hours.

If Fraz-Urb'luu dies, these effects fade over the course of 1d10 days.

MADNESS OF FRAZ-URB'LUU

If a creature goes mad in Fraz-Urb'luu's lair or within line of sight of the demon lord, roll on the Madness of Fraz-Urb'luu table to determine the nature of the madness, which is a character flaw that lasts until cured. See the *Dungeon Master's Guide* for more on madness.

MADNESS OF FRAZ-URB'LUU

d100	Flaw (lasts until cured)
01–20	"I never let anyone know the truth about my actions or intentions, even if doing so would be beneficial to me."
21–40	"I have intermittent hallucinations and fits of catatonia."
41–60	"My mind wanders as I have elaborate fantasies that have no bearing on reality. When I return my focus to the world, I have a hard time remembering that it was just a daydream."
61–80	"I convince myself that things are true, even in the face of overwhelming evidence to the contrary."
81–00	"My perception of reality doesn't match anyone else's. It makes me prone to violent delusions that make no sense to anyone else."

Graz'zt

The appearance of the Dark Prince is a warning that not all beautiful things are good. Standing nearly nine feet tall, Graz'zt strikes the perfect figure of untamed desire, every plane and curve of his body, every glance of his burning eyes, promising a mixture of pleasure and pain. A subtle wrongness pervades his beauty, from the cruel cast of his features to the six fingers on each hand and six toes on each foot. Graz'zt can also transform himself at will, appearing in any humanoid form that pleases him, or his onlookers, all equally tempting in their own ways.

Graz'zt surrounds himself with the finest of things and the most attractive of servants, and he adorns himself in silks and leathers both striking and disturbing in their workmanship. His lair, and those of his cultists, are pleasure palaces where nothing is forbidden, save moderation or kindness.

The dark Prince of Pleasure considers restriction the only sin, and takes what he wants. Cults devoted to him are secret societies of indulgence, often using their debauchery to subjugate others through blackmail, addiction, and manipulation. They frequently wear alabaster masks with ecstatic expressions and ostentatious dress and body ornamentation to their secret assignations.

Although he prefers charm and subtle manipulation, Graz'zt is capable of terrible violence when provoked. He wields the greatsword Angdrelve, also called Wave of Sorrow, its wavy, razor-edged blade dripping acid at his command.

Graz'zt's Lair

Graz'zt's principal lair is his Argent Palace, a grandiose structure in the city of Zelatar, found within his abyssal domain of Azzatar. Graz'zt's maddening influence radiates outward in a tangible ripple, warping reality around him. Given enough time in a single location, Graz'zt can twist it with his madness. Graz'zt's lair is a den of ostentation and hedonism. It is adorned with finery and decorations so decadent that even the wealthiest of mortals would blush at the excess. Within Graz'zt's lairs, followers, thralls, and subjects alike are forced to slake Graz'zt's thirst for pageantry and pleasure.

Lair Actions

On initiative count 20 (losing initiative ties), Graz'zt can take a lair action to cause one of the following effects; he can't use the same effect two rounds in a row:

- Graz'zt casts the *command* spell on every creature of his choice in the lair. He needn't see each one, but he must be aware that an individual is in the lair to target that creature. He issues the same command to all the targets.
- Smooth surfaces within the lair become as reflective as a polished mirror. Until a different lair action is used, creatures within the lair have disadvantage on Dexterity (Stealth) checks made to hide.

Regional Effects

The region containing Graz'zt's lair is warped by his magic, creating one or more of the following effects:

- Flat surfaces within 1 mile of the lair that are made of stone or metal become highly reflective, as though polished to a shine. These surfaces become supernaturally mirrorlike.
- Wild beasts within 6 miles of the lair break into frequent conflicts and coupling, mirroring the behavior that occurs during their mating seasons.
- If a humanoid spends at least 1 hour within 1 mile of the lair, that creature must succeed on a DC 23 Wisdom saving throw or descend into a madness determined by the Madness of Graz'zt table. A creature that succeeds on this saving throw can't be affected by this regional effect again for 24 hours.

If Graz'zt dies, these effects fade over the course of 1d10 days.

Madness of Graz'zt

If a creature goes mad in Graz'zt's lair or within line of sight of the demon lord, roll on the Madness of Graz'zt table to determine the nature of the madness, which is a character flaw that lasts until cured. See the *Dungeon Master's Guide* for more on madness.

Madness of Graz'zt

d100	Flaw (lasts until cured)
01–20	"Nothing is more important to me than admiring my own reflection. Anyone who doesn't appreciate my beauty is a fool."
21–40	"Sex is a great solution to all of life's problems. Why doesn't anyone else get this?"
41–60	"My appetite for delicious, pleasurable substances knows no bounds. I'll do anything to get more."
61–80	"Rumors spread easily, and I know many of them. Who cares if they're true?"
81–90	"To properly honor my dark, beautiful lord, I must prepare intricate, debauched rituals."
91–00	"Anyone who doesn't do exactly what I say deserves no happiness."

GRAZ'ZT

Large fiend (demon, shapechanger), chaotic evil

Armor Class 20 (natural armor)
Hit Points 346 (33d10 + 165)
Speed 40 ft.

STR	DEX	CON	INT	WIS	CHA
22 (+6)	15 (+2)	21 (+5)	23 (+6)	21 (+5)	26 (+8)

Saving Throws Dex +9, Con +12, Wis +12
Skills Deception +15, Insight +12, Perception +12, Persuasion +15
Damage Resistances cold, fire, lightning
Damage Immunities poison; bludgeoning, piercing, and slashing that is nonmagical
Condition Immunities charmed, exhaustion, frightened, poisoned
Senses truesight 120 ft., passive Perception 22
Languages all, telepathy 120 ft.
Challenge 24 (62,000 XP)

Shapechanger. Graz'zt can use his action to polymorph into a form that resembles a Medium humanoid, or back into his true form. Aside from his size, his statistics are the same in each form. Any equipment he is wearing or carrying isn't transformed.

Innate Spellcasting. Graz'zt's spellcasting ability is Charisma (spell save DC 23). He can innately cast the following spells, requiring no material components:

At will: *charm person, crown of madness, detect magic, dispel magic, dissonant whispers*

3/day each: *counterspell, darkness, dominate person, sanctuary, telekinesis, teleport*
1/day each: *dominate monster, greater invisibility*

Legendary Resistance (3/Day). If Graz'zt fails a saving throw, he can choose to succeed instead.

Magic Resistance. Graz'zt has advantage on saving throws against spells and other magical effects.

Magic Weapons. Graz'zt's weapon attacks are magical.

Actions

Multiattack. Graz'zt attacks twice with Wave of Sorrow.

Wave of Sorrow (Greatsword). *Melee Weapon Attack:* +13 to hit, reach 10 ft., one target. *Hit:* 20 (4d6 + 6) slashing damage plus 10 (3d6) acid damage.

Teleport. Graz'zt magically teleports, along with any equipment he is wearing or carrying, up to 120 feet to an unoccupied space he can see.

Legendary Actions

Graz'zt can take 3 legendary actions, choosing from the options below. Only one legendary action option can be used at a time and only at the end of another creature's turn. Graz'zt regains spent legendary actions at the start of his turn.

Attack. Graz'zt attacks once with Wave of Sorrow.
Dance, My Puppet! One creature charmed by Graz'zt that Graz'zt can see must use its reaction to move up to its speed as Graz'zt directs.
Sow Discord. Graz'zt casts *crown of madness* or *dissonant whispers*.
Teleport. Graz'zt uses his Teleport action.

JUIBLEX

Called the Faceless Lord and the Oozing Hunger in ancient grimoires, Juiblex is demon lord of slime and ooze, a noxious creature that doesn't care about the plots and schemes of others of its kind. It exists only to consume, digesting and transforming living matter into more of itself.

A true horror, Juiblex is a mass of bubbling slime, swirling black and green, with glaring red eyes floating and shifting within it. It can rise up like a 20-foot hill, lashing out with dripping pseudopods to drag victims into its bulk. Those consumed by Juiblex are obliterated.

Only the truly insane worship Juiblex and tend to its slimes and oozes. Those who offer themselves up to the demon lord are engulfed by it and become vaguely humanoid, sentient oozes. The bodies of these former flesh-and-blood creatures form Juiblex's extended physical body, while the demon lord slowly digests and savors their identities over time.

JUIBLEX'S LAIR

Juiblex's principal lair is known as the Slime Pits, a realm that Juiblex shares with Zuggtmoy. This layer of the Abyss, which is also known as Shedaklah, is a bubbling morass of oozing, fetid sludge. Its landscape is covered in vast expanses of caustic and unintelligent slimes, and strange organic forms rise from the oceans of molds and oozes at Juiblex's command.

LAIR ACTIONS

On initiative count 20 (losing initiative ties), Juiblex can take a lair action to cause one of the following effects; it can't use the same effect two rounds in a row:

- Juiblex slimes a square area of ground it can see within the lair. The area can be up to 10 feet on a side. The slime lasts for 1 hour or until it is burned away with fire. When the slime appears, each creature in that area must succeed on a DC 21 Strength saving throw or become restrained. When a creature enters the area for the first time on a turn or ends its turn there, that creature must make the same save.

  A restrained creature is stuck as long as it remains in the slimy area or until it breaks free. The restrained creature, or another creature that can reach it, can use its action to try to break free and must succeed on a DC 21 Strength check.

  If the slime is set on fire, it burns away after 1 round. Any creature that starts its turn in the burning slime takes 22 (4d10) fire damage.

- Juiblex slimes a square area of ground it can see within the lair. The area can be up to 10 feet on a side. The slime lasts for 1 hour or until it is burned away with fire. When the slime appears, each creature on it must succeed on a DC 21 Dexterity saving throw or fall prone and slide 10 feet in a random direction determined by a d8 roll. When a creature enters the area for the first time on a turn or ends its turn there, that creature must make the same save.

  If the slime is set on fire, it burns away after 1 round. Any creature that starts its turn in the burning slime takes 22 (4d10) fire damage.

- A green slime (see the *Dungeon Master's Guide*) appears on a spot on the ceiling that Juiblex chooses within the lair. The slime disintegrates after 1 hour.

REGIONAL EFFECTS

The region containing Juiblex's lair is warped by its magic, creating one or more of the following effects:

- Small bodies of water, such as ponds or wells, within 1 mile of the lair turn highly acidic, corroding any object that touches them.
- Surfaces within 6 miles of the lair are frequently covered by a thin film of slime, which is slick and sticks to anything that touches it.
- If a humanoid spends at least 1 hour within 1 mile of the lair, that creature must succeed on a DC 18 Wisdom saving throw or descend into a madness determined by the Madness of Juiblex table. A creature that succeeds on this saving throw can't be affected by this regional effect again for 24 hours.

If Juiblex dies, these effects fade over the course of 1d10 days.

MADNESS OF JUIBLEX

If a creature goes mad in Juiblex's lair or within line of sight of the demon lord, roll on the Madness of Juiblex table to determine the nature of the madness, which is a character flaw that lasts until cured. See the *Dungeon Master's Guide* for more on madness.

MADNESS OF JUIBLEX

d100	Flaw (lasts until cured)
01–20	"I must consume everything I can!"
21–40	"I refuse to part with any of my possessions."
41–60	"I'll do everything I can to get others to eat and drink beyond their normal limits."
61–80	"I must possess as many material goods as I can."
81–00	"My personality is irrelevant. I am defined by what I consume."

JUIBLEX

Huge fiend (demon), chaotic evil

Armor Class 18 (natural armor)
Hit Points 350 (28d12 + 168)
Speed 30 ft.

STR	DEX	CON	INT	WIS	CHA
24 (+7)	10 (+0)	23 (+6)	20 (+5)	20 (+5)	16 (+3)

Saving Throws Dex +7, Con +13, Wis +12
Skills Perception +12
Damage Resistances cold, fire, lightning
Damage Immunities poison; bludgeoning, piercing, and slashing that is nonmagical
Condition Immunities blinded, charmed, deafened, exhaustion, frightened, grappled, paralyzed, petrified, poisoned, prone, restrained, stunned, unconscious
Senses truesight 120 ft., passive Perception 22
Languages all, telepathy 120 ft.
Challenge 23 (50,000 XP)

Foul. Any creature, other than an ooze, that starts its turn within 10 feet of Juiblex must succeed on a DC 21 Constitution saving throw or be poisoned until the start of the creature's next turn.

Innate Spellcasting. Juiblex's spellcasting ability is Charisma (spell save DC 18, +10 to hit with spell attacks). Juiblex can innately cast the following spells, requiring no material components:

At will: *acid splash* (17th level), *detect magic*
3/day each: *blight, contagion, gaseous form*

Legendary Resistance (3/Day). If Juiblex fails a saving throw, it can choose to succeed instead.

Magic Resistance. Juiblex has advantage on saving throws against spells and other magical effects.

Magic Weapons. Juiblex's weapon attacks are magical.

Regeneration. Juiblex regains 20 hit points at the start of its turn. If it takes fire or radiant damage, this trait doesn't function at the start of its next turn. Juiblex dies only if it starts its turn with 0 hit points and doesn't regenerate.

Spider Climb. Juiblex can climb difficult surfaces, including upside down on ceilings, without needing to make an ability check.

ACTIONS

Multiattack. Juiblex makes three acid lash attacks.

Acid Lash. *Melee Weapon Attack:* +14 to hit, reach 10 ft., one target. *Hit:* 21 (4d6 + 7) acid damage. Any creature killed by this attack is drawn into Juiblex's body, and the corpse is obliterated after 1 minute.

Eject Slime (Recharge 5–6). Juiblex spews out a corrosive slime, targeting one creature that it can see within 60 feet of it. The target must make a DC 21 Dexterity saving throw. On a failure, the target takes 55 (10d10) acid damage. Unless the target avoids taking any of this damage, any metal armor worn by the target takes a permanent –1 penalty to the AC it offers, and any metal weapon it is carrying or wearing takes a permanent –1 penalty to damage rolls. The penalty worsens each time a target is subjected to this effect. If the penalty on an object drops to –5, the object is destroyed.

LEGENDARY ACTIONS

Juiblex can take 3 legendary actions, choosing from the options below. Only one legendary action option can be used at a time and only at the end of another creature's turn. Juiblex regains spent legendary actions at the start of its turn.

Acid Splash. Juiblex casts *acid splash.*
Attack. Juiblex makes one acid lash attack.
Corrupting Touch (Costs 2 Actions). *Melee Weapon Attack:* +14 to hit, reach 10 ft., one creature. *Hit:* 21 (4d6 + 7) poison damage, and the target is slimed. Until the slime is scraped off with an action, the target is poisoned, and any creature, other than an ooze, is poisoned while within 10 feet of the target.

ORCUS

Orcus is the Demon Prince of Undeath, known as the Blood Lord. He takes some pleasure in the sufferings of the living, but far prefers the company and service of the undead. His desire is to see all life quenched and the multiverse transformed into a vast necropolis populated solely by undead creatures under his command.

Orcus rewards those who spread death in his name by granting them a small portion of his power. The least of these become ghouls and zombies who serve in his legions, while his favored servants are the cultists and necromancers who murder the living and then manipulate the dead, emulating their dread master.

Orcus is a bestial creature of corruption with a diseased, decaying look. He has the lower torso of a goat, and a humanoid upper body with a corpulent belly swollen with rot. Great bat wings sprout from his shoulders, and his head is like the skull of a goat, the flesh nearly rotted from it. In one hand, he wields the legendary *Wand of Orcus*, which is described in chapter 7 of the *Dungeon Master's Guide*.

ORCUS'S LAIR

Orcus makes his lair in the fortress city of Naratyr, which is on Thanatos, the layer of the Abyss that he rules. Surrounded by a moat fed by the River Styx,

Naratyr is an eerily quiet and cold city, its streets often empty for hours at a time. The central castle of bone has interior walls of flesh and carpets made of woven hair. The city contains wandering undead, many of which are engaged in continuous battles with one another.

LAIR ACTIONS

On initiative count 20 (losing initiative ties), Orcus can take a lair action to cause one of the following effects; he can't use the same effect two rounds in a row:

- Orcus's voice booms throughout the lair. His utterance causes one creature of his choice to be subjected to *power word kill* (save DC 23). Orcus needn't see the creature, but he must be aware that the individual is in the lair.
- Orcus causes up to six corpses within the lair to rise as skeletons, zombies, or ghouls. These undead obey his telepathic commands, which can reach anywhere in the lair.
- Orcus causes skeletal arms to rise from an area on the ground in a 20-foot square that he can see. They last until the next initiative count 20. Each creature in that area when the arms appear must succeed on a DC 23 Strength saving throw or be restrained until the arms disappear or until Orcus releases them (no action required).

Regional Effects

The region containing Orcus's lair is warped by Orcus's magic, creating one or more of the following effects:

- Dead beasts periodically animate as undead mockeries of their former selves. Skeletal and zombie versions of local wildlife are commonly seen in the area.
- The air becomes filled with the stench of rotting flesh, and buzzing flies grow thick within the region, even when there is no carrion to be found.
- If a humanoid spends at least 1 hour within 1 mile of the lair, that creature must succeed on a DC 23 Wisdom saving throw or descend into a madness determined by the Madness of Orcus table. A creature that succeeds on this saving throw can't be affected by this regional effect again for 24 hours.

If Orcus dies, these effects fade over the course of 1d10 days.

Madness of Orcus

If a creature goes mad in Orcus's lair or within line of sight of the demon lord, roll on the Madness of Orcus table to determine the nature of the madness, which is a character flaw that lasts until cured. See the *Dungeon Master's Guide* for more on madness.

Madness of Orcus

d100	Flaw (lasts until cured)
01–20	"I often become withdrawn and moody, dwelling on the insufferable state of life."
21–40	"I am compelled to make the weak suffer."
41–60	"I have no compunction against tampering with the dead in my search to better understand death."
61–80	"I want to achieve the everlasting existence of undeath."
81–00	"I am awash in the awareness of life's futility."

Orcus

Huge fiend (demon), chaotic evil

Armor Class 17 (natural armor), 20 with the *Wand of Orcus*
Hit Points 405 (30d12 + 210)
Speed 40 ft., fly 40 ft.

STR	DEX	CON	INT	WIS	CHA
27 (+8)	14 (+2)	25 (+7)	20 (+5)	20 (+5)	25 (+7)

Saving Throws Dex +10, Con +15, Wis +13
Skills Arcana +12, Perception +12
Damage Resistances cold, fire, lightning
Damage Immunities necrotic, poison; bludgeoning, piercing, and slashing that is nonmagical
Condition Immunities charmed, exhaustion, frightened, poisoned
Senses truesight 120 ft., passive Perception 22
Languages all, telepathy 120 ft.
Challenge 26 (90,000 XP)

Wand of Orcus. The wand has 7 charges, and any of its properties that require a saving throw have a save DC of 18. While holding it, Orcus can use an action to cast *animate dead, blight,* or *speak with dead.* Alternatively, he can expend 1 or more of the wand's charges to cast one of the following spells from it: *circle of death* (1 charge), *finger of death* (1 charge), or *power word kill* (2 charges). The wand regains 1d4 + 3 charges daily at dawn.

While holding the wand, Orcus can use an action to conjure undead creatures whose combined average hit points don't exceed 500. These undead magically rise up from the ground or otherwise form in unoccupied spaces within 300 feet of Orcus and obey his commands until they are destroyed or until he dismisses them as an action. Once this property of the wand is used, the property can't be used again until the next dawn.

Innate Spellcasting. Orcus's spellcasting ability is Charisma (spell save DC 23, +15 to hit with spell attacks). He can innately cast the following spells, requiring no material components:

At will: *chill touch* (17th level), *detect magic*
3/day each: *create undead, dispel magic*
1/day: *time stop*

Legendary Resistance (3/Day). If Orcus fails a saving throw, he can choose to succeed instead.

Magic Resistance. Orcus has advantage on saving throws against spells and other magical effects.

Magic Weapons. Orcus's weapon attacks are magical.

Master of Undeath. When Orcus casts *animate dead* or *create undead,* he chooses the level at which the spell is cast, and the creatures created by the spells remain under his control indefinitely. Additionally, he can cast *create undead* even when it isn't night.

Actions

Multiattack. Orcus makes two *Wand of Orcus* attacks.

Wand of Orcus. *Melee Weapon Attack:* +19 to hit, reach 10 ft., one target. *Hit:* 21 (3d8 + 8) bludgeoning damage plus 13 (2d12) necrotic damage.

Tail. *Melee Weapon Attack:* +16 to hit, reach 10 ft., one target. *Hit:* 21 (3d8 + 8) piercing damage plus 9 (2d8) poison damage.

Legendary Actions

Orcus can take 3 legendary actions, choosing from the options below. Only one legendary action option can be used at a time and only at the end of another creature's turn. Orcus regains spent legendary actions at the start of his turn.

Tail. Orcus makes one tail attack.
A Taste of Undeath. Orcus casts *chill touch* (17th level).
Creeping Death (Costs 2 Actions). Orcus chooses a point on the ground that he can see within 100 feet of him. A cylinder of swirling necrotic energy 60 feet tall and with a 10-foot radius rises from that point and lasts until the end of Orcus's next turn. Creatures in that area have vulnerability to necrotic damage.

YEENOGHU

The Beast of Butchery appears as a great battle-scarred gnoll, towering 14 feet tall. Yeenoghu is the Gnoll Lord, and his creations are made in his twisted image. When the demon lord hunted across the Material Plane, packs of hyenas followed in his wake. Those that ate of great Yeenoghu's kills became gnolls, emulating their master's ways. Few others worship the Beast of Butchery, but those who do tend to take on a gnoll-like aspect, hunched over, and filing their teeth down to points.

Yeenoghu wants nothing more than slaughter and senseless destruction. The gnolls are his instruments, and he drives them to ever-greater atrocities in his name. Yeenoghu takes pleasure in causing fear before death, and he sows sorrow and despair through destroying beloved things. He doesn't parlay; to meet him is to do battle with him—unless he becomes bored. The Beast of Butchery has a long rivalry with Baphomet, the Horned King, and the two demon lords and their followers attack one another on sight.

The Gnoll Lord is covered in matted fur and taut, leathery hide, his face like a grinning predator's skull. Patchwork armor made of discarded shields and breastplates is lashed onto his body with heavy chains, decorated by the flayed skins of his foes. He wields a triple-headed flail called the Butcher, which he can summon into his hand at will, although he is as likely to tear his prey apart with his bare hands before ripping out its throat with his teeth.

YEENOGHU'S LAIR

Yeenoghu's lair in the Abyss is called the Death Dells, its barren hills and ravines serving as one great hunting ground, where he pursues captured mortals in a cruel game. Yeenoghu's lair is a place of blood and death, populated by gnolls, hyenas, and ghouls, and there are few structures or signs of civilization on his layer of the Abyss.

LAIR ACTIONS

On initiative count 20 (losing initiative ties), Yeenoghu can take a lair action to cause one of the following effects; he can't use the same effect two rounds in a row:

- Yeenoghu causes an iron spike—5 feet tall and 1 inch in diameter—to burst from the ground at a point he can see within 100 feet of him. Any creature in the space where the spike emerges must make a DC 24 Dexterity saving throw. On a failed save, the creature takes 27 (6d8) piercing damage and is restrained by being impaled on the spike. A creature can use an action to remove itself (or a creature it can reach) from the spike, ending the restrained condition.

- Each gnoll or hyena that Yeenoghu can see can use its reaction to move up to its speed.
- Until the next initiative count 20, all gnolls and hyenas within the lair are enraged, causing them to have advantage on melee weapon attack rolls and causing attack rolls to have advantage against them.

REGIONAL EFFECTS

The region containing Yeenoghu's lair is warped by his magic, creating one or more of the following effects:

- Within 1 mile of the lair, large iron spikes grow out of the ground and stone surfaces. Yeenoghu impales the bodies of the slain on these spikes.
- Predatory beasts within 6 miles of the lair become unusually savage, killing far more than what they need for food. Carcasses of prey are left to rot in an unnatural display of wasteful slaughter.
- If a humanoid spends at least 1 hour within 1 mile of the lair, that creature must succeed on a DC 17 Wisdom saving throw or descend into a madness determined by the Madness of Yeenoghu table. A creature that succeeds on this saving throw can't be affected by this regional effect again for 24 hours.

If Yeenoghu dies, these effects fade over the course of 1d10 days.

MADNESS OF YEENOGHU

If a creature goes mad in Yeenoghu's lair or within line of sight of the demon lord, roll on the Madness of Yeenoghu table to determine the nature of the madness, which is a character flaw that lasts until cured. See the *Dungeon Master's Guide* for more on madness.

MADNESS OF YEENOGHU

d100	Flaw (lasts until cured)
01–20	"I get caught up in the flow of anger, and try to stoke others around me into forming an angry mob."
21–40	"The flesh of other intelligent creatures is delicious!"
41–60	"I rail against the laws and customs of civilization, attempting to return to a more primitive time."
61–80	"I hunger for the deaths of others, and am constantly starting fights in the hope of seeing bloodshed."
81–00	"I keep trophies from the bodies I have slain, turning them into adornments."

YEENOGHU

Huge fiend (demon), chaotic evil

Armor Class 20 (natural armor)
Hit Points 333 (23d12 + 184)
Speed 50 ft.

STR	DEX	CON	INT	WIS	CHA
29 (+9)	16 (+3)	23 (+8)	15 (+3)	24 (+7)	15 (+2)

Saving Throws Dex +10, Con +15, Wis +14
Skills Intimidation +9, Perception +14
Damage Resistances cold, fire, lightning
Damage Immunities poison; bludgeoning, piercing, and slashing that is nonmagical
Condition Immunities charmed, exhaustion, frightened, poisoned
Senses truesight 120 ft., passive Perception 24
Languages all, telepathy 120 ft.
Challenge 24 (62,000 XP)

Innate Spellcasting. Yeenoghu's spellcasting ability is Charisma (spell save DC 17, +9 to hit with spell attacks). He can innately cast the following spells, requiring no material components:

At will: *detect magic*
3/day each: *dispel magic, fear, invisibility*
1/day: *teleport*

Legendary Resistance (3/Day). If Yeenoghu fails a saving throw, he can choose to succeed instead.

Magic Resistance. Yeenoghu has advantage on saving throws against spells and other magical effects.

Magic Weapons. Yeenoghu's weapon attacks are magical.

Rampage. When Yeenoghu reduces a creature to 0 hit points with a melee attack on his turn, Yeenoghu can take a bonus action to move up to half his speed and make a bite attack.

ACTIONS

Multiattack. Yeenoghu makes three flail attacks. If an attack hits, he can cause it to create an additional effect of his choice or at random (each effect can be used only once per Multiattack):

1. The attack deals an extra 13 (2d12) bludgeoning damage.
2. The target must succeed on a DC 17 Constitution saving throw or be paralyzed until the start of Yeenoghu's next turn.
3. The target must succeed on a DC 17 Wisdom saving throw or be affected by the *confusion* spell until the start of Yeenoghu's next turn.

Flail. *Melee Weapon Attack:* +16 to hit, reach 15 ft., one target. *Hit:* 15 (1d12 + 9) bludgeoning damage.

Bite. *Melee Weapon Attack:* +16 to hit, reach 10 ft., one target. *Hit:* 14 (1d10 + 9) piercing damage.

LEGENDARY ACTIONS

Yeenoghu can take 3 legendary actions, choosing from the options below. Only one legendary action option can be used at a time and only at the end of another creature's turn. Yeenoghu regains spent legendary actions at the start of his turn.

Charge. Yeenoghu moves up to his speed.
Swat Away. Yeenoghu makes a flail attack. If the attack hits, the target must succeed on a DC 24 Strength saving throw or be pushed 15 feet in a straight line away from Yeenoghu. If the saving throw fails by 5 or more, the target falls prone.
Savage (Costs 2 Actions). Yeenoghu makes a bite attack against each creature within 10 feet of him.

ZUGGTMOY

The Demon Queen of Fungi, Lady of Rot and Decay, Zuggtmoy is an alien creature whose only desire is to infect the living with spores, transforming them into her mindless servants and, eventually, into decomposing hosts for the mushrooms, molds, and other fungi that she spawns.

Utterly inhuman, Zuggtmoy can mold her fungoid form into an approximation of a humanoid shape, including the skeletal-thin figure depicted in grimoires and ancient art, draped and veiled in mycelia and lichen. Indeed, much of her appearance and manner, and that of her servants, is a soulless mockery of mortal life and its many facets.

Zuggtmoy's cultists often follow her unwittingly. Most are fungi-infected to some degree, whether through inhaling her mind-controlling spores or being transformed to the point where flesh and fungus become one. Such cultists are fungal extensions of the Demon Queen's will. Their devotion might begin with the seemingly harmless promises offered by exotic spores and mushrooms, but quickly consumes them, body and soul.

ZUGGTMOY'S LAIR

Zuggtmoy's principal lair is her palace on Shedaklah. It consists of two dozen mushrooms of pale yellow and rancid brown. These massive fungi are some of the largest in existence. They are surrounded by a field of acidic puffballs and poisonous vapors. The mushrooms are all interconnected by bridges of shelf-fungi, and countless chambers have been hollowed out inside their rubbery, fibrous stalks.

LAIR ACTIONS

On initiative count 20 (losing initiative ties), Zuggtmoy can take a lair action to cause one of the following effects; she can't use the same effect two rounds in a row:

- Zuggtmoy causes four gas spores or violet fungi (see the *Monster Manual*) to appear in unoccupied spaces that she chooses within the lair. They vanish after 1 hour.
- Up to four plant creatures that are friendly to Zuggtmoy and that Zuggtmoy can see can use their reactions to move up to their speed and make one weapon attack.
- Zuggtmoy uses either her Infestation Spores or her Mind Control Spores, centered on a mushroom or other fungus within her lair, instead of on herself.

REGIONAL EFFECTS

The region containing Zuggtmoy's lair is warped by her magic, creating one or more of the following effects:

- Molds and fungi grow on surfaces within 6 miles of the lair, even where they would normally find no purchase.
- Plant life within 1 mile of the lair becomes infested with parasitic fungi, slowly mutating as it is overwhelmed.

- If a humanoid spends at least 1 hour within 1 mile of the lair, that creature must succeed on a DC 17 Wisdom saving throw or descend into a madness determined by the Madness of Zuggtmoy table. A creature that succeeds on this saving throw can't be affected by this regional effect again for 24 hours.

If Zuggtmoy dies, these effects fade over the course of 1d10 days.

MADNESS OF ZUGGTMOY

If a creature goes mad in Zuggtmoy's lair or within line of sight of the demon lord, roll on the Madness of Zuggtmoy table to determine the nature of the madness, which is a character flaw that lasts until cured. See the *Dungeon Master's Guide* for more on madness.

MADNESS OF ZUGGTMOY

d100	Flaw (lasts until cured)
01–20	"I see visions in the world around me that others do not."
21–40	"I periodically slip into a catatonic state, staring off into the distance for long stretches at a time."
41–60	"I see an altered version of reality, with my mind convincing itself that things are true even in the face of overwhelming evidence to the contrary."
61–80	"My mind is slipping away, and my intelligence seems to wax and wane."
81–00	"I am constantly scratching at unseen fungal infections."

ZUGGTMOY

Large fiend (demon), chaotic evil

Armor Class 18 (natural armor)
Hit Points 304 (32d10 + 128)
Speed 30 ft.

STR	DEX	CON	INT	WIS	CHA
22 (+6)	15 (+2)	18 (+4)	20 (+5)	19 (+4)	24 (+7)

Saving Throws Dex +9, Con +11, Wis +11
Skills Perception +11
Damage Resistances cold, fire, lightning
Damage Immunities poison; bludgeoning, piercing, and slashing that is nonmagical
Condition Immunities charmed, exhaustion, frightened, poisoned
Senses truesight 120 ft., passive Perception 21
Languages all, telepathy 120 ft.
Challenge 23 (50,000 XP)

Innate Spellcasting. Zuggtmoy's spellcasting ability is Charisma (spell save DC 22). She can innately cast the following spells, requiring no material components:

At will: *detect magic, locate animals or plants, ray of sickness*
3/day each: *dispel magic, ensnaring strike, entangle, plant growth*
1/day each: *etherealness, teleport*

Legendary Resistance (3/Day). If Zuggtmoy fails a saving throw, she can choose to succeed instead.

Magic Resistance. Zuggtmoy has advantage on saving throws against spells and other magical effects.

Magic Weapons. Zuggtmoy's weapon attacks are magical.

ACTIONS

Multiattack. Zuggtmoy makes three pseudopod attacks.

Pseudopod. *Melee Weapon Attack:* +13 to hit, reach 10 ft., one target. *Hit:* 15 (2d8 + 6) bludgeoning damage plus 9 (2d8) poison damage.

Infestation Spores (3/Day). Zuggtmoy releases spores that burst out in a cloud that fills a 20-foot-radius sphere centered on her, and it lingers for 1 minute. Any flesh-and-blood creature in the cloud when it appears, or that enters it later, must make a DC 19 Constitution saving throw. On a successful save, the creature can't be infected by these spores for 24 hours. On a failed save, the creature is infected with a disease called the spores of Zuggtmoy and also gains a random form of madness (determined by rolling on the Madness of Zuggtmoy table) that lasts until the creature is cured of the disease or dies. While infected in this way, the creature can't be reinfected, and it must repeat the saving throw at the end of every 24 hours, ending the infection on a success. On a failure, the infected creature's body is slowly taken over by fungal growth, and after three such failed saves, the creature dies and is reanimated as a spore servant if it's a type of creature that can be (see the "Myconids" entry in the *Monster Manual*).

Mind Control Spores (Recharge 5–6). Zuggtmoy releases spores that burst out in a cloud that fills a 20-foot-radius sphere centered on her, and it lingers for 1 minute. Humanoids and beasts in the cloud when it appears, or that enter it later, must make a DC 19 Wisdom saving throw. On a successful save, the creature can't be infected by these spores for 24 hours. On a failed save, the creature is infected with a disease called the influence of Zuggtmoy for 24 hours. While infected in this way, the creature is charmed by her and can't be reinfected by these spores.

REACTIONS

Protective Thrall. When Zuggtmoy is hit by an attack, one creature within 5 feet of Zuggtmoy that is charmed by her must use its reaction to be hit by the attack instead.

LEGENDARY ACTIONS

Zuggtmoy can take 3 legendary actions, choosing from the options below. Only one legendary action option can be used at a time and only at the end of another creature's turn. Zuggtmoy regains spent legendary actions at the start of her turn.

Attack. Zuggtmoy makes one pseudopod attack.
Exert Will. One creature charmed by Zuggtmoy that she can see must use its reaction to move up to its speed as she directs or to make a weapon attack against a target that she designates.

D

*Mad as hatters, every one of them.
No derro has ever been sane, but neither
is every form of madness a hindrance.*

Derro

Derro slink through the subterranean realms, seeking places that are safe from the perils of the Underdark. Equal parts fearful and vicious, bands of these dwarf-kin prey on those weaker than themselves, while giving simpering obeisance to any creatures they deem more powerful. Wild-haired, haggard, shuddering, and shabbily dressed, a lone derro seems a pitiable creature, but when a cackling, spitting, growling, howling horde of them attacks, the sight inspires both fear and revulsion.

Madness and Sorcery. Fractious in groups and individually weak, derro would have been driven to extinction long ago but for two elements of their character. They have an inborn tendency toward paranoia, a peculiarity that serves them well as they navigate the dangers of the Underdark and its societies. They also have a stronger-than-normal tendency to develop sorcerous power. Individuals who do so become their leaders, known as savants. The derro consider these sorcerers to be specially blessed by their deity, Diirinka.

Forgotten Duergar. Grandiose fantasies and rampant fanaticism have obscured the true origin of the derro, even among themselves. Most dwarves don't recognize derro as kin, but the legends that the derro tell about their race and the story that the duergar believe share a grain of truth.

According to the duergar, the derro are descended from dwarves of a clan that was left behind when the others escaped the mind flayers' rule. They eventually also got away, but not before becoming demented and contorted.

The derro tell their own story of flight and survival in the Underdark, and the mind flayers aren't always the enemy. Laduguer and Deep Duerra don't feature in their mythic history. Instead they tell of two brothers, Diirinka and Diinkarazan, and of how Diirinka cleverly betrayed his sibling so that he could steal magical power from the evil they escaped. The danger the brothers are said to face in this legend varies, depending on whatever foe the savants want to lead their people against, yet the essence of the story remains the same: a lesson of survival at any price and an example of how deceitfulness and cruelty can be virtues.

Derro

Small humanoid (derro), chaotic evil

Armor Class 13 (leather armor)
Hit Points 13 (3d6 + 3)
Speed 30 ft.

STR	DEX	CON	INT	WIS	CHA
10 (+0)	14 (+2)	12 (+1)	11 (+0)	5 (−3)	9 (−1)

Skills Stealth +4
Senses darkvision 120 ft., passive Perception 7
Languages Dwarvish, Undercommon
Challenge 1/4 (50 XP)

Magic Resistance. The derro has advantage on saving throws against spells and other magical effects.

Sunlight Sensitivity. While in sunlight, the derro has disadvantage on attack rolls, as well as on Wisdom (Perception) checks that rely on sight.

ACTIONS

Hooked Spear. *Melee Weapon Attack:* +2 to hit, reach 5 ft., one target. *Hit:* 3 (1d6) piercing damage. If the target is Medium or smaller, the derro can choose to deal no damage and knock it prone.

Light Crossbow. *Ranged Weapon Attack:* +4 to hit, range 80/320 ft., one target. *Hit:* 6 (1d8 + 2) piercing damage.

Derro Madness

All derro suffer from a form of madness that most often manifests as mania and paranoia, but other mental afflictions and strange tics also commonly affect them. Derro take little notice of odd behavior in their ranks, except when an individual displays the characteristics of a savant. They believe the strange behavior of savants arises because those leaders carry messages from Diirinka. You can use the Derro Madness table to generate one or more odd qualities for a derro NPC.

Derro Madness

d20	Oddity
1	Never bathes or changes clothes
2	Frets with hair or mustache
3	Speaks to someone who isn't there
4	Walks backward whenever possible
5	Never looks others in the eye
6	Gnashes teeth after each sentence
7	Spits out half of each mouthful of food and drink
8	Insults everyone when first addressing them
9	Touches whomever he or she speaks to
10	Sees the spirits of the dead leaving their bodies
11	Faints when first subjected to bright light
12	Frequently licks their palms
13	Hears voices
14	Terrified of writing
15	Tastes objects
16	Stands too close to others
17	Breathes loudly
18	Drools constantly
19	Mumbles when speaking
20	Hops from place to place

Derro Savant

Small humanoid (derro), chaotic evil

Armor Class 13 (leather armor)
Hit Points 36 (8d6 + 8)
Speed 30 ft.

STR	DEX	CON	INT	WIS	CHA
9 (−1)	14 (+2)	12 (+1)	11 (+0)	5 (−3)	14 (+2)

Skills Stealth +4
Senses darkvision 120 ft., passive Perception 7
Languages Dwarvish, Undercommon
Challenge 3 (700 XP)

Magic Resistance. The derro savant has advantage on saving throws against spells and other magical effects.

Spellcasting. The derro savant is a 5th-level spellcaster. Its spellcasting ability is Charisma (spell save DC 12, +4 to hit with spell attacks). The derro knows the following sorcerer spells:

Cantrips (at will): *acid splash, mage hand, message, prestidigitation, ray of frost*
1st level (4 slots): *burning hands, chromatic orb, sleep*
2nd level (3 slots): *invisibility, spider climb*
3rd level (2 slots): *lightning bolt*

Sunlight Sensitivity. While in sunlight, the derro savant has disadvantage on attack rolls, as well as on Wisdom (Perception) checks that rely on sight.

Actions

Quarterstaff. *Melee Weapon Attack:* +1 to hit, reach 5 ft., one target. *Hit:* 2 (1d6 − 1) bludgeoning damage.

DEVILS

Devils scheme and fight to reach the top of the infernal hierarchy of the Nine Hells. Several devils are introduced here, some that have a place in the social order and others that stand apart from it.

ABISHAI

Each abishai was once a mortal who somehow won Tiamat's favor before death and, as a reward, found its soul transformed into a hideous devil to serve at her pleasure in the Nine Hells.

Emissaries of Doom. Tiamat deploys abishais as emissaries, sending them to represent her interests in the Hells and across the multiverse. Some have simple tasks, such as delivering a message to cultists or taking charge of worshipers to carry out a sensitive mission. Others have greater responsibilities, such as leading large groups, assassinating targets, and serving in armies. In all cases, abishais are fanatically loyalty to Tiamat, ready to lay down their lives if needed.

Outsiders in Hell. Abishais stand outside the normal hierarchy of the Nine Hells, having their own chain of command and ultimately answering to Tiamat (and Asmodeus, when the dark lord chooses to use them). Other archdevils can command abishais to work for them, but most archdevils do so rarely, since it is never clear whether an abishai follows Tiamat's orders or Asmodeus's. There is inherent risk in countermanding an order given by Tiamat, but interfering with Asmodeus's plans invites certain destruction.

BLACK ABISHAI

Expert assassins and infiltrators, black abishais can weave shadows to mask their presence, allowing them to reach a location from where they can deliver a fatal strike to their targets.

Tiamat is a force of Chaos bound to a place of Law. Are abishai her servants or her jailers?

BLACK ABISHAI
Medium fiend (devil), lawful evil

Armor Class 15 (natural armor)
Hit Points 58 (9d8 + 18)
Speed 30 ft., fly 40 ft.

STR	DEX	CON	INT	WIS	CHA
14 (+2)	17 (+3)	14 (+2)	13 (+1)	16 (+3)	11 (+0)

Saving Throws Dex +6, Wis +6
Skills Perception +6, Stealth +6
Damage Resistances cold; bludgeoning, piercing, and slashing from nonmagical attacks that aren't silvered
Damage Immunities acid, fire, poison
Condition Immunities poisoned
Senses darkvision 120 ft., passive Perception 16
Languages Draconic, Infernal, telepathy 120 ft.
Challenge 7 (2,900 XP)

Devil's Sight. Magical darkness doesn't impede the abishai's darkvision.

Magic Resistance. The abishai has advantage on saving throws against spells and other magical effects.

Magic Weapons. The abishai's weapon attacks are magical.

Shadow Stealth. While in dim light or darkness, the abishai can take the Hide action as a bonus action.

ACTIONS

Multiattack. The abishai makes three attacks: two with its scimitar and one with its bite.

Scimitar. *Melee Weapon Attack:* +6 to hit, reach 5 ft., one target. *Hit:* 6 (1d6 + 3) slashing damage.

Bite. *Melee Weapon Attack:* +6 to hit, reach 5 ft., one target. *Hit:* 8 (1d10 + 3) piercing damage plus 9 (2d8) acid damage.

Creeping Darkness (Recharge 6). The abishai casts *darkness* at a point within 120 feet of it, requiring no components. Wisdom is its spellcasting ability for this spell. While the spell persists, the abishai can move the area of darkness up to 60 feet as a bonus action.

BLUE ABISHAI

Seekers of forgotten lore and lost relics, blue abishais are the most cunning and learned of their kind. Their research into occult subjects gleaned from tomes and grimoires plundered from across the multiverse enables them to become accomplished spellcasters. They use their magic to devastate their mistress's enemies.

GREEN ABISHAI

The envoys of Tiamat's armies, green abishais represent the god's interests in the Nine Hells and beyond. Their keen senses make them adept at discovering secrets and other sensitive information, while their diplomatic skills and their magic ensure that they can manipulate even the shrewdest opponents.

RED ABISHAI

Red abishais have no equals among the abishais when it comes to leadership ability and raw power. They can invoke Tiamat's authority to bend even dragons to their will. Red abishais lead other devils into battle or take charge of troublesome cults to ensure that they continue to carry out Tiamat's commands. A red abishai cuts a fearsome figure, and that sight can be inspiring to the abishai's allies, filling them with a fanatical willingness to fight.

WHITE ABISHAI

Though they are the least of their kind, white abishais fight with a reckless fury, making them ideally suited for bolstering the ranks of Tiamat's armies. White abishais fight without fear, becoming whirlwinds of destruction on the battlefield.

BLUE ABISHAI

Medium fiend (devil), lawful evil

Armor Class 19 (natural armor)
Hit Points 195 (26d8 + 78)
Speed 30 ft., fly 50 ft.

STR	DEX	CON	INT	WIS	CHA
15 (+2)	14 (+2)	17 (+3)	22 (+6)	23 (+6)	18 (+4)

Saving Throws Int +12, Wis +12
Skills Arcana +12
Damage Resistances cold; bludgeoning, piercing, and slashing from nonmagical attacks that aren't silvered
Damage Immunities fire, lightning, poison
Condition Immunities poisoned
Senses darkvision 120 ft., passive Perception 16
Languages Draconic, Infernal, telepathy 120 ft.
Challenge 17 (18,000 XP)

Devil's Sight. Magical darkness doesn't impede the abishai's darkvision.

Magic Resistance. The abishai has advantage on saving throws against spells and other magical effects.

Magic Weapons. The abishai's weapon attacks are magical.

Spellcasting. The abishai is a 13th-level spellcaster. Its spellcasting ability is Intelligence (spell save DC 20, +12 to hit with spell attacks). The abishai has the following wizard spells prepared:

Cantrips (at will): *friends, mage hand, message, minor illusion, shocking grasp*
1st level (4 slots): *chromatic orb, disguise self, expeditious retreat, magic missile, charm person, thunderwave*
2nd level (3 slots): *darkness, mirror image, misty step*
3rd level (3 slots): *dispel magic, fear, lightning bolt*
4th level (3 slots): *dimension door, greater invisibility, ice storm*
5th level (2 slots): *cone of cold, wall of force*
6th level (1 slot): *chain lightning*
7th level (1 slot): *teleport*

ACTIONS

Multiattack. The abishai makes two attacks: one with its quarterstaff and one with its bite.

Quarterstaff. *Melee Weapon Attack:* +8 to hit, reach 5 ft., one target. *Hit:* 5 (1d6 + 2) bludgeoning damage, or 6 (1d8 + 2) bludgeoning damage if used with two hands.

Bite. *Melee Weapon Attack:* +8 to hit, reach 5 ft., one target. *Hit:* 13 (2d10 + 2) piercing damage plus 14 (4d6) lightning damage.

D

Green Abishai

Medium fiend (devil), lawful evil

Armor Class 18 (natural armor)
Hit Points 187 (25d8 + 75)
Speed 30 ft., fly 40 ft.

STR	DEX	CON	INT	WIS	CHA
12 (+1)	17 (+3)	16 (+3)	17 (+3)	12 (+1)	19 (+4)

Saving Throws Int +8, Cha +9
Skills Deception +9, Insight +6, Perception +6, Persuasion +9
Damage Resistances cold; bludgeoning, piercing, and slashing from nonmagical attacks that aren't silvered
Damage Immunities fire, poison
Condition Immunities poisoned
Senses darkvision 120 ft., passive Perception 16
Languages Draconic, Infernal, telepathy 120 ft.
Challenge 15 (13,000 XP)

Devil's Sight. Magical darkness doesn't impede the abishai's darkvision.

Innate Spellcasting. The abishai's innate spellcasting ability is Charisma (spell save DC 17). It can innately cast the following spells, requiring no material components:

At will: *alter self, major image*
3/day each: *charm person, detect thoughts, fear*
1/day each: *confusion, dominate person, mass suggestion*

Magic Resistance. The abishai has advantage on saving throws against spells and other magical effects.

Magic Weapons. The abishai's weapon attacks are magical.

Actions

Multiattack. The abishai makes two attacks, one with its claws and one with its longsword, or it casts one spell from its Innate Spellcasting trait and makes one claw attack.

Longsword. *Melee Weapon Attack:* +6 to hit, reach 5 ft., one target. *Hit:* 5 (1d8 + 1) slashing damage, or 6 (1d10 + 1) slashing damage if used with two hands.

Claws. *Melee Weapon Attack:* +8 to hit, reach 5 ft., one target. *Hit:* 12 (2d8 + 3) piercing damage. If the target is a creature, it must succeed on a DC 16 Constitution saving throw or take 11 (2d10) poison damage and become poisoned for 1 minute. The poisoned target can repeat the saving throw at the end of each of its turns, ending the effect on itself on a success.

Red Abishai

Medium fiend (devil), lawful evil

Armor Class 22 (natural armor)
Hit Points 255 (30d8 + 120)
Speed 30 ft., fly 50 ft.

STR	DEX	CON	INT	WIS	CHA
23 (+6)	16 (+3)	19 (+4)	14 (+2)	15 (+2)	19 (+4)

Saving Throws Str +12, Con +10, Wis +8
Skills Intimidation +10, Perception +8
Damage Resistances cold; bludgeoning, piercing, and slashing from nonmagical attacks that aren't silvered
Damage Immunities fire, poison
Condition Immunities poisoned
Senses darkvision 120 ft., passive Perception 18
Languages Draconic, Infernal, telepathy 120 ft.
Challenge 19 (22,000 XP)

Devil's Sight. Magical darkness doesn't impede the abishai's darkvision.

Magic Resistance. The abishai has advantage on saving throws against spells and other magical effects.

Magic Weapons. The abishai's weapon attacks are magical.

Actions

Multiattack. The abishai can use its Frightful Presence. It also makes three attacks: one with its morningstar, one with its claw, and one with its bite.

Morningstar. *Melee Weapon Attack:* +12 to hit, reach 5 ft., one target. *Hit:* 10 (1d8 + 6) piercing damage.

Claw. *Melee Weapon Attack:* +12 to hit, reach 5 ft., one target. *Hit:* 17 (2d10 + 6) slashing damage.

Bite. *Melee Weapon Attack:* +12 to hit, reach 5 ft., one target. *Hit:* 22 (5d10 + 6) piercing damage plus 38 (7d10) fire damage.

Frightful Presence. Each creature of the abishai's choice that is within 120 feet and aware of it must succeed on a DC 18 Wisdom saving throw or become frightened of it for 1 minute. A creature can repeat the saving throw at the end of each of its turns, ending the effect on itself on a success. If a creature's saving throw is successful or the effect ends for it, the creature is immune to the abishai's Frightful Presence for the next 24 hours.

Incite Fanaticism. The abishai chooses up to four of its allies within 60 feet of it that can see it. For 1 minute, each of those allies makes attack rolls with advantage and can't be frightened.

Power of the Dragon Queen. The abishai targets one dragon it can see within 120 feet of it. The dragon must make a DC 18 Charisma saving throw. A chromatic dragon makes this save with disadvantage. On a successful save, the target is immune to the abishai's Power of the Dragon Queen for 1 hour. On a failed save, the target is charmed by the abishai for 1 hour. While charmed in this way, the target regards the abishai as a trusted friend to be heeded and protected. This effect ends if the abishai or its companions deal damage to the target.

WHITE ABISHAI

GREEN ABISHAI

RED ABISHAI

WHITE ABISHAI

Medium fiend (devil), lawful evil

Armor Class 15 (natural armor)
Hit Points 68 (8d8 + 32)
Speed 30 ft., fly 40 ft.

STR	DEX	CON	INT	WIS	CHA
16 (+3)	11 (+0)	18 (+4)	11 (+0)	12 (+1)	13 (+1)

Saving Throws Str +6, Con +7
Damage Resistances bludgeoning, piercing, and slashing from nonmagical attacks that aren't silvered
Damage Immunities cold, fire, poison
Condition Immunities poisoned
Senses darkvision 120 ft., passive Perception 11
Languages Draconic, Infernal, telepathy 120 ft.
Challenge 6 (2,300 XP)

Devil's Sight. Magical darkness doesn't impede the abishai's darkvision.

Magic Resistance. The abishai has advantage on saving throws against spells and other magical effects.

Magic Weapons. The abishai's weapon attacks are magical.

Reckless. At the start of its turn, the abishai can gain advantage on all melee weapon attack rolls during that turn, but attack rolls against it have advantage until the start of its next turn.

ACTIONS

Multiattack. The abishai makes two attacks: one with its longsword and one with its claw.

Longsword. *Melee Weapon Attack:* +6 to hit, reach 5 ft., one target. *Hit:* 7 (1d8 + 3) slashing damage, or 8 (1d10 + 3) slashing damage if used with two hands.

Claw. *Melee Weapon Attack:* +6 to hit, reach 5 ft., one target. *Hit:* 8 (1d10 + 3) slashing damage.

Bite. *Melee Weapon Attack:* +6 to hit, reach 5 ft., one target. *Hit:* 5 (1d4 + 3) piercing damage plus 3 (1d6) cold damage.

REACTIONS

Vicious Reprisal. In response to taking damage, the abishai makes a bite attack against a random creature within 5 feet of it. If no creature is within reach, the abishai moves up to half its speed toward an enemy it can see, without provoking opportunity attacks.

D

Amnizu

Amnizus lead the infernal legions into battle and command guardians at the gateways to the Hells. Amnizus are arrogant, bullying, and ruthless, but they're also highly intelligent tacticians and unfailingly loyal—qualities that the hellish archdukes value.

Guarding the River Styx. Some amnizus perform the critical task of watching over the River Styx from fortresses along the river's blighted banks, where it flows through Dis and Stygia. Souls arriving in the form of lemures have no personalities or memories; they're driven only by the desire to commit evil. The amnizus that patrol here drill the rules of the Nine Hells into the new arrivals' pitiful brains and marshal the lemures into legions.

Variant: Devil Summoning

Some amnizus have an action that allows them to summon other devils.

Summon Devil (1/Day). The amnizu summons 2d4 bearded devils or 1d4 barbed devils. A summoned devil appears in an unoccupied space within 60 feet of the amnizu, acts as an ally of the amnizu, and can't summon other devils. It remains for 1 minute, until the amnizu dies, or until its summoner dismisses it as an action.

Amnizu

Medium fiend (devil), lawful evil

Armor Class 21 (natural armor)
Hit Points 202 (27d8 + 81)
Speed 30 ft., fly 40 ft.

STR	DEX	CON	INT	WIS	CHA
11 (+0)	13 (+1)	16 (+3)	20 (+5)	12 (+1)	18 (+4)

Saving Throws Dex +7, Con +9, Wis +7, Cha +10
Skills Perception +7
Damage Resistances cold; bludgeoning, piercing, and slashing from nonmagical attacks that aren't silvered
Damage Immunities fire, poison
Condition Immunities charmed, poisoned
Senses darkvision 120 ft., passive Perception 17
Languages Common, Infernal, telepathy 1,000 ft.
Challenge 18 (20,000 XP)

Devil's Sight. Magical darkness doesn't impede the amnizu's darkvision.

Innate Spellcasting. The amnizu's innate spellcasting ability is Intelligence (spell save 19, +11 to hit with spell attacks). The amnizu can innately cast the following spells, requiring no material components:

At will: *charm person, command*
3/day each: *dominate person, fireball*
1/day each: *dominate monster, feeblemind*

Magic Resistance. The amnizu has advantage on saving throws against spells and other magical effects.

Actions

Multiattack. The amnizu uses Poison Mind. It also makes two attacks: one with its whip and one with its Disruptive Touch.

Taskmaster Whip. *Melee Weapon Attack:* +11 to hit, reach 10 ft., one target. *Hit:* 10 (2d4 + 5) slashing damage plus 33 (6d10) force damage.

Disruptive Touch. *Melee Spell Attack:* +11 to hit, reach 5 ft., one target. *Hit:* 44 (8d10) necrotic damage.

Poison Mind. The amnizu targets one or two creatures that it can see within 60 feet of it. Each target must succeed on a DC 19 Wisdom saving throw or take 26 (4d12) necrotic damage and be blinded until the start of the amnizu's next turn.

Forgetfulness (Recharge 6). The amnizu targets one creature it can see within 60 feet of it. That creature must succeed on a DC 18 Intelligence saving throw or become stunned for 1 minute. A stunned creature repeats the saving throw at the end of each of its turns, ending the effect on itself on a success. If the target is stunned for the full minute, it forgets everything it sensed, experienced, and learned during the last 5 hours.

Reactions

Instinctive Charm. When a creature within 60 feet of the amnizu makes an attack roll against it, and another creature is within the attack's range, the attacker must make a DC 19 Wisdom saving throw. On a failed save, the attacker must target the creature that is closest to it, not including the amnizu or itself. If multiple creatures are closest, the attacker chooses which one to target. If the saving throw is successful, the attacker is immune to the amnizu's Instinctive Charm for 24 hours.

Hellfire Engine

Hellfire engines are semiautonomous bringers of destruction. Amnizus and other devilish generals hold them in reserve until they are needed to repel an incursion by demons or crusading mortals, but occasionally one of these mechanical and magical hybrids gets loose, driven berserk by its need to destroy.

Many Forms, One Purpose. Hellfire engines take many forms, but all of them have one purpose: to mow down foes in waves. They are incapable of subtlety or trickery, but their destructive capability is immense.

Soul Trapping. Mortal creatures slain by hellfire engines are doomed to join the infernal legions in mere hours unless powerful magic-wielders intervene on their behalf. The archdukes would like nothing better than to modify this magic so it works against demons, too, but that discovery has eluded them so far.

Constructed Nature. A hellfire engine doesn't require air, food, drink, or sleep.

HELLFIRE ENGINE
Huge construct, lawful evil

Armor Class 18 (natural armor)
Hit Points 216 (16d12 + 112)
Speed 40 ft.

STR	DEX	CON	INT	WIS	CHA
20 (+5)	16 (+3)	24 (+7)	2 (−4)	10 (+0)	1 (−5)

Saving Throws Dex +8, Wis +5, Cha +0
Damage Resistances cold, psychic; bludgeoning, piercing, and slashing from nonmagical attacks that aren't silvered
Damage Immunities fire, poison
Condition Immunities charmed, deafened, exhaustion, frightened, paralyzed, poisoned, unconscious
Senses darkvision 120 ft., passive Perception 10
Languages understands Infernal but can't speak
Challenge 16 (15,000 XP)

Immutable Form. The hellfire engine is immune to any spell or effect that would alter its form.

Magic Resistance. The hellfire engine has advantage on saving throws against spells and other magical effects.

ACTIONS

Flesh-Crushing Stride. The hellfire engine moves up to its speed in a straight line. During this move, it can enter Large or smaller creatures' spaces. A creature whose space the hellfire engine enters must make a DC 18 Dexterity saving throw. On a successful save, the creature is pushed 5 feet to the nearest space out of the hellfire engine's path. On a failed save, the creature falls prone and takes 28 (8d6) bludgeoning damage.

If the hellfire engine remains in the prone creature's space, the creature is also restrained until it's no longer in the same space as the hellfire engine. While restrained in this way, the creature, or another creature within 5 feet of it, can make a DC 18 Strength check. On a success, the creature is shunted to an unoccupied space of its choice within 5 feet of the hellfire engine and is no longer restrained.

Hellfire Weapons. The hellfire engine uses one of the following options:

Bonemelt Sprayer. The hellfire engine spews acidic flame in a 60-foot cone. Each creature in the cone must make a DC 20 Dexterity saving throw, taking 11 (2d10) fire damage plus 18 (4d8) acid damage on a failed save, or half as much damage on a successful one. Creatures that fail the saving throw are drenched in burning acid and take 5 (1d10) fire damage plus 9 (2d8) acid damage at the end of their turns. An affected creature or another creature within 5 feet of it can take an action to scrape off the burning fuel.

Lightning Flail. *Melee Weapon Attack:* +11 to hit, reach 15 ft., one creature. *Hit:* 18 (3d8 + 5) bludgeoning damage plus 22 (5d8) lightning damage. Up to three other creatures of the hellfire engine's choice that it can see within 30 feet of the target must each make a DC 20 Dexterity saving throw, taking 22 (5d8) lightning damage on a failed save, or half as much damage on a successful one.

Thunder Cannon. The hellfire engine targets a point within 120 feet of it that it can see. Each creature within 30 feet of that point must make a DC 20 Dexterity saving throw, taking 27 (5d10) bludgeoning damage plus 13 (2d12) thunder damage on a failed save, or half as much damage on a successful one.

If the chosen option kills a creature, the creature's soul rises from the River Styx as a lemure in Avernus in 1d4 hours. If the creature isn't revived before then, only a *wish* spell or killing the lemure and casting *true resurrection* on the creature's original body can restore it to life. Constructs and devils are immune to this effect.

MERREGON

The souls of fallen soldiers, mercenaries, and body-guards who served evil without reservation often find everlasting servitude in the Nine Hells as merregons. These faceless foot soldiers are the hells' legionnaires, tasked with protecting the realm and its rulers against intruders.

Masks of Uniformity. Merregons have no individuality, and hence no need for faces. Every merregon legionnaire has a metal mask bolted to its head. Markings on the mask indicate the only elements of the wearer's identity that matter: its commander and the layer of the Nine Hells it serves.

Fearless Obedience. Because of their unshakable loyalty, merregons form the backbone of many devils' protective retinues. They shrink from no task, no matter how dangerous. Unless ordered to fall back, they retreat from no fight.

Merregons can't speak, and their telepathy is one-to-one. Their orderly ranks are easily confused if you slay their shouting masters.

MERREGON
Medium fiend (devil), lawful evil

Armor Class 16 (natural armor)
Hit Points 45 (6d8 + 18)
Speed 30 ft.

STR	DEX	CON	INT	WIS	CHA
18 (+4)	14 (+2)	17 (+3)	6 (−2)	12 (+1)	8 (−1)

Damage Resistances cold; bludgeoning, piercing, and slashing from nonmagical attacks that aren't silvered
Damage Immunities fire, poison
Condition Immunities frightened, poisoned
Senses darkvision 60 ft., passive Perception 11
Languages understands Infernal but can't speak, telepathy 120 ft.
Challenge 4 (1,100 XP)

Devil's Sight. Magical darkness doesn't impede the merregon's darkvision.

Magic Resistance. The merregon has advantage on saving throws against spells and other magical effects.

ACTIONS

Multiattack. The merregon makes two halberd attacks, or if an allied fiend of challenge rating 6 or higher is within 60 feet of it, the merregon makes three halberd attacks.

Halberd. *Melee Weapon Attack:* +6 to hit, reach 10 ft., one target. *Hit:* 9 (1d10 + 4) slashing damage.

Heavy Crossbow. *Ranged Weapon Attack:* +4 to hit, range 100/400 ft., one target. *Hit:* 7 (1d10 + 2) piercing damage.

REACTIONS

Loyal Bodyguard. When another fiend within 5 feet of the merregon is hit by an attack, the merregon causes itself to be hit instead.

Narzugon

Paladins who make deals with devils and carry their twisted sense of honor into the afterlife are especially valuable to the archdukes of the Nine Hells, who want unquestioning champions to lead their legions in war. These narzugons, wielding lances of hellfire and riding nightmare steeds like horrific perversions of knights errant, roam across the infernal layers and other planes to carry out the will of their masters.

NARZUGON
Medium fiend (devil), lawful evil

Armor Class 20 (plate armor, shield)
Hit Points 112 (15d8 + 45)
Speed 30 ft.

STR	DEX	CON	INT	WIS	CHA
20 (+5)	10 (+0)	17 (+3)	16 (+3)	14 (+2)	19 (+4)

Saving Throws Dex +5, Con +8, Cha +9
Skills Perception +7
Damage Resistances acid, cold; bludgeoning, piercing, and slashing from nonmagical attacks that aren't silvered
Damage Immunities fire, poison
Condition Immunities charmed, frightened, poisoned
Senses darkvision 120 ft., passive Perception 17
Languages Common, Infernal, telepathy 120 ft.
Challenge 13 (10,000 XP)

Diabolical Sense. The narzugon has advantage on Wisdom (Perception) checks made to perceive good-aligned creatures.

Infernal Tack. The narzugon wears spurs that are part of *infernal tack*, which allow it to summon its nightmare companion.

Magic Resistance. The narzugon has advantage on saving throws against spells and other magical effects.

ACTIONS

Multiattack. The narzugon uses its Infernal Command or Terrifying Command. It also makes three hellfire lance attacks.

Hellfire Lance. *Melee Weapon Attack:* +10 to hit, reach 10 ft., one target. *Hit:* 11 (1d12 + 5) piercing damage plus 16 (3d10) fire damage. If this damage kills a creature, the creature's soul rises from the River Styx as a lemure in Avernus in 1d4 hours. If the creature isn't revived before then, only a *wish* spell or killing the lemure and casting *true resurrection* on the creature's original body can restore it to life. Constructs and devils are immune to this effect.

Infernal Command. Each ally of the narzugon within 60 feet of it can't be charmed or frightened until the end of the narzugon's next turn.

Terrifying Command. Each creature that isn't a fiend within 60 feet of the narzugon that can hear it must succeed on a DC 17 Charisma saving throw or become frightened of it for 1 minute. A creature can repeat the saving throw at the end of each of its turns, ending the effect on itself on a success. A creature that makes a successful saving throw is immune to this narzugon's Terrifying Command for 24 hours.

Healing (1/Day). The narzugon, or one creature it touches, regains up to 100 hit points.

Death in Hellfire. A narzugon's lances are forged in hellfire. The soul of anyone killed by such a lance is shunted to the River Styx for rebirth as a lemure. Each lance is unique to its owner, bearing the marks of both the narzugon and its master.

Nightmare Riders. Each narzugon claims a nightmare as its mount. These nightmares are bound by *infernal tack* (see the sidebar) and must respond to summons and commands from the wearer of the spurs.

MAGIC ITEM: INFERNAL TACK
Wondrous item, legendary (requires attunement by a creature of evil alignment)

A narzugon binds a nightmare to its service with *infernal tack*, which consists of a bridle, bit, reins, saddle, stirrups, and spurs. A nightmare equipped with *infernal tack* must serve whoever wears the spurs until the wearer dies or the tack is removed.

You can use an action to call a nightmare equipped with *infernal tack* by clashing the spurs together or scraping them through blood. The nightmare appears at the start of your next turn, within 20 feet of you. It acts as your ally and takes its turn on your initiative count. It remains for 1 day, until you or it dies, or until you dismiss it as an action. If the nightmare dies, it reforms in the Nine Hells within 24 hours, after which you can summon it again.

The tack doesn't conjure a nightmare from thin air; one must first be subdued so the tack can be placed on it. No nightmare accepts this forced servitude willingly, but some eventually form strong loyalties to their masters and become true partners in evil.

Nupperibo

No soul is turned away from the Nine Hells, but the truly worthless—those whose evil acts in life arose from carelessness and sloth more than anything else—are suitable only to become nupperibos. These pitiful creatures shuffle mindlessly across the landscape: blind, bloated from unquenchable hunger, and groping for whatever scraps of fetid matter or swarming vermin they can scoop into their groaning mouths.

Nauseating Bulk. Individually, nupperibos are pathetic, but they're rarely alone and can be dangerous when gathered into packs. They herd together into throngs that can clog a vital passage or an entire valley. Clouds of stinging insects, stirges, and other vermin surround them in a terrifying, reeking sheath that torments any non-devil that draws near.

Hunger Unending. A nupperibo knows nothing but the hunger that propels it on a blind quest for anything to devour. Once it senses a potential meal, it pursues that prey tirelessly until the food is consumed, the nupperibo is slain, or some other morsel crosses the fiend's path and distracts it.

Slavish Obedience. With no interest of its own beyond the need to consume, a nupperibo obeys unthinkingly any command it receives telepathically from another devil. This blind loyalty makes them the easiest of infernal troops to lead into battle, but their presence in a legion does nothing to elevate its general's status.

A lemure emerges from the Styx wiped of memory, yet the patterns of evil it performed in life remain indelibly inscribed upon its soul. Those who lacked ambition cannot climb the hierarchical ladder of the Hells. They instead step down, becoming nupperibos.

Nupperibo

Medium fiend (devil), lawful evil

Armor Class 13 (natural armor)
Hit Points 11 (2d8 + 2)
Speed 20 ft.

STR	DEX	CON	INT	WIS	CHA
16 (+3)	11 (+0)	13 (+1)	3 (−4)	8 (−1)	1 (−5)

Skills Perception +1
Damage Resistances acid, cold; bludgeoning, piercing, and slashing from nonmagical attacks that aren't silvered
Damage Immunities fire, poison
Condition Immunities blinded, charmed, frightened, poisoned
Senses blindsight 10 ft. (blind beyond this radius), passive Perception 11
Languages understands Infernal but can't speak
Challenge 1/2 (100 XP)

Cloud of Vermin. Any creature, other than a devil, that starts its turn within 20 feet of the nupperibo must make a DC 11 Constitution saving throw. A creature within the areas of two or more nupperibos makes the saving throw with disadvantage. On a failure, the creature takes 2 (1d4) piercing damage.

Hunger-Driven. In the Nine Hells, the nupperibos can flawlessly track any creature that has taken damage from any nupperibo's Cloud of Vermin within the previous 24 hours.

Actions

Bite. *Melee Weapon Attack:* +5 to hit, reach 5 ft., one target. *Hit:* 6 (1d6 + 3) piercing damage.

Orthon

When an archduke of the Nine Hells needs a creature tracked, found, and either done away with or captured, the task usually falls to an orthon. Orthons are infernal bounty hunters, tireless in their pursuit of their quarry across the multiverse.

Unseen and All-Seeing. Orthons are infamous for their sharp senses. Because an orthon can become invisible at will, its quarry is often unaware of being hunted until the orthon strikes. The orthon's invisibility can be disrupted when the devil is attacked, however, so a strong counterattack is often the best defense against it.

A Sporting Chance. Orthons value the challenge of the chase and the thrill of one-on-one combat above all else. An orthon's first loyalty is to its archduke, but if it has no immediate assignment, an orthon might work for anyone who offers it the promise of a worthy struggle against a lethal foe. Because they travel widely, orthons are unequaled as guides through the layers of the Nine Hells.

Orthon
Large fiend (devil), lawful evil

Armor Class 17 (half plate)
Hit Points 105 (10d10 + 50)
Speed 30 ft., climb 30 ft.

STR	DEX	CON	INT	WIS	CHA
22 (+6)	16 (+3)	21 (+5)	15 (+2)	15 (+2)	16 (+3)

Saving Throws Dex +7, Con +9, Wis +6
Skills Perception +10, Stealth +11, Survival +10
Damage Resistances cold; bludgeoning, piercing, and slashing from nonmagical attacks that aren't silvered
Damage Immunities fire, poison
Condition Immunities charmed, exhaustion, poisoned
Senses darkvision 120 ft., truesight 30 ft., passive Perception 20
Languages Common, Infernal, telepathy 120 ft.
Challenge 10 (5,900 XP)

Invisibility Field. The orthon can use a bonus action to become invisible. Any equipment the orthon wears or carries is also invisible as long as the equipment is on its person. This invisibility ends immediately after the orthon makes an attack roll or is hit by an attack.

Magic Resistance. The orthon has advantage on saving throws against spells and other magical effects.

Actions

Infernal Dagger. *Melee Weapon Attack:* +10 to hit, reach 5 ft., one target. *Hit:* 11 (2d4 + 6) slashing damage, and the target must make a DC 17 Constitution saving throw, taking 22 (4d10) poison damage on a failed save, or half as much damage on a successful one. On a failure, the target is also poisoned for 1 minute. The poisoned target can repeat the saving throw at the end of each of its turns, ending the effect on itself on a success.

Brass Crossbow. *Ranged Weapon Attack:* +7 to hit, range 100/400 ft., one target. *Hit:* 14 (2d10 + 3) piercing damage, plus one of the following effects:

1. **Acid.** The target must make a DC 17 Constitution saving throw, taking an additional 17 (5d6) acid damage on a failed save, or half as much damage on a successful one.
2. **Blindness (1/Day).** The target takes 5 (1d10) radiant damage. In addition, the target and all other creatures within 20 feet of it must each make a successful DC 17 Dexterity saving throw or be blinded until the end of the orthon's next turn.
3. **Concussion.** The target and each creature within 20 feet of it must make a DC 17 Constitution saving throw, taking 13 (2d12) thunder damage on a failed save, or half as much damage on a successful one.
4. **Entanglement.** The target must make a successful DC 17 Dexterity saving throw or be restrained for 1 hour by strands of sticky webbing. A restrained creature can escape by using an action to make a successful DC 17 Dexterity or Strength check. Any creature other than an orthon that touches the restrained creature must make a successful DC 17 Dexterity saving throw or become similarly restrained.
5. **Paralysis (1/Day).** The target takes 22 (4d10) lightning damage and must make a successful DC 17 Constitution saving throw or be paralyzed for 1 minute. The paralyzed target can repeat the saving throw at the end of each of its turns, ending the effect on itself on a success.
6. **Tracking.** For the next 24 hours, the orthon knows the direction and distance to the target, as long as it's on the same plane of existence. If the target is on a different plane, the orthon knows which one, but not the exact location there.

Reactions

Explosive Retribution. When it is reduced to 15 hit points or fewer, the orthon causes itself to explode. All other creatures within 30 feet of it must each make a DC 17 Dexterity saving throw, taking 9 (2d8) fire damage plus 9 (2d8) thunder damage on a failed save, or half as much damage on a successful one. This explosion destroys the orthon, its infernal dagger, and its brass crossbow.

D

DEVILS: ARCHDEVILS

At the top of the hierarchy of the Nine Hells stand the archdevils, a vicious and backbiting group made up of the Hells' elite devils. They include the various lords, the nobles who owe them fealty, and some exiles and outcasts who have fallen out of favor. Favor in the Nine Hells shifts like the wind, and the fortunes of the great and mighty rise and fall at the whims of their betters. Many dread names are included in the rolls of the archdevils; the few described here are among those that adventurers are most likely to encounter.

Wish Fulfillment. All devils seek control over mortal souls, so they offer enticements to tempt mortals into making unwise bargains. Archdevils, possessing the true power of the Nine Hells, can fulfill nearly any desire (within the limits of a *wish* spell) requested by the mortals they bind to their infernal contracts. Archdevils always fulfill the letter of the wish, rewarding desperate mortals with a twisted interpretation of their desires. In exchange for this gift, the devil expects and receives total power over a soul and usually claims it upon the mortal's death. An archdevil can't fulfill its own wish.

Bael, Geryon, Hutijin, Moloch—they are pawns. Even the lords of layers such as Zariel and Mammon are merely more powerful pieces. Archdevils may make dramatic moves, but it is Asmodeus who plays the game best.

BAEL
Large fiend (devil), lawful evil

Armor Class 18 (plate)
Hit Points 189 (18d10 + 90)
Speed 30 ft.

STR	DEX	CON	INT	WIS	CHA
24 (+7)	17 (+3)	20 (+5)	21 (+5)	24 (+7)	24 (+7)

Saving Throws Dex +9, Con +11, Int +11, Cha +13
Skills Intimidation +13, Perception +13, Persuasion +13
Damage Resistances cold; bludgeoning, piercing, and slashing from nonmagical attacks that aren't silvered
Damage Immunities fire, poison
Condition Immunities charmed, exhaustion, frightened, poisoned
Senses truesight 120 ft., passive Perception 23
Languages all, telepathy 120 ft.
Challenge 19 (22,000 XP)

Dreadful. Bael can use a bonus action to appear dreadful until the start of his next turn. Each creature, other than a devil, that starts its turn within 10 feet of Bael must succeed on a DC 22 Wisdom saving throw or be frightened until the start of the creature's next turn.

Innate Spellcasting. Bael's innate spellcasting ability is Charisma (spell save DC 21, +13 to hit with spell attacks). He can innately cast the following spells, requiring no material components:

At will: *alter self* (can become Medium when changing his appearance), *animate dead*, *charm person*, *detect magic*, *inflict wounds* (as an 8th-level spell), *invisibility* (self only), *major image*
3/day each: *counterspell*, *dispel magic*, *fly*, *suggestion*, *wall of fire*
1/day each: *dominate monster*, *symbol* (stunning only)

Legendary Resistance (3/Day). If Bael fails a saving throw, he can choose to succeed instead.

Magic Resistance. Bael has advantage on saving throws against spells and other magical effects.

Magic Weapons. Bael's weapon attacks are magical.

Regeneration. Bael regains 20 hit points at the start of his turn. If he takes cold or radiant damage, this trait doesn't function at the start of his next turn. Bael dies only if he starts his turn with 0 hit points and doesn't regenerate.

ACTIONS

Multiattack. Bael makes two melee attacks.

Hellish Morningstar. *Melee Weapon Attack:* +13 to hit, reach 20 ft., one target. *Hit:* 16 (2d8 + 7) piercing damage plus 13 (3d8) necrotic damage.

Infernal Command. Each ally of Bael's within 60 feet of him can't be charmed or frightened until the end of his next turn.

Teleport. Bael magically teleports, along with any equipment he is wearing and carrying, up to 120 feet to an unoccupied space he can see.

LEGENDARY ACTIONS

Bael can take 3 legendary actions, choosing from the options below. Only one legendary action option can be used at a time and only at the end of another creature's turn. Bael regains spent legendary actions at the start of his turn.

Attack (Cost 2 Actions). Bael attacks once with his hellish morningstar.
Awaken Greed. Bael casts *charm person* or *major image*.
Infernal Command. Bael uses his Infernal Command action.
Teleport. Bael uses his Teleport action.

BAEL

With the Blood War raging for eons and no end in sight, opportunities abound for ambitious archdevils to win fame, glory, and power in the ongoing struggle against the demons. Duke Bael, one of Mammon's most important vassals, has won fame and acclaim for his victories. Charged with leading sixty-six companies of barbed devils, Bael has proven to be a tactical genius, earning esteem for himself and his master as a result of victory after victory over the abyssal host. Mammon relies on Bael, because of his battle acumen, to safeguard his holdings. Mammon has never been ousted during a time when so many other archdevils have lost their positions, which is a testament to Bael's skill on the battlefield.

For his accomplishments, as well as for the hue of his skin, Baal has been granted the title of Bronze General. His accolades notwithstanding, Bael has had a difficult time navigating the quagmire of infernal politics. His critics call him naive, though never to his face. His primary interest has always been leading soldiers in battle, so he finds it frustrating to have his ambitions of ascending to a higher rank constantly stymied by politically shrewd rivals.

Bael prefers to make servants out of his adversaries, and mortals bound to his service earn their wretched place by falling victim to Bael's superior stratagems. Bael gladly spares the lives of those he defeats, but only if they pledge their souls and service to him. Although he is willing to corrupt almost any being in this way, he always destroys any demons he defeats.

Bael also welcomes mortals into his service if they can provide him with an advantage in his own politicking. He recruits savvy individuals and relies on them to represent his interests at Mammon's court, which leaves Bael free to pursue his battle lust.

Despite his lack of interest in affairs outside battle, or perhaps because of it, Bael has gained a small following of cultists. Those who worship at his altar call him the King of Hell, and the most deluded believe that he is the lord of all devils. In arcane circles, certain writings, such as the dreaded *Book of Fire*, say that Bael revealed the *invisibility* spell to the world, though some scholars of magic hotly refute such claims. Bael is sometimes depicted as a toad, a cat, a male human, or some combination of these forms, though none of these images reflect his true appearance.

GERYON

Geryon is locked in an endless struggle with Levistus for control of Stygia. The two have fought each other for centuries, each displacing the other innumerable times. Currently, Geryon occupies an odd position in the infernal hierarchy. Although Levistus still claims lordship over Stygia, he has been trapped in an enormous block of ice at the command of Asmodeus. For his part, Geryon marshals his followers and seeks to discover the means to replace his hated rival.

Among the archdevils, Geryon and Zariel are especially known for martial prowess. He is a ferocious hunter and a relentless tracker. Other devils command legions and bid their followers to battle their enemies. Geryon loves the feeling of flesh and steel being sundered beneath his claws, and the taste of his foes' blood.

His ferocity serves him well in Stygia's frozen waste, but it has also limited his ability to collect souls and forge an effective hierarchy. Sages who study the Nine Hells believe that the battle for control of Stygia is a test staged by Asmodeus in hopes of purging the worst impulses from both Geryon and Levistus, or at the very least opening the door for a competent replacement for both to rise from the ranks.

GERYON'S LAIR

Geryon has recently reclaimed his ancient fortress, Coldsteel, a sprawling complex that rises from the ice and snow at the center of Stygia. He roams the passages of this place, scattering the ice devils and minotaur slaves he took from Baphomet, raging against Asmodeus's betrayal while spitting oaths of vengeance and hatching mad schemes to reclaim his standing from Levistus.

Lair Actions. On initiative count 20 (losing initiative ties), Geryon can take a lair action to cause one of the following effects; he can't use the same effect two rounds in a row:

- Geryon causes a blast of cold to burst from the ground at a point he can see within 120 feet of him. The cold fills a cube, 10 feet on each side, centered on that point. Each creature in that area must succeed on a DC 21 Constitution saving throw or take 28 (8d6) cold damage.
- Geryon targets one creature he can see within 60 feet of him. The target must succeed on a DC 21 Wisdom saving throw or become restrained for 1 minute. The target can end the effect on itself if it deals any damage to one or more of its allies.
- Geryon casts the *banishment* spell.

Which is less worthy: the archdevil who leads a layer while being trapped in a block of ice, or the archdevil who can't outmaneuver a frozen adversary?

Regional Effects. The region containing Geryon's lair is warped by his magic, creating one or more of the following effects:

- Intelligent creatures within 1 mile of the lair frequently see shimmering portals leading to places they consider safe. Passing through a portal always deposits a traveler somewhere in Stygia.
- Freezing strong winds howl around the area within 1 mile of the lair.
- Howls and screams fill the air within 1 mile of the lair. Any creature that finishes a short or long rest in this area must succeed on a DC 21 Wisdom saving throw or derive no benefit from the rest.

If Geryon dies, these effects fade over the course of 1d10 days.

> ### VARIANT: SOUND THE HORN
>
> Geryon can have an action that allows him to summon enslaved minotaurs.
>
> ***Sound the Horn (1/Day).*** Geryon blows his horn, which causes 5d4 minotaurs to appear in unoccupied spaces of his choice within 600 feet of him. The minotaurs roll initiative when they appear. They remain until they die or Geryon uses an action to dismiss any or all of them.

GERYON
Huge fiend (devil), lawful evil

Armor Class 19 (natural armor)
Hit Points 300 (24d12 + 144)
Speed 30 ft., fly 50 ft.

STR	DEX	CON	INT	WIS	CHA
29 (+9)	17 (+3)	22 (+6)	19 (+4)	16 (+3)	23 (+6)

Saving Throws Dex +10, Con +13, Wis +10, Cha +13
Skills Deception +13, Intimidation +13, Perception +10
Damage Resistances bludgeoning, piercing, and slashing from nonmagical attacks that aren't silvered
Damage Immunities cold, fire, poison
Condition Immunities charmed, exhaustion, frightened, poisoned
Senses truesight 120 ft., passive Perception 20
Languages all, telepathy 120 ft.
Challenge 22 (41,000 XP)

Innate Spellcasting. Geryon's innate spellcasting ability is Charisma (spell save DC 21). He can innately cast the following spells, requiring no material components:

At will: *alter self* (can become Medium when changing his appearance), *detect magic*, *geas*, *ice storm*, *invisibility* (self only), *locate object*, *suggestion*, *wall of ice*
1/day each: *divine word*, *symbol* (pain only)

Legendary Resistance (3/Day). If Geryon fails a saving throw, he can choose to succeed instead.

Magic Resistance. Geryon has advantage on saving throws against spells and other magical effects.

Magic Weapons. Geryon's weapon attacks are magical.

Regeneration. Geryon regains 20 hit points at the start of his turn. If he takes radiant damage, this trait doesn't function at the start of his next turn. Geryon dies only if he starts his turn with 0 hit points and doesn't regenerate.

ACTIONS

Multiattack. Geryon makes two attacks: one with his claws and one with his stinger.

Claws. *Melee Weapon Attack:* +16 to hit, reach 15 ft., one target. *Hit:* 23 (4d6 + 9) slashing damage. If the target is Large or smaller, it is grappled (DC 24) and restrained until the grapple ends. Geryon can grapple one creature at a time. If the target is already grappled by Geryon, the target takes an extra 27 (6d8) slashing damage.

Stinger. *Melee Weapon Attack:* +16 to hit, reach 20 ft., one creature. *Hit:* 14 (2d4 + 9) piercing damage, and the target must succeed on a DC 21 Constitution saving throw or take 13 (2d12) poison damage and become poisoned until it finishes a short or long rest. The target's hit point maximum is reduced by an amount equal to half the poison damage it takes. If its hit point maximum drops to 0, it dies. This reduction lasts until the poisoned condition is removed.

Teleport. Geryon magically teleports, along with any equipment he is wearing and carrying, up to 120 feet to an unoccupied space he can see.

LEGENDARY ACTIONS

Geryon can take 3 legendary actions, choosing from the options below. Only one legendary action option can be used at a time and only at the end of another creature's turn. Geryon regains spent legendary actions at the start of his turn.

Infernal Glare. Geryon targets one creature he can see within 60 feet of him. If the target can see Geryon, the target must succeed on a DC 23 Wisdom saving throw or become frightened of Geryon until the end of its next turn.
Swift Sting (Costs 2 Actions). Geryon attacks with his stinger.
Teleport. Geryon uses his Teleport action.

What price would you put on your life? How much then, for your soul? Bargain with Hutijin, and it will cost you both. I hope it is worth it.

HUTIJIN

Politics in the Nine Hells are anything but predictable. Alliances form all the time, but most wind up unraveling due to treachery. Nevertheless, for all their backbiting and betrayal, the devils do occasionally display loyalty, offering unwavering service to their masters. One such example is Hutijin, a duke of Cania and loyal servant of Mephistopheles.

Across the Hells, Hutijin's name fills lesser devils with fear and loathing, for this duke commands two companies of pit fiends, which make up Cania's aristocracy. With such soldiers under his command, Hutijin can easily crush any rival who gets in his way, while also providing Mephistopheles with security against armies that might seek to contest his dominion. Hutijin has amassed enough power to challenge the lord of Cania, but he has never wavered in his support for his master—suggesting, perhaps, that Mephistopheles has some hold over him.

Outside the Nine Hells, Hutijin is a relatively obscure figure, known only to the most learned infernal scholars. He has no cults of his own, and his servants are few in number. The reason is simple: Hutijin hates mortals. When summoned from the Hells, he repays the instigator with a long and agonizing death.

Mephistopheles forbids Hutijin from making too many forays into the Material Plane, since the duke's absence leaves him vulnerable to his rivals. Other archdevils know how much Hutijin despises mortals and have secretly disseminated the means to call him from the Nine Hells in the hope of distracting the archdevil long enough for them to assail Mephistopheles. Hutijin sends devils into the Material Plane to eradicate mention of his name and destroy those who have learned of him, but the summonings still occur. When called from his post, he negotiates as quickly as he can, usually closing a deal with little cost to the summoner. However, once the deal has been struck, Hutijin repays the interruption with death.

D

Hutijin

Large fiend (devil), lawful evil

Armor Class 19 (natural armor)
Hit Points 200 (16d10 + 112)
Speed 30 ft., fly 60 ft.

STR	DEX	CON	INT	WIS	CHA
27 (+8)	15 (+2)	25 (+7)	23 (+6)	19 (+4)	25 (+7)

Saving Throws Dex +9, Con +14, Wis +11
Skills Intimidation +14, Perception +11
Damage Resistances cold; bludgeoning, piercing, and slashing from nonmagical attacks that aren't silvered
Damage Immunities fire, poison
Condition Immunities charmed, exhaustion, frightened, poisoned
Senses truesight 120 ft., passive Perception 21
Languages all, telepathy 120 ft.
Challenge 21 (33,000 XP)

Infernal Despair. Each creature within 15 feet of Hutijin that isn't a devil makes saving throws with disadvantage.

Innate Spellcasting. Hutijin's innate spellcasting ability is Charisma (spell save DC 22). He can innately cast the following spells, requiring no material components:

At will: *alter self* (can become Medium when changing his appearance), *animate dead*, *detect magic*, *hold monster*, *invisibility* (self only), *lightning bolt*, *suggestion*, *wall of fire*
3/day: *dispel magic*
1/day each: *heal*, *symbol* (hopelessness only)

Legendary Resistance (3/Day). If Hutijin fails a saving throw, he can choose to succeed instead.

Magic Resistance. Hutijin has advantage on saving throws against spells and other magical effects.

Magic Weapons. Hutijin's weapon attacks are magical.

Regeneration. Hutijin regains 20 hit points at the start of his turn. If he takes radiant damage, this trait doesn't function at the start of his next turn. Hutijin dies only if he starts his turn with 0 hit points and doesn't regenerate.

Actions

Multiattack. Hutijin makes four attacks: one with his bite, one with his claw, one with his mace, and one with his tail.

Bite. *Melee Weapon Attack:* +15 to hit, reach 5 ft., one target. *Hit:* 15 (2d6 + 8) piercing damage. The target must succeed on a DC 22 Constitution saving throw or become poisoned. While poisoned in this way, the target can't regain hit points, and it takes 10 (3d6) poison damage at the start of each of its turns. The poisoned target can repeat the saving throw at the end of each of its turns, ending the effect on itself on a success.

Claw. *Melee Weapon Attack:* +15 to hit, reach 10 ft., one target. *Hit:* 17 (2d8 + 8) slashing damage.

Mace. *Melee Weapon Attack:* +15 to hit, reach 5 ft., one target. *Hit:* 15 (2d6 + 8) bludgeoning damage.

Tail. *Melee Weapon Attack:* +15 to hit, reach 10 ft., one target. *Hit:* 19 (2d10 + 8) bludgeoning damage.

Teleport. Hutijin magically teleports, along with any equipment he is wearing and carrying, up to 120 feet to an unoccupied space he can see.

Reactions

Fearful Voice (Recharge 5–6). In response to taking damage, Hutijin utters a dreadful word of power. Each creature within 30 feet of him that isn't a devil must succeed on a DC 22 Wisdom saving throw or become frightened of him for 1 minute. A creature can repeat the saving throw at the end of each of its turns, ending the effect on itself on a success. A creature that saves against this effect is immune to Hutijin's Fearful Voice for 24 hours.

Legendary Actions

Hutijin can take 3 legendary actions, choosing from the options below. Only one legendary action option can be used at a time and only at the end of another creature's turn. Hutijin regains spent legendary actions at the start of his turn.

Attack. Hutijin attacks once with his mace.
Lightning Storm (Costs 2 Actions). Hutijin releases lightning in a 20-foot radius. All other creatures in that area must each make a DC 22 Dexterity saving throw, taking 18 (4d8) lightning damage on a failed save, or half as much damage on a successful one.
Teleport. Hutijin uses his Teleport action.

MOLOCH

Exiled from the Nine Hells, Moloch would do anything
to reclaim his position. Long ago, Moloch earned his
place among the other archdevils through the glory he
won driving demons out of the Nine Hells. Asmodeus
rewarded him by elevating Moloch to the rulership
of Malbolge.

For eons, Moloch ruled his domain, vying against the
other archdevils as he sought still greater power. This
animosity worked in Asmodeus's favor, since Asmodeus
knew that Moloch's scheming helped keep the other
archdevils in check. The arrangement began to unravel,
however, when Moloch took the night hag named Mal-
agard for his advisor. Her words were poison, and gradually she convinced Moloch to direct his efforts to topple
Asmodeus. Although the conspiracy nearly succeeded,
it was thwarted. Moloch was stripped of his station and
sentenced to death—and only the timely use of a planar
portal allowed him to escape.

Moloch wasted no time in preparing for his return.
He amassed an army of devils and monsters and left
them to make final preparations for invading the Nine
Hells, while he ventured to a distant Material Plane in
the hope of finding an artifact that would ensure his
success. While there, he became trapped, leaving his
armies at the mercy of his enemies. In short order they
were destroyed.

Now, Moloch has been rendered nearly powerless
after his last failure. He endlessly schemes of ways to
return to his former status, but every time he enters the
Nine Hells, he is demoted to an imp and can't regain his
normal powers until he leaves. Thus, he lives a split existence, sometimes scheming in Malbolge or other layers of the Hells and at other times wandering the planes
searching for magical might or secrets that might help
him win back his title.

Rumors suggest that he can often be found in Sigil,
where he bargains with yugoloths to build yet another
army with which he might invade Malbolge and wrest
the throne from Glasya. Bereft as he is, he has little to
offer in exchange, so he might bargain with mortals to
gain their aid in acquiring coin, jewels, and other riches
in return for knowledge about the Nine Hells and the
other planes.

Most of Moloch's cultists have switched allegiance
to one of the other archdevils, but idols constructed to
honor him still stand in deep dungeons, their jeweled
eyes and the remnants of power they hold drawing monstrous worshipers and unwise adventurers into places
where his foul influence remains.

MOLOCH

Large fiend (devil), lawful evil

Armor Class 19 (natural armor)
Hit Points 253 (22d10 + 132)
Speed 30 ft.

STR	DEX	CON	INT	WIS	CHA
26 (+8)	19 (+4)	22 (+6)	21 (+5)	18 (+4)	23 (+6)

Saving Throws Dex +11, Con +13, Wis +11, Cha +13
Skills Deception +13, Intimidation +13, Perception +11
Damage Resistances cold; bludgeoning, piercing, and slashing from nonmagical attacks that aren't silvered
Damage Immunities fire, poison
Condition Immunities charmed, exhaustion, frightened, poisoned
Senses darkvision 120 ft., passive Perception 21
Languages all, telepathy 120 ft.
Challenge 21 (33,000 XP)

Innate Spellcasting. Moloch's innate spellcasting ability is Charisma (spell save DC 21). He can innately cast the following spells, requiring no material components:

At will: *alter self* (can become Medium when changing his appearance), *animate dead*, *burning hands* (as a 7th-level spell), *confusion*, *detect magic*, *fly*, *geas*, *major image*, *stinking cloud*, *suggestion*, *wall of fire*
1/day each: *flame strike*, *symbol* (stunning only)

Legendary Resistance (3/Day). If Moloch fails a saving throw, he can choose to succeed instead.

Magic Resistance. Moloch has advantage on saving throws against spells and other magical effects.

Magic Weapons. Moloch's weapon attacks are magical.

Regeneration. Moloch regains 20 hit points at the start of his turn. If he takes radiant damage, this trait doesn't function at the start of his next turn. Moloch dies only if he starts his turn with 0 hit points and doesn't regenerate.

ACTIONS

Multiattack. Moloch makes three attacks: one with his bite, one with his claw, and one with his whip.

Bite. *Melee Weapon Attack:* +15 to hit, reach 5 ft., one target. *Hit:* 26 (4d8 + 8) piercing damage.

Claw. *Melee Weapon Attack:* +15 to hit, reach 10 ft., one target. *Hit:* 17 (2d8 + 8) slashing damage.

Many-Tailed Whip. *Melee Weapon Attack:* +15 to hit, reach 30 ft., one target. *Hit:* 13 (2d4 + 8) slashing damage plus 11 (2d10) lightning damage. If the target is a creature, it must succeed on a DC 24 Strength saving throw or be pulled up to 30 feet in a straight line toward Moloch.

Breath of Despair (Recharge 5–6). Moloch exhales in a 30-foot cube. Each creature in that area must succeed on a DC 21 Wisdom saving throw or take 27 (5d10) psychic damage, drop whatever it is holding, and become frightened for 1 minute. While frightened in this way, a creature must take the Dash action and move away from Moloch by the safest available route on each of its turns, unless there is nowhere to move, in which case it needn't take the Dash action. If the creature ends its turn in a location where it doesn't have line of sight to Moloch, the creature can repeat the saving throw. On a success, the effect ends.

Teleport. Moloch magically teleports, along with any equipment he is wearing and carrying, up to 120 feet to an unoccupied space he can see.

LEGENDARY ACTIONS

Moloch can take 3 legendary actions, choosing from the options below. Only one legendary action option can be used at a time and only at the end of another creature's turn. Moloch regains spent legendary actions at the start of his turn.

Stinking Cloud. Moloch casts *stinking cloud*.
Teleport. Moloch uses his Teleport action.
Whip. Moloch makes one attack with his whip.

Moloch obsesses over power he lost rather than thinking of the power he could gain elsewhere in the planes.

What a pity he so wastes his potential.

D

I actually admire Titivilus. If he weren't so remorselessly evil, he'd be an excellent administrator of the Balance.

TITIVILUS

The gloomy Lord of the Second, Dispater, rules from his iron palace, seeming to hide surrounded by its labyrinthine corridors, iron walls, diabolical traps, and monstrous servants. So intense is his paranoia that he almost never travels farther than the sprawling city that lies outside his magnificent palace. Dispater knows he has enemies on all sides—enemies who would do to him what has been done to the likes of Geryon, Moloch, and so many others.

Dispater is correct to fear, but the true threat comes not from without. The lord's great error was allowing himself to be seduced by Titivilus, who beguiled his way into being the primary advisor in Dispater's household.

Although he is inferior in physical strength and power when compared to other archdevils, Titivilus compensates with cunning. A shrewd and calculating politician, he has clawed his way up through the ranks to become the second-most powerful fiend in Dis, entirely by saying just the right thing at the right time to get what he wanted. Charming and pleasant, he is a master at negotiation, able to twist words in such a way as to leave his victims confused and believing they have found a friend in Titivilus. Through these skills, Titivilus has manipulated everyone along his path to power, either to win them over to his cause or to remove them as a threat.

Since gaining his position, Titivilus has convinced Dispater that countless plots are being hatched against him and that Asmodeus himself seeks to remove Dispater from power. In response, Dispater has withdrawn to his palace and left day-to-day decisions to Titivilus, while also authorizing him to answer and negotiate bargains with mortals who attempt to summon Dispater. Titivilus now represents his master and speaks with his voice, a turn of events that leads some to whisper that either Titivilus is Dispater in disguise, or that Titivilus has removed the archduke and replaced him altogether.

Titivilus recognizes the inherent precariousness of his position. After all, Dispater's acceptance of his plans and his advice can last only so long before some other plotter steps in and reveals the truth. For insurance, Titivilus has begun recruiting outsiders to deal with problem devils, to insulate himself against criticism, and, above all, to create complications that he can solve so as to reinforce his value in the eyes of his master. Titivilus finds adventurers well suited to the tasks he needs performed and recruits them directly or through intermediaries, expending them later as his plans require.

TITIVILUS

Medium fiend (devil), lawful evil

Armor Class 20 (natural armor)
Hit Points 127 (17d8 + 51)
Speed 40 ft., fly 60 ft.

STR	DEX	CON	INT	WIS	CHA
19 (+4)	22 (+6)	17 (+3)	24 (+7)	22 (+6)	26 (+8)

Saving Throws Dex +11, Con +8, Wis +11, Cha +13
Skills Deception +13, Insight +11, Intimidation +13, Persuasion +13
Damage Resistances cold; bludgeoning, piercing, and slashing from nonmagical attacks that aren't silvered
Damage Immunities fire, poison
Condition Immunities charmed, exhaustion, frightened, poisoned
Senses darkvision 120 ft., passive Perception 16
Languages all, telepathy 120 ft.
Challenge 16 (15,000 XP)

Innate Spellcasting. Titivilus's innate spellcasting ability is Charisma (spell save DC 21). He can innately cast the following spells, requiring no material components:

At will: *alter self, animate dead, bestow curse, confusion, major image, modify memory, nondetection, sending, suggestion*
3/day each: *greater invisibility* (self only), *mislead*
1/day each: *feeblemind, symbol* (discord or sleep only)

Legendary Resistance (3/Day). If Titivilus fails a saving throw, he can choose to succeed instead.

Magic Resistance. Titivilus has advantage on saving throws against spells and other magical effects.

Magic Weapons. Titivilus's weapon attacks are magical.

Regeneration. Titivilus regains 10 hit points at the start of his turn. If he takes cold or radiant damage, this trait doesn't function at the start of his next turn. Titivilus dies only if he starts his turn with 0 hit points and doesn't regenerate.

Ventriloquism. Whenever Titivilus speaks, he can choose a point within 60 feet; his voice emanates from that point.

ACTIONS

Multiattack. Titivilus makes one sword attack and uses his Frightful Word once.

Silver Sword. *Melee Weapon Attack:* +9 to hit, reach 5 ft., one target. *Hit:* 8 (1d8 + 4) slashing damage, or 9 (1d10 + 4) slashing damage if used with two hands, plus 16 (3d10) necrotic damage. If the target is a creature, its hit point maximum is reduced by an amount equal to half the necrotic damage it takes.

Frightful Word. Titivilus targets one creature he can see within 10 feet of him. The target must succeed on a DC 21 Wisdom saving throw or become frightened of him for 1 minute. While frightened in this way, the target must take the Dash action and move away from Titivilus by the safest available route on each of its turns, unless there is nowhere to move, in which case it needn't take the Dash action. The target can repeat the saving throw at the end of each of its turns, ending the effect on itself on a success.

Teleport. Titivilus magically teleports, along with any equipment he is wearing and carrying, up to 120 feet to an unoccupied space he can see.

Twisting Words. Titivilus targets one creature he can see within 60 feet of him. The target must succeed on a DC 21 Charisma saving throw or become charmed by Titivilus for 1 minute. The charmed target can repeat the saving throw if Titivilus deals any damage to it. A creature that succeeds on the saving throw is immune to Titivilus's Twisting Words for 24 hours.

LEGENDARY ACTIONS

Titivilus can take 3 legendary actions, choosing from the options below. Only one legendary action option can be used at a time and only at the end of another creature's turn. Titivilus regains spent legendary actions at the start of his turn.

Assault (Costs 2 Actions). Titivilus attacks with his silver sword or uses his Frightful Word.
Corrupting Guidance. Titivilus uses Twisting Words. Alternatively, he targets one creature charmed by him that is within 60 feet of him; that charmed target must make a DC 21 Charisma saving throw. On a failure, Titivilus decides how the target acts during its next turn.
Teleport. Titivilus uses his Teleport action.

D

ZARIEL

Zariel rules Avernus, the first layer of the Nine Hells. Once a mighty angel charged with watching the tides of the Blood War, she succumbed to the plane's corrupting influence and fell from grace. She recently reclaimed her position as archdevil of Avernus after the cautious Bel proved inadequate at marshaling his forces to launch offensives against the encroaching demons. Now Bel advises her and helps her manage the war, though many whisper that her true agenda is vengeance against Asmodeus, and her true plan is to drive him from the Nine Hells.

All who enter and exit the Nine Hells must pass through Avernus, so the infernal armies muster on this layer. Here, the amnizus guard the citadels overlooking the River Styx, much of the fighting of the Blood War takes place, and devils gather to invade the Abyss. Anyone hoping to reach the lower layers must first contend with the darkness of this layer and the myriad threats it houses. Zariel manages it all and has the ultimate say over who comes and goes.

Given her role in the Blood War, Zariel is keenly interested in collecting souls from the greatest warriors on the Material Plane and securing their loyalty. She bargains hard, and mortals end up worse for dealing with her, because she holds all the cards. A bargain with Zariel is eternal; there is little hope of wriggling out of it. However, she does expect the best from her servants, and so she allows her mortal followers to live out their lives, ever honing their talents, so she can put them to the best use when she finally calls in their debts. As a result, Zariel's servants are universally effective, disciplined, and dangerous.

ZARIEL

Large fiend (devil), lawful evil

Armor Class 21 (natural armor)
Hit Points 580 (40d10 + 360)
Speed 50 ft., fly 150 ft.

STR	DEX	CON	INT	WIS	CHA
27 (+8)	24 (+7)	28 (+9)	26 (+8)	27 (+8)	30 (+10)

Saving Throws Int +16, Wis +16, Cha +18
Skills Intimidation +18, Perception +16
Damage Resistances cold, fire, radiant; bludgeoning, piercing, and slashing from nonmagical attacks that aren't silvered
Damage Immunities necrotic, poison
Condition Immunities charmed, exhaustion, frightened, poisoned
Senses darkvision 120 ft., passive Perception 26
Languages all, telepathy 120 ft.
Challenge 26 (90,000 XP)

Devil's Sight. Magical darkness doesn't impede Zariel's darkvision.

Fiery Weapons. Zariel's weapon attacks are magical. When she hits with any weapon, the weapon deals an extra 36 (8d8) fire damage (included in the weapon attacks below).

Innate Spellcasting. Zariel's innate spellcasting ability is Charisma (spell save DC 26). She can innately cast the following spells, requiring no material components:

At will: *alter self* (can become Medium when changing her appearance), *detect evil and good*, *fireball*, *invisibility* (self only), *wall of fire*
3/day each: *blade barrier*, *dispel evil and good*, *finger of death*

Legendary Resistance (3/Day). If Zariel fails a saving throw, she can choose to succeed instead.

Magic Resistance. Zariel has advantage on saving throws against spells and other magical effects.

Regeneration. Zariel regains 20 hit points at the start of her turn. If she takes radiant damage, this trait doesn't function at the start of her next turn. Zariel dies only if she starts her turn with 0 hit points and doesn't regenerate.

ACTIONS

Multiattack. Zariel attacks twice with her longsword or with her javelins. She can substitute Horrid Touch for one of these attacks.

Longsword. *Melee Weapon Attack:* +16 to hit, reach 10 ft., one target. *Hit:* 17 (2d8 + 8) slashing damage, or 19 (2d10 + 8) slashing damage if used with two hands, plus 36 (8d8) fire damage.

Javelin. *Melee or Ranged Weapon Attack:* +16 to hit, range 30/120 ft., one target. *Hit:* 15 (2d6 + 8) piercing damage plus 36 (8d8) fire damage.

Horrid Touch (Recharge 5–6). *Melee Weapon Attack:* +16 to hit, reach 10 ft., one target. *Hit:* 44 (8d10) necrotic damage, and the target is poisoned for 1 minute. While poisoned in this way, the target is also blinded and deafened. The target can repeat the saving throw at the end of each of its turns, ending the effect on itself on a success.

Teleport. Zariel magically teleports, along with any equipment she is wearing and carrying, up to 120 feet to an unoccupied space she can see.

LEGENDARY ACTIONS

Zariel can take 3 legendary actions, choosing from the options below. Only one legendary action option can be used at a time and only at the end of another creature's turn. Zariel regains spent legendary actions at the start of her turn.

Immolating Gaze (Costs 2 Actions). Zariel turns her magical gaze toward one creature she can see within 120 feet of her and commands it to combust. The target must succeed on a DC 26 Wisdom saving throw or take 22 (4d10) fire damage.
Teleport. Zariel uses her Teleport action.

Zariel's Lair

Zariel makes her lair in a basalt citadel that rises up in Avernus. From nearly a mile away, one can hear the screams and moans coming from the burned victims chained to the stronghold's wall, the dying remains of those who failed to impress the archdevil. The stronghold, covering five square miles, is surrounded by walls reinforced with high turrets. Devils of all kinds crawl over the structure, ensuring that no intruders breach their defenses.

Lair Actions. On initiative count 20 (losing initiative ties), Zariel can take a lair action to cause one of the following effects; she can't use the same effect two rounds in a row:

- Zariel casts *major image* four times at its lowest level, targeting different areas with the spell. Zariel prefers to create images of intruders' loved ones being burned alive. Zariel doesn't need to concentrate on the spells, which end on initiative count 20 of the next round. Each creature that can see these illusions must succeed on a DC 26 Wisdom saving throw or become frightened of the illusion for 1 minute. A frightened creature can repeat the saving throw at the end of each of its turns, ending the effect on itself on a success.
- Zariel casts her innate *fireball* spell.

Regional Effects. The region containing Zariel's lair is warped by her magic, which creates one or more of the following effects:

- The area within 9 miles of the lair is filled with screaming voices and the stench of burning meat.
- Once every 60 feet within 1 mile of the lair, 10-foot-high gouts of flame rise from the ground. Any creature or object that touches the flame takes 7 (2d6) fire damage, though it can take this damage no more than once per round.
- The area within 2 miles, but no closer than 500 feet, of the lair is filled with smoke, which causes the area to be heavily obscured. The smoke can't be cleared away.

If Zariel dies, these effects fade over the course of 1d10 days.

> *Do not pity the fallen angel.*
> *Fallen angels survive the fall.*
> *How many other souls did*
> *Zariel bring down with her?*

Drow

Whether they are found in Underdark cities, the darkened passages between them, or in the dreaded Demonweb Pits, drow stand as one of the most insidious threats to surface-dwellers. Devoted to Lolth, the dark elves obey her often-contradictory commands and live in fear of her wrath. Some attain great power and influence through cunning, talent, or subterfuge, evoking fear from the lesser drow who serve them.

Drow Arachnomancer

Medium humanoid (elf), chaotic evil

Armor Class 15 (studded leather)
Hit Points 162 (25d8 + 50)
Speed 30 ft., climb 30 ft.

STR	DEX	CON	INT	WIS	CHA
11 (+0)	17 (+3)	14 (+2)	19 (+4)	14 (+2)	16 (+3)

Saving Throws Con +7, Int +9, Cha +8
Skills Arcana +9, Nature +9, Perception +7, Stealth +8
Damage Resistances poison
Senses blindsight 10 ft., darkvision 120 ft., passive Perception 17
Languages Elvish, Undercommon, can speak with spiders
Challenge 13 (10,000 XP)

Change Shape (Recharges after a Short or Long Rest). The drow can use a bonus action to magically polymorph into a giant spider, remaining in that form for up to 1 hour. It can revert to its true form as a bonus action. Its statistics, other than its size, are the same in each form. It can speak and cast spells while in giant spider form. Any equipment it is wearing or carrying in humanoid form melds into the giant spider form. It can't activate, use, wield, or otherwise benefit from any of its equipment. It reverts to its humanoid form if it dies.

Fey Ancestry. The drow has advantage on saving throws against being charmed, and magic can't put the drow to sleep.

Innate Spellcasting. The drow's innate spellcasting ability is Charisma (spell save DC 16). It can innately cast the following spells, requiring no material components:

At will: *dancing lights*
1/day each: *darkness, faerie fire, levitate* (self only)

Spellcasting. The drow is a 16th-level spellcaster. Its spellcasting ability is Charisma (spell save DC 16, +8 to hit with spell attacks). It regains its expended spell slots when it finishes a short or long rest. It knows the following warlock spells:

Cantrips (at will): *chill touch, eldritch blast, mage hand, poison spray*
1st–5th level (3 5th-level slots): *conjure animals* (spiders only), *crown of madness, dimension door, dispel magic, fear, fly, giant insect, hold monster, insect plague, invisibility, vampiric touch, web, witch bolt*
1/day each: *dominate monster, etherealness, eyebite*

Spider Climb. The drow can climb difficult surfaces, including upside down on ceilings, without needing to make an ability check.

Sunlight Sensitivity. While in sunlight, the drow has disadvantage on attack rolls, as well as on Wisdom (Perception) checks that rely on sight.

Web Walker. The drow ignores movement restrictions caused by webbing.

Actions

Multiattack. The drow makes two poisonous touch attacks or two bite attacks. The first of these attacks that hits each round deals an extra 26 (4d12) poison damage to the target.

Poisonous Touch (Humanoid Form Only). *Melee Weapon Attack:* +8 to hit, reach 5 ft., one target. *Hit:* 28 (8d6) poison damage.

Bite (Giant Spider Form Only). *Melee Weapon Attack:* +7 to hit, reach 5 ft., one target. *Hit:* 12 (2d8 + 3) piercing damage, and the target must make a DC 15 Constitution saving throw, taking 26 (4d12) poison damage on a failed save, or half as much damage on a successful one. If the poison damage reduces the target to 0 hit points, the target is stable but poisoned for 1 hour, even after regaining hit points, and is paralyzed while poisoned in this way.

Web (Giant Spider Form Only; Recharge 5–6). *Ranged Weapon Attack:* +8 to hit, range 30/60 ft., one target. *Hit:* The target is restrained by webbing. As an action, the restrained target can make a DC 15 Strength check, bursting the webbing on a success. The webbing can also be attacked and destroyed (AC 10; hp 5; vulnerability to fire damage; immunity to bludgeoning, poison, and psychic damage).

D

Drow mages can be quite learned and skilled in magic. Some of them can even cast my spells.

DROW ARACHNOMANCER

Drow spellcasters who seek to devote themselves wholly to the Spider Queen sometimes walk the dark path of the arachnomancer. By offering up body and soul to Lolth, they gain tremendous power and a supernatural connection to the ancient spiders of the Demonweb Pits, channeling magic from that dread place.

DROW FAVORED CONSORT

Nearly all priestesses of Lolth, including the powerful matron mothers, take attractive drow as their consorts. Often these individuals serve no purpose beyond pleasure, breeding, or both, but sometimes consorts can gain the ear of their priestess and be relied on to provide useful advice. No position of consort is assured for long; priestesses are infamous for being fickle with their favor, which are they are especially glad to lavish on a consort who combines beauty with magical might.

DROW FAVORED CONSORT

Medium humanoid (elf), neutral evil

Armor Class 15 (18 with *mage armor*)
Hit Points 225 (30d8 + 90)
Speed 30 ft.

STR	DEX	CON	INT	WIS	CHA
15 (+2)	20 (+5)	16 (+3)	18 (+4)	15 (+2)	18 (+4)

Saving Throws Dex +11, Con +9, Cha +10
Skills Acrobatics +11, Athletics +8, Perception +8, Stealth +11
Senses darkvision 120 ft., passive Perception 18
Languages Elvish, Undercommon
Challenge 18 (20,000 XP)

Fey Ancestry. The drow has advantage on saving throws against being charmed, and magic can't put the drow to sleep.

Innate Spellcasting. The drow's innate spellcasting ability is Charisma (spell save DC 18). It can innately cast the following spells, requiring no material components:

At will: *dancing lights*
1/day each: *darkness, faerie fire, levitate* (self only)

Spellcasting. The drow is a 11th-level spellcaster. Its spellcasting ability is Intelligence (spell save DC 18, +10 to hit with spell attacks). It has the following wizard spells prepared:

Cantrips (at will): *mage hand, message, poison spray, shocking grasp, ray of frost*

1st level (4 slots): *burning hands, mage armor, magic missile, shield*
2nd level (3 slots): *gust of wind, invisibility, misty step, shatter*
3rd level (3 slots): *counterspell, fireball, haste*
4th level (3 slots): *dimension door, Otiluke's resilient sphere*
5th level (2 slots): *cone of cold*
6th level (1 slot): *chain lightning*

Sunlight Sensitivity. While in sunlight, the drow has disadvantage on attack rolls, as well as on Wisdom (Perception) checks that rely on sight.

War Magic. When the drow uses its action to cast a spell, it can make one weapon attack as a bonus action.

ACTIONS

Multiattack. The drow makes three scimitar attacks.

Scimitar. *Melee Weapon Attack:* +11 to hit, reach 5 ft., one target. *Hit:* 8 (1d6 + 5) slashing damage plus 18 (4d8) poison damage. In addition, the target has disadvantage on the next saving throw it makes against a spell the drow casts before the end of the drow's next turn.

Hand Crossbow. *Ranged Weapon Attack:* +11 to hit, range 30/120 ft., one target. *Hit:* 8 (1d6 + 5) piercing damage, and the target must succeed on a DC 13 Constitution saving throw or be poisoned for 1 hour. If the saving throw fails by 5 or more, the target is also unconscious while poisoned in this way. The target regains consciousness if it takes damage or if another creature takes an action to shake it.

D

DROW HOUSE CAPTAIN

Medium humanoid (elf), neutral evil

Armor Class 16 (chain mail)
Hit Points 162 (25d8 + 50)
Speed 30 ft.

STR	DEX	CON	INT	WIS	CHA
14 (+2)	19 (+4)	15 (+2)	12 (+1)	14 (+2)	13 (+1)

Saving Throws Dex +8, Con +6, Wis +6
Skills Perception +6, Stealth +8
Senses darkvision 120 ft., passive Perception 16
Languages Elvish, Undercommon
Challenge 9 (5,000 XP)

Battle Command. As a bonus action, the drow targets one ally he can see within 30 feet of him. If the target can see or hear the drow, the target can use its reaction to make one melee attack or to take the Dodge or Hide action.

Fey Ancestry. The drow has advantage on saving throws against being charmed, and magic can't put the drow to sleep.

Innate Spellcasting. The drow's innate spellcasting ability is Charisma (spell save DC 13). He can innately cast the following spells, requiring no material components:

At will: *dancing lights*
1/day each: *darkness, faerie fire, levitate* (self only)

Sunlight Sensitivity. While in sunlight, the drow has disadvantage on attack rolls, as well as on Wisdom (Perception) checks that rely on sight.

ACTIONS

Multiattack. The drow makes three attacks: two with his scimitar and one with his whip or his hand crossbow.

Scimitar. *Melee Weapon Attack:* +8 to hit, reach 5 ft., one target. *Hit:* 7 (1d6 + 4) slashing damage plus 14 (4d6) poison damage.

Whip. *Melee Weapon Attack:* +8 to hit, reach 10 ft., one target. *Hit:* 6 (1d4 + 4) slashing damage. If the target is an ally, it has advantage on attack rolls until the end of its next turn.

Hand Crossbow. *Ranged Weapon Attack:* +8 to hit, range 30/120 ft., one target. *Hit:* 7 (1d6 + 4) piercing damage, and the target must succeed on a DC 13 Constitution saving throw or be poisoned for 1 hour. If the saving throw fails by 5 or more, the target is also unconscious while poisoned in this way. The target regains consciousness if it takes damage or if another creature takes an action to shake it.

REACTIONS

Parry. The drow adds 3 to his AC against one melee attack that would hit him. To do so, the drow must see the attacker and be wielding a melee weapon.

DROW INQUISITOR

Medium humanoid (elf), neutral evil

Armor Class 16 (breastplate)
Hit Points 143 (22d8 + 44)
Speed 30 ft.

STR	DEX	CON	INT	WIS	CHA
11 (+1)	15 (+2)	14 (+2)	16 (+3)	21 (+5)	20 (+5)

Saving Throws Con +7, Wis +10, Cha +10
Skills Insight +10, Perception +10, Religion +8, Stealth +7
Condition Immunities frightened
Senses darkvision 120 ft., passive Perception 20
Languages Elvish, Undercommon
Challenge 14 (11,500 XP)

Discern Lie. The drow knows when she hears a creature speak a lie in a language she knows.

Fey Ancestry. The drow has advantage on saving throws against being charmed, and magic can't put the drow to sleep.

Innate Spellcasting. The drow's innate spellcasting ability is Charisma (spell save DC 18). She can innately cast the following spells, requiring no material components:

At will: *dancing lights, detect magic*
1/day each: *clairvoyance, darkness, detect thoughts, dispel magic, faerie fire, levitate* (self only), *suggestion*

Magic Resistance. The drow has advantage on saving throws against spells and other magical effects.

Spellcasting. The drow is a 12th-level spellcaster. Her spellcasting ability is Wisdom (spell save DC 18, +10 to hit with spell attacks). She has the following cleric spells prepared:

Cantrips (at will): *guidance, message, poison spray, resistance, thaumaturgy*
1st level (4 slots): *bane, cure wounds, inflict wounds*
2nd level (3 slots): *blindness/deafness, silence, spiritual weapon*
3rd level (3 slots): *bestow curse, dispel magic, magic circle*
4th level (3 slots): *banishment, divination, freedom of movement*
5th level (2 slots): *contagion, dispel evil and good, insect plague*
6th level (1 slot): *harm, true seeing*

Sunlight Sensitivity. While in sunlight, the drow has disadvantage on attack rolls, as well as on Wisdom (Perception) checks that rely on sight.

ACTIONS

Multiattack. The drow makes three death lance attacks.

Death Lance. *Melee Weapon Attack:* +10 to hit, reach 5 ft., one target. *Hit:* 8 (1d6 + 5) piercing damage plus 18 (4d8) necrotic damage. The target's hit point maximum is reduced by an amount equal to the necrotic damage it takes. This reduction lasts until the target finishes a long rest. The target dies if its hit point maximum is reduced to 0.

DROW HOUSE CAPTAIN

Each drow noble house entrusts the leadership of its military forces to a house captain, a position normally held by the matriarch's first or second son. The house captain commands the drow and slaves making up the family's army and has made extensive study of strategy and tactics to become an effective leader in battle.

DROW INQUISITOR

Drow expect treachery. After all, the Spider Queen encourages it. A certain amount of backstabbing and double-crossing can be managed, but too much can undermine an entire community. To keep some semblance of order and to root out traitors, drow priestesses employ inquisitors. Chosen from the ranks of the priesthood, these female drow possess authority equaled only by the matrons of the noble houses. Anyone they decide is at odds with the hierarchy faces torture and usually an excruciating death.

Many creatures enjoy torture, but the dark elves have made it into an exquisite art.

> ### VARIANT: YOCHLOL SUMMONING
> Some drow inquisitors have an action that allows them to summon a demon.
> ***Summon Demon (1/Day).*** The drow attempts to magically summon a yochlol, with a 50 percent chance of success. If the attempt fails, the drow takes 5 (1d10) psychic damage. Otherwise, the summoned demon appears in an unoccupied space within 60 feet of its summoner, acts as an ally of its summoner, and can't summon other demons. It remains for 10 minutes, until it or its summoner dies, or until its summoner dismisses it as an action.

DROW MATRON MOTHER

Medium humanoid (elf), neutral evil

Armor Class 17 (half plate)
Hit Points 262 (35d8 + 105)
Speed 30 ft.

STR	DEX	CON	INT	WIS	CHA
12 (+1)	18 (+4)	16 (+3)	17 (+3)	21 (+5)	22 (+6)

Saving Throws Con +9, Wis +11, Cha +12
Skills Insight +11, Perception +11, Religion +9, Stealth +10
Condition Immunities charmed, frightened, poisoned
Senses darkvision 120 ft., passive Perception 21
Languages Elvish, Undercommon
Challenge 20 (25,000 XP)

Fey Ancestry. The drow has advantage on saving throws against being charmed, and magic can't put the drow to sleep.

Innate Spellcasting. The drow's innate spellcasting ability is Charisma (spell save DC 20). She can innately cast the following spells, requiring no material components:

At will: *dancing lights, detect magic*
1/day each: *clairvoyance, darkness, detect thoughts, dispel magic, faerie fire, levitate* (self only), *suggestion*

Lolth's Fickle Favor. As a bonus action, the matron can bestow the Spider Queen's blessing on one ally she can see within 30 feet of her. The ally takes 7 (2d6) psychic damage but has advantage on the next attack roll it makes until the end of its next turn.

Magic Resistance. The drow has advantage on saving throws against spells and other magical effects.

Spellcasting. The drow is a 20th-level spellcaster. Her spellcasting ability is Wisdom (spell save DC 19, +11 to hit with spell attacks). The drow has the following cleric spells prepared:

Cantrips (at will): *guidance, mending, resistance, sacred flame, thaumaturgy*
1st level (4 slots): *bane, command, cure wounds, guiding bolt*
2nd level (3 slots): *hold person, silence, spiritual weapon*
3rd level (3 slots): *bestow curse, clairvoyance, dispel magic, spirit guardians*
4th level (3 slots): *banishment, death ward, freedom of movement, guardian of faith*
5th level (3 slots): *contagion, flame strike, geas, mass cure wounds*
6th level (2 slots): *blade barrier, harm*
7th level (2 slots): *divine word, plane shift*
8th level (1 slot): *holy aura*
9th level (1 slot): *gate*

Sunlight Sensitivity. While in sunlight, the drow has disadvantage on attack rolls, as well as on Wisdom (Perception) checks that rely on sight.

ACTIONS

Multiattack. The matron mother makes two demon staff attacks or three tentacle rod attacks.

Demon Staff. *Melee Weapon Attack:* +10 to hit, reach 5 ft., one target. *Hit:* 7 (1d6 + 4) bludgeoning damage, or 8 (1d8 + 4) bludgeoning damage if used with two hands, plus 14 (4d6) psychic damage. In addition, the target must succeed on a DC

19 Wisdom saving throw or become frightened of the drow for 1 minute. The frightened target can repeat the saving throw at the end of each of its turns, ending the effect on itself on a success.

Tentacle Rod. *Melee Weapon Attack:* +9 to hit, reach 15 ft., one target. *Hit:* 3 (1d6) bludgeoning damage. If the target is hit three times by the rod on one turn, the target must succeed on a DC 15 Constitution saving throw or suffer the following effects for 1 minute: the target's speed is halved, it has disadvantage on Dexterity saving throws, and it can't use reactions. Moreover, on each of its turns, it can take either an action or a bonus action, but not both. At the end of each of its turns, it can repeat the saving throw, ending the effect on itself on a success.

Summon Servant (1/Day). The drow magically summons a retriever or a yochlol. The summoned creature appears in an unoccupied space within 60 feet of its summoner, acts as an ally of its summoner, and can't summon other demons. It remains for 10 minutes, until it or its summoner dies, or until its summoner dismisses it as an action.

LEGENDARY ACTIONS

The drow can take 3 legendary actions, choosing from the options below. Only one legendary action option can be used at a time and only at the end of another creature's turn. The drow regains spent legendary actions at the start of her turn.

Demon Staff. The drow makes one attack with her demon staff.
Compel Demon (Costs 2 Actions). An allied demon within 30 feet of the drow uses its reaction to make one attack against a target of the drow's choice that she can see.
Cast a Spell (Costs 1–3 Actions). The drow expends a spell slot to cast a 1st-, 2nd-, or 3rd-level spell that she has prepared. Doing so costs 1 legendary action per level of the spell.

Drow Matron Mother

At the head of each drow noble house sits a matron mother, an influential priestess of Lolth charged with carrying out the god's will while also advancing the interests of the family. Matron mothers embody the scheming and treachery associated with the Queen of Spiders. Each stands at the center of a vast conspiratorial web, with demons, drow, spiders, and slaves positioned between them and their enemies. Although matron mothers command great power, that power depends on maintaining the Spider Queen's favor, and the dark god sometimes capriciously takes back what she has given. The stat block here represents a matron mother at the height of her power.

Drow Shadowblade

Drow shadowblades steal down the darkened passages of the Underdark, bound on errands of mayhem. Ruthless killers, shadowblades find employment with a noble house, usually involving the elimination of a rival in another house. Shadowblades also protect enclaves and Underdark cities from enemies and track down thieves who make off with prized treasures. In whatever role they serve, they move undetected until the moment they attack. And then they are the last thing their victims see.

A shadowblade harnesses a dark magic that is said to arise from a fiendish ritual in which the drow kills a lesser demon and mystically prevents it from reforming in the Abyss. This ritual creates a shadow demon and infuses the drow with shadow magic.

Matron mother is a strange title for a cruel tyrant, but given what drow consider to be a goddess, perhaps we shouldn't be surprised.

> ## Variant: Shadow Demon Summoning
> Some drow shadowblades have an action that allows them to summon a demon.
>
> ***Summon Shadow Demon (1/Day).*** The drow attempts to magically summon a shadow demon with a 50 percent chance of success. If the attempt fails, the drow takes 5 (1d10) psychic damage. Otherwise, the summoned demon appears in an unoccupied space within 60 feet of its summoner, acts as an ally of its summoner, and can't summon other demons. It remains for 10 minutes, until it or its summoner dies, or until its summoner dismisses it as an action.

Drow Shadowblade
Medium humanoid (elf), neutral evil

Armor Class 17 (studded leather)
Hit Points 150 (20d8 + 60)
Speed 30 ft.

STR	DEX	CON	INT	WIS	CHA
14 (+2)	21 (+5)	16 (+3)	12 (+1)	14 (+2)	13 (+1)

Saving Throws Dex +9, Con +7, Wis +6
Skills Perception +6, Stealth +9
Senses darkvision 120 ft., passive Perception 16
Languages Elvish, Undercommon
Challenge 11 (7,200 XP)

Fey Ancestry. The drow has advantage on saving throws against being charmed, and magic can't put the drow to sleep.

Innate Spellcasting. The drow's innate spellcasting ability is Charisma (spell save DC 13). It can innately cast the following spells, requiring no material components:

At will: *dancing lights*
1/day each: *darkness, faerie fire, levitate* (self only)

Shadow Step. While in dim light or darkness, the drow can teleport as a bonus action up to 60 feet to an unoccupied space it can see that is also in dim light or darkness. It then has advantage on the first melee attack it makes before the end of the turn.

Sunlight Sensitivity. While in sunlight, the drow has disadvantage on attack rolls, as well as on Wisdom (Perception) checks that rely on sight.

Actions

Multiattack. The drow makes two attacks with its shadow sword. If either attack hits and the target is within 10 feet of a 5-foot cube of darkness created by the shadow sword on a previous turn, the drow can dismiss that darkness and cause the target to take 21 (6d6) necrotic damage. The drow can dismiss darkness in this way no more than once per turn.

Shadow Sword. *Melee Weapon Attack:* +9 to hit, reach 5 ft., one target. *Hit:* 8 (1d6 + 5) piercing damage plus 10 (3d6) necrotic damage and 10 (3d6) poison damage. The drow can then fill an unoccupied 5-foot cube within 5 feet of the target with magical darkness, which remains for 1 minute.

Hand Crossbow. *Ranged Weapon Attack:* +9 to hit, range 30/120 ft., one target. *Hit:* 8 (1d6 + 5) piercing damage, and the target must succeed on a DC 13 Constitution saving throw or be poisoned for 1 hour. If the saving throw fails by 5 or more, the target is also unconscious while poisoned in this way. The target regains consciousness if it takes damage or if another creature takes an action to shake it.

DUERGAR

The cruel duergar plot not only to defeat other dwarves, but to cast down the entire dwarven pantheon in revenge for their being abandoned and left to be enslaved by mind flayers. To this end, duergar train warriors to fulfill a variety of roles.

DUERGAR DESPOT

Medium humanoid (dwarf), lawful evil

Armor Class 21 (natural armor)
Hit Points 119 (14d8 + 56)
Speed 25 ft.

STR	DEX	CON	INT	WIS	CHA
20 (+5)	5 (–3)	19 (+4)	15 (+2)	14 (+2)	13 (+1)

Saving Throws Con +8, Wis +6
Damage Immunities poison
Condition Immunities charmed, exhaustion, frightened, paralyzed, poisoned
Senses darkvision 120 ft., passive Perception 12
Languages Dwarvish, Undercommon
Challenge 12 (8,400 XP)

Innate Spellcasting (Psionics). The duergar despot's innate spellcasting ability is Intelligence (spell save DC 12). It can cast the following spells, requiring no components:

At will: *mage hand, minor illusion*
1/day each: *counterspell, misty step, stinking cloud*

Magic Resistance. The duergar has advantage on saving throws against spells and other magical effects.

Psychic Engine. When the duergar despot suffers a critical hit or is reduced to 0 hit points, psychic energy erupts from its frame to deal 14 (4d6) psychic damage to each creature within 5 feet of it.

Sunlight Sensitivity. While in sunlight, the duergar despot has disadvantage on attack rolls, as well as on Wisdom (Perception) checks that rely on sight.

ACTIONS

Multiattack. The despot makes two iron fist attacks and two stomping foot attacks. It can replace up to four of these attacks with uses of its Flame Jet.

Iron Fist. *Melee Weapon Attack:* +9 to hit, reach 5 ft., one target. *Hit:* 14 (2d8 + 5) bludgeoning damage. If the target is a Large or smaller creature, it must make a successful DC 17 Strength saving throw or be thrown up to 30 feet away in a straight line. The target lands prone and then takes 10 (3d6) bludgeoning damage.

Stomping Foot. *Melee Weapon Attack:* +9 to hit, reach 5 ft., one target. *Hit:* 9 (1d8 + 5) bludgeoning damage, or 18 (3d8 + 5) to a prone target.

Flame Jet. The duergar spews flames in a line 100 feet long and 5 feet wide. Each creature in the line must make a DC 16 Dexterity saving throw, taking 18 (4d8) fire damage on a failed save, or half as much damage on a successful one.

DUERGAR DESPOT

Duergar despots replace parts of their bodies with mechanical devices that they control through their psionic abilities.

DUERGAR HAMMERER

The hammerer is a digging machine with a duergar strapped inside it—typically a punishment for those whose work ethic wavers. The machine's mechanism transforms the captive duergar's pain into energy that powers the device, which is typically used to dig tunnels and repel invaders.

DUERGAR KAVALRACHNI

The kavalrachni are duergar cavalry, trained to fight while riding steeders.

DUERGAR MIND MASTER

The feared duergar mind masters usually operate as spies, both inside and beyond a duergar stronghold. Their psionically augmented abilities enable them to see through illusions with ease and shrink down to miniature size to spy on their targets.

DUERGAR HAMMERER

Medium construct, lawful evil

Armor Class 17 (natural armor)
Hit Points 33 (6d8 + 6)
Speed 20 ft.

STR	DEX	CON	INT	WIS	CHA
17 (+3)	7 (–2)	12 (+1)	5 (–3)	5 (–3)	5 (–3)

Damage Immunities poison
Condition Immunities charmed, exhaustion, frightened, paralyzed, petrified, poisoned
Senses darkvision 60 ft., passive Perception 7
Languages understands Dwarvish but can't speak
Challenge 2 (450 XP)

Engine of Pain. Once per turn, a creature that attacks the hammerer can target the duergar trapped in it. The attacker has disadvantage on the attack roll. On a hit, the attack deals an extra 5 (1d10) damage to the hammerer, and the hammerer can respond by using its Multiattack with its reaction.

Siege Monster. The hammerer deals double damage to objects and structures.

ACTIONS

Multiattack. The hammerer makes two attacks: one with its claw and one with its hammer.

Claw. *Melee Weapon Attack:* +5 to hit, reach 5 ft., one target. *Hit:* 6 (1d6 + 3) bludgeoning damage.

Hammer. *Melee Weapon Attack:* +5 to hit, reach 5 ft., one target. *Hit:* 10 (2d6 + 3) bludgeoning damage.

DUERGAR
MIND MASTER

Absence of light results in darkness. So, what results from the absence of Good? The Underdark is a place with very little of either.

DUERGAR MIND MASTER
Medium humanoid (dwarf), lawful evil

Armor Class 14 (leather armor)
Hit Points 39 (6d8 + 12)
Speed 25 ft.

STR	DEX	CON	INT	WIS	CHA
11 (+0)	17 (+3)	14 (+2)	15 (+2)	10 (+0)	12 (+1)

Saving Throws Wis +2
Skills Perception +2, Stealth +5
Damage Resistances poison
Senses darkvision 120 ft., truesight 30 ft., passive Perception 12
Languages Dwarvish, Undercommon
Challenge 2 (450 XP)

Duergar Resilience. The duergar has advantage on saving throws against poison, spells, and illusions, as well as to resist being charmed or paralyzed.

Sunlight Sensitivity. While in sunlight, the duergar has disadvantage on attack rolls, as well as on Wisdom (Perception) checks that rely on sight.

ACTIONS

Multiattack. The duergar makes two melee attacks. It can replace one of those attacks with a use of Mind Mastery.

Mind-Poison Dagger. *Melee Weapon Attack:* +5 to hit, reach 5 ft., one target. *Hit:* 5 (1d4 + 3) piercing damage and 10 (3d6) psychic damage, or 1 piercing damage and 14 (4d6) psychic damage while reduced.

Invisibility (Recharge 4–6). The duergar magically turns invisible for up to 1 hour or until it attacks, it casts a spell, it uses its Reduce, or its concentration is broken (as if concentrating on a spell). Any equipment the duergar wears or carries is invisible with it.

Mind Mastery. The duergar targets one creature it can see within 60 feet of it. The target must succeed on a DC 12 Intelligence saving throw, or the duergar causes it to use its reaction either to make one weapon attack against another creature the duergar can see or to move up to 10 feet in a direction of the duergar's choice. Creatures that can't be charmed are immune to this effect.

Reduce (Recharges after a Short or Long Rest). For 1 minute, the duergar magically decreases in size, along with anything it is wearing or carrying. While reduced, the duergar is Tiny, reduces its weapon damage to 1, and makes attacks, checks, and saving throws with disadvantage if they use Strength. It gains a +5 bonus to all Dexterity (Stealth) checks and a +5 bonus to its AC. It can also take a bonus action on each of its turns to take the Hide action.

DUERGAR KAVALRACHNI
Medium humanoid (dwarf), lawful evil

Armor Class 16 (scale mail, shield)
Hit Points 26 (4d8 + 8)
Speed 25 ft.

STR	DEX	CON	INT	WIS	CHA
14 (+2)	11 (+0)	14 (+2)	11 (+0)	10 (+0)	9 (–1)

Damage Resistances poison
Senses darkvision 120 ft., passive Perception 10
Languages Dwarvish, Undercommon
Challenge 2 (450 XP)

Cavalry Training. When the duergar hits a target with a melee attack while mounted on a female steeder, the steeder can make one melee attack against the same target as a reaction.

Duergar Resilience. The duergar has advantage on saving throws against poison, spells, and illusions, as well as to resist being charmed or paralyzed.

Sunlight Sensitivity. While in sunlight, the duergar has disadvantage on attack rolls, as well as on Wisdom (Perception) checks that rely on sight.

ACTIONS

Multiattack. The duergar makes two war pick attacks.

War Pick. *Melee Weapon Attack:* +4 to hit, reach 5 ft., one target. *Hit:* 6 (1d8 + 2) piercing damage plus 5 (2d4) poison damage.

Heavy Crossbow. *Ranged Weapon Attack:* +2 to hit, range 100/400 ft., one target. *Hit:* 5 (1d10) piercing damage.

Shared Invisibility (Recharges after a Short or Long Rest). The duergar magically turns invisible for up to 1 hour or until it attacks, it casts a spell, or its concentration is broken (as if concentrating on a spell). Any equipment the duergar wears or carries is invisible with it. While the invisible duergar is mounted on a female steeder, the steeder is invisible as well. The invisibility ends early on the steeder immediately after it attacks.

Duergar Screamer

A duergar screamer is a construct that uses sonic energy to grind rock into dust. Duergar accused of spreading gossip or plotting against their superiors are trapped within one of these devices, their beards shorn and their ongoing agony channeled into psionic energy that powers the screamer.

Duergar Soulblade

Soulblades are duergar warriors whose mastery of psionics allows them to manifest blades of psychic energy to slice apart their foes.

Duergar Screamer

Medium construct, lawful evil

Armor Class 15 (natural armor)
Hit Points 38 (7d8 + 7)
Speed 20 ft.

STR	DEX	CON	INT	WIS	CHA
18 (+4)	7 (−2)	12 (+1)	5 (−3)	5 (−3)	5 (−3)

Damage Immunities poison
Condition Immunities charmed, exhaustion, frightened, paralyzed, petrified, poisoned
Senses darkvision 60 ft., passive Perception 7
Languages understands Dwarvish but can't speak
Challenge 3 (700 XP)

Engine of Pain. Once per turn, a creature that attacks the screamer can target the duergar trapped in it. The attacker has disadvantage on the attack roll. On a hit, the attack deals an extra 11 (2d10) damage to the screamer, and the screamer can respond by using its Multiattack with its reaction.

Actions

Multiattack. The screamer makes one drill attack and uses its Sonic Scream.

Drill. *Melee Weapon Attack:* +6 to hit, reach 5 ft., one target. *Hit:* 10 (1d12 + 4) piercing damage.

Sonic Scream. The screamer emits destructive energy in a 15-foot cube. Each creature in that area must succeed on a DC 11 Strength saving throw or take 7 (2d6) thunder damage and be knocked prone.

Duergar Soulblade

Medium humanoid (dwarf), lawful evil

Armor Class 14 (leather armor)
Hit Points 18 (4d8)
Speed 25 ft.

STR	DEX	CON	INT	WIS	CHA
11 (+0)	16 (+3)	10 (+0)	11 (+0)	10 (+0)	12 (+1)

Damage Resistances poison
Senses darkvision 120 ft., passive Perception 10
Languages Dwarvish, Undercommon
Challenge 1 (200 XP)

Duergar Resilience. The duergar has advantage on saving throws against poison, spells, and illusions, as well as to resist being charmed or paralyzed.

Create Soulblade. As a bonus action, the duergar can create a shortsword-sized, visible blade of psionic energy. The weapon appears in the duergar's hand and vanishes if it leaves the duergar's grip, or if the duergar dies or is incapacitated.

Innate Spellcasting (Psionics). The duergar's innate spellcasting ability is Wisdom (spell save DC 12, +4 to hit with spell attacks). It can innately cast the following spells, requiring no components:

At will: *blade ward, true strike*
3/day each: *jump, hunter's mark*

Sunlight Sensitivity. While in sunlight, the duergar has disadvantage on attack rolls, as well as on Wisdom (Perception) checks that rely on sight.

Actions

Soulblade. *Melee Weapon Attack:* +5 to hit, reach 5 ft., one target. *Hit:* 6 (1d6 + 3) force damage, or 10 (2d6 + 3) force damage while enlarged. If the soulblade has advantage on the attack roll, the attack deals an extra 3 (1d6) force damage.

Enlarge (Recharges after a Short or Long Rest). For 1 minute, the duergar magically increases in size, along with anything it is wearing or carrying. While enlarged, the duergar is Large, doubles its damage dice on Strength-based weapon attacks (included in the attacks), and makes Strength checks and Strength saving throws with advantage. If the duergar lacks the room to become Large, it attains the maximum size possible in the space available.

Invisibility (Recharges after a Short or Long Rest). The duergar magically turns invisible for up to 1 hour or until it attacks, it casts a spell, it uses its Enlarge, or its concentration is broken (as if concentrating on a spell). Any equipment the duergar wears or carries is invisible with it.

You think dwarves are dour and unpleasant? Wait until you meet a duergar.

DUERGAR STONE GUARD

DUERGAR STONE GUARD

The stone guard are elite duergar troops, deployed in small numbers to bolster war bands of regulars or organized into elite strike forces for specific missions.

DUERGAR STONE GUARD

Medium humanoid (dwarf), lawful evil

Armor Class 18 (chain mail, shield)
Hit Points 39 (6d8 + 12)
Speed 25 ft.

STR	DEX	CON	INT	WIS	CHA
18 (+4)	11 (+0)	14 (+2)	11 (+0)	10 (+0)	9 (−1)

Damage Resistances poison
Senses darkvision 120 ft., passive Perception 10
Languages Dwarvish, Undercommon
Challenge 2 (450 XP)

Duergar Resilience. The duergar has advantage on saving throws against poison, spells, and illusions, as well as to resist being charmed or paralyzed.

Phalanx Formation. The duergar has advantage on attack rolls and Dexterity saving throws while standing within 5 feet of a duergar ally wielding a shield.

Sunlight Sensitivity. While in sunlight, the duergar has disadvantage on attack rolls, as well as on Wisdom (Perception) checks that rely on sight.

ACTIONS

King's Knife (Shortsword). *Melee Weapon Attack:* +6 to hit, reach 5 ft., one target. *Hit:* 7 (1d6 + 4) piercing damage, or 11 (2d6 + 4) piercing damage while enlarged.

Javelin. *Melee or Ranged Weapon Attack:* +6 to hit, reach 5 ft. or range 30/120 ft., one target. *Hit:* 7 (1d6 + 4) piercing damage, or 11 (2d6 + 4) piercing damage while enlarged.

Enlarge (Recharges after a Short or Long Rest). For 1 minute, the duergar magically increases in size, along with anything it is wearing or carrying. While enlarged, the duergar is Large, doubles its damage dice on Strength-based weapon attacks (included in the attacks), and makes Strength checks and Strength saving throws with advantage. If the duergar lacks the room to become Large, it attains the maximum size possible in the space available.

Invisibility (Recharges after a Short or Long Rest). The duergar magically turns invisible for up to 1 hour or until it attacks, it casts a spell, it uses its Enlarge, or its concentration is broken (as if concentrating on a spell). Any equipment the duergar wears or carries is invisible with it.

Duergar Warlord

Medium humanoid (dwarf), lawful evil

Armor Class 20 (plate mail, shield)
Hit Points 75 (10d8 + 30)
Speed 25 ft.

STR	DEX	CON	INT	WIS	CHA
18 (+4)	11 (+0)	17 (+3)	12 (+1)	12 (+1)	14 (+2)

Damage Resistances poison
Senses darkvision 120 ft., passive Perception 11
Languages Dwarvish, Undercommon
Challenge 6 (2,300 XP)

Duergar Resilience. The duergar has advantage on saving throws against poison, spells, and illusions, as well as to resist being charmed or paralyzed.

Sunlight Sensitivity. While in sunlight, the duergar has disadvantage on attack rolls, as well as on Wisdom (Perception) checks that rely on sight.

Actions

Multiattack. The duergar makes three hammer or javelin attacks and uses Call to Attack, or Enlarge if it is available.

Psychic-Attuned Hammer. *Melee Weapon Attack:* +7 to hit, reach 5 ft., one target. *Hit:* 9 (1d10 + 4) bludgeoning damage, or 15 (2d10 + 4) bludgeoning damage while enlarged, plus 5 (1d10) psychic damage.

Javelin. *Melee or Ranged Weapon Attack:* +7 to hit, reach 5 ft. or range 30/120 ft., one target. *Hit:* 7 (1d6 + 4) piercing damage, or 11 (2d6 + 4) piercing damage while enlarged.

Call to Attack. Up to three allied duergar within 120 feet of this duergar that can hear it can each use their reaction to make one weapon attack.

Enlarge (Recharges after a Short or Long Rest). For 1 minute, the duergar magically increases in size, along with anything it is wearing or carrying. While enlarged, the duergar is Large, doubles its damage dice on Strength-based weapon attacks (included in the attacks), and makes Strength checks and Strength saving throws with advantage. If the duergar lacks the room to become Large, it attains the maximum size possible in the space available.

Invisibility (Recharge 4–6). The duergar magically turns invisible for up to 1 hour or until it attacks, it casts a spell, it uses its Enlarge, or its concentration is broken (as if concentrating on a spell). Any equipment the duergar wears or carries is invisible with it.

Reactions

Scouring Instruction. When an ally that the duergar can see makes a d20 roll, the duergar can roll a d6 and the ally can add the number rolled to the d20 roll by taking 3 (1d6) psychic damage. A creature immune to psychic damage can't be affected by Scouring Instruction.

DUERGAR WARLORD

A warlord is cunning, inspiring, and cruel in equal parts. A skilled warrior who leads duergar into battle, the warlord can use spikes of psionic energy to compel duergar warriors to fight harder.

DUERGAR XARRORN

The xarrorn are specialists who construct weapons using a mixture of alchemy and psionics.

DUERGAR XARRORN

Medium humanoid (dwarf), lawful evil

Armor Class 18 (plate mail)
Hit Points 26 (4d8 + 8)
Speed 25 ft.

STR	DEX	CON	INT	WIS	CHA
16 (+3)	11 (+0)	14 (+2)	11 (+0)	10 (+0)	9 (−1)

Damage Resistances poison
Senses darkvision 120 ft., passive Perception 10
Languages Dwarvish, Undercommon
Challenge 2 (450 XP)

Duergar Resilience. The duergar has advantage on saving throws against poison, spells, and illusions, as well as to resist being charmed or paralyzed.

Sunlight Sensitivity. While in sunlight, the duergar has disadvantage on attack rolls, as well as on Wisdom (Perception) checks that rely on sight.

ACTIONS

Fire Lance. *Melee Weapon Attack:* +5 to hit (with disadvantage if the target is within 5 feet of the duergar), reach 10 ft., one target. *Hit:* 9 (1d12 + 3) piercing damage plus 3 (1d6) fire damage, or 16 (2d12 + 3) piercing damage plus 3 (1d6) fire damage while enlarged.

Fire Spray (Recharge 5–6). From its fire lance, the duergar shoots a 15-foot cone of fire or a line of fire 30 feet long and 5 feet wide. Each creature in that area must make a DC 12 Dexterity saving throw, taking 10 (3d6) fire damage on a failed save, or half as much damage on a successful one.

Enlarge (Recharges after a Short or Long Rest). For 1 minute, the duergar magically increases in size, along with anything it is wearing or carrying. While enlarged, the duergar is Large, doubles its damage dice on Strength-based weapon attacks (included in the attacks), and makes Strength checks and Strength saving throws with advantage. If the duergar lacks the room to become Large, it attains the maximum size possible in the space available.

Invisibility (Recharges after a Short or Long Rest). The duergar magically turns invisible for up to 1 hour or until it attacks, it casts a spell, it uses its Enlarge, or its concentration is broken (as if concentrating on a spell). Any equipment the duergar wears or carries is invisible with it.

EIDOLON

The gods have many methods for protecting sites they deem holy. One servant they rely on often to do so is the eidolon, a ghostly spirit bound by a sacred oath to safeguard a place of import to the divine. Forged from the souls of those who had proven their unwavering devotion, eidolons stalk temples and vaults, places where miracles have been witnessed and relics enshrined, to ensure that no enemy can gain a foothold against the gods' cause through defilement or violence within these sites. If an enemy with such intent sets foot inside a warded location, the eidolon plunges into a graven vessel, a statue specially prepared to house the souls of these protectors. The eidolon then animates the effigy and uses the borrowed body to drive out the intruders bent on plundering the relics it is charged with guarding.

Sacred Guardians. Creating an eidolon requires a spirit of fanatical devotion—that of an individual who, in life, served with unwavering faithfulness. Upon death, a god might reward such a follower with everlasting service in the protection of a holy site. An eidolon has no purpose beyond guarding the place it was assigned to and never leaves.

Animated Statues. An eidolon has few methods for protecting itself beyond its ability to awaken its sacred vessels. When a foe enters, the eidolon leaps into action by merging its body with one of several statues at the site. After doing so, the eidolon controls the construct as if it was its own body and uses its fists to drive back intruders, smashing and crushing anything it can reach.

Undead Nature. An eidolon doesn't require air, food, drink, or sleep.

It's not just gods that have the power to bind spirits to their idols. Beings such as archdevils can do it with the souls of their cultists. Moloch, for instance.

EIDOLON

Medium undead, any alignment

Armor Class 9
Hit Points 63 (18d8 − 18)
Speed 0 ft., fly 40 ft. (hover)

STR	DEX	CON	INT	WIS	CHA
7 (−2)	8 (−1)	9 (−1)	14 (+2)	19 (+4)	16 (+3)

Saving Throws Wis +8
Skills Perception +8
Damage Resistances acid, fire, lightning, thunder; bludgeoning, piercing, and slashing from nonmagical attacks
Damage Immunities cold, necrotic, poison
Condition Immunities charmed, exhaustion, frightened, grappled, paralyzed, petrified, poisoned, prone, restrained
Senses darkvision 60 ft., passive Perception 18
Languages the languages it knew in life
Challenge 12 (8,400 XP)

Incorporeal Movement. The eidolon can move through other creatures and objects as if they were difficult terrain. It takes 5 (1d10) force damage if it ends its turn inside an object other than a sacred statue.

Sacred Animation (Recharge 5–6). When the eidolon moves into a space occupied by a sacred statue, the eidolon can disappear, causing the statue to become a creature under the eidolon's control. The eidolon uses the sacred statue's statistics in place of its own.

Turn Resistance. The eidolon has advantage on saving throws against any effect that turns undead.

ACTIONS

Divine Dread. Each creature within 60 feet of the eidolon that can see it must succeed on a DC 15 Wisdom saving throw or be frightened of it for 1 minute. While frightened in this way, the creature must take the Dash action and move away from the eidolon by the safest available route at the start of each of its turns, unless there is nowhere for it to move, in which case the creature also becomes stunned until it can move again. A frightened target can repeat the saving throw at the end of each of its turns, ending the effect on itself on a success. If a target's saving throw is successful or the effect ends for it, the target is immune to any eidolon's Divine Dread for the next 24 hours.

SACRED STATUE

Large construct, as the eidolon's alignment

Armor Class 19 (natural armor)
Hit Points 95 (10d10 + 40)
Speed 25 ft.

STR	DEX	CON	INT	WIS	CHA
19 (+4)	8 (−1)	19 (+4)	14 (+2)	19 (+4)	16 (+3)

Saving Throws Wis +8
Damage Resistances acid, fire, lightning; bludgeoning, piercing, and slashing from nonmagical attacks
Damage Immunities cold, necrotic, poison
Condition Immunities charmed, exhaustion, frightened, paralyzed, petrified, poisoned
Senses darkvision 60 ft., passive Perception 14
Languages the languages the eidolon knew in life

False Appearance. While the statue remains motionless, it is indistinguishable from a normal statue.

Ghostly Inhabitant. The eidolon that enters the sacred statue remains inside it until the statue drops to 0 hit points, the eidolon uses a bonus action to move out of the statue, or the eidolon is turned or forced out by an effect such as the *dispel evil and good* spell. When the eidolon leaves the statue, it appears in an unoccupied space within 5 feet of the statue.

Inert. When not inhabited by an eidolon, the statue is an object.

ACTIONS

Multiattack. The statue makes two slam attacks.

Slam. *Melee Weapon Attack:* +8 to hit, reach 10 ft., one target. *Hit:* 43 (6d12 + 4) bludgeoning damage.

Rock. *Ranged Weapon Attack:* +8 to hit, range 60 ft./240 ft., one target. *Hit:* 37 (6d10 + 4) bludgeoning damage.

ELADRIN

Eladrin dwell in the verdant splendor of the Feywild. They are related to the elves found on the Material Plane, and resemble them in both their love of beauty and the value they place on personal freedom. But where other elves can temper their wild impulses, eladrin are creatures ruled by emotion—and because of their unique magical nature, they undergo physical changes to match their changes in temperament.

The eladrin have spent centuries in the Feywild, and most of them have become fey creatures as a result. Some of them are still humanoid, similar in that respect to their other elven kin. The eladrin presented here are of the fey variety.

Creatures of Passion. The magic flowing through eladrin responds to their emotional state by transforming them into different seasonal aspects, with behaviors and capabilities that change with their forms. Some eladrin might remain in a particular aspect for years, while others run through the emotional spectrum each week.

Lovers of Beauty. Regardless of the aspect they express, eladrin love beauty and surround themselves with lovely things. Eladrin try to possess any objects they find striking. They might seek to own a painting, a statue, or a glittering jewel. When they encounter people of comely form or luminous spirit, they use their magic to delight those folk or, in the case of evil eladrin, to abduct them.

AUTUMN ELADRIN

Eladrin often enter the autumn season when they are overcome by feelings of goodwill. In this aspect, they defuse conflicts and alleviate suffering by using their magic to heal, to cure, and to relieve any ailment that might afflict the people who come to them for aid. They tolerate no violence in their presence and move quickly to settle disputes, to ensure that peace continues to reign.

SPRING ELADRIN

Their hearts filled with joy, spring eladrin cavort through their sylvan realms, their songs and laughter filling the air. These playful eladrin beguile other creatures to fill them with the joy of spring. Their antics can lead other creatures into danger and make mischief for them.

SUMMER ELADRIN

When they are angered, eladrin enter the season of summer, a burning, tempestuous state that transforms them into aggressive warriors eager to vent their wrath. Their magic responds to their fury and amplifies their fighting ability, which helps them move with astonishing quickness and strike with terrible force.

WINTER ELADRIN

When sorrow distresses eladrin, they enter the winter season, becoming figures of melancholy and bitterness. Frozen tears drop from their cheeks, and their palpable sadness emanates from them as bitter cold.

CHANGEABLE NATURE

Whenever one of the eladrin presented here finishes a long rest, it can associate itself with a different season, provided it isn't incapacitated. When the eladrin makes this change, it uses the stat block of the new season, rather than its old stat block. Any damage the eladrin sustained in its original form applies to the new form, as do any conditions or other ongoing effects affecting it.

AUTUMN ELADRIN
Medium fey (elf), chaotic neutral

Armor Class 19 (natural armor)
Hit Points 127 (17d8 + 51)
Speed 30 ft.

STR	DEX	CON	INT	WIS	CHA
12 (+1)	16 (+3)	16 (+3)	14 (+2)	17 (+3)	18 (+4)

Skills Insight +7, Medicine +7
Damage Resistances bludgeoning, piercing, and slashing from nonmagical attacks
Senses darkvision 60 ft., passive Perception 13
Languages Common, Elvish, Sylvan
Challenge 10 (5,900 XP)

Enchanting Presence. Any non-eladrin creature that starts its turn within 60 feet of the eladrin must make a DC 16 Wisdom saving throw. On a failed save, the creature becomes charmed by the eladrin for 1 minute. On a successful save, the creature becomes immune to any eladrin's Enchanting Presence for 24 hours.

Whenever the eladrin deals damage to the charmed creature, the creature can repeat the saving throw, ending the effect on itself on a success.

Fey Step (Recharge 4–6). As a bonus action, the eladrin can teleport up to 30 feet to an unoccupied space it can see.

Innate Spellcasting. The eladrin's innate spellcasting ability is Charisma (spell save DC 16). It can innately cast the following spells, requiring no material components:

At will: *calm emotions, sleep*
3/day each: *cure wounds* (as a 5th-level spell), *lesser restoration*
1/day each: *greater restoration, heal, raise dead*

Magic Resistance. The eladrin has advantage on saving throws against spells and other magical effects.

ACTIONS

Longsword. Melee Weapon Attack: +5 to hit, reach 5 ft., one target. Hit: 5 (1d8 + 1) slashing damage, or 6 (1d10 + 1) slashing damage if used with two hands, plus 18 (4d8) psychic damage.

Longbow. Ranged Weapon Attack: +7 to hit, range 150/600 ft., one target. Hit: 7 (1d8 + 3) piercing damage plus 18 (4d8) psychic damage.

REACTIONS

Foster Peace. If a creature charmed by the eladrin hits with an attack roll while within 60 feet of the eladrin, the eladrin magically causes the attack to miss, provided the eladrin can see the attacker.

*To be not just ruled by emotions,
but physically changed by them?
Better to have no emotions at all.*

SPRING ELADRIN

Medium fey (elf), chaotic neutral

Armor Class 19 (natural armor)
Hit Points 127 (17d8 + 51)
Speed 30 ft.

STR	DEX	CON	INT	WIS	CHA
14 (+2)	16 (+3)	16 (+3)	18 (+4)	11 (+0)	18 (+4)

Skills Deception +8, Persuasion +8
Damage Resistances bludgeoning, piercing, and slashing from
 nonmagical attacks
Senses darkvision 60 ft., passive Perception 10
Languages Common, Elvish, Sylvan
Challenge 10 (5,900 XP)

Fey Step (Recharge 4–6). As a bonus action, the eladrin can
teleport up to 30 feet to an unoccupied space it can see.

Innate Spellcasting. The eladrin's innate spellcasting ability is
Charisma (spell save DC 16). It can innately cast the following
spells, requiring no material components:

At will: *charm person, Tasha's hideous laughter*
3/day each: *confusion, enthrall, suggestion*
1/day each: *hallucinatory terrain, Otto's irresistible dance*

Joyful Presence. Any non-eladrin creature that starts its turn
within 60 feet of the eladrin must make a DC 16 Wisdom saving
throw. On a failed save, the creature becomes charmed by the
eladrin for 1 minute. On a successful save, the creature becomes immune to any eladrin's Joyful Presence for 24 hours.

 Whenever the eladrin deals damage to the charmed creature,
it can repeat the saving throw, ending the effect on itself on
a success.

Magic Resistance. The eladrin has advantage on saving throws
against spells and other magical effects.

ACTIONS

Multiattack. The eladrin makes two weapon attacks. The
eladrin can cast one spell in place of one of these attacks.

Longsword. *Melee Weapon Attack:* +6 to hit, reach 5 ft., one target. *Hit:* 6 (1d8 + 2) slashing damage, or 7 (1d10 + 2) slashing
damage if used with two hands, plus 4 (1d8) psychic damage.

Longbow. *Ranged Weapon Attack:* +7 to hit, range 150/600 ft.,
one target. *Hit:* 7 (1d8 + 3) piercing damage plus 4 (1d8) psychic damage.

SUMMER ELADRIN

Medium fey (elf), chaotic neutral

Armor Class 19 (natural armor)
Hit Points 127 (17d8 + 51)
Speed 50 ft.

STR	DEX	CON	INT	WIS	CHA
19 (+4)	21 (+5)	16 (+3)	14 (+2)	12 (+1)	18 (+4)

Skills Athletics +8, Intimidation +8
Damage Resistances bludgeoning, piercing, and slashing from
 nonmagical attacks
Senses darkvision 60 ft., passive Perception 9
Languages Common, Elvish, Sylvan
Challenge 10 (5,900 XP)

Fearsome Presence. Any non-eladrin creature that starts its turn
within 60 feet of the eladrin must make a DC 16 Wisdom saving
throw. On a failed save, the creature becomes frightened of the
eladrin for 1 minute. A creature can repeat the saving throw
at the end of each of its turns, ending the effect on itself on a
success. If a creature's saving throw is successful or the effect
ends for it, the creature is immune to any eladrin's Fearsome
Presence for the next 24 hours.

Fey Step (Recharge 4–6). As a bonus action, the eladrin can
teleport up to 30 feet to an unoccupied space it can see.

Magic Resistance. The eladrin has advantage on saving throws
against spells and other magical effects.

ACTIONS

Multiattack. The eladrin makes two weapon attacks.

Longsword. *Melee Weapon Attack:* +8 to hit, reach 5 ft., one target. *Hit:* 13 (2d8 + 4) slashing damage, or 15 (2d10 + 4) slashing damage if used with two hands, plus 4 (1d8) fire damage.

Longbow. *Ranged Weapon Attack:* +9 to hit, range 150/600
ft., one target. *Hit:* 14 (2d8 + 5) piercing damage plus 4 (1d8)
fire damage.

REACTIONS

Parry. The eladrin adds 3 to its AC against one melee attack
that would hit it. To do so, the eladrin must see the attacker
and be wielding a melee weapon.

WINTER ELADRIN

Medium fey (elf), chaotic neutral

Armor Class 19 (natural armor)
Hit Points 127 (17d8 + 51)
Speed 30 ft.

STR	DEX	CON	INT	WIS	CHA
11 (+0)	10 (+0)	16 (+3)	18 (+4)	17 (+3)	13 (+1)

Damage Resistances cold; bludgeoning, piercing, and slashing from nonmagical attacks
Senses darkvision 60 ft., passive Perception 13
Languages Common, Elvish, Sylvan
Challenge 10 (5,900 XP)

Fey Step (Recharge 4–6). As a bonus action, the eladrin can teleport up to 30 feet to an unoccupied space it can see.

Innate Spellcasting. The eladrin's innate spellcasting ability is Intelligence (spell save DC 16). It can innately cast the following spells, requiring no material components:

At will: *fog cloud, gust of wind*
1/day each: *cone of cold, ice storm*

Magic Resistance. The eladrin has advantage on saving throws against spells and other magical effects.

Sorrowful Presence. Any non-eladrin creature that starts its turn within 60 feet of the eladrin must make a DC 13 Wisdom saving throw. On a failed save, the creature becomes charmed by the eladrin for 1 minute. While charmed in this way, the creature has disadvantage on ability checks and saving throws. The charmed creature can repeat the saving throw at the end of each of its turns, ending the effect on itself on a success. If a creature's saving throw is successful or the effect ends for it, the creature is immune to any eladrin's Sorrowful Presence for the next 24 hours.

   Whenever the eladrin deals damage to the charmed creature, it can repeat the saving throw, ending the effect on itself on a success.

ACTIONS

Longsword. *Melee Weapon Attack:* +4 to hit, reach 5 ft., one target. *Hit:* 4 (1d8) slashing damage, or 5 (1d10) slashing damage if used with two hands.

Longbow. *Ranged Weapon Attack:* +4 to hit, range 150/600 ft., one target. *Hit:* 4 (1d8) piercing damage.

REACTIONS

Frigid Rebuke. When the eladrin takes damage from a creature the eladrin can see within 60 feet of it, the eladrin can force that creature to succeed on a DC 16 Constitution saving throw or take 11 (2d10) cold damage.

SPRING ELADRIN

SUMMER ELADRIN

WINTER ELADRIN

ELDER ELEMENTALS

On their native planes, elementals sweep across the weird and tempestuous landscape. Some possess greater power, gained by feeding on their lesser kin and adding the essence of creatures they have devoured to their own until they become something extraordinary. When summoned, these elder elementals manifest as beings of apocalyptic capability, entities whose mere existence promises destruction.

Deadly When Summoned. The methods for summoning elder elementals remain hidden in forbidden tomes or inscribed on the walls of lost temples raised to honor the Elder Elemental Eye. Only casters of superlative skill have even the faintest chance of calling forth one of these monsters, and the spellcaster is often destroyed by the effort. Thus, only the most unhinged and nihilistic members of Elemental Evil cults attempt such a summoning, in the hope of hastening the world toward some cataclysmic end.

Elemental Nature. An elder elemental doesn't require air, food, drink, or sleep.

LEVIATHAN

Gargantuan elemental, neutral

Armor Class 17
Hit Points 328 (16d20 + 160)
Speed 40 ft., swim 120 ft.

STR	DEX	CON	INT	WIS	CHA
30 (+10)	24 (+7)	30 (+10)	2 (−4)	18 (+4)	17 (+3)

Saving Throws Wis +10, Cha +9
Damage Resistances bludgeoning, piercing, and slashing from nonmagical attacks
Damage Immunities acid, poison
Condition Immunities exhaustion, grappled, paralyzed, petrified, poisoned, prone, restrained, stunned
Senses darkvision 60 ft., passive Perception 14
Languages —
Challenge 20 (25,000 XP)

Legendary Resistance (3/Day). If the leviathan fails a saving throw, it can choose to succeed instead.

Partial Freeze. If the leviathan takes 50 cold damage or more during a single turn, the leviathan partially freezes; until the end of its next turn, its speeds are reduced to 20 feet, and it makes attack rolls with disadvantage.

Siege Monster. The leviathan deals double damage to objects and structures (included in Tidal Wave).

Water Form. The leviathan can enter a hostile creature's space and stop there. It can move through a space as narrow as 1 inch wide without squeezing.

ACTIONS

Multiattack. The leviathan makes two attacks: one with its slam and one with its tail.

Slam. *Melee Weapon Attack:* +16 to hit, reach 20 ft., one target. *Hit:* 15 (1d10 + 10) bludgeoning damage plus 5 (1d10) acid damage.

Tail. *Melee Weapon Attack:* +16 to hit, reach 20 ft., one target. *Hit:* 16 (1d12 + 10) bludgeoning damage plus 6 (1d12) acid damage.

Tidal Wave (Recharge 6). While submerged, the leviathan magically creates a wall of water centered on itself. The wall is up to 250 feet long, up to 250 feet high, and up to 50 feet thick.

When the wall appears, all other creatures within its area must each make a DC 24 Strength saving throw. A creature takes 33 (6d10) bludgeoning damage on failed save, or half as much damage on a successful one.

At the start of each of the leviathan's turns after the wall appears, the wall, along with any other creatures in it, moves 50 feet away from the leviathan. Any Huge or smaller creature inside the wall or whose space the wall enters when it moves must succeed on a DC 24 Strength saving throw or take 27 (5d10) bludgeoning damage. A creature takes this damage no more than once on a turn. At the end of each turn the wall moves, the wall's height is reduced by 50 feet, and the damage creatures take from the wall on subsequent rounds is reduced by 1d10. When the wall reaches 0 feet in height, the effect ends.

A creature caught in the wall can move by swimming. Because of the force of the wave, though, the creature must make a successful DC 24 Strength (Athletics) check to swim at all during that turn.

LEGENDARY ACTIONS

The leviathan can take 3 legendary actions, choosing from the options below. Only one legendary action option can be used at a time and only at the end of another creature's turn. The leviathan regains spent legendary actions at the start of its turn.

Slam (Costs 2 Actions). The leviathan makes one slam attack.
Move. The leviathan moves up to its speed.

> *To rise like a phoenix from the ashes—so many use that quaint colloquialism. Little do they know about the true horror of such a rebirth.*

LEVIATHAN

A towering wall of water that drags ships down to the ocean's depths and washes away coastal settlements—that phenomenon typifies the destruction a leviathan can unleash on the world. When called forth, a leviathan arises from a large body of water to form an immense serpent-shaped creature.

PHOENIX

Releasing a phoenix from the Inner Planes creates an explosion of fire that spreads across the sky. An enormous fiery bird forms in the center of the flames and smoke—an elder elemental possessed by a need to burn everything to ash. The phoenix rarely stays in one place for long as it strives to transform the world into an inferno.

PHOENIX
Gargantuan elemental, neutral

Armor Class 18
Hit Points 175 (10d20 + 70)
Speed 20 ft., fly 120 ft.

STR	DEX	CON	INT	WIS	CHA
19 (+4)	26 (+8)	25 (+7)	2 (–4)	21 (+5)	18 (+4)

Saving Throws Wis +10, Cha +9
Damage Resistances bludgeoning, piercing, and slashing from nonmagical attacks
Damage Immunities fire, poison
Condition Immunities exhaustion, grappled, paralyzed, petrified, poisoned, prone, restrained, stunned
Senses darkvision 60 ft., passive Perception 15
Languages —
Challenge 16 (15,000 XP)

Fiery Death and Rebirth. When the phoenix dies, it explodes. Each creature within 60-feet of it must make a DC 20 Dexterity saving throw, taking 22 (4d10) fire damage on a failed save, or half as much damage on a successful one. The fire ignites flammable objects in the area that aren't worn or carried.

The explosion destroys the phoenix's body and leaves behind an egg-shaped cinder that weighs 5 pounds. The cinder is blazing hot, dealing 21 (6d6) fire damage to any creature that touches it, though no more than once per round. The cinder is immune to all damage, and after 1d6 days, it hatches a new phoenix.

Fire Form. The phoenix can move through a space as narrow as 1 inch wide without squeezing. Any creature that touches the phoenix or hits it with a melee attack while within 5 feet of it takes 5 (1d10) fire damage. In addition, the phoenix can enter a hostile creature's space and stop there. The first time it enters a creature's space on a turn, that creature takes 5 (1d10) fire damage. With a touch, the phoenix can also ignite flammable objects that aren't worn or carried (no action required).

Flyby. The phoenix doesn't provoke opportunity attacks when it flies out of an enemy's reach.

Illumination. The phoenix sheds bright light in a 60-foot radius and dim light for an additional 30 feet.

Legendary Resistance (3/Day). If the phoenix fails a saving throw, it can choose to succeed instead.

Siege Monster. The phoenix deals double damage to objects and structures.

ACTIONS

Multiattack. The phoenix makes two attacks: one with its beak and one with its fiery talons.

Beak. *Melee Weapon Attack:* +13 to hit, reach 15 ft., one target. *Hit:* 15 (2d6 + 8) fire damage. If the target is a creature or a flammable object, it ignites. Until a creature takes an action to douse the fire, the target takes 5 (1d10) fire damage at the start of each of its turns.

Fiery Talons. *Melee Weapon Attack:* +13 to hit, reach 15 ft., one target. *Hit:* 17 (2d8 + 8) fire damage.

LEGENDARY ACTIONS

The phoenix can take 3 legendary actions, choosing from the options below. Only one legendary action option can be used at a time and only at the end of another creature's turn. The phoenix regains spent legendary actions at the start of its turn.

Peck. The phoenix makes one beak attack.
Move. The phoenix moves up to its speed.
Swoop (Costs 2 Actions). The phoenix moves up to its speed and attacks with its fiery talons.

ELDER TEMPEST

Terrifying storms manifest in the body of the elder tempest. A being carved from clouds, wind, rain, and lightning, the elder tempest assumes the shape of a serpent that slithers through the sky. The tempest drowns the land beneath it with rain and stabs the earth with lances of lightning. Punishing winds scream around it as it flies, feeding the chaos it creates.

ELDER TEMPEST
Gargantuan elemental, neutral

Armor Class 19
Hit Points 264 (16d20 + 96)
Speed 0 ft., fly 120 ft. (hover)

STR	DEX	CON	INT	WIS	CHA
23 (+6)	28 (+9)	23 (+6)	2 (−4)	21 (+5)	18 (+4)

Saving Throws Wis +12, Cha +11
Damage Resistances bludgeoning, piercing, and slashing from nonmagical attacks
Damage Immunities lightning, poison, thunder
Condition Immunities exhaustion, grappled, paralyzed, petrified, poisoned, prone, restrained, stunned
Senses darkvision 60 ft., passive Perception 15
Languages —
Challenge 23 (50,000 XP)

Air Form. The tempest can enter a hostile creature's space and stop there. It can move through a space as narrow as 1 inch wide without squeezing.

Flyby. The tempest doesn't provoke opportunity attacks when it flies out of an enemy's reach.

Legendary Resistance (3/Day). If the tempest fails a saving throw, it can choose to succeed instead.

Living Storm. The tempest is always at the center of a storm 1d6 + 4 miles in diameter. Heavy precipitation in the form of either rain or snow falls there, causing the area to be lightly obscured. Heavy rain also extinguishes open flames and imposes disadvantage on Wisdom (Perception) checks that rely on hearing.

In addition, strong winds swirl in the area covered by the storm. The winds impose disadvantage on ranged attack rolls. The winds extinguish open flames and disperse fog.

Siege Monster. The tempest deals double damage to objects and structures.

ACTIONS

Multiattack. The tempest makes two attacks with its thunderous slam.

Thunderous Slam. *Melee Weapon Attack:* +16 to hit, reach 20 ft., one target. *Hit:* 23 (4d6 + 9) thunder damage.

Lightning Storm (Recharge 6). All other creatures within 120 feet of the tempest must each make a DC 20 Dexterity saving throw, taking 27 (6d8) lightning damage on a failed save, or half as much damage on a successful one. If a target's saving throw fails by 5 or more, the creature is also stunned until the end of its next turn.

LEGENDARY ACTIONS

The tempest can take 3 legendary actions, choosing from the options below. Only one legendary action option can be used at a time and only at the end of another creature's turn. The tempest regains spent legendary actions at the start of its turn.

Move. The tempest moves up to its speed.
Lightning Strike (Costs 2 Actions). The tempest can cause a bolt of lightning to strike a point on the ground anywhere under its storm. Each creature within 5 feet of that point must make a DC 20 Dexterity saving throw, taking 16 (3d10) lightning damage on a failed save, or half as much damage on a successful one.
Screaming Gale (Costs 3 Actions). The tempest releases a blast of thunder and wind in a line that is 1 mile long and 20 feet wide. Objects in that area take 22 (4d10) thunder damage. Each creature there must succeed on a DC 21 Dexterity saving throw or take 22 (4d10) thunder damage and be flung up to 60 feet in a direction away from the line. If a thrown target collides with an immovable object, such as a wall or floor, the target takes 3 (1d6) bludgeoning damage for every 10 feet it was thrown before impact. If the target would collide with another creature instead, that other creature must succeed on a DC 19 Dexterity saving throw or take the same damage and be knocked prone.

ZARATAN

When a zaratan is summoned from the Elemental Plane of Earth, the ground rises up to take the shape of what looks like a hulking, armored reptile, its shell composed of the landscape from which it arose. The zaratan plods across the land, each step sending shock waves through the ground severe enough to unsettle structures. Dim-witted, the zaratan lurches onward, expressing its rage through its trumpeting calls and the occasional boulder or blast of debris it spews from its cavernous maw. If seriously injured, the zaratan slowly retracts its appendages to gain shelter beneath its impervious shell, biding its time until it recovers and can resume its march.

ZARATAN
Gargantuan elemental, neutral

Armor Class 21 (natural armor)
Hit Points 307 (15d20 + 150)
Speed 40 ft., swim 40 ft.

STR	DEX	CON	INT	WIS	CHA
30 (+10)	10 (+0)	30 (+10)	2 (–4)	21 (+5)	18 (+4)

Saving Throws Wis +12, Cha +11
Damage Vulnerabilities thunder
Damage Resistances cold, fire, lightning; bludgeoning, piercing, and slashing from nonmagical attacks
Damage Immunities poison
Condition Immunities exhaustion, paralyzed, petrified, poisoned, stunned
Senses darkvision 60 ft., tremorsense 60 ft., passive Perception 15
Languages —
Challenge 22 (41,000 XP)

Earth-Shaking Movement. As a bonus action after moving at least 10 feet on the ground, the zaratan can send a shock wave through the ground in a 120-foot-radius circle centered on itself. That area becomes difficult terrain for 1 minute. Each creature on the ground that is concentrating must succeed on a DC 25 Constitution saving throw or the creature's concentration is broken.

The shock wave deals 100 thunder damage to all structures in contact with the ground in the area. If a creature is near a structure that collapses, the creature might be buried; a creature within half the distance of the structure's height must make a DC 25 Dexterity saving throw. On a failed save, the creature takes 17 (5d6) bludgeoning damage, is knocked prone, and is trapped in the rubble. A trapped creature is restrained, requiring a successful DC 20 Strength (Athletics) check as an action to escape. Another creature within 5 feet of the buried creature can use its action to clear rubble and grant advantage on the check. If three creatures use their actions in this way, the check is an automatic success. On a successful save, the creature takes half as much damage and doesn't fall prone or become trapped.

Legendary Resistance (3/Day). If the zaratan fails a saving throw, it can choose to succeed instead.

Magic Weapons. The zaratan's weapon attacks are magical.

Siege Monster. The elemental deals double damage to objects and structures (included in Earth-Shaking Movement).

ACTIONS

Multiattack. The zaratan makes two attacks: one with its bite and one with its stomp.

Bite. *Melee Weapon Attack:* +17 to hit, reach 20 ft., one target. *Hit:* 28 (4d8 + 10) piercing damage.

Stomp. *Melee Weapon Attack:* +17 to hit, reach 20 ft., one target. *Hit:* 26 (3d10 + 10) bludgeoning damage.

Spit Rock. *Ranged Weapon Attack:* +17 to hit, range 120 ft./240 ft., one target. *Hit:* 31 (6d8 + 10) bludgeoning damage.

Spew Debris (Recharge 5–6). The zaratan exhales rocky debris in a 90-foot cube. Each creature in that area must make a DC 25 Dexterity saving throw. A creature takes 33 (6d10) bludgeoning damage on a failed save, or half as much damage on a successful one. A creature that fails the save by 5 or more is knocked prone.

LEGENDARY ACTIONS

The zaratan can take 3 legendary actions, choosing from the options below. Only one legendary action option can be used at a time and only at the end of another creature's turn. The zaratan regains spent legendary actions at the start of its turn.

Stomp. The zaratan makes one stomp attack.
Move. The zaratan moves up to its speed.
Spit (Costs 2 Actions). The zaratan uses Spit Rock.
Retract (Costs 2 Actions). The zaratan retracts into its shell. Until it takes its Emerge action, it has resistance to all damage, and it is restrained. The next time it takes a legendary action, it must take its Revitalize or Emerge action.
Revitalize (Costs 2 Actions). The zaratan can use this option only if it is retracted in its shell. It regains 52 (5d20) hit points. The next time it takes a legendary action, it must take its Emerge action.
Emerge (Costs 2 Actions). The zaratan emerges from its shell and uses Spit Rock. It can use this option only if it is retracted in its shell.

E

ELEMENTAL MYRMIDONS

Elemental myrmidons are elementals conjured and bound by magic into ritually created suits of plate armor. In this form, they possess no recollection of their former existence as free elementals. They exist only to follow the commands of their creators.

AIR ELEMENTAL MYRMIDON

Medium elemental, neutral

Armor Class 18 (plate)
Hit Points 117 (18d8 + 36)
Speed 30 ft., fly 30 ft. (hover)

STR	DEX	CON	INT	WIS	CHA
18 (+4)	14 (+2)	14 (+2)	9 (−1)	10 (+0)	10 (+0)

Damage Resistances lightning, thunder; bludgeoning, piercing, and slashing from nonmagical attacks
Damage Immunities poison
Condition Immunities paralyzed, petrified, poisoned, prone
Senses darkvision 60 ft., passive Perception 10
Languages Auran, one language of its creator's choice
Challenge 7 (2,900 XP)

Magic Weapons. The myrmidon's weapon attacks are magical.

ACTIONS

Multiattack. The myrmidon makes three flail attacks.

Flail. *Melee Weapon Attack:* +7 to hit, reach 5 ft., one target. *Hit:* 8 (1d8 + 4) bludgeoning damage.

Lightning Strike (Recharge 6). The myrmidon makes one flail attack. On a hit, the target takes an extra 18 (4d8) lightning damage, and the target must succeed on a DC 13 Constitution saving throw or be stunned until the end of the myrmidon's next turn.

EARTH ELEMENTAL MYRMIDON

Medium elemental, neutral

Armor Class 18 (plate)
Hit Points 127 (17d8 + 51)
Speed 30 ft.

STR	DEX	CON	INT	WIS	CHA
18 (+4)	10 (+0)	17 (+3)	8 (−1)	10 (+0)	10 (+0)

Damage Resistances bludgeoning, piercing, and slashing from nonmagical attacks
Damage Immunities poison
Condition Immunities paralyzed, petrified, poisoned, prone
Senses darkvision 60 ft., passive Perception 10
Languages Terran, one language of its creator's choice
Challenge 7 (2,900 XP)

Magic Weapons. The myrmidon's weapon attacks are magical.

ACTIONS

Multiattack. The myrmidon makes two maul attacks.

Maul. *Melee Weapon Attack:* +7 to hit, reach 5 ft., one target. *Hit:* 11 (2d6 + 4) bludgeoning damage.

Thunderous Strike (Recharge 6). The myrmidon makes one maul attack. On a hit, the target takes an extra 16 (3d10) thunder damage, and the target must succeed on a DC 14 Strength saving throw or be knocked prone.

Fire Elemental Myrmidon

Medium elemental, neutral

Armor Class 18 (plate)
Hit Points 123 (19d8 + 38)
Speed 40 ft.

STR	DEX	CON	INT	WIS	CHA
13 (+1)	18 (+4)	15 (+2)	9 (−1)	10 (+0)	10 (+0)

Damage Resistances bludgeoning, piercing, and slashing from nonmagical attacks
Damage Immunities fire, poison
Condition Immunities paralyzed, petrified, poisoned, prone
Senses darkvision 60 ft., passive Perception 10
Languages Ignan, one language of its creator's choice
Challenge 7 (2,900 XP)

Illumination. The myrmidon sheds bright light in a 20-foot radius and dim light in a 40-foot radius.

Magic Weapons. The myrmidon's weapon attacks are magical.

Water Susceptibility. For every 5 feet the myrmidon moves in 1 foot or more of water, it takes 2 (1d4) cold damage.

Actions

Multiattack. The myrmidon makes three scimitar attacks.

Scimitar. *Melee Weapon Attack:* +7 to hit, reach 5 ft., one target. *Hit:* 7 (1d6 + 4) slashing damage.

Fiery Strikes (Recharge 6). The myrmidon uses Multiattack. Each attack that hits deals an extra 5 (1d10) fire damage.

Water Elemental Myrmidon

Medium elemental, neutral

Armor Class 18 (plate)
Hit Points 127 (17d8 + 51)
Speed 40 ft., swim 40 ft.

STR	DEX	CON	INT	WIS	CHA
18 (+4)	14 (+2)	15 (+3)	8 (−1)	10 (+0)	10 (+0)

Damage Resistances acid; bludgeoning, piercing, and slashing from nonmagical attacks
Damage Immunities poison
Condition Immunities paralyzed, petrified, poisoned, prone
Senses darkvision 60 ft., passive Perception 10
Languages Aquan, one language of its creator's choice
Challenge 7 (2,900 XP)

Magic Weapons. The myrmidon's weapon attacks are magical.

Actions

Multiattack. The myrmidon makes three trident attacks.

Trident. *Melee or Ranged Weapon Attack:* +7 to hit, reach 5 ft. or range 20/60 ft., one target. *Hit:* 7 (1d6 + 4) piercing damage, or 8 (1d8 + 4) piercing damage if used with two hands to make a melee attack.

Freezing Strikes (Recharge 6). The myrmidon uses Multiattack. Each attack that hits deals an extra 5 (1d10) cold damage. A target that is hit by one or more of these attacks has its speed reduced by 10 feet until the end of the myrmidon's next turn.

GIFF

It's easy to spot the giff in a room: a group of 7-foot-tall, hippopotamus-headed humanoids attired in gaudy military uniforms, with gleaming pistols and muskets on display. These spacefaring mercenaries are renowned for their martial training and their love of explosives.

Military Organization. Every aspect of giff society is organized along military lines. From birth until death, every giff has a military rank. It must follow orders from those of superior rank, and it can give orders to those of lower rank. Promotions don't depend on age but are granted by a superior as a reward for valor. Giff are devoted to their children, even as most of their education is geared toward fighting and war.

Mercenaries Extraordinaire. Giff are in high demand as warriors for hire, but they insist on serving in units composed entirely of giff; a giff hiring itself out individually is unheard of. Giff refuse to fight other giff, and will never agree to a contract unless it stipulates that they can sit out a battle rather than wage war against their kin. A giff prizes the reputation of its unit above its own life. Life is fleeting, but the regiment endures for generations or even centuries.

A Whiff of Gunpowder. Muskets and grenades are the favorite weapons of every giff. The bigger the boom, the brighter the flash, and the thicker the smoke it produces, the more giff love a weapon. Their skill with gunpowder is another reason for their popularity as mercenaries. Giff revel in the challenge of building a bomb big enough to level a fortification. They gladly accept payment in kegs of gunpowder in preference to gold, gems, or other currency.

No Honor in Magic. Some giff become wizards, clerics, and other kinds of spellcasters, but they're so infrequent that most giff mercenary units have no magical capability. Typical giff are as smart as the average human, but their focus on military training to the exclusion of all other areas of study can make them seem dull-witted to those who have more varied interests.

GIFF
Medium humanoid, lawful neutral

Armor Class 16 (breastplate)
Hit Points 60 (8d8 + 24)
Speed 30 ft.

STR	DEX	CON	INT	WIS	CHA
18 (+4)	14 (+2)	17 (+3)	11 (+0)	12 (+1)	12 (+1)

Senses passive Perception 11
Languages Common
Challenge 3 (700 XP)

Headfirst Charge. The giff can try to knock a creature over; if the giff moves at least 20 feet in a straight line that ends within 5 feet of a Large or smaller creature, that creature must succeed on a DC 14 Strength saving throw or take 7 (2d6) bludgeoning damage and be knocked prone.

Firearms Knowledge. The giff's mastery of its weapons enables it to ignore the loading property of muskets and pistols.

ACTIONS

Multiattack. The giff makes two pistol attacks.

Longsword. *Melee Weapon Attack:* +6 to hit, reach 5 ft., one target. *Hit:* 8 (1d8 + 4) slashing damage, or 9 (1d10 + 4) slashing damage if used with two hands.

Musket. *Ranged Weapon Attack:* +4 to hit, range 40/120 ft., one target. *Hit:* 7 (1d12 + 2) piercing damage.

Pistol. *Ranged Weapon Attack:* +4 to hit, range 30/90 ft., one target. *Hit:* 7 (1d10 + 2) piercing damage.

Fragmentation Grenade (1/day). The giff throws a grenade up to 60 feet. Each creature within 20 feet of the grenade's detonation must make a DC 15 Dexterity saving throw, taking 17 (5d6) piercing damage on a failed save, or half as much damage on a successful one.

GUNPOWDER BY THE KEG

Aside from their personal gunpowder weapons, giff ships and mercenary companies carry spare gunpowder in kegs. In an emergency, or any time a large explosion is needed, a whole keg can be detonated. A giff lights the fuse on the keg and can then throw the keg up to 15 feet as part of the same action. The keg explodes at the start of the giff's next turn. Each creature within 20 feet of the exploding keg must make a DC 12 Dexterity saving throw. On a failed save, a creature takes 24 (7d6) fire damage and is knocked prone. On a successful save, a creature takes half as much damage and isn't knocked prone.

Every other keg of gunpowder within 20 feet of an exploding keg has a 50 percent chance of also exploding. Check each keg only once per turn, no matter how many other kegs explode around it.

What would become of this multiverse if githyanki didn't guard the Astral Plane from the illithid menace? What would reality become if beings of thought ruled the plane of thought?

GITH

The descendants of an ancient people—so old their original name has been lost—have turned against each other, becoming vicious enemies divided over mortality, purpose, and the machinations of their leaders. The bellicose githyanki terrorize the Astral Plane, raiding into other worlds to plunder the multiverse of its magic and riches. The githzerai live apart from the rest of the cosmos, content within the confines of their fortresses floating through the chaos of Limbo. Although the two groups of gith despise each other, their hatred for the mind flayers from whom they escaped endures, and both githyanki and githzerai are dedicated to hunting their ancestral foes.

GITHYANKI GISH
Medium humanoid (gith), lawful evil

Armor Class 17 (half plate)
Hit Points 123 (19d8 + 38)
Speed 30 ft.

STR	DEX	CON	INT	WIS	CHA
17 (+3)	15 (+2)	14 (+2)	16 (+3)	15 (+2)	16 (+3)

Saving Throws Con +6, Int +7, Wis +6
Skills Insight +6, Perception +6, Stealth +6
Senses passive Perception 16
Languages Gith
Challenge 10 (5,900 XP)

Innate Spellcasting (Psionics). The githyanki's innate spellcasting ability is Intelligence (spell save DC 15, +7 to hit with spell attacks). It can innately cast the following spells, requiring no components:

At will: *mage hand* (the hand is invisible)
3/day each: *jump, misty step, nondetection* (self only)
1/day each: *plane shift, telekinesis*

Spellcasting. The githyanki is an 8th-level spellcaster. Its spellcasting ability is Intelligence (spell save DC 15, +7 to hit with spell attacks). The githyanki has the following wizard spells prepared:

Cantrips (at will): *blade ward, light, message, true strike*
1st level (4 slots): *expeditious retreat, magic missile, sleep, thunderwave*
2nd level (3 slots): *blur, invisibility, levitate*
3rd level (3 slots): *counterspell, fireball, haste*
4th level (2 slots): *dimension door*

War Magic. When the githyanki uses its action to cast a spell, it can make one weapon attack as a bonus action

ACTIONS

Multiattack. The githyanki makes two longsword attacks.

Longsword. *Melee Weapon Attack:* +7 to hit, reach 5 ft., one target. *Hit:* 7 (1d8 + 3) slashing damage, or 8 (1d10 + 3) slashing damage if used with two hands, plus 18 (4d8) psychic damage.

GITHYANKI GISH

Their keen minds and psionic gifts allow the githyanki to master magic. Gish blend their magical abilities with swordplay to become dangerous foes in battle. Their specialized capabilities make them well suited for assassination, raiding, and espionage.

GITHYANKI KITH'RAK

The githyanki's militarized culture assigns ranks and responsibilities to its citizens. Groups of ten warriors follow the commands of the sarths (githyanki warriors), while ten sarths obey the commands of the mighty kith'rak. These champions earn their status through torturous training and psionic testing until they can command the respect of their underlings.

GITHYANKI KITH'RAK
Medium humanoid (gith), lawful evil

Armor Class 18 (plate)
Hit Points 180 (24d8 + 72)
Speed 30 ft.

STR	DEX	CON	INT	WIS	CHA
18 (+4)	16 (+3)	17 (+3)	16 (+3)	15 (+2)	17 (+3)

Saving Throws Con +7, Int +7, Wis +6
Skills Intimidation +7, Perception +6
Senses passive Perception 16
Languages Gith
Challenge 12 (8,400 XP)

Innate Spellcasting (Psionics). The githyanki's innate spellcasting ability is Intelligence (spell save DC 15, +7 to hit with spell attacks). It can innately cast the following spells, requiring no components:

At will: *mage hand* (the hand is invisible)
3/day each: *blur, jump, misty step, nondetection* (self only)
1/day each: *plane shift, telekinesis*

Rally the Troops. As a bonus action, the githyanki can magically end the charmed and frightened conditions on itself and each creature of its choice that it can see within 30 feet of it.

ACTIONS

Multiattack. The githyanki makes three greatsword attacks.

Greatsword. *Melee Weapon Attack:* +8 to hit, reach 5 ft., one target. *Hit:* 11 (2d6 + 4) slashing damage plus 17 (5d6) psychic damage.

REACTIONS

Parry. The githyanki adds 4 to its AC against one melee attack that would hit it. To do so, the githyanki must see the attacker and be wielding a melee weapon.

G

GITHYANKI GISH

GITHYANKI
SUPREME COMMANDER

GITHYANKI
KITH'RAK

GITHYANKI SUPREME COMMANDER

Medium humanoid (gith), lawful evil

Armor Class 18 (plate)
Hit Points 187 (22d8 + 88)
Speed 30 ft.

STR	DEX	CON	INT	WIS	CHA
19 (+4)	17 (+3)	18 (+4)	16 (+3)	16 (+3)	18 (+4)

Saving Throws Con +9, Int +8, Wis +8
Skills Insight +8, Intimidation +9, Perception +8
Senses passive Perception 18
Languages Gith
Challenge 14 (11,500 XP)

Innate Spellcasting (Psionics). The githyanki's innate spellcasting ability is Intelligence (spell save DC 16, +8 to hit with spell attacks). It can innately cast the following spells, requiring no components:

At will: *mage hand* (the hand is invisible)
3/day each: *jump, levitate* (self only), *misty step, nondetection* (self only)
1/day each: *Bigby's hand, mass suggestion, plane shift, telekinesis*

ACTIONS

Multiattack. The githyanki makes two greatsword attacks.

Silver Greatsword. *Melee Weapon Attack:* +12 to hit, reach 5 ft., one target. *Hit:* 14 (2d6 + 7) slashing damage plus 17 (5d6) psychic damage. On a critical hit against a target in an astral body (as with the *astral projection* spell), the githyanki can cut the silvery cord that tethers the target to its material body, instead of dealing damage.

REACTIONS

Parry. The githyanki adds 5 to its AC against one melee attack that would hit it. To do so, the githyanki must see the attacker and be wielding a melee weapon.

LEGENDARY ACTIONS

The githyanki can take 3 legendary actions, choosing from the options below. Only one legendary action option can be used at a time and only at the end of another creature's turn. The githyanki regains spent legendary actions at the start of its turn.

Attack (2 Actions). The githyanki makes a greatsword attack.
Command Ally. The githyanki targets one ally it can see within 30 feet of it. If the target can see or hear the githyanki, the target can make one melee weapon attack using its reaction and has advantage on the attack roll.
Teleport. The githyanki magically teleports, along with any equipment it is wearing and carrying, to an unoccupied space it can see within 30 feet of it. It also becomes insubstantial until the start of its next turn. While insubstantial, it can move through other creatures and objects as if they were difficult terrain. If it ends its turn inside an object, it takes 16 (3d10) force damage and is moved to the nearest unoccupied space.

G

Githyanki Supreme Commander

Supreme commanders lead the githyanki armies, each one commanding ten kith'raks, who in turn lead the rest of their forces. Most supreme commanders ride red dragons into battle.

Githzerai Anarch

The most powerful of the githzerai, anarchs lead communities and maintain the adamantine citadels that serve as strong points in planes beyond Limbo. They have formidable psionic capabilities, able to manipulate the unformed substance of their adopted plane with a thought. These rare githzerai are sages and mystics, and their word is law.

An Anarch's Lair

In Limbo, githzerai anarchs create islands of tranquility in the otherwise turbulent plane. By directing its psionic power, an anarch can give form to formless substance, creating mountains, lakes, and structures of any composition to serve as a foundation for a githzerai community.

Lair Actions. An anarch can use lair actions. On initiative count 20 (losing initiative ties), the anarch can take a lair action to cause one of the following effects; the anarch can't use the same effect two rounds in a row:

- The anarch casts the *lightning bolt* spell (at 5th level), but the anarch can change the damage type from lightning to cold, fire, psychic, radiant, or thunder. If the spell deals damage other than fire or lightning, it doesn't ignite flammable objects.
- The anarch casts the *creation* spell (as a 9th-level spell) using the unformed substance of Limbo instead of shadow material. If used in Limbo, the object remains until the anarch's concentration is broken, regardless of its composition. If the anarch moves more than 120 feet from the object, its concentration breaks.
- The anarch can magically move an object it can see within 150 feet of it by making a Wisdom check with advantage. The DC depends on the object's size: DC 5 for Tiny, DC 10 for Small, DC 15 for Medium, DC 20 for Large, and DC 25 for Huge or larger.

Regional Effects. The region containing an anarch's lair is warped by its presence, which creates one or more of the following effects:

- In Limbo, the anarch can spend 10 minutes stabilizing a 5-mile area centered on it, causing the unformed substance to take whatever inanimate form the anarch chooses. During that process, the anarch determines the shape and composition of the forms created.
- The anarch stabilizes any object created in Limbo and brought to the Material Plane for as long as the anarch remains within 1 mile of it (no action required).

If the anarch dies, these effects end after 1d6 rounds. All formed substance becomes a chaotic churn of energy and matter, unraveling into unformed substance that dissipates 1d6 rounds later.

> *The githzerai are a check on the githyanki and the illithids. The githyanki are a check on the githzerai and the illithids. Thus, three unequal forces enforce the Balance.*

Githzerai Anarch

Medium humanoid (gith), lawful neutral

Armor Class 20
Hit Points 144 (17d8 + 68)
Speed 30 ft., fly 40 ft. (hover)

STR	DEX	CON	INT	WIS	CHA
16 (+3)	21 (+5)	18 (+4)	18 (+4)	20 (+5)	14 (+2)

Saving Throws Str +8, Dex +10, Int +9, Wis +10
Skills Arcana +9, Insight +10, Perception +10
Senses passive Perception 20
Languages Gith
Challenge 16 (15,000 XP)

Innate Spellcasting (Psionics). The anarch's innate spellcasting ability is Wisdom (spell save DC 18, +10 to hit with spell attacks). It can innately cast the following spells, requiring no components:

At will: *mage hand* (the hand is invisible)
3/day each: *feather fall, jump, see invisibility, shield, telekinesis*
1/day each: *globe of invulnerability, plane shift, teleportation circle, wall of force*

Psychic Defense. While the anarch is wearing no armor and wielding no shield, its AC includes its Wisdom modifier.

Actions

Multiattack. The anarch makes three unarmed strikes.

Unarmed Strike. *Melee Weapon Attack:* +10 to hit, reach 5 ft., one target. *Hit:* 14 (2d8 + 5) bludgeoning damage plus 18 (4d8) psychic damage.

Legendary Actions

The anarch can take 3 legendary actions, choosing from the options below. Only one legendary action option can be used at a time and only at the end of another creature's turn. The anarch regains spent legendary actions at the start of its turn.

Strike. The anarch makes one unarmed strike.
Teleport. The anarch magically teleports, along with any equipment it is wearing and carrying, to an unoccupied space it can see within 30 feet of it.
Change Gravity (Costs 3 Actions). The anarch casts the *reverse gravity* spell. The spell has the normal effect, except that the anarch can orient the area in any direction and creatures and objects fall toward the end of the area.

GITHZERAI ENLIGHTENED

GITHZERAI ANARCH

GITHZERAI ENLIGHTENED

Githzerai never stop training. They spend long hours in meditation to transcend the limits of their forms and to apprehend the nature of reality. Zerths who complete the next tier of their training become one of the githzerai known as the enlightened.

GITHZERAI ENLIGHTENED

Medium humanoid (gith), lawful neutral

Armor Class 18
Hit Points 112 (15d8 + 45)
Speed 30 ft.

STR	DEX	CON	INT	WIS	CHA
14 (+2)	19 (+4)	16 (+3)	17 (+3)	19 (+4)	13 (+1)

Saving Throws Str +6, Dex +8, Int +7, Wis +8
Skills Arcana +7, Insight +8, Perception +8
Senses passive Perception 18
Languages Gith
Challenge 10 (5,900 XP)

Innate Spellcasting (Psionics). The githzerai's innate spellcasting ability is Wisdom (spell save DC 16, +8 to hit with spell attacks). It can innately cast the following spells, requiring no components:

At will: *mage hand* (the hand is invisible)
3/day each: *blur, expeditious retreat, feather fall, jump, see invisibility, shield*
1/day each: *haste, plane shift, teleport*

Psychic Defense. While the githzerai is wearing no armor and wielding no shield, its AC includes its Wisdom modifier.

ACTIONS

Multiattack. The githzerai makes three unarmed strikes.

Unarmed Strike. *Melee Weapon Attack:* +8 to hit, reach 5 ft., one target. *Hit:* 13 (2d8 + 4) bludgeoning damage plus 13 (3d8) psychic damage.

Temporal Strike (Recharge 6). *Melee Weapon Attack:* +8 to hit, reach 5 ft., one creature. *Hit:* 13 (2d8 + 4) bludgeoning damage plus 52 (8d12) psychic damage. The target must succeed on a DC 16 Wisdom saving throw or move 1 round forward in time. A target moved forward in time vanishes for the duration. When the effect ends, the target reappears in the space it left or in an unoccupied space nearest to that space if it's occupied.

G

I suspect gray renders owe their origin to the neogi, since they are often in their company. Those that appear in the wilderness are likely castaways from frustrated neogi masters.

GRAY RENDER

A curious impulse drives the gray render. Despite its hulking form and terrible appetite, it wants most of all to bond with an intelligent creature and, once bonded, give its life to protect that creature. Great strength and a savage nature enable gray renders to be fierce guardians, but they lack even a shred of cunning.

A Spreading Plague. Gray renders reproduce by forming nodules on their bodies that, upon reaching maturity, break off to begin life as young gray renders. These monstrosities feel no obligation to their young, and they have no inclination to gather with others of their kind.

Chaotic Allies. As a side effect of its breeding, each gray render has an overpowering need to bond with an intelligent creature. When it encounters a suitable master, the render sings to it—a weird, warbling cry accompanied by scratching at the earth and a show of deference. Once it forms the bond, the render serves its master in all things.

Although this bond can be a great benefit, renders are inherently chaotic. In a battle, a render fights with all the savagery it can muster and never willingly harms its master, but outside battle, a gray render might present considerable difficulty for its master's associates. It might follow its master even after being told to stay put, destroy its master's house, burrow holes in the side of a ship, kill horses, attack when it feels jealous, and more. A gray render might be a boon companion, but it is always an unpredictable one.

The Gray Render Quirks table presents possible quirks for gray renders that can be generated randomly or selected as desired.

GRAY RENDER QUIRKS

d12	Quirk
1	Hates horses and other mounts
2	Roars loudly when its bonded creature is touched by another creature
3	Likes to snuggle
4	Uproots and chews on trees
5	Has terrific and eye-watering flatulence
6	Brings offerings of meat to its bonded creature
7	Compulsively digs up the ground
8	Attacks carts and wagons as if they were terrible monsters
9	Howls when it rains
10	Whines piteously in the dark
11	Buries treasure it finds
12	Chases birds, leaping into the air to catch them, heedless of the destruction it causes

GRAY RENDER

Large monstrosity, chaotic neutral

Armor Class 19 (natural armor)
Hit Points 189 (18d10 + 90)
Speed 30 ft.

STR	DEX	CON	INT	WIS	CHA
19 (+4)	13 (+1)	20 (+5)	3 (−4)	6 (−2)	8 (−1)

Saving Throws Str +8, Con +9
Skills Perception +2
Senses darkvision 60 ft., passive Perception 12
Languages —
Challenge 12 (8,400 XP)

ACTIONS

Multiattack. The gray render makes three attacks: one with its bite and two with its claws.

Bite. *Melee Weapon Attack:* +8 to hit, reach 5 ft., one target. *Hit:* 17 (2d12 + 4) piercing damage. If the target is Medium or smaller, the target must succeed on a DC 16 Strength saving throw or be knocked prone.

Claws. *Melee Weapon Attack:* +8 to hit, reach 10 ft., one target. *Hit:* 13 (2d8 + 4) slashing damage, plus 7 (2d6) bludgeoning damage if the target is prone.

REACTIONS

Bloody Rampage. When the gray render takes damage, it makes one attack with its claws against a random creature within its reach, other than its master.

Why does the howler sing? Doing so causes its prey to flee, and surely stealth would make for better hunting in howling Pandemonium. There is only one answer: the creature can taste fear.

HOWLER

A far-off wail precedes the sight of a howler. Even at a distance, one's mind cringes at the sound and fills with horror at the realization that the noise is drawing closer. When howlers go on the prowl, courage isn't enough to stand up against them, and even one's sanity is at risk.

Prowlers from Pandemonium. These nightmare creatures, native to Pandemonium, can also be found on most of the Lower Planes, because of the many fiends that capture them and train them as war hounds. Howlers can be domesticated, after a fashion, but they respond only to brutal training during which they are forced to recognize the trainer as the pack's undisputed leader. A trained pack then follows its leader without hesitation. Howler packs course over the battlefields of the Blood War and also serve evil mortals who have the power and the savagery to command their loyalty.

Brutal Hunters. Howlers rely on speed, numbers, and their mind-numbing howl to corner prey before they tear it apart. The howl floods the minds of its victims, making complex thought impossible. They can do little more than stare in horror and stumble around the battlefield in a search for safety. Any task more demanding than that is beyond their capability. Fiends especially prize howlers for this reason, because for a few crucial moments in a battle, their howls can neutralize an enemy's ability to use spells and other powers.

HOWLER
Large fiend, chaotic evil

Armor Class 16 (natural armor)
Hit Points 90 (12d10 + 24)
Speed 40 ft.

STR	DEX	CON	INT	WIS	CHA
17 (+3)	16 (+3)	15 (+2)	5 (−3)	20 (+5)	6 (−2)

Skills Perception +8
Damage Resistances cold, fire, lightning; bludgeoning, piercing, and slashing from nonmagical attacks
Condition Immunities frightened
Senses darkvision 60 ft., passive Perception 15
Languages understands Abyssal but can't speak
Challenge 8 (3,900 XP)

Pack Tactics. A howler has advantage on attack rolls against a creature if at least one of the howler's allies is within 5 feet of the creature and the ally isn't incapacitated.

ACTIONS

Multiattack. The howler makes two bite attacks.

Rending Bite. *Melee Weapon Attack:* +6 to hit, reach 5 ft., one target. *Hit:* 10 (2d6 + 3) piercing damage, plus 22 (4d10) psychic damage if the target is frightened. This attack ignores damage resistance.

Mind-Breaking Howl (Recharge 6). The howler emits a keening howl in a 60-foot cone. Each creature in that area that isn't deafened must succeed on a DC 16 Wisdom saving throw or be frightened until the end of the howler's next turn. While a creature is frightened in this way, its speed is halved, and it is incapacitated. A target that successfully saves is immune to the Mind-Breaking Howl of all howlers for the next 24 hours.

Imagine a hive of ants the size of horses, but the ants are wearing armor. Then exterminate them.

KRUTHIKS

Kruthiks are chitin-covered reptiles that hunt in packs and nest in sprawling subterranean warrens. They are attracted to sources of heat, such as dwarven forges and pools of molten lava, and carve out lairs as close to such locations as possible. As they burrow through the earth, they leave behind tunnels—evidence that is often the first clue to the nearby presence of a kruthik hive. Kruthiks also make use of preexisting underground chambers, incorporating them into their lairs when they can.

Kruthiks communicate with one another through a series of hisses and chittering noises. These sounds can often be heard in advance of a kruthik attack. Whenever their lair is invaded, kruthik guards send out an alarm by rapidly tapping the stone floor with their sharp legs.

Sharp Senses. In addition to having an acute sense of smell, kruthiks can see in the dark and can detect vibrations in the earth around them. They take the scent of their own dead as a warning and avoid areas where many other kruthiks have died. Slaying a sufficient number of kruthiks in one area might cause the remaining hive members to move elsewhere.

Sharper Weapons. Although they can feed on carrion, kruthiks prefer live prey. They kill enemies by impaling them on their spiked limbs, then grind up the flesh and bones with mandibles strong enough to chew rock. When several kruthiks gang up on a single foe, they become frenzied and even more lethal.

Shared Lair. Kruthiks abide the presence of constructs, elementals, oozes, and undead, and use such creatures to help guard their hive. Kruthiks are smart enough to barricade some tunnels and dig new ones that keep their neighbors away from their eggs.

YOUNG KRUTHIK

Kruthiks hatch from eggs laid by female adults. Each egg is about the size of an adult human's head and hatches within a month. Tiny kruthik hatchlings are harmless, rarely stray far from the nest, and feed primarily on offal and one another. Within a month, the survivors become young kruthiks large enough to hunt and defend themselves.

YOUNG KRUTHIK
Small monstrosity, unaligned

Armor Class 16 (natural armor)
Hit Points 9 (2d6 + 2)
Speed 30 ft., burrow 10 ft., climb 30 ft.

STR	DEX	CON	INT	WIS	CHA
13 (+1)	16 (+3)	13 (+1)	4 (−3)	10 (+0)	6 (−2)

Senses darkvision 30 ft., tremorsense 60 ft.,
  passive Perception 10
Languages Kruthik
Challenge 1/8 (25 XP)

Keen Smell. The kruthik has advantage on Wisdom (Perception) checks that rely on smell.

Pack Tactics. The kruthik has advantage on an attack roll against a creature if at least one of the kruthik's allies is within 5 feet of the creature and the ally isn't incapacitated.

Tunneler. The kruthik can burrow through solid rock at half its burrowing speed and leaves a 2½-foot-diameter tunnel in its wake.

ACTIONS

Stab. *Melee Weapon Attack:* +5 to hit, reach 5 ft., one target. *Hit:* 5 (1d4 + 3) piercing damage.

ADULT KRUTHIK

It takes six months of steady eating for a young kruthik to reach adult size. The natural life span of an adult kruthik is roughly seven years.

Adult kruthiks grow spiky protrusions on their legs and can fling these dagger-sized spikes at enemies beyond the reach of their claws.

KRUTHIK HIVE LORD

A hive lord rules each kruthik hive. When the hive lord dies, the surviving members of the hive abandon their lair and search for a new one. When a suitable location is found, the largest kruthik in the hive undergoes a metamorphosis, forming a cocoon around itself and emerging several weeks later as a hive lord—a bigger and smarter kruthik with the ability to spray digestive acid from its maw. The hive lord claims the largest chamber of the lair and keeps several adult kruthiks nearby as bodyguards.

> Other creatures that abide in hives serve a purpose in the natural world. Bees pollinate flowers. Termites make earth out of wood. Kruthiks, by contrast, slay societies. Perhaps that function is just as necessary.

KRUTHIK HIVE LORD

Large monstrosity, unaligned

Armor Class 20 (natural armor)
Hit Points 102 (12d10 + 36)
Speed 40 ft., burrow 20 ft., climb 40 ft.

STR	DEX	CON	INT	WIS	CHA
19 (+4)	16 (+3)	17 (+3)	10 (+0)	14 (+2)	10 (+0)

Senses darkvision 60 ft., tremorsense 60 ft., passive Perception 12
Languages Kruthik
Challenge 5 (1,800 XP)

Keen Smell. The kruthik has advantage on Wisdom (Perception) checks that rely on smell.

Pack Tactics. The kruthik has advantage on an attack roll against a creature if at least one of the kruthik's allies is within 5 feet of the creature and the ally isn't incapacitated.

Tunneler. The kruthik can burrow through solid rock at half its burrowing speed and leaves a 10-foot-diameter tunnel in its wake.

ACTIONS

Multiattack. The kruthik makes two stab attacks or two spike attacks.

Stab. *Melee Weapon Attack:* +7 to hit, reach 10 ft., one target. *Hit:* 9 (1d10 + 4) piercing damage.

Spike. *Ranged Weapon Attack:* +6 to hit, range 30/120 ft., one target. *Hit:* 7 (1d6 + 4) piercing damage.

Acid Spray (Recharge 5–6). The kruthik sprays acid in a 15-foot cone. Each creature in that area must make a DC 14 Dexterity saving throw, taking 22 (4d10) acid damage on a failed save, or half as much damage on a successful one.

ADULT KRUTHIK

Medium monstrosity, unaligned

Armor Class 18 (natural armor)
Hit Points 39 (6d8 + 12)
Speed 40 ft., burrow 20 ft., climb 40 ft.

STR	DEX	CON	INT	WIS	CHA
15 (+2)	16 (+3)	15 (+2)	7 (−2)	12 (+1)	8 (−1)

Senses darkvision 60 ft., tremorsense 60 ft., passive Perception 11
Languages Kruthik
Challenge 2 (450 XP)

Keen Smell. The kruthik has advantage on Wisdom (Perception) checks that rely on smell.

Pack Tactics. The kruthik has advantage on an attack roll against a creature if at least one of the kruthik's allies is within 5 feet of the creature and the ally isn't incapacitated.

Tunneler. The kruthik can burrow through solid rock at half its burrowing speed and leaves a 5-foot-diameter tunnel in its wake.

ACTIONS

Multiattack. The kruthik makes two stab attacks or two spike attacks.

Stab. *Melee Weapon Attack:* +5 to hit, reach 5 ft., one target. *Hit:* 6 (1d6 + 3) piercing damage.

Spike. *Ranged Weapon Attack:* +5 to hit, range 20/60 ft., one target. *Hit:* 5 (1d4 + 3) piercing damage.

Marut

The nigh-unstoppable inevitables serve a singular purpose: they enforce contracts forged in the Hall of Concordance in the city of Sigil. Primus, the leader of the modrons, created maruts and other inevitables to bring order to dealings between planar folk. Many creatures, including yugoloths, will enter into a contract with inevitables if asked.

Cosmic Enforcers. The Hall of Concordance is an embassy of pure law in Sigil, the City of Doors. In the hall, two parties who agree to mutual terms—and who pay the requisite gold to the Kolyarut, a mechanical engine of absolute jurisprudence—can have their contract chiseled onto a sheet of gold that is placed in the chest of a marut. From that moment until the contract is fulfilled, the marut is bound to enforce its terms and to punish any party who breaks them. A marut resorts to lethal force only when a contract calls for it, when the contract is fully broken, or when the marut is attacked.

Word Is Law. Inevitables care nothing for the spirit of an agreement, only the letter. A marut enforces what is written, not what was meant by or supposed to be understood from the writing. The Kolyarut rejects contracts that contain vague, contradictory, or unenforceable terms. Beyond that, it doesn't care whether both parties understand what they're agreeing to. A small army of solicitors waits outside the Hall of Concordance, eager to sell their expertise in the crafting or vetting of contracts.

Constructed Nature. A marut doesn't require air, food, drink, or sleep.

Marut

Large construct (inevitable), lawful neutral

Armor Class 22 (natural armor)
Hit Points 432 (32d10 + 256)
Speed 40 ft., fly 30 ft. (hover)

STR	DEX	CON	INT	WIS	CHA
28 (+9)	12 (+1)	26 (+8)	19 (+4)	15 (+2)	18 (+4)

Saving Throws Int +12, Wis +10, Cha +12
Skills Insight +10, Intimidation +12, Perception +10
Damage Resistances thunder; bludgeoning, piercing, and slashing from nonmagical attacks
Damage Immunities poison
Condition Immunities charmed, frightened, paralyzed, poisoned, unconscious
Senses darkvision 60 ft., passive Perception 20
Languages all but rarely speaks
Challenge 25 (75,000 XP)

Immutable Form. The marut is immune to any spell or effect that would alter its form.

Innate Spellcasting. The marut's innate spellcasting ability is Intelligence (spell save DC 20). The marut can innately cast the following spell, requiring no material components.

At will: *plane shift* (self only)

Legendary Resistance (3/Day). If the marut fails a saving throw, it can choose to succeed instead.

Magic Resistance. The marut has advantage on saving throws against spells and other magical effects.

Actions

Multiattack. The marut makes two slam attacks.

Unerring Slam. *Melee Weapon Attack:* automatic hit, reach 5 ft., one target. *Hit:* 60 force damage, and the target is pushed up to 5 feet away from the marut if it is Huge or smaller.

Blazing Edict (Recharge 5–6). Arcane energy emanates from the marut's chest in a 60-foot cube. Every creature in that area takes 45 radiant damage. Each creature that takes any of this damage must succeed on a DC 20 Wisdom saving throw or be stunned until the end of the marut's next turn.

Justify. The marut targets up to two creatures it can see within 60 feet of it. Each target must succeed on a DC 20 Charisma saving throw or be teleported to a teleportation circle in the Hall of Concordance in Sigil. A target fails automatically if it is incapacitated. If either target is teleported in this way, the marut teleports with it to the circle.

After teleporting in this way, the marut can't use this action again until it finishes a short or long rest.

MEAZEL

In places where the Shadowfell washes against the shores of the Material Plane dwell meazels, hateful hermits who left behind their old lives to contemplate their misery in shadow. Now evil burns in their hearts, and they resent any intrusion into their suffering.

Hateful Hermit. Meazels are all that remain of people who fled into the Shadowfell to escape their mortal existence. There the darkness transformed them, and their bitterness made them twisted and cruel. Now, they loiter near Shadowfell crossings to waylay travelers who venture too close to their lairs.

Divide and Conquer. The stain of darkness responsible for the existence of meazels imparts to them magical powers that allow them to move through shadows with ease. Merely stepping into one pool of darkness allows a meazel to move to another one. They use this talent to ambush creatures, snatching them around the throat with their strangling cords and then stepping away. Meazels also use this ability to ferry their victims to isolated spots and then leave the hapless souls to the designs of whatever horrors lurk there.

Creatures that are drawn through the shadows by meazels are cursed by the meazels' baleful magic. The curse acts as a beacon; sorrowsworn, undead, and other terrors sense where they are located and descend on the stranded victims to tear them apart.

MEAZEL

Medium humanoid (meazel), neutral evil

Armor Class 13
Hit Points 35 (10d8 – 10)
Speed 30 ft.

STR	DEX	CON	INT	WIS	CHA
8 (–1)	17 (+3)	9 (–1)	14 (+2)	13 (+1)	10 (+0)

Skills Perception +3, Stealth +5
Senses darkvision 120 ft., passive Perception 13
Languages Common
Challenge 1 (200 XP)

Shadow Stealth. While in dim light or darkness, the meazel can take the Hide action as a bonus action.

ACTIONS

Garrote. *Melee Weapon Attack:* +5 to hit, reach 5 ft., one target of the meazel's size or smaller. *Hit:* 6 (1d6 + 3) bludgeoning damage, and the target is grappled (escape DC 13 with disad-

vantage). Until the grapple ends, the target takes 10 (2d6 + 3) bludgeoning damage at the start of each of the meazel's turns. The meazel can't make weapon attacks while grappling a creature in this way.

Shortsword. *Melee Weapon Attack:* +5 to hit, reach 5 ft., one target. *Hit:* 6 (1d6 + 3) piercing damage, plus 3 (1d6) necrotic damage.

Shadow Teleport (Recharge 5–6). The meazel, any equipment it is wearing or carrying, and any creature it is grappling teleport to an unoccupied space within 500 feet of it, provided that the starting space and the destination are in dim light or darkness. The destination must be a place the meazel has seen before, but it need not be within line of sight. If the destination space is occupied, the teleportation leads to the nearest unoccupied space.

Any other creature the meazel teleports becomes cursed by shadow for 1 hour. Until this curse ends, every undead and every creature native to the Shadowfell within 300 feet of the cursed creature can sense it, which prevents that creature from hiding from them.

NAGPA

Long ago, the Raven Queen cursed a cabal of thirteen powerful wizards for meddling in a ritual that would have helped avert a war between the gods. She stripped them of their beauty, turning them into scabrous, bird-like monstrosities. The nagpas now plot as they ever did, but they now strive to bring about terrible, world-shaking calamities so they can pry secrets and power from the wreckage their conspiracies create.

The nagpas fear the Raven Queen and do their best to avoid her and her agents. When it's impossible to do so, they become cringing, fawning things, eager to please and thereby escape the cold gaze of the being who brought them so low. All of the original thirteen remain alive, thanks to their cunning and their willingness to do whatever is necessary to survive.

Looters of Civilization. The curse the Raven Queen placed on the nagpas restricts the ways in which they can acquire new lore and magical power, barring them from any source except for the ruins left behind from fallen civilizations and great calamities. For this reason, nagpas turn their efforts to bringing about such ends, so they can loot the libraries, plunder the vaults, and gather up secrets of arcane lore from the wreckage.

Puppet Masters. Nagpas work in the shadows, manipulating events to bring about ruin. As accomplished magic-users, they can bring to bear an array of spells to make agents of other creatures, influencing their decisions in subtle ways and pulling on strings to make them into unwitting accomplices in their own destruction. Nagpas show great patience in their plots and have several schemes working simultaneously, each at different stages of completion, so if one plan goes awry, they can shift their focus to another. Typically, nagpas only show their handiwork and emerge from the shadows when they can deliver a finishing blow and then revel in the grand devastation their plotting brought about.

NAGPA

Medium humanoid (nagpa), neutral evil

Armor Class 19 (natural armor)
Hit Points 187 (34d8 + 34)
Speed 30 ft.

STR	DEX	CON	INT	WIS	CHA
9 (−1)	15 (+2)	12 (+1)	23 (+6)	18 (+4)	21 (+5)

Saving Throws Int +12, Wis +10, Cha +11
Skills Arcana +12, Deception +11, History +12, Insight +10, Perception +10
Senses truesight 120 ft., passive Perception 20
Languages Common plus up to five other languages
Challenge 17 (18,000 XP)

Corruption. As a bonus action, the nagpa targets one creature it can see within 90 feet of it. The target must make a DC 20 Charisma saving throw. An evil creature makes the save with disadvantage. On a failed save, the target is charmed by the nagpa until the start of the nagpa's next turn. On a successful save, the target becomes immune to the nagpa's Corruption for the next 24 hours.

Paralysis (Recharge 6). As a bonus action, the nagpa forces each creature within 30 feet of it to succeed on a DC 20 Wisdom saving throw or be paralyzed for 1 minute. A paralyzed target can repeat the saving throw at the end of each of its turns, ending the effect on itself on a success. Undead and constructs are immune to this effect.

Spellcasting. The nagpa is a 15th-level spellcaster. Its spellcasting ability is Intelligence (spell save DC 20, +12 to hit with spell attacks). A nagpa has the following wizard spells prepared:

Cantrips (at will): *chill touch, fire bolt, mage hand, message, minor illusion*
1st level (4 slots): *charm person, detect magic, protection from evil and good, witch bolt*
2nd level (3 slots): *hold person, ray of enfeeblement, suggestion*
3rd level (3 slots): *counterspell, fireball, fly*
4th level (3 slots): *confusion, hallucinatory terrain, wall of fire*
5th level (2 slots): *dominate person, dream, geas*
6th level (1 slot): *circle of death, disintegrate*
7th level (1 slot): *etherealness, prismatic spray*
8th level (1 slot): *feeblemind*

ACTIONS

Staff. *Melee Weapon Attack:* +8 to hit, reach 5 ft., one target. *Hit:* 9 (2d6 + 2) bludgeoning damage.

NIGHTWALKER

The Negative Plane is a place of darkness and death, anathema to all living things. Yet there are those who would tap into its fell power, to use its energy for sinister ends. Most often, when such individuals approach the midnight realm, they find they are unequal to the task. Those not destroyed outright are sometimes drawn inside the plane and replaced by nightwalkers, terrifying undead creatures that devour all life they encounter.

Mighty Spawn. One can reach the Negative Plane from the Shadowfell, much in the same way that it is possible to step from the Material Plane into the Shadowfell in a place where the barrier between the planes is thin.

Stepping into the Negative Plane is tantamount to suicide, since the plane sucks the life and soul from such audacious creatures and annihilates them at once. Those few who survive the effort do so by sheer luck or by harnessing some rare form of magic that protects them against the hostile atmosphere. They soon discover, however, that they can't leave as easily as they arrived. For each creature that enters the plane, a nightwalker is released to take its place. In order for a trapped creature to escape, the released nightwalker must be lured back to the Negative Plane by offerings of life for it to devour. If the nightwalker is destroyed, the trapped creature has no hope of escape.

Beings of Anti-Life. One can discern the nature of creatures trapped in the Negative Plane from the sites that nightwalkers frequent. Generally, a nightwalker on the Material Plane is attracted to elements of the world associated with the creature responsible for its creation. Such interest doesn't indicate a willingness to engage with the world; nightwalkers exist to make life extinct and never to serve living things.

Undead Nature. A nightwalker doesn't require air, food, drink, or sleep.

NIGHTWALKER

Huge undead, chaotic evil

Armor Class 14
Hit Points 297 (22d12 + 154)
Speed 40 ft., fly 40 ft.

STR	DEX	CON	INT	WIS	CHA
22 (+6)	19 (+4)	24 (+7)	6 (−2)	9 (−1)	8 (−1)

Saving Throws Con +13
Damage Resistances acid, cold, fire, lightning, thunder; bludgeoning, piercing, and slashing from nonmagical attacks
Damage Immunities necrotic, poison
Condition Immunities exhaustion, frightened, grappled, paralyzed, petrified, poisoned, prone, restrained
Senses darkvision 120 ft., passive Perception 9
Languages —
Challenge 20 (25,000 XP)

Annihilating Aura. Any creature that starts its turn within 30 feet of the nightwalker must succeed on a DC 21 Constitution saving throw or take 14 (4d6) necrotic damage and grant the nightwalker advantage on attack rolls against it until the start of the creature's next turn. Undead are immune to this aura.

Life Eater. A creature reduced to 0 hit points from damage dealt by the nightwalker dies and can't be revived by any means short of a *wish* spell.

ACTIONS

Multiattack. The nightwalker uses Enervating Focus twice, or it uses Enervating Focus and Finger of Doom, if available.

Enervating Focus. *Melee Weapon Attack:* +12 to hit, reach 15 ft., one target. *Hit:* 28 (5d8 + 6) necrotic damage. The target must succeed on a DC 21 Constitution saving throw or its hit point maximum is reduced by an amount equal to the necrotic damage taken. This reduction lasts until the target finishes a long rest.

Finger of Doom (Recharge 6). The nightwalker points at one creature it can see within 300 feet of it. The target must succeed on a DC 21 Wisdom saving throw or take 26 (4d12) necrotic damage and become frightened until the end of the nightwalker's next turn. While frightened in this way, the creature is also paralyzed. If a target's saving throw is successful, the target is immune to the nightwalker's Finger of Doom for the next 24 hours.

OBLEX

By experimenting on the slimes, jellies, and puddings that infest the depths of the Underdark, mind flayers created a special breed of ooze, the oblex—a slime capable of assaulting the minds of other creatures. Cunning hunters, these pools of jelly stalk prey, searching for the memories they so desperately crave. When oblexes feed on those thoughts, sometimes killing their victims, they can form weird copies of their prey, which help them to harvest even more victims for their dark masters.

Memory Eaters. Oblexes feed on thoughts and memories. The sharper the mind, the better the meal, so oblexes hunt obviously intelligent targets such as wizards and other spellcasters. When suitable fare comes within reach, an oblex draws its body up to engulf its victim. As it withdraws, it plunders the creature's mind, leaving its prey befuddled and confused.

Ooze Nature. An oblex doesn't require sleep.

OBLEX SPAWN

An oblex devours memories not only to sustain its existence, but also to spawn new oblexes. Each time it fully drains the memories of a victim, it gains the creature's personality—now twisted by the oblex's foul nature. The more memories an oblex steals, the larger it becomes, until it must shed a personality it has absorbed or else go insane. This act spawns a new oblex.

ADULT AND ELDER OBLEXES

Newly formed oblexes lack the capabilities of their older kin. They seek only to feed on memories and grow until they can impersonate their victims.

Older oblexes, called adults and elders, have eaten so many memories that they can form duplicates of the creatures they have devoured from the substance of their bodies, sending them off to lure prey into their clutches, while remaining tethered to the slime by long tendrils of goo. These duplicated creatures are indistinguishable from their victims except for a faint sulfurous smell. Oblexes use these duplicates to lure prey into danger or to infiltrate settlements so they can feed on superior victims.

OBLEX SPAWN

Tiny ooze, lawful evil

Armor Class 13
Hit Points 18 (4d4 + 8)
Speed 20 ft.

STR	DEX	CON	INT	WIS	CHA
8 (−1)	16 (+3)	15 (+2)	14 (+2)	11 (+0)	10 (+0)

Saving Throws Int +4, Cha +2
Condition Immunities blinded, charmed, deafened, exhaustion, prone
Senses blindsight 60 ft. (blind beyond this distance), passive Perception 12
Languages —
Challenge 1/4 (50 XP)

Amorphous. The oblex can move through a space as narrow as 1 inch wide without squeezing.

Aversion to Fire. If the oblex takes fire damage, it has disadvantage on attack rolls and ability checks until the end of its next turn.

ACTIONS

Pseudopod. Melee Weapon Attack: +5 to hit, reach 5 ft., one target. Hit: 5 (1d4 + 3) bludgeoning damage plus 2 (1d4) psychic damage.

An oblex wants memories, but not to serve any end of its own making. Oblexes are hungry for memories and personalities because they are empty without such nourishment. In this way they serve their creators, the illithids. An oblex in the range of an elder brain's powers provides everything necessary for the mind flayers to find choice victims.

Adult Oblex

Medium ooze, lawful evil

Armor Class 14
Hit Points 75 (10d8 + 30)
Speed 20 ft.

STR	DEX	CON	INT	WIS	CHA
8 (−1)	19 (+4)	16 (+3)	19 (+4)	12 (+1)	15 (+2)

Saving Throws Int +7, Cha +5
Skills Deception +5, Perception +4, plus one of the following: Arcana +7, History +7, Nature +7, or Religion +7
Condition Immunities blinded, charmed, deafened, exhaustion, prone
Senses blindsight 60 ft. (blind beyond this distance), passive Perception 14
Languages Common plus two more languages
Challenge 5 (1,800 XP)

Amorphous. The oblex can move through a space as narrow as 1 inch wide without squeezing.

Aversion to Fire. If the oblex takes fire damage, it has disadvantage on attack rolls and ability checks until the end of its next turn.

Innate Spellcasting. The oblex's innate spellcasting ability is Intelligence (spell save DC 15). It can innately cast the following spells, requiring no components:

3/day each: *charm person* (as 5th-level spell), *color spray*, *detect thoughts*, *hold person* (as 3rd-level spell)

Sulfurous Impersonation. As a bonus action, the oblex can extrude a piece of itself that assumes the appearance of one Medium or smaller creature whose memories it has stolen. This simulacrum appears, feels, and sounds exactly like the creature it impersonates, though it smells faintly of sulfur. The oblex can impersonate 1d4 + 1 different creatures, each one tethered to its body by a strand of slime that can extend up to 120 feet away. For all practical purposes, the simulacrum is the oblex, meaning that the oblex occupies its space and the simulacrum's space simultaneously. The slimy tether is immune to damage, but it is severed if there is no opening at least 1 inch wide between the oblex's main body and the simulacrum. The simulacrum disappears if the tether is severed.

Actions

Multiattack. The oblex makes one pseudopod attack and uses Eat Memories.

Pseudopod. *Melee Weapon Attack:* +7 to hit, reach 5 ft., one target. *Hit:* 7 (1d6 + 4) bludgeoning damage plus 5 (2d4) psychic damage.

Eat Memories. The oblex targets one creature it can see within 5 feet of it. The target must succeed on a DC 15 Wisdom saving throw or take 18 (4d8) psychic damage and become memory drained until it finishes a short or long rest or until it benefits from the *greater restoration* or *heal* spell. Constructs, oozes, plants, and undead succeed on the save automatically.

While memory drained, the target must roll a d4 and subtract the number rolled from any ability check or attack roll it makes. Each time the target is memory drained beyond the first, the die size increases by one: the d4 becomes a d6, the d6 becomes a d8, and so on until the die becomes a d20, at which point the target becomes unconscious for 1 hour. The effect then ends.

When an oblex causes a target to become memory drained, the oblex learns all the languages the target knows and gains all its proficiencies, except for any saving throw proficiencies.

ELDER OBLEX

Huge ooze, lawful evil

Armor Class 16
Hit Points 115 (10d12 + 50)
Speed 20 ft.

STR	DEX	CON	INT	WIS	CHA
15 (+2)	16 (+3)	21 (+5)	22 (+6)	13 (+1)	18 (+4)

Saving Throws Int +10, Cha +8
Skills Arcana +10, Deception +8, History +10, Nature +10, Perception +5, Religion +10
Condition Immunities blinded, charmed, deafened, exhaustion, prone
Senses blindsight 60 ft. (blind beyond this distance), passive Perception 15
Languages Common plus six more
Challenge 10 (5,900 XP)

Amorphous. The oblex can move through a space as narrow as 1 inch wide without squeezing.

Aversion to Fire. If the oblex takes fire damage, it has disadvantage on attack rolls and ability checks until the end of its next turn.

Innate Spellcasting. The oblex's innate spellcasting ability is Intelligence (spell save DC 18). It can innately cast the following spells, requiring no material components:

At will: *charm person* (as 5th-level spell), *detect thoughts, hold person*
3/day each: *confusion, dimension door, dominate person, fear, hallucinatory terrain, hold monster, hypnotic pattern, telekinesis*

Sulfurous Impersonation. As a bonus action, the oblex can extrude a piece of itself that assumes the appearance of one Medium or smaller creature whose memories it has stolen. This simulacrum appears, feels, and sounds exactly like the creature it impersonates, though it smells faintly of sulfur. The oblex can impersonate 2d6 + 1 different creatures, each one tethered to its body by a strand of slime that can extend up to 120 feet away. For all practical purposes, the simulacrum is the oblex, meaning the oblex occupies its space and the simulacrum's space simultaneously. The slimy tether is immune to damage, but it is severed if there is no opening at least 1 inch wide between the oblex's main body and the simulacrum. The simulacrum disappears if the tether is severed.

ACTIONS

Multiattack. The elder oblex makes two pseudopod attacks and uses Eat Memories.

Pseudopod. *Melee Weapon Attack:* +7 to hit, reach 10 ft., one target. *Hit:* 17 (4d6 + 3) bludgeoning damage plus 7 (2d6) psychic damage.

Eat Memories. The oblex targets one creature it can see within 5 feet of it. The target must succeed on a DC 18 Wisdom saving throw or take 44 (8d10) psychic damage and become memory drained until it finishes a short or long rest or until it benefits from the *greater restoration* or *heal* spell. Constructs, oozes, plants, and undead succeed on the save automatically.

While memory drained, the target must roll a d4 and subtract the number rolled from any ability check or attack roll it makes. Each time the target is memory drained beyond the first, the die size increases by one: the d4 becomes a d6, the d6 becomes a d8, and so on until the die becomes a d20, at which point the target becomes unconscious for 1 hour. The effect then ends.

When an oblex causes a target to become memory drained, the oblex learns all the languages the target knows and gains all its proficiencies, except any saving throw proficiencies.

OGRES

Ogres are infamously dim-witted, but with enough time and patience, some of them can be trained to carry out specialized missions in battle. The names they are given—the battering ram, the bolt launcher, the chain brute, and the howdah—reflect their particular functions. These jobs are simple, but they're tailored to take advantage of an ogre's strengths.

OGRE BATTERING RAM

An ogre battering ram carries an enormous club used primarily for bashing doors into kindling, but which also works well for smashing foes. These ogres are drilled in two simple tasks: rushing forward to shatter enemy fortifications, and using their weapons to force an advancing enemy to halt.

OGRE BOLT LAUNCHER

A bolt launcher carries a gigantic crossbow—a weapon so large it's essentially an ogre-held ballista. An ogre bolt launcher can load this immense weapon and loose its deadly missile as quickly as a dwarf handles a crossbow. The bolts are so large that few ogres can carry more than a half-dozen at a time, but bolt launchers have been known to uproot small trees or tear beams out of buildings and launch those when their ammunition runs low.

OGRE BATTERING RAM
Large giant, chaotic evil

Armor Class 14 (ring mail)
Hit Points 59 (7d10 + 21)
Speed 40 ft.

STR	DEX	CON	INT	WIS	CHA
19 (+4)	8 (−1)	16 (+3)	5 (−3)	7 (−2)	7 (−2)

Senses darkvision 60 ft., passive Perception 8
Languages Common, Giant
Challenge 4 (1,100 XP)

Siege Monster. The ogre deals double damage to objects and structures.

ACTIONS

Bash. *Melee Weapon Attack:* +6 to hit, reach 5 ft., one target. *Hit:* 15 (2d10 + 4) bludgeoning damage, and the ogre can push the target 5 feet away if the target is Huge or smaller.

Block the Path. Until the start of the ogre's next turn, attack rolls against the ogre have disadvantage, it has advantage on the attack roll it makes for an opportunity attack, and that attack deals an extra 16 (3d10) bludgeoning damage on a hit. Also, each enemy that tries to move out of the ogre's reach without teleporting must succeed on a DC 14 Strength saving throw or have its speed reduced to 0 until the start of the ogre's next turn.

OGRE BOLT LAUNCHER
Large giant, chaotic evil

Armor Class 13 (hide armor)
Hit Points 59 (7d10 + 21)
Speed 40 ft.

STR	DEX	CON	INT	WIS	CHA
19 (+4)	12 (+1)	16 (+3)	5 (−3)	7 (−2)	7 (−2)

Senses darkvision 60 ft., passive Perception 8
Languages Common, Giant
Challenge 2 (450 XP)

ACTIONS

Fist. *Melee Weapon Attack:* +6 to hit, reach 5 ft., one target. *Hit:* 9 (2d4 + 4) bludgeoning damage.

Bolt Launcher. *Ranged Weapon Attack:* +3 to hit, range 120/480 ft., one target. *Hit:* 17 (3d10 + 1) piercing damage.

OGRE CHAIN BRUTE

An ogre chain brute wields a great spiked chain. It swings this chain with both hands in a wide circle around itself to knock foes off their feet. Alternatively, it can swing the chain in a crushing overhead smash that's nearly impossible to block or deflect.

OGRE HOWDAH

The most unusual of the specialized ogres, the howdah carries a palisaded wooden fort on its back. The fort is big enough to serve as a fighting platform for up to four small humanoids. Ogre howdahs are most often seen bearing goblins equipped with bows and spears into battle, but they could just as easily transport kobolds, deep gnomes, or other humanoids of similar size.

OGRE CHAIN BRUTE

Large giant, chaotic evil

Armor Class 11 (hide armor)
Hit Points 59 (7d10 + 21)
Speed 40 ft.

STR	DEX	CON	INT	WIS	CHA
19 (+4)	8 (–1)	16 (+3)	5 (–3)	7 (–2)	7 (–2)

Senses darkvision 60 ft., passive Perception 8
Languages Common, Giant
Challenge 3 (700 XP)

ACTIONS

Fist. *Melee Weapon Attack:* +6 to hit, reach ft., one target. *Hit:* 9 (2d4 + 4) bludgeoning damage.

Chain Sweep. The ogre swings its chain, and every creature within 10 feet of it must make a DC 14 Dexterity saving throw. On a failed saving throw, a creature takes 8 (1d8 + 4) bludgeoning damage and is knocked prone. On a successful save, the creature takes half as much damage and isn't knocked prone.

Chain Smash (Recharge 6). *Melee Weapon Attack:* +6 to hit, reach 10 ft., one target. *Hit:* 13 (2d8 + 4) bludgeoning damage, and the target must succeed on a DC 14 Constitution saving throw or be knocked unconscious for 1 minute. The unconscious target repeats the saving throw if it takes damage and at the end of each of its turns, ending the effect on itself on a success.

OGRE HOWDAH

Large giant, chaotic evil

Armor Class 13 (breastplate)
Hit Points 59 (7d10 + 21)
Speed 40 ft.

STR	DEX	CON	INT	WIS	CHA
19 (+4)	8 (–1)	16 (+3)	5 (–3)	7 (–2)	7 (–2)

Senses darkvision 60 ft., passive Perception 8
Languages Common, Giant
Challenge 2 (450 XP)

Howdah. The ogre carries a compact fort on its back. Up to four Small creatures can ride in the fort without squeezing. To make a melee attack against a target within 5 feet of the ogre, they must use spears or weapons with reach. Creatures in the fort have three-quarters cover against attacks and effects from outside it. If the ogre dies, creatures in the fort are placed in unoccupied spaces within 5 feet of the ogre.

ACTIONS

Mace. *Melee Weapon Attack:* +6 to hit, reach 5 ft., one target. *Hit:* 11 (2d6 + 4) bludgeoning damage.

RETRIEVER

The retriever is a potent, spider-like construct conceived and built by the drow for one original purpose—to prowl the Abyss and capture demons for the drow to enslave or use in their rituals. The automatons proved so effective and so fearsome that they now perform many different missions.

Demon-Infused. Although each retriever is a metal-and-magic construct, it houses the imprisoned spirit of a bebilith. Most of the demon's intellect has been distilled away, leaving only its cruelty and cunning.

Lethal Collectors. Though they were created to operate only in the Abyss, retrievers are sometimes dispatched when a powerful drow needs some creature or object captured and brought back alive and intact. Only under the rarest of circumstances is a retriever handed over or sold to a non-drow, since the dark elves don't want to take the chance that the construct will be turned against them.

RETRIEVER
Large construct, lawful evil

Armor Class 19 (natural armor)
Hit Points 210 (20d10 + 100)
Speed 40 ft., climb 40 ft.

STR	DEX	CON	INT	WIS	CHA
22 (+6)	16 (+3)	20 (+5)	3 (−4)	11 (+0)	4 (−3)

Saving Throws Dex +8, Con +10, Wis +5
Skills Perception +5, Stealth +8
Damage Immunities necrotic, poison, psychic; bludgeoning, piercing, and slashing from nonmagical attacks that aren't adamantine
Condition Immunities charmed, exhaustion, frightened, paralyzed, poisoned
Senses blindsight 30 ft., darkvision 60 ft., passive Perception 15
Languages understands Abyssal, Elvish, and Undercommon but can't speak
Challenge 14 (11,500 XP)

Faultless Tracker. The retriever is given a quarry by its master. The quarry can be a specific creature or object the master is personally acquainted with, or it can be a general type of creature or object the master has seen before. The retriever knows the direction and distance to its quarry as long as the two of them are on the same plane of existence. The retriever can have only one such quarry at a time. The retriever also always knows the location of its master.

Innate Spellcasting. The retriever's innate spellcasting ability is Wisdom (spell save DC 13). The retriever can innately cast the following spells, requiring no material components.

3/day each: *plane shift* (only self and up to one incapacitated creature, which is considered willing for the spell), *web*

ACTIONS

Multiattack. The retriever makes two foreleg attacks and uses its force or paralyzing beam once, if available.

Foreleg. *Melee Weapon Attack:* +11 to hit, reach 10 ft., one target. *Hit:* 15 (2d8 + 6) slashing damage.

Force Beam. The retriever targets one creature it can see within 60 feet of it. The target must make a DC 16 Dexterity saving throw, taking 27 (5d10) force damage on a failed save, or half as much damage on a successful one.

Paralyzing Beam (Recharge 5–6). The retriever targets one creature it can see within 60 feet of it. The target must succeed on a DC 18 Constitution saving throw or be paralyzed for 1 minute. The paralyzed target can repeat the saving throw at the end of each of its turns, ending the effect on itself on a success.

If the paralyzed creature is Medium or smaller, the retriever can pick it up as part of the retriever's move and walk or climb with it at full speed.

SALAMANDER, FROST

Frost salamanders are natives of the Plane of Ice, also called the Frostfell, which rests between the Plane of Air and the Plane of Water. Frost salamanders especially like to hunt warm-blooded creatures. They sometimes travel to frigid climes on the Material Plane by wandering through planar gates.

Devourers of Heat. The frost salamanders' aggression appetite for any heat source leads them to attack settlements they come across. They might mistake the fire of a forge or a campfire for a large, tasty meal, drawing them to attack expeditions and settlements that other predators would avoid. Azers sometimes venture into the Frostfell, where they use large fires to lure frost salamanders into traps to kill them and collect their hides and fangs for use in crafting weapons and armor.

False Refuge. Although frost salamanders can burrow their way through loose soil, they prefer to dig into the ice. They roll around in piles of broken chunks of ice, allowing it to scratch their backs as they grind it down. This habit leads them to create extensive networks of ice caves, becoming ever larger as they claw fresh chunks of ice from the walls of their lairs.

A frost salamander that dwells in a lair for a while carves out enough space to allow a small army to camp within. Inexperienced travelers who come across these caves see them as a welcome shelter, though they are anything but. Frost salamanders greedily devour any prey foolhardy enough to try sleeping in their lairs.

On rare occasions, frost giants capture and tame these creatures, using them to burrow into the ice to help create outposts and fortresses.

FROST SALAMANDER
Huge elemental, unaligned

Armor Class 17 (natural armor)
Hit Points 168 (16d12 + 64)
Speed 60 ft., burrow 40 ft., climb 40 ft.

STR	DEX	CON	INT	WIS	CHA
20 (+5)	12 (+1)	18 (+4)	7 (−2)	11 (+0)	7 (−2)

Saving Throws Con +8, Wis +4
Skills Perception +4
Damage Vulnerabilities fire
Damage Immunities cold
Senses darkvision 60 ft., tremorsense 60 ft., passive Perception 14
Languages Primordial
Challenge 9 (5,000 XP)

Burning Fury. When the salamander takes fire damage, its Freezing Breath automatically recharges.

ACTIONS

Multiattack. The salamander makes five attacks: four with its claws and one with its bite.

Claws. *Melee Weapon Attack:* +9 to hit, reach 10 ft., one target. *Hit:* 8 (1d6 + 5) piercing damage.

Bite. *Melee Weapon Attack:* +9 to hit, reach 15 ft., one target. *Hit:* 9 (1d8 + 5) piercing damage and 5 (1d10) cold damage.

Freezing Breath (Recharge 6). The salamander exhales chill wind in a 60-foot cone. Each creature in that area must make a DC 17 Constitution saving throw, taking 44 (8d10) cold damage on a failed save, or half as much damage on a successful one.

SHADAR-KAI

In the perpetual gloom of the Shadowfell lives a society that serves the Raven Queen. They were brought into that dusky realm in ages past, so long ago that they're now perfectly adapted to that cheerless environment, both physically and mentally.

Soul Custodians. Shadar-kai watch over both the Shadowfell and the material world, scouting out choice souls and tragedies that might please their deity. They are rumored to be able to coax worldly events along tragic paths for her amusement. The Raven Queen is famously cryptic even to her most devoted followers, however. The shadar-kai's efforts are rewarded only with vague omens they interpret as best they can.

Blighted Elves. Shadar-kai were once elves, but eons of exposure to the debilitating influence of the Shadowfell has left them joyless and mournful. In that realm, they have the appearance of withered elves: pale hair, wrinkled gray skin, and swollen joints give them a corpselike aspect. They appear more youthful while on other planes, but their skin always retains its deathly pallor. They dress in dark cloaks and heavy veils, detest mirrors, and avoid keeping things that remind them of their age.

GLOOM WEAVER

Although a formidable fighter, a gloom weaver is often content to remain hidden in the shadows, watching with rapt attention as its very presence affects its victims. Its dark energy weighs down the heart, causing those within its oppressive aura to feel the approach of death. This torment alone is enough to please its master, the Raven Queen, but should it be detected, a gloom weaver uses its shadow magic to reduce its enemies to ghastly corpses.

SHADOW DANCER

Those who have fought shadow dancers describe the experience as similar to fighting a living darkness. Every dim alcove and darkened nook is a place from where the lithe and acrobatic shadow dancers can emerge to ambush their prey. Using this tactic, they attack their enemies from all angles with a flurry of entangling chains that hold fast and corrupt the flesh. When their quarry is helpless, others move in to help dispatch the prey. Then they loot the corpse for trinkets, anything colorful and lively to gaze at after they return to the gloom of the Shadowfell.

SOUL MONGER

Wracked with despair over the loss of memories of a brighter time, soul mongers now crave the vitality of others. The aching void within a soul monger radiates outward, manifesting as an unbearable weight that drains the vigor of anyone unfortunate enough to be in its presence. Those who have escaped the onslaught of a soul monger can hardly shake the memory of the sound it makes—the moan of a tortured soul, lost in a bottomless well of tragedy.

GLOOM WEAVER

Medium humanoid (elf), neutral

Armor Class 14 (17 with *mage armor*)
Hit Points 104 (16d8 + 32)
Speed 30 ft.

STR	DEX	CON	INT	WIS	CHA
11 (+0)	18 (+4)	14 (+2)	15 (+2)	12 (+1)	18 (+4)

Saving Throws Dex +8, Con +6
Damage Immunities necrotic
Condition Immunities charmed, exhaustion
Senses darkvision 60 ft., passive Perception 11
Languages Common, Elvish
Challenge 9 (5,000 XP)

Burden of Time. Beasts and humanoids, other than shadar-kai, have disadvantage on saving throws while within 10 feet of the gloom weaver.

Fey Ancestry. The gloom weaver has advantage on saving throws against being charmed, and magic can't put it to sleep.

Innate Spellcasting. The gloom weaver's innate spellcasting ability is Charisma (spell save DC 16, +8 to hit with spell attacks). It can innately cast the following spells, requiring no material components:

At will: *arcane eye, mage armor, speak with dead*
1/day each: *arcane gate, bane, compulsion, confusion, true seeing*

Spellcasting. The gloom weaver is a 12th-level spellcaster. Its spellcasting ability is Charisma (spell save DC 16, +8 to hit with spell attacks). It regains its expended spell slots when it finishes a short or long rest. It knows the following warlock spells:

Cantrips (at will): *chill touch* (3d8 damage), *eldritch blast* (3 beams, +4 bonus to each damage roll), *minor illusion, prestidigitation*
1st–5th level (3 5th-level slots): *armor of Agathys, blight, darkness, dream, invisibility, fear, hypnotic pattern, major image, contact other plane, vampiric touch, witch bolt*

ACTIONS

Multiattack. The gloom weaver makes two spear attacks and casts one spell that takes 1 action to cast.

Shadow Spear. *Melee Weapon Attack:* +8 to hit, reach 5 ft., one target. *Hit:* 7 (1d6 + 4) piercing damage, or 8 (1d8 + 4) piercing damage if used with two hands, plus 26 (4d12) necrotic damage.

REACTIONS

Misty Escape (Recharges after a Short or Long Rest). When the gloom weaver takes damage, it turns invisible and teleports up to 60 feet to an unoccupied space it can see. It remains invisible until the start of its next turn or until it attacks or casts a spell.

SHADOW DANCER

GLOOM WEAVER

SOUL MONGER

SHADOW DANCER

Medium humanoid (elf), neutral

Armor Class 15 (studded leather)
Hit Points 71 (13d8 + 13)
Speed 30 ft.

STR	DEX	CON	INT	WIS	CHA
12 (+1)	16 (+3)	13 (+1)	11 (+0)	12 (+1)	12 (+1)

Saving Throws Dex +6, Cha +4
Skills Stealth +6
Damage Resistances necrotic
Condition Immunities charmed, exhaustion
Senses darkvision 60 ft., passive Perception 11
Languages Common, Elvish
Challenge 7 (2,900 XP)

Fey Ancestry. The shadow dancer has advantage on saving throws against being charmed, and magic can't put it to sleep.

Shadow Jump. As a bonus action, the shadow dancer can teleport up to 30 feet to an unoccupied space it can see. Both the space it teleports from and the space it teleports to must be in dim light or darkness. The shadow dancer can use this ability between the weapon attacks of another action it takes.

ACTIONS

Multiattack. The shadow dancer makes three spiked chain attacks.

Spiked Chain. *Melee Weapon Attack:* +6 to hit, reach 10 ft., one target. *Hit:* 10 (2d6 + 3) piercing damage, and the target must succeed on a DC 14 Dexterity saving throw or suffer one additional effect of the shadow dancer's choice:

- The target is grappled (escape DC 14) if it is a Medium or smaller creature. Until the grapple ends, the target is restrained, and the shadow dancer can't grapple another target.
- The target is knocked prone.
- The target takes 22 (4d10) necrotic damage.

Soul Monger

Medium humanoid (elf), neutral

Armor Class 15 (studded leather)
Hit Points 123 (19d8 + 38)
Speed 30 ft.

STR	DEX	CON	INT	WIS	CHA
8 (−1)	17 (+3)	14 (+2)	19 (+4)	15 (+3)	13 (+1)

Saving Throws Dex +7, Wis +7, Cha +5
Skills Perception +7
Damage Immunities necrotic, psychic
Condition Immunities charmed, exhaustion, frightened
Senses darkvision 60 ft., passive Perception 17
Languages Common, Elvish
Challenge 11 (7,200 XP)

Fey Ancestry. The soul monger has advantage on saving throws against being charmed, and magic can't put it to sleep.

Innate Spellcasting. The soul monger's innate spellcasting ability is Intelligence (spell save DC 16, +8 to hit with spell attacks). It can innately cast the following spells, requiring no material components:

At will: *chill touch* (3d8 damage), *poison spray* (3d12 damage)
1/day each: *bestow curse, chain lightning, finger of death, gaseous form, phantasmal killer, seeming*

Magic Resistance. The soul monger has advantage on saving throws against spells and other magical effects.

Soul Thirst. When the soul monger reduces a creature to 0 hit points, the soul monger can gain temporary hit points equal to half the creature's hit point maximum. While the soul monger has temporary hit points from this ability, it has advantage on attack rolls.

Weight of Ages. Any beast or humanoid, other than a shadar-kai, that starts its turn within 5 feet of the soul monger has its speed reduced by 20 feet until the start of that creature's next turn.

Actions

Multiattack. The soul monger makes two phantasmal dagger attacks.

Phantasmal Dagger. *Melee Weapon Attack:* +7 to hit, reach 5 ft., one target. *Hit:* 13 (4d4 + 3) piercing damage plus 19 (3d12) necrotic damage, and the target has disadvantage on saving throws until the start of the soul monger's next turn.

Wave of Weariness (Recharge 4–6). The soul monger emits weariness in a 60-foot cube. Each creature in that area must make a DC 16 Constitution saving throw. On a failed save, a creature takes 45 (10d8) psychic damage and suffers 1 level of exhaustion. On a successful save, it takes 22 (5d8) psychic damage.

Some children have imaginary friends that their parents can't see. Sometimes those invisible friends aren't imaginary.

SKULK

Skulks are the soulless shells of travelers who became lost in the Shadowfell, wandering its gray wastes until they lost all sense of self. They are so devoid of identity that they have become permanently invisible. Only children can see a skulk without the help of a mirror or a special candle. On the rare occasions when a skulk is visible, it appears as a drab, featureless, hairless humanoid.

Summoned Servants. A skulk can be summoned from the Shadowfell by performing a ritual. If the creature is given a portion of the summoner's identity, the skulk is bound to obey the summoner's commands for 30 days. If a skulk is visible, an astute observer might deduce who summoned it, because a skulk assumes a vague likeness of its master.

Cruel and chaotic, skulks carry out their orders in the most violent manner possible. A summoned skulk can't return to the Shadowfell until it dies, so it has every motivation to throw itself into creating bloodshed and mayhem.

Hollow Lives. After killing a person in the material world, a skulk sometimes takes up a silent imitation of that person's life. In extreme cases, skulks have invaded villages, killed all the occupants, and turned the places into seeming ghost towns, where flavorless food is prepared daily, colorless clothes are hung up to dry, and livestock is shifted from pen to pen until it starves.

SKULK
Medium humanoid, chaotic neutral

Armor Class 14
Hit Points 18 (4d8)
Speed 30 ft.

STR	DEX	CON	INT	WIS	CHA
6 (−2)	19 (+4)	10 (+0)	10 (+0)	7 (−2)	1 (−5)

Saving Throws Con +2
Skills Stealth +8
Damage Immunities radiant
Condition Immunities blinded
Senses darkvision 120 ft., passive Perception 8
Languages understands Common but can't speak
Challenge 1/2 (100 XP)

Fallible Invisibility. The skulk is invisible. This invisibility can be circumvented by three things:

- The skulk appears as a drab, smooth-skinned humanoid if its reflection can be seen in a mirror or on another surface.
- The skulk appears as a dim, translucent form in the light of a candle made of fat rendered from a corpse whose identity is unknown.
- Humanoid children, aged 10 and under, can see through this invisibility.

Trackless. The skulk leaves no tracks to indicate where it has been or where it's headed.

ACTIONS

Claws. *Melee Weapon Attack:* +6 to hit, reach 5 ft., one target. *Hit:* 6 (1d4 + 4) slashing damage. If the skulk has advantage on the attack roll, the target also takes 7 (2d6) necrotic damage.

S

IN THE SHADOWFELL AND ELSEWHERE IN THE MULTIVERSE,
THE CURSE OF UNDEATH THREATENS TO OVERWHELM ALL LIFE.

Skull Lord

The skull lords have claimed vast regions of the Shadowfell as their dominion. From these blighted lands, they wage war against their rivals, commanding hordes of undead in a bid to establish dominance. Yet skull lords always prove to be their own worst enemies; as a combined being born from three hateful individuals, they constantly plot against themselves.

Creatures of Betrayal. Infighting and treachery brought the skull lords into existence. The first of them appeared in the aftermath of Vecna's bid to conquer the world of Greyhawk, after the vampire Kas betrayed Vecna and took his eye and hand. In the confusion resulting from this turn of events, Vecna's warlords turned against each other, and the dark one's plans were dashed. In a rage, Vecna gathered up his generals and captains and bound them in groups of three, fusing them into undead abominations cursed to fight among themselves for all time. Since the first skull lords were exiled into shadow, others have joined them, typically after being created from other leaders who betrayed their masters.

Undead Nature. A skull lord doesn't require air, food, drink, or sleep.

Skull Lord

Medium undead, lawful evil

Armor Class 18 (plate)
Hit Points 105 (14d8 + 42)
Speed 30 ft.

STR	DEX	CON	INT	WIS	CHA
14 (+2)	16 (+3)	17 (+3)	16 (+3)	15 (+2)	21 (+5)

Skills Athletics +7, History +8, Perception +12, Stealth +8
Damage Resistances cold, necrotic; bludgeoning, piercing, and slashing from nonmagical attacks
Damage Immunities poison
Condition Immunities blinded, charmed, deafened, exhaustion, frightened, poisoned, stunned, unconscious
Senses darkvision 60 ft., passive Perception 22
Languages all the languages it knew in life
Challenge 15 (13,000 XP)

Legendary Resistance (3/Day). If the skull lord fails a saving throw, it can choose to succeed instead.

Master of the Grave. While within 30 feet of the skull lord, any undead ally of the skull lord makes saving throws with advantage, and that ally regains 1d6 hit points whenever it starts its turn there.

Evasion. If the skull lord is subjected to an effect that allows it to make a Dexterity saving throw to take only half the damage, the skull lord instead takes no damage if it succeeds on the saving throw, and only half damage if it fails.

Spellcasting. The skull lord is a 13th-level spellcaster. Its spellcasting ability is Charisma (spell save DC18, +10 to hit with spell attacks). The skull lord knows the following sorcerer spells:

Cantrips (at will): *chill touch, fire bolt, mage hand, poison spray, ray of frost, shocking grasp*
1st level (4 slots): *magic missile, expeditious retreat, thunderwave*
2nd level (3 slots): *mirror image, scorching ray*
3rd level (3 slots): *fear, haste*
4th level (3 slots): *dimension door, ice storm*
5th level (2 slots): *cloudkill, cone of cold*
6th level (1 slot): *eyebite*
7th level (1 slot): *finger of death*

Actions

Multiattack. The skull lord makes three bone staff attacks.

Bone Staff. *Melee Weapon Attack:* +8 to hit, reach 5 ft., one target. *Hit:* 7 (1d8 + 3) bludgeoning damage plus 14 (4d6) necrotic damage.

Legendary Actions

The skull lord can take 3 legendary actions, choosing from the options below. Only one legendary action option can be used at a time and only at the end of another creature's turn. The skull lord regains spent legendary actions at the start of its turn.

Bone Staff (Costs 2 Actions). The skull lord makes a bone staff attack.
Cantrip. The skull lord casts a cantrip.
Move. The skull lord moves up to its speed without provoking opportunity attacks.
Summon Undead (Costs 3 Actions). Up to five skeletons or zombies appear in unoccupied spaces within 30 feet of the skull lord and remain until destroyed. Undead summoned in this way roll initiative and act in the next available turn. The skull lord can have up to five undead summoned by this ability at a time.

SORROWSWORN

The Shadowfell's pervasive melancholy sometimes gives rise to strange incarnations of the plane's bleak nature. The sorrowsworn embody the forms of suffering that are inherent to the shadowy landscape, and they visit horror on those who stumble into their midst.

Emotion Given Form. Each sorrowsworn personifies a different aspect of despair or distress. Some are manifestations of anger; others are loneliness given physical form. Their nature provides a clue both to understanding how they become more powerful and to overcoming them. Giving in to the negative emotions that the sorrowsworn represent causes these entities to grow deadlier. Fighting against these emotions can weaken them and drive them away.

THE ANGRY

Relying on violence to sustain their existence, the Angry grow more powerful when their foes fight back. If a creature opts not to attack, though, the Angry becomes confused, and its attacks weaken. Each of the Angry has two heads, which bicker with each other until they find something else on which they can vent their wrath.

THE HUNGRY

Horrid beasts with grasping claws and yawning mouths, the Hungry do whatever is necessary to sate their appetites. These greedy devourers consume all life and energy they encounter, stuffing their maws with flesh and drinking in their victims' screams. When they finish, they lurch away while their bright eyes resume the search for something else to consume.

THE LONELY

The sorrow of isolation afflicts many creatures that lurk in the Shadowfell, but the need for companionship is never manifested more dramatically than in the Lonely. When these sorrowsworn spot other creatures, they feel keenly the need for interaction and so they launch their harpoon-like arms to drag their victims close.

THE LOST

The Shadowfell turns visitors around until they become marooned in its twisted landscape. The Lost are representations of the anxiety and fear that people experience when they can't find their way. These sorrowsworn appear as desperate and panicked things.

The Lost try to embrace any creatures they can reach, attempting to find solace in the contact. Aside from the horror of being embraced by such a thing, the victim experiences a flood of fear and panic as its mind buckles under the fury of this assault. The harder the victims' allies fight for release, the worse the experience becomes.

THE WRETCHED

Horrid little monsters, the Wretched gather in large packs to scour the Shadowfell for prey. These pitiful entities subsist on life force, so when they find a creature, they surge forward to sink their fangs into their victims and drink deep of their life energy and their fear.

THE ANGRY
Medium monstrosity, neutral evil

Armor Class 18 (natural armor)
Hit Points 255 (30d8 + 120)
Speed 30 ft.

STR	DEX	CON	INT	WIS	CHA
17 (+3)	10 (+0)	19 (+4)	8 (−1)	13 (+1)	6 (−2)

Skills Perception +6
Damage Resistances bludgeoning, piercing, and slashing while in dim light or darkness
Senses darkvision 60 ft., passive Perception 16
Languages Common
Challenge 13 (10,000 XP)

Two Heads. The Angry has advantage on Wisdom (Perception) checks and on saving throws against being blinded, charmed, deafened, frightened, stunned, or knocked unconscious.

Rising Anger. If another creature deals damage to the Angry, the Angry's attack rolls have advantage until the end of its next turn, and the first time it hits with a hook attack on its next turn, the attack's target takes an extra 19 (3d12) psychic damage.

On its turn, the Angry has disadvantage on attack rolls if no other creature has dealt damage to it since the end of its last turn.

ACTIONS

Multiattack. The Angry makes two hook attacks.

Hook. *Melee Weapon Attack:* +8 to hit, reach 5 ft., one target. *Hit:* 16 (2d12 + 3) piercing damage.

The Hungry

Medium monstrosity, neutral evil

Armor Class 17 (natural armor)
Hit Points 225 (30d8 + 90)
Speed 30 ft.

STR	DEX	CON	INT	WIS	CHA
19 (+4)	10 (+0)	17 (+3)	6 (−2)	11 (+0)	6 (−2)

Damage Resistances bludgeoning, piercing, and slashing while in dim light or darkness
Senses darkvision 60 ft., passive Perception 10
Languages Common
Challenge 11 (7,200 XP)

Life Hunger. If a creature the Hungry can see regains hit points, the Hungry gains two benefits until the end of its next turn: it has advantage on attack rolls, and its bite deals an extra 22 (4d10) necrotic damage on a hit.

Actions

Multiattack. The Hungry makes two attacks: one with its bite and one with its claws.

Bite. *Melee Weapon Attack:* +8 to hit, reach 5 ft., one target. *Hit:* 8 (1d8 + 4) piercing damage plus 13 (3d8) necrotic damage.

Claws. *Melee Weapon Attack:* +8 to hit, reach 10 ft., one target. *Hit:* 18 (4d6 + 4) slashing damage. If the target is Medium or smaller, it is grappled (escape DC 16) and restrained until the grapple ends. While grappling a creature, the Hungry can't attack with its claws.

The Lonely

Medium monstrosity, neutral evil

Armor Class 16 (natural armor)
Hit Points 112 (15d8 + 45)
Speed 30 ft.

STR	DEX	CON	INT	WIS	CHA
16 (+3)	12 (+1)	17 (+3)	6 (−2)	11 (+0)	6 (−2)

Damage Resistances bludgeoning, piercing, and slashing while in dim light or darkness
Senses darkvision 60 ft., passive Perception 10
Languages Common
Challenge 9 (5,000 XP)

Psychic Leech. At the start of each of the Lonely's turns, each creature within 5 feet of it must succeed on a DC 15 Wisdom saving throw or take 10 (3d6) psychic damage.

Thrives on Company. The Lonely has advantage on attack rolls while it is within 30 feet of at least two other creatures. It otherwise has disadvantage on attack rolls.

Actions

Multiattack. The Lonely makes one harpoon arm attack and uses Sorrowful Embrace.

Harpoon Arm. *Melee Weapon Attack:* +7 to hit, reach 60 ft., one target. *Hit:* 21 (4d8 + 3) piercing damage, and the target is grappled (escape DC 15) if it is a Large or smaller creature. The Lonely has two harpoon arms and can grapple up to two creatures at once.

Sorrowful Embrace. Each creature grappled by the Lonely must make a DC 15 Wisdom saving throw. A creature takes 18 (4d8) psychic damage on a failed save, or half as much damage on a successful one. In either case, the Lonely pulls each creature grappled by it up to 30 feet straight toward it.

The Lost

Medium monstrosity, neutral evil

Armor Class 15 (natural armor)
Hit Points 78 (12d8 + 24)
Speed 30 ft.

STR	DEX	CON	INT	WIS	CHA
17 (+3)	12 (+1)	15 (+2)	6 (−2)	7 (−2)	5 (−3)

Skills Athletics +6
Damage Resistances bludgeoning, piercing, and slashing while in dim light or darkness
Senses darkvision 60 ft., passive Perception 8
Languages Common
Challenge 7 (2,900 XP)

Actions

Multiattack. The Lost makes two arm spike attacks.

Arm Spike. *Melee Weapon Attack:* +6 to hit, reach 5 ft., one target. *Hit:* 14 (2d10 + 3) piercing damage.

Embrace. *Melee Weapon Attack:* +6 to it, reach 5 ft., one target. *Hit:* 25 (4d10 + 3) piercing damage, and the target is grappled (escape DC 14) if it is a Medium or smaller creature. Until the grapple ends, the target is frightened, and it takes 27 (6d8) psychic damage at the end of each of its turns. The Lost can embrace only one creature at a time.

Reactions

Tightening Embrace. If the Lost takes damage while it has a creature grappled, that creature takes 18 (4d8) psychic damage.

The Wretched

Small monstrosity, neutral evil

Armor Class 15 (natural armor)
Hit Points 10 (4d6 − 4)
Speed 40 ft.

STR	DEX	CON	INT	WIS	CHA
7 (−2)	12 (+1)	9 (−1)	5 (−3)	6 (−2)	5 (−3)

Damage Resistances bludgeoning, piercing, and slashing while in dim light or darkness
Senses darkvision 60 ft., passive Perception 8
Languages —
Challenge 1/4 (50 XP)

Wretched Pack Tactics. The Wretched has advantage on an attack roll against a creature if at least one of the Wretched's allies is within 5 feet of the creature and the ally isn't incapacitated. The Wretched otherwise has disadvantage on attack rolls.

Actions

Bite. *Melee Weapon Attack:* +3 to hit, reach 5 ft., one target. *Hit:* 6 (1d10 + 1) piercing damage, and the Wretched attaches to the target. While attached, the Wretched can't attack, and at the start of each of the Wretched's turns, the target takes 6 (1d10 + 1) necrotic damage.

The attached Wretched moves with the target whenever the target moves, requiring none of the Wretched's movement. The Wretched can detach itself by spending 5 feet of its movement on its turn. A creature, including the target, can use its action to detach a Wretched.

S

STAR SPAWN

The Material Plane represents only one small part of the multiverse. Beyond the best-known planes of existence lie realms that are lethal to mortal life. Some are so hostile that even a moment's contact with such a place is enough to plunge a mortal mind into madness. Yet beings do exist that are native to these realms: beings that are eternally hungering, searching, warring, sometimes dreaming. These Elder Evils are far older than most of the mortal races and always horrific to humanoid minds.

However much they might desire to enter and dominate the Material Plane, the Elder Evils are unable or unwilling to leave their realms. Some are imprisoned in their dimensions by external forces, some are inextricably bound to their home realities, and others simply can't find any way out.

Heralds of Doom. The creatures known as star spawn are the heralds, servants, foot soldiers, and lieutenants of the Elder Evils, capable of taking on forms that can journey to the Material Plane. They arrive most often in the wake of a comet—or perhaps such a phenomenon merely signals that star spawn are in the vicinity and available for communication. When the signs are right, warlocks and cultists hasten to gather together, read aloud their blasphemous texts, and conduct the mind-searing rituals that guide the blazing star spawn into the world.

STAR SPAWN GRUE

Fanged and lipless, the ever-grinning, madly staring grue lopes about on spindly legs and long arms. Bristles and spines project from odd patches of its pallid skin, and it's long fingers end in broken and dirty nails. Grues are the weakest of the star spawn. A host of writhing, scrambling grues typically accompanies more powerful star spawn. Their constant chittering and shrieking produces discordant psychic energy that disrupts thought patterns in other creatures. Intelligent creatures experience flashing colors, hallucinations, disorientation, and waves of hopelessness when they find themselves near a group of star spawn grues.

STAR SPAWN HULK

The hulk is the largest of the known star spawn. Though ogre-like in stature, the hulk's glistening translucent skin reveals a muscled form devoid of an ogre's fat. Pale and seemingly lidless eyes glare balefully from a face distorted by too many teeth and too little nose.

Hulks are seldom encountered without a commanding seer nearby. A hulk appears to have little will of its own, other than to protect its master.

STAR SPAWN GRUE
Small aberration, neutral evil

Armor Class 11
Hit Points 17 (5d6)
Speed 30 ft.

STR	DEX	CON	INT	WIS	CHA
6 (−2)	13 (+1)	10 (+0)	9 (−1)	11 (+0)	6 (−2)

Damage Immunities psychic
Senses darkvision 60 ft., passive Perception 10
Languages Deep Speech
Challenge 1/4 (50 XP)

Aura of Madness. Creatures within 20 feet of the grue that aren't aberrations have disadvantage on saving throws, as well as on attack rolls against creatures other than a star spawn grue.

ACTIONS

Confounding Bite. *Melee Weapon Attack:* +3 to hit, reach 5 ft., one target. *Hit:* 6 (2d4 + 1) piercing damage, and the target must succeed on a DC 10 Wisdom saving throw or attack rolls against it have advantage until the start of the grue's next turn.

STAR SPAWN HULK
Large aberration, chaotic evil

Armor Class 16 (natural armor)
Hit Points 136 (13d10 + 65)
Speed 30 ft.

STR	DEX	CON	INT	WIS	CHA
20 (+5)	8 (−1)	21 (+5)	7 (−2)	12 (+1)	9 (−1)

Saving Throws Dex +3, Wis +5
Skills Perception +5
Damage Resistances bludgeoning, piercing, and slashing from nonmagical attacks
Condition Immunities charmed, frightened
Senses darkvision 60 ft., passive Perception 15
Languages Deep Speech
Challenge 10 (5,900 XP)

Psychic Mirror. If the hulk takes psychic damage, each creature within 10 feet of the hulk takes that damage instead; the hulk takes none of the damage. In addition, the hulk's thoughts and location can't be discerned by magic.

ACTIONS

Multiattack. The hulk makes two slam attacks. If both attacks hit the same target, the target also takes 9 (2d8) psychic damage and must succeed on a DC 17 Constitution saving throw or be stunned until the end of the target's next turn.

Slam. *Melee Weapon Attack:* +9 to hit, reach 10 ft., one target. *Hit:* 14 (2d8 + 5) bludgeoning damage.

Reaping Arms (Recharge 5–6). The hulk makes a separate slam attack against each creature within 10 feet of it. Each creature that is hit must also succeed on a DC 17 Dexterity saving throw or be knocked prone.

Star Spawn Larva Mage

A larva mage is a nightmarish combination of a mortal body and otherworldly substance. When a powerful cultist of a wormlike entity such as Kyuss or Kezef—usually a warlock or other spellcaster—contacts the comet-borne emissary of an Elder Evil, the emissary can merge with a mortal consciousness to create a larva mage. None of the original cultist's personality survives the transformation, so what emerges is wholly alien.

The cultists who blaspheme reality by calling out to Elder Evils often speak of a Far Realm from which these entities hail. In truth, there is no one place or space from which they come. There is the multiverse of things that are, and there is the multiverse of things that shouldn't be.

STAR SPAWN LARVA MAGE
Medium aberration, chaotic evil

Armor Class 16 (natural armor)
Hit Points 168 (16d8 + 96)
Speed 30 ft.

STR	DEX	CON	INT	WIS	CHA
17 (+3)	12 (+1)	23 (+6)	18 (+4)	12 (+1)	16 (+3)

Saving Throws Dex +6, Wis +6, Cha +8
Skills Perception +6
Damage Resistances cold; bludgeoning, piercing, and slashing from nonmagical attacks
Damage Immunities psychic
Condition Immunities charmed, frightened, paralyzed, petrified, poisoned, restrained
Senses darkvision 60 ft., passive Perception 16
Languages Deep Speech
Challenge 16 (15,000 XP)

Innate Spellcasting. The larva mage's innate spellcasting ability is Charisma (spell save DC 16, +8 to hit with spell attacks). It can innately cast the following spells, requiring no material components:

At will: *eldritch blast* (3 beams, +3 bonus to each damage roll), *minor illusion*
3/day: *dominate monster*
1/day: *circle of death*

Return to Worms. When the larva mage is reduced to 0 hit points, it breaks apart into a **swarm of insects** in the same space. Unless the swarm is destroyed, the larva mage reforms from it 24 hours later.

ACTIONS

Slam. *Melee Weapon Attack:* +8 to hit, reach 10 ft., one target. *Hit:* 7 (1d8 + 3) bludgeoning damage, and the target must succeed on a DC 19 Constitution saving throw or be poisoned until the end of its next turn.

Plague of Worms (Recharge 6). Each creature other than a star spawn within 10 feet of the larva mage must succeed on a DC 19 Dexterity saving throw or take 22 (5d8) necrotic damage and be blinded and restrained by masses of swarming worms. The affected creature takes 22 (5d8) necrotic damage at the start of each of the larva mage's turns. The creature can repeat the saving throw at the end of each of its turns, ending the effect on itself on a success.

REACTIONS

Feed on Weakness. When a creature within 20 feet of the larva mage fails a saving throw, the larva mage gains 10 temporary hit points.

LEGENDARY ACTIONS

The larva mage can take 3 legendary actions, choosing from the options below. Only one legendary action option can be used at a time and only at the end of another creature's turn. The larva mage regains spent legendary actions at the start of its turn.

Cantrip (Costs 2 Actions). The larva mage casts one cantrip.
Slam (Costs 2 Actions). The larva mage makes one slam attack.
Feed (Costs 3 Actions). Each creature restrained by the larva mage's Plague of Worms takes 13 (3d8) necrotic damage, and the larva mage gains 6 temporary hit points.

S

Stars don't spawn these creatures. Such beautiful lights shouldn't be blamed for such balefulness.

Star Spawn Mangler

A mangler is a low-slung, creeping horror with multiple gangly arms. A mangler most often has six arms, but one can have any number from four to eight. Manglers creep along the ground or the walls, sticking to shadows, hiding in spots that seem too shallow or well-lit to conceal anything. They appear smaller than their true size, thanks to their hunched posture and emaciated frame. Cultists summon these creatures to serve as guards and assassins, two roles at which they excel.

Star Spawn Mangler

Medium aberration, chaotic evil

Armor Class 14
Hit Points 71 (13d8 + 13)
Speed 40 ft., climb 40 ft.

STR	DEX	CON	INT	WIS	CHA
8 (−1)	18 (+4)	12 (+1)	11 (+0)	12 (+1)	7 (−2)

Saving Throws Dex +7, Con +4
Skills Stealth +7
Damage Resistances cold
Damage Immunities psychic
Condition Immunities charmed, frightened, prone
Senses darkvision 60 ft., passive Perception 11
Languages Deep Speech
Challenge 5 (1,800 XP)

Ambush. On the first round of each combat, the mangler has advantage on attack rolls against a creature that hasn't taken a turn yet.

Shadow Stealth. While in dim light or darkness, the mangler can take the Hide action as a bonus action.

Actions

Multiattack. The mangler makes two claw attacks.

Claw. *Melee Weapon Attack:* +7 to hit, reach 5 ft., one target. *Hit:* 8 (1d8 + 4) slashing damage. If the attack roll has advantage, the target also takes 7 (2d6) psychic damage.

Flurry of Claws (Recharge 4–6). The mangler makes six claw attacks against one target. Either before or after these attacks, it can move up to its speed as a bonus action without provoking opportunity attacks.

Star Spawn Seer

Medium aberration, neutral evil

Armor Class 17 (natural armor)
Hit Points 153 (18d8 + 72)
Speed 30 ft.

STR	DEX	CON	INT	WIS	CHA
14 (+2)	12 (+1)	18 (+4)	22 (+6)	19 (+4)	16 (+3)

Saving Throws Dex +6, Int +11, Wis +9, Cha +8
Skills Perception +9
Damage Resistances cold; bludgeoning, piercing, and slashing from nonmagical attacks
Damage Immunities psychic
Condition Immunities charmed, frightened
Senses darkvision 60 ft., passive Perception 19
Languages Common, Deep Speech, Undercommon
Challenge 13 (10,000 XP)

Out-of-Phase Movement. The seer can move through other creatures and objects as if they were difficult terrain. Each creature it moves through takes 5 (1d10) psychic damage; no creature can take this damage more than once per turn. The seer takes 5 (1d10) force damage if it ends its turn inside an object.

Actions

Multiattack. The seer makes two comet staff attacks or uses Psychic Orb twice.

Comet Staff. *Melee Weapon Attack:* +11 to hit, reach 5 ft., one target. *Hit:* 9 (1d6 + 6) bludgeoning damage, or 10 (1d8 + 6) bludgeoning damage if used with two hands, plus 18 (4d8) psychic damage, and the target must succeed on a DC 19 Constitution saving throw or be incapacitated until the end of its next turn.

Psychic Orb. *Ranged Spell Attack:* +11 to hit, range 120 feet, one target. *Hit:* 27 (5d10) psychic damage.

Collapse Distance (Recharge 6). The seer warps space around a creature it can see within 30 feet of it. That creature must make a DC 19 Wisdom saving throw. On a failed save, the target, along with any equipment it is wearing or carrying, is magically teleported up to 60 feet to an unoccupied space the seer can see, and all other creatures within 10 feet of the target's original space each takes 39 (6d12) psychic damage. On a successful save, the target takes 19 (3d12) psychic damage.

Reactions

Bend Space. When the seer would be hit by an attack, it teleports, exchanging positions with another star spawn it can see within 60 feet of it. The other star spawn is hit by the attack instead.

Star Spawn Seer

A star spawn seer is most often encountered as the leader of a cult that worships one or more of the Elder Evils. Usually, the seer is the only cult member that grasps the full extent of the horror the cult is venerating.

An entity that appears as a star spawn seer in the Material Plane usually arrives as something different—something disembodied. When a warlock or other spellcaster establishes communication with it, the seer-entity takes control of the mortal's form and spirit, transforming it into a star spawn seer. Whoever the seer once was largely vanishes beneath the corpulent bulk of tumorous skin than builds up in strange whorls all over the seer's body. Hands become bulky, flipper-like appendages capable of grasping their strange staffs—formed of some blend of flesh, bone, and star stuff—but clumsy and painful when used to manipulate other things.

A star spawn seer is almost always accompanied by one or more star spawn hulks. Although the hulk is a worthy combatant in its own right, it's also a vital part of a tactic often used by seers. When a seer deals psychic damage to a hulk, the hulk isn't hurt, while the effect ricochets off the hulk and expands to assault other creatures.

The seer's goal is to tap the energy sources and master the rites that will enable it to extend a bridge between the vulnerable sanity of the Material Plane and the squirming madness of an Elder Evil's prison.

Elder Evil Blessings

Through generations of study and grim practice, the disciples of certain Elder Evils have mastered the ability to bestow supernatural gifts on minions they select for the privilege. Any creature that serves a cult of Elder Evil, including a star spawn, can be given one of these rewards—usually as compensation for faithful service, but sometimes as a chance for a creature that breached the cult's laws to redeem itself. The following powers are unique to specific cults, and typically a creature has no more than one of them.

Cult of Borem of the Lake of Boiling Mud

Borem's Embrace (1/Day). The cultist touches one creature within 5 feet of it. The target must succeed on a DC 15 Dexterity saving throw or be coated in sticky, steaming mud. While it is coated in this way, the target's speed is halved, it can't use reactions, and it takes 10 (3d6) fire damage at the start of its turns. The effect lasts for 1 minute, until the cultist is incapacitated or dies, or until the target is immersed in water.

Cult of Atropus the World Born Dead

Gaze of Corruption (Recharge 6). The cultist targets one creature it can see within 30 feet of it. The target must succeed on a DC 15 Constitution saving throw or take 16 (3d10) necrotic damage and be poisoned for 1 minute. The poisoned target can repeat the saving throw at the end of each of its turns, ending the effect on itself on a success.

Cult of Haask the Voice of Hargut

Haask's Presence (1/Day). The cultist transforms into a Tiny, leech-like being and teleports onto the shoulder of a humanoid that it can see within 30 feet of it. The targeted humanoid must succeed on a DC 15 Charisma saving throw or be charmed by the cultist. While the target is charmed, the cultist has control of it on the target's next turn. At the end of that turn, the cultist teleports to an unoccupied space it can see within 30 feet of it and returns to its normal form. The cultist can't be targeted directly by any attack or other effect while it's in the slug-like form, but it is subject to areas of effect as normal.

Cult of Tyranthraxus the Flamed One

Radiant Flames (1/Day). Multihued flame surrounds the cultist for 1 minute, until the cultist is incapacitated or dies, or until the cultist extinguishes the flame (no action required). While inflamed, the cultist has telepathy with a range of 30 feet, and it can teleport as a bonus action up to 30 feet to an unoccupied space it can see. In addition, every creature that starts its turn within 5 feet of the cultist must make a DC 15 Dexterity saving throw, taking 16 (3d10) radiant damage on a failed save, or half as much damage on a successful one.

Cult of Tharizdun the Chained God

Tharizdun's Spark (Recharge 6). As a bonus action, the cultist touches a simple or martial weapon or a natural weapon, if it has one. The next creature hit by the touched weapon must succeed on a DC 15 Wisdom saving throw or experience short-term madness for 10 minutes. Consult the Short-Term Madness table (see "Madness Effects" in chapter 8 of the *Dungeon Master's Guide*) to determine the form of the madness. The affected creature can repeat the saving throw at the end of each minute, ending the effect on itself on a success.

ELDER EVILS

Exactly who or what the Elder Evils are remains in dispute among the rare sources of knowledge about them. Few creatures in the multiverse have any awareness of these beings, and no one can claim to know them all.

Some Elder Evils are called gods, primordials, or fiends. Yet some scholars versed in esoteric mysteries insist they are none of these, but in fact are beings set apart from what mortals consider reality. Some Elder Evils are alleged to be creatures of the Far Realm, while others are thought to be trapped in a particular plane or world, or held in check somehow by wandering stars, imprisoned in the vastness of the night sky.

The names given to these terrible entities include such strange descriptions as Ityak-Ortheel the Elf-Eater, Dendar the Night Serpent, Borem of the Lake of Boiling Mud, Kezef the Chaos Hound, Zargon the Returner, Camnod the Unseen, Holashner the Hunger Below, Piscaethces the Blood Queen, Shothotugg the Eater of Worlds, Y'chak the Violet Flame, Bolothamogg Who Watches from Beyond the Stars, Hargut of the Gray Pestilence, Haask the Voice of Hargut, Ragnorra the Mother of Monsters, the Hulks of Zoretha, Kyuss the Worm That Walks, Tharizdun the Elder Elemental Eye, Atropus the World Born Dead, Pandorym the Utter Annihilation, Haemnathuun the Blood Lord, Maram of the Great Spear, Tyranthraxus the Flamed One, the unnamed Queen of Chaos, and Father Llymic, the Alien Thought Given Flesh.

The extent to which these beings have power beyond their native environments varies, as do notions of their relative strength. But they are all forces of corruption and evil. Nothing good can come from their influence. No bargain made with them ends in anything other than madness, plague, death, or worse.

STEEDERS

Giant hunting spiders, steeders prowl the depths of the Underdark. Most steeders are encountered in the company of duergar.

Female Dominance. Female steeders grow larger and stronger than males, and the female often devours the male after breeding. In captivity, males are used as draft animals, while females serve as steeds in battle.

Lone Predators. Steeders consider other steeders as enemies and attempt to tear apart perceived threats. Their duergar handlers must stable steeders separate from one another and place blinders on them when they're put to work to keep them from attacking each other.

Low Cunning. Steeders are intelligent enough to learn simple hand signals and vocal commands, but even a domesticated steeder can turn against its handler. Training these beasts requires a rider to bond with the steeder, a process that begins shortly after the creature hatches. The rider stays with the steeder as it grows to full size, working throughout that time to channel the beast's predatory instincts.

Deadly Hunters. Rather than spinning webs, steeders excrete a viscous substance from their legs. This goo allows them to creep along walls and ceilings and to grapple prey.

> *Steeders resemble spiders as much as worgs resemble wolves. The creatures may appear similar, but steeders are more than mere vermin.*

FEMALE STEEDER

Large monstrosity, unaligned

Armor Class 14 (natural armor)
Hit Points 30 (4d10 + 8)
Speed 30 ft., climb 30 ft.

STR	DEX	CON	INT	WIS	CHA
15 (+2)	16 (+3)	14 (+2)	2 (−4)	10 (+0)	3 (−4)

Skills Stealth +7, Perception +4
Senses darkvision 120 ft., passive Perception 14
Languages —
Challenge 1 (200 XP)

Spider Climb. The steeder can climb difficult surfaces, including upside down on ceilings, without needing to make an ability check.

Extraordinary Leap. The distance of the steeder's long jumps is tripled; every foot of its walking speed that it spends on the jump allows it to move 3 feet.

ACTIONS

Bite. *Melee Weapon Attack:* +5 to hit, reach 5 ft., one target. *Hit:* 7 (1d8 + 3) piercing damage plus 9 (2d8) poison damage.

Sticky Leg. *Melee Weapon Attack:* +5 to hit, reach 5 ft., one Medium or smaller creature. *Hit:* The target is stuck to the steeder's leg and grappled until it escapes (escape DC 12). The steeder can have only one creature grappled at a time.

MALE STEEDER

Medium monstrosity, unaligned

Armor Class 12 (natural armor)
Hit Points 13 (2d8 + 4)
Speed 30 ft., climb 30 ft.

STR	DEX	CON	INT	WIS	CHA
15 (+2)	12 (+1)	14 (+2)	2 (−4)	10 (+0)	3 (−4)

Skills Stealth +5, Perception +4
Senses darkvision 120 ft., passive Perception 14
Languages —
Challenge 1/4 (50 XP)

Spider Climb. The steeder can climb difficult surfaces, including upside down on ceilings, without needing to make an ability check.

Extraordinary Leap. The distance of the steeder's long jumps is tripled; every foot of its walking speed that it spends on the jump allows it to jump 3 feet.

ACTIONS

Bite. *Melee Weapon Attack:* +4 to hit, reach 5 ft., one target. *Hit:* 6 (1d8 + 2) piercing damage plus 4 (1d8) poison damage.

Sticky Leg. *Melee Weapon Attack:* +4 to hit, reach 5 ft., one Small or Tiny creature. *Hit:* The target is stuck to the steeder's leg and grappled until it escapes (escape DC 12). The steeder can have only one creature grappled at a time.

STEEL PREDATOR

A steel predator is a merciless machine with one purpose: to locate and kill its target regardless of distance and obstacles.

Modron Engineering. Steel predators are created by a particular hexton modron, using a machine located in the city of Sigil. It wasn't always headquartered in the City of Doors, however. On its original home, the plane of Mechanus, the ingenious hexton was lauded for its invention—until it turned its creations against its superiors. Steel predators wreaked havoc across the modron hierarchy until the rogue hexton was trapped and exiled. Now it operates a shop in Sigil where, for a steep price, anyone can commission the manufacture of a steel predator.

Assassins on Demand. To create a steel predator, the hexton's machine must be fed something that identifies the predator's target, such as a lock of hair, a well-worn glove, or a much-used weapon. The moment the newly manufactured steel predator emerges, it bounds away in search of its prey. It senses the location of its target across planar boundaries, but such detection is accurate only to within a thousand yards; to close the remaining distance, the steel predator locates its prey by sight and smell.

Once battle is joined, the predator ignores every other threat to attack its target, unless other creatures prevent it from reaching the target. In that case, it does what it must to fulfill its mission.

Rogue Killers. If all goes according to plan, a steel predator slays its target and then voluntarily returns to Sigil, where it's broken down into parts that can be used in another steel predator. Battle damage can cause this instinct to fail, however, causing the steel predator to linger in the area, hunting and killing other creatures that resemble its target, that fit the target's general description, or that simply live nearby. Such rogues become the most dangerous of predators.

Constructed Nature. A steel predator doesn't require air, food, drink, or sleep.

STEEL PREDATOR

Large construct, lawful evil

Armor Class 20 (natural armor)
Hit Points 207 (18d10 + 108)
Speed 40 ft.

STR	DEX	CON	INT	WIS	CHA
24 (+7)	17 (+3)	22 (+6)	4 (−3)	14 (+2)	6 (−2)

Skills Perception +7, Stealth +8, Survival +7
Damage Resistances cold, lightning, necrotic, thunder
Damage Immunities poison, psychic; bludgeoning, piercing, and slashing from nonmagical attacks
Condition Immunities charmed, exhaustion, frightened, paralyzed, petrified, poisoned, stunned
Senses blindsight 30 ft., darkvision 60 ft., passive Perception 17
Languages understands Modron and the language of its owner but can't speak
Challenge 16 (15,000 XP)

Innate Spellcasting. The steel predator's innate spellcasting ability is Wisdom. The steel predator can innately cast the following spells, requiring no components:

3/day each: *dimension door* (self only), *plane shift* (self only)

Magic Resistance. The steel predator has advantage on saving throws against spells and other magical effects.

Magic Weapons. The steel predator's weapon attacks are magical.

ACTIONS

Multiattack. The steel predator makes three attacks: one with its bite and two with its claw.

Bite. *Melee Weapon Attack:* +12 to hit, reach 5 ft., one target. *Hit:* 14 (2d6 + 7) piercing damage.

Claw. *Melee Weapon Attack:* +12 to hit, reach 5 ft., one target. *Hit:* 16 (2d8 + 7) slashing damage.

Stunning Roar (Recharge 5–6). The steel predator emits a roar in a 60-foot cone. Each creature in that area must make a DC 19 Constitution saving throw. On a failed save, a creature takes 27 (5d10) thunder damage, drops everything it's holding, and is stunned for 1 minute. On a successful save, a creature takes half as much damage. The stunned creature can repeat the saving throw at the end of each of its turns, ending the effect on itself on a success.

STONE CURSED

The stone cursed are spawned through a foul alchemical ritual performed on a humanoid that has been turned to stone. The ritual, which requires a mixture of basilisk blood and the ashes from the burned feathers of a cockatrice, awakens a dim echo of the petrified victim's spirit, animating the statue and turning it into a useful guardian.

Lingering Spirits. The stone cursed possess a malevolent drive to slay the living, yet they are utterly loyal to whoever performed the ritual to animate them, and they obey that being's orders to the best of their ability.

In combat, stony claws that drip with thick, gray sludge emerge from a stone cursed's fingers. This alchemical sludge transforms those slashed by the claws into statues.

A Strange Harvest. As part of the ritual used to create a stone cursed, a fist-sized obsidian skull forms within the creature's torso. The skull isn't visible while the stone cursed is active, but when it is slain, the statue shatters and the skull clatters to the ground. Because it is the nexus for the alchemy used to create these horrors, a dim echo of the original victim's memories resonates within the skull. A skilled magic-wielder can attempt to extract memories from it to gain insight into the victim's past or find lore that otherwise would be lost.

Constructed Nature. A stone cursed doesn't require air, food, drink, or sleep.

CRYPTIC WHISPERS

Even though creatures transformed into stone cursed are long dead, a vague whisper of their memories lives on in the obsidian skull embedded within the stone cursed's body. At the end of a short rest, a character can make a DC 20 Intelligence (Arcana) check to attempt to extract a memory from the skull—a memory that is a response to a verbal question posed by the character to the skull. Once this check is made, whether it succeeds or fails, the skull can't be used in this manner again.

STONE CURSED
Medium construct, lawful evil

Armor Class 17 (natural armor)
Hit Points 19 (3d8 + 4)
Speed 10 ft.

STR	DEX	CON	INT	WIS	CHA
16 (+3)	5 (−3)	14 (+2)	5 (−3)	8 (−1)	7 (−2)

Damage Vulnerabilities bludgeoning
Damage Immunities poison
Condition Immunities charmed, exhaustion, frightened, petrified, poisoned
Senses passive Perception 9
Languages the languages it knew in life
Challenge 1 (200 XP)

Cunning Opportunist. The stone cursed has advantage on the attack rolls of opportunity attacks.

False Appearance. While the stone cursed remains motionless, it is indistinguishable from a normal statue.

ACTIONS

Petrifying Claws. *Melee Weapon Attack:* +5 to hit, reach 5 ft., one target. *Hit:* 8 (1d10 + 3) slashing damage, or 14 (2d10 + 3) slashing damage if the attack roll had advantage. If the target is a creature, it must succeed on a DC 12 Constitution saving throw, or it begins to turn to stone and is restrained until the end of its next turn, when it must repeat the saving throw. The effect ends if the second save is successful; otherwise the target is petrified for 24 hours.

SWORD WRAITH

When a glory-obsessed warrior dies in battle without earning the honor it desperately sought, its valor-hungry spirit might haunt the battlefield as a sword wraith.

Brooding Spirits. The most likely spots for encountering sword wraiths are scenes of ancient ambushes, battlefields where soldiers were felled by magic with no chance to fight back, and sites where enemies were hemmed in and slaughtered without quarter.

Honor Above All. Sword wraiths fly into a rage if anyone questions their valor. Conversely, they are easily appeased by praise. Little pleases them more than hearing a ballad performed in their honor. Towns located near ancient battlefields hold annual festivals of remembrance to keep sword wraiths there placated.

Undead Nature. A sword wraith doesn't require air, food, drink, or sleep.

SWORD WRAITH COMMANDER
Medium undead, lawful evil

Armor Class 18 (breastplate, shield)
Hit Points 127 (15d8 + 60)
Speed 30 ft.

STR	DEX	CON	INT	WIS	CHA
18 (+4)	14 (+2)	18 (+4)	11 (+0)	12 (+1)	14 (+2)

Skills Perception +4
Damage Resistances necrotic; bludgeoning, piercing, and slashing from nonmagical attacks
Damage Immunities poison
Condition Immunities exhaustion, frightened, poisoned, unconscious
Senses darkvision 60 ft., passive Perception 14
Languages the languages it knew in life
Challenge 8 (3,900 XP)

Martial Fury. As a bonus action, the sword wraith can make one weapon attack, which deals an extra 9 (2d8) necrotic damage on a hit. If it does so, attack rolls against it have advantage until the start of its next turn.

Turning Defiance. The sword wraith and any other sword wraiths within 30 feet of it have advantage on saving throws against effects that turn undead.

ACTIONS

Multiattack. The sword wraith makes two weapon attacks.

Longsword. *Melee Weapon Attack:* +7 to hit, reach 5 ft., one target. *Hit:* 8 (1d8 + 4) slashing damage, or 9 (1d10 + 4) slashing damage if used with two hands.

Longbow. *Ranged Weapon Attack:* +5 to hit, range 150/600 ft., one target. *Hit:* 6 (1d8 + 2) piercing damage.

Call to Honor (1/Day). To use this action, the sword wraith must have taken damage during the current combat. If the sword wraith can use this action, it gives itself advantage on attack rolls until the end of its next turn, and 1d4 + 1 sword wraith warriors appear in unoccupied spaces within 30 feet of it. The warriors last until they drop to 0 hit points, and they take their turns immediately after the commander's turn on the same initiative count.

SWORD WRAITH WARRIOR
Medium undead, lawful evil

Armor Class 16 (chain shirt, shield)
Hit Points 45 (6d8 + 18)
Speed 30 ft.

STR	DEX	CON	INT	WIS	CHA
18 (+4)	12 (+1)	17 (+3)	6 (−2)	9 (−1)	10 (+0)

Damage Resistances necrotic; bludgeoning, piercing, and slashing from nonmagical attacks
Damage Immunities poison
Condition Immunities exhaustion, frightened, poisoned, unconscious
Senses darkvision 60 ft., passive Perception 9
Languages the languages it knew in life
Challenge 3 (700 XP)

Martial Fury. As a bonus action, the sword wraith can make one weapon attack. If it does so, attack rolls against it have advantage until the start of its next turn.

ACTIONS

Longsword. *Melee Weapon Attack:* +6 to hit, reach 5 ft., one target. *Hit:* 8 (1d8 + 4) slashing damage, or 9 (1d10 + 4) slashing damage if used with two hands.

Longbow. *Ranged Weapon Attack:* +3 to hit, range 150/600 ft., one target. *Hit:* 5 (1d8 + 1) piercing damage.

TORTLES

Tortles are omnivorous, turtle-like humanoids with shells that cover most of their bodies. Tortles have a saying: "We wear our homes on our backs." Consequently, tortles feel little need to stay put for long.

An adult tortle stands about 6 feet tall and weighs between 450 and 500 pounds. Males and females are nearly identical in size and appearance.

Temporary Towns. A tortle settlement is primarily used as a kind of moot, where tortles can socialize with one another and trade with strangers. Tortles don't regard these settlements as places worth defending with their lives, and they abandon a settlement when it no longer serves their needs.

A Life of Wandering. Most tortles like to see how other creatures live and discover new customs. The urge to procreate doesn't kick in until the end of a tortle's life, and a tortle can spend decades away from its native land without feeling homesick.

Tortles view the world as a place of everyday wonder. They live for the chance to hear a soft wind blowing through palm trees, to watch a frog croaking on a lily pad, or to stand in a crowded marketplace.

TORTLE
Medium humanoid (tortle), lawful good

Armor Class 17 (natural)
Hit Points 22 (4d8 + 4)
Speed 30 ft.

STR	DEX	CON	INT	WIS	CHA
15 (+2)	10 (+0)	12 (+1)	11 (+0)	13 (+1)	12 (+1)

Skills Athletics +4, Survival +3
Senses passive Perception 11
Languages Aquan, Common
Challenge 1/4 (50 XP)

Hold Breath. The tortle can hold its breath for 1 hour.

ACTIONS

Claws. *Melee Weapon Attack:* +4 to hit, reach 5 ft., one target. *Hit:* 4 (1d4 + 2) slashing damage.

Quarterstaff. *Melee Weapon Attack:* +4 to hit, reach 5 ft., one target. *Hit:* 5 (1d6 + 2) bludgeoning damage, or 6 (1d8 + 2) bludgeoning damage if used with two hands.

Light Crossbow. *Ranged Weapon Attack:* +2 to hit, range 80/320 ft., one target. *Hit:* 4 (1d8) piercing damage.

Shell Defense. The tortle withdraws into its shell. Until it emerges, it gains a +4 bonus to AC and has advantage on Strength and Constitution saving throws. While in its shell, the tortle is prone, its speed is 0 and can't increase, it has disadvantage on Dexterity saving throws, it can't take reactions, and the only action it can take is a bonus action to emerge.

TORTLE DRUID
Medium humanoid (tortle), lawful neutral

Armor Class 17 (natural)
Hit Points 33 (6d8 + 6)
Speed 30 ft.

STR	DEX	CON	INT	WIS	CHA
14 (+2)	10 (+0)	12 (+1)	11 (+0)	15 (+2)	12 (+1)

Skills Animal Handling +4, Nature +2, Survival +4
Senses passive Perception 12
Languages Aquan, Common
Challenge 2 (450 XP)

Hold Breath. The tortle can hold its breath for 1 hour.

Spellcasting. The tortle is a 4th-level spellcaster. Its spellcasting ability is Wisdom (spell save DC 12, +4 to hit with spell attacks). It has the following druid spells prepared:

Cantrips (at will): *druidcraft, guidance, produce flame*
1st level (4 slots): *animal friendship, cure wounds, speak with animals, thunderwave*
2nd level (3 slots): *darkvision, hold person*

ACTIONS

Claws. *Melee Weapon Attack:* +4 to hit, reach 5 ft., one target. *Hit:* 4 (1d4 + 2) slashing damage.

Quarterstaff. *Melee Weapon Attack:* +4 to hit, reach 5 ft., one target. *Hit:* 5 (1d6 + 2) bludgeoning damage, or 6 (1d8 + 2) bludgeoning damage if used with two hands.

Shell Defense. The tortle withdraws into its shell. Until it emerges, it gains a +4 bonus to AC and has advantage on Strength and Constitution saving throws. While in its shell, the tortle is prone, its speed is 0 and can't increase, it has disadvantage on Dexterity saving throws, it can't take reactions, and the only action it can take is a bonus action to emerge.

Trolls

Trolls that are nearly obliterated but survive and regenerate from mere scraps of flesh can display bizarre mutations. One of these warped trolls is especially likely to arise if the creature regenerates in the presence of magical emanations, planar energy, disease, or death on a vast scale, or if its body was damaged by elemental forces. These mutated forms can also be produced and shaped by the ritual magic of evil spellcasters.

Dire Troll

Huge giant, chaotic evil

Armor Class 15 (natural armor)
Hit Points 172 (15d12 + 75)
Speed 40 ft.

STR	DEX	CON	INT	WIS	CHA
22 (+6)	15 (+2)	21 (+5)	9 (–1)	11 (+0)	5 (–3)

Saving Throws Wis +5, Cha +2
Skills Perception +5
Damage Resistances bludgeoning, piercing, and slashing from nonmagical attacks
Condition Immunities frightened, poisoned
Senses darkvision 60 ft., passive Perception 15
Languages Giant
Challenge 13 (10,000 XP)

Keen Senses. The troll has advantage on Wisdom (Perception) checks that rely on smell or sight.

Regeneration. The troll regains 10 hit points at the start of its turn. If the troll takes acid or fire damage, it regains only 5 hit points at the start of its next turn. The troll dies only if it is hit by an attack that deals 10 or more acid or fire damage while the troll has 0 hit points.

Actions

Multiattack. The troll makes five attacks: one with its bite and four with its claws.

Bite. *Melee Weapon Attack:* +11 to hit, reach 10 ft., one target. *Hit:* 10 (1d8 + 6) piercing damage plus 5 (1d10) poison damage.

Claws. *Melee Weapon Attack:* +11 to hit, reach 10 ft., one target. *Hit:* 16 (3d6 + 6) slashing damage.

Whirlwind of Claws (Recharge 5–6). Each creature within 10 feet of the troll must make a DC 19 Dexterity saving throw, taking 44 (8d10) slashing damage on a failed save, or half as much damage on a successful one.

Dire Troll

Trolls kill and eat almost anything—including, in rare cases, other trolls. This cannibalism has the effect of causing the troll to grow to an unusually large size. These dire trolls crave more and more troll flesh to fuel their continued growth.

Dire trolls also increase their size by grafting flesh and organs onto themselves. When a slab of quivering troll flesh is bound against a fresh wound on the dire troll, its regenerative capacity incorporates the new mass into its own musculature. Even more horrifying are the multiple arms, eyes, claws, and other organs that a dire troll tears from its victims and grafts onto itself. Over time, these creatures can accumulate many limbs.

> ### Vaprak the Destroyer
>
> Although trolls are hardly devout and seldom ponder spiritual questions, they do fear and venerate the entity known as Vaprak the Destroyer. As with many lesser deities, Vaprak's true nature is something of a mystery, but it is always portrayed as a horrid, misshapen, greenish creature strongly resembling a troll. It's given to fits of mindless destruction and is constantly paranoid about the plots and ambitions of other deities.
>
> Among trolls, Vaprak is believed to devour those on the brink of death, but only if the troll is already cooked or digested (slain by fire or acid). Otherwise, the god spits the soul back into the world to regenerate a new body, no matter how little of its previous form remained. Thus, only trolls slain by acid or fire remain dead, because only those are consumed by Vaprak.

ROT TROLL

A troll that is infused with waves of necrotic energy as it regenerates can develop a symbiotic relationship with that deathly power. The troll's body withers, and its flesh falls away from the body as quickly as it forms. Eventually a rot troll becomes unable to regenerate, though it still heals normally. The creature courses with necrotic energy that flows out of its withered form. Simply standing near a rot troll exposes other creatures to its lethal emanations.

SPIRIT TROLL

A troll blasted with psychic energy can take a nonphysical form when it regenerates. Its psyche survives, but the body of a spirit troll is as insubstantial as shadow. The troll might be unaware of the transition—it still moves and attacks with teeth and claws as it always did—but now it strikes at its victim's mind.

SPIRIT TROLL
Large giant, chaotic evil

Armor Class 17 (natural armor)
Hit Points 97 (15d10 + 15)
Speed 30 ft.

STR	DEX	CON	INT	WIS	CHA
1 (−5)	17 (+3)	13 (+1)	8 (−1)	9 (−1)	16 (+3)

Skills Perception +3
Damage Resistances acid, cold, fire, lightning, thunder
Damage Immunities bludgeoning, piercing, and slashing from nonmagical attacks
Condition Immunities exhaustion, grappled, paralyzed, petrified, prone, restrained, unconscious
Senses darkvision 60 ft., passive Perception 13
Languages Giant
Challenge 11 (7,200 XP)

Incorporeal Movement. The troll can move through other creatures and objects as if they were difficult terrain. It takes 5 (1d10) force damage if it ends its turn inside an object.

Regeneration. The troll regains 10 hit points at the start of each of its turns. If the troll takes psychic or force damage, this trait doesn't function at the start of the troll's next turn. The troll dies only if it starts its turn with 0 hit points and doesn't regenerate.

ACTIONS

Multiattack. The troll makes three attacks: one with its bite and two with its claws.

Bite. *Melee Weapon Attack:* +7 to hit, reach 5 ft., one creature. *Hit:* 19 (3d10 + 3) psychic damage, and the target must succeed on a DC 15 Wisdom saving throw or be stunned for 1 minute. The stunned target can repeat the saving throw at the end of each of its turns, ending the effect on itself on a success.

Claws. *Melee Weapon Attack:* +7 to hit, reach 5 ft., one creature. *Hit:* 14 (2d10 + 3) psychic damage.

ROT TROLL
Large giant, chaotic evil

Armor Class 16 (natural armor)
Hit Points 138 (12d10 + 72)
Speed 30 ft.

STR	DEX	CON	INT	WIS	CHA
18 (+4)	13 (+1)	22 (+6)	5 (−3)	8 (−1)	4 (−3)

Skills Perception +3
Damage Immunities necrotic
Senses darkvision 60 ft., passive Perception 13
Languages Giant
Challenge 9 (5,000 XP)

Rancid Degeneration. At the end of each of the troll's turns, each creature within 5 feet of it takes 11 (2d10) necrotic damage, unless the troll has taken acid or fire damage since the end of its last turn.

ACTIONS

Multiattack. The troll makes three attacks: one with its bite and two with its claws.

Bite. *Melee Weapon Attack:* +8 to hit, reach 5 ft., one target. *Hit:* 7 (1d6 + 4) piercing damage plus 16 (3d10) necrotic damage.

Claws. *Melee Weapon Attack:* +8 to hit, reach 5 ft., one target. *Hit:* 11 (2d6 + 4) slashing damage plus 5 (1d10) necrotic damage.

SPIRIT TROLL

VENOM TROLL

A troll ravaged by massive doses of poison might mutate into a venom troll. Lingering poison infuses its blood and tissue, and poison leaks from its pores to coat its fangs and claws. These creatures are especially dangerous in close combat, because poison drips off their flesh and sprays out from every wound they receive.

VENOM TROLL

Large giant, chaotic evil

Armor Class 15 (natural armor)
Hit Points 94 (9d10 + 45)
Speed 30 ft.

STR	DEX	CON	INT	WIS	CHA
18 (+4)	13 (+1)	20 (+5)	7 (−2)	9 (−1)	7 (−2)

Skills Perception +2
Damage Immunities poison
Condition Immunities poisoned
Senses darkvision 60 ft., passive Perception 12
Languages Giant
Challenge 7 (2,900 XP)

Keen Smell. The troll has advantage on Wisdom (Perception) checks that rely on smell.

Poison Splash. When the troll takes damage of any type but psychic, each creature within 5 feet of the troll takes 9 (2d8) poison damage.

Regeneration. The troll regains 10 hit points at the start of each of its turns. If the troll takes acid or fire damage, this trait doesn't function at the start of the troll's next turn. The troll dies only if it starts its turn with 0 hit points and doesn't regenerate.

ACTIONS

Multiattack. The troll makes three attacks: one with its bite and two with its claws.

Bite. *Melee Weapon Attack:* +7 to hit, reach 5 ft., one target. *Hit:* 7 (1d6 + 4) piercing damage plus 4 (1d8) poison damage, and the creature is poisoned until the start of the troll's next turn.

Claws. *Melee Weapon Attack:* +7 to hit, reach 5 ft., one target. *Hit:* 11 (2d6 + 4) slashing damage plus 4 (1d8) poison damage.

Venom Spray (Recharge 6). The troll slices itself with a claw, releasing a spray of poison in a 15-foot cube. The troll takes 7 (2d6) slashing damage (this damage can't be reduced in any way). Each creature in the area must make a DC 16 Constitution saving throw. On a failed save, a creature takes 18 (4d8) poison damage and is poisoned for 1 minute. On a successful save, the creature takes half as much damage and isn't poisoned. A poisoned creature can repeat the saving throw at the end of each of its turns, ending the effect on itself on a success.

Vampiric Mist

In billowing clouds of fog lurk vampiric mists, the wretched remnants of vampires that were prevented from finding rest. Indistinguishable from the mists they lurk within, they strike unseen and undetected to bleed their victims dry.

Former Vampires. Vampiric mists, sometimes called crimson mists, are all that remain of vampires who couldn't return to their burial places after being defeated or suffering some mishap. Denied the restorative power of these places, the vampires' bodies dissolve into mist. The transformation strips the intelligence and personality from them until only an unholy, insatiable thirst for blood remains.

Blood Thief. Indistinguishable from fog aside from the charnel reek it exudes, a vampiric mist descends on a creature and causes the blood in its body to ooze through the creature's pores or spill out from its eyes, nose, and mouth. This blood wafts out from the victim like crimson smoke, which the mist then consumes. The feeding causes no pain or discomfort to the victim, so vampiric mists can feed on sleepers without waking them. The more a mist feeds, the redder it gets, such that it turns pink, then red, and finally a deep scarlet hue that rains blood droplets wherever it goes.

Attracted to Blood. Like sharks in water, vampiric mists can scent blood from up to a mile away. Any injury, no matter how small, might catch their attention and draw them toward their victims. In battle, a mist focuses its attacks on injured targets, since open wounds are a more ready source of blood.

Undead Nature. A vampiric mist doesn't require air or sleep.

Vampiric Mist

Medium undead, chaotic evil

Armor Class 13
Hit Points 30 (4d8 + 12)
Speed 0 ft., fly 30 ft. (hover)

STR	DEX	CON	INT	WIS	CHA
6 (−2)	16 (+3)	16 (+3)	6 (−2)	12 (+1)	7 (−2)

Saving Throws Wis +3
Damage Resistances acid, cold, lightning, necrotic, thunder; bludgeoning, piercing, and slashing from nonmagical attacks
Damage Immunities poison
Condition Immunities charmed, exhaustion, grappled, paralyzed, petrified, poisoned, prone, restrained
Senses darkvision 60 ft., passive Perception 11
Languages —
Challenge 3 (700 XP)

Life Sense. The mist can sense the location of any creature within 60 feet of it, unless that creature's type is construct or undead.

Forbiddance. The mist can't enter a residence without an invitation from one of the occupants.

Misty Form. The mist can occupy another creature's space and vice versa. In addition, if air can pass through a space, the mist can pass through it without squeezing. Each foot of movement in water costs it 2 extra feet, rather than 1 extra foot. The mist can't manipulate objects in any way that requires fingers or manual dexterity.

Sunlight Hypersensitivity. The mist takes 10 radiant damage whenever it starts its turn in sunlight. While in sunlight, the mist has disadvantage on attack rolls and ability checks.

Actions

Life Drain. The mist touches one creature in its space. The target must succeed on a DC 13 Constitution saving throw (undead and constructs automatically succeed), or it takes 10 (2d6 + 3) necrotic damage, the mist regains 10 hit points, and the target's hit point maximum is reduced by an amount equal to the necrotic damage taken. This reduction lasts until the target finishes a long rest. The target dies if its hit point maximum is reduced to 0.

YUGOLOTHS

Mercenaries that ply their trade throughout the Lower Planes and in other realms, yugoloths have a reputation for effectiveness that is matched only by their desire for ever more wealth. Although yugoloths aren't especially loyal and typically try to exploit every potential loophole in a contract, they undertake any task for which they are hired, no matter how despicable. Yugoloths come in a wide variety of forms, including those described in the *Monster Manual* and the six creatures presented here.

CANOLOTH

Canoloths prefer to enter into contracts to guard valuable treasures and important locations. They always do exactly as asked—never any more, never any less.

With senses sharp enough to pinpoint the locations of nearby invisible creatures, canoloths respond unfailingly to any threat to their charges. Furthermore, they emit a magical distortion field that prevents creatures close to them from teleporting.

Canoloths confront intruders with swift and terrible force, projecting long, spiny tongues to grab their foes and drag them close. What happens next depends on the contract. Unless instructed to kill, a canoloth merely holds onto its prisoner, but if given the order to do so, it tears its prey limb from limb.

Canoloths are fundamentally lazy creatures. Given no reason to attack, they rarely rise to the bait.

CANOLOTH
Medium fiend (yugoloth), neutral evil

Armor Class 16 (natural armor)
Hit Points 120 (16d8 + 48)
Speed 50 ft.

STR	DEX	CON	INT	WIS	CHA
18 (+4)	10 (+0)	17 (+3)	5 (−3)	17 (+3)	12 (+1)

Skills Investigation +3, Perception +9
Damage Resistances cold, fire, lightning; bludgeoning, piercing, and slashing from nonmagical attacks
Damage Immunities acid, poison
Condition Immunities poisoned
Senses darkvision 60 ft., truesight 120 ft., passive Perception 19
Languages Abyssal, Infernal, telepathy 60 ft.
Challenge 8 (3,900 XP)

Dimensional Lock. Other creatures can't teleport to or from a space within 60 feet of the canoloth. Any attempt to do so is wasted.

Magic Resistance. The canoloth has advantage on saving throws against spells and other magical effects.

Magic Weapons. The canoloth's weapon attacks are magical.

Uncanny Senses. The canoloth can't be surprised while it isn't incapacitated.

ACTIONS

Multiattack. The canoloth makes two attacks: one with its tongue or its bite and one with its claws.

Bite. *Melee Weapon Attack:* +7 to hit, reach 5 ft., one target. *Hit:* 25 (6d6 + 4) piercing damage.

Claws. *Melee Weapon Attack:* +7 to hit, reach 5 ft., one target. *Hit:* 15 (2d10 + 4) slashing damage.

Tongue. *Ranged Weapon Attack:* +7 to hit, range 30 ft., one target. *Hit:* 17 (2d12 + 4) piercing damage. If the target is Medium or smaller, it is grappled (escape DC 15), pulled up to 30 feet toward the canoloth, and restrained until the grapple ends. The canoloth can grapple one target at a time with its tongue.

DHERGOLOTH

Dhergoloths rush into battle like whirlwinds of destruction, lashing out with five sets of claws, which extend from their squat, barrel-shaped bodies. They take contracts to put down uprisings, clear out rabble, and eliminate scouts and skirmishers, and they revel in the butchery they create, their unhinged laughter rising above their victims' screams.

Since dhergoloths are little more than dumb brutes, employers must use caution when instructing these fiends. They can handle simple orders that don't take a lot of time to resolve. When given anything complex to do, they either forget what they're told or don't listen in the first place, and then bungle the task that was set for them.

A dhergoloth's head doesn't turn along with its furiously spinning torso, and its torso can spin a different direction from its dancing legs. I'd like to vivisect one at some point to find out how this can be.

DHERGOLOTH
Medium fiend (yugoloth), neutral evil

Armor Class 15 (natural armor)
Hit Points 119 (14d8 +56)
Speed 30 ft.

STR	DEX	CON	INT	WIS	CHA
17 (+3)	10 (+0)	19 (+4)	7 (–2)	10 (+0)	9 (–1)

Saving Throws Str +6
Damage Resistances cold, fire, lightning; bludgeoning, piercing, and slashing from nonmagical attacks
Damage Immunities acid, poison
Condition Immunities poisoned
Senses blindsight 60 ft., darkvision 60 ft., passive Perception 10
Languages Abyssal, Infernal, telepathy 60 ft.
Challenge 7 (2,900 XP)

Innate Spellcasting. The dhergoloth's innate spellcasting ability is Charisma (spell save DC 10). It can innately cast the following spells, requiring no material components:

At will: *darkness, fear*
3/day: *sleep*

Magic Resistance. The dhergoloth has advantage on saving throws against spells and other magical effects.

Magic Weapons. The dhergoloth's weapon attacks are magical.

ACTIONS

Multiattack. The dhergoloth makes two claw attacks.

Claw. *Melee Weapon Attack:* +6 to hit, reach 5 ft., one target. *Hit:* 12 (2d8 + 3) slashing damage.

Flailing Claws (Recharge 5–6). The dhergoloth moves up to its walking speed in a straight line and targets each creature within 5 feet of it during its movement. Each target must succeed on a DC 14 Dexterity saving throw or take 22 (3d12 + 3) slashing damage.

Teleport. The dhergoloth magically teleports, along with any equipment it is wearing or carrying, up to 60 feet to an unoccupied space it can see.

HYDROLOTH

Medium fiend (yugoloth), neutral evil

Armor Class 15
Hit Points 135 (18d8 + 54)
Speed 20 ft., swim 40 ft.

STR	DEX	CON	INT	WIS	CHA
12 (+1)	21 (+5)	16 (+3)	19 (+4)	10 (+0)	14 (+2)

Skills Insight +4, Perception +4
Damage Vulnerabilities fire
Damage Resistances cold, lightning; bludgeoning, piercing, and slashing from nonmagical attacks
Damage Immunities acid, poison
Condition Immunities poisoned
Senses blindsight 60 ft., darkvision 60 ft., passive Perception 14
Languages Abyssal, Infernal, telepathy 60 ft.
Challenge 9 (5,000 XP)

Amphibious. The hydroloth can breathe air and water.

Innate Spellcasting. The hydroloth's innate spellcasting ability is Intelligence (spell save DC 16). It can innately cast the following spells, requiring no material components:

At will: *darkness, detect magic, dispel magic, invisibility* (self only), *water walk*
3/day each: *control water, crown of madness, fear, phantasmal killer, suggestion*

Magic Resistance. The hydroloth has advantage on saving throws against spells and other magical effects.

Magic Weapons. The hydroloth's weapon attacks are magical.

Secure Memory. The hydroloth is immune to the waters of the River Styx as well as any effect that would steal or modify its memories or detect or read its thoughts.

Watery Advantage. While submerged in liquid, the hydroloth has advantage on attack rolls.

ACTIONS

Multiattack. The hydroloth makes two melee attacks. In place of one of these attacks, it can cast one spell that takes 1 action to cast.

Claws. *Melee Weapon Attack:* +9 to hit, reach 5 ft., one target. *Hit:* 14 (2d8 + 5) slashing damage.

Bite. *Melee Weapon Attack:* +9 to hit, reach 5 ft., one target. *Hit:* 16 (2d10 + 5) piercing damage.

Steal Memory (1/Day). The hydroloth targets one creature it can see within 60 feet of it. The target takes 4d6 psychic damage, and it must make a DC 16 Intelligence saving throw. On a successful save, the target becomes immune to this hydroloth's Steal Memory for 24 hours. On a failed save, the target loses all proficiencies, it can't cast spells, it can't understand language, and if its Intelligence and Charisma scores are higher than 5, they become 5. Each time the target finishes a long rest, it can repeat the saving throw, ending the effect on itself on a success. A *greater restoration* or *remove curse* spell cast on the target ends this effect early.

Teleport. The hydroloth magically teleports, along with any equipment it is wearing or carrying, up to 60 feet to an unoccupied space it can see.

HYDROLOTH

Like the thought-stealing waters of the River Styx they inhabit, hydroloths filch the memories of creatures they attack, stealing away their thoughts for delivery to whatever master they happen to serve. Hydroloths are skilled at finding lost things, especially those that have been swallowed up in the deeps.

For amphibious assaults or underwater conflicts, hydroloths have no equal among yugoloths. They sometimes hire themselves out to attack and scuttle ships and raid coastal settlements.

MERRENOLOTH

The grim, gaunt captains of the ferries on the River Styx, merrenoloths have total command of their vessels, ensuring that their passengers reach their destinations safely. Sometimes merrenoloths can be coaxed away from the Lower Planes to captain other vessels, affording those ships and crews the same protection.

Whenever a merrenoloth takes on a contract to captain a ship, it bonds with the vehicle to make sure nothing goes awry with it during the journey. A merrenoloth can navigate its ship safely through the worst storms, always stays on course, and never runs afoul of the myriad hazards that can thwart lesser captains.

A merrenoloth can hold its own in a fight, but it prefers to avoid combat when possible. In fact, it typically specifies in its contracts that it is under no obligation to fight. A merrenoloth's first duty is always to its vessel.

Lair Actions

Any ship a merrenoloth is contracted to captain becomes the creature's lair. When fighting on the ship, the merrenoloth can invoke its ability to take lair actions. On initiative count 20 (losing initiative ties), the merrenoloth can take one lair action to cause one of the following effects; it can't use the same effect two rounds in a row:

- The ship regains 22 (4d10) hit points.
- A strong wind propels the ship, increasing its speed by 30 feet until initiative count 20 on the next round.
- The air within 60 feet of the ship is filled with howling wind. Until initiative count 20 on the next round, that area is difficult terrain, and when a Medium or smaller creature flies into that area or starts its turn flying there, it must succeed on a DC 13 Strength saving throw or be knocked prone.

Regional Effects

A merrenoloth imbues its vessel with powerful magic that creates one or more of the following effects:

- The ship doesn't sink even if its hull is breached.
- The ship always stays on course to the destination the merrenoloth names.
- Creatures the merrenoloth chooses to take on the ship aren't discomfited by wind or weather, though this effect doesn't protect against damage.

If the merrenoloth dies, these effects fade over the course of 1d6 hours.

Merrenoloth

Medium fiend (yugoloth), neutral evil

Armor Class 13
Hit Points 40 (9d8)
Speed 30 ft., swim 40 ft.

STR	DEX	CON	INT	WIS	CHA
8 (−1)	17 (+3)	10 (+0)	17 (+3)	14 (+2)	11 (+0)

Saving Throws Dex +5, Int +5
Skills History +5, Nature +5, Perception +4, Survival +4
Damage Resistances cold, fire, lightning; bludgeoning, piercing, and slashing from nonmagical attacks
Damage Immunities acid, poison
Condition Immunities poisoned
Senses blindsight 60 ft., darkvision 60 ft., passive Perception 14
Languages Abyssal, Infernal, telepathy 60 ft.
Challenge 3 (700 XP)

Innate Spellcasting. The merrenoloth's innate spellcasting ability is Intelligence (spell save DC 13). It can innately cast the following spells, requiring no material components:

At will: *charm person, darkness, detect magic, dispel magic, gust of wind*
3/day: *control water*
1/day: *control weather*

Magic Resistance. The merrenoloth has advantage on saving throws against spells and other magical effects.

Magic Weapons. The merrenoloth's weapon attacks are magical.

Teleport. As a bonus action, the merrenoloth magically teleports, along with any equipment it is wearing or carrying, up to 60 feet to an unoccupied space it can see.

Actions

Multiattack. The merrenoloth uses Fear Gaze once and makes one oar attack.

Oar. Melee Weapon Attack: +5 to hit, reach 5 ft., one target. Hit: 8 (2d4 + 3) slashing damage.

Fear Gaze. The merrenoloth targets one creature it can see within 60 feet of it. The target must succeed on a DC 13 Wisdom saving throw or become frightened of the merrenoloth for 1 minute. The frightened target can repeat the saving throw at the end of each of its turns, ending the effect on itself on a success.

Oinoloth

Grim specters of death, oinoloths bring pestilence wherever they go. To armies who recognize their awful forms, their mere appearance causes soldiers to break ranks and flee, lest they succumb to one of the awful plagues that oinoloths let loose.

Oinoloths provide the ultimate solution to thorny problems, usually by killing everyone involved. They are hired as a last resort, when a siege has gone on too long or an army has proved too strong to overcome. Once summoned, oinoloths stalk the killing field, poisoning the ground and sickening creatures they encounter. Sometimes they might be hired to lift the very plagues they spread, but the price for such work is high, and the effort turns the creatures they save into debilitated wrecks.

Oinoloth

Medium fiend (yugoloth), neutral evil

Armor Class 17 (natural armor)
Hit Points 126 (12d10 + 60)
Speed 40 ft.

STR	DEX	CON	INT	WIS	CHA
19 (+4)	17 (+3)	18 (+4)	17 (+3)	16 (+3)	19 (+4)

Saving Throws Con +8, Wis +7
Skills Deception +8, Intimidation +8, Perception +7
Damage Resistances cold, fire, lightning; bludgeoning, piercing, and slashing from nonmagical attacks
Damage Immunities acid, poison
Condition Immunities poisoned
Senses blindsight 60 ft., darkvision 60 ft., passive Perception 17
Languages Abyssal, Infernal, telepathy 60 ft.
Challenge 12 (8,400 XP)

Bringer of Plagues (Recharge 5–6). As a bonus action, the oinoloth blights the area within 30 feet of it. The blight lasts for 24 hours. While blighted, all normal plants in the area wither and die, and the number of hit points restored by a spell to a creature in that area is halved.

Furthermore, when a creature moves into the blighted area or starts its turn there, that creature must make a DC 16 Constitution saving throw. On a successful save, the creature is immune to the oinoloth's Bringer of Plagues for the next 24 hours. On a failed save, the creature takes 14 (4d6) necrotic damage and is poisoned.

The poisoned creature can't regain hit points. After every 24 hours that elapse, the poisoned creature can repeat the saving throw. On a failed save, the creature's hit point maximum is reduced by 5 (1d10). This reduction lasts until the poison ends, and the target dies if its hit point maximum is reduced to 0. The poison ends after the creature successfully saves against it three times.

Innate Spellcasting. The oinoloth's innate spellcasting ability is Charisma (spell save DC 16). It can innately cast the following spells, requiring no material components:

At will: *darkness, detect magic, dispel magic, invisibility* (self only)
1/day each: *feeblemind, globe of invulnerability, wall of fire, wall of ice*

Magic Resistance. The oinoloth has advantage on saving throws against spells and other magical effects.

Magic Weapons. The oinoloth's weapon attacks are magical.

Actions

Multiattack. The oinoloth uses its Transfixing Gaze and makes two claw attacks.

Claw. *Melee Weapon Attack:* +8 to hit, reach 5 ft., one target. *Hit:* 14 (3d6 + 4) slashing damage plus 22 (4d10) necrotic damage.

Corrupted Healing (Recharge 6). The oinoloth touches one willing creature within 5 feet of it. The target regains all its hit points. In addition, the oinoloth can end one disease on the target or remove one of the following conditions from it: blinded, deafened, paralyzed, or poisoned. The target then gains 1 level of exhaustion, and its hit point maximum is reduced by 7 (2d6). This reduction can be removed only by a *wish* spell or by casting *greater restoration* on the target three times within the same hour. The target dies if its hit point maximum is reduced to 0.

Teleport. The oinoloth magically teleports, along with any equipment it is wearing or carrying, up to 60 feet to an unoccupied space it can see.

Transfixing Gaze. The oinoloth targets one creature it can see within 30 feet of it. The target must succeed on a DC 16 Wisdom saving throw against this magic or be charmed until the end of the oinoloth's next turn. While charmed in this way, the target is restrained. If the target's saving throw is successful, the target is immune to the oinoloth's gaze for the next 24 hours.

YAGNOLOTH

Anyone who would contract yugoloths for a task usually ends up dealing with a yagnoloth. Cunning negotiators, these strange fiends handle the writing of contracts for all of their kind. Once a yagnoloth is hired, it communicates its employer's desires to the fiends it commands.

Although they are entrusted with leading lesser yugoloths, yagnoloths ultimately take their orders from arcanaloths and ultroloths. Aside from their superiors, yagnoloths have full authority over and expect obedience from the fiends under their command. A yagnoloth follows the dictates in a contract it negotiated, but it is certain to have included a loophole to escape its obligation if the situation warrants.

A yagnoloth has one arm of human size and one giant-sized arm, and it always covers one or the other with a long cape. During negotiations, the yagnoloth uncovers its human arm and uses it to draft and sign contracts. When a show of force is necessary or when combat is joined, it shifts its cape to reveal its brutally powerful giant appendage.

YAGNOLOTH

Large fiend (yugoloth), neutral evil

Armor Class 17 (natural armor)
Hit Points 147 (14d10 + 70)
Speed 40 ft.

STR	DEX	CON	INT	WIS	CHA
19 (+4)	14 (+2)	21 (+5)	16 (+3)	15 (+2)	18 (+4)

Saving Throws Dex +6, Int +7, Wis +6, Cha +8
Skills Deception +8, Insight +6, Perception +6, Persuasion +8
Damage Resistances cold, fire, lightning; bludgeoning, piercing, and slashing from nonmagical attacks
Damage Immunities acid, poison
Condition Immunities poisoned
Senses blindsight 60 ft., darkvision 60 ft., passive Perception 16
Languages Abyssal, Infernal, telepathy 60 ft.
Challenge 11 (7,200 XP)

Innate Spellcasting. The yagnoloth's innate spellcasting ability is Charisma (spell save DC 16). It can innately cast the following spells, requiring no material components:

At will: *darkness, detect magic, dispel magic, invisibility* (self only), *suggestion*
3/day: *lightning bolt*

Magic Resistance. The yagnoloth has advantage on saving throws against spells and other magical effects.

Magic Weapons. The yagnoloth's weapon attacks are magical.

ACTIONS

Multiattack. The yagnoloth makes one massive arm attack and one electrified touch attack, or it makes one massive arm attack and teleports before or after the attack.

Electrified Touch. *Melee Weapon Attack:* +8 to hit, reach 5 ft., one target. *Hit:* 27 (6d8) lightning damage.

Massive Arm. *Melee Weapon Attack:* +8 to hit, reach 15 ft., one target. *Hit:* 23 (3d12 + 4) bludgeoning damage. If the target is a creature, it must succeed on a DC 16 Constitution saving throw or become stunned until the end of the yagnoloth's next turn.

Life Leech. The yagnoloth touches one incapacitated creature within 15 feet of it. The target takes 36 (7d8 + 4) necrotic damage, and the yagnoloth gains temporary hit points equal to half the damage dealt. The target must succeed on a DC 16 Constitution saving throw, or its hit point maximum is reduced by an amount equal to the damage taken. This reduction lasts until the target finishes a long rest, and the target dies if its hit point maximum is reduced to 0.

Battlefield Cunning (Recharge 4–6). Up to two allied yugoloths within 60 feet of the yagnoloth that can hear it can use their reactions to make one melee attack each.

Teleport. The yagnoloth magically teleports, along with any equipment it is wearing or carrying, up to 60 feet to an unoccupied space it can see.

Appendix: Monster Lists

Stat Blocks by Creature Type

Stat Blocks by Challenge Rating

CREATURES BY ENVIRONMENT

ARCTIC CREATURES

Creatures	Challenge (XP)
Vampiric mist	3 (700 XP)
The Lost	7 (2,900 XP)
Frost salamander	9 (5,000 XP)
Winter eladrin	10 (5,900 XP)
Boneclaw	12 (8,400 XP)
Dire troll	13 (10,000 XP)
Nightwalker	20 (25,000 XP)
Elder tempest	23 (50,000 XP)

COASTAL CREATURES

Creatures	Challenge (XP)
Tortle	1/4 (50 XP)
Skulk	1/2 (100 XP)
Tortle druid	2 (450 XP)
Merrenoloth, vampiric mist	3 (700 XP)
Canoloth	8 (3,900 XP)
The Lonely	9 (5,000 XP)
Balhannoth, spirit troll	11 (7,200 XP)
Eidolon	12 (8,400 XP)
Wastrilith	13 (10,000 XP)
Blue abishai, nagpa	17 (18,000 XP)
Leviathan	20 (25,000 XP)
Elder tempest	23 (50,000 XP)

DESERT CREATURES

Creatures	Challenge (XP)
Young kruthik	1/8 (25 XP)
Meazel, stone cursed	1 (200 XP)
Adult kruthik, berbalang	2 (450 XP)
Dybbuk	4 (1,100 XP)
Kruthik hive lord	5 (1,800 XP)
The Lost	7 (2,900 XP)
Howler	8 (3,900 XP)
Rot troll, the Lonely	9 (5,000 XP)
Githyanki gish, githzerai enlightened, orthon, summer eladrin	10 (5,900 XP)
Boneclaw, eidolon, githyanki kith'rak, oinoloth	12 (8,400 XP)
Githyanki supreme commander, retriever	14 (11,500 XP)
Skull lord	15 (13,000 XP)
Phoenix	16 (15,000 XP)
Nagpa	17 (18,000 XP)
Nightwalker	20 (25,000 XP)
Zaratan	22 (41,000 XP)

FOREST CREATURES

Creatures	Challenge (XP)
Skulk	1/2 (100 XP)
Bronze scout, choker, meazel	1 (200 XP)
Vampiric mist	3 (700 XP)
Iron cobra, stone defender	4 (1,100 XP)
Oaken bolter	5 (1,800 XP)
Shadow dancer, the Lost, venom troll	7 (2,900 XP)

Creatures	Challenge (XP)
Corpse flower	8 (3,900 XP)
Rot troll	9 (5,000 XP)
Autumn eladrin, spring eladrin, summer eladrin, winter eladrin	10 (5,900 XP)
Spirit troll, the Hungry	11 (7,200 XP)
Eidolon, gray render	12 (8,400 XP)
Dire troll	13 (10,000 XP)
Retriever	14 (11,500 XP)
Nagpa	17 (18,000 XP)
Zaratan	22 (41,000 XP)

GRASSLAND CREATURES

Creatures	Challenge (XP)
Bronze scout, meazel	1 (200 XP)
Ogre bolt launcher, ogre howdah	2 (450 XP)
Ogre chain brute, sword wraith warrior, vampiric mist	3 (700 XP)
Iron cobra, ogre battering ram, stone defender	4 (1,100 XP)
Oaken bolter	5 (1,800 XP)
Howler, sword wraith commander	8 (3,900 XP)
Spring eladrin	10 (5,900 XP)
Eidolon	12 (8,400 XP)
Cadaver collector	14 (11,500 XP)
Zaratan	22 (41,000 XP)
Elder tempest	23 (50,000 XP)

HILL CREATURES

Creatures	Challenge (XP)
Bronze scout, meazel	1 (200 XP)
Ogre bolt launcher, ogre howdah	2 (450 XP)
Ogre chain brute	3 (700 XP)
Iron cobra, ogre battering ram, stone defender	4 (1,100 XP)
Oaken bolter	5 (1,800 XP)
Howler	8 (3,900 XP)
Gray render	12 (8,400 XP)
Dire troll	13 (10,000 XP)
Zaratan	22 (41,000 XP)
Elder tempest	23 (50,000 XP)

MOUNTAIN CREATURES

Creatures	Challenge (XP)
Young kruthik	1/8 (25 XP)
Derro, star spawn grue	1/4 (50 XP)
Bronze scout, choker, duergar soulblade, meazel, stone cursed	1 (200 XP)
Adult kruthik, duergar hammerer, duergar kavalrachni, duergar mind master, duergar stone guard, duergar xarrorn, ogre bolt launcher, ogre howdah	2 (450 XP)

Creatures	Challenge (XP)
Duergar screamer, ogre chain brute, vampiric mist	3 (700 XP)
Iron cobra, ogre battering ram, stone defender	4 (1,100 XP)
Kruthik hive lord, oaken bolter	5 (1,800 XP)
Duergar warlord	6 (2,300 XP)
The Lost	7 (2,900 XP)
The Lonely	9 (5,000 XP)
Githyanki gish, githzerai enlightened	10 (5,900 XP)
Balhannoth	11 (7,200 XP)
Duergar despot, eidolon, githyanki kith'rak	12 (8,400 XP)
Dire troll, star spawn seer	13 (10,000 XP)
Githyanki supreme commander	14 (11,500 XP)
Phoenix, star spawn larva mage	16 (15,000 XP)
Red abishai	19 (22,000 XP)
Zaratan	22 (41,000 XP)
Elder tempest	23 (50,000 XP)

Swamp Creatures

Creatures	Challenge (XP)
Oblex spawn, star spawn grue, the Wretched	1/4 (50 XP)
Skulk	1/2 (100 XP)
Meazel	1 (200 XP)
Sword wraith warrior, vampiric mist	3 (700 XP)
Adult oblex, allip	5 (1,800 XP)
Maurezhi, the Lost, venom troll	7 (2,900 XP)
Corpse flower	8 (3,900 XP)
Rot troll	9 (5,000 XP)
Elder oblex, sword wraith commander	10 (5,900 XP)
Spirit troll	11 (7,200 XP)
Star spawn seer, wastrilith	13 (10,000 XP)
Nabassu, skull lord	15 (13,000 XP)
Nagpa	17 (18,000 XP)
Nightwalker	20 (25,000 XP)

Underdark Creatures

Creatures	Challenge (XP)
Young kruthik	1/8 (25 XP)
Derro, male steeder, oblex spawn, the Wretched	1/4 (50 XP)
Skulk	1/2 (100 XP)
Choker, duergar soulblade, female steeder, meazel	1 (200 XP)
Adult kruthik, duergar hammerer, duergar kavalrachni, duergar mind master, duergar stone guard, duergar xarrorn	2 (450 XP)
Derro savant, duergar screamer, vampiric mist	3 (700 XP)
Adult oblex, kruthik hive lord	5 (1,800 XP)
Duergar warlord	6 (2,300 XP)

Creatures	Challenge (XP)
Armanite, dhergoloth, shadow dancer, the Lost, venom troll	7 (2,900 XP)
Canoloth, howler	8 (3,900 XP)
Drow house captain, gloom weaver, rot troll, the Lonely	9 (5,000 XP)
Elder oblex, orthon	10 (5,900 XP)
Alkilith, balhannoth, drow shadowblade, soul monger, spirit troll, the Hungry	11 (7,200 XP)
Duergar despot, oinoloth	12 (8,400 XP)
Dire troll, drow arachnomancer, the Angry, wastrilith	13 (10,000 XP)
Drow inquisitor, retriever	14 (11,500 XP)
Nabassu, skull lord	15 (13,000 XP)
Nagpa	17 (18,000 XP)
Drow favored consort, sibriex	18 (20,000 XP)
Drow matron mother, nightwalker	20 (25,000 XP)
Zaratan	22 (41,000 XP)

Underwater Creatures

Creatures	Challenge (XP)
Wastrilith	13 (10,000 XP)
Leviathan	20 (25,000 XP)

Urban Creatures

Creatures	Challenge (XP)
Oblex spawn, the Wretched	1/4 (50 XP)
Skulk	1/2 (100 XP)
Meazel, stone cursed	1 (200 XP)
Giff, vampiric mist	3 (700 XP)
Deathlock, dybbuk	4 (1,100 XP)
Adult oblex, allip	5 (1,800 XP)
White abishai	6 (2,300 XP)
Black abishai, maurezhi, shadow dancer, the Lost	7 (2,900 XP)
Canoloth, corpse flower, deathlock mastermind	8 (3,900 XP)
Gloom weaver, the Lonely	9 (5,000 XP)
Elder oblex, githyanki gish, githzerai enlightened, orthon	10 (5,900 XP)
Alkilith, soul monger, the Hungry, yagnoloth	11 (7,200 XP)
Boneclaw, eidolon, githyanki kith'rak	12 (8,400 XP)
Star spawn seer, the Angry	13 (10,000 XP)
Githyanki supreme commander	14 (11,500 XP)
Green abishai, nabassu	15 (13,000 XP)
Steel predator	16 (15,000 XP)
Blue abishai, nagpa	17 (18,000 XP)
Red abishai	19 (22,000 XP)